Hearts in Peril

A Suspenseful Romance Collection

Alison Reid

Hearts in Peril – A Suspenseful Romance Collection

by Alison Reid

ISBN: 978-1-7644837-8-0

First edition

Independently published

Introduction to...

Hearts in Peril

A Suspenseful Romance Collection

Fear. Suspicion. Desire.

In **Hearts in Peril**, love doesn't arrive quietly—it crashes into lives already scarred by loss, betrayal, and danger. These are stories where hearts are tested under pressure, trust is fragile, and every choice carries consequences.

From the tension of hidden secrets to the thrill of life-threatening stakes, these romances prove that love is at its most powerful when it faces the impossible. The men are protective, determined, and occasionally reckless; the women are resilient, courageous, and unwilling to surrender their hearts without a fight.

Each story in this collection is a standalone romance, written in the spirit of classic Mills & Boon with a modern edge. You'll find second chances, slow-burning chemistry, emotional suspense, and high-stakes situations that make every moment between hero and heroine charged with intensity.

Whether you're drawn to passion sparked in the aftermath of grief, love surviving betrayal, or the thrill of romance entwined with danger, **Hearts in Peril** invites you to immerse yourself in a world where love is never simple—but always worth the risk.

Enjoy the journey, and prepare for hearts to be tested, desires to ignite, and love to triumph against the odds.

Table of Contents

Collide

Alison Reid

A complete standalone romance

Previously published individually

Chapter One

The sharp, citrus bite of lemon cleaner filled Sarah's tiny Bondi apartment as she swept the cloth across the kitchen counter, letting the familiar rhythm settle her nerves. Late-afternoon sunlight spilled through the windows in warm golden stripes, softening the edges of her cluttered thoughts. Cleaning wasn't just a chore for her—it was a reset button, a way to clear out more than crumbs and fingerprints.

Her phone buzzed.

She glanced over, expecting a reminder or a message from work.

Damian.

Her hand hesitated. She hadn't expected to hear from him—not today, not after days of vague excuses and half-hearted texts. Maybe he'd finally decided to talk about where they stood. Maybe he'd finally stop dodging the real conversations.

With a tiny prickle of unease, she opened the message.

Sorry babe, not interested in a platonic relationship—we're done.

Sarah blinked, then huffed out a humourless laugh. Babe? As if that word ever meant anything coming from him.

She wasn't heartbroken—far from it. More…annoyed. Damian had been a question mark in her mind for weeks, a man she couldn't quite trust. Well, that mystery was solved. Rolling her eyes, she tapped out her reply.

Well, I'm glad I didn't sleep with you then, jerk.

She tossed her phone onto the couch with a satisfying little thud and went back to wiping down the counter. Some men were just a waste of perfectly good time.

Nearly an hour passed before her phone buzzed again. She almost ignored it—expecting Damian, trying to justify himself or toss out another petty insult. But when she glanced at the screen, her stomach dropped.

Sarah, I'm so sorry. Just caught Damian in bed with Melissa.

Melissa.

Derek's Melissa.

A cold weight settled in her chest. She could shrug off Damian's stupidity, but Derek… Derek was different. He'd been head over heels for Melissa—confident she was his forever. *And she'd done this? With Damian?*

Her fingers flew across the screen.

Oh, Derek, I'm so sorry—I know how much you loved her. Are you okay? Where are you?

His reply came fast.

At the bar in Bondi, drowning my sorrows.

That made her pulse kick. Derek didn't cope well with heartbreak. He felt deeply, reacted quickly, and sometimes made choices he regretted later.

Stay where you are. You shouldn't be alone right now. I'm coming—don't move.

A beat of silence passed before the next message appeared.

I should have fallen in love with you, you're the best.

Sarah froze. Her breath caught in her throat. She knew it wasn't real—not really. Grief, shock, alcohol… they twisted words.

Please, Derek. Don't do anything until I get there. Promise me.

I promise.

She snatched her keys off the hook and rushed for the door, a knot of fear tightening in her chest.

Derek needed her. And she wasn't about to let him face this alone.

Sarah practically jogged down the crowded Bondi streets, weaving between tourists and locals as her heart thudded beneath her ribs. When she burst into the bar, her breath caught—Derek was still there. Slumped over the counter, shoulders bowed, fingers wrapped around a nearly empty whiskey glass. Relief washed over her, but it was thin, fragile.

"Hey," she murmured, sliding onto the stool beside him. "Come on, let's get you out of here."

Derek lifted his head, eyes glassy and unfocused. A slow, crooked grin tugged at his lips. "Sarah… my beautiful, loyal Sarah." His hand groped for hers. "Why didn't I see it before?"

She drew her hand back gently. "You're drunk, Derek. Let's go home."

Instead of standing, he tipped back the last swallow of whiskey, slammed the glass onto the counter, and lurched toward the exit. Sarah hurried after him, a cold knot tightening in her stomach.

"Derek, wait—let me call you a ride."

"I can drive." He was already fumbling with his car keys.

Sarah grabbed his wrist, holding tight. "No, you can't. You've had way too much."

He turned to her with a lazy, lopsided smile. The scent of whiskey rolled off him in waves. "You're cute when you're bossy," he drawled, leaning closer. "Maybe I really should've fallen in love with you. You actually take care of me."

Her throat tightened. "Derek, please. Don't start this."

"Why not?" He scrubbed a hand through his messy hair, his voice deepening. "You're gorgeous. You're smart. And you give a damn about me. Unlike her."

His jaw clenched. "Maybe if I'd been with you, I wouldn't be out here drinking like a fool."

Sarah swallowed the ache forming in her chest. She knew these words were soaked in alcohol and heartbreak—not truth. Derek, for all his charm, was spiralling.

"I'm flattered," she said softly, "but you're only saying that because you're drunk."

He smirked. "Drunk words, sober thoughts." His fingers brushed her cheek, featherlight, sending an unwelcome warmth through her skin. "If I kissed you right now… would you stop me?"

Sarah steadied herself. "Yes."

For a heartbeat, something in his eyes flickered—hurt? —but it vanished behind a chuckle. "Guess I had that coming."

Then, before she could react, he staggered toward the exit.

"Derek, wait!" She followed him, quick and desperate.

But he was already unlocking his car.

"Derek, please," she begged, stepping in front of the driver's door. "Let me call a ride. Let's just go home."

He paused, the dim streetlights catching on the raw grief in his eyes. Reaching out, he tucked a loose strand of hair behind her ear—an intimate gesture that made her breath hitch. "You really are the best," he whispered. "Too good for me."

She caught his wrist, gripping tighter this time. "Then don't make me watch you do something stupid."

For a moment—just a moment—she thought she'd reached him. His shoulders sagged. His jaw twitched. His eyes glossed with something like regret.

Then he exhaled sharply. "The only stupid thing I've done tonight is fall in love with a cheating bitch." And he yanked open the car door.

"No!" Sarah jumped in front of it again. "Derek, you're not thinking straight—"

But he was already sliding into the driver's seat, hands locking around the wheel. The engine roared to life, the vibration rattling through the pavement.

Panic burst through her. "Derek, please!"

His gaze snapped to her, dark and wounded. "Get in," he said, voice rough, "or stay here."

Her pulse slammed against her ribs. She couldn't let him drive alone—not like this, not when he was one wrong decision away from disaster.

She yanked open the passenger door and climbed in, heart hammering. As soon as her seatbelt clicked, Derek tore onto the road, the tyres screaming against the asphalt as the night swallowed them whole.

Then Derek lifted his phone and made a call.

Sarah's breath caught.

A man answered on the next ring, calm and unsuspecting. "Hey, Derek."

"She betrayed me, Jason." Derek's voice was rough, shredded with rage and heartbreak. "I can't believe she slept with him." His words broke off.

Sarah's pulse hammered. His hand strangled the steering wheel, knuckles bone-white.

"Derek," she whispered, leaning toward him, "please. Driving like this won't solve anything."

But he didn't hear her. His jaw was clenched so tightly the muscles jumped. His eyes—red, burning, lost—locked onto hers instead of the road.

"Why, Sarah?" His voice cracked. "Why would she do that to me?"

His gaze stayed on her, desperate and searching.

"Derek—watch the road!" Sarah cried.

A blaring horn split the night.

Derek snapped forward, swearing as he jerked the wheel. The car skidded violently to the right, tyres screaming over the slick pavement as they narrowly missed the headlights barrelling toward them.

Sarah slammed a hand against the dashboard, heart punching her ribs. "Derek, slow down—please—"

And then the sky opened.

Rain hammered the car in a relentless torrent, pounding against the windshield so hard the wipers smeared more than they cleared. The world outside dissolved into streaks of white and shadow, headlights smudged, road lines vanishing.

Sarah sucked in a sharp breath. Her hands clenched the seat. "Derek, you have to slow down!"

But he only laughed—a broken, bitter sound that made her stomach twist. His fingers trembled as he gripped the wheel.

"I loved her," he said, voice wrecked. "I was going to marry her. I would've given her everything."

Sarah reached out and touched his arm—lightly, carefully—hoping to anchor him. "I know you did, Derek. I know."

His entire body was taut beneath her hand; muscles coiled with anguish.

The rain intensified, pelting the car in sheets. The road shimmered dangerously, water pooling across the asphalt. The tyres hydroplaned for half a second—long enough for Sarah's breath to lock tight in her chest.

"Derek, please—pull over," she pleaded, her voice breaking. "This won't help. It won't make the hurt go away."

For the first time since they'd gotten in the car, something flickered across his face—pain, exhaustion, clarity fighting through the haze. His grip eased just a fraction. His shoulders shook with a long, unsteady exhale.

"Okay…" His voice dropped, hoarse. "I'm sorry, Sarah." He dragged a trembling hand through his hair. "I shouldn't have driven. It was stupid. So bloody stupid."

Sarah's throat tightened. This was the Derek she knew beneath the chaos—the one who cared deeply, even when he was falling apart.

He nodded once, almost to himself, as if trying to steady the storm inside him. "I'll pull over."

Relief flooded through her so fast she felt dizzy, her shoulders sagging as she finally exhaled.

Then—

The tyres slammed into a slick patch of water.

The car jolted violently sideways.

Derek's hands shot to the wheel, knuckles bloodless as he wrestled for control. "Shit—"

The car skidded, fishtailing as the rain intensified, pounding the windshield in blinding sheets. The road vanished beneath a smear of water, headlights, and shadow.

Sarah's breath hitched. "Derek—!"

But he was already fighting the skid, his arms locked, breath ragged. Panic shredded through his voice. "It's fine—I've got it, I've got it—"

He didn't.

The tyres lost their grip.

The world lurched, the car spinning sideways.

Headlights appeared—too close. Too bright. Too fast.

A horn ripped through the storm, sharp and terrified.

Metal screamed. The collision slammed into them like a sledgehammer.

Sarah's world exploded.

The impact threw her forward, the airbag erupting into her chest with brutal force. Her seatbelt snapped tight, biting into her ribs. The deafening crunch of steel folding in on itself swallowed every other sound.

Shattered glass burst around her like icy shrapnel.

A burst of white-hot pain shot through the side of her head.

Somewhere next to her—muffled, distant, as if through water—Derek was shouting her name, his voice raw with fear.

Sarah tried to respond, tried to move, but the world around her smeared and tilted, colours bleeding into darkness.

Her vision flickered.

The chaos dimmed.

And then—

Blackness swallowed everything.

Chapter Two

The antiseptic sting of the hospital corridor clung to the air, sharp and unforgiving. Jason Olander paced the length of the hallway, each footstep echoing back at him like a reminder he couldn't outrun. His mind kept replaying Derek's frantic call, every word carved into him with razor precision.

"She betrayed me, Jason. I can't believe she slept with him."

And then—faint, distressed, unmistakably female:

"Derek, please, driving like this won't solve anything."

A beat. Then Derek's voice, cracked and wild:

"Why, Sarah?!"

The line had gone dead after that. Jason had tried calling back again and again, each unanswered ring tightening the dread in his gut.

Now, under the glare of the fluorescent lights, dread had grown into something heavier—like a vice around his ribs, squeezing.

He stopped when a doctor approached—middle-aged, kind eyes, grim expression.

"Mr. Olander?"

Jason's throat tightened. This was it.

"Yes?" The word scraped out of him.

"I'm very sorry… but your brother didn't make it. His injuries were too severe."

The world seemed to tilt. Jason staggered back, catching the wall with his palm. For a moment, he couldn't breathe. *Didn't make it.* The words rang in his head, hollow and devastating.

Derek. His little brother. Twenty-five. Reckless, stubborn, full of life. Gone.

Five years ago, they'd buried their parents after a plane crash tore their world apart. Jason had sworn he'd protect what little family he had left.

But he hadn't been there tonight.

"Would you like to see him?" the doctor asked quietly.

Jason nodded because speaking suddenly felt impossible.

The trauma bay was cold—too bright, too sterile. Machines beeped in steady, indifferent rhythms. The hum of the fluorescent lights felt like mockery.

And Derek lay there.

Still. Silent. Peaceful in a way that hurt to look at.

Jason stepped closer, his heartbeat a thunderous echo in his ears. Derek's face wasn't twisted in pain; he looked almost asleep. But that stillness—that unnatural quiet—told the truth.

Jason's breath hitched. Memories crushed in: Derek laughing at something stupid, Derek calling him for help, Derek insisting he was fine when he wasn't.

And the bitter truth—Jason hadn't been around much lately. Work had swallowed him. Derek had been dealing with… something. Something Jason had brushed off, promising, *"We'll talk soon."*

There would be no soon.

Regret surged through him like acid, burning its way into every corner of his chest.

Then—slowly—regret sharpened. Hardened.

Turned into rage.

His mind flashed to the last call. To Derek's broken voice. To the woman's voice in the background—soft, pleading.

Sarah.

The betrayal. The cheating. The panic in Derek's voice. The way he'd sounded moments before everything went horribly wrong.

Jason's jaw clenched, anger building with terrifying clarity.

She had been there.

She had been with him.

She had pushed him to this edge. Hadn't she?

If she hadn't betrayed him…

If she hadn't hurt him…

If she hadn't been in that car—

The grief in his chest twisted hard enough to steal his breath.

Jason curled his hand into a fist. He didn't know the full truth—not yet. But he would. He had to.

And when he found out exactly what part Sarah played in Derek's final moments…

She would pay for it.

He couldn't do this. Not right now.

The walls felt as if they were closing in on him, the air too thin, too sharp in his lungs.

He needed answers.

Jason stepped out of the room where Derek now lay still and impossibly quiet, his legs moving on instinct alone. His thoughts were a violent storm—rage, disbelief, grief—each one crashing into the next. He barely registered the nurses rushing past, the chaotic urgency of the emergency department surging around him.

Until he saw her.

Sarah.

She lay on a stretcher, pale and streaked with blood, her lashes fluttering in a ghost of consciousness. A trauma team surrounded her, working in swift, coordinated motions, but Jason barely noticed their hands, their equipment, their urgency. His gaze tunnelled in on her—fragile, broken, surviving.

His chest clamped tight.

Who the hell was this woman?

What had she done to Derek?

His brother was dead. And she—this woman whose voice he'd heard pleading in the background—was still breathing.

Why?

Had she ever cared about Derek at all? Or had he been nothing more than a stepping stone, an inconvenience, another casualty of her selfishness? The questions burned like acid, feeding the fury rising in him.

A voice broke through the haze.

"Sir? Are you alright?"

Jason blinked. A nurse stood before him; concern etched in her expression. He forced something resembling composure.

"I'm fine." The lie was stiff, brittle.

She hesitated, then glanced down at her clipboard. "Are you Sarah Pratt's next of kin?"

The world seemed to pause.

Then cold resolve settled over him like armour.

"Yes," he said, his voice flat.

Her brows lifted slightly, but she accepted it without comment. "She's in critical condition. We're doing everything we can."

"Is she going to make it?" Jason asked, surprising himself with how steady he sounded.

"We hope so," the nurse replied, offering a practiced, reassuring smile before hurrying away.

Jason nodded absently, though beneath the veneer of calm his emotions churned violently. Grief. Fury. Something darker. Something he refused to name.

But one truth crystallised with chilling clarity:

He needed Sarah to survive.

Not out of mercy.

Not out of compassion.

But because she was the only one who could tell him what happened.

She was the key to the truth—and to the justice he intended to deliver.

He moved to the edge of the trauma bay, drawn in despite every instinct screaming at him to turn away. The room was a flurry of motion under the harsh fluorescent lights, every shadow sharp and unforgiving.

Monitors beeped in steady, urgent rhythms.

A doctor issued clipped commands.

Nurses adjusted IV lines, checked vitals, wiped blood from trembling skin.

The air was thick with antiseptic and the faint metallic sting of blood.

Sarah lay motionless amid the chaos, her skin ghostly against the stark white sheets. Bandages covered fresh wounds, red blossoming through the gauze. An oxygen mask hugged her face, fogging faintly with each fragile breath she managed.

Jason's pulse hammered, a primal reaction he couldn't contain. Every instinct warred within him—rage demanding justice, grief demanding answers, disbelief demanding explanations.

A nurse glanced toward him briefly, her eyes soft with empathy—and then she was gone again, swallowed by the urgency of saving Sarah's life.

Time stretched. Seconds felt like minutes, minutes like hours. Jason stood frozen, forced to watch as the woman he blamed for Derek's death hovered between life and death herself.

Powerless.

Helpless.

The cold reality settled over him like a shroud:

He couldn't touch her.

Couldn't question her.

Couldn't demand the truth.

Not yet.

All he could do was watch—and wait—while the woman who held the answers to his brother's final moments fought for her own life beneath the relentless glow of hospital lights.

Chapter Three

Sarah drifted in and out of consciousness, caught between jagged shards of pain and suffocating darkness. Shadows pulsed at the edges of her mind—voices rising and falling like distant waves—but she couldn't hold onto any of them. Everything felt muted, far away, as if she were submerged deep underwater, sinking faster with every heartbeat.

A rhythmic beeping cut through the void.

Fast. Uneven. Urgent.

"Sarah, stay with us!"

A voice sliced through the fog—firm, commanding, laced with fear.

She tried to answer, but her body refused to obey. Her limbs were heavy, foreign. Her head throbbed with a sharp, relentless ache that made thought impossible. She forced her eyes open, just for a heartbeat.

Blinding fluorescent lights.

Blurred figures in scrubs moving with frantic, precise urgency.

The world spun.

"She's got a collapsed lung!" someone shouted, voice strained with alarm.

Hands pressed against her body. Gloves. Cold metal. More voices—layered, urgent, overlapping.

The pain crashed into her all at once. A crushing pressure pinned her chest, each breath shallow and weaker than the one before. She tried to inhale, but the air wouldn't come. Her vision narrowed, darkness creeping inward like a closing fist.

No—she couldn't let go.

Not yet.

"She's fading!" another voice cut through the chaos. "We're losing her—get the chest tube in, now!"

Cold fear seized her, sharp and paralysing, but she couldn't move. Couldn't speak. Could barely cling to consciousness.

A hand closed around hers—warm, steady, anchoring her to the world.

"Sarah, can you hear me?"

The voice was closer now, softer but strained with urgency.

She tried to swallow, though her throat felt like sandpaper. Somehow, a whisper scraped out. "What...?"

"Stay with me, Sarah." The voice trembled—doctor, nurse, stranger—she couldn't tell. "You were in an accident. You're in hospital. You're going to be okay."

An accident...?

The words floated through her fogged mind, too heavy to grasp. Panic should have surged, but exhaustion smothered it, dulling everything to a slow, distant ache.

Nothing made sense.

Nothing connected.

A stabbing pain speared through her ribs when she tried to shift, ripping a broken cry from her raw throat.

"She's in distress," someone yelled. "We need to intubate—now!"

No—no, she didn't want that—she wanted to ask what happened, to beg them to stop—

But the world was slipping away again, faster this time.

The voices faded.

The pain ebbed into nothing.

The warmth on her hand drifted out of reach.

And then—

Silence.

Darkness.

Oblivion.

Jason paced the hospital's waiting area, a caged storm barely held together by thin threads of restraint. Every tick of the clock scraped against his nerves, stretching the minutes into something unbearable. His jaw ached from clenching, his foot tapping out a relentless, uneven rhythm against the cold tile. Questions—sharp, vicious, unending—swarmed his mind.

When the doctor finally approached, her expression marked by exhaustion and gravity, his breath caught. He straightened instantly, a knot of fear twisting deep in his gut.

"Mr. Olander?" she asked, her tone steady but cautious.

He gave a sharp nod, pulse pounding so hard it felt like it rattled his ribs.

"We've stabilised Sarah," she began. "She sustained multiple injuries—she's still unconscious. We had to intubate her due to a collapsed lung. There are several fractured ribs, extensive bruising, and a head laceration that required stitches."

Her words hit him like blows—each one precise, clinical, merciless. He absorbed them, but they felt strangely distant, muffled beneath the violent tangle of emotions tearing through him.

Anger.

Grief.

Helplessness.

And beneath it all, to his disgust—relief.

She was alive.

Derek wasn't.

His hands curled into fists, nails biting into his palms.

"Will she be okay?" he asked, though the question came out rough, almost guttural.

The doctor's expression softened just slightly. "It's too early to know. Until she wakes, we can't assess neurological function or the full extent of her injuries."

Jason went rigid. If she never woke up…

Then he would never know.

Never know why Derek ended the night dead while she survived.

Never know what happened in that car.

Never know what she did.

Derek was gone.

And the only person who might have answers lay unconscious behind a hospital door.

The doctor continued, "We're monitoring her closely. She's stable for now, but the next twenty-four hours are critical."

His chest tightened, breath coming shallow. Everything unsaid, everything unresolved, pressed down on him like a physical weight.

"Do you want to see her?" she asked quietly.

"Yes."

No hesitation. No doubt.

"Come with me."

Jason followed her down the sterile, too-bright corridor. The fluorescent lights hummed overhead, casting an unforgiving white sheen on everything they touched. The sharp scent of antiseptic clung to the air, seeping into his lungs with every breath. His steps felt heavy, each one pulling him deeper into a reality he wasn't ready for.

Collapsed lung.

Fractured ribs.

Head wound.

The words echoed in his skull, jagged and relentless.

At the door, the doctor paused, her voice cautious. "She's still unconscious," she reminded him. "But she's stable."

Jason barely registered the reassurance.

He stepped past her, into the room—

and into the sight of the woman who might hold the truth…

or the guilt.

The sight of Sarah lying motionless in the hospital bed hit him like a gut punch.

She looked impossibly small beneath the tangle of wires and monitors, fragile and exposed. Her skin was pale, almost ghostly, the dark sweep of her lashes stark against the bruising along her cheekbone. A thick bandage wrapped tightly around her forehead, contrasting sharply with the deep purple swelling that marred her temple. Each shallow rise and fall of her chest was laboured, only made possible by the tubes keeping her alive.

Jason exhaled shakily, running a hand over his face as he stepped closer. The steady, mechanical beeping of the monitors filled the silence, each pulse a grim reminder of how delicate her existence had become.

He froze at the edge of the bed, fingers twitching at his sides. He wanted—needed—to touch her, to confirm that she was real, that she was alive. But the sight of her like this, broken and vulnerable, made his stomach churn.

Anger flared, hot and sharp.

She had survived.

Derek hadn't.

A muscle in his jaw twitched as he stared down at her, scanning her face for answers she couldn't give. What had happened in that car? Had she betrayed Derek? Was she the reason his brother was gone?

His fists clenched so tightly his knuckles whitened.

He needed to know.

He needed her to wake up.

He needed the truth.

And he wouldn't rest until he had it.

Chapter Four

Sarah's eyelids fluttered open, the harsh fluorescent light overhead forcing her to squint. A dull, persistent ache pulsed through her body, each breath shallow and laboured. The steady beep of a heart monitor echoed in the room, mingling with the low hum of machines that hummed like distant, indifferent witnesses.

She blinked, letting her vision swim into focus. White walls. Sterile scent. An IV line taped to her arm.

A hospital.

Her stomach knotted. *Why am I in a hospital?*

"Oh my God, you're awake!" A warm, relieved voice pierced the haze.

Sarah turned her head with a soft wince. A woman in scrubs stood beside her bed, a bright, reassuring smile lighting her face.

"You gave us quite a scare," the nurse said gently. "How are you feeling?"

Sarah tried to speak, but her throat was dry and raw. She swallowed, forcing out a whisper. "I… I don't know."

"That's okay," the nurse said, producing a cup of water and guiding a straw to her lips. The cool liquid soothed her parched throat, but it did nothing to quell the uneasy flutter twisting in her stomach. Something was… off.

"What… happened?" Sarah rasped.

The nurse's smile faltered. "Let me get the doctor."

She returned only moments later with a young woman in a crisp white coat, serious and calm. Pulling up a chair beside the bed, the doctor studied her with steady eyes.

"Sarah," she began carefully, "I'm Dr. Carter. You're at St. Vincent's Hospital. You were in a car accident. You've been unconscious for two days."

A car accident. Unconscious.

The words hung in the air, heavy, alien, and uncomfortably final. Sarah's brow furrowed as she searched her mind for a fragment, a spark, anything—but there was only blankness.

"I… I don't remember that," she admitted, panic creeping into her voice.

Dr. Carter nodded, her gaze calm but probing. "That's not unusual. Head injuries can cause memory loss. Sometimes it returns gradually. Sometimes… it doesn't."

Sarah's breath caught. *Not at all?*

The room seemed to shrink around her, the sterile lights glaring down like accusatory eyes. She wanted to ask more, to demand answers—but the questions wouldn't form. Only fear and emptiness filled the space where memories should have been.

"Let's start with something simple," Dr. Carter said gently. "Can you tell me your name?"

Sarah hesitated for a heartbeat before answering, her voice weak. "Sarah Anne Pratt."

The doctor's lips curved in an encouraging smile. "Good. That's a great sign."

"Do you know what year it is?"

Her mind felt sluggish, foggy. After a pause, she whispered, "2025?"

Dr. Carter nodded. "And do you remember where you live?"

"Bondi," Sarah said slowly, testing the words.

Another approving nod. "That's all good, Sarah. Your general memory seems intact, but it's possible the accident itself is blocked out due to the trauma." She paused, then asked, "Can you tell me the last thing you remember?"

Sarah frowned, racking her brain. The last thing… what was it?

Flickers of memory flashed—her apartment, the scent of lemon cleaner, a buzzing phone… Damian.

And then nothing.

Her stomach twisted as she struggled to grasp the fragments. "Friday afternoon… I was home, cleaning," she admitted, voice uncertain. "And… I don't know. It's fuzzy."

Dr. Carter offered a calm, reassuring smile. "That's okay. Don't force it. Your brain is still healing."

Sarah inhaled sharply, wincing as pain knotted through her ribs. The beeping of the monitors quickened with her rising anxiety.

She didn't remember the accident.

Didn't remember how she got here.

Didn't remember—

Her chest tightened. A sudden, suffocating fear clenched her heart.

"Did anyone else… get hurt?" Her voice was barely more than a whisper, yet the urgency was undeniable.

Dr. Carter's expression remained neutral, too neutral, but something flickered in her gaze—something unreadable.

"There was a young man in the car with you," she said carefully. "He was driving."

Sarah's throat went dry. "Is he… okay?"

The doctor hesitated, a fraction of a second too long. Her face softened, voice quieter, almost fragile. "I'm so sorry, Sarah… Derek didn't make it."

The words landed like a physical blow, hollow and devastating.

Sarah blinked, struggling to comprehend. No. That wasn't right. Derek had been here. Alive. Laughing. Breathing. Loving.

Her breath caught. "Derek…" The name felt foreign on her tongue, a stranger's word in her mouth.

The room seemed to tilt. Pressure coiled in her chest, climbing to her throat.

"No," she choked, shaking her head. "No, that's not—"

But the doctor's gaze remained steady, unyielding.

A single tear slipped down Sarah's cheek, followed by another. Her chest constricted under the weight of grief, each inhale trembling and shallow.

"No…" The word came out fragile, broken, barely audible.

It couldn't be real. It didn't feel real.

Derek had been here moments ago—alive, present. And now… nothing.

A sob tore through her, raw and ragged. Her trembling hand flew to her face, but it did nothing to stem the flood of tears cascading down.

The doctor exhaled softly, gentle yet firm. "I'm so sorry," she murmured. "Just rest now."

She stepped back, leaving Sarah alone in the unbearable silence.

Sarah stared at the ceiling, vision blurred, body numb.

Derek was gone.

And she was still here.

The room seemed to shrink around her. Machines beeped, fluorescent lights hummed overhead—but it all blurred into a muffled haze, lost beneath the deafening silence swallowing her whole. The only thing she could feel was absence.

Derek's absence.

The space he should have filled was now cold and hollow, an ache so sharp it stole her breath.

Her fingers curled into the hospital sheets, trembling as she tried to anchor herself to something—anything—solid. But there was nothing to hold on to. Nothing but quiet. Nothing but loss. Nothing but the fragments of memories she couldn't reach.

She was alone.

And she didn't even remember why.

Her thoughts drifted, scattered, and unmoored, until something surfaced—faint but stinging.

Damian.

Friday.

He had broken up with her, hadn't he? She could almost hear his voice—sharp, tired, final. A blur of harsh words. A door closing. Was that why she'd been with Derek? Was that why her mind had sought refuge in his warmth, his easy kindness? The details hovered just out of reach, but the idea made a painful sort of sense. Even if it felt wrong. Even if she couldn't recall the moment itself.

The emptiness inside her stretched wider.

Not just because of Derek.

But because everything else—the memories, the accident, her purpose, her footing—had slipped through her fingers.

Gone.

Lost.

Like smoke dissolving before she could grasp it.

Her chest tightened at another truth; one she didn't need memory to remember:

She had no one.

Her father—gone before she ever knew him. Just a shadow in photographs.

Her mother—buried two years ago, leaving a hollow so deep nothing had ever filled it.

No siblings. No aunts, no uncles.

No family at all.

Untethered. Adrift. A single thread fraying in the middle of a vast, indifferent world.

Sarah had always survived. Losing her parents so young had forced her to stand on her own long before she was ready. Independence had become her strength, her armour—but also her isolation. It kept her safe, but it kept her alone. Derek… he'd been one of the rare few she'd allowed past her guard.

And now he was gone too.

Her eyes fluttered shut, exhaustion pulling at her like a riptide. The ache in her chest swelled, pressing hard against her ribs, suffocating her breath by breath. The crushing weight of heartbreak. The silence that made her ears ring. The emptiness that seemed to expand without end.

It was all too much.

Too heavy.

Too vast.

The world felt enormous—wide and echoing and unbearably empty—and she felt impossibly small within it, a single fragile point swallowed by grief.

Chapter Five

Jason arrived at the hospital Monday afternoon; his stomach tied in knots. The staff had informed him that Sarah was awake. Finally. Maybe now he could get some answers.

Inside, he immediately spotted the same doctor from Friday night. She saw him and approached, her expression a mixture of professionalism and cautious concern.

"You're here to see Sarah?" she asked.

"Yes," he said, his voice tight.

She hesitated, then continued. "I need to let you know—she's on the mend, but she doesn't remember the accident."

Jason's eyes narrowed. "What do you mean?"

"She has short-term memory loss," the doctor explained. "She can recall events leading up to the hours before the accident, but nothing about the incident itself."

How convenient.

His jaw clenched, suspicion curling like a hot knife through his gut. She remembered everything—except the one thing that mattered most. The one thing that could confirm what really happened that night.

"How long will that last?" His voice was low, edged with doubt.

"It's difficult to predict," she admitted. "For many patients, memory returns within days or weeks as the brain heals. But with head trauma, there's always a risk of lingering gaps."

Jason exhaled sharply, the uncertainty gnawing at him. It fed the tangle of grief, anger, and fear already suffocating him.

Her expression softened. "Mr. Olander, Sarah's injuries were significant. She'll need to stay here for at least two weeks for monitoring and treatment. After that, she shouldn't be alone—she'll require assistance during her recovery."

Jason stiffened. He hadn't thought that far ahead.

"Will you be the one looking after her?" the doctor asked gently.

A muscle in his jaw twitched. He knew nothing about Sarah's life—who she leaned on, who she trusted. Yet the thought of leaving her in someone else's care, before he had answers, stirred a deep unease in his chest.

"I… don't know," he admitted, his voice tight.

The doctor nodded, unshaken. "If necessary, we can arrange home health services or alternative care options to ensure she has the support she needs."

Jason barely registered her words. His mind had already spiralled back—Derek, the accident, the woman lying in that hospital bed, whose role in his brother's death remained maddeningly unclear.

"Don't push her for memories," the doctor added softly. "Let them return naturally."

Jason's gaze hardened. Naturally or not, he would know the truth. One way or another.

Jason stood just outside Sarah Pratt's hospital room; his hand pressed against the cold metal of the doorframe. His thoughts raced, a storm of grief, confusion, and rage swirling with no outlet. Every instinct told him to step back, to avoid facing her, but another part of him burned to know the truth.

The doctor's words echoed in his mind: *Don't push Sarah for memories. Let them come back naturally.*

How could he stand by? How could he not demand answers?

Questions clawed at him relentlessly. Did she remember the accident—or was that memory gone, buried under trauma? Did she remember everything that led up to it? Or was she hiding the truth behind her hazy recollection? Did she remember cheating on Derek?

Jason's jaw clenched, fists balling at his sides. Every part of him had resisted coming here, dreading this confrontation. And yet, here he was. He hated seeing her. Hated being near her. Hated that she was the reason Derek was gone—the reason his brother had spiralled, reckless and heartbroken, until the unthinkable happened.

Derek's words haunted him still, sharp, and raw: *"She betrayed me, Jason. I can't believe she slept with him."*

And then Derek was gone. Dead. Leaving Jason to drown in unanswered questions, a gnawing anger that had no release. Now, Sarah was alive—broken, fragile, confused—and standing there was like looking into a mirror reflecting everything that had shattered around him. She was the embodiment of all the pieces of Derek's life he couldn't put back together.

And still… he had to be here. He couldn't walk away. He couldn't pretend it didn't matter. The truth mattered. He needed answers. He needed to know why Derek had fallen apart. Why his brother had died.

Late at night, when the apartment was silent, Jason allowed himself the full weight of it—the grief, the guilt, the helplessness. Tears would come unbidden, stinging his eyes, his chest tight with the ache of loss. He had always been the protector, the older brother who carried the responsibility of keeping Derek safe after their parents' deaths. Losing him felt like failing in the one duty he had ever truly held sacred.

Taking a deep, steadying breath, Jason pushed open the door.

Sarah lay motionless in the hospital bed, her pale face delicate yet hauntingly beautiful, even in her fragility. Auburn hair spilled across the pillow in soft, tangled waves, a vivid contrast to the stark white sheets. The breathing tube was gone, leaving only the gentle rise and fall of her chest as proof of life. The bulky bandage that had wrapped her head was replaced by a smaller patch over the stitched wound. She looked fragile—like a porcelain figure, fractured and painstakingly pieced back together.

Despite her vulnerability, she seemed at peace, unaware of the storm raging in Jason's chest. It was as if the world had paused just outside the room, and the chaos of their lives hadn't yet reached her.

Jason hesitated, breath catching. For a moment, he couldn't ignore how beautiful she was. Timeless, magnetic—her full lips, the gentle curve of her cheek, the soft waves of her hair. His mind betrayed him with thoughts he didn't want to have, visions of lips he imagined kissing hers, though they unsettled him. She had been Derek's. And now, the sight of her stirred something dangerously complicated inside him.

No. He had to stay focused.

The doctor's words echoed in his mind: *Take it slow. Let her memories resurface naturally.* But following them felt impossible. How could he let her lie there while questions burned through him like fire? Why had Derek been in so much pain? Why had Sarah been involved? Why had his brother's trust and love ended in devastation?

And yet, deep down, he knew the truth in those words. Despite the simmering rage, despite the desperate need for answers, it wasn't his choice. It wasn't about him. It was about Sarah. Derek had loved her, trusted her, believed in her. And she had been at the centre of a pain Jason could barely comprehend.

How could he reconcile it all? The love Derek had held for her. The destruction it had wrought. The betrayal he felt now, standing at her bedside. His hatred for her seemed almost disloyal to Derek's memory, yet he couldn't help it. He needed to understand. He needed to see, to hear, to know.

Jason cleared his throat softly, careful not to startle her. "Sarah?"

Her eyelids fluttered open, and for a brief instant, confusion clouded her gaze. Then her eyes met his—dreamy blue, almond-shaped, and devastatingly alive. Jason felt an ache stir in his chest, a pang of something he couldn't name, twisting sharply through the remnants of his control.

Chapter Six

Sarah's gaze lifted from the stark whiteness of the hospital bed, drawn to the figure standing beside her. Her breath hitched as her eyes fell on him—the most striking man she had ever seen.

He was tall, his broad shoulders filling the space with quiet authority. Strength radiated from him—not just in muscle, but in the subtle, unshakable presence of someone who had endured and carried the weight of the world. His dark brown hair was slightly tousled, a few careless strands brushing his forehead, the rest swept back with effortless precision, framing a face that seemed carved from memory and something else—dangerous, compelling.

But it was his eyes that held her. Forest green, deep and unreadable, as if they carried centuries of unspoken truths. When they met hers, the world contracted, gravity shifting. She felt herself pulled into them; into a storm she had no hope of navigating.

Her gaze drifted to his jawline, sharp and resolute, and then to his lips—full, firm, carrying a restraint that made them all the more magnetic. Every feature demanded attention—not loudly, but with a quiet insistence that made her hyper-aware of herself, of every breath, every rapid beat of her heart.

For a heartbeat, the world blurred. Reality softened at the edges until only he existed. His face etched itself into her mind, startling in its clarity. And then a sudden, wrenching recognition hit her.

He looked like an older Derek.

Her throat went dry. The thought hovered there, fragile, and uncertain. "Hello… do I know you?" she whispered, voice trembling.

Jason's chest tightened. Words escaped before he could stop them, precise, soft, restrained. "I'm Jason," he said, steady, almost painfully calm. "Derek's brother."

The name landed in the room like a weight. Sarah's expression flickered—pain, raw and unguarded, cutting through the fragility she tried to maintain. Her eyes glistened, tears clinging stubbornly to their edges.

"Derek…" she breathed, the name heavy on her tongue, voice cracking as she gripped the sheets as though holding herself together. Jason's jaw clenched.

She's good, he thought—but the sorrow in her gaze gave him pause. It wasn't an act. It felt painfully, achingly real.

"I… I'm so sorry," she added, voice thick with emotion, a whisper meant to bridge worlds she hadn't yet touched.

Jason felt an involuntary jolt of sympathy, only for it to be replaced instantly by the anger that burned through him. She had caused Derek's death. She was the reason his brother was gone. He had to remember that.

And yet… the depth of her grief mirrored his own, reflecting back at him in a way that stole the breath from his chest.

He exhaled slowly, forcing his voice steady. "Thank you. I'm sorry too." The words felt foreign, heavy with necessity, precise in their measured restraint.

Sarah hesitated, her fingers curling around the edge of the hospital sheet. Her gaze flickered to his face, searching for judgment, anger, or understanding. "I— I can't remember what happened," she admitted, her voice a fragile whisper, raw in its sincerity.

Jason froze for a heartbeat; caught between the urge to demand answers and the careful restraint he knew he had to maintain. *Don't show your hand. Not yet.* His jaw tightened, and he forced his face into a mask of calm, though beneath it a storm raged—grief, rage, confusion, and the faint, dangerous tug of something he didn't want to admit.

The silence between them thickened, each second stretching like a taut wire. He watched her chest rise and fall, noticed the way her lashes swept across her pale cheeks, the faint tremor in her hand as it rested on the sheet. He wanted to reach out, to steady her—but he didn't. He couldn't.

"You've been unconscious for two days," he finally said, voice low and measured. "I've been getting updates on your condition." He paused, letting the words hang. Then, carefully, he added, "How are you feeling?"

Sarah exhaled slowly, a soft, rattling sound. "My ribs… they're really sore. My head still hurts." She forced a small smile, but it didn't quite reach her eyes. Her vulnerability tugged at something deep inside him—a mixture of empathy and frustration he hadn't intended to feel.

Jason nodded once, deliberately slow, and lowered himself into the chair beside her bed. He moved with control, each gesture precise, almost wary, as though leaning too far forward might tip the balance of this fragile moment. "How long had you known Derek?"

"Six months," Sarah replied, shifting slightly against the pillows, the faintest wince crossing her face. "Not that long, but… we hit it off straight away. I met him through a friend."

She had no idea how much Jason already knew about Derek's life—about Melissa, about the people who had shaped his brother's final days. But that didn't matter. It wasn't Sarah's place to tell him.

Jason studied her quietly, his eyes sharp, reading every micro-expression. Derek had never mentioned a Sarah to him. And yet here she was, lying fragile and exposed in a hospital bed, tangled in the aftermath of his brother's final, tragic moments.

He leaned back slightly, letting his posture seem relaxed while his gaze remained intense. "Were you close?"

Sarah didn't hesitate. "Yes." The word fell softly, yet it carried weight. Heavy meaning lingered in it, unspoken. Jason wasn't sure what kind—trust, affection, love—but he noted it anyway.

She thought she and Derek were close. She had confided in him, spent more time with him than Melissa ever did. Melissa had always been distant—always complaining, always pushing Derek away. Sarah had never understood why he loved her so much.

But love made people do foolish things.

Jason's eyes flicked to her, noting the curve of her jaw, the subtle warmth of her expression, the quiet strength in her voice. She was striking, undeniably so. Under different circumstances, that beauty might have disarmed him. But nothing mattered now. Because Derek was gone, and she was still here.

He pushed back in the chair, the motion deliberate, controlled. "I should let you rest."

Sarah lifted her gaze to him, her blue eyes soft, filled with a quiet sincerity that made something ache in his chest. "Thank you… for coming to see me," she said. Her voice was steady, though laced with emotion. "I'm really sorry about Derek. He will be missed… I'll miss him very much."

Her words were simple, but they carried a weight he hadn't expected. For a moment, he wanted to doubt her, to find an excuse to turn and leave with his anger intact. But as he looked at her, he realised with a sinking certainty—she meant every word.

Jason's jaw tightened, his throat constricting with emotion he refused to name. "Yeah," he said gruffly. "He will be missed."

Without another word, he rose, lingering only long enough to feel the fragile, raw humanity in the woman before him. And then he turned, letting the door close behind him, the soft click echoing like a punctuation mark to the fragile truth they both carried.

Jason had told himself he'd stay away. That once she was discharged, he could wash his hands of her—for good. Their lives would separate cleanly, the way they should have from the beginning. But the lie sat bitter on his tongue every time he repeated it.

Because he kept coming back.

Every second day for the past two weeks, he found himself standing at her bedside. Some days he brought flowers. Other days he brought nothing but the tight coil of emotions he refused to unravel. They talked about everything except the one thing that mattered most—Derek.

They talked about the weather. Her physical therapy. The book she was trying to read but couldn't concentrate on. They even talked about the kids she taught—stories that softened her features, made her eyes brighten with something warm and gentle.

But they never talked about Derek.

Jason told himself it was strategy.

That he was waiting for her memory to snap back into place.

Waiting for the truth to slip—unguarded, unfiltered—from her lips.

But deep down, beneath the anger and the grief, he knew better. Something in her presence unsettled him, tugged at him in ways he wished he could ignore.

One afternoon, as the pale winter sunlight slanted through the blinds and dust motes shimmered in the quiet room, he finally broached the subject that had been gnawing at him for days.

"The doctors think you'll be ready to go home soon."

Sarah blinked as if waking from a faraway thought. "Yes," she murmured. "I'm... looking forward to getting out."

Her voice held a quiet hope, but also something fragile—like she wasn't entirely sure what waited for her outside these walls.

Jason's chest tightened. She had no family. No siblings. No parents. No partner. No one to help her through the confusion and pain she couldn't remember. Her life was built around her classroom, around sticky-fingered hugs and children's laughter—not around people who could catch her when she fell.

"The doctors say you should have someone with you. At least someone checking in." His voice came out softer than he intended, almost careful. "How are you planning to manage?"

Sarah exhaled slowly, her fingers tracing absent circles on her blanket. "They're arranging for a nurse to stop by. Just to make sure everything's okay." She tried to sound matter of fact, but he heard what she didn't say. *I'm used to doing things alone.*

Jason hesitated. He had already made up his mind before he walked into the room but seeing her now—so composed on the surface yet clearly fragile underneath—doubt whispered at the edges of his resolve.

Still, he pressed on.

"I think you should come home with me."

The words left him more firmly than he'd intended. "Derek would have wanted me to take care of you. He wouldn't have wanted you to be alone."

Sarah froze. Her breath hitched.

Her eyes lifted to his, wide and uncertain.

"Home… with you?" she repeated slowly, as if trying to feel the shape of the words before accepting them. "I don't think…"

Her voice faltered, the rest slipping away as confusion clouded her expression.

Jason stepped closer, lowering his voice. "I know it's a lot. And I know you probably don't want my help."

Christ, I don't even know if I want to help you.

"But you don't have to decide right now. Just… think about it."

Her fingers tightened around the blanket, knuckles pale as she searched for stability. Vulnerability radiated from her—quiet, unintentional, disarming.

A long silence stretched between them, thick with everything unsaid.

Finally, she nodded.

"I'll think about it," she whispered. "But you don't have to do that."

Jason swallowed the bitterness rising in his throat and managed to keep his voice even. "Derek obviously cared about you," he said carefully, though the words scraped like sandpaper.

Loved you more than you deserved, you treacherous bitch.

"He wouldn't have wanted me to neglect you."

Sarah lowered her gaze, twisting the blanket between her fingers in a slow, unconscious rhythm. "Derek was a wonderful person," she murmured, her voice trembling with sincerity.

Jason nodded, forcing a steady breath. "Yeah. He was."

He hesitated, then added, "That's why I think you should come home with me."

Before she could respond, the door swung open, and a young male nurse stepped in, clipboard in hand, moving with an easy confidence that immediately set Jason on edge.

His spine stiffened. Every instinct screamed at him—*watch her, protect her, don't let anyone get close.*

The nurse's voice, warm and familiar, reached Sarah first. "Good afternoon, Sarah," he said, a practiced smile lighting his face.

Sarah returned it, a little too sweetly. "Hello, Peter," she said, her tone casual, almost fond.

Jason's jaw tightened, fingers curling into fists at his sides. He didn't like the way she looked at Peter, the small tilt of her head, the way her eyes softened around him.

Peter leaned in a fraction too close as he checked her vitals, his hand brushing hers more than necessary. His smile lingered, easy and practiced, but it made Jason's blood boil in a way he didn't expect. Irritation twisted through him, raw and unfamiliar.

It shouldn't matter; he told himself. Peter was just a nurse. Sarah—his brother's lover, the woman tangled in the tragedy of Derek's death—was nothing to him.

And yet, the sight of Peter's hand lightly skimming Sarah's wrist sent something sharp and possessive crawling up his spine. Jealousy, plain and undeniable.

Peter finally straightened, stepping back with a professional smile. "I'll be right back with your medication," he said, his tone smooth, lingering just a heartbeat too long on her before he turned to leave.

Jason's gaze followed him out, unblinking, a storm simmering beneath the surface. *I don't like that guy. Not one damn bit.*

The room fell quiet once Peter left, save for the faint hum of the monitors. Sarah's voice, soft and tentative, cut through the tension.

"Okay," she said, looking up at him, her eyes clear and steady. "I'll come home with you."

Jason's chest tightened, the words striking a nerve he didn't want to admit existed. He forced himself to remain composed, even as a flicker of relief—and something more complicated—rippled through him.

"Thank you," she added softly, her tone sincere, almost vulnerable. "I really appreciate it."

Jason didn't answer immediately. He nodded once, sharply, as if that alone was enough, stuffing his hands into his pockets. He fought to ignore the pull he felt toward her, the tension coiling through his chest, the way her presence made him aware of his own rapid heartbeat.

This isn't about her, he reminded himself, the thought like a mantra. *It's about Derek.*

His jaw clenched, and he looked away, forcing himself to remember why he was here. Every flicker of attraction, every surge of protectiveness had to be buried beneath the weight of his grief, beneath the memory of his brother.

Because Derek had loved her. And Derek was gone.

Everything else—the pull, the anger, the unbidden warmth—didn't matter. Not yet.

Chapter Seven

Sarah sat in the wheelchair near the nurse's station, her fingers curled tightly around the arms of the chair. Her stomach fluttered with nerves, a low hum of anxiety she couldn't shake. She had agreed to go with Jason—Derek wouldn't have wanted her to be alone—but the thought of leaving the safety of the hospital, of stepping into the unknown with him, left her unsettled.

Jason Olander was an enigma. Kind, in his own way, yet distant. Attentive, yet guarded. She couldn't quite place him, couldn't decide whether she should feel grateful for his presence—or wary. Being around him made her feel something unfamiliar, something that made her pulse quicken, her chest tighten in a way that scared her almost as much as it drew her in.

As she waited, Peter crouched beside her, holding out her new phone. Her old one had been lost in the accident, another small reminder of the chaos that had upended her life.

"I put my number in," he said with a playful grin. "Call me if you need anything."

Sarah hesitated, then smiled faintly. Peter's kindness was a lifeline, a tether to normalcy in a world that suddenly felt alien. "Thank you, Peter. That's very sweet of you."

But then a shadow fell over them.

Sarah's pulse skipped. She looked up—and there he was. Jason.

"Morning, Sarah," his deep voice cut through the moment, cool and measured, yet with an undertone that hinted at intensity. "You all ready to go?"

Her breath caught slightly. He was impossibly tall, effortlessly composed in dark jeans and a fitted button-up, his green eyes sharp, assessing, flicking between her and Peter with quiet authority. There was something about the way he carried himself that made it impossible to look away, something that made her simultaneously tense and strangely comforted.

Ignoring Jason's arrival, Peter gave her wheelchair a light push. "Let's get you outside."

Jason followed closely behind, silent, predatory in his calm. The hospital doors swung open, letting in the crisp afternoon air, scented with coffee and the distant hum of city life. Sarah blinked against the light, the breeze brushing her hair across her face.

Peter stopped at the curb and stepped in to help her rise. Sarah placed her hands on the armrests, slowly straightening, every movement cautious and deliberate. As she did, Peter leaned in, pressing a quick, friendly kiss to her cheek. "Take care, Sarah."

Jason's fists clenched at his sides, the tight coil of irritation rising like fire in his chest. *Every man in a fifty-kilometre radius? Is she a magnet?* Or does she even notice? He could feel it—the heat, the sharp edge of jealousy he couldn't quite explain.

Sarah smiled, polite and warm. "You, too, Peter."

Before Jason could respond, he closed the distance, palm sliding to the small of her back as he guided her toward the sleek black BMW parked at the curb. The warmth of her body seeped through the thin fabric of her dress, sharp and distracting against the cool bite of his frustration. She stiffened, just slightly, but didn't pull away. His fingers twitched instinctively before he wrenched himself back from the edge of feeling, forcing his focus where it belonged.

It shouldn't feel like this—not with her.

Focus.

He opened the passenger door, his touch firm but careful as he helped her inside. Sarah sank into the leather seat with a soft exhale, hands clutching the edge as if it were an anchor in this strange, new world. Jason closed the door behind her, the click of the latch sounding unnervingly final.

Sliding into the driver's seat, he started the engine, the low growl vibrating through the car. The ride out of the hospital was quiet, heavy with tension. Words hovered unspoken between them, their absence pressing against the edges of the car like the city outside pressing in.

Sarah kept her hands folded in her lap, eyes fixed on the passing scenery, but she could feel him watching her. Jason's grip on the steering wheel was steady, controlled, but the tightness in his jaw, the tension in his shoulders, betrayed the storm beneath.

Every stoplight, every turn, every subtle glance was a battle of restraint—for him, for her, for the memory of the brother she had lost, and the questions neither of them could yet speak aloud.

And in that quiet, suspended ride, Sarah with a shiver that this journey wasn't just about getting home—it was about navigating the fragile, volatile web of grief, anger, and unspoken truths that tied them together.

Fifteen minutes later, Jason eased the car into the underground parking of a towering high-rise. The space smelled faintly of concrete and tires, the echo of distant footsteps and the hum of ventilation filling the cavernous structure. He barely spared a glance at Sarah's wide-eyed expression as he swung open her door.

"Welcome home," he said, his voice low and controlled, as he helped her out. His hand brushed hers briefly, a small, grounding contact that made her pulse quicken despite herself.

Home. The word felt heavy in her mind. Home. Somehow, she knew—before even stepping inside—that this wouldn't feel like the safe, comforting place the word usually conjured.

The private elevator slid open smoothly, and Jason gestured for her to step in first. The doors glided shut behind them, enclosing them in a hushed, metallic cocoon. Sarah's fingers pressed lightly against the railing, her chest tight with a mix of anticipation and unease.

When the elevator doors finally opened, sunlight poured into a sleek, modern penthouse, spilling across the pale hardwood floors like liquid gold. Sarah stepped out cautiously, her breath catching at the sight.

Floor-to-ceiling windows stretched the full length of the living room, framing an impossibly beautiful view of Sydney Harbour. The Opera House's iconic sails glinted in the afternoon sun, and the steel curves of the Harbour Bridge seemed impossibly elegant against the shimmering water. Boats dotted the harbour, each one a tiny, moving jewel.

"You live here?" she whispered, the words escaping before she could stop them.

Jason's smirk faded as he watched her take in the space, so small, so fragile amidst the expanse of glass and steel. She looked like a bird in a cage, and he wasn't sure whether to protect her or leave her to fend for herself. Either way, she didn't belong here.

She followed him, her gaze darting across the open plan living area, drinking in every detail. A massive charcoal-grey sectional faced a marble fireplace, its sleek, minimalist design offset by the warmth of a large abstract painting hung above.

Hardwood floors gleamed under recessed lighting, and a glass coffee table sat neatly centred, reflecting the sunlight in shards of brilliance.

To the right, an elegant dining area featured a long oak table surrounded by black leather chairs beneath a sculptural pendant light. Beyond it, the kitchen was a study in contrast: dark cabinetry, white marble countertops, and stainless-steel appliances that gleamed like polished armour. Every detail screamed wealth, refinement, and control—the same qualities she felt radiating from Jason himself.

"Your bedroom is down this hallway," he said, leading her past a sleek black grand piano positioned near the windows. Its glossy surface caught the light, reflecting fragments of the harbour outside.

Sarah's fingers twitched at her sides, her curiosity fighting the prudence drilled into her by the accident, by Derek, by Jason. She ached to run her hands over the smooth, polished keys, to feel the music under her fingertips. Would she even get the chance? And more importantly—would Jason allow it?

The hallway stretched ahead, long and quiet, flanked by doors she assumed led to other bedrooms or perhaps an office. Jason's steps were silent, deliberate, measured. Sarah followed, the soft click of her heels against the hardwood sounding louder than it should have, echoing in the otherwise still space.

Finally, he stopped at the last door on the right. He pushed it open without ceremony, the subtle shift of air whispering into the room.

"This is yours," he said simply.

Sarah stepped inside, her heart skipping a beat.

The guest bedroom was just as luxurious as the rest of the penthouse. A king-sized bed, dressed in crisp white linens, commanded the space, flanked by minimalist nightstands that seemed almost sculptural in their simplicity. A plush navy-blue armchair sat near a smaller set of floor-to-ceiling windows, offering another breathtaking view of Sydney Harbour. Sunlight pooled across the polished hardwood floor, soft lighting adding warmth to the otherwise pristine room. It was spacious yet inviting, a balance of sophistication and comfort that made her feel both small and oddly protected.

Jason moved toward a second door and pushed it open. "There's an en-suite bathroom here."

Sarah peered inside, her breath catching. The space was vast and immaculate: a glass-enclosed rainfall shower beside a deep soaking tub, all set against walls of flawless white marble. A long vanity with double sinks gleamed under soft recessed lighting, gold accents gleaming like quiet luxury. Even the towels were plush, neatly folded, almost impossibly perfect.

"You have everything you need?" Jason asked, his tone flat, unreadable.

Sarah turned back to face him, still taking in the room. "This is… more than I expected."

Jason's gaze lingered on her for a beat, cool and measured. "Derek wouldn't have wanted you to be uncomfortable."

The mention of Derek sent a familiar ache twisting through her chest. Her throat tightened, and she ran a hand along the soft bedding, letting the luxurious fabric slip through her fingers. "Thank you, Jason. I'll try not to be too much trouble. I should be out of your hair in a couple of weeks."

He studied her silently, those green eyes sharp and unreadable, as if weighing every word. After a moment, he gave a short nod and turned toward the door.

"There's no rush. Get some rest," he said evenly, but the subtle tension in his tone made her wonder if there was more behind the words than he let on.

He paused at the door, glancing back. "I'll take you to your apartment later today so you can pick up some clothes, okay?"

Sarah's voice was quiet but steady. "Yes. Thank you."

Jason inclined his head once, then stepped out, closing the door softly behind him.

Silence enveloped the room, leaving Sarah standing in the middle of a life that didn't feel like hers, surrounded by a view too grand, too breathtaking, for the heaviness in her heart. She let out a slow breath, trying to steady the whirl of emotions—grief, relief, anxiety—all competing at once.

Needing a moment to herself, she stepped into the en-suite bathroom. The warm spray of the rainfall shower enveloped her, washing away some of the lingering exhaustion from the past week, soothing her sore ribs and aching muscles. Steam filled the room, curling around her like a protective cocoon.

By the time she emerged, wrapped in a plush towel, her eyelids felt impossibly heavy. She paused for a moment, letting the quiet sink in, then, without bothering to change, she climbed onto the king-sized bed. She curled into herself, the soft sheets and comforting weight of the duvet surrounding her and let sleep claim her almost instantly.

Later that afternoon, a soft knock echoed from Sarah's bedroom door. Jason paused, hand hovering, his pulse quickening slightly despite his best efforts to stay composed. When there was no answer, he hesitated, then pushed the door open gently, careful not to startle her.

His breath caught for a fraction of a second.

Sarah lay on top of the bed, wrapped in nothing but a towel, the soft fabric clinging to the curves of her body. Her auburn hair tumbled over the pillows in damp, tousled waves, strands curling at the ends from the shower. Her skin glowed in the soft light, and even in this private, unguarded moment, she looked effortless—stunning in a way that made the air feel thick with something he couldn't name.

Jason clenched his jaw, forcing a tight-lipped exhale. Focus. He had no business lingering here, no right to let his gaze wander. She was vulnerable, she was fragile, and above all, she was Derek's past. Not his.

For a long, painful beat, he just stood there, frozen by the contradiction of it all: her beauty and innocence, the woman he thought had destroyed his brother, and the undeniable pull she held over him. He could feel it—the same gravity that had drawn Derek in, that had led to so much heartbreak. And for a terrifying moment, he wondered if he was about to fall into the same trap.

The rational part of him won—or at least forced a semblance of control. He stepped back, closing the door softly behind him. His knuckles rapped against the wood a little louder this time. "Sarah? You awake?"

A faint shuffle answered him, then the door cracked open. She appeared, hair still damp and tousled from sleep, eyes heavy with drowsiness, cheeks slightly flushed. A tentative, uncertain smile tugged at her lips.

Jason forced his own smile, keeping his voice even, masking the tightness in his chest. "I thought I'd take you to get some clothes now."

She nodded, that same quiet smile lingering. "No problem," she murmured softly. "I won't be long."

As she disappeared into the bathroom to change, Jason ran a hand through his hair, exhaling sharply. The thought of going to her apartment—the life she had known before Derek's death—felt disorienting. He was stepping into her world, a world he had no right to understand, yet he needed to see it. Needed to understand her, and through her, perhaps a glimpse of Derek's final days.

His mind churned, circling questions he had been asking himself since the accident. How much had she mattered to Derek? Was she a fleeting presence, or had she been the heart of his world? Could seeing her life, her apartment, trigger the memories she'd lost? Could it reveal the truth he so desperately needed?

Ten minutes later, she returned, now dressed in the same black dress she had worn the night of the accident. Jason's eyes flicked over her, taking in the way she fiddled nervously with the hem, small gestures betraying the uncertainty she carried. She was close—so close he could smell the faint trace of her shampoo, soft and comforting, a scent that made his chest tighten for reasons he had no right to feel. He clenched his jaw, resisting the urge to brush a damp strand of hair from her cheek. *Focus, Jason. This isn't about you.*

She stood in the doorway, posture rigid, gaze slightly averted. For a moment, Jason saw just how delicate she was—not the dangerous, seductive woman he sometimes imagined, but fragile, broken, and unguarded. It stirred something inside him, something he had no permission to acknowledge.

The silence stretched, thick and heavy, the distance between them charged with unspoken tension. Finally, she lifted her eyes, offering him a soft nod. "Let's go."

Jason inclined his head once, forcing his voice steady. "Alright."

And together, they stepped into the world beyond the penthouse, each lost in their own thoughts, carrying grief, curiosity, and a fragile thread of trust that neither of them fully understood yet.

Chapter Eight

They left the penthouse together, stepping into the cool stillness of the underground carpark. Their footsteps echoed off the concrete, the space quiet enough that every sound—her soft breaths, the faint scrape of his shoes—felt amplified. Jason stayed close but not too close, watching the way Sarah moved.

She lowered herself into the passenger seat carefully, every motion controlled, her body betraying the lingering pain she tried so hard to hide. He saw it anyway—the slight grimace she tried to mask, the way she braced her hand against the door for balance. It twisted at something in him, something he refused to examine.

He shut her door gently and rounded the hood, climbing into the driver's seat. Once the engine hummed to life, silence settled between them. Thick. Heavy. Uncomfortable.

Jason didn't break it.

He couldn't.

His thoughts drifted—inevitably—to Derek. To his brother's laugh, his brother's stubbornness, the night of the accident. The darkness that had swallowed Jason whole ever since. Rage flickered low in his chest, a familiar burn, but sitting beside Sarah quieted something in him too, and he hated that he noticed.

The city passed by in a blur through the windshield: busy streets, crowds of people, the shifting glow of late afternoon light. After a long stretch of silence and tension, the air changed—the faint tang of salt drifting in through the cracked window.

Bondi.

The rhythm of the ocean whispered from a distance, soothing and relentless all at once. But the calm didn't touch Jason. His chest stayed tight, every muscle drawn taut with restrained emotion.

He parked the black BMW near a row of modest apartment buildings overlooking the beach. Sunlight shimmered off the water, waves rolling in perfect rhythm to the shore. Children laughed in the distance, a dog barked, the world kept moving—oblivious to the hollow ache that had carved itself into Jason's life.

"Here we are," he said quietly, nodding toward the complex.

It wasn't flashy or grand. In fact, it was simple—washed-out walls, a narrow staircase, a row of mailboxes that had seen better days. But the location? It was priceless. A small, humble slice of paradise. The kind of place that belonged to someone who valued beauty over luxury. Someone like Sarah.

Jason climbed out of the car and circled around to her side, offering a steady hand as she stepped out. She accepted it hesitantly, her fingers cool against his palm before she pulled away to adjust her balance.

Her silence clung to her like a second skin. She walked ahead of him, shoulders drawn, gaze downcast—not because she didn't want him there, but because every step seemed to take a piece of strength she didn't have much left of.

They climbed the stairs slowly. A soft breeze washed over them, carrying the familiar scent of saltwater, sunscreen, and something faintly floral—coming from her. The approach to her apartment felt strange, almost intimate, like he was stepping into a chapter of her life he had no right to read.

At the door, she fumbled with her keys. The sound of metal clinking against metal echoed too loudly in the narrow hallway. Her hands trembled slightly— not enough for most people to notice, but Jason saw. He saw everything.

Finally, with a soft click, the lock turned. She pushed the door open, and the small creak of the hinges seemed to split the silence between them cleanly in two.

And then...

The small, beachside apartment opened up before them—warm, lived-in, personal. A stark contrast to Jason's cold, pristine penthouse. A glimpse into who she was before the accident.

A glimpse Jason wasn't sure he was ready for.

Jason paused at the threshold, taking in the space. It was small, simple, unpretentious—a cozy living room with a compact kitchen tucked off to the side. A few framed art prints softened the walls, each hinting at her personality in quiet, careful strokes. No luxury. No excess. No sign she'd ever lived any other life but this one.

It was just... her.

"Do you rent?" Jason asked casually, though a tightness tugged at his voice, betraying the tension coiled beneath.

Sarah's lips curved into a faint, wistful smile. "No, I own it. My mother had life insurance, so I used it to buy the apartment." Her gaze dipped to the floor, the shadow of old grief settling over her features.

Jason shifted, discomfort rippling through him. He couldn't shake the need to understand her—her life, her choices, her connection to Derek. This space was quiet, grounded, almost painfully ordinary… and it still didn't give him the answers gnawing at him.

He looked toward the windows, the glimmer of the beach stretching just beyond the glass. "It's nice," he murmured, though the word felt too small, too pale, to describe the stillness here.

Sarah's eyes tracked around the room, her expression soft but threaded with a quiet ache. "It's… home." When she met his gaze, something fragile flickered there—a loneliness she tried to hide but couldn't quite bury. "Thank you for bringing me," she added, her voice barely above a breath.

Jason nodded, his throat tight. "Take a few minutes to grab what you need. I'll wait here. If you need help, just call out."

As she disappeared down the short hallway, Jason stayed rooted to the spot, his gaze drifting around the room. It was personal—soft blankets, neatly stacked books, a faint lavender scent lingering in the air. But there were no pictures of Derek. No mementos. No trace of a relationship, not even a hint of a man ever sharing this space.

The absence hit him harder than he expected.

Sarah emerged from the bedroom a few minutes later with a small bag, packed neatly but lightly. She'd kept it simple—just enough clothes for a couple of weeks. She knew this stay at Jason's penthouse was temporary, an obligation he carried because of Derek. Nothing more.

"I'm ready," she said quietly, holding out the bag.

Jason took it, surprised by its weight—or lack of it. His brow creased. "You're sure you have everything?"

She offered a small nod. "Yes. I should be okay to come home in a couple of weeks."

Jason hesitated, studying her face with a searching intensity, as if he could pull the truth straight from her skin. "Have you remembered anything about the accident?" he asked gently.

Sarah's shoulders dipped. She shook her head, frustration edging her voice. "No… sorry. I wish I could. I want to know what happened, too." Her fingers toyed nervously with the hem of her dress, a small gesture that spoke louder than her words.

It was Monday, and the apartment lay in a soft hush, the kind that settled into corners and wrapped around her like a thin veil. Sarah sat curled on the couch, her thoughts scattered and restless. Jason had left early that morning—*just a few hours at the office*, he'd said—but she was still reeling from what she'd learned the day before.

He was a CEO.

Of a major tech company in Sydney.

The revelation had surprised her more than it should have. She had only known Derek for six months—a handful of coffees, a few shared jokes, a growing friendship that had been natural and easy—but he had never spoken much about his family. He'd hinted at an older brother, but he'd never mentioned the scale of Jason's world, or the pressure he lived under. She now wondered what else she hadn't known, what pieces of Derek's life she had only glimpsed without ever seeing the full picture.

Her gaze drifted to the coffee table where a small white card rested, stark and quiet—the details of Derek's funeral. *Tomorrow.* The word hollowed something inside her.

Jason had told her last night, his voice controlled but his grief barely contained.

She had nodded. Tried to be strong.

She wasn't.

The news had struck her harder than she expected. Six months wasn't long— not compared to the years others had shared with him—but in that time, Derek had become a bright spot in her life, someone she trusted, someone she laughed with, someone who made her feel seen. And now he was gone.

And the worst part was… she couldn't remember the last moments she'd spent with him. Couldn't recall the sound of his voice in the car, the words he'd said, the expression on his face. Those memories—so few to begin with—had been stolen from her, leaving only empty spaces where answers should have been.

Regret twisted inside her.

She had meant to open up to him more.

To tell him what his friendship meant.

To stop holding back out of fear or hesitation.

But now that chance was gone.

Tomorrow, she would have to stand among the people who had truly known him—his family, his childhood friends, the ones who had loved him for years—and she would feel like an outsider. She wasn't sure what hurt more, losing him, or feeling like she didn't have the right to grieve as deeply as she did.

She rose from the couch, her movements slow, and crossed the room to the window. The city buzzed below her—cars weaving through traffic, people moving with purpose, the world continuing without pause. She felt disconnected from all of it, as though she were standing on the outside looking in, trapped behind the glass.

Her palm pressed lightly to the cool windowpane.

What happened that day?

She reached for the memories again, desperation clawing at the edges of her mind. But the harder she tried, the faster they slipped away—like mist dispersing in sunlight.

The emptiness in her mind terrified her.

Six months of friendship, gone in an instant.

And the final minutes—the ones that mattered most—were sealed behind a wall she couldn't break.

She turned away from the window, needing something solid beneath her hands. Her eyes fell on the piano, its glossy surface reflecting the soft afternoon light. A small breath escaped her—part relief, part longing.

She walked toward it and sat down, her fingers hovering over the keys. For a moment, she hesitated. Then the first notes drifted into the air—fragile, searching.

Music had always been her refuge.

Her mother's encouragement.

Hours of practice that once felt tedious but now offered comfort.

A connection to a part of her life untouched by tragedy.

As she played, her breathing steadied. The melody spread through the room, filling the silence, smoothing the jagged edges of her thoughts. Here, she didn't need to explain her grief or justify it. She didn't need to remember the accident or confront tomorrow.

For a little while, the music held her together.

For a little while, she wasn't falling apart.

The lift doors slid open with a soft whisper, and Jason stepped into the penthouse—only to be met by the unmistakable swell of music drifting through the space. He stopped mid-stride.

Piano.

Not just someone tapping out a tune.

Not a hesitant, uncertain melody.

This was *beautiful*—fluid, aching, precise. The kind of music that slipped under the skin and pulled something tight in the chest.

Drawn in despite himself, Jason followed the sound through the open living space. When he reached the living room, he froze.

Sarah sat at the grand piano, her back straight, her eyes closed as if the world beyond the keys didn't exist. Her fingers glided effortlessly, each note delivered with the confidence of someone who had spent years—decades—learning how to make emotion audible. The melody rose and fell, delicate and haunting, filling his home with a kind of beauty it had never known.

For a long moment, Jason didn't move. He hardly breathed.

He'd always considered the penthouse too quiet, too polished, too empty. But now… it felt alive. Like the music had seeped into the walls, softening something inside him he had tried so damn hard to keep locked away.

He didn't want to break the moment.

Didn't want her to stop.

For the first time in days, his grief quieted. His anger eased. And in its place was something he wasn't ready to name.

The last notes drifted into the air, humming softly before dissolving into silence. Sarah's lashes fluttered open—then widened when she saw him standing there, watching her.

She jolted to her feet, startled and embarrassed, moving too quickly.

Pain tore through her, sharp and unforgiving.

"Aah—" The sound escaped before she could smother it.

Jason reacted instantly, crossing the room in two long strides. He caught her before she stumbled, his hands firm around her arms, steadying her with a gentleness that startled them both.

"Easy," he murmured, his voice low, soothing. "Careful."

He guided her to the couch, lowering her down slowly, as though she might shatter if he wasn't cautious. Her fingers clutched his forearms for balance—warm, fragile, trembling. Jason felt his muscles tense beneath her touch, a jolt of heat he tried to ignore.

She shivered, and he noticed.

"Thank you," she whispered, breathless, her eyes lifting to his.

He sat beside her, not too close but not far enough to hide the intensity in his gaze.

"When did you learn to play?" he asked, his voice rougher than he intended. "You're... incredible."

A faint flush touched her cheeks as she looked down at her hands. "My mother taught me. And her mother taught her. It was our thing." She smiled softly. "It always felt natural. I loved it."

Jason nodded slowly, his gaze dropping to her fingers—slender, elegant, made for the keys.

"It's a shame you don't play more often."

She gave a small laugh. "I play a little at the kindergarten, but... my audience prefers songs about rainbows and dinosaurs. Classical music is a hard sell."

Jason's lips twitched. "I can imagine."

"I did manage to turn Für Elise into a sing-along once," she added, her tone playful.

He actually laughed—quiet, genuine. It felt strange in his chest, that small moment of levity. Foreign. But welcome.

The laughter faded, replaced by something heavier. Something charged.

Her fingers still rested lightly against his arm—she hadn't pulled away. Maybe she hadn't even noticed. But he had. Every point of contact. Every soft breath she drew. Every slow lift of her lashes.

The room dimmed around them, shadows soft and warm, highlighting the curve of her cheek, the auburn shimmer in her hair, the vulnerability in her eyes.

Jason's heartbeat kicked hard against his ribs.

This was wrong.

She was Derek's friend.

She was staying here because she needed help.

He had no right to feel anything.

But God—he felt *something.*

Too much.

He stood abruptly, putting space between them. A breath. A barrier.

"I should… check some emails," he said, the words stiff, unconvincing even to his own ears.

Sarah blinked up at him, the faintest flicker of disappointment crossing her face before she masked it. "Oh. Right. Of course."

Jason nodded once, then turned away—before he could do something he would regret, something he wouldn't be able to take back.

But as he walked toward the hallway, the music she had played lingered in the air.

It followed him.

Clung to him.

Settled under his skin.

And no matter how hard he tried, it wouldn't let him go.

Chapter Nine

The day of the funeral arrived, heavy and suffocating, a grey sky pressing down on the city as if the world itself mourned. Sarah dressed with deliberate care in a simple black dress, the fabric hugging her slender frame in a way that felt almost constricting, a reminder of the fragility she couldn't escape. She wore no makeup—today, it seemed unnecessary, even wrong. Her bag was stuffed with tissues, though she hoped she wouldn't need them all.

Taking a deep breath, she stepped into the living room, where Jason waited. He stood near the window, his back rigid, shoulders squared, the city sprawling below him like a silent witness. He didn't move when she entered, didn't acknowledge her presence immediately. When he finally turned, his face was unreadable, sculpted in that mask of controlled calm he always wore.

But his eyes betrayed him.

For the briefest heartbeat, something raw and unguarded flickered there. Shock, sorrow, perhaps a glimpse of the anger he rarely let anyone see. He took her in—the simplicity of her black dress, the absence of artifice, the way her hands clutched the strap of her bag. She was delicate, exposed, and painfully human.

"You're ready?" His voice was low, steady, but the tightness in his jaw gave away the strain beneath.

She nodded, swallowing past the lump in her throat. "Yes."

He didn't respond immediately, only studied her with an intensity that made her feel simultaneously scrutinized and oddly protected. Jason's eyes searched hers as if looking for a truth she couldn't give. For a moment, the silence was unbearable, and then, with a quiet authority, he turned toward the door. "Let's go."

The drive to the cemetery was suffocating. The air inside the car was thick with tension, each inhale a reminder of everything unspoken between them. Sarah stared out the window at the blur of city streets, her stomach twisting with anxiety. She didn't know how people would react—would they stare, whisper, blame her?

Jason said nothing, his hands gripping the wheel so tightly his knuckles gleamed white. His jaw was set, the rigid posture of a man bracing himself for the storm outside and the one still roiling inside.

When they arrived, a sea of mourners dressed in black filled the cemetery, their movements hushed, faces solemn, voices carrying quiet condolences that seemed distant to Sarah. Her chest tightened as she spotted Derek's framed photo by the casket—his smiling face frozen in time, a cruel reminder of everything she had lost.

Jason moved through the crowd with careful politeness, nodding, shaking hands, murmuring thanks, but his mind was elsewhere, caught in the relentless loop of anger, guilt, and grief. Every glance at the coffin, stark and immovable, dragged him back into the night that had changed everything.

Beside him, Sarah sat on the folding chair with her back straight, hands folded tightly in her lap. She didn't fidget, didn't glance around at the mourners, only stared ahead at the coffin as if willing herself not to crumble. But Jason saw the tension in her shoulders, the subtle tightening of her fingers as they clutched the fabric of her dress. Knuckles whitening. The faint tremor of someone holding back tears.

The cuts along her arms and legs—fading now, still healing—were reminders of that night, the night that had stolen Derek from them both. She had survived; he had not. And though logic screamed that she hadn't intended this, the ache of loss twisted into a sharper, rawer edge each time Jason looked at her.

He exhaled slowly, forcing himself to focus as the service began. The priest's voice was calm, steady, offering words meant to console, but Jason felt nothing. Only the hollow, gnawing weight of what was lost—and the quiet, unspoken questions he couldn't yet voice.

When Derek's friends and colleagues stepped forward, recounting stories of his humour, his loyalty, the way he could light up a room, Jason felt his throat tighten as though it were filled with stone. Each memory, each fond anecdote, hammered home the truth he could barely accept: his brother had been larger than life, fearless in the pursuit of happiness, untethered by hesitation—and now he was gone.

Sarah barely moved beside him, but when someone spoke of Derek's generosity, a shaky breath escaped her lips. Jason's gaze flicked to her, noting the subtle tremor of her fingers as they clenched tighter in her lap, the way her shoulders tensed, the almost imperceptible quiver of her jaw. Tears traced silent paths down her pale cheeks, glistening in the soft light of the cemetery.

Did she remember something? Did the ghost of guilt stir within her?

She should feel guilty.

The thought came unbidden, heavy and unforgiving, and instead of pushing it away, Jason let it simmer, feeding the storm of grief and rage that had been coiled inside him for so long.

Then, the officiant called his name.

Jason stood, feeling the taut weight of all those watching settle across his shoulders. The crowd's eyes followed him with quiet expectation, yet he couldn't prepare a speech. How do you encapsulate a life like Derek's? How do you string together words for someone who lived too fast and too fully, someone who was gone far too soon?

He exhaled slowly, gripping the edges of the podium, letting his gaze drift over the mourners before settling finally on the coffin.

"My brother was reckless," he began, his voice rough, carrying the raw edges of grief. "Impulsive. Stubborn as hell." A sad, fleeting smile tugged at the corners of his mouth before fading. "But he was also kind. Loyal. And he loved without hesitation."

His gaze flickered toward Sarah for a fraction of a second before he forced himself to look away, the sight of her so close, so painfully alive, igniting a turmoil he couldn't name.

"He wasn't perfect, but he lived," he continued, each word measured, each pause weighted. His throat tightened, and he swallowed hard, the taste of salt and bitter grief rising in his mouth. "And he should still be here."

The final words hung in the air, jagged and raw, piercing the quiet like a blade. Jason barely managed to step away from the podium before the grief clawed at his chest, his fists clenching so tightly at his sides that his nails dug into his palms. His body trembled slightly, a physical echo of the storm roiling inside him, and he struggled to keep his composure as the ache of Derek's absence pressed down, relentless and unyielding.

When he returned to his seat, Sarah remained motionless, her gaze fixed ahead, her face hidden beneath the veil of silent tears. She didn't speak, didn't reach for him. And yet, her presence was a weight beside him—heavy, unspoken, a reminder of everything lost, of everything he still didn't understand. He could feel it pressing against him, a quiet accusation, a fragile plea.

When the funeral ended, Jason led her toward his car, the gravel crunching underfoot the only sound in the subdued chaos of the departing mourners. But Sarah suddenly froze, her body stiffening as if rooted to the spot. Jason followed her gaze, noting the sharp intake of her breath.

A man held a crying woman, his arm wrapped protectively around her, his hand firm at her back. The scene was ordinary, domestic, yet Sarah's reaction was anything but.

Jason looked down at her, watching her expression shift—hurt, surprise, something else he couldn't name. Confusion? Recognition? Her fingers tightened at the fabric of her dress, knuckles whitening, as if she were trying to ground herself against a memory she couldn't quite reach.

"What's wrong?" he asked, keeping his voice steady, though tension coiled in his chest.

She startled at his words, blinking rapidly before glancing up at him, eyes wide and searching. "I'm… not sure," she admitted, her voice small, fragile.

Jason studied her carefully, sensing layers of emotion beneath her words—grief alone didn't explain the sudden rigidity, the way her body seemed to hum with unspoken awareness. "Do you know them?" he pressed gently.

She hesitated, her eyes flickering toward the couple before returning to his. "Yes. That's… Melissa and Damian."

The names meant nothing to Jason, but her reaction did. Something buried deep stirred in her—a memory on the edge of consciousness, just out of reach. "Do you remember something?" he asked, his tone softer now, almost pleading.

She met his gaze, tear-streaked and sorrowful, but shook her head. "No," she whispered, frustration lacing her words. "I wish I did."

"Who are they?" Jason asked, his voice low, controlled, but with an edge of urgency.

"Friends," she replied quickly, too quickly, her tone clipped. There was hesitation in the pause, as if she were debating how much to reveal—or conceal. Jason's gut tightened. Something wasn't right.

Before he could press further, Melissa and Damian's attention shifted toward Sarah. Guilt flickered across their faces, brief and sharp, before Damian tightened his hold on Melissa and began leading her toward the parking lot.

Sarah's breath hitched beside him, and Jason could feel the tension radiating off her in waves. Her hands gripped his arm for a brief instant—so slight, so fleeting—but enough to make his jaw clench.

"Why is Damian with Melissa?" she murmured, more to herself than to him, her voice trembling despite her attempt at calm.

Jason didn't have an answer. But watching the couple retreat, one thing became painfully clear: Sarah wasn't just another grieving friend. She was part of this puzzle—whether she remembered it or not—and the answers she might hold could change everything.

He kept his gaze on her, on the tight line of her shoulders, the way her lips pressed together as if holding back more than words could express. And for the first time since the funeral began, he felt the raw pull of urgency—not just for Derek's memory, but for the truth she carried, buried deep within the fragments of her own mind.

The drive back to the apartment was heavy with silence. The city passed by in a blur of muted lights and shadows, the soft hum of the engine the only sound between them. Jason stole glances at Sarah from time to time, noting the furrow of her brow, the way her lower lip caught between her teeth, the subtle tremor of her hands resting in her lap. Confusion, uncertainty, grief—all of it etched across her face. She was trying to grasp something just out of reach, and it made him uneasy.

She didn't speak, and he didn't push—not yet.

His hands tightened around the wheel, knuckles white as his mind replayed the funeral scene over and over. Melissa and Damian. The guilt in their eyes. The way they had turned and left the moment Sarah looked their way. Something didn't fit. Something was off.

And at the centre of it, whether she admitted it or not, was her.

When they pulled up to the apartment, Sarah moved without a word, disappearing into her room. Jason lingered in the living room, torn between giving her space and checking on her. He exhaled slowly, his chest tight with a mixture of frustration and concern and started toward his own room.

Then he heard it.

A muffled, raw sob, trembling and unrestrained, seeping from the walls between them. His chest constricted.

He froze, hands clenched at his sides, unsure what to do, unsure if he had the right to cross that boundary. But the sound—the vulnerability, the heartbreak—pulled at something deep within him, overriding every caution.

He knocked softly, waiting a beat before nudging the door open. There she was, standing in the middle of her room, eyes red-rimmed, cheeks blotchy, shoulders trembling. She didn't speak. He didn't need words.

He reached for her, pulling her into his arms.

She didn't resist.

Her fingers dug into the fabric of his shirt, clutching him like a lifeline as she buried her face against his chest. Her body shook with the force of her grief, and Jason exhaled, forcing his anger, his doubt, all of it to the back of his mind. None of it mattered in this moment.

They needed this. They needed someone.

So, he held her. Tightened his arms around her as if letting go would shatter them both. The room faded, leaving only the rhythm of their breaths and the quiet thrum of raw emotion between them.

When her sobs finally slowed, she pulled back slightly, just enough to look up at him. Her tear-streaked face was inches from his, eyes glistening, fragile and unguarded. Her lips trembled, as if words were trapped there, unspoken.

"Thank you," she whispered.

Jason said nothing. He simply looked at her—really looked—taking in the curve of her jaw, the softness of her expression, the way the vulnerability in her eyes made his chest tighten even further.

He should have stepped back. Should have maintained the distance, reminded himself of every reason this was a bad idea. But every instinct told him not to move, not to break the fragile connection that had formed between them.

And before his mind could warn him, before caution could claim him, he lowered his head.

Their lips met.

A kiss that neither of them had anticipated, yet one they couldn't pull away from, even if they wanted to.

It was soft at first—tentative, almost a question—but when she responded, it deepened. The kiss carried the weight of grief, the pull of shared loss, the tension of unspoken truths. It was reckless, wrong, impossible. And yet, in that fragile, fleeting moment, it was exactly what they both needed.

The world seemed to stop. Time slowed, the air thick with something neither of them could name. It wasn't careful or hesitant—it was raw, desperate, edged with the ache of sorrow neither could articulate. Each movement was a silent plea to feel, to touch, to connect with something that wasn't pain.

Jason's arms wrapped around her, firm yet mindful of her injuries, holding her like she might shatter if he let go. Her fingers clutched at the fabric of his shirt, anchoring herself as though he was the only solid thing in a world that had fractured. He felt her warmth, soft and electric, searing through the tension he had built around his heart.

The kiss shifted, urgent, searching—frantic even. She tilted her head, pressing closer, letting herself drown in him, and Jason let her—because, God help him, he was drowning too. The lines between grief, guilt, and desire blurred, leaving only the raw pulse of need that neither could deny.

She wasn't supposed to feel like this. He wasn't supposed to feel like this. It was wrong. It was dangerous. And yet, in the heat of it, it felt unbearably right.

Then, as suddenly as it began, it ended.

Jason tore himself away, breathless, staring at her with a shock that left his chest tight and his mind spinning. The air between them was electric, charged with the weight of what had just happened. Neither spoke. Neither moved. But the storm was already brewing.

His pulse hammered in his ears, his heart ragged, breath mingling with hers for one brief, fleeting moment before separation became reality. His hands itched to pull her back, to press the kiss further, to claim what he shouldn't. But then reality slammed into him like a cold fist:

What the hell had he just done?

She was tied to Derek. She was part of the tragedy he couldn't forgive. And yet… he had kissed her. Needed her. Wanted her.

Disgust churned in his stomach—not just at himself, but at the betrayal of everything he believed, everything he had promised himself.

His jaw tightened, his hands balling into fists, trembling with the effort to restrain the chaos inside him. He needed space—needed distance before he did something even more catastrophic.

Without a word, he stepped back, as if burned, and turned on his heel. His movements were stiff, precise, each step measured to prevent him from losing control, from throwing reason to the wind. He reached the door and closed it quietly behind him—but the sound did nothing to quiet the truth gnawing at his mind.

He had kissed her.

In his room, the anger and confusion hit him in waves. He ripped off his tie, yanked at the buttons of his shirt, shaking with a need to shed the weight of what had just happened. His chest heaved, breaths sharp, uneven. Every nerve in his body screamed at him—this was wrong, catastrophic, insane.

And yet… her lips still lingered on his. Her taste, sweet, maddening, a memory that burned hotter than guilt, hotter than grief.

He turned to the mirror, and the reflection that stared back was a stranger—haunted, furious, conflicted. His hand trembled as he pressed it against the glass, as if trying to physically hold himself together. He wanted to scream, to hit something, to erase the taste, the feel, the memory.

But he couldn't.

He had kissed her. He had wanted to.

And worst of all…

He wanted to do it again.

Chapter Ten

The next morning, Sarah stepped into the kitchen, her stomach growling as she scanned the cupboards and fridge. She moved almost mechanically, grabbing a few pieces of fruit, a slice of toast, and a cup of coffee. She had lingered in her room until she was certain Jason had left for work, unwilling—too anxious—to face him after what had happened the night before.

Her mind kept circling back to the kiss—its intensity, its suddenness, the way it had left so many questions hanging in the air like smoke. The memory of his lips pressed against hers, firm yet gentle, haunted her. It was impossible to ignore, yet equally impossible to decipher. The confusion weighed heavily, pressing down on her chest, and the silence between them now seemed louder than any words could ever be. She knew she couldn't hide forever, but the thought of confronting him—or being confronted—made her stomach twist.

She had never been kissed like that before. Damian's kisses had been fleeting, perfunctory, leaving no mark, no echo. Jason's kiss had been different—raw, consuming, and unsettlingly intimate. Her pulse had raced, her breath had hitched, and for the first time in months, she felt unmoored, unsteady in ways she didn't fully understand. It had shifted something inside her, leaving her emotions tangled, vulnerable, and wide open. Everything felt altered, as if the ground beneath her had tilted on its axis, and she didn't know how to find her footing.

She set her mug down on the counter, running a hand through her hair as if the simple motion could steady her. Then came the knock at the door. Sarah froze, heart hammering in her chest. She hadn't expected anyone—no visitors were planned. Her fingers lingered on the edge of the countertop, the mug cold beneath her touch.

Hesitant, she walked slowly to the door, her bare feet barely making a sound on the hardwood floor. Peering through the peephole, she saw a woman standing there—mid-fifties, with kind eyes and a warm, reassuring smile. Something about her presence was immediately calming, though Sarah couldn't shake the residual tension coiling in her chest.

The woman lifted her hand in a small wave, the gesture polite but purposeful. Sarah blinked, momentarily torn between curiosity and caution.

Sarah opened the door, startled by the unexpected knock. "Hello?"

The woman smiled warmly, her eyes crinkling with genuine kindness. "Hello, I'm Margaret Healy. I live across the hall. Jason mentioned he had a friend staying and thought I'd come by to introduce myself."

Sarah blinked, still uncertain, but something about Margaret's gentle tone put her slightly at ease. "Oh, um… nice to meet you. I'm Sarah. Please, come in."

Margaret stepped inside with a graceful ease, her presence immediately calming. "Thank you, dear. It's lovely to meet you. I just wanted to make sure you're settling in okay." She moved toward the couch and sat down, crossing her legs comfortably, as if she had been visiting a friend for years rather than minutes.

Sarah felt a small flutter of relief at the prospect of company, the quiet apartment feeling less oppressive. She perched on the opposite couch, folding her hands neatly in her lap. "Thank you—that's very kind of you, Mrs Healy."

"Oh, please, call me Margaret," she said with a warm laugh that softened her words. "My husband, Patrick, and I are very fond of Jason. He's like family to us."

Sarah smiled faintly, her lips tugging up just enough to acknowledge the kindness. "He is lovely. He's letting me stay here while I recover from an accident."

Margaret's expression softened as she nodded, her gaze lingering on Sarah's healing cuts and faint bruises. "Yes… I know about poor Derek. We were at the funeral yesterday, but we didn't want to intrude. How are you holding up, dear?"

Sarah hesitated for a moment, brushing a stray strand of hair from her face. "I'm… getting stronger every day," she said softly, her voice tinged with fragility.

Margaret's eyes softened with sympathy. "Were you close to Derek?" she asked gently.

Sarah's throat tightened as she thought back. "Not for long… I'd only known him for six months, but we got along well. He was very kind… and generous with his time. I met him through my friend Melissa—she was dating him. He was lovely. I can't believe he's gone."

Margaret nodded solemnly, her hand reaching out briefly to rest over Sarah's in quiet support. "Yes… it's terrible. And poor Jason… he has no more family. His parents past five years ago, so it's just been him and Derek."

"That's… sad," Sarah murmured, her voice barely above a whisper. Her hands twisted nervously in her lap. "I know what it's like to feel alone. I lost my mother two years ago—she had a stroke, very sudden." Her voice faltered, tears threatening to spill, but she blinked them back.

Margaret's heart ached at the confession. "Oh, dear… I'm so sorry. That must have been devastating." She reached out again, gently touching Sarah's arm.

Sarah's lips curved into a faint, grateful smile. "Thank you… it's been hard." She paused, then offered, "Would you like some coffee? I just made a pot."

"Oh, that would be lovely, dear," Margaret said, settling back with a contented sigh.

They sat together, the aroma of freshly brewed coffee curling through the apartment and spent over an hour talking. Stories flowed easily—some light-hearted, some tinged with sadness—and Sarah found herself relaxing for the first time in days. Margaret's calm presence was like a balm, easing the loneliness that had wrapped around her since the accident.

Eventually, Margaret stretched and stood, brushing imaginary dust from her skirt. "I'd better go," she said with a small sigh. "Patrick is probably wondering where I've gotten to."

Sarah's smile was genuine this time. "Thank you for coming by Margaret. It was really nice to talk."

"It was my pleasure, dear," Margaret replied warmly. "By the way, we're having a little gathering on Friday—just a few friends. Jason will be there. Would you like to come?"

Sarah hesitated, uncertainty warring with the small spark of curiosity. "I… I don't know. I shouldn't intrude."

"Oh, please," Margaret urged, her smile gentle but persuasive. "It's just casual, nothing formal. It would be lovely to have you there."

Sarah thought for a moment, then nodded slowly. "Okay… if Jason is fine with it, I'll come. Thank you."

"Jason will be delighted," Margaret said with a grin. "Wonderful! I'm looking forward to seeing you there."

As Margaret left, Sarah closed the door behind her, a small sense of ease settling in her chest. For the first time in days, the apartment felt less like a place to recover and more like a space she could inhabit. The visit had reminded her that, even amid grief and uncertainty, connection—however brief or unexpected—could make the world seem a little less heavy.

Later that evening, Sarah decided to cook dinner for herself—and for Jason. It was the least she could do after he had let her stay in his apartment while she recovered, the quiet generosity of his actions weighing on her more than she cared to admit.

The kitchen was serene, almost meditative, as she moved about, chopping vegetables and stirring sauces. The rhythmic motions gave her a small sense of control, a grounding she hadn't felt since the accident. The lingering ache in her ribs and the soreness threading through her body reminded her of how fragile she still was, but she deliberately avoided the painkillers Jason had offered. She didn't want to become dependent; she had read too many cautionary stories, and the thought of losing herself to them was frightening.

She prepared a simple, hearty meal: roast chicken with vegetables, creamy mashed potatoes, and a small, crisp salad. The smell of roasting herbs filled the apartment, warm and inviting, and for the first time in days, she allowed herself a quiet sense of pride. Even if it was a small gesture, cooking felt like something tangible she could do for someone who had done so much for her.

As she set the table, Sarah's mind wandered to Jason. The memory of their kiss lingered, a ghost she couldn't shake. She pressed her lips together, shaking her head slightly. She had no illusions—Jason was helping her because of Derek, because it was the right thing to do. And yet… the warmth of his arms, the heat of that moment, refused to fade. She had to push the thought down, bury it under reason. It wasn't fair to herself, or to him, to indulge it.

By eight o'clock, the meal was ready. Jason still hadn't returned. A flicker of unease pricked at her chest—a fleeting, sharp pang of jealousy at the thought of him being elsewhere, perhaps with someone else. She chastised herself immediately. It wasn't rational. He wasn't hers, and she had no claim over him.

Sarah ate alone, the silence of the apartment wrapping around her like a heavy blanket. Each bite was deliberate, almost ritualistic, a way of filling the empty hours and distracting herself from the whirlpool of conflicting emotions inside. She set aside a plate in the oven, hoping Jason might be hungry when he returned—a small offering of thanks that required no words.

After cleaning up, she lingered in the quiet, listening to the hum of the refrigerator, the distant rumble of traffic, the occasional gull outside her window. When she finally climbed into bed, exhaustion weighed on her, but not enough to quiet her thoughts. Her mind kept replaying fleeting moments from the day, fragments of memory, and the taste of that kiss that had left her heart racing.

She closed her eyes, willing herself to sleep, but the tension lingered, a subtle undercurrent she couldn't yet name. Jason wasn't just Derek's brother. He was complicated, infuriating, and impossibly magnetic—and she didn't know how to navigate that truth. For now, all she could do was lie there, letting the quiet of the apartment cradle her into an uneasy rest.

Jason got home at nine o'clock that night. He was tired—bone-deep tired— and famished. He'd lingered at the office far longer than necessary, deliberately avoiding Sarah, needing a few more hours of distance from the memory of their kiss. The memory lingered like a brand against his chest, both maddening and irresistible. He still couldn't make sense of it, and part of him resented himself for it.

The moment he stepped into the apartment, the smell of roast chicken hit him. Rich, warm, and comforting, it wrapped around him in a way that made him pause. For an instant, he was somewhere else—his mother in the kitchen, the faint hum of conversation, the clatter of dishes. He hadn't had anything like that in years, not since his parents died. His stomach growled, breaking through the fog of his grief and frustration, and for a fraction of a second, a small spark of warmth stirred in his chest.

He moved toward the kitchen, still caught in the haze of the scent, and noticed a note lying neatly on the counter, written in Sarah's careful, precise handwriting:

Jason,

I hope you don't mind I cooked dinner. It's in the oven if you're hungry.

Sarah

Jason's eyes lingered on the note longer than he expected. Something about the simplicity of it—her thoughtfulness, the quiet effort behind it—hit him harder than he wanted to admit. He opened the oven, finding a plate of roast chicken, golden vegetables, and creamy mashed potatoes, perfectly cooked.

It was just dinner.

And yet, it felt like so much more.

He shook his head, trying to push the feelings aside. *Stop. She's the enemy. You can't have these feelings. She caused Derek's death.* The words echoed in his mind, but the ache in his chest refused to ease. He couldn't stop replaying her face, the softness of her body when she'd clung to him, the way her lips had felt against his. Every detail haunted him, unrelenting.

He clenched his fists, the heat of frustration coiling in his gut. This isn't supposed to happen. *She's part of the chaos, part of the grief, and yet... she's everything I can't stop thinking about.* The memory of the kiss—soft, desperate, and achingly perfect—kept creeping back, uninvited, unshakable.

With a long, controlled exhale, he took the plate from the oven. The comforting aroma followed him to the kitchen bench, and for the first time in hours, he allowed himself a small reprieve. He ate slowly, savouring each bite. The food was simple, yet it was exactly what he needed after a day that had left him frayed at the edges. Damn, he thought, *she knows how to cook.*

When the plate was empty, he loaded it into the dishwasher and paused, his gaze returning to Sarah's note. The words were modest, almost casual—but beneath them lay a kindness that was impossible to ignore. Jason grabbed a pen and scrawled a single, curt addition at the bottom:

Thank you.

He exhaled again, heavier this time, as if releasing some of the tension coiled in his chest. His mind was still a storm of thoughts—questions he didn't want answers to, emotions he refused to name, and Sarah, always Sarah, at the centre of it all.

He went to his room, took a quick shower to wash away the lingering day, and collapsed onto his bed. The exhaustion should have brought sleep, but it didn't. His mind spun with memories, what-ifs, and the relentless pull of desire he shouldn't feel. And as he lay there in the quiet darkness, one truth was unavoidable: she was everywhere he looked, even when she wasn't, and he had no idea how to make it stop.

Chapter Eleven

Thursday morning, Sarah finally decided she couldn't avoid Jason any longer. She would shove the kiss to the back of her mind and pretend nothing had changed, even though her heart stubbornly insisted otherwise. She refused to dwell on it—not now. Not while she still wasn't ready to face what it meant.

As she stepped into the kitchen, the faint hiss of the coffee machine broke the quiet, grounding her in the present. Jason was already there, standing at the counter, his posture relaxed yet taut, the green of his eyes catching the light as he looked up at her. For a fraction of a second, they met, and then he looked away, leaving a charged silence hanging between them.

"Morning," Sarah said, forcing cheer into her voice. If she acted normal, maybe it would feel normal.

Jason gave a small nod, expression unreadable. "Morning. Coffee?"

She hesitated only briefly, then nodded. "Yes, please."

He reached for another mug, fingers brushing hers for the briefest moment as he passed it to her. The touch was fleeting, almost accidental—but it sparked something in her chest, a warmth that made her heart hitch. She quickly looked away, pretending to inspect the counter, but she could feel the ghost of his touch lingering, teasing at the edges of her resolve.

"How do you take it?" he asked, curiosity threading his voice.

Sarah blinked, caught off guard by the question. "Black, one sugar," she replied softly, noticing for the first time how little she actually knew about him, or how little he knew about her.

Jason froze for a heartbeat, as if the simplicity of the answer unsettled him. He'd been so wrapped up in anger and resentment, in the image of Sarah as his brother's betrayer, that he hadn't allowed himself to consider her as just… Sarah. But now, in the gentle light of morning, standing here with her, so real and unguarded, he felt a subtle shift stirring within him.

It wasn't just that she wasn't what he had imagined. She wasn't only that. The anger and bitterness still lingered, but mingled now with a new, confusing sense of intrigue. She had depth, history, kindness—a softness that unsettled him in ways he wasn't ready to understand.

He cleared his throat and leaned against the counter, careful to mask the tension in his shoulders. "I wasn't sure if you'd be awake."

"I'm usually up early," she said, taking a small sip from her cup, her gaze tracing the rim as if to delay looking at him.

Jason didn't respond right away. He lifted his coffee, took a slow sip, and allowed himself to glance at her once more. The sight of her—small, vulnerable, yet quietly composed—kept him caught between the urge to reach out and the need to hold back.

Sarah let out a quiet breath, determined to steer the conversation into safer waters. "Margaret came by yesterday," she said, watching for his reaction.

His brow lifted slightly. "Yeah?"

"She invited me to the party on Friday."

For the briefest moment, his expression darkened, subtle enough that she almost questioned it.

"And?"

"I told her I'd come… but only if you were okay with it." Her voice was careful, measured, carrying the weight of her hesitation.

Jason's fingers tightened around his mug, knuckles whitening slightly. "You don't need my permission, Sarah."

"I know," she said softly, a trace of nervousness in her tone. "I just… don't want to make things awkward for you."

He exhaled slowly, a low, controlled sound that carried more than words could reveal. "Margaret wouldn't have invited you if she didn't want you there. It's fine."

The warmth of his tone soothed her unease slightly, yet there was something beneath it—a quiet tension, an unspoken current of emotion she couldn't name. She nodded, keeping her voice light. "Okay."

For a moment, they stood there, the room filled with the gentle hum of the coffee machine and the unspoken weight of the morning, each aware of the fragile balance between them. The sunlight streaming through the window caught the edges of Sarah's hair, softening her features, and Jason found himself staring longer than he intended, as if trying to memorise her in that quiet moment.

A heavy silence settled, stretching uncomfortably. Sarah had thought she could pretend nothing had changed, that she could shove the kiss and the lingering heat of the night into the back of her mind. But standing here in the soft morning light, with Jason a mere metre away, she realised how impossible that was. Every small movement, every glance, felt loaded, full of a tension neither of them dared to name.

She set her mug down and cleared her throat, her voice just above a whisper. "Is it okay if I cook dinner again?" She hesitated, unsure if he'd appreciate her taking over his kitchen.

Jason's gaze flickered to her, something softening in his eyes, a quiet warmth that unsettled him more than it should. "Yeah, that's fine. I'd like that."

Relief brushed her features. "Okay. Just to check—you're not allergic to anything?"

"No," he replied, voice flat but steady.

"Good. I'll leave it in the oven for you," she added, assuming he'd be late again.

Jason surprised her by saying, "I'll be home earlier tonight."

"Oh. Okay." She turned to leave, but a sharp twinge in her ribs caused her to wince.

His frown deepened instantly. "Still bad?"

"It's getting better," she replied quickly, trying to mask the discomfort. But the edge in her voice betrayed her.

He studied her, silent and intense, as if weighing whether to push further. In the end, he didn't, but the concern lingered in his eyes, and it unnerved her in a way she couldn't explain.

"Have a good day," she said softly, her voice still carrying the remnants of tension between them.

"You too," he murmured, but the words hung heavy, unsaid things swirling between them.

Sarah exited the kitchen, but Jason lingered, fingers drumming against the counter, thoughts in turmoil. It hit him then—he didn't really know her. Not truly. His brother had loved her, but Jason had only ever glimpsed the edges of her life, the pieces that intersected with Derek's. And now, here she was, a woman with her own history, her own scars, her own quiet strength.

The realisation gnawed at him, leaving him restless. He had been so consumed by anger, confusion, and grief that he had failed to see her as anything but Derek's love, the girl caught in the wreckage of his brother's life. But now—now he saw her differently. She wasn't just a symbol of heartbreak or betrayal. She was Sarah. Someone who had endured pain, who had survived, who was brave enough to show kindness in the midst of loss.

His mind replayed her earlier words about cooking dinner, the way she had offered a small gesture of care despite everything. It was both brave and heartbreaking, and it sparked something inside him he couldn't ignore. Curiosity, yes—but also a deep, restless need to understand her, to see her for who she truly was.

The thought struck him suddenly, with startling clarity: what better way to learn more about her than over a meal? To see the woman behind the grief, behind the history he had clung to so tightly.

Jason grabbed his coat, moving decisively. He couldn't stay on the sidelines anymore, couldn't continue watching from a distance while the questions—and the pull—between them grew.

He stepped toward the elevator, a plan forming in his mind. It wasn't complicated, but it required courage—and a willingness to face whatever this connection with Sarah might bring.

For the first time that morning, he allowed himself a small, determined smile. He wasn't going to wait. Not this time.

Jason got home at six, and the moment he stepped through the door, the rich, mouthwatering aroma of steak sizzling on the stove hit him. Warm, savoury, and familiar in a way that made him pause, it was almost like a whisper of normalcy, a fleeting reprieve from the chaos of the past days.

He walked into the kitchen and froze for just a heartbeat. Sarah stood there, fully absorbed in her task, earbuds in place, lips moving softly as she hummed and sang along to the music. Her voice was gentle, yet clear and full of life, carrying a subtle warmth that drew him in without warning.

Jason hesitated, watching her. She moved with ease, with a grace and confidence he hadn't noticed before. There was a quiet calm about her, a rhythm to her movements that made her seem untouchably herself, separate from the shadows of his grief and anger. For the first time, he saw Sarah—not as the woman tied to his brother's memory, not as the one who had been entwined in heartbreak, but as someone entirely herself. And that realisation unsettled him in a way he hadn't expected.

It wasn't until she turned and caught sight of him that she paused, a faint blush creeping up her neck as she pulled the earbuds free.

"Hey," she said, voice warm, soft, tinged with surprise. "Dinner's almost ready."

Jason's lips curved into a small, genuine smile, the kind he rarely allowed himself. For a moment, the distance between them seemed to shrink. Her presence here—so effortless, so real—made him forget the world outside the kitchen.

"It smells amazing," he said, stepping closer, the tension in his chest easing just slightly.

"Thanks," she replied, her smile softening as she turned back to the stove. "I hope you're hungry."

"I'm starving," he admitted, shrugging off his jacket and letting it drop over a chair. "Looks like you're in your element."

She chuckled, glancing at him briefly before returning her attention to the sizzling steak. "I've always liked cooking. It's… therapeutic, I guess. My mother taught me—always said I needed to know how to look after myself."

Jason leaned against the counter, studying her. There was something magnetic about the way she moved—comfortable, confident, yet quietly reserved. A subtle vulnerability lingered beneath the surface, and it drew him in like gravity.

"Did you always like singing?" he asked, almost without thinking.

Sarah paused, glancing at him over her shoulder. Her eyes softened, and a small, almost shy smile tugged at her lips. "Yeah. Ever since I was little, I guess. My mum's the only one who's ever really heard me."

Jason nodded slowly, struck by the quiet intimacy of her confession. She was strong, capable, yet there was a delicate edge to her, a part of her she didn't show freely. The paradox intrigued him more than he cared to admit.

"Maybe you should sing more often," he murmured, his voice low, almost hesitant.

Sarah tilted her head, unreadable for a moment, before a faint smile curved her lips. "Oh, I don't know… I don't think I'm that good," she said, and for a beat, it was almost like she was considering it seriously for the first time.

The silence that followed was comfortable, a rare ease settling over the space between them. No words were needed to acknowledge the subtle connection forming, the quiet understanding that passed in glances and small movements.

"You have time to have a shower if you want before I serve," she said casually, almost as if she hadn't noticed the tension in the air.

Jason raised an eyebrow, a small chuckle escaping him. "A shower? You really know how to treat a guy, don't you?"

Sarah's cheeks coloured slightly, a soft lift at the corners of her lips as she continued tending to the steak. "It's not like I'm offering a five-star massage," she teased lightly. "But I figured you'd appreciate a minute to relax before dinner."

He hesitated, torn between exhaustion and the magnetic pull of her presence. The idea of a hot shower was tempting, yes—but lingering here, in this warm, calm kitchen with her, felt equally impossible to resist.

"I might take you up on that," he said after a beat, stepping toward the hall. "Thanks."

"Of course," she replied, returning her attention to the sizzling steak, her movements fluid, almost hypnotic.

Jason paused in the doorway for a moment, letting his gaze linger, silently acknowledging the small but undeniable shift in how he felt about her. And for the first time in days, he allowed himself to think—not of anger, not of loss— but of something else. Something softer, something he couldn't quite name.

Jason nodded and walked down the hallway to the bathroom, his mind racing as he peeled off his shirt and let the warm water cascade over him. The heat was a welcome relief, but it did little to calm the storm of thoughts swirling in his head. There was something about the ease with which Sarah moved in her own world, the quiet confidence that seemed to radiate from her, that unsettled him. Warmth and mystery intertwined in her presence, pulling at him in a way he couldn't quite name. He wanted to know more—about her, about the layers she kept hidden, about the life she had lived before all of this.

He finished his shower quickly, tension easing from his muscles but not from his mind. Wrapping a towel around his waist, he dressed in jeans and a soft tee shirt, every movement mechanical yet aware, his thoughts still drifting back to her.

When he stepped into the kitchen, he found her at the stove, pulling the steak from the pan and arranging it on a plate with a quiet elegance. The golden light from the overhead fixture caught the shine of her hair as it fell across her shoulders, framing her face in soft shadows. She moved with a fluidity that made everything else—the apartment, the chaos of his mind—fade into the background. For a fleeting moment, she looked up at him, their eyes meeting for a brief second before she focused on the plate, and something tightened in his chest.

"Just in time," she said, her voice soft, easy, almost musical. "Go ahead, sit down. I'll get everything plated."

Jason swallowed, the pull of something unfamiliar—gratitude, admiration, maybe even desire—curling in his chest. He crossed to the table, taking a seat, watching her as she worked. Every motion she made, deliberate yet unhurried, seemed to draw him further in, until it was impossible to look away.

"Thank you," he murmured as she placed the plate of steak Diane and vegetables before him. The aroma was rich and inviting, but it was her presence that truly filled the space. "This looks amazing."

She gave a small nod, sliding into the chair across from him, her eyes briefly flicking toward his. "I hope you like it," she said, her tone carrying a subtle warmth that made him pause mid-bite.

For several minutes, the only sounds were the gentle clink of silverware against plates and the quiet hiss of the stove cooling in the background. Jason ate slowly, savouring each bite—not just the food, but the rare, grounding sensation of calm in her company. For the first time in days, he let himself relax, the tension that had been coiled tight between them finally loosening.

He realised, almost reluctantly, that he was genuinely enjoying her presence. He wasn't thinking about the past, the anger, the grief, or the tangled emotions that had plagued him. He was just here, with her. Just... present.

When they both pushed their plates aside, the silence stretched again. Sarah began to rise, perhaps to clear the table, but Jason reached out, his hand lightly resting on her arm. The touch was deliberate but gentle, a silent request for her to pause.

"Sit for a little while," he said, his voice low, carrying a rare vulnerability. "I realised this morning... I don't really know much about you."

Chapter Twelve

Sarah froze, the weight of his words sinking in. Her heart fluttered with a mix of nervous anticipation and relief she hadn't expected. She'd spent so long hiding behind a mask of normalcy, pretending her past didn't exist, pretending the grief and loss weren't always there just beneath the surface. And now—Jason was asking her to let him in. To see her. Did she want that? Could she?

She hesitated, glancing down at her hands before settling back into her chair, trying to steady the sudden rush of emotions. "I'm a kindergarten teacher in Bondi," she began, her voice low, almost tentative. "I'm twenty-five… no siblings. My parents… they're gone."

Jason didn't respond, didn't comment. He already knew much of it from the investigator he had employed, but he let her speak, letting the words hang between them. There was something compelling about her openness, the quiet bravery it took to share pieces of herself.

She swallowed, her gaze dropping to the table. "I play the piano. I love to cook, and I… enjoy singing. Reading, jogging—though I can't run properly until I'm fully healed. And I love kids. That's why I became a teacher, I guess… it feels like something I'm meant to do."

Jason felt a curiosity stir, but his usual walls immediately went up. He forced himself to ask the next question, careful not to sound too probing. "Friends? Boyfriends?"

Her eyes flicked away briefly, tracing the rim of her glass as if it could anchor her. "I have friends," she said softly, almost reluctantly, "but none that I'm really close to." The words carried a quiet regret, a hint of vulnerability he hadn't expected. Something about her tone made his chest tighten. He opened his mouth to ask more but paused as she shifted the conversation.

"And you?" she asked, her voice gentle, curious, encouraging him to share without pushing.

Jason's throat tightened. He wasn't used to talking about himself like this—not with anyone, and certainly not with someone like Sarah, who seemed capable of seeing straight through him, seeing the parts of him he usually hid.

"Not much to tell," he said, his tone clipped, protective, like he could somehow keep her from uncovering too much too soon. He hesitated, then let his guard drop just a fraction. "I'm thirty-two. No family left. CEO. Friends… yes, but no one I'd call close. Derek was… he was my best friend."

Her eyes softened instantly, and before he could stop her, her hand reached out, brushing lightly against his arm. The warmth of her touch hit him like a jolt—comforting, grounding, and utterly disarming all at once. He wasn't used to that kind of unguarded kindness. He wasn't sure how to respond.

"It's okay," he murmured, quieter now, as if saying it aloud could somehow make the hurt more bearable. He offered her a half-smile, though it didn't quite reach his eyes. "I can't sing, can't play piano, and I'm not much of a cook. I guess… I'm kind of a work in progress."

Sarah let out a small, understanding laugh, soft and warm, like sunlight spilling into a dark room. The sound was enough to chip away at the tension coiling between them.

"Everyone's a work in progress, Jason," she said, her eyes locking with his. There was something in her gaze—something that saw him, really saw him—that made his chest ache in ways he didn't expect. Humbling, terrifying, but… strangely freeing.

For a long moment, neither of them spoke. The silence stretched, but this time, it wasn't uncomfortable or heavy. It was gentle, easy, a quiet acknowledgment of trust and understanding. In that pause, Jason realised something he hadn't let himself admit before: he wanted to know her—not just pieces of her, but all of her. And for the first time, he felt the faintest hope that maybe… she wanted the same.

She stood, gathering the dirty plates, and Jason found himself following her into the kitchen without thinking. The silence between them was comfortable, yet charged, as they worked side by side, stacking dishes and wiping counters. The mundane task felt strangely intimate, the space between them shrinking with every glance, every subtle brush of their hands.

Once the kitchen was tidy, Jason lingered in the doorway, his gaze fixed on her. There was a pull inside him he couldn't name—a quiet, insistent tug that made the air between them feel electric.

"Would you… play the piano for me?" His voice was lower than usual, almost a whisper, a request that carried something more than the music itself—a need, a longing, a fragile trust.

Sarah paused, her hands resting on the counter. Her eyes softened as she met his, and for the first time, Jason wondered if she sensed the unspoken layers behind the question.

"Okay," she said simply, a faint smile tugging at her lips.

They moved into the living room. Jason sank onto the couch, his hands loosely resting on his knees, while Sarah approached the grand piano. The dimmed lights reflected off the polished wood, bathing the space in a soft, intimate glow.

"Any requests?" she asked, fingers hovering over the keys, ready to play.

Jason hesitated, then smiled faintly. "Do you know 'River Flows in You'?"

She nodded, her eyes lifting briefly to meet his. "By Yiruma, yes."

Jason leaned back, his gaze distant. "It was my mother's favourite… the piano, actually, is hers," he added quietly, almost as if saying it aloud made the memory more real.

Sarah felt the subtle weight in his words, a delicate ache that seemed to settle over the room. She nodded, letting her fingers find the keys, the notes trembling under her touch like a whispered acknowledgment of memory and loss.

With a soft exhale, she began to play. The melody floated through the room, each note delicate, haunting, brimming with unspoken emotion. Jason closed his eyes, letting the music carry him back—his mother's laughter, her hands gliding over these same keys, the warmth of her presence in moments long past. A tightness gripped his chest, and before he could stop it, a single tear slipped down his cheek.

Sarah, lost in the music, felt her own heart swell. The raw, quiet grief that lingered behind his calm exterior reached out to her, and she felt a resonance, a connection that went beyond words. When the final notes faded into the soft silence, she realised her eyes were misty too.

Jason rose, moving toward her as if pulled by some invisible force. He took her hand gently, and she allowed him to guide her upright. Without speaking, he drew her close, holding her as though letting go was unthinkable. Their bodies aligned, the warmth of her against him grounding something that had been fragile and aching inside him.

They stayed like that for minutes, neither needing words. Just the quiet inhale and exhale of each other's breath, the softness of skin against skin, the subtle weight of mutual understanding.

"That was beautiful," Jason murmured, his voice husky with restrained emotion. He pulled back slightly to meet her eyes, searching them, reading her, still feeling the tremor of something unspoken between them. "Thank you, Sarah."

She nodded, breath shallow, a faint warmth colouring her cheeks. She didn't speak, didn't need to.

Jason's gaze roamed her face, lingering on the curve of her lips, the soft line of her jaw, the pulse in her neck. He could feel the faint rise and fall of her chest against him. A powerful, unbidden urge to kiss her gripped him, sharp and insistent, but he held back.

And she didn't move either.

Time seemed to stretch, holding them suspended in that fragile, electric moment. The past, the future, the weight of unsaid words—all of it disappeared. It was just them: two people, standing close enough to feel every shiver, every quiet heartbeat, every small, intimate breath. And in that suspended space, the connection between them hummed, undeniable and consuming.

Sarah knew this was madness. No man had ever stirred her like this—not with just a look, a touch, a fleeting moment of shared breath. The way Jason's eyes had held hers, as if he could see the parts of her, she wasn't sure anyone should, was too intense. Too dangerous. Too consuming.

She needed to stop this before she lost herself entirely. Before desire clouded every thought and left her unmoored.

Taking a deliberate step back, she broke the spell. "You're welcome," she whispered, her voice trembling just slightly, betraying the storm she fought to contain. The air between them seemed to pulse, thick with everything left unsaid. After a heartbeat, she added, quieter still, "I think it's time for bed."

Jason's jaw tightened, and for a fleeting second, she saw the war inside him— the longing, the restraint, the pull toward her he clearly struggled to resist. He wanted to say something. To bridge the space, she had put between them. To close the distance that suddenly felt unbearable. But he didn't. Instead, he gave a slow nod, his gaze lingering on hers far longer than it should, before he finally stepped back, releasing her.

She felt the weight of his eyes as she retreated, and it pressed against her chest like a tangible force. Her own pulse thundered in her ears, and a whisper of doubt—or was it desire? —flitted across her mind. What the hell was happening to them? Why did he draw her in so completely? Why did she want him so badly when every rational thought screamed that this was reckless, that it was dangerous?

By the time she reached her room, her body still hummed from the intensity of the moment, her mind spinning in circles she didn't want to explore. The pull between them was undeniable, and it left her breathless, her heart racing in ways she hadn't expected.

As she closed the door behind her, shutting out the dim light of the living room, one thought echoed in her mind, chilling and thrilling all at once: Jason Olander wasn't just dangerous—he was a force she couldn't ignore, and somehow, she didn't want to.

Chapter Thirteen

The party was set to begin at seven, and Sarah took her time getting ready. It had been ages since she had attended a gathering like this, and she wanted to look her best—not for anyone in particular, but for herself. After washing and drying her long auburn hair, she let it fall in soft, natural waves that brushed her shoulder blades. A touch of makeup highlighted her blue eyes, giving them a subtle sparkle, while a hint of blush and a sweep of lip colour brought warmth to her features.

That morning, Jason had mentioned he would be late and would meet her at the party when he arrived. At first, she hadn't thought much of it. But as she slid into the form-fitting red dress and stepped into matching heels, a flutter of nerves crept through her. Would he notice the change? Would he approve? She wasn't supposed to care, but a small, stubborn part of her hoped he would.

By five past seven, she found herself at Margaret's door, heart racing in a mix of anticipation and unease. She knocked once, softly. Music and laughter spilled from inside, mingling with the low hum of conversation.

The door swung open, and Margaret's radiant smile immediately put her at ease. "Oh, Sarah, I'm so glad you could make it! Don't you look lovely."

Beside her, an older gentleman with neatly combed white hair and a gentle smile stepped forward. Margaret gestured toward him. "This is my husband, Patrick."

Patrick extended his hand warmly. "Hello, Sarah. Margaret has told me all about you."

Sarah shook his hand, smiling. "All good things, I hope."

"Of course," Margaret said with a playful twinkle in her eye. "Come in, let me introduce you to everyone."

As Sarah stepped inside, the scene unfolded like a painting. Elegantly dressed guests mingled in small groups, laughter and clinking glasses filling the air. The warm glow of ambient lighting cast golden highlights across the room, and the scent of something rich and savory drifted from the dining area. Margaret's easy presence made Sarah feel welcome, soothing the nerves she hadn't realised had tightened in her chest.

Margaret guided her deeper into the room, past a cluster of women discussing art and fashion, and toward a group of younger guests. "Oh, let me introduce you," she said cheerfully. "This is Daniel, Thomas, and Liam. They're Patrick's business associates' sons."

The three men turned as Margaret spoke, their gazes briefly lingering on Sarah. Dressed in red, she didn't exactly blend in, but she felt a flicker of confidence instead of discomfort.

Daniel, tall with sandy blond hair and a charming smile, stepped forward first. "Nice to meet you, Sarah. I don't think I've seen you at one of Margaret's parties before."

"No, this is my first one," Sarah admitted with a small, polite smile.

"Well, then I'd say you're already the most stunning guest here," he said smoothly, his blue eyes twinkling.

Sarah chuckled, shaking her head. "That's quite a compliment."

Thomas, dark-haired with a lean, athletic build, smirked. "Daniel's laying it on thick, but he's not wrong."

Liam, the quietest of the three, observed her over the rim of his glass, eyes thoughtful. After a slow sip, he asked, "Are you here with someone?"

Sarah hesitated, aware that Jason hadn't arrived yet. "Just a friend," she said vaguely, her voice light.

Daniel's grin widened. "Then I hope you'll save a dance for me later."

Sarah smiled politely, unsure how to respond. Before she could answer, Margaret laughed, looping her arm through Sarah's. "Now, now, boys, don't overwhelm her. Let her enjoy the evening."

As Sarah followed Margaret further into the room, her nerves began to settle. The laughter, the music, the hum of conversation—it was all comforting, a small respite from the swirl of emotions she carried. For the first time that evening, she allowed herself to enjoy the moment, to feel normal, if only for a little while.

As Margaret steered her away, Sarah could still feel their eyes on her. A flush of warmth crept over her, and for the first time in a long while, she felt... happy.

Almost instinctively, her thoughts drifted to Jason. She found herself wondering what he would think when he saw her tonight—if he'd notice the way the dress hugged her, or the subtle shine in her eyes, or the nervous excitement she tried to mask.

Jason didn't get home until eight, delayed by a late Teams meeting with Europe. Exhausted, but eager to reach the party, he took a quick shower before dressing carefully—black trousers paired with a sleek, silk shirt. As he buttoned the cuffs, he paused, glancing around the quiet, dimly lit penthouse.

Sarah wasn't here.

He hadn't realised how much he'd come to expect her presence—the soft sound of her voice, the little spark in her eyes when she saw him, the way she made the place feel alive. Now, the rooms seemed emptier, colder, lacking the warmth she carried naturally.

Shaking off the thought, he grabbed his keys and headed out to Margaret and Patrick's.

The moment he stepped inside, Margaret's voice cut through the hum of conversation. "Oh, there you are, Jason!" She beckoned him in, lowering her tone but keeping a teasing edge. "Sarah's a big hit—the boys are falling over themselves."

Sarah? A big hit?

Jason's steps faltered. The words echoed in his mind louder than they should have. He hadn't expected that, and a strange, unwelcome twist of possessiveness settled in his chest. He forced a smirk. "Is that so?"

Margaret chuckled softly, eyes twinkling. "Oh, yes. I don't think she's had a moment to herself since she arrived. The boys seem to have taken quite a liking to her."

Jason's jaw tightened involuntarily. He scanned the room, fighting the tug of irritation rising in his chest, and finally spotted her.

She was radiant. The red dress clung to her curves in all the right places, the auburn waves of her hair catching the soft glow of the chandelier. She laughed at something one of the men beside her said, her expression open, effortless, magnetic.

So, this was what Margaret meant.

A sharp twist of jealousy shot through him, hot and undeniable. His chest constricted, and he felt the almost irrational urge to storm across the room and stake his claim. Every instinct screamed at him that seeing her like this—so admired, so desired—shouldn't affect him. And yet, it did.

He swallowed, forcing his jaw to unclench and his expression to remain neutral. But inside, a storm was building, dark and possessive.

Why did it bother him so much?

Because it wasn't just admiration she drew—it was attention from anyone but him. And that thought made his heart pound, his mind reel with a mix of desire and frustration.

He studied her for a moment longer. Her laughter, her easy grace, the way she leaned slightly toward one of the men—it should have been harmless. It was, objectively, nothing. But seeing her in that red dress, alive and radiant, completely herself… it stirred something deep, raw, and unrelenting in him.

Jason clenched his fists at his sides, forcing himself to breathe.

He couldn't let it show.

But he also knew, with a certainty that made his chest tighten, that he didn't like it. Not one bit.

Just as he took a step toward her, the tall blond next to her—Daniel, if he remembered correctly—grinned, reached for her hand, and spun her effortlessly into his arms. Jason froze, a sharp twist of irritation—and something darker—curling through him. Before he could react, Daniel swept her toward the dance floor, guiding her into the midst of swaying couples, his hand settling possessively on the small of her back.

Jason's fingers curled into tight fists at his sides, nails biting into his palms.

He didn't like this. Not one damn bit.

He stalked toward Liam and Thomas, planting himself nearby as his gaze followed every move Daniel made with Sarah. His jaw clenched, his entire body taut, like a coiled spring.

"Hey, Jason. How's it going?" Thomas said, voice cheerful, lifting his glass in a casual greeting.

"I'm good, thanks. You?" Jason replied, his tone neutral, too tight.

"Great." Thomas's gaze drifted to the dance floor, a smirk tugging at his lips. "Ah, you've already noticed the best-looking woman in the room."

Jason's jaw tightened further, but he said nothing, forcing himself to maintain control.

Liam, usually quiet and unobtrusive, finally spoke, his tone careful but teasing. "Sorry, mate. Daniel's already staked a claim."

Jason let out a short, humourless laugh. There was nothing funny about it. He watched Daniel hold Sarah close, his hand lingering a second too long on her waist. The knot in his chest tightened, a mix of possessiveness, frustration, and something he wasn't ready to name.

"Is that so?" he murmured, his voice deceptively calm, though every fibre of him screamed otherwise.

He couldn't stop the flicker of jealousy that shot through him as he saw Sarah laugh, her attention fixed on someone else. And with it came a thought he refused to fully admit he didn't like seeing her with anyone but him.

Thomas chuckled, shaking his head. "Yeah, he's been glued to her since she walked in. Can't really blame him."

Jason could. And he did. Every instinct in him bristled at the sight.

The song faded, and Daniel finally stepped back as Sarah pulled away. He leaned in, murmuring something close to her ear that made her stiffen before she excused herself and headed toward the bathroom.

Jason's eyes followed her retreating figure, a protective, almost primal urge flaring within him. The way she moved—graceful, unaware of the storm she left in her wake—made his chest tighten further.

Moments later, Daniel wandered over, his smug grin impossible to miss. "Hey, Jason, how are you?"

Jason's gaze didn't waver, his expression neutral but sharp. "Good. I see you've met Sarah."

The three men exchanged quick, startled glances. Thomas was the first to break the silence, his tone tinged with surprise. "You… you know her?"

Jason's lips pressed into a thin line, his green eyes locking on Daniel's for a long, unreadable beat. The words he didn't say hung heavy in the air: *Don't touch her. Don't look at her like that. She's mine.*

Jason smirked, taking quiet satisfaction in their surprise. His reply was measured, cool, but carried an unmistakable edge. "Yes. She's staying with me." There was no need for further explanation—his tone left the statement undeniable.

Daniel froze, drink halfway to his lips, eyes widening in disbelief. "Wait—she's... yours?" His voice held a mixture of shock and something darker, but Jason didn't bother figuring out what.

Jason didn't flinch. "No, Daniel. She's not my girl." His gaze sharpened, words dropping like ice. "She was in the car when my brother died."

The air shifted instantly. Thomas's eyes widened, while Liam remained quiet, watching, absorbing the sudden tension.

Daniel's expression changed, confusion giving way to understanding, though unease lingered in his features. "Oh," he muttered, the playful glint in his eyes replaced by something softer. "That's why she said her ribs were sore."

Jason's nod was curt, deliberate, the weight of his words settling over them like a shadow. "Yes."

Liam, curious despite the charged atmosphere, finally spoke. "Was she... Derek's girl?"

Jason paused, weighing the answer carefully. His voice was steady, but a subtle edge betrayed the tension coiled inside him. "I don't know. She can't remember the accident, and the doctors told me not to push for details."

Daniel leaned in slightly, his grin returning, but now it carried a knowing undertone. "So, she's not with anyone, then?"

Jason felt the stir of irritation but kept his voice calm, almost deceptively so. "As far as I know, she's unattached."

Thomas, always the observer, raised an eyebrow, intrigued but holding back. "How long has she been staying with you?" His tone was casual but probing enough to ruffle Jason's patience.

"A week," Jason replied, words clipped, his gaze narrowing slightly as he redirected the focus.

Daniel, oblivious to the shift in atmosphere, leaned in, eyes glinting with amusement. "And you haven't made a move? Are you blind, mate?"

Jason's body tensed, a flash of frustration surging beneath his calm exterior. "It's not that simple," he said, his voice firmer than intended, a warning laced beneath the words.

Thomas, sensing the rising tension, chuckled softly but wisely chose not to press further.

Daniel, ever the provocateur, grinned brazenly, undeterred. "So… you're cool if I go for it then?"

Jason's jaw tightened, a surge of possessiveness and something unnameable knotting his stomach. "It's not my call," he muttered, his tone low, sharp, warning enough to hint at boundaries Daniel didn't yet fully understand.

Just then, a familiar presence approached. Jason turned instinctively, his pulse quickening as Sarah came into view. Her smile was bright, warm, effortlessly drawing him in, and her eyes locked on his with that disarming openness that always left him off balance.

"Hello, Jason," she greeted, her voice soft but radiant, and in that single glance, she seemed to claim the room without realising it.

Thomas, ever the observer, nudged Daniel with a teasing grin. "I don't think you have a hope in hell." His amusement was palpable, a silent acknowledgment of the tension crackling in the air.

Daniel shot back with overconfidence, though Jason's steady gaze made him falter slightly. "We'll see," he said, voice cocky but forced, his certainty brushing against the invisible wall Jason had erected around Sarah.

Jason's eyes never left Sarah, the subtle protective edge in his gaze unmistakable. In that moment, the room seemed to shrink, the noise and laughter fading into the background. It was just her, him, and the unspoken understanding that no one else could—or would—claim her.

He stepped forward slightly, his presence grounding and quiet, as if the air itself had shifted around them. His voice, low and warm, cut through the hum of the party. "Hello, Sarah. How are you? Not overdoing it, I hope?"

Sarah laughed, a soft, lilting sound that carried a lightness he hadn't realised he was craving. But beneath it, Jason caught something more genuine, something unguarded in her smile, and it made his chest tighten in a way that was at once thrilling and alarming.

Before he could respond further, Daniel, sensing opportunity, slid his arm around her waist, drawing her slightly closer. Jason's pulse spiked. Sarah's subtle stiffening did not go unnoticed, and his hands curled into fists at his sides. He took a step forward, ready to intervene, but stopped himself, forcing his control back, though he couldn't shake the sting of possessiveness—or was it jealousy?

"I've been looking after her, Jas. She's in good hands," Daniel said smoothly, his tone deliberately possessive.

Jason's jaw tightened, but before he could answer, Margaret appeared, her energy radiant as always. "Sarah, I hear you play the piano!" she exclaimed, her eyes sparkling with excitement.

Sarah turned to her, and Daniel's arm fell away, his claim on her instantly evaporating. "Yes, I do," she said softly, a trace of regret in her voice, as if she wished she hadn't drawn that attention.

Jason's expression softened, a hint of pride lighting his features. "She plays beautifully. I've been lucky enough to hear her," he said, his voice carrying quiet admiration that resonated deeper than mere praise.

Margaret's face glowed. "Oh, you simply must play for us, Sarah. Please!" she urged, her enthusiasm impossible to resist.

Sarah hesitated, the blush rising along her neck as her uncertainty surfaced. "Oh, I don't know… there are a lot of people here."

Margaret's eyes swept across the gathering, sparkling with encouragement. "Oh, come now," she said, her voice lively and persuasive. "It's just music— your music. We'd love it."

Sarah exhaled softly, giving in, though the tension in her posture remained. "Okay… I hope I don't make a fool of myself."

Jason stepped closer, closing the small space between them, his hands resting gently on her shoulders. His touch was grounding, steady, and his voice softened, full of quiet reassurance. "You won't," he murmured, the weight of his words carrying an unspoken strength that made her heart skip a beat.

She looked up at him, meeting his gaze, and for a fleeting moment, the world outside their bubble seemed to vanish. A small, shy smile curved her lips, layered with something unspoken, a silent acknowledgment of the tension between them that neither dared name aloud.

Taking a steadying breath, Sarah broke the moment with Jason and turned toward Margaret. "Alright… do you have a request?"

Margaret's eyes lit up with delight. "Oh, wonderful! Do you know Clair de Lune?"

Sarah nodded, a small smile playing at her lips. "By Claude Debussy?"

"That's the one!" Margaret said, her excitement palpable as she gently guided Sarah toward the piano, the soft click of heels against the polished floor marking the beginning of a moment that would linger in more ways than one.

A faint blush coloured Sarah's cheeks as she settled at the piano, her fingers hovering over the keys for a heartbeat. Doubt flickered in her eyes, a whisper of uncertainty, but when they met Jason's steady gaze, the weight of his quiet support grounded her. His presence, silent yet powerful, gave her the courage to begin.

Her fingers pressed down on the keys, and the first notes of Clair de Lune flowed like liquid silver through the room. The melody was delicate yet achingly emotional, each note rising and falling with an effortless grace that seemed to suspend time. Conversations dimmed, laughter faded—the guests fell into a hushed reverence, caught in the spell of her music.

Jason stood a few feet away, rooted in place. The haunting beauty of her playing stole his breath. He had heard her before, but now, with the soft glow of the chandelier highlighting the waves of her auburn hair and the intensity in her eyes, it felt different—intimate, almost sacred. Every note seemed to reach inside him, stirring something quiet and unrelenting.

Her hands moved with a confident precision, yet there was vulnerability in the gentle rise and fall of each chord. Jason's chest tightened as he watched, mesmerised not just by her talent but by the woman herself—strong, delicate, luminous, and entirely present in this moment.

When the final note faded into silence, there was a pause so profound that it felt as if the room were holding its breath. Then, applause erupted, warm and genuine, echoing off the walls. Sarah's fingers lingered over the last keys, her heart racing from the rush of performing, the adrenaline mingling with a quiet sense of pride.

But it wasn't the clapping that made her chest flutter—it was the way Jason was looking at her. His green eyes were soft, filled with admiration, and for the first time in a long while, Sarah felt truly seen. The blush deepened across her cheeks as a small, tentative smile tugged at her lips. His gaze held her, unbroken and unwavering, a silent affirmation that in this moment, nothing else mattered.

Chapter Fourteen

The party continued well into the early hours, music thumping, laughter echoing through the ornate rooms, glasses clinking in rhythm with the beat. The air was thick with the mingling scents of wine, perfume, and polished wood, a heady cocktail that made every sound and movement seem sharper, more vivid. Sarah, radiant and carefree, had fallen into an easy conversation with Daniel. Her laughter rang like bells—light, unrestrained, utterly unlike the careful, measured smiles she'd worn around Jason in the past.

Jason watched from across the room, every instinct screaming at him as he gripped his beer bottle tighter than necessary. Daniel leaned closer, his hand brushing against Sarah's arm in a gesture that should have been trivial. But the effect was immediate—a punch to Jason's chest that left him momentarily breathless. He hated it. Hated the way it seemed so effortless, the way Sarah's eyes lit up when she looked at Daniel, the way her whole attention tilted toward him as though Jason didn't exist.

He forced himself to take a slow, deliberate breath, to mask the storm coiling in his gut. He told himself it was just concern, nothing more. Yet, with every laugh, every tilt of her head toward Daniel, every shimmer of light catching in her hair, the knot in his chest tightened. It wasn't just concern. No, it was something deeper—an urgent, undeniable pull, a fear he hadn't fully admitted even to himself. The thought that he might have let something precious slip through his fingers, something he hadn't realised he wanted until now, made his stomach twist.

Jason shifted his weight, trying to shake off the heat rising in his veins. Then, as if sensing him, Sarah glanced over and met his eyes. Her warm smile cut through the chaos inside him, and for a heartbeat, the room slowed. Everything else—the laughter, the music, even Daniel—faded to the edges of his awareness. For a single, fleeting moment, it felt like just the two of them existed in that space.

But then Daniel spoke again, his voice smooth and confident, cutting through the brief calm like a knife. Jason felt irritation spike anew, sharp and unwelcome. Daniel's charm, his ease, his effortless presence in Sarah's orbit—it was infuriating. Jason's fists clenched, and a low, restless heat pooled in his chest, a mix of frustration, desire, and the gnawing certainty that he couldn't stay on the sidelines any longer.

Every glance, every laugh, every subtle touch between Daniel and Sarah hammered at him. And yet, as he watched her, Jason's mind wandered back to that night—the crash, Derek, the story he'd told himself about betrayal and blame. He had framed Sarah as the reason for his brother's reckless end, wrapped it in anger and grief to keep himself sane.

But now, seeing her laugh freely, the tension between them dissolving in the glow of the party lights, Jason realised how incomplete that story had been. She wasn't the woman he had imagined. She was warm, kind, and entirely present. Her loyalty, her laughter, the subtle way she carried herself—it all spoke of someone who could never have intentionally caused harm. He blinked, uncertainty prickling at the edges of his control. Had he been wrong? Could it be that the truth was far more complicated than his grief had allowed him to see?

The thought unsettled him, left a jagged edge in his chest, but it also fuelled a new determination. He couldn't linger in the shadows, watching. He couldn't ignore the pull he felt, the need to know her fully, beyond the filtered fragments of the past. Not when every instinct, every heartbeat, demanded action.

Taking a steadying breath, Jason pushed aside the swirl of jealousy, doubt, and unresolved grief. One step, then another, each heavier than the last, carried him across the polished floor toward Sarah. His focus narrowed, the room compressing into the space between them. When Daniel's eyes flicked to him, Jason met the gaze with a silent, unspoken challenge, then let it go, fixing his attention solely on her.

"Sarah," he said, his voice firm yet carrying a vulnerability that betrayed more than he intended. "Would you like to dance?"

Sarah's eyes widened briefly in surprise, but her smile softened, warm and inviting. She studied him for a heartbeat, as if weighing the invitation, before nodding. "I'd love to," she said, her voice carrying a gentle certainty that made Jason feel—unexpectedly—anchored.

He held out his hand, and she took it without hesitation, a small, fleeting smile brushing her lips as they made their way to the dance floor. Out of the corner of his eye, Jason caught Daniel's gaze, sharp and dark with quiet animosity, like coiled lightning ready to strike. But he didn't flinch. Not now. Not with Sarah in his arms.

Jason's hands settled at her waist, feeling the soft, familiar curve of her body against him. She rested her hands lightly on his shoulders, steady but delicate. The moment their bodies aligned, a wave of warmth swept through him, displacing everything else—the chatter, the music, the crowded room—all of it blurring into insignificance.

Her breath hitched slightly as they swayed to the rhythm, a subtle echo of the nervousness he felt mirrored in her. The tension between them wasn't the old, sharp kind—it was fragile, tentative, but electric, a silent understanding forming with every step.

He drank in her presence—the gentle scent of her hair, the soft press of her skin, the faint rise and fall of her chest. Every detail drew him closer, each one whispering that he never wanted to let this moment go. For the first time, he realised he wasn't just attracted to her. He was captivated.

The world around them dissolved. Every laugh, every distant conversation, every weight of expectation vanished. There was only Sarah, only this fragile, intoxicating closeness. A heat spread through Jason, a quiet fire that burned just beneath the surface, and he didn't fight it. He simply felt—alive, present, tethered to her in a way he hadn't anticipated.

When the song ended, Jason reluctantly released her, his hands lingering on her waist a fraction longer than necessary. She stepped back, a subtle pull of disappointment tugging at him as their connection slipped away.

Sarah looked up, her eyes soft but unreadable, edged with a quiet hesitation. "I think I should go. It's getting late."

Jason's chest tightened, though he forced a nod, unwilling—or perhaps unable—to voice how much he didn't want the night to end. "I'll leave too," he said, his tone carrying a reluctant softness.

They moved toward Margaret and Patrick to say their goodbyes. Margaret greeted them warmly, eyes sparkling with genuine gratitude. "Thank you both for coming, and Sarah, your piano performance was simply enchanting."

"It was my pleasure," Sarah replied, her voice gentle, her smile luminous. "Thank you for such a lovely evening."

As they turned to the trio of men near the door, Sarah's calm composure returned, but there was a subtle steel beneath it. "It's time for us to go," she said, soft but firm.

Daniel, leaning casually against the wall, straightened instantly, his expression shifting from relaxed confidence to mild frustration. "Not yet?" he said, voice smooth, playful, yet edged with something more—a challenge. "There's still time. Stay a little longer."

Sarah's gaze flicked briefly to Jason, a quiet question in her eyes. Then, with a polite but unyielding smile, she answered, "I'm afraid I really must go." Her tone was gentle, but the finality in her words hung like a blade between them.

Daniel didn't let the moment pass. "Can I call you?" His voice lingered in the air, a subtle challenge, his confidence unwavering.

Sarah hesitated just long enough to maintain her composure, then nodded, taking his phone and typing her number in quickly, efficiently. A trace of unease fluttered through her, though she didn't show it.

Daniel leaned in, brushing a light kiss across her cheek. "Thanks for a wonderful night, Sarah," he said, voice smooth, his gaze lingering, sharp and deliberate, cutting through the polite formality. Then, with a silent, almost daring glance at Jason, he stepped back, the unspoken challenge clear.

Jason's stomach knotted, a hot tension coiling low in his chest. He didn't like the way Daniel looked at her—like he had a chance, like he could stake a claim Jason wasn't willing to share. His jaw tightened, the simmering possessiveness rising, but he forced himself to stay calm, to mask the fire roiling beneath the surface.

Because in the end, it was her eyes he wanted—not anyone else's.

After the final round of goodbyes, Sarah and Jason made their way back to his apartment. The walk was silent but comfortable, the air between them charged with something unspoken. As they entered the living room, Sarah paused, something pulling her to stay there, just a little longer.

She turned to him, her smile soft, her eyes warm. In that moment, time seemed to slow, everything else fading into the background, leaving only the two of them in the quiet space of the room.

"Sarah..." Jason's voice was low, a whisper that carried both a question and a confession.

Neither of them knew who moved first—maybe it didn't matter. One moment there was distance, the next it dissolved as though it had never existed at all.

Then they were in each other's arms.

The world seemed to tilt, gravity pulling them together with a force neither of them had the strength—or the will—to resist.

His lips claimed hers, warm and firm, a kiss that wasn't rushed or frantic but deliberate, reverent… as if he were memorising her mouth one slow breath at a time. It wasn't just lips meeting; it was a release. A surrender. A confession of every unspoken feeling that had burned between them since the moment they met.

She melted into him instantly, her body softening against his, fitting into him as if she'd been made for that space. Her fingers slid into his thick, silky hair, tightening as she drew him closer, desperate to erase every second they'd spent fighting this magnetic pull.

Jason's hands found her waist, large and warm, his grip both possessive and careful. His thumbs stroked lazy circles against her skin, igniting little sparks that shot straight through her. The taste of her—sweet, familiar, dangerously addictive—made his head spin.

The kiss deepened.

Their tongues met in a slow, sensual rhythm, a teasing push and pull that rolled like heat through their bodies. It wasn't gentle anymore. It was hungry, charged, a simmering want that had finally broken free of restraint.

Her breath trembled against his lips, and when his mouth drifted from hers— trailing a path along the soft line of her jaw—her entire body shivered. He kissed lower, down her throat, each touch sending a wave of warmth through her. She tilted her head back in wordless invitation, her fingers gripping his shoulders, holding on as though he was the only solid thing in a world that kept shifting beneath her feet.

Jason's heartbeat thundered in his ears. Every inhale was filled with her—her scent, her warmth, her small, breathless sounds that wrapped around him and pulled him deeper.

Nothing else existed.

There was no past.

No grief.

No suspicions.

No reason to stop.

Only her. Only them. Only this fierce, undeniable connection neither one could shut out any longer.

And in that moment, something inside Jason snapped—quietly, irrevocably.

He didn't care about his doubts. He didn't care about the pieces of the story that didn't make sense. All he knew—deep in his bones—was that he wanted her. Wanted her more fiercely, more desperately, than he had ever wanted anyone.

Still kissing her, he slid his arms beneath her and lifted her effortlessly. She gasped softly against his mouth, clinging to him as he carried her through the apartment. Each step was slow, intentional, the air humming with anticipation and heat.

When they reached his bedroom, he lowered her to the bed with a gentleness that stole her breath. He hovered over her, the dim light casting shadows across his face, his hand brushing the curve of her cheek.

And then it hit him.

Derek.

The memory slammed into him—his brother's laugh, the last argument, the phone call, the grief that had swallowed him whole. Guilt clawed its way up his spine. *Was this a betrayal? Was he crossing a line he'd promised himself he never would?*

For one suspended second, he froze.

But then Sarah's fingers brushed through his hair again—soft, hesitant, so full of trust it cracked something in him. She looked up at him with those wide, honest eyes. No lies. No manipulations. Just a woman who was hurting, just like him.

Something inside him shifted.

The weight of his anger loosened.

The certainty of his blame faltered.

Maybe he had been wrong.

Maybe she wasn't the villain he had turned her into.

Maybe she was the only person who understood this pain.

"Jason…" she whispered, her voice barely a breath. A plea. A promise. A surrender.

And just like that, whatever remained of his resolve shattered.

He lowered his mouth to hers again—deeper, fiercer—letting himself fall. Letting himself feel. Letting her in.

Chapter Fifteen

Jason pulled back, breathing hard, his gaze fixed on Sarah as though he couldn't quite believe she was real. For a beat, he hesitated—then his fingers found the hem of his shirt, and he lifted it over his head in one fluid motion. He stripped the rest of his clothes until only his boxers remained, the low light catching on the hard lines of his chest and the tension running through his shoulders.

He eased down beside her, the space between them humming, charged with everything they hadn't been able to say out loud. His hand reached for hers, warm and steady, his thumb stroking lightly over her knuckles. He searched her eyes, silently giving her the chance to pull away.

But Sarah didn't. She moved closer—just a breath, just enough—her fingers brushing his bare skin. The simple touch sent a shiver through him, a tremor he couldn't hide.

No words passed between them. They didn't need any. The silence held their truths far better than language ever could.

Jason slid his arms around her, drawing her against him as his mouth found hers again—slow, searching, aching. His hand traced the length of her spine, following the zipper of her dress. He eased it down with deliberate care, kissing her deeply as inch by inch of warm, soft skin was revealed beneath his fingers.

With her quiet help, he pushed the dress from her shoulders. It slipped down her body in a lazy glide, pooling at her ankles before he swept it away, barely sparing it a glance. His attention was entirely, fiercely, on her.

He unhooked her bra next, letting it fall away. Then he gently guided her onto her back, propping himself on his elbow as his gaze roamed her body with open, reverent hunger.

"You're beautiful," he murmured, his voice low and rough, as though the words scraped up from somewhere deep.

A soft smile touched her lips. She cupped his face, pulling him down into another kiss—this one urgent, molten, filled with all the longing she'd tried so hard to ignore.

Then she pushed him onto his back, straddling him with slow, electrifying confidence. Her hands slid over his chest, feeling the warmth, the strength, the way his muscles tightened beneath her touch. A deep groan vibrated through him, his head tipping back slightly as she explored him.

Leaning down, she brushed lingering kisses along his neck, then lower, tracing the defined lines of his chest with her tongue. She circled one nipple with a teasing flick before sucking gently, rewarded with his sharp intake of breath. She moved to the other, lingering just long enough to draw another low, helpless sound from him.

"Sarah…" Jason rasped, the need in his voice unmistakable.

A wicked, breathless smile curved her lips as she kissed down the ridges of his abdomen. Sliding further, she hooked her fingers into the waistband of his boxers, peeling them away inch by inch before tugging them down his legs and tossing them aside.

His erection stood hard, thick, waiting for her. Heat flooded her, her pulse stuttering as she wrapped her hand around him, stroking once—slow, deliberate, devastating. His breath hissed out, his entire body tensing beneath her touch.

She leaned forward, flicking her tongue across the sensitive tip, tasting him. Jason's hands balled into fists at his sides, fighting for control.

"Sarah…" he groaned again, raw, pleading.

She took him into her mouth—slowly at first, savouring every inch, every reaction. His hips jerked, his breath shattering. She drew him deeper, her lips and tongue working in a slow, torturous rhythm, retreating only to take him again, each movement wringing another strangled sound from him.

Jason's fingers finally gave in, sliding into her hair, tightening as pleasure surged through him. His breaths came ragged, uneven, his restraint fraying with every passing second.

"Enough," he growled, his voice rough and barely controlled.

Before she could answer, he grabbed her shoulders and pulled her up in one fierce, instinctive motion. Their bodies collided, his mouth capturing hers in a hot, consuming kiss that left no doubt—no hesitation—no distance at all.

In that moment, nothing else mattered.

Not the past.

Not the consequences.

Only this—only them—caught in the wildfire they could no longer outrun.

His mouth claimed hers again—desperate, consuming—before he rolled her onto her back, his body covering hers in one fluid, powerful motion. The weight of him pressed her into the mattress, surrounding her, matching the fierce, hungry fire pulsing between them.

Propped on one elbow, he held her gaze, his eyes dark and molten, his breath rough against her cheek. His free hand drifted down the soft curve of her stomach, his fingers teasing, tracing, exploring. He reached the edge of her panties, pausing just long enough to make her pulse stutter—then he slipped lower, brushing lightly over the heat of her core.

Sarah's breath caught, her lips parting on a soft, helpless moan. Jason swallowed the sound with a deep, intoxicating kiss as his fingers explored her—slow, sure, relentless. The slick warmth of her drove him wild, and his touch matched the rising urgency between them, building her higher, drawing her toward the edge with every deliberate stroke.

He lowered his mouth to her breast, teasing the tight peak with his tongue before taking it fully into his mouth. A shudder tore through her, pleasure arching her spine as his tongue and fingers worked in perfect, devastating harmony—stroking, circling, pressing, coaxing her higher and higher until—

She broke.

A strangled cry escaped her as her body arched into him, her release crashing through her in blinding, pulsing waves. She trembled, breathless, undone beneath him.

Jason lifted his head, his lips grazing the shell of her ear, his voice thick with raw, urgent need.

"I want you. Now."

Her breath came in soft, uneven gasps as she pulled him closer, her body still trembling, still burning for him.

"Yes… please, Jason," she whispered, her voice trembling with desire. "I need you."

Reaching toward the bedside table, Jason fumbled for a condom with hands that shook from restraint and urgency. He tore it open and rolled it on, breathing hard, while Sarah slid her panties down her legs. The scrap of lace fell to the floor, forgotten, her movements unhurried and inviting. When she looked up at him, her eyes were smoky with desire.

As Jason moved over her, she parted her thighs in silent invitation, guiding him between them with a gentle, trembling touch. His body settled over hers, warm and solid, their skin brushing in a way that made her pulse trip.

The thick, hard length of him pressed against her entrance, sliding through her slick heat but not yet pushing in. The teasing made her gasp softly, her nails digging into his shoulders as she wrapped her legs around his hips, urging him closer.

He exhaled shakily.

"Sarah… God."

And then he pushed forward—slow, powerful, deliberate—filling her inch by devastating inch until he was buried deep inside her.

A soft, breathless moan escaped her lips.

"Jason…"

Her tight heat closed around him, and for a moment he stilled, eyes squeezing shut as he fought for control.

"God, Sarah…" his voice was a rasp, a broken confession. "You feel like heaven."

He pulled back almost entirely, sliding out until she trembled from the loss, then thrust back in with exquisite slowness, savouring every pulse, every clench of her body around him. She gasped, arching up to meet him, her fingers threading through his hair, her lips seeking his.

He lowered himself, bracing on his elbows as he kissed her—deeply, hungrily— while his hips set a rhythm that was unhurried, consuming. Each stroke was deliberate, each movement dragging another helpless moan from her. Their bodies synced effortlessly, as though they had been made for this—made for each other.

The tension tightened between them, a delicious coil drawing them closer and closer to the edge.

Jason's control broke first.

With a low, guttural sound, he gripped her hips and drove into her harder, faster, his rhythm taking on a fierce, desperate intensity. Heat spiralled, their breaths tangled, the room echoing with the soft slap of skin against skin and the desperate sounds spilling from both of them.

"Jason," Sarah whimpered, her voice trembling, needy. "Please…"

He dropped his forehead to hers, breath ragged.

"Sarah…" he gasped, losing himself completely in the way she clung to him, in the way her body welcomed him, squeezed him, consumed him.

The pleasure built—sharp, overwhelming, impossible to hold back.

With a broken, gasping cry, Sarah shattered first. Her body arched, tightening around him in pulsing waves that dragged him under with her.

Jason thrust deep one last time, a guttural groan ripping from his throat as he surrendered utterly, his release crashing through him with blinding force.

For a long, breathless moment, neither of them moved. They stayed tangled together, his weight warm and comforting over her, their breaths mingling in the soft, charged silence.

The world outside ceased to exist.

All that remained was the shared heat of their bodies, the thrum of their racing hearts—and the unspoken connection that now felt impossible to ignore.

Finally, Jason rolled onto his back, bringing Sarah with him, holding her close as if he could somehow anchor both of them in this moment. Their hearts pounded in unison, a shared rhythm that made the silence between them feel alive. She nestled against his chest, warm and soft, her body still humming with the aftermath of their passion. His fingers traced slow, lazy circles along the curve of her spine, every touch lingering, memorising the way her skin responded. He pressed a gentle kiss to her hair, inhaling the faint scent of shampoo and her natural warmth.

"I don't think I'll ever get enough of you," he murmured, his voice thick with wonder and exhaustion, rough around the edges from exertion and emotion.

A slow, satisfied smile curved Sarah's lips as she pressed herself closer, whispering against the hollow of his throat, "Good."

Jason chuckled softly, the sound low and private, tightening his hold on her, as if letting her slip even slightly would fracture something fragile and precious between them. They lay tangled together, limbs intertwined, the rest of the world falling away, shrinking until it didn't exist. The room felt warmer, quieter, cocooned in the soft light of early morning filtering through the curtains.

Their breathing was uneven, ragged at first, then gradually settling into something steadier. Jason's mind reeled, trying to make sense of the intensity of what had just passed between them. It wasn't just desire, not merely lust or heat—it was something deeper, something that carved its way into his chest and soul. Being with Sarah felt like standing on the edge of something vast and terrifying yet exhilarating. She made him feel things he hadn't dared to feel in years.

Sarah broke the silence first, her voice barely above a whisper, trembling with awe and vulnerability. "That... that was intense. I've never felt anything like it." Her fingers wandered across his chest in absent-minded, delicate patterns, tracing each contour as though she wanted to memorise him as he had memorised her.

Jason tilted his head, brushing a stray lock of hair from her face. His touch lingered, warm and gentle, as if he wanted to imprint himself on her. "I'm glad," he murmured softly, his voice low, sincere. "You were incredible." His eyes held hers, admiration and something softer, more fragile shining within them.

Sarah exhaled, resting her head against his chest, her fingers tightening slightly around his arm. The rise and fall of his chest beneath her cheek was hypnotic, grounding, a quiet anchor in a world that had been spinning too fast for far too long. She felt safe, desired, and profoundly connected in a way that went far beyond the physical.

Jason let out a slow, contented breath, closing his eyes for a moment, feeling her warmth pressed against him. Every worry, every ache of grief or frustration, seemed to fade in this shared cocoon of quiet intimacy. The heat of their bodies, the rhythm of their hearts, the lingering touch of lips and fingertips—it all spoke louder than words ever could.

Jason felt the moment shift as her breathing softened, deepened. Her body melted into his, her limbs relaxing against him as sleep pulled her under. He hesitated, a battle flickering in his chest. A part of him wanted to stay exactly as he was—with her curled against him, warm and trusting—refusing to move even an inch. But another part, the careful, disciplined part, urged him to slip away before the weight of reality crashed back in.

Still, he moved slowly, gently, easing himself out from beneath her with painstaking care. She didn't stir, not even when the mattress lifted slightly. She simply sighed, settling deeper into the pillow.

Jason stood at the edge of the bed; breath caught in his throat.

She was lying on her stomach now, golden skin illuminated by the soft glow of the bedside lamp he hadn't turned off. Her hair fanned across the pillow in a dark halo, long strands brushing her cheek. One arm was tucked beneath her, the other reaching lazily across the sheets as though searching for him even in sleep.

He felt something tighten low in his chest—sharp, unfamiliar.

Peace.

That was the only word for the strange, steady warmth spreading through him. He hadn't felt it in years. Maybe not since before his parents died, not since Derek's voice stopped filling the silence. And now, watching her sleep, so beautiful, so unguarded…

He wanted this moment to stretch on forever.

He knew it wouldn't. He wasn't naïve. But God, if he could freeze time, he would.

They woke before dawn, wrapped in the stillness of early morning. The world outside was dark and silent, as though it too was suspended between breaths. Their bodies were warm beneath the tangled sheets, their breathing soft and synchronised.

For a moment, neither spoke. Neither moved.

Then, as if guided by instinct rather than thought, they reached for each other at the same time.

Sarah shifted closer, her hand sliding over his chest with quiet tenderness. Jason cupped her cheek, brushing his thumb along her lower lip before pulling her into his embrace. There was no hesitation, no awkwardness—only a deep, unspoken understanding that this was exactly where they needed to be.

This time, their intimacy held a different kind of power.

Gentler. Deeper. More real.

Jason traced his fingertips down the length of her spine, slow and reverent. Each delicate touch drew a soft sigh from her, her body arching into him, seeking more. He leaned in, pressing a lingering kiss to her lips—unhurried, as though he wanted to savour every second. She kissed him back with the same tender hunger, her hand sliding to his jaw, holding him close.

The quiet ache between them built gradually, steadily, as they explored each other with soft touches and whispered breaths. Jason kissed the curve of her neck, the slope of her shoulder, the spot just beneath her ear that made her tremble. Sarah ran her fingers through his hair, down the solid muscles of his back, her touch light but sure.

When they joined again, it was slow—so slow it stole their breath. Their bodies moved in perfect harmony, a rhythm born not of urgency but intimacy. He cradled her face as he kissed her, as if trying to tell her everything he hadn't yet said. She held him tightly, her legs curling around him, her whispered moans soft in the dim light.

It felt like more than pleasure. More than desire.

It felt like truth.

By the time the first streaks of morning light crept through the window, painting soft gold across their bodies, they were still wrapped together—foreheads touching, breaths mingling.

Jason couldn't stop touching her.

Her body fit against his in a way that felt terrifyingly right. Every time her breath hitched when he traced slow circles along her hip, or her fingers fluttered against his chest, something inside him pulled tighter, sinking deeper.

And then, drawn by a heat that never truly faded, they found each other again.

This time, they moved even more slowly, savouring each touch, each gasp, each shiver. Jason explored her with a tenderness that bordered on worship, kissing down her throat, along her collarbone, across the delicate skin of her stomach. Sarah arched beneath him, breathless, her hands clutching him like she wanted to anchor herself to him.

But restraint couldn't hold them for long.

Passion surged—wild and consuming—sweeping through them in a rush too powerful to control. Their movements grew urgent, desperate, their bodies moving in a fevered rhythm that stole all thought. Their pleasure built together, fast and unstoppable, until it consumed them completely.

When it finally crashed over them, they clung to each other—shaking, breathless, lost.

Silence settled again. Not cold, not empty.

Warm. Comforting. Safe.

Jason wrapped his arms around her, holding her tightly against his chest. She curved into him, her breath feathering against his neck. He kissed her temple, her forehead, the tip of her nose—each kiss soft, lingering, a silent admission of everything he couldn't yet speak aloud.

He didn't want to let her go.

Every time he touched her, every time he kissed her, the realisation pushed deeper into him, carving itself into his heart.

He never wanted this to end.

Chapter Sixteen

The sunlight filtered through the half-open blinds, casting a warm glow on the bed where Sarah lay beside him. Her body, tangled in the sheets, was the picture of contentment. Jason, still half-dazed from the passion of the night, could feel the softness of her skin against his as he slowly shifted beside her. He glanced down at her peaceful face, her hair splayed out in a wild mess, and a small smile tugged at his lips.

He couldn't remember the last time he'd felt this… content. This whole. It was as if time had stopped, and everything in his world had narrowed down to this one moment, to Sarah.

She stirred slightly, her lashes fluttering as she began to wake. Her eyes met his, and for a moment, neither of them spoke—words weren't necessary. They just shared a look, a quiet understanding of what had passed between them, of how they had connected in a way neither of them could have predicted.

"Morning," Jason murmured, his voice thick with sleep and something deeper, something more.

Sarah smiled softly, reaching out to trace his jaw with her fingers. "Morning," she replied, her voice a gentle whisper, still tinged with the remnants of sleep.

Jason's heart skipped a beat at the intimacy of the moment, the closeness they now shared. He leaned in, pressing a kiss on her forehead, his lips lingering for just a second longer than necessary.

"You're beautiful," he whispered again, as though he couldn't say it enough.

She chuckled softly, her hand reaching up to cup his face. "You keep saying that you will give me a big head."

"I don't believe that," he replied with a smirk.

Sarah's heart fluttered at his words, a warmth spreading through her chest. She pulled him closer, kissing him slowly, lingeringly, savouring the feel of his lips on hers.

But eventually, the quiet peace of the morning began to pull them both out of their sleepy haze. Jason reluctantly pulled away from her, though his eyes remained locked on hers as he got out of bed. "I'm going to make us breakfast. You need to rest."

Sarah's eyes followed him as he moved toward the door. "Breakfast? Are you sure? I didn't think you can cook."

"I can cook breakfast," Jason said, flashing her a grin. "Besides, after last night…" He paused, turning back toward her. "I think I owe you a proper breakfast."

A playful smirk tugged at Sarah's lips. "Well, I look forward to your culinary skills."

Jason chuckled softly and disappeared into the kitchen, the sound of pots and pans clanging soon filling the air.

Sarah lay back on the bed for a moment, her mind drifting as she listened to Jason's movements. She felt completely at ease, something she hadn't realised she had been missing in her life. Her thoughts turned to the intimacy they had shared, how every kiss, every touch had felt like it was meant to be. There was a deep connection between them, one that transcended the physical. She could feel it in every quiet moment, in every laugh they shared, in the way they moved together so naturally.

As Jason worked, she eventually got up and made her way into the kitchen, a smile tugging at her lips as she leaned against the door frame, watching him. He was humming softly to himself as he flipped a pancake, looking every bit the man she had come to know in such a short time. His confidence, the way he moved, the care he put into everything he did—it all made her heart swell.

"Need some help?" she asked, her voice light.

Jason looked up, his grin widening when he saw her standing there. "Sure, you can keep me company. But no cooking. I've got this."

Sarah walked over to him, standing close as she reached for the coffee pot, pouring herself a cup. She leaned against the counter, her eyes never leaving him as he continued to cook.

"You look good in the kitchen," she teased. "Didn't take you for a breakfast chef."

He glanced at her over his shoulder. "I have a lot of hidden skills."

Her grin grew wider. "I'm starting to learn," she replied softly.

Jason set the plate of pancakes down on the table, and they sat together, the quiet intimacy of the moment settled over them. They ate, laughed, and shared stories about their lives—small things, nothing too deep, but all of it made them feel closer. The kind of connection that only deepened with time.

As the day wore on, they found themselves outdoors, walking hand in hand through a nearby park. It was a beautiful day, the sun high in the sky, casting a gentle warmth over everything. They walked in easy silence, only speaking occasionally, exchanging playful remarks or comments about the world around them.

Jason loved the ease with which they could be together. There was no pressure, no awkwardness. Just them, enjoying each other's company, letting the world move around them.

They found a bench and sat, Sarah leaning against him as he wrapped his arm around her shoulders, pulling her close. The quiet sound of birds in the trees and the distant chatter of passersby filled the air, but it was the gentle hum of their own contentment that filled the silence between them.

"Do you ever think about what comes next?" Sarah asked after a long pause, her voice soft, almost as though she were testing the waters.

Jason glanced down at her, sensing the vulnerability in her words. "What do you mean?"

"I mean…" She hesitated, searching for the right words. "I don't know. What happens after this? After last night?"

Jason felt his heart beat a little faster, but he squeezed her hand, his fingers gently caressing hers. "I don't know," he admitted, "but I'm not afraid of it. Whatever happens, whatever comes next—I want to face it with you."

Sarah's smile softened, and she kissed him gently on the lips, a promise in the simple act. "Me too."

They spent the rest of the day wrapped up in each other's presence, their connection growing deeper with every laugh, every kiss, every quiet moment shared. And as the sun began to set, casting a golden hue over everything, they knew that no matter what the future held, this moment, this day, would stay with them forever.

The week slipped by in a peaceful blur—soft, steady, almost unreal in its simplicity. Jason's days hadn't changed: the same meetings, the same calls, the same endless grind of decisions and responsibilities. But something inside him had shifted. Work was no longer the only thing anchoring him. Every morning, when he dragged himself out of bed, it wasn't the office he thought of.

It was her.

Coming home to Sarah had become the quiet pulse that carried him through the hours.

Each evening, the moment he opened the door, the weight of the day loosened its hold. Warm light, the soft hum of music, the scent of something simmering on the stove—roasted chicken, crusty bread, a pot of her favourite soup. It wasn't just the food. It was the intention behind it. The way she poured herself into the little things, filling spaces he hadn't realised were empty until she touched them.

And then there was Sarah herself—standing by the stove, curled up with a book, or padding across the room in bare feet, always greeting him with a gentle smile that made him forget, for just a moment, how hard the world could be.

"You're home early," she'd say, warmth softening her voice.

Jason would loosen his tie, gaze lingering on her face. "Just wanted to get back to you."

It always felt like he was understating the truth.

Dinner was easy, comfortable—her laughter drifting over the table, his voice roughening when she leaned forward to listen. She told him about the small things that coloured her day: the recipe she'd tried, the chapter that made her cry, the sunset that had turned the sky molten gold. He told her the truth he rarely told anyone—the frustrations he carried, the things that kept him up at night. And she listened. Really listened. As if nothing he said was ever too much.

Afterward, they would drift to the couch. Sarah curled beside him with natural familiarity, fitting into the curve of his body as if she had always been meant to be there. Sometimes they watched a movie. Sometimes they talked. Sometimes they simply existed together, fingers intertwined, breaths syncing, the silence warmer than any words.

And the nights…

The nights were their own kind of sanctuary.

In the dark, with their bodies tangled under the sheets, the world fell away. Sometimes their touches were slow, reverent; sometimes urgent, hungry. But always, always real. When it was over, he held her close, his face buried in the soft place where her neck met her shoulder, her hand drifting through his hair in a rhythm that soothed him more than sleep ever had.

Every morning, he woke to her—soft, drowsy, sunlight caught in her hair. Every morning, something deep in him whispered the same truth.

He could get used to this.

He was getting used to this.

And it terrified him in a way nothing else ever had.

One night, as they lay entangled, Jason brushed a strand of hair from her cheek. She tilted her face into his hand, instinctively, like she trusted his touch without thinking.

"You've made this week… incredible," he said quietly.

Sarah's smile was soft, sleepy. Her fingers traced lazy circles on his chest. "It's just us," she murmured. "Funny how the simplest things feel like everything with the right person."

His chest tightened. He didn't know how to answer that, so he didn't. He simply pulled her closer, letting her warmth settle into him.

The days that followed settled into a rhythm so gentle, so effortless, it felt like a life beginning to take shape. A life he hadn't realised he wanted until she was in it.

A life he didn't know he could lose.

And then came Friday.

Friday, when he left work early.

Friday, when everything still felt right.

Friday—

when one moment shattered the world they'd built

and nothing was ever the same again.

Chapter Seventeen

Friday afternoon, as the sun filtered through the curtains, Sarah was startled by the sharp ring of the intercom, breaking the quiet of the day. She glanced toward it, hesitation creeping in before she stepped forward, pressing the button.

"Hello?"

"Miss Pratt," came the concierge's crisp, professional voice. "There is a Daniel down here to see you."

Sarah's breath caught. Daniel? What on earth was he doing here? Her stomach twisted as a flood of questions rushed through her mind. She hadn't spoken to him since the party—hadn't even thought about him. And yet, here he was, standing in the lobby of Jason's apartment building.

A sense of unease settled over her. This isn't right. She couldn't let him come up. Jason wasn't home, and she had no interest in creating unnecessary tension for Jason.

"I'll come down to meet him," she said quickly, keeping her voice neutral despite the nerves coiling in her stomach. "Tell him I'll be down soon."

"Very good, Miss Pratt," the concierge replied before the line clicked off.

Sarah exhaled, bracing herself. She didn't know what Daniel wanted, but she wasn't about to let this spiral into something messy. Jason knew she had given Daniel her new number, but she had never expected him to actually show up here.

Stepping into the elevator, she smoothed her hands down her clothes, trying to shake the unsettled feeling growing in her chest. When the doors slid open, she stepped into the lobby and at once spotted Daniel waiting by the entrance, hands in his pockets, his signature confident smile in place.

"Hello, Daniel," she greeted cautiously. "What brings you here?"

"Hi, gorgeous," he said smoothly, leaning down to kiss her cheek.

Sarah stiffened. *Gorgeous?* She had never encouraged that, and his casual affection sent warning bells through her mind.

"I wanted to see if you'd go out with me tomorrow night," he continued, his tone light, as if this were the most natural thing in the world.

Sarah blinked at him, caught off guard. Did he think she was available?

"Thank you for the offer, Daniel, but Jason and I are dating now." Her voice was firm, unwavering.

Daniel's smirk faltered. He exhaled, rubbing the back of his neck as he took a step back. "Oh… I was afraid of that."

Sarah offered a polite but pointed smile. "I'm really sorry, but it's only recent." She turned slightly toward the entrance, subtly signalling that their conversation was over.

Daniel hesitated for a second, then let out a small chuckle. "Okay, I know when I'm beat."

Sarah turned to face him one last time, ready to say goodbye with a smile—when suddenly, Daniel grabbed her upper arms and pulled her in, crushing his lips against hers.

Her body went rigid.

Shock slammed into her first—cold and blinding—followed instantly by a wave of disgust and white-hot fury.

For a heartbeat she couldn't move, couldn't breathe, her mind struggling to catch up with what had just happened. Then the spell broke.

She shoved Daniel hard, sending him stumbling back. Her eyes burned with outrage, her voice shaking with the force of it.

"Daniel! Don't you ever do that again."

She took a step back, jaw tight, breath trembling. "I'm not a cheater. Not now, not ever."

He had the audacity to look apologetic; his hands raised in surrender. "Sorry, sorry. It won't happen again." He took a step back, his smile turning sad. "Be happy, Sarah."

She clenched her jaw, taking a steadying breath. "Thank you, Daniel."

She watched him walk away, shaking her head, anger simmering beneath her skin.

As she turned and headed toward the elevator, one thought took over her mind—

She had to tell Jason. *Before he heard it from someone else.*

Friday felt like every other Friday—until Jason decided he was done pretending work mattered more than she did.

It had been another week of relentless meetings, back-to-back calls, and the constant hum of pressure he'd grown far too used to. But tonight, for the first time in a long time, he didn't want to stay late, or bury himself in spreadsheets, or chase distractions that kept him from feeling too much.

Tonight, he wanted to go home early.

Because home meant Sarah.

She had cooked for him every night this week, sliding so seamlessly into the rhythm of his life that he barely recognised the version of himself he'd been before her—quiet, empty, untouched by the warmth she brought with her soft laugh and gentle presence. He hadn't realised how lonely he'd been until she started filling the silence.

Tonight, he wanted to give something back.

Take her out. Make her feel special. Let her rest for once.

As he drove, she occupied every corner of his thoughts—the sparkle in her eyes when she teased him, the soft give of her body when she curled into his arms, the way her voice felt like a balm after a hard day. A smile tugged at his mouth, unrestrained and easy.

He pictured her at the door, startled and delighted when he showed up early. He could already imagine her biting her lip, pretending to protest that she didn't mind cooking, that it was no trouble, that he didn't need to spoil her.

But he would insist.

He'd take her to that little Italian place she mentioned—the one that reminded her of home, the one she spoke of with that wistful smile he couldn't get out of his head.

He wanted to see that smile again.

He wanted her.

God, he wanted her.

And wanting her felt like standing at the edge of something dangerous and beautiful.

He turned the corner toward his building just as the light ahead shifted to red, forcing him to brake.

The moment the car rolled to a stop, he saw them.

Daniel.

And Sarah.

Jason's stomach twisted so sharply he almost doubled over.

They were stepping out of the entrance together. She was smiling—smiling—up at Daniel, her hair catching the late-afternoon sunlight, her expression soft and open in a way Jason had begun to think was meant for him alone.

He leaned forward unconsciously, breath suspended.

And then it happened.

Daniel reached for Sarah and pulled her into him and dipped his head and pressed his mouth to hers.

Jason's breath hitched like someone had smashed a fist straight into his ribs. For a split second he forgot how to inhale entirely.

The light flicked to green.

But Jason didn't move.

His knuckles blanched as he tightened his grip on the steering wheel, every muscle in his body locking up as the image seared itself into his mind. Daniel's hands. Daniel's mouth. Sarah—still, so still.

The world around him dissolved into a smear of movement and colour as he forced the car forward on autopilot, but inside his head, nothing moved at all.

The kiss looped again.

And again.

A cruel reel he couldn't shut off, no matter how desperately he tried.

By the time he pulled into the parking garage, Jason's pulse thundered in his ears, his stomach a churning mess of jealousy, anger, and disbelief.

Why had Daniel been there?

Why had he kissed her?

And—most painfully—*why hadn't she pushed him away?*

It hadn't been casual. It hadn't been friendly.

A sharp, gnawing pain coiled in his chest, twisting like a knife.

Was she seeing him? Was she cheating on me?

He'd seen the way Daniel looked at Sarah before—like she belonged to him. And Sarah… that smile at the party. Had he been blind? Had he ignored the signs that were staring him in the face all along?

Doubt slithered in, insidious and relentless.

She cheated on Derek.

Jason had forced himself to reject the thought before. No. It wasn't true. It couldn't be true.

But now… he wasn't so sure.

Derek's last words echoed in his mind.

"She betrayed me, Jason. I can't believe she slept with him."

He hadn't wanted to believe it. He'd told himself Sarah wasn't capable of that. But Derek had died that night—heartbroken, reckless, destroyed. Because of her.

Jason's jaw clenched. His breath came in ragged bursts.

No… Sarah wouldn't do that. She couldn't.

Would she?

The question lodged in his skull, a cold, relentless weight that poisoned everything—his trust, his certainty, even his feelings for her.

And then it hit him like a lightning strike.

I'm in love with Sarah.

The realisation should have stunned him, should have left him breathless. Instead, all he felt was the acidic burn of betrayal curling in his gut.

And then the second, crueler truth cut through the fog:

She fooled me. Just like she fooled Derek.

First Derek. Now him. And probably Daniel too.

His stomach twisted, bile rising like molten lead.

He had let himself believe in her. Trust her. Care for her.

And now? He was just another name on her list.

A serial cheater.

Jason's hands clenched the steering wheel until his knuckles whitened as he pulled into his parking spot. His jaw ached from how tightly he was grinding his teeth, his body trembling with barely contained rage.

No.

She wasn't going to do this to him.

Not him.

He wasn't Derek.

He wasn't going to crumble. He wasn't going to give her the satisfaction of knowing she'd hurt him.

Not this time.

Jason pushed open the car door, his muscles taut with fury—not just at her, but at himself. How had he let it happen? How had he fallen for her lies, just like Derek had?

Was this some twisted game to her? Did she enjoy watching men stumble at her feet?

His chest ached, but he shoved it aside.

She wasn't going to break him. Not like she had broken Derek.

She is the reason my brother is dead.

The thought cut through him like fire, igniting a storm of anger beneath his skin. Derek had loved her. Believed in her. And she had destroyed him.

Jason's breath came in sharp, uneven bursts as he strode toward the elevator, every step coiled with tension.

Well, she was going to find out exactly how he felt about her.

The elevator doors slid open with a soft chime, and he stepped inside, each movement deliberate, controlled, yet brimming with barely restrained fury.

And then he saw her.

Standing barefoot in his living room, bathed in the soft glow of the lamp, Sarah's face lit up the moment she saw him.

"Jason." Her voice was warm, familiar, filled with the trust and affection she had always carried for him. She stepped forward, slipping her arms around his neck, expecting the easy, familiar embrace they once shared.

He didn't move.

Not a muscle. Not a flicker of recognition. His body was rigid, arms hanging at his sides like lifeless weights.

Confusion flickered across her face. "Is something wrong?"

His voice came cold, clipped, emotionless. "It's time for you to leave."

Sarah blinked, stunned, letting out a nervous laugh as she searched his face. "What? Jason… what are you talking about?"

"I want you gone."

The warmth drained from her expression. "Jason, if—if something happened, we can talk—"

"There's nothing to talk about." His words were sharp, each syllable cutting through the fragile hope in her eyes. "You should've never been here."

Hurt tightened her chest, and her brows furrowed. "I don't understand. If this is about me staying here, I can go back to my apartment tomorrow—"

"No." His gaze was hard, merciless. "Now."

Her stomach dropped. "Now?"

Jason exhaled sharply, a controlled frustration simmering beneath his words. "You heard me."

Her heart raced, panic threading through her voice. "Jason, please—"

"You and me?" He let out a humourless, bitter laugh. "It was never real."

The floor seemed to tilt beneath her.

"What… what are you saying?" she whispered, her voice trembling.

He met her gaze with unflinching coldness. "I used you, Sarah."

Her breath hitched.

And then—

The final blow.

"It was just a way to punish you for my brother's death."

Sarah flinched as though he had struck her across the face.

"No," she choked out, shaking her head violently. "Derek's death wasn't my fault! Why would you even think that?"

Jason's jaw clenched, rigid and unyielding. "Because it is."

Tears welled in her eyes, blurring the world around her. "Jason… I thought—" Her voice cracked, splintering under the weight of heartbreak. "I thought you loved me."

His silence was sharper than any blade.

The man who had once held her through every fear, who had whispered promises against her skin, who had kissed her like she was his entire world—was now looking at her as though she were nothing.

"You mean nothing to me, Sarah." His words were stone-cold, deliberate, leaving no room for doubt.

The declaration shattered her completely. She staggered back, hands trembling as if her very body couldn't hold the weight of it.

"You're lying," she whispered, barely audible, a desperate plea.

Jason's gaze met hers, unflinching, void of any warmth. "I'm not."

A sob tore through her, raw and ragged, as she wrapped her arms around herself, trying in vain to hold together the pieces of her breaking heart.

"Are you telling me…" Her voice shook violently, cracking under the weight of disbelief. "You… you slept with me just because you thought I caused Derek's death? That I drove him to—"

Jason didn't flinch. Didn't blink. Didn't hesitate.

"Yes."

Her chest tightened, the air caught in her lungs, suffocating.

"You upset him that night. You pushed him. He got behind the wheel because of you. It was your fault."

Sarah swayed where she stood, knees threatening to buckle, the world tilting around her. Every word was a hammer, crushing her from the inside out.

Jason turned away, his voice void of any humanity, detached.

"Get out."

Her lips trembled. "Jason, please—"

He didn't look back.

"Don't come back."

The door to his bedroom closed with a final, echoing thud.

The sound shattered the fragile remnants of her courage.

Sarah froze, the silence pressing in, suffocating, as if the air itself had been stolen from her lungs.

And then the sobs came—raw, ragged, unstoppable—ripping through her chest as she sank to the floor. She curled in on herself, trembling, broken, in the very place she had once felt safest.

The living room, once warm and familiar, had become a tomb of her heartache.

Chapter Eighteen

Sarah sat in stunned silence, her body pressed against the cold floor, every nerve raw. She couldn't move. Couldn't think. Couldn't breathe. Hours—or maybe only minutes—passed, but time had lost all meaning.

The door Jason had disappeared behind felt miles away, and yet every fibre of her being was fixed on it. The man she had loved. The man she had trusted. The man who had just told her she meant nothing.

"You mean nothing to me, Sarah."

The words reverberated in her skull like a hammer, each one striking harder than the last. She squeezed her eyes shut, shaking her head violently, willing them to vanish. But they clung to her, gnawing, suffocating.

"It was just a way to punish you for my brother's death."

Her chest heaved. Fresh tears burned down her cheeks.

No.

No, no, no.

That couldn't be true. Derek's death wasn't her fault.

Fragments of that night surfaced, jagged and incomplete. She still couldn't remember everything—pieces blurred by grief and trauma—but one truth burned bright: she hadn't hurt Derek. He had cared about her, trusted her. He had been her friend. Would he have believed she was capable of destroying him if he truly knew her?

A sob clawed its way up her throat, raw and ragged. Jason had believed she was guilty. Jason had used her.

Her hands trembled violently as she forced herself to her feet, her movements shaky and uneven. She stumbled into the spare room, grabbing clothes with frantic desperation, shoving them into a bag as if the faster she packed, the faster she could escape the pain.

Every item she had brought to his apartment—the place she had once called home for a few short weeks—was reduced to chaos in her arms, crammed into the bag in mere minutes.

The weight of it hit her all at once. The finality. The betrayal. Her stomach turned as she gripped the zipper, her breath jagged. *Was this real? Had he truly meant what he said?*

Her heart screamed no, but the memory of that cold, merciless look in his eyes offered no comfort. He didn't love her. He never had.

A broken, strangled sound escaped her lips as she closed her bag. The noise seemed deafening in the emptiness of the apartment.

And then, without another glance, she walked out—her heart fractured, her trust shattered, leaving behind everything she had once held dear.

By the time Sarah reached the lobby, her eyes were swollen, her limbs heavy, as if the weight of betrayal had seeped into her bones. Her entire body felt hollow, drained—not just of energy, but of the part of herself she had entrusted to Jason.

She had no plan. No destination. Only a desperate need to escape.

As she stumbled toward the exit, a gentle voice cut through the haze.

"Sarah?"

Before she could even register it, Margaret appeared at her side, her face etched with concern.

Sarah opened her mouth, but no words came. Her throat felt raw, her voice lost to the sobs clawing at her chest.

Margaret took one look at her tear-streaked face, her expression softening. "Oh, sweetheart…"

That single note of warmth and care cracked something deep inside Sarah. A fresh, shuddering sob tore through her, and her knees nearly gave way.

Without hesitation, Margaret guided her to an armchair in the corner, sitting close, hands enveloping Sarah's trembling ones. Her touch was steady, grounding, a quiet lifeline in the storm.

Sarah's body shook as she tried to catch her breath, her words barely audible. "Jason… he thinks I've done something terrible… but I swear I haven't… I didn't…" Her voice broke completely, choking on the weight of disbelief, her fingers clutching at the fabric of her dress like a lifeline.

Margaret tightened her hold, murmuring gently, "Oh, sweetheart… tell me what happened."

Sarah shook her head, unable to speak the truth. How could she explain that the man she had loved, the one she had trusted with her entire heart, had just shattered it beyond recognition?

"He thinks I…" she whispered, swallowing hard as fresh tears cascaded down her cheeks. "I can't believe he actually thinks that of me."

Margaret's face tightened with concern, her thumb tracing soothing circles across Sarah's back. "Where are you going?" she asked softly.

Sarah wiped at her cheeks, though the tears continued to fall. "Back home," she murmured. "I… I need to go."

Margaret frowned, hesitating. "Sweetheart, maybe you should stay somewhere nearby tonight—just until you feel better—"

"No." Sarah shook her head, her voice firm despite the trembling. "I can't stay here."

Margaret's eyes searched hers, a flicker of worry in her gaze. "Are you sure?"

Sarah managed a small, trembling smile—fragile but determined. "Thank you, Margaret. It's been… lovely knowing you."

Something in the quiet weight of her words made Margaret's stomach drop. There was a finality in her tone, a subtle, chilling acceptance that pressed against the older woman's chest.

"Sarah—"

Before she could finish, Sarah reached for Margaret's hands, gripping them tightly. Her gaze, raw and desperate, searched Margaret's with an intensity that stole her breath.

"Look after Jason for me," she whispered, voice breaking.

Margaret's throat tightened at the plea.

"Please," Sarah added, wavered with unspoken emotion. "Make sure he's okay."

The depth of heartbreak in her voice left Margaret's chest aching. She hesitated for only a moment before nodding, her own voice barely above a whisper. "I promise."

Sarah exhaled shakily, a small nod as if that single reassurance was enough.

Then, without another word, she turned toward the exit.

Margaret watched her go, her fingers clenching at her sides as Sarah's figure moved toward the doors. For a heartbeat, it seemed as if she might turn back, might offer one last plea, one final goodbye.

But she didn't.

She squared her shoulders, took a measured breath, and stepped out.

Without looking back.

Margaret's eyes lingered on the empty doorway long after she had gone, a hollow ache settling deep in her chest. Something told her this wasn't just Sarah leaving Jason's apartment.

She was leaving—for good.

Steam curled around Jason, fogging the mirror, turning his reflection into a ghost of himself. His skin stung from the scalding water, but no heat could chase away the cold gnawing at his chest. Every muscle in his body ached, tension coiled so tightly that simply standing felt like a battle.

He gripped the edges of the sink, knuckles white, breaths ragged. Water droplets clung to his lashes like unshed tears, tracing lines down his face. He forced himself to meet his reflection, but the man staring back looked hollow, broken—a man who had just made the worst mistake of his life.

He had convinced himself it was necessary. Pushing Sarah away, cutting her out like a wound that refused to heal, would somehow balance the scales for Derek. That inflicting even a fraction of his own pain on her would serve some cruel, twisted justice.

Instead, all he felt was emptiness. Like his heart had been ripped out and trampled.

Her face burned behind his eyes—the disbelief, the hurt, the rawness in her voice as she asked *why*. The fragile trust in her gaze, shattered in an instant. Jason squeezed his eyes shut, but it was useless. She clung to him, etched into his bones, into the very air he breathed.

And beneath the anger, beneath the grief and the walls he had spent years building, something dark and corrosive stirred.

Regret.

A sharp knock at the door jolted him from his thoughts. He ran a hand down his face, tasting the metallic tang of frustration and guilt. He wasn't in the mood for anyone. But if it was Margaret, it meant something was wrong.

Bracing himself, he turned from the mirror, every step toward the door heavy, deliberate, carrying the weight of everything he had just lost.

Margaret stood in the doorway, her face stormy, eyes blazing.

"What did you do to that girl?" she demanded, storming past him into the apartment.

Jason exhaled sharply, shutting the door behind her. "Margaret, don't get involved."

"Don't get involved?" she echoed, incredulous, hands on her hips. "That poor girl walked out of here looking like her whole world just ended! And you're telling me not to get involved?"

Jason's jaw clenched, guilt clawing at him. "It's none of your business," he snapped.

Margaret scoffed, stepping closer, jabbing a finger into his chest. "The hell it isn't! I care about that girl. And I care about you, even when you're being a damn fool. So, I'll ask you again—what did you do to her?"

The words escaped him before he could stop them. "She is the reason my brother is dead."

Margaret froze, her expression shifting from fury to shock, then disbelief. "You can't believe that," she said, her voice quieter now but resolute. "How could she be? There is no way on this earth that girl was responsible for your brother's death. No way."

"She is," Jason insisted, voice hard as he sank onto the couch, running a hand through his hair, trying to erase Sarah's tear-streaked face from his mind.

"Do you want the gory details, Margaret?" he scoffed. "Did she run to you for sympathy?"

"No, she didn't," Margaret replied, crossing her arms, her tone firm.

Jason blinked, thrown off.

"She didn't tell me anything," Margaret continued, stepping closer. "All she said was that you think she did something horrible, and she can't believe you believe it. And do you know what else, Jason? She made me promise to make sure *you're* okay."

Jason's throat went dry. "She—she what?"

"Yes," Margaret said, steel beneath her calm. "She made me promise." Her voice softened, but the conviction didn't fade. "Does that sound like a girl who could destroy a life and walk away? Does that sound like someone capable of causing death?"

Jason opened his mouth, but nothing came out.

Margaret shook her head gently. "I don't even want to know what you think she did, because I won't believe it. I'm here for you, Jason, but don't make yourself believe a lie. That girl has a heart of gold."

Without another word, she turned and left, leaving Jason alone with the suffocating silence of his own thoughts.

Doubt slithered in, unwelcome and insistent.

Was he wrong?

No. He couldn't be.

He had seen Daniel kissing her. The betrayal, the heartbreak—it had sent Derek spiralling.

Jason's jaw clenched, forcing himself to hold onto that certainty.

Sarah had to be responsible.

…Hadn't she?

Sarah took an Uber back to her Bondi apartment, her body numb, her heart anything but. The moment she stepped inside, the weight of everything she had been holding together snapped. She didn't bother turning on a light. She didn't even take off her shoes. She simply staggered to her bedroom, collapsed onto the bed, and folded into herself as the sobs tore loose.

She buried her face in the pillow, but nothing could muffle the hollow, aching sound of her heartbreak. Every breath felt fractured. Every thought circled back to the same brutal truth:

Jason believed she had killed his brother.

That thought alone was enough to break her all over again.

The weekend scraped by painfully, every hour stretching like a lifetime. Jason didn't call—not that she had expected him to—but some naïve, stubborn shard of hope inside her had still waited for the phone to ring. Every time it stayed silent, the hurt dug deeper.

It wasn't just that he'd pushed her away.

It was that he had meant it.

Every cold word. Every accusation.

He had looked at her like she was a monster.

She wished she could remember more from that night. Fragments surfaced, blurry and jagged, but never enough. And without her old phone—lost in the wreck—she had nothing. No messages, no call logs, nothing to prove to him that she and Derek had only ever been friends. His phone had vanished too.

Two phones. Two lives shattered. No proof left behind.

By Monday morning, she hadn't slept more than a handful of hours. Her ribs still twinged when she breathed too deeply, her body reminding her of an accident she barely remembered. Her heart, however, reminded her of everything she wished she could forget.

But she had been off work for four weeks. She couldn't hide forever.

She got dressed mechanically, her movements stiff and slow, and took the bus to the school. As she walked through the gates, the familiar courtyard felt foreign, as if it belonged to a life she'd left behind months ago.

The principal welcomed her back warmly, relief softening her features. "We're so grateful you're feeling better," she said, her tone gentle.

Sarah nodded, but the words slid past her like water. Sitting in that office, listening to encouragement, praise, and an invitation to return to routine, felt suffocating. Her chest tightened with every passing second.

She couldn't go back. Not to the classroom. Not to the same routine. Not to the life she'd lived before everything imploded.

She had already made her decision long before she forced herself through the school gates.

"I've decided to take some time away," she said softly, surprised by how steady her voice sounded. "To travel. I just… I need a fresh start."

She watched the principal's expression shift—first surprise, then disappointment, then something gentler. Compassion. Understanding.

"Are you sure, Sarah? You're a wonderful teacher. We'd love to have you back."

A faint smile tugged at Sarah's lips, fragile but sincere. "I know. And I'm grateful. But I can't go back to my old life. Not right now."

The principal nodded after a long moment. "Then promise me one thing— don't disappear forever. You'll always have a place here."

Her throat tightened. "Thank you," she whispered.

When she walked back down the hallway, the school felt like a snapshot from another lifetime—a version of her who no longer existed.

Outside, the morning sun was bright, almost mocking in its warmth. The weight on her shoulders was still there, heavy and cold, but beneath it, something else stirred.

Not relief exactly.

But direction.

She didn't know where she would go next.

She only knew she couldn't stay.

Chapter Nineteen

The weeks dragged on for Jason, each day heavier, each night longer. Misery had settled into him like a second skin—tight, suffocating, impossible to peel off. He hated how lost he felt. How hollow. How furious.

But the fury wasn't reserved for Sarah.

It was for himself.

For the gnawing uncertainty he couldn't shake, no matter how many times he replayed the facts he thought he knew. For the questions that whispered in the quiet moments, refusing to stay buried.

Margaret's words echoed in his mind endlessly.

She made me promise to make sure you were okay.

Why would Sarah say that?

Why would she care?

If she was guilty—if she had really betrayed Derek—why wouldn't she have fought back? Why wouldn't she have screamed, denied, begged him to believe her? Why wouldn't she have defended herself instead of walking away with nothing but devastation in her eyes?

Unless…

Unless she had cared about him far more than he had allowed himself to believe.

But he shut that thought down. Hard.

He had heard his brother's voice on the phone that night.

He had seen Daniel kiss her.

There was nothing innocent about any of it.

No—Sarah wasn't shattered because she loved him.

She was shattered because she was guilty.

…Right?

Jason wasn't sure anymore. And that terrified him.

Two Fridays after he'd sent her away—two weeks of silence, tension, and doubt—Jason sat at his desk pretending to work when the intercom buzzed sharply.

"Yes?" he said, more clipped than intended.

His secretary's voice came through. "There are two police officers here to see you, sir. They said it's about your brother."

A cold weight dropped into his stomach. *Now what? After all this time?*

"Send them in."

The officers entered his office with practiced solemnity. Jason stood, shaking their hands. One produced a sealed evidence bag.

"Mr. Olander, these are some personal effects recovered from your brother's vehicle. They were never claimed."

Jason stared at the bag—at the ghost of his brother held in clear plastic—before quietly accepting it. "Thank you."

The officers offered brief condolences and left him alone.

He sank back into his chair, the evidence bag resting on his desk like it was waiting to explode. His fingers brushed the edge of the seal, but he didn't open it.

He was afraid of what he might find.

Or what he wouldn't.

He shoved the bag aside, deciding to face it later—maybe tonight, once the numbness set in.

After work, he carried the package home and left it on the kitchen bench. He stepped into the shower, cranking the water until steam filled the room. But not even scalding heat could loosen the tension coiled inside him. His thoughts ran in circles—Derek, Sarah, the kiss, the doubts he hated himself for having.

Just as he stepped out of the bathroom, towel around his waist, a firm knock rattled the front door.

What now?

He dragged a clean shirt on and opened it.

Margaret stood there, hands on hips, eyes sharp with determination.

"Jason," she said, "you're coming to our gathering tonight. And before you say anything—I won't take no for an answer."

He exhaled sharply. "Margaret, I'm not in the mood for people."

Her expression softened only a fraction. "It's been two weeks. And if I don't keep my promise, I'll feel like I'm failing her."

Sarah again. *Always Sarah.*

Jason scrubbed a hand through his damp hair. Margaret's stubbornness was legendary; he knew resistance was pointless.

"Fine," he muttered. "I'll come by."

Margaret gave a curt nod, satisfied, and left without another word.

Jason delayed for an hour—enough time to hope she'd forget, which he knew she wouldn't. Because Margaret didn't let things go.

And if he didn't show up, she'd be back. Probably with backup.

So, with a resigned breath and a heart that felt heavier than ever, he grabbed his keys and headed out.

Jason stepped into the room, his gaze snapping to Daniel, who stood amid their friends, drink in hand, laughter spilling effortlessly. A surge of anger coiled in Jason's chest, muscles tensing, fists clenching at his sides.

Daniel's eyes lit up as he noticed him. "Jason! Where's Sarah?" he called, a cocky smirk tugging at his lips.

Jason's vision narrowed, a red haze creeping over the edges.

Unfazed, Daniel continued, leaning back slightly. "Did Sarah mention our little… encounter?"

A muscle in Jason's jaw twitched. His teeth ground together.

Daniel chuckled, oblivious. "You should've seen her face when I kissed her. She was livid."

Thomas raised an eyebrow. "What did you do, Romeo?"

Daniel shrugged, feigning innocence. "Dropped by a couple of weeks ago, asked her out. She turned me down—said you two were together."

Jason's breaths grew sharp, deliberate, trying to keep control as heat and confusion battled in his chest.

Liam frowned. "So why the hell did you kiss her?"

Daniel let out a dramatic sigh. "She wouldn't even let me into the apartment. Thought it was inappropriate. So… I went for it."

He let out a low whistle. "Man, if looks could kill. She was furious. Told me, 'I'm no cheater.'"

Jason froze, the words hammering through his mind.

Confusion crashed into him, twisting through the rage he had carried for weeks. His heart pounded, every beat echoing with the weight of realisation.

It didn't line up with what he had believed. Not at all.

Liam shook his head. "I'm surprised she didn't slap you, you arrogant prick."

Daniel laughed. "I got out before she could."

Thomas smirked. "So, Jason, where is she? Keeping her locked away so Daniel can't get to her?"

The laughter around him grated, sharp and hollow against Jason's fraying composure.

Sarah had pushed Daniel away. She had been furious. She had said, *I'm no cheater.*

So why had he believed the worst of her?

When he finally spoke, his voice was low, taut with restrained fury and disbelief. "I need to go."

Without waiting for a response, he turned sharply, every muscle coiled and strode out. The weight of his mistake pressed down on him like a vice.

Had he been wrong about Sarah?

Oh God… what if he had been?

He headed straight to his apartment, the evidence bag from the police sitting exactly where he'd left it on the kitchen counter. For a long moment he just stared at it, his hands trembling before he even touched the seal.

Finally, he forced himself to open it.

Two mobile phones.

A gold lighter.

Sunglasses.

And a small velvet ring box.

His breath stalled.

"No…" he whispered, barely a sound.

He lifted the box with unsteady fingers and opened it.

A diamond solitaire stared up at him—a clean, brilliant stone meant for a life-changing question. The kind you only buy when you're absolutely sure.

Derek had been planning to propose.

To Sarah?

His stomach dropped. His pulse hammered against his ribs. None of it made sense. Derek had never hinted at anything. Nothing about it fit.

So, if it wasn't Sarah…

Then who?

Had Jason really convinced himself of her guilt so blindly that he'd never even considered another possibility?

Shame burned hot beneath his skin.

He reached for the phones, desperate for answers. Both were dead. He plugged them in, pacing until the screens finally flickered to life. Derek's phone he recognised instantly. But the other one…

It had to be Sarah's.

His throat tightened as he picked it up. The lock screen opened without a code—just like her. Trusting. Uncomplicated. The kind of woman who offered honesty without even thinking to guard it.

He scrolled until he found a thread with someone named Damian. The final messages punched him in the chest:

Damian: Sorry babe, not interested in a platonic relationship—we're done.

Sarah: Well, I'm glad I didn't sleep with you then, jerk.

Jason let out a harsh breath. Dumped over text for wanting boundaries? Only an idiot treated a woman like that.

He kept scrolling.

Then he saw it—messages between Derek and Sarah.

And with every line, the blood drained from his face.

Derek: Sarah, I'm so sorry. Just caught Damian in bed with Melissa.

Sarah: Oh Derek, I'm so sorry—I know how much you loved Melissa.

Loved.

Derek had loved *Melissa.*

Not Sarah.

Jason's chest constricted so fast he had to sit down. He scrolled further, dread twisting inside him.

Sarah: Are you okay, Derek? Where are you?

Derek: At the bar in Bondi, drowning my sorrows.

Sarah: Stay where you are, you shouldn't be alone. I'll be there soon… don't move.

Derek: I should have fallen in love with you, you're the best.

Sarah: Please Derek, don't do anything until I get there… promise me, please.

Derek: I promise.

Jason stared at the phone, unable to breathe.

And then another memory hit him—Damian and Melissa at the funeral, the way they couldn't meet Sarah's eyes, their faces pinched with guilt. At the time, he'd thought it was guilt for *him*.

No.

They'd been feeling guilty for Sarah.

For what *they* had done to Derek.

His vision blurred for a moment.

My God... what have I done?

Sarah hadn't been hiding anything.

She hadn't betrayed anyone.

She had been trying to help Derek—trying to get to him before he did something stupid.

She had been loyal.

She had been kind.

And Jason had thrown accusation after accusation at her because he refused to see what was right in front of him.

A sick, cold wave of regret washed over him.

Sarah... she'll never forgive me.

How could she?

He gripped the edge of the counter, knuckles white, the truth cutting deeper than any lie ever could.

How could I have been so unbelievably, unforgivably wrong?

His fingers trembled as he reached for Derek's phone. He hesitated, staring at the black screen. If he'd been wrong about Sarah—catastrophically wrong— then what else had he blinded himself to?

With a breath that shuddered through him, he typed in Derek's birthday.

For a heartbeat, nothing happened.

Then—

Unlocked.

Jason's stomach twisted.

He opened Melissa's messages first, bracing himself, but nothing could've prepared him for the flood of affectionate texts:

I love you, babe.

Miss you already, babe.

Can't wait to see you tonight.

Each line hit him like a blow.

Every word was proof.

Proof that Derek had been in love.

Proof that Melissa had lied.

Proof that Sarah had *nothing* to do with his brother's heartbreak.

A slow, bitter anger rose in him—anger at Melissa for her betrayal, anger at Damian for being involved, anger at himself most of all. Melissa had been the one responsible for Derek's downward spiral. She was the one whose guilt had been written all over her face at the funeral. And he'd completely missed it.

Because he'd been too focused on condemning Sarah.

God, what have I done?

"How am I supposed to fix this?" he whispered, his voice breaking in the empty room. "How do I even begin to ask her to forgive me?"

The question hung heavy in the air, tormenting him as he stared at the phone—at the evidence that shattered everything he thought he knew.

He was still clutching it when a sharp knock jolted him upright.

Margaret.

He barely managed to get to the door before opening it. The moment she saw him—pale, stricken, devastated—her expression softened from impatience into something like worry.

"Jason," she said carefully, "why are you still here?" She paused, eyes scanning his face. "What happened?"

Jason exhaled a ragged breath and dragged a shaking hand through his hair. When he finally spoke, his voice was raw, thick with remorse. "Margaret… I've made a terrible mistake."

He covered his face with both hands, shoulders sagging beneath the crushing weight of guilt.

He didn't have to say her name.

Margaret gently touched his shoulder. "Go to her, Jason. She loves you."

His head snapped up, desperate, wounded. "Do you really think so?"

She smiled softly, knowingly. "Of course. I saw it the first time I met her. Every time someone mentioned your name, she lit up like it meant something."

Jason let out a low, broken sound. "She'll hate me now."

"Maybe," Margaret said with a small shrug. "But love doesn't switch off because someone makes a mistake. Love breeds forgiveness."

She stepped back, seeing the shift in his eyes—the moment determination overtook fear.

"Good luck," she said gently as she turned to leave. "Go get your girl."

Jason didn't waste another second. He snatched his keys off the counter and bolted for the door, adrenaline surging through him. The drive to Sarah's Bondi apartment felt both impossibly long and terrifyingly fast, every red light a personal attack, every slow car a barrier between him and the woman he'd failed.

By the time he reached her building, his pulse was a wild, unsteady drumbeat. He didn't bother calming himself; he couldn't. Not now. Not when everything depended on this.

He raced up the stairs and knocked—hard, urgent, almost frantic.

The door opened.

But it wasn't Sarah.

A stranger stood in the doorway—a man, mid-thirties, relaxed, curious, completely unfamiliar. "Yeah? Can I help you?"

Jason's breath caught. "I'm looking for Sarah."

The man blinked, then shook his head. "Sorry, no Sarah here."

That didn't make sense. Jason's brows drew together. "Are you sure? Sarah—she lived here."

"Not anymore," the man said gently. "I only moved in last weekend."

The words landed like a punch to the chest.

Jason stepped back a fraction, the hallway tilting. Last weekend.

She'd already left by then. Already packed up. Already walked away.

She was gone.

For a moment, he couldn't breathe. His mistake—the unforgivable way he'd treated her—hadn't just hurt her. It had driven her out of the city. Out of reach. Out of his life.

He had no idea where she'd gone.

Panic clawed at his ribs. He hadn't asked for her new mobile number—he'd always just called the apartment phone. He'd never needed her direct contact, never thought he would.

God, how had he been so careless?

"How the hell do I find you?" he whispered under his breath, more to himself than to the man still standing there.

Then the answer slammed into him.

The real estate agent.

They would have her forwarding details, her application, her next-of-kin contact—something.

He turned sharply back to the man. "Which real estate agency handled your lease?"

The guy rattled off the name, slightly startled by the urgency in Jason's voice.

Jason managed a strained, breathless, "Thanks," before sprinting back down the hall.

He didn't have a plan.

He only had hope.

And he wasn't losing her without a fight.

Chapter Twenty

Sarah stepped into the dimly lit piano bar, the low murmur of conversation blending seamlessly with the warm thrum of a jazz melody humming through the speakers. The scent of aged whiskey, polished wood, and the faint spice of cologne drifted through the room—familiar now, almost comforting. A world away from the chaos she'd left behind.

"Hey, Sarah," her boss called from behind the bar.

She glanced over with a soft smile. "Hey, Megan."

After she'd decided not to return to teaching, her Bondi apartment had been rented out within days. She spent the next few weeks drifting from town to town, hoping distance would soften the sharp edges of her heartbreak.

But heartbreak had a long reach.

Even now—two months later—Jason lived in the quiet spaces of her thoughts. He lingered in the pauses between breaths, in the lingering chords of every love song she played. She missed him with an ache that had settled deep in her bones. She still loved him. God, she probably always would.

Melbourne had been her chance to start fresh. And the job at this exclusive piano bar had felt like a lifeline the moment it fell into her lap. The atmosphere, the quiet luxury, the grand piano—it was the closest thing to peace she'd found since the accident. Music had always been her language, her refuge. Here, it became her livelihood.

She slipped onto the piano stool, fingers brushing the cool ivory keys. The soft buzz of expectation washed over her, grounding her. She drew a slow breath, exhaled, and began to play.

A gentle melody filled the room, warm and rich, curling around conversations like a familiar embrace. She had her nightly setlist, but she welcomed requests. She loved watching how people responded—the way a single song could spark a memory, evoke a forgotten longing, draw out a smile or a tear. Music connected strangers in ways words never could.

Tonight, like every night, she let the melody speak for her. It was easier than trying to put her broken heart into sentences.

Throughout the evening, as usual, a few men drifted closer, offering compliments, flirtatious smiles, drinks she politely declined. She never encouraged any of it. She wasn't ready. She didn't know if she ever would be.

Because she'd crossed cities, changed jobs, rebuilt her life piece by piece… and still, one truth refused to let her go:

She loved Jason.

Deeply. Completely. Quietly.

Some days, she convinced herself she was moving on. Other days, one small memory—a look, a touch, a laugh—would unravel all the progress she'd made.

Like now.

She finished a slow, wistful melody, the final note lingering in the air like a held breath. She lifted her hands from the keys just as a voice cut through the room— sharp, familiar, impossible.

"Sarah!"

Her heart stuttered.

She turned, breath catching in her throat.

Margaret.

Sarah's heart skipped, a sharp jolt that nearly stole her breath as she watched the older woman weave through the tables, her expression unreadable beneath the dim amber lights. For a moment, Sarah forgot how to breathe.

"Hello, Margaret." Her smile came automatically—genuine but shaded with caution. "What brings you here?"

Margaret reached her, and instinct pulled Sarah to her feet. Their embrace was warm, familiar, and painfully bittersweet. It had been months since she'd seen her—months since she'd seen anyone connected to the life she had abandoned in Sydney.

When Margaret pulled back, she studied Sarah with a mother's eye, gaze sweeping her face. "You look tired."

Sarah let out a soft laugh, hoping humour would diffuse the tension coiled tight in her chest. "That's hospitality for you. Late nights, too much music, not nearly enough sleep."

The look Margaret gave her said she didn't believe a word of it.

Without another comment, Margaret gently guided her toward a nearby table where Patrick—steady, reliable Patrick—was already seated. His familiar nod made something twist inside her.

She sat, folding her hands to keep them from shaking.

Margaret didn't ease into it. "What are you doing in Melbourne?"

Sarah opened her mouth, then closed it again. Finally, she sighed. "After everything that happened, I needed space. I got this job about a month ago." She lifted her chin, trying to shift the spotlight. "What about you? What brings you here?"

"Visiting friends," Margaret said with a small smile. But her expression sobered almost immediately. "Sarah… Jason has been looking for you."

Everything inside her went still.

Her breath faltered, her pulse stumbling as old wounds pulsed awake. She shook her head quickly—too quickly. "Please don't tell him where I am."

Margaret frowned, leaning in. "Why not? He regrets what happened."

Sarah traced the rim of her glass, unable to meet her eyes. "He said things that don't just disappear, Margaret." Her voice was calm, but the pain embedded within it was raw and unmistakable.

Margaret's brow softened. "Sarah, love… the only thing that can't be undone is death. Everything else? It can be mended if you let it."

The words struck like a dull blade—deep, familiar, and unwelcome.

Margaret sighed. "Jason isn't doing well."

Sarah's head snapped up before she could stop herself. Panic and longing collided in her chest. "What do you mean?"

A slow, knowing sadness filled Margaret's eyes. "You still care. Anyone can see that."

Sarah's jaw clenched. She didn't respond—couldn't. Caring felt like betrayal… of her pride, of her healing, of the distance she had forced between them.

Margaret continued gently, "He barely eats. He's lost weight. He doesn't sleep. He's running himself into the ground."

A sharp ache bloomed inside her. Images of Jason rose unbidden—the warmth of his laugh, the heat of his gaze, the feel of his hands on her waist. Memories she had tried so hard to bury clawed their way to the surface.

And now he was unraveling.

She hated that it mattered. Hated that her heart still tightened at the thought of him hurting. Hated that part of her still loved him with a depth she wished she could forget.

Margaret reached across the table and closed her hand over Sarah's, her touch steady and kind. "I won't tell him unless you want me to. But I'm asking you— please let me."

Sarah's throat burned. Tears pricked her eyes, blurring the room into soft shapes. She swallowed hard, fighting for composure.

When she finally spoke, it was barely a whisper.

"Okay, Margaret." She wiped quickly at her cheek. "But… he probably won't care."

Patrick, silent until now, leaned forward, his voice low and unwavering.

"Believe me, Sarah—he will care."

Jason stepped into his apartment on Friday afternoon, the weight of exhaustion pressing down on him like an anchor, dragging him into a sea of regret. Two months. Two long, torturous months since Sarah left—no, since he had thrown her out.

The apartment felt hollow, the air stale and lifeless. It was exactly as he had left it that morning, but it no longer felt like home. Not without her. Four walls, a ceiling, a floor—it had all the structure of a home, but none of the warmth. Every surface seemed to echo the absence of her laughter, the empty space where her presence had once softened everything.

He ran a hand through his hair, frustration and self-recrimination clawing at his chest. He had tried everything—every avenue, every lead—but she had vanished. The real estate agent refused to give her new address or even a phone number, citing privacy laws. Daniel had been no help, deleting her number the moment she'd told him she was dating Jason, out of some misguided attempt at loyalty.

Desperation had driven him further. He had hired a private investigator, but so far, nothing. No sightings. No messages. No whispers. Nothing. And that terrified him. Sarah wasn't the type to disappear. She stayed. She fought. She loved fiercely. But he had pushed her so hard, hurt her so deeply, that she hadn't looked back.

Jason sank onto the couch, staring at the empty space where she used to sit, curled up with a book, fingers idly playing with the hem of her dress as she laughed at something he had said. God, he could still hear it—that soft, musical laugh that had once unravelled all the tension in his chest. Now, all he had was silence.

He had to find her. Even if she never forgave him, even if she wanted nothing to do with him, she needed to know how sorry he was. She needed to understand that pushing her away had been the worst, most selfish mistake of his life.

His chest ached, a dull, relentless pain that refused to loosen its grip. He loved her. God, he loved her. And yet, instead of holding her close, he had thrown her away. He had told her she meant nothing, when in truth, she had been everything.

Jason leaned forward, elbows on his knees, head in his hands.

God, I'm an idiot.

The memories came crashing in, unbidden and unrelenting. He saw her smile, lighting up a room without even trying. Felt her warmth when she wrapped her arms around him at the door after work, melting away the stress of the day with a simple, effortless embrace. Tasted the meals she had cooked, each small, thoughtful gesture a reflection of her love and care. She had always been that way—giving, kind, endlessly patient, endlessly understanding.

And worst of all, he remembered how she had felt in his arms when they made love—perfect, inevitable, like she had been meant to be there all along.

But she was gone. And the silence she had left behind was deafening.

All because he had been a coward. All because he hadn't listened to his heart. He hadn't given her a chance to defend herself.

You could have just talked to her—about Derek, about Daniel.

But he hadn't. Because deep down, he had been terrified of what he might hear. Terrified that she had loved Derek. That she still did. That she might have been drawn to Daniel.

But she wasn't, was she?

He knew that now.

She had never been in love with Derek. She had never wanted Daniel. She had only ever been honest with him, open in ways that made trust feel effortless. If he had asked, truly asked, she would have told him everything. He would have known.

Even if he couldn't bear the truth about Derek, why hadn't he let her explain about Daniel? Because he had been afraid. Afraid that she might care for someone else, afraid that she might not be wholly his in the way he had imagined, the way he had needed her to be.

And now?

Now, he had lost her anyway.

The thought pressed into him, suffocating and unyielding. Two months without her had carved a cavern in his chest—an ache so constant it felt like part of his anatomy now. No amount of work, no distraction, no self-punishment could fill the void she'd left. She was out there somewhere, breathing, living, changing… and he wasn't part of any of it. Every day that passed tightened the chain of his regret until it felt like it was strangling him from the inside out.

Jason closed his eyes and let the grief wash over him, hot and relentless. He didn't know how he would find her. He didn't know if she would ever want to see his face again. But one truth burned through the fog of misery with absolute, desperate clarity: he would not stop until he had tried.

He exhaled sharply and pushed himself off the couch. His body felt heavy, every muscle stiff with exhaustion—not just from lack of sleep, but from two months of carrying guilt like a lead weight strapped to his spine. He started toward the bedroom, planning to take a shower, hoping the water might rinse away even a fraction of the weariness clinging to him.

But as he reached the doorway, something glimmered on the dresser. Something small. Familiar. Devastating.

Sarah's bracelet.

A simple silver chain with a tiny charm—a book, because she loved to read. Carrying her stories, her dreams, her softness. Her mother had given it to her; he remembered the quiet pride in her voice the night she told him.

She must have forgotten it in the chaos of that awful night.

Jason stepped closer, each movement slow, reverent, as if approaching something holy—or fragile enough to shatter. He reached out, his fingers brushing the cool metal, and his breath caught in his throat. The charm swung slightly, tapping against his skin, and the sound felt like a punch straight to the gut.

She had taken everything else. Every dress, every book, every trace of herself from his home.

But she had forgotten this.

Left this.

Left *him*.

His chest tightened as fresh pain surged through him, sharper than before. He curled his fingers around the bracelet, gripping it so tightly it bit into his palm, leaving small crescents in his skin. He welcomed the sting.

Jason shut his eyes. He could still see her smile behind them. Still hear her voice. Still feel her warmth.

He had to find her.

He had to make this right.

Because losing her forever?

That wasn't an option.

His phone rang.

Jason stared at it, torn. He wasn't in the mood to talk to anyone—not now, not when his thoughts were a tangled mess of regret, longing, and self-loathing. But when he glanced at the screen and saw Margaret's name, his brow furrowed.

Why was she calling? She was supposed to be in Melbourne visiting friends. Maybe she needed someone to let a tradesman into her apartment.

With a reluctant sigh, he answered. "Hello, Margaret. Are you having a good time?"

Her next words slammed into him like a physical blow.

"Jason, I've found her."

Every part of him froze. His breath caught, his heart threatened to stop altogether.

"Sarah?" His voice was barely a whisper, fragile and disbelieving.

"Yes. In Melbourne, Jason." Margaret's excitement crackled through the phone, but he barely registered it.

His grip on the phone tightened so hard his knuckles whitened. "How is she? Is she… okay?"

"She looks thinner than she was, and a little tired, but otherwise, she's fine."

Jason closed his eyes, guilt crashing over him like a tidal wave. Thinner. Tired. Had she been hurting all this time, quietly, silently? Had she been suffering as much as he had?

Of course she had. *You broke her. You pushed her away. You told her she meant nothing to you.*

His throat tightened, and he swallowed hard. "Did you tell her I was looking for her?"

"Yes," Margaret said carefully. "At first, she didn't want you to know where she was."

His heart plummeted.

She didn't want him. She didn't want to be found. She wanted nothing to do with him.

But then Margaret's words came, sharp and hopeful: "We convinced her to let us tell you."

Jason exhaled sharply, relief surging through him like electricity. There was still a chance. She hadn't erased him completely.

"Where is she?" His voice was urgent now, raw with desperation.

"She's working in a piano bar. I'll send you the address."

He ran a hand through his hair, heart hammering in his chest. "Thank you, Margaret. Thank you… thank you so much."

There was a pause, and then her voice returned, firm and unwavering.

"Don't screw this up, Jason."

"I won't," he promised, voice low but resolute. "I swear."

A minute later, his phone dinged with a message. His pulse raced as he grabbed it, slightly trembling. Margaret had sent the address of the piano bar.

For the first time in two months, hope flared in his chest. Real, blinding hope.

His hands clenched around the phone. *This was it. He finally knew where she was.*

Without hesitation, he opened his airline app, searching for flights. The next available one left in four hours. He booked it without a second thought.

Jason didn't hesitate. He was going to Melbourne.

And he wasn't coming back without Sarah.

Chapter Twenty-One

Late Saturday afternoon, Jason stepped into the piano bar, his pulse hammering in his ears. The air was thick with the scent of aged wood, warm whiskey, and a faint trace of perfume—comforting and foreign all at once. Dim light spilled from vintage sconces, casting long shadows across the room, while a soft jazz melody floated from the stage, weaving through the quiet hum of conversation.

His eyes scanned the patrons—couples leaning into each other over glasses of wine, solitary drinkers lost in thought, a group near the stage laughing at a joke he couldn't hear. But he wasn't here for any of them.

He was here for her.

A tightening in his stomach made each step toward the bar feel heavier than the last. The bartender, a woman with sharp green eyes and a commanding presence, looked up from polishing a glass. Her gaze measured him, wary and calculating.

"What can I get you?" she asked, voice smooth but edged with suspicion.

Jason swallowed, forcing his own voice to stay steady. "I'm looking for Sarah Pratt."

At the mention of her name, her expression flickered—surprise, caution, protectiveness. He couldn't tell which it was, and he didn't dare guess.

"Why?" she asked, eyes narrowing slightly.

Jason met her gaze without hesitation. "I'm a friend from Sydney." He extended a hand. "Jason Olander."

Recognition sparked in her eyes—whether from Sarah's stories, warnings, or both, he couldn't be sure. After a tense pause, she offered her hand.

"Megan," she said, her tone cautious but polite.

"Nice to meet you, Megan," Jason replied, keeping his smile light, though his heart raced.

Megan studied him a moment longer, her eyes flicking to the stage, then back to him. Finally, she relented. "Sarah doesn't start work for another hour."

Jason exhaled slowly, the words catching somewhere between relief and frustration. One hour. After two months of searching, of despair and longing, what was another sixty minutes?

"In that case," he said, pressing his hands against the bar, "I'll have a lemonade."

Megan nodded, pouring the drink with precise, deliberate movements before sliding it across to him. Jason murmured a quiet thanks, taking the glass and moving toward a secluded table at the back of the room. He sank into the chair, fingers tightening around the cool rim of the glass, the ice clinking softly.

He let out a slow breath, his mind racing and still. Two months of absence, two months of regret, and now—here he was, so close he could almost see her before she even arrived.

Now, all that remained was waiting.

Waiting for the woman he loved.

Waiting for the chance to make right what he had broken.

Every tick of the clock, every note of the piano, made his heart pound faster. He could do this. He had to.

Sarah walked into the piano bar five minutes before her shift, the soft click of her heels barely audible over the low murmur of conversation. She smoothed the front of her simple black dress, fingers tracing the fabric almost absentmindedly as her gaze swept the room. Same patrons, same dim lighting, same calm that had become her sanctuary. Behind the piano, she didn't have to think about the past—not about Jason, not about Derek, not about anything that still ached in her chest. Only the music mattered here.

Making her way to the bar, she offered Megan a small, polite smile. "Hi, Megan."

"Hey, Sarah," Megan replied, her eyes lingering on her longer than usual. There was something in that look—a flicker of curiosity, maybe concern, maybe warning—that made Sarah pause mid-step.

"What?" she asked, narrowing her eyes.

Megan hesitated, biting her lip. "Nothing... just... you have an audience tonight."

Sarah frowned, but before she could press for clarification, the soft background music faded, signalling the start of her set. A flutter of anticipation—or was it anxiety? —skipped through her chest.

She pushed aside Megan's cryptic remark, crossing the room to the grand piano. Sliding onto the bench, she drew in a steadying breath, letting her fingers hover over the ivory keys for a heartbeat, feeling the weight of expectation and possibility all at once.

And then, with a quiet exhale, she began to play.

The first notes spilled into the room like a warm tide, sweeping away the tension in her shoulders, the lingering ache in her heart. In that moment, she was entirely absorbed, lost in the one thing that never let her down, the one language that could carry the unspoken pieces of herself she couldn't yet voice.

Jason spotted her the second she walked in.

For a moment, he forgot how to breathe.

She was breathtaking.

Her long auburn hair cascaded down her back, catching the dim light of the bar, gleaming like molten copper. The simple black dress hugged her slender frame, understated yet impossibly elegant, swaying with each step as if the room itself conspired to follow her. The sight of her stabbed through his chest, a sharp, hollow ache that stole his breath and left his limbs heavy.

God, I've missed you.

She didn't see him. Not yet. She moved with quiet confidence, nodding at familiar faces, exchanging soft words with Megan, her presence calm yet magnetic, until she reached the grand piano.

Jason remained frozen in his seat, fingers tightening around the cool glass in his hand. His heart pounded like a relentless drum, a chaotic rhythm that mirrored the storm of nerves and longing coursing through him. He had imagined this moment for months—every possible scenario played in his mind—but now, with her only a few feet away, every carefully rehearsed line dissolved into static.

She settled onto the piano bench, straight and poised, her shoulders squared but relaxed. He watched, mesmerised, as her fingers hovered over the keys, lingering for a brief, almost imperceptible hesitation before the first note floated into the air.

The music wrapped around the room, rich, aching, and alive.

Jason swallowed hard.

She was always like this when she played—completely absorbed, every note a fragment of her soul, every melody a story he had longed to read. She had the power to make a room disappear, to make the world outside vanish with nothing but the press of a key. And now… she had made him vanish into the shadows of his own regret.

Would she even care that he was here? Would she look up and see the same ache that had gnawed at him for the past two months?

Doubt coiled in his chest like a living thing.

Why would she? He had been cruel. He had pushed her away, made her believe she was nothing when, in truth, she had been everything. And seeing her now—so beautiful, so achingly familiar—he realised that no amount of longing could undo the damage he had done.

She looked thinner. The sight tightened his stomach. Had she been eating? Sleeping? Had his cruelty left a mark deeper than he had ever imagined?

He stayed frozen, eyes fixed on her, heart pounding, afraid that a single movement—too deep a breath, a shift of his gaze—might shatter the fragile spell of this moment.

How would she react when she finally saw him?

Anger? Hurt? Indifference?

Would she walk away before he could say everything—the truth, the apologies, the confessions he had rehearsed a thousand times in his mind?

Jason exhaled slowly, forcing himself to stay grounded. He had come too far to leave now. He wouldn't leave until she knew.

He didn't approach her during breaks. A hurried conversation amidst the clinking of glasses and murmurs of strangers wouldn't suffice—not for the words he needed to speak, not for the truth he needed her to hear.

So, he waited.

For three long hours, he remained in the shadows, eyes never leaving her. Every note, every delicate nuance of her music, every glance she cast away from him only deepened the ache in his chest and strengthened his resolve.

When the final song ended and the last lingering note faded into silence, Sarah rose from the piano, gathering her things with quiet, graceful efficiency.

Jason's pulse raced, his hands curling into fists at his sides.

This was it.

No more waiting. No more hesitation.

It was time.

Sarah made her way to the bar, exchanging a few quiet words with Megan. The low hum of conversation, the clinking of glasses, the soft jazz weaving through the room—it was all familiar, a comforting rhythm she had come to rely on. She reached for a glass of water, her fingers brushing the cool surface, ready to take a sip—

Then Megan subtly tilted her head, eyes flicking toward the entrance.

Sarah turned.

And the world stopped.

Her breath caught in her throat, her fingers tightening around the glass as her gaze locked onto him. Jason.

For a heartbeat, she thought she was imagining it. That her mind had conjured some cruel illusion after months of aching absence. But no—there he was. Broad shoulders, storm-grey eyes fixed on her, standing with a quiet intensity that made everything else fade. Jason Olander, standing in her bar.

Shock hit first, freezing her mid-motion. Then, almost immediately, a surge of something dangerously close to longing threatened to unravel her. Her chest tightened. Her pulse raced. But she forced it down, hard. Vulnerability, desire, regret—she shoved it all into the corners of her mind, out of reach. She had survived two months without him; she could survive a few minutes more.

Her expression hardened into a mask of calm.

Jason's jaw tightened almost imperceptibly, his eyes searching hers as if trying to find some trace of the woman he had once held close. But she wouldn't let him see. Not now. Not the trembling, the yearning, the nights spent replaying their past.

She straightened her spine, voice steady, even as her stomach twisted. "Why are you here, Jason?"

Calm. Controlled. Unreadable.

Inside, however, she was shaking.

Jason took a step forward but stopped the instant she stiffened. "I had to see you," he said, voice low, edged with raw desperation.

"Well," she replied, flat, detached, every word measured, "you've seen me. Now you can leave."

She turned sharply, a move to walk away, but his hand shot out instinctively, closing gently around her wrist.

"Please," he murmured. Raw, pleading, vulnerable. "Let me explain."

Her breath hitched. She froze, heart pounding. Then she looked down at his hand on her wrist.

He immediately let go, careful not to push too hard.

Sarah's jaw clenched. A long pause passed, heavy with tension. Finally, she spoke, quiet, deliberate. "Okay. But not here."

Jason exhaled slowly, relief flickering faintly in his chest.

"Where?"

She tilted her head, considering. "Where are you staying?"

She wasn't taking him to her apartment. She needed an escape route—needed to be able to leave the moment she wanted to.

"The Ritz-Carlton, not far from here," he said.

Sarah studied him for a long moment, then nodded. "Okay."

"My car's in the car park."

"Okay."

She followed him outside; her arms crossed tightly over her chest as if bracing herself. Jason opened the passenger door for her, and after a brief hesitation, she slid in without a word.

Jason risked a glance at her as he drove, knuckles white against the steering wheel. Sarah sat rigid in the passenger seat, her posture straight, hands clutching the strap of her purse, eyes fixed on the passing streetlights. The fleeting glow painted shifting shadows across her delicate features, emphasising the sharp line of her jaw and the tight press of her lips.

She was a world away from the woman he had once held in his arms—the woman who had looked at him with warmth, trust, and unspoken love. Now, there was only distance, a wall of ice and restraint he wasn't sure he could penetrate.

The silence between them was heavy, suffocating. He wanted to speak, to fill the space with something—anything—but every word that came to mind felt hopelessly inadequate. This wasn't a car conversation. It wasn't a space for rushing, for forced explanations.

So, he drove, each turn measured, each stoplight a reminder that he had to be patient. And yet, he stole glances at her whenever he could, searching for even a flicker of the Sarah he had lost, some sign that she might still be the same woman who had once trusted him with her heart.

When they arrived at the Ritz-Carlton, the valet took his car, and they moved through the grand entrance together. Jason's gaze flicked to her again, but her face remained unreadable, fixed ahead as if she were guarding herself against the world—and him.

He swallowed, the ache in his throat sharp and bittersweet, and led her across the marble floors. The soft lighting of the lobby glimmered against the polished surfaces, the faint scent of lilies hanging in the air, but his senses barely registered it. All that mattered was her—every controlled movement, every tight grip on her purse, every subtle tension in her shoulders.

He pressed the elevator button, and the doors slid open with a gentle chime. Sarah hesitated for a heartbeat, then stepped inside, her restraint almost palpable.

Jason followed, pressing the button for his floor. As the doors closed, sealing them in the small, intimate space, the weight of everything left unsaid pressed down between them.

At least she was here. At least she hadn't walked away. At least she was willing to listen.

And that—tenuous as it was—was all the hope he needed to keep going.

Once inside his suite, Sarah moved directly to the large windows, her back to him, staring out at the glittering lights of Melbourne. The city shimmered like a thousand tiny stars, but Jason's world had narrowed to the space between them.

Jason swallowed hard, his chest tight, heart clenching with a mix of longing and guilt.

"Sarah—"

"Say what you came to Melbourne to say, Jason." Her voice was calm, measured, but the edge of steel in it made him pause. "I don't know how it's going to make a difference. I mean nothing to you, remember?"

The words stabbed him, sharp and unyielding.

Jason exhaled roughly, his voice low, hoarse with emotion. "You mean more to me than anything, Sarah. I lied. I was blind with anger. And I was so, so wrong."

"You nearly destroyed me." Her voice remained even, but the quiet pain beneath it cut him deeper than any accusation ever could. "You thought I did unspeakable things."

"I know," he said, throat tight, voice breaking slightly. "And I was wrong."

"Why did you accuse me?" Her hands curled into fists at her sides, knuckles whitening.

Jason ran a hand through his hair, frustration, and remorse tangling in his chest. "I saw you with Daniel. That Friday. I was… jealous. Foolishly, destructively jealous."

A bitter laugh escaped Sarah. "I was going to tell you, Jason. Daniel came to your apartment, but I didn't even let him up. It wouldn't have been right without you there. And when he kissed me, I was furious. He knew it."

Jason swallowed hard, the weight of truth heavy on his tongue. "I know. He told me."

"That still doesn't explain why you thought I had anything to do with Derek's death," she said softly, voice steady but trembling under the surface. "I don't remember that night fully, but in my heart, I would never have hurt him. He was kind to me. I liked him."

Jason stepped closer, closing the space, careful not to crowd her. He studied her profile—her jaw tight, her shoulders tense, the way she fought to contain every ripple of emotion.

"I know that too," he murmured, his voice barely above a whisper.

From his pocket, he drew out a phone and held it toward her. Slowly, cautiously, she glanced down. Their fingers brushed as she took it, and a tiny spark of electricity flared at the contact. She gasped softly and jerked her hand away.

Jason's heart sank. Instinctively, he reached out, resting a hand lightly on her shoulder, a silent plea for understanding, for forgiveness.

Sarah froze, her jaw tightening, eyes flashing. "Don't touch me."

His hand dropped immediately, and he took a small step back, leaving space between them, the tension stretching taut in the room.

The silence that followed was heavy, electric—a fragile pause between them, filled with everything they hadn't said, everything they still felt.

She turned to face him, her blue eyes blazing with a mix of pain and frustration. "Why did you think I caused his death, Jason? Why?"

He exhaled slowly, rubbing a hand over his face, the weight of two months of guilt pressing down on him. "That night… Derek called me. He said someone he cared about had slept with another guy." His voice was hoarse, raw with regret. "Then I heard you in the background, telling him to stop driving erratically. And then he said… 'Why, Sarah?'" Jason swallowed hard, his throat tight. "I thought… I thought he was asking you why you cheated on him."

Sarah's breath hitched. Her eyes widened in shock, her chest rising and falling rapidly as she processed his words.

He raised his hands quickly, as if surrendering, guilt written in every line of his face. "I know now it wasn't you. It was Melissa."

Her expression faltered, confusion giving way to sorrow. "Melissa cheated on Derek?" she repeated, voice quiet, numbly echoing his revelation. Then her gaze softened, sorrow threading through her features. "Oh… he really loved her." She shook her head slowly, swallowing hard. "Poor Derek… he didn't deserve that."

"She cheated with Damian," Jason added quietly, his voice almost a whisper.

Sarah's head snapped up, eyes narrowing, brows furrowed in disbelief. "Damian?" she murmured, shaking her head as if trying to reconcile the fragments. "Melissa… slept with Damian?"

Then, almost to herself, her voice softened, a thread of understanding weaving through it. "That's why they were together at the funeral… that explains the guilt on their faces."

"Yes," Jason confirmed gently, watching as the realisation settled over her like a fragile dawn.

She moved slowly to the couch, sinking onto it as if the weight of the revelation had physically exhausted her. Her hands clasped in her lap, her mind piecing together fragments of the past, the accident, the betrayal.

"Damian broke up with me the day of the accident," she murmured, staring at her hands. "That's the last thing I remember… until I woke up in the hospital."

Jason sat beside her, careful not to crowd her, giving her the space she clearly needed. His chest ached at the distant, haunted look in her eyes—the trace of all the pain he had caused.

"I am so, so sorry, Sarah," he said, voice thick with remorse. "You didn't deserve anything I said. I… I regret it more than I can ever put into words. You mean everything to me." His hand brushed against hers for a fleeting second before retreating, unable to bear the thought of imposing. "I feel sick thinking about how much I hurt you."

Sarah's voice was quiet, steady, but laced with raw honesty that made his chest constrict. "I've never been hurt by anyone as much as you hurt me."

A long, careful breath followed, her fingers tightening around themselves as she steadied herself. Then, softly, she added, "But… I forgive you."

Jason's heart jolted as if struck by lightning. Hope ignited in him, bright and fierce, like a match struck in the dark. His breath hitched, his chest loosening slightly for the first time in months, as if the weight crushing him had finally lifted, even if just a little.

She stood, and he rose immediately, his body moving before his mind could catch up. Every step he took toward her was urgent, desperate—he needed to close the distance, to feel her warmth, to make sure this wasn't some cruel mirage.

But before his hands could reach her, she took a deliberate step back.

"No." Her voice was quiet but firm, resolute, cutting through him like a knife.

Jason froze mid-step, his chest tightening.

"I said I forgive you," she continued, meeting his gaze with an intensity that left him raw. "But that doesn't mean I'm coming back."

The flicker of hope he had clung to—the fragile thread of possibility—snapped, replaced by a sharp, aching hollow in his chest.

"Sarah—" His throat constricted, words sticking in his mouth.

She shook her head, a mask of calm determination hiding the storm beneath. "Goodbye, Jason."

The finality in her voice shattered something deep inside him, splintering the fragile pieces of his hope.

Before he could respond, before he could even process the enormity of what was happening, she turned. Her movements were measured, controlled, almost ritualistic—the kind of composure born from pain so deep it had hardened her resolve. The kind she refused to show him.

Jason's pulse thundered in his ears. No. This couldn't be it.

"Sarah," he called, voice low, trembling, barely more than a whisper.

She didn't pause.

Desperation clawed at his chest. He stepped forward, hands reaching, grasping at air as if the mere act of trying could pull her back. "Please, Sarah... don't go."

For the briefest fraction of a second, she hesitated. Her fingers lingered on the door handle, her shoulders rising and falling with a breath he could not hear. His heart leapt—was there still a chance?

But then, just as quickly, she moved again. She didn't turn, didn't glance back.

Jason's throat tightened, his voice breaking under the weight of unsaid words, emotions too raw to be contained. He had come this far, bared his soul, confessed his guilt, laid his heart at her feet. And still—he wasn't enough.

He let the words tumble out, ragged, desperate, the confession he had saved for every moment since she left:

"I love you."

Sarah stilled. For a heartbeat, the world seemed suspended between them. Jason held his breath, listening, hoping, praying.

But she didn't turn. She didn't speak.

Then, as if time itself had finally exhaled, she opened the door and stepped through it. Quietly, deliberately. And the door closed softly behind her.

Leaving Jason alone, frozen, drowning in the silence she left in her wake.

He sank to his knees, the echo of her absence pressing into him, relentless. The words hung in the air—unanswered, unclaimed, impossible to retrieve.

Chapter Twenty-Two

I love you.

Those three words looped in her mind, relentless, like a haunting melody she couldn't escape. No matter how many times she tried to push them away, they clung to her.

I love you.

Sarah exhaled sharply, gripping the edge of her kitchen counter until her knuckles turned white, her fingers trembling with the effort of holding herself together.

I love you.

Her hands tightened further, the cold, unyielding surface biting into her skin. The sensation grounded her, but it didn't dull the ache in her chest—the ache that had never fully healed.

I love you too, Jason… but you hurt me.

She squeezed her eyes shut, willing herself to shut it all out: the memories, the heartbreak, the raw ache clawing its way up from deep inside. She had been fine before tonight. She had convinced herself she was stronger, that she had moved on.

But the moment he had spoken those words, the fragile walls she had built cracked, splintering under the weight of longing and fear.

Could she trust him again?

Could she dare to open her heart, knowing how deeply he had wounded her before?

A shaky breath escaped her lips as the past pressed in like a phantom she couldn't shake. The nights she had cried herself to sleep. The mornings she had forced herself out of bed, pretending she didn't miss him. The careful, painstaking walls she had erected to keep him out—and to keep herself safe.

Then, like a whisper through the storm, another thought crept in—quieter, softer, but impossible to ignore.

What if he doesn't hurt me again?

What if he means it this time?

What if I walk away, and spend the rest of my life regretting it?

Her pulse thundered in her ears, fear, and hope colliding in a fierce, uncontrollable rhythm. She had spent too long letting fear dictate her choices.

The decision came with sudden, irrevocable clarity.

With trembling hands, she grabbed her keys and phone. Her heart raced like a drum as she opened the ride share app, each second stretching into an eternity while she waited for the car to arrive.

She didn't know what would happen next. She didn't know if she was ready for what awaited her—or if she could survive another heartbreak.

But for the first time in months, she felt alive again.

And that was enough.

Jason stared blankly at the amber liquid swirling in his glass. His second pour. Maybe his third. He wasn't counting. Didn't want to.

What was the point?

The whiskey burned as it slid down his throat, but the fire was nothing compared to the raw, relentless ache in his chest—the hollow, gnawing regret that no amount of alcohol could dull.

He had lost her.

Sarah.

The only woman he had ever truly loved.

And there was no one to blame but himself.

His grip tightened around the glass, knuckles white. How had he been so blind? So stupid? So arrogantly sure of his assumptions that he'd ignored the truth glaring at him every damn day? He had pushed her away, built walls of pride and anger, and now… she was gone.

Jason ran a hand through his hair, exhaling sharply. The hotel room pressed down on him like a tomb—stale air, empty walls, and the echo of his mistakes. He couldn't escape the memories:

Her blue eyes that night, shimmering with hurt he had caused.

The tremble in her voice when she said, *I forgive you.*

The step back she took when he reached for her.

I forgive you… but that doesn't mean I'm coming back.

His stomach twisted, a cold, sick hollow settling deep inside him. He wanted her. Needed her. And he wasn't about to give up—not now, not ever.

With a sharp clink, he pushed the glass aside. It felt final, a punctuation mark on the self-inflicted chaos of the past months. He had ruined everything, but one thing was crystal clear: he wasn't walking away.

She might hate him. She might never forgive him.

But he had to try.

Jason rose to his feet, heart hammering, every muscle taut with resolve. He would see her again. He would make her listen—even if it took every ounce of him.

Because Sarah was it for him.

And he sure as hell wasn't losing her without a fight.

A sharp knock at the door made him flinch. His jaw clenched. Not now.

"Go away," he barked, voice rough, raw with exhaustion.

Another knock, firmer, insistent.

His patience snapped. He yanked himself upright, rubbing a hand over his face. Whoever it was needed to leave him alone.

He flung the door open—and froze.

Sarah.

For a moment, he thought he was imagining her—as if his desperate heart had finally betrayed him.

But she was real. Standing there, in front of him, breath catching, chest rising and falling with the weight of unspoken words and withheld emotions.

His throat went dry. "Sarah—"

She met his gaze, piercing and steady. Quiet, deliberate. "Say it again."

His chest tightened. She had heard him. She had heard *him* say the words he'd kept locked away for months, the words that had haunted every restless night.

He looked straight into her eyes. "I love you," he said, voice rough, raw, trembling with sincerity.

Her breath hitched. Lashes fluttered as though bracing against the weight of his confession.

Jason didn't move. He couldn't. He waited, silently, holding himself back, praying she would speak, that she would give him any sign that it was real.

Then, finally, she did.

"I love you too."

His heart nearly stopped.

Before reason could catch up, before fear could retreat, his hands found her shoulders. He pulled her into the room, into his arms, just as the door swung shut behind her.

And then—he kissed her.

Sarah melted into him, fingers tangling in his shirt, clinging like she was afraid to let go. God, he had missed this. The taste of her. The warmth of her body pressed against his. The way she fit in his arms as if she'd always belonged there.

But he needed more.

He bent down, arms sliding under her thighs, lifting her effortlessly into his embrace. A soft gasp escaped her lips, but she didn't protest. She wrapped her arms around his neck, hands threading through his hair, holding on like the world could shatter outside and it wouldn't matter.

He carried her to the couch, seating her on his lap. His lips never left hers—soft, desperate, demanding. He couldn't stop. Wouldn't stop.

She was home.

Finally, he drew back, resting his forehead against hers, breaths mingling in the charged air between them. "I'm sorry, Sarah," he murmured, voice thick with emotion.

Her fingers traced along his jaw, soft and grounding, before rising to cover his lips, silencing him.

"No," she whispered. "No more apologies. Just tell me again."

His eyes blazed with need and devotion. "I love you," he said, raw, unguarded, every syllable carrying the weight of months of regret and longing. "More than anything."

A soft, trembling breath left her lips—a fragile sound that sent a shiver racing through him. His hands cupped her face, thumbs brushing along her cheekbones as if memorising every inch of her. Without hesitation, he kissed her again—deep, lingering, unrelenting.

He poured everything into that kiss: his love, his remorse, his silent vow never to let her go again.

Sarah clung to him, fingers digging into his shirt, anchoring herself to him and to the moment. The world outside disappeared—the past, the pain, the fear—all dissolved in the warmth and weight of his embrace.

When they finally parted, they didn't move. Foreheads pressed together, breaths mingling, hearts racing in tandem.

"I've missed you," she whispered, voice breaking.

A low chuckle rumbled from deep within him, a sound thick with relief and longing. "Believe me, I've missed you more." His gaze softened, every look and every inch of his body conveying what words could never capture.

She brushed her fingers over his cheek. "Then don't let me go again."

"Never," he promised, tightening his hold. And then he kissed her again, slow, claiming, as if memorising every curve, every line, every inch of her.

When they finally broke apart, Jason studied her face, committing each emotion to memory—the flicker of vulnerability, the glimmer of hope, the fierce spark of love that had never truly died.

"I love you, Jason," she murmured.

He drew a shaky breath, hands still cupping her face. "I love you, too. Always."

Sarah leaned into him, head resting on his shoulder, lips trailing soft, lingering kisses along his neck, up to his ear. A shiver ran through him. He could feel her desire, pressing against him, and the heat pooled low in his belly.

Then, in the faintest, breathless whisper—the words that unraveled him completely—she said:

"Make love to me, Jason."

A deep, guttural sound escaped his chest. He didn't need to hear it twice.

In one swift movement, he lifted her into his arms, his grip firm yet reverent, as if she were something precious—something he would never let slip through his fingers again.

Their eyes met, and for a moment, the world stilled. No past, no pain, no regrets. Just them. Then, with a shared understanding, he carried her to the bedroom where they planned to show each other exactly how much love still burned between them.

They undressed in record time, clothes flying in every direction, discarded in their urgency. The moment they were bare, their bodies collided, mouths fusing, hands roaming, as if touching each other was the only way to breathe again.

They tumbled onto the bed, limbs tangling, desperate to make up for every second they had been apart.

Sarah straddled Jason, her thighs framing his hips, her breath coming in soft, needy pants as she positioned herself over him. Their eyes locked, a silent storm of emotion passing between them, then, with one smooth motion, she sank down onto him, taking him deep inside her.

A mutual groan of satisfaction filled the room, the pleasure so intense it stole their breath. Jason's fingers dug into her hips as he let his head fall back, his jaw tight, struggling for control.

"Sarah… you feel like heaven," he murmured, his voice rough with desire.

Sarah gasped at the sensation of him stretching her, filling her so completely. "Jason… I've missed you so much," she whispered breathlessly, bracing her hands on his chest as she started to move.

He growled low in his throat, his hands sliding up her body, fingers kneading her breasts, thumbs teasing her hardened nipples. She moaned, arching into his touch, rolling her hips in slow, tantalising circles that made him curse under his breath.

His grip tightened on her waist, guiding her movements as he thrust up to meet her, their bodies moving in perfect sync. The slow, torturous rhythm built between them, each thrust, each roll of her hips pushing them higher.

Jason sat up suddenly, wrapping his arms around her, pressing his mouth to the hollow of her throat as he drove deeper into her. Sarah cried out, clutching at his shoulders, her head falling back as waves of pleasure crashed over her.

"You're mine," he whispered against her skin, his voice raw, almost desperate.

"Yes," she gasped, burying her fingers in his hair, holding him to her. "Yours."

Their rhythm grew frantic, fevered, the need to reach the edge consuming them both. Jason flipped her onto her back in one swift motion, pinning her beneath him, never breaking their connection as he thrust into her with deep, relentless strokes.

Sarah met him thrust for thrust, her nails biting into his back, her cries of pleasure filling the room. The pressure built to an unbearable peak, the pleasure coiling tighter and tighter until—

"Jason!" she shattered beneath him, her body trembling as waves of ecstasy crashed through her.

Jason followed a heartbeat later, groaning her name as he thrust deep one final time, his body shaking with the force of his release.

For a long moment, they simply lay there, tangled together, their hearts pounding in unison. Then Jason rolled to the side, pulling Sarah into his arms, holding her close as their breathing slowly steadied.

"I love you," she whispered against his chest, her voice soft, sated.

Jason pressed a kiss to the top of her head, tightening his hold on her. "And I'll never let you go again."

A long time later, they lay tangled in each other's arms, bodies warm beneath the soft glow of the bedside lamp. The quiet hum of their breathing filled the room, punctuated only by the occasional creak of the bed settling. Jason's fingers traced slow, lazy circles along Sarah's arm, his touch light and absentminded, as if memorising every inch of her.

"You know," he murmured, his voice hushed, intimate, "I fell in love with you the first day I spoke to you in the hospital. I didn't realise it at the time."

Sarah tilted her head, brows lifting in surprise. "Really?"

Jason nodded, a small smirk tugging at the corner of his lips. "Yeah. I think I realised a little later. Remember that male nurse who came in? The one who was a little too friendly with you?"

Sarah frowned, then let out a soft laugh. "Oh, Peter? He was just being nice."

Jason scoffed, rolling his eyes. "Nice? I wanted to strangle him."

She propped herself on one elbow, studying him with an amused tilt of her head. "Seriously?"

"Dead serious." His fingers stilled on her arm as he met her gaze. "I hated how easily he made you smile. And that was before I even understood why I cared so much."

A slow, teasing smile curved Sarah's lips. "So, what you're saying is… you were jealous?"

Jason groaned, tipping his head back against the pillow. "Don't start."

Sarah giggled, resting her head against his chest, her fingers tracing idle patterns along the firm planes of his torso. "Well, for what it's worth," she murmured, voice soft, "the first time I saw you, I thought you were the most strikingly handsome man I'd ever met."

Jason glanced down at her, amusement flickering in his dark eyes. "Strikingly handsome, huh?"

Sarah lifted her head slightly, her gaze gentle, almost shy. "I think I fell for you the first time I saw you, too."

Jason chuckled, the sound vibrating warmly against her cheek. "Love at first sight?"

She exhaled a small, wistful laugh. "Something like that."

His expression softened, tenderness overtaking the teasing glint in his eyes. He tucked a stray strand of hair behind her ear, his fingers lingering against her skin. "I'll spend the rest of my life making sure you never regret it."

Sarah's lips curved into a smile, soft and full of warmth. She leaned in, pressing a gentle kiss to his, sealing his promise in the quiet intimacy of their embrace.

For a while, neither of them spoke, content to simply exist in the stillness, the unspoken understanding between them heavier than words. Then Jason's voice broke the quiet, low, and thoughtful. "Did you know Derek was going to propose to Melissa?"

Sarah stiffened slightly, tilting her head to meet his gaze. "No," she murmured, her voice soft. "I knew he loved her—he told me. But he never mentioned a proposal."

Jason exhaled, jaw tightening, silence stretching as though he were weighing memories he could never change.

Sarah's tone softened, tender yet tinged with sadness. "I met Derek through Melissa, you know. He was a good guy. One of the best." She paused, her fingers brushing against his chest, tracing gentle patterns. "He was the one who told me not to trust Damian."

Jason's brows drew together in surprise. "Really?"

She nodded. "Yeah. He never liked him. Said there was something… off about him, something he couldn't quite put his finger on."

Jason's jaw hardened. "Well, he was right, wasn't he?"

"Yes," she said simply, pressing a soft kiss to his chest.

He tightened his arm around her, drawing her closer, his voice low and measured. "I read yours and Derek's messages on your phone. I know you tried to save him, but he was just too far gone. He was obviously shattered by what Melissa and Damian did—I don't think he would have intentionally put you in danger."

Sarah exhaled, a faint shiver running through her as her fingers traced delicate patterns along his chest. "I know that," she admitted quietly. "I still don't remember that day. The doctor said I may never remember."

Jason studied her face; concern etched into every line. "Does that worry you?"

She hesitated, then shook her head, a fragile smile tugging at her lips. "To be honest… I don't think I want to remember."

He said nothing at first, simply watching her, absorbing the weight of her words, the quiet bravery in her choice. Then, slowly, deliberately, he bent down and kissed her, deep and tender, letting every ounce of love, regret, and reassurance flow into it. A kiss that said she didn't have to carry the past alone. She didn't have to remember. All that mattered was moving forward—together.

When they finally parted, their foreheads resting against each other, breaths mingling in the quiet room, Sarah whispered, "I just want us… from now on."

Jason's lips curved into a soft, unwavering smile. "From now on," he promised, tightening his arms around her as if he could shield her from the world—and from anything that had ever hurt her.

Jason reluctantly left Sarah in Melbourne on Monday morning, giving her time to organise her move back to Sydney. Every day without her had felt like a year, every minute a reminder of how empty his world had been. But finally, the week was over, and he was home.

As soon as the elevator doors slid open, the familiar, comforting scent of roast chicken wrapped around him, and his chest clenched. Sarah. She was here. She was home.

Without a second thought, he dropped his briefcase and strode toward the kitchen.

And there she was.

She turned just as he reached her, her eyes lighting up, a smile spreading across her face. Before she could say a word, he swept her into his arms, lifting her off the ground and spinning her around.

"Jason—" she laughed, breathless, clutching his shoulders.

He silenced her with a deep, desperate kiss, as if the world itself had conspired to keep them apart until this exact moment. He pressed his forehead to hers, letting the warmth of her presence sink into his bones.

"Marry me, Sarah," he whispered, his voice raw, trembling with the weight of everything he felt.

Her breath hitched, her fingers clutching at his arms. "Jason…"

"Marry me," he repeated, his hands gripping hers with a fierce urgency. "I want to come home to you every single day. I want to wake up with you, fall asleep with you, love you without hesitation, without fear. I love you."

Tears welled in her eyes, and her vision blurred, but she could still see the truth in his gaze, the vulnerability he rarely let anyone witness. It was all real—this man, her Jason, had fought his way back to her with a love that refused compromise.

Her heart swelled. She lifted a trembling hand to his face, fingertips brushing over the rough stubble on his jaw. "Are you sure?" she whispered. "You're not just saying this because you're afraid to lose me?"

Jason exhaled, pressing his forehead to hers, his voice thick with emotion. "I've never been surer of anything in my life. I love you, Sarah. I love you so much it terrifies me. But the only thing that scares me more is the thought of living without you."

A tear slid down her cheek. Jason caught it gently with his thumb, his touch tender enough to make her heart ache.

"I want a life with you," he continued, his voice a soft, desperate promise. "Not just stolen moments, not love wrapped in fear or regret. Everything. A home, a family, a future with you. I want to love you every single day for the rest of my life."

Sarah let out a shaky laugh, overwhelmed by the depth of his words, the purity of his love. "Yes," she breathed, a smile breaking through her tears. "Yes, Jason."

His heart raced, his grip tightening as if afraid she might vanish. He crushed her to him, their lips meeting in a kiss so deep, so full of love and relief, that it left them both trembling. She melted into him, her arms wrapping tightly around his neck, grounding them both in the certainty of their forever.

When they finally broke apart, their foreheads remained pressed together, breaths mingling in the quiet kitchen.

"You just made me the happiest man alive," Jason murmured, a rare, unguarded smile lighting his face.

Sarah laughed softly, brushing her fingers through his hair. "Then I guess that makes me the luckiest woman."

He kissed her again—slow, lingering, deliberate—sealing his promise in the warmth of their embrace.

Their forever had just begun.

Epilogue

14 months later....

The sun dipped low over Sydney Harbour, casting golden hues across the sky as a soft breeze carried the scent of salt and blooming jasmine. From their balcony, Sarah watched the waves roll against the shore, her fingers absently tracing the rim of her champagne flute.

Behind her, Jason wrapped his arms around her waist, pulling her against his chest. She leaned into him, tilting her head back to meet his gaze.

"Happy anniversary, Mrs. Olander," he murmured, pressing a kiss to her temple.

She smiled, warmth spreading through her chest at the sound of her new name. "Happy anniversary, Mr. Olander."

It still felt surreal. A year ago, she had been standing in this very spot, hesitating, wondering if she could truly let herself believe in this love. Now, she was his wife, wearing the ring that symbolised everything they had fought for—everything they had survived.

Jason reached for her hand, lacing their fingers together as he rested his chin on her shoulder. "You know, I had a whole speech planned for tonight."

"Oh?" She turned slightly, arching a brow. "And what did it say?"

"Something about how this has been the best year of my life. How waking up beside you every morning is a privilege I'll never take for granted. And how I love you more today than I did yesterday, and somehow, I know I'll love you even more tomorrow."

Sarah's breath hitched. Even after all this time, he still had the power to make her heart race.

"You don't need a speech for that, Jason," she whispered, turning fully in his arms. "I already know."

His lips curved. "Yeah?"

"Yeah." She brushed her fingers against his jaw, gazing up at the man who had once broken her, only to put her back together stronger than before.

He kissed her then, slow, and deep, as if savouring the moment.

And then, with a mischievous glint in his eyes, he pulled away just enough to murmur, "I do have one more thing for you."

Before she could ask, he reached into his pocket and pulled out a small velvet box.

Her breath caught. "Jason…"

"Open it."

With slightly trembling hands, she lifted the lid, revealing a delicate gold necklace. Dangling from it was a tiny, intricate charm—the shape of a key.

"A key?" she asked, glancing up at him with curiosity.

He smiled. "Not just any key. It's a replica of the one to our new home. The place where we will hopefully start our family." He lifted the necklace and fastened it around her neck, letting his fingers linger against her skin. "It's a reminder that no matter where life takes us, you'll always have the key to my heart."

Tears pricked her eyes, but she didn't try to stop them. Instead, she threw her arms around him, burying her face against his chest.

"I love you," she whispered, the words coming as easily as breathing.

Jason tightened his hold on her, pressing a kiss into her hair. "I love you more."

Sarah pulled back slightly, her hands still resting on his chest, her heart pounding at what she was about to say.

"There's something else," she murmured, her voice shaky but filled with quiet excitement.

Jason frowned slightly, his thumb brushing over her cheek. "What is it?"

She took a deep breath, then placed his hand gently over her stomach.

"I'm pregnant."

Jason froze. For a moment, he just stared at her, as if his brain hadn't fully processed the words. Then, his eyes widened, his breath hitching.

"You're—" His voice cracked, and he swallowed hard. "You're serious?"

A soft laugh escaped her, tears filling her eyes. "Yes."

His hand trembled against her stomach, his gaze dropping as if he could somehow see the tiny life growing inside her. When he looked back up, raw emotion filled his eyes.

"I—" He exhaled sharply, then cupped her face, kissing her deeply, passionately, reverently.

When he finally pulled back, he rested his forehead against hers, his voice thick with emotion.

"We're having a baby," he whispered, as if saying it aloud would make it more real.

Sarah nodded, her own tears slipping free. "Yes, we are."

A choked laugh rumbled in his chest as he pulled her close, holding her tightly.

"This is the best anniversary gift you could have ever given me," he murmured against her hair.

Sarah smiled, her heart full.

And as the sun dipped below the horizon, casting the sky in brilliant shades of pink and gold, she knew—this was only going to get better.

Eight months later, their new home was quiet, bathed in the soft golden light of the late afternoon sun. Outside, a gentle breeze rustled the leaves, and the scent of freshly cut grass drifted in through the open windows.

Jason stood in the doorway of the nursery, leaning against the frame, watching the love of his life hold their newborn son.

Sarah sat in the plush rocking chair, cradling the tiny bundle in her arms, humming softly as she gazed down at him. Their son's little fingers curled around hers, his dark lashes fluttering as he dozed peacefully against her chest.

Jason's heart clenched, overwhelmed by the sight of them. He had never known this kind of happiness was possible—that love could be this deep, this all-consuming.

"Hey," he murmured, stepping into the room.

Sarah looked up, her smile soft, glowing with the quiet joy of motherhood. "Hey."

Jason crouched beside her, brushing his knuckles lightly over their son's downy cheek. "He's perfect."

Sarah nodded, her eyes shining with unshed tears. "He is."

Jason swallowed hard, his voice rough with emotion. "I still can't believe he's ours."

Sarah shifted slightly, turning to face him. "Do you think Derek would've liked his namesake?" she asked, her voice barely above a whisper.

Jason exhaled, his throat tightening. He looked down at his son—Derek Alexander Olander—and felt the weight of the name settle in his chest.

"He would've loved him," Jason said, his voice thick. "And he would've spoiled him rotten."

Sarah smiled, though a tear slipped down her cheek. "I like to think he's watching over him."

Jason reached out, gently wiping the tear away. "I know he is."

For a long moment, they sat in silence, just the three of them, wrapped in the warmth of love and memory.

Then, their son stirred, making a soft, sleepy noise. Jason chuckled. "He's got my temper; I can already tell."

Sarah laughed, "you don't have a temper."

Leaning into Jason as he pressed a kiss to her temple. "Well, let's hope he gets my patience."

Jason grinned. "As long as he gets your heart, I think we'll be just fine."

Sarah looked up at him, love shining in her eyes. "We already are."

Jason leaned in and kissed her—slow, lingering, full of every promise he had ever made.

And in that quiet moment, with their son nestled between them, their love felt infinite.

The End

Mended Hearts

Alison Reid

A complete standalone romance

Previously published individually

Prologue

Ten Years Ago…

The courtroom was too cold.

Savannah Blake sat shivering in the witness box, though it had nothing to do with the air conditioning—and everything to do with the way her world had cracked open and never quite fit back together.

The oak-panelled walls pressed in like a tomb. Murmurs from the gallery blurred into static, drowned beneath the roar of her pulse. She clutched the edge of her seat like it might anchor her to something solid.

But nothing felt solid anymore.

Not since the night everything fell apart.

Not since Tyler died.

Not since they took him away.

Her gaze drifted—unwilling, unstoppable—to the defence table.

Jace Calloway.

He sat frozen beside his lawyer, fists clenched on the table. His face was pale, bruised, scraped from the arrest. His expression unreadable.

Except his eyes.

Dark. Wounded. Locked on her like a lifeline.

Savannah blinked hard. It hurt just to look at him.

He was the boy who used to carry her books in sixth grade. Who kissed her under the fireworks when she was sixteen. Who made her laugh when everything else felt heavy. Who knew every scar on her heart and never turned away.

The boy her brother had loved like family.

And now they were saying he'd killed Tyler.

The prosecutor stepped forward, heels silent on the polished floor. Her voice was steady, calm—almost kind.

"Miss Blake, on the night your brother, Tyler Blake, was murdered… did Jace Calloway argue with him?"

Savannah flinched. The words landed like a slap.

She hadn't wanted to testify. Had begged not to. She was eighteen—barely holding it together, torn in half by grief that hadn't stopped since the night of the sirens.

But the DA insisted: You're the only one who saw them together that night. The only one who can tell the truth.

But what if she didn't know the truth?

She remembered the raised voices. The slammed door. Tyler's anger. Jace's hurt.

But not what came next.

And Jace—her Jace—could never have done what they accused him of.

Could he?

Her throat closed. Tears burned behind her eyes. The courtroom swam.

Tyler had loved Jace. Trusted him.

So had she.

So did she.

"Miss Blake?" the prosecutor repeated, sharper now. "Did Jace Calloway argue with your brother that night?"

Savannah opened her mouth.

No sound came.

Her gaze locked with Jace's—and in his eyes, she saw no anger. No blame. Only that quiet, desperate plea:

Tell them the truth. Remember who I am.

And yet…

And yet…

"Yes," she whispered. "Yes, he did."

Three words.

Just three.

But they crashed through the courtroom like gunfire.

She felt it—rippling through the gallery, shifting the air. Jace's eyes closed for one beat, just long enough for something to break behind them.

His shoulders didn't flinch. But she felt it.

Felt the fracture like it was her own.

And she knew—she had just destroyed him.

The silence that followed was unbearable.

She had spoken what they wanted to hear.

What they believed was truth.

But deep in her chest, something twisted and cried out:

What if I'm wrong?

What if she'd just condemned the only boy she had ever loved?

What if she had betrayed them both?

Chapter One

The shift had been long—twelve gruelling hours of blood, noise, and relentless grief. Savannah Blake stepped out of the trauma bay into the cooling air of the hospital parking lot, where the orange dusk bled into a velvet night. The automatic doors sighed shut behind her, sealing away the chaos for another day. For a moment, she just stood there, shoulders tense, chest heavy, letting the quiet press in after the storm.

Above her, the sky stretched wide and bruised, streaked with fading light and the hush of everything unspoken. Clouds hung low and scattered, touched by the last traces of sunlight, casting golden streaks across the horizon like the remnants of a forgotten fire. It should have been beautiful. It was beautiful. But Savannah barely noticed.

Her dark hair, still twisted into a low bun, had loosened during the shift, damp strands curling against her temples and the curve of her neck. She reached up and tugged out the elastic, fingers running through tangled waves as she rolled her shoulders, trying to shake off the tension buried deep in her muscles like rusted nails. Even after nearly a decade in trauma care, it hadn't gotten easier. The dying. The screaming. The pleading looks from people who believed she could save everyone. Some days, she believed that too.

Even exhaustion couldn't hide the striking figure she cut—tall, strong, graceful in a way that came from years of learning to carry pain without spilling it. Her sun-kissed skin glowed faintly beneath the parking lot lights, the navy of her scrubs clinging to her—stained with effort, memory, and something unspoken. Her eyes, nearly black in the dim light, carried a weight that made strangers look twice—not just because she was beautiful, but because there was something fractured beneath the surface. Something unfinished.

She didn't notice the glances. She never did.

Beauty had always been an irrelevant truth in Savannah's life—like sorrow, or survival. Something constant. Something endured. Something that never saved her.

She crossed the lot in slow, measured steps, gravel crunching beneath her worn sneakers. Her Jeep sat in the far corner, its dark frame familiar, coated in the dust and memory of Cedar Ridge. She clicked the key fob, and the locks chirped in response, the sound too loud in the quiet.

The motion was automatic.

Routine.

But nothing about Savannah's life had ever truly been routine. Not since she was three years old and woke in the middle of the night to smoke curling through the hallway, the scent of burning paper and screams she couldn't understand. Her biological parents had died in that fire—both of them gone before she even learned to write her name. All she remembered was a stuffed bear clutched to her chest and the ache of arms that never held her again.

She grew up in another home, under another name for a while, before becoming a Blake. Her adoptive parents had been warm, generous, the kind of people who made soup from scratch and knew the names of every neighbour within a mile. They loved her. And she loved them. But twelve years ago, a rainy road and an overturned semi-truck stole them away too.

And Tyler…

God. Tyler.

Her older brother. Her protector. Her safe place in a world that had taken everything else. He'd taught her how to ride a bike, how to fish, how to throw a punch hard enough to make a boy think twice. He had been the only real constant in her life—and Jace Calloway had taken him away.

Allegedly.

Her heart still tripped over that word. Still caught in the ache between grief and doubt.

Jace had been her everything once. First love. First heartbreak. First betrayal. They had grown up on the same back roads, kissed under the same bleachers, whispered dreams in the same quiet fields. They'd made plans. They'd made promises.

And then everything shattered.

Now, there was no one left. No family. No safety net. Just Savannah.

She lived alone now, in a farmhouse haunted by silence. Shadows stretched across floorboards that creaked beneath old ghosts. She worked too much. Slept too little. Some nights, she drank wine on the porch, it was the only thing that stilled her hands.

But she stayed. She endured. She showed up for strangers the way no one had ever shown up for her.

Because someone had to.

Because if she didn't—who would? That thought followed her like a shadow as she climbed into the Jeep with stiff limbs and a tired sigh. The cabin was dark, the air inside stale from the day's heat. She let the keys dangle from her fingers for a moment, staring through the windshield as the shadows lengthened across the pavement.

Then her phone buzzed against the centre console.

She glanced down.

Did you hear?

He's back.

Cassidy's name lit the screen like a flare in the dark.

Savannah stared at the message, her breath catching mid-inhale. For three full seconds, everything inside her went still. Her chest tightened around the slow, unwanted truth.

Jace Calloway.

The name hit her like a punch—sharp and sudden and too damn familiar.

Jace Calloway.

Her mind reeled.

There were names that lost meaning with time—names that blurred at the edges and softened with distance. But not his. Never his. That name had weight. History. Blood. It didn't just stir a memory; it cracked open a vault of everything she had spent ten years trying to seal shut.

Ten years disappeared in a blink.

The hospital vanished. The hiss of sliding doors, the fluorescent hum, even the distant chatter of nurses on their break—all of it dropped away like scenery in a bad dream.

The world narrowed to silence.

And in that silence came the sound that still haunted her dreams.

The echo of a gavel.

Her voice, young and breaking.

Her heartbeat thudding like a drumbeat in her ears.

Yes, he did.

Three words.

Three syllables that shattered more than one life.

She hadn't spoken the words since the trial. Not since the courtroom pressed in, the walls closing, her voice trembling on the stand. Eighteen, unravelling. And Jace—already halfway gone.

Her throat went dry, and she swallowed hard against the rush of guilt that surged like bile.

She hadn't heard his name in years. Not since the trial. Not since the verdict. Not since the day they led him away in cuffs, and she watched the boy she loved vanish behind a door she couldn't follow.

In the weeks that followed, she'd buried him in the same way she buried Tyler. No funeral, no flowers. Just silence. Just the ache of a heart too shattered to form new words.

She had buried Jace deep—beneath rage, beneath sorrow, beneath a determination to survive the impossible.

But ghosts have long memories. And some names refuse to stay buried.

Her fingers trembled as she locked the phone and shoved it into her bag, the screen going black, but its message lingering like smoke. Her pulse still pounded like a war drum in her chest. Her limbs felt weightless, like she could float away if she didn't hold tight to the steering wheel.

She didn't want to know where he was now. Didn't want to know what he looked like, how prison had shaped his face, whether he still wore that small, crooked smile that once made her knees go weak.

She didn't want to know why he was back in Cedar Ridge.

Because knowing would make it real.

And real meant pain.

She didn't want to ask if prison had changed him—if it had carved hard edges into the boy who used to cradle her face like she was something holy. She didn't want to picture his hands—those hands that once traced poetry across her skin—curled into fists. Didn't want to imagine his shoulders hunched, his knuckles bruised, his voice grown hoarse from silence.

She didn't want to wonder if he still remembered the way she used to laugh—wild and unguarded—or the way her voice cracked when she gave him everything. Every piece of her. Heart, soul, body.

But she remembered.

She remembered everything.

The scratch of his flannel shirt against her bare skin.

The tremble in her own hands as she reached for him.

The sound of the wind rustling the grass around them, as the stars wheeled overhead like they had paused just to watch.

The world had gone impossibly still when she whispered that she was ready—and meant it.

No candles. No rehearsed lines. Just two teenagers wrapped in something fierce and fragile and utterly unforgettable.

It was the summer before everything shattered.

They'd gone down to the lake, where the water lapped the shore like a secret and the tall grass whispered around their ankles. He'd brought a blanket, a beat-up thermos of hot chocolate, and that quiet smile that always said he knew her better than anyone else ever would.

They'd talked for hours. About the future. About the past. About who they were and who they were afraid to become.

She told him she wanted to be a trauma nurse. He told her he wasn't sure who he was without her.

And somewhere between a laugh and a soft hush of wind, he kissed her.

Not like a boy experimenting. Not like a kid fumbling through firsts.

But like someone who saw her.

Every piece of her.

He kissed her like she was fire and water and something eternal.

And when they made love—slow, uncertain, reverent—it wasn't about lust. It was about trust. It was about the quiet promise they had written between them long before that night. A promise that they would always choose each other. Even when the world tried to pull them apart.

Afterward, he held her for hours. Whispered that nothing would ever touch her as long as he was breathing. That she was his whole world. That he'd never let her go.

And she had believed him.

God help her, she still wanted to believe him.

Even now.

Because some memories don't fade. They become part of you. They nest inside your bones, tucked between ribs and heartbeat, impossible to dig out without breaking something vital.

When they took Jace away, they didn't just take her first love.

They took her future.

For ten years, she hadn't let another man touch her. Not really. She'd dated. Pretended. Smiled when she was supposed to. But no one else came close. No one else made her feel like Jace did—like she was seen, known, wanted for more than just the curve of her body or the name on her badge.

Every man since had felt like a placeholder. Every kiss, every glance, a quiet betrayal of what her heart still clung to. So, she never gave herself to anyone else.

She told herself she was broken. Unworthy of love. Unwilling to try.

But the truth was worse.

She still loved him.

At twenty-eight, after everything—after silence and prison bars and years of learning to live without him—her heart still beat to the rhythm of his name. Like muscle memory. Like destiny. Like a curse she could never outrun.

She hated that about herself.

Hated that her body still remembered the sound of his voice. That her soul still leaned toward the echo of a love that might have been built on a lie.

Because if he did it—if he killed Tyler—then every part of her that still longed for him made her a traitor.

To her brother's memory.

To herself.

She lived in the in-between now. Too loyal to forget her brother. Too in love to forget Jace.

And it was killing her.

She started the engine with a shaky hand, headlights flaring into the deepening dark. Gravel crunched beneath her tyres as she pulled out of the parking lot, her grip white-knuckled on the wheel.

She didn't look back.

She couldn't.

Because looking back meant hope.

And hope was dangerous.

Some ghosts belonged to the past.

But some?

Some had a way of following you home.

Chapter Two

Her farmhouse sat just outside Cedar Ridge, tucked at the edge of the woods where silence pressed in like a secret. It had once been a place of comfort, of laughter and second chances. Left to her and Tyler after their adoptive parents' deaths, it had been a symbol of starting over. Now, it was just hers—emptier, quieter, lonelier. A house that creaked at night and held more memories than she had strength to face.

The crooked oak tree out front reached its gnarled limbs over the weathered roof, a sentry bent with age, still standing watch. The porch light flickered weakly, casting dull yellow halos over the gravel as Savannah Blake turned into the drive, her headlights cutting through the gloom.

She didn't expect to see anything.

But then—

Something moved.

The beam of light swept across the steps and landed on the silhouette of a man— broad shoulders, stillness like a statue, a shadow carved out of her past.

She hit the brakes, hard. The Jeep jerked forward with a grunt, tyres crunching on loose gravel.

Her pulse detonated.

No.

It couldn't be.

But it was.

Jace.

Sitting on her porch like no time had passed. Like he hadn't been ripped from her life, from the town, from her heart. Like he hadn't been locked behind bars while she stood on a witness stand with tears in her throat and betrayal in her bones.

Her breath punched from her lungs. A sound—part gasp, part curse, all disbelief.

He stood slowly as she climbed out of the Jeep, every inch of his body uncoiling like he'd been waiting there for hours. For years.

He looked almost exactly the same.

And completely different.

The boy was gone. The man who stood before her now was harder, darker, shaped by years that had left their fingerprints behind. His black hair was longer, messy from wind or worry, brushed back with the careless effort of someone who didn't look in mirrors anymore. His face was leaner, more angular, and the stubble on his jaw only deepened the shadows on his face.

But his eyes—those steel-blue eyes—were unmistakable.

Still full of ghosts.

Even now looking at her like she was a home he'd lost.

She didn't move. Couldn't.

The porch light buzzed above them. The trees whispered behind.

And then—

"Hi," he said, voice low and rough, like gravel after a rainstorm. "It's been a while."

Her throat tightened, but she forced her voice to work. "Not long enough."

His jaw flexed. He nodded once, like he'd earned that.

"I just—I needed to talk to you."

She barked a humourless laugh. "You shouldn't be here."

"I didn't have anywhere else to go."

She took a step closer, boots crunching on gravel, the porch looming between them like a line drawn in sand. "You had choices when you came back to town. You didn't have to come here."

"You think I wanted to?" His voice cracked into something bitter. "Trust me, Blake, this was the last place I thought I'd see again."

Blake.

Not Savvy.

Not baby or beautiful or the hundred soft names he used to say like prayers against her skin.

No. He used her last name like a blade.

Good. Let it cut.

Her arms folded across her chest, a barrier against the storm building between them. "Then why did you come?"

He looked away for the first time, jaw tight, eyes hard. "Because I didn't kill your brother. And someone out there knows I didn't."

The air went still.

It was like the world held its breath.

The words dropped between them like glass.

She should have laughed.

She almost did—a sharp, breathless sound caught in the back of her throat. "Ten years too late for that revelation, don't you think?"

"I didn't come to beg for forgiveness," he said, voice hoarse with unshed truths. "I came back because someone out there wants the truth to stay buried. And if I was framed—then you could be next."

Her blood ran cold.

"What the hell are you talking about?"

"I know how it sounds." He stepped closer, but not enough to touch. "You don't believe me. I get it. But something's happening. Things aren't what they seemed back then. They never were."

Her hands balled into fists. "You don't get to come back into my life with vague warnings and conspiracy theories. You don't get to talk about Tyler. You don't get to act like you care."

"I never stopped caring." His voice dropped, ragged. "I never stopped trying to protect you."

His words hit like a blow to the chest.

She staggered back a step.

Lightning cracked on the horizon—silent and electric—flashing white through the trees like a warning shot. The air changed. Charged. The smell of coming rain hung thick between them.

She shook her head slowly. "Don't. Just… don't."

"I don't want anything from you, Savannah." Her name on his lips sounded broken. "But I had to come. I had to warn you. Someone doesn't want the truth coming out. And if they went after Tyler to shut him up... what makes you think they'd stop now?"

Silence.

Long. Heavy.

Painful.

She swallowed hard, her throat thick with the things she wouldn't say. "You don't get to protect me anymore."

"I never stopped."

She hated him.

She hated that she didn't hate him enough.

"Leave," she whispered. "Tonight. Don't come back."

He didn't argue.

Didn't plead.

Instead, he reached into his coat pocket and pulled out a folded piece of paper. It was old—creased, yellowed, smudged with fingerprints and rain. The ink was fading, the edges torn. A relic. A secret. A story no one had told yet.

He held it out.

"Read it," he said. "Then decide."

She didn't take it.

So, he placed it gently on the top step—like it might bite, or burn, or beg.

Then he walked past her.

Close enough for her to feel the heat of him. Close enough for memories to rise like smoke—his arms, her brother's voice, the sirens, the trial, the night that never stopped replaying.

His scent clung to the air—familiar, faded. Like a campfire that burned out years ago.

She didn't turn around.

Couldn't.

Her heart beat too loudly in her ears.

The rain started as he disappeared into the night—soft at first, then steady.

She stared at the folded paper, the ink already beginning to blur beneath the drops. Her fingers trembled as she reached down, hesitating.

Afraid.

But she picked it up.

And yet—she didn't go inside.

Because sometimes the past didn't knock.

Sometimes, it sat on your front porch and waited.

He didn't look at her as he walked past.

Couldn't.

If he did, he might not keep walking.

And he had to. For her sake. For his.

But he felt her—God, he felt her.

Like gravity, pulling at the edges of him, insistent and unrelenting. Her presence hit him before his boots even touched the first step. It lived in the air, in the silence, in the trembling hush of the moment.

And when he passed close enough to catch the soft brush of her breath against his arm, it was like time folded in on itself—collapsing years into seconds, memories into muscle.

She was right there.

And still impossibly far away.

Her perfume lingered—subtle, clean. A little citrus. A little warmth. Her. The same scent she wore back when they were kids pretending not to fall in love. Back when she used to run barefoot through the fields and steal his baseball cap and tell him he'd never be as fast as her.

Back when her laughter came easy, and her eyes still trusted him.

That scent hit him like a sucker punch to the gut.

Even now she wore it.

After all this time.

After everything.

He swallowed hard. The back of his throat burned with it. With the memory of holding her in the dark, of whispering promises into her hair. With the way she used to tuck her head beneath his chin and breathe like he was the only thing tethering her to the world.

He kept his pace steady. Measured. Controlled.

Even though every cell in his body screamed to stop.

To turn around.

To look at her one more time, just to make sure she was real and not some grief-spun hallucination conjured by guilt and rain and too many nights spent dreaming of what he'd lost.

God, she was so beautiful.

She always had been.

But now… now there was something quieter about it. Something earned. Not the careless glow of youth, but the hard-won grace of a woman who had endured more than her fair share of pain—and still stood tall.

Life had carved edges into her. Sharpened her. Softened her. Made her dangerous in a different way.

He'd fallen in love with her before he even knew what love meant. When she was all sunburned cheeks and smart-mouth sass. She'd rolled her eyes at him in homeroom. Stolen his dessert at lunch. Tripped him in gym and then helped him up with a smirk that said she'd do it again.

And somewhere between that first punch and their first kiss behind the library, he was hers.

Completely.

And he'd let her wreck him. Happily.

Because back then, it had been simple. Back then, she was everything.

He could still feel her eyes on him. The silence between them stretched like wire—taut, humming with things unsaid.

I'm sorry.

I still love you.

I didn't kill him.

He didn't say any of it. Not now. Maybe not ever.

He didn't look back.

Didn't trust himself to.

But he knew she was standing there. Knew it in the ache under his ribs. In the phantom warmth brushing the space between them.

She hadn't gone inside.

And he hadn't stopped walking.

Maybe that was the only way they knew how to survive each other now.

From opposite sides of everything they'd lost.

Chapter Three

Savannah didn't sleep.

She tried—God, she tried. Tossed and turned until the sheets twisted around her like restraints, the mattress unfamiliar beneath a body that refused to rest. Her skin was too hot, then too cold. She kicked off the blanket, pulled it back up. Counted her breaths. Counted the hours. Counted all the ways her life had unravelled since Jace Calloway stepped back onto her porch.

Her body was exhausted, but her mind… her mind was a storm. Sleep refused her.

Every time her eyes drifted shut, he was there.

Jace.

Standing on her porch like some ghost summoned by old pain. His voice soft, low, roughened by time—saying her name like it still meant something. Like ten years and a manslaughter conviction hadn't burned it to ash.

Savvy.

He hadn't said it aloud. But she'd heard it anyway.

Felt it.

Like a whisper pulled from another life. And somehow, that was worse. Because it meant he still remembered. Still saw her through the same lens. Still believed he had the right.

And despite everything—despite the ache of betrayal, the suffocating grief, the grave she still visited every year on Tyler's birthday—some part of her responded. Some part of her curled around that name like it had been waiting for it all this time.

The memories came uninvited, a slow bleed through the cracks in her armour. Her brother's laugh. The blood. The sirens. Her own screaming. The prosecutor's voice. The cold, echoing courtroom. Her words.

Yes, he did.

Then silence.

Ten years of it.

Until now.

When dawn finally broke, it didn't bring relief. Just the pale gold edge of another day she didn't know how to survive. Light spilled across the ridge line, seeping into the mist and crawling over the trees like fingers reaching for something that could no longer be touched.

She gave up.

Dragged herself out of bed with limbs that felt boneless. Hollow. She padded barefoot to the kitchen, the floorboards cold beneath her heels.

The first thing she did was make coffee—strong, black, bitter enough to ground her.

The second was stare at the crumpled piece of paper Jace had left behind.

It sat on the counter like it had always been there. Like it belonged there. Like it wasn't a hand grenade disguised as paper. Like it hadn't waited a decade to be read.

The edges were frayed. Dampness had warped it, curling the corners inward. The folds were deep, sharp—creased by too many hands. Too many years. Ink bled into the fibres in places, turning letters into shadows.

It felt alive somehow. Heavy. As if it had absorbed the grief it carried.

She stared at it for a long time. Pacing the length of the kitchen. Once. Twice. Again. Every lap felt like a countdown.

She made it to six before she finally stopped. Chest tight. Mouth dry.

Her fingers hovered over the paper. Not touching. Just trembling in its orbit.

And then, with a sudden burst of frustration and pain—she grabbed it.

Like it might hurt less if she tore it open fast. Like that could make any of it easier.

She unfolded it slowly anyway, careful despite her anger. As if reverence could make it less damning.

Water stains mottled the paper, blooming like bruises. The writing was smudged, but it was his. She'd know it anywhere.

Tyler's handwriting.

Familiar. Slanted. Sloppy in a way only brothers could get away with. The same lettering that used to scribble "Save me one, Sav" on her cupcakes. The same tilt that labelled VHS tapes with dumb nicknames and left notes on her textbooks when he borrowed cash.

She didn't realise she was crying until the first tear hit the page.

It felt like he was close. Like he'd just left the room and would be back in a second to ruffle her hair and steal her coffee.

Her knees gave a little, and she sank onto the nearest stool, the page trembling in her grip like her hands weren't her own.

And then—heart in her throat—she began to read.

Savvy,

If you're reading this, it means I got in deeper than I should've. I messed up. But I swear to you, I was trying to fix it. I thought I could take them down myself. Thought I could be the hero. But now I'm scared. Not for me—for you.

If something happens to me... it wasn't an accident.

Trust Jace. He doesn't know everything, but he never stopped watching your back. Even when I didn't deserve him.

Don't trust Cassidy. Not with this. Not until you're sure.

I love you. Don't hate me forever.

Ty.

The words sank like stones in her chest.

She read it again. And again.

Until they blurred.

Trust Jace.

Don't trust Cassidy.

The coffee sat untouched on the counter. Her stomach curled into itself, nausea tightening her core like a vice. It didn't make sense. It couldn't make sense.

Cassidy had held her hand the day of the funeral. Slept on her couch after the trial. Helped her move. Helped her breathe.

Cassidy had been the only thing standing between Savannah and complete collapse.

And Tyler hadn't trusted her.

Her throat burned. No. It wasn't possible. She couldn't believe that. Not yet.

And Jace… God, Jace.

What if he'd been telling the truth?

What if she'd sent an innocent man to prison?

Her entire world tilted on its axis. Every memory shifted. Every truth warped.

She folded the letter slowly now, with shaking fingers. No anger this time. Just heartbreak.

She tucked it into the back pocket of her jeans like it was sacred. Like it could anchor her to something real.

Then she grabbed her keys and drove into town, the paper pressed against her spine, her pulse pounding like a war drum beneath her ribs.

Because everything she thought she knew—

Might have been a lie.

Cassidy's boutique sat neatly between the flower shop and Dot's Diner on Main Street. Quaint, polished, perfect—just like everything Cassidy touched. The window display boasted summer dresses in soft blush tones, linen trousers on minimalist mannequins, and artfully scattered flower petals. It looked like a place untouched by grief. Untouched by guilt. Untouched by truth.

Inside, soft acoustic guitar drifted from hidden speakers, blending with the familiar scent of lavender, eucalyptus, and sun-warmed wood. Sunlight spilled through the large windows, casting golden bars across the wide-plank floor. Everything was curated. Controlled.

Cassidy stood behind the counter, tapping something into her tablet. Her platinum hair was swept into a loose, glossy knot. Her makeup was flawless in soft taupes and pinks. A silver scarf tied at her neck gave her the kind of effortless glamour Savannah had never had time—or patience—for.

Her eyes lit up as Savannah walked in. "Hey, stranger! You look like you've wrestled a storm."

Savannah didn't smile. She walked straight to the counter, boots heavy on the floor, and planted her hands flat against the surface. Her voice came low. Controlled. Icy.

"I did. His name is Jace Calloway."

Cassidy froze. The light drained from her expression like a dimmer switch flipped too fast.

"I heard the rumour. He's really back?" she said, voice almost a whisper.

"I saw him." Savannah's throat tightened. "He showed up at my house."

Cassidy's mouth opened, but no words came. Her shoulders went stiff.

"What did he want?"

"To talk." Savannah didn't blink. "He says he's innocent. Says someone else killed Tyler."

The words hit like a thrown stone. Cassidy's knuckles went white against the counter. Her body was perfectly still—but her eyes moved too fast, flicking over Savannah like she could search for weaknesses in her face.

"And… do you believe him?"

A beat of silence. Then another.

"I didn't," Savannah said, slowly. "Not until I read Tyler's letter."

Cassidy straightened. "What letter?"

Savannah's voice dropped into something harder. Sharper. She pulled the letter out of her pocket and held it up.

"This letter. The one Tyler left me. I didn't even know it existed. But he wrote it, Cassidy. And in it, he said two things."

Her hands trembled slightly as she held up two fingers, her body vibrating with restraint.

"One—he was scared. Said he was in over his head. And two… he said not to trust you."

Cassidy didn't react. Not right away.

Then she blinked, too quickly, and looked down. "Savannah—"

"He said the only person I could trust was Jace." Her voice cracked around the edges, but she didn't stop. "And I don't know what that means yet. I don't know what you're hiding. But Tyler knew something. Something big enough to write this. Big enough to warn me."

Cassidy's lips parted. Her hand fluttered at her side like a broken wing. "In danger… from who? Why would he say that about me?"

Savannah stepped closer, her voice tight. "I'm trying to figure that out. But he was afraid. And Tyler wasn't the kind of guy to scare easily."

Cassidy stared down at the countertop. When she spoke again, her voice was barely audible. "Savannah…"

"You told me you didn't know anything," she said. "You swore to me. But if Tyler said not to trust you…"

"I don't know why he would say that," Cassidy cut in, her voice rising. "That's insane. I've been your best friend since middle school."

"I know," Savannah whispered. "That's what makes this so damn hard."

Cassidy's eyes filled with tears, but none fell. Her jaw clenched, her voice thinned into steel. "You're going to trust him? After everything?"

Savannah didn't speak.

"I stayed," Cassidy said. "When the whole damn town turned its back on you, I stayed. I brought you groceries. Sat with you at the courthouse. I held you when you cried yourself sick after the trial."

Savannah flinched at that—but just barely.

"He shattered you," Cassidy hissed.

"I remember," Savannah said. Quiet. Steady. Devastating.

The silence between them expanded, stretching wide and brittle.

"I remember everything," she added. "That's why I can't ignore this."

Cassidy came around the counter fast, reached for her arm. Her grip wasn't rough—but it was desperate.

"Savannah don't do this. Don't let him back in. Not after what he did. You don't know what he's capable of."

Savannah looked down at Cassidy's hand. Then slowly—coldly—into her eyes.

"No," she said. "But maybe I didn't know what you were capable of either."

Cassidy recoiled like she'd been slapped.

She opened her mouth, tried to speak—but nothing came.

Savannah stepped back, every inch of her shaking, but steady somehow.

And for the first time in years, she went to walk out of Cassidy's boutique not knowing who she could trust…

—but knowing exactly who she couldn't.

She'd barely taken two steps toward the door when the bell above it jingled.

A sheriff's deputy entered, hat low over his eyes, his uniform damp from the drizzle outside. His hand rested on the grip of his sidearm—not threatening, but alert. Like a man preparing for something he couldn't name.

"Miss Blake?" he asked.

Savannah turned. "Yes?"

"There's been an incident at your property," he said. "I'm going to need you to come with me."

Savannah's stomach dropped. "An… incident?"

The word didn't sound like a break-in. It didn't sound like vandalism.

No. It sounded personal.

And it felt like a message.

One meant just for her.

"Yes, one of your neighbours called it in."

Maybe the past wasn't done with her yet.

Chapter Four

Ten minutes later, Savannah gripped the steering wheel of her Jeep tighter than she meant to. Her fingers ached from the strain, knuckles white, tendons pulled tight like piano wire. She could barely feel them anymore.

Ahead, the sheriff's cruiser wound steadily down the backroad toward her farmhouse, kicking up dry dust and loose gravel that pinged softly against her windshield. The road, once familiar and quiet, felt different now—too narrow, too still. Like it was holding its breath.

The spinning lights atop the patrol car pulsed red and blue in silence. No sirens. Just the flicker of warning, painting the trees in jarring bursts of colour—danger, danger, danger—as if the woods themselves had seen something they couldn't unsee.

She followed mechanically, wheels bumping over potholes and ruts, but the jostling barely registered. Her mind was moving too fast, darting between questions she didn't want the answers to.

She had only been gone an hour.

One hour.

As they rounded the last curve, her heart twisted—expecting the worst, begging for it not to come.

At first glance, everything looked… normal. The house stood just as she'd left it, sun glinting off the tin roof, the porch sagging slightly at the corner like always. The crooked oak tree stood sentinel out front, casting its long shadow across the steps.

But then—

The cruiser slowed.

Then stopped.

And the moment she saw why, her breath ripped free like a scream swallowed too late.

She slammed the Jeep into park. Threw open the door. Her boots hit gravel with a crunch that sounded too loud. Too final. Like the start of something she couldn't stop.

"Miss Blake—stay in your vehicle!" the deputy shouted, urgency laced through his command. One hand hovered near his sidearm as he hurried after her.

But she didn't hear him.

Didn't stop.

Couldn't.

Her blood was roaring in her ears, drowning everything else out.

She crossed the gravel in three fast strides, heart hammering, pulse a wildfire behind her ribs. And then—

She saw it.

The front window.

Her window.

Defaced in thick, angry slashes of red—YOU DON'T WANT TRUTH—the words smeared across the glass like a scream made visible. The letters were crude, uneven, ragged with fury. They took up nearly the entire pane, the strokes so deep and heavy that they'd left splatter trails down the siding.

She froze at the foot of the steps. Her stomach lurched violently.

At first, she thought it was paint.

Please let it be paint.

But then the wind shifted—and the scent hit her.

Metallic. Sharp. Rotting.

Blood.

Savannah stumbled backward, a hand flying to her mouth. The bile came fast and hot, rising in her throat like acid. The porch tilted slightly in her vision. The sky pressed down.

She hadn't felt this way since—

Since the night Tyler died.

Since the sirens. The trial. The scream that never really stopped.

Her body remembered before her mind did—how panic rolled like a wave and left you breathless in its wake. How the past could punch its way back into the present without warning. How grief could smell like rust.

Her knees buckled, but she didn't fall.

Not this time.

She reached—almost without thinking—for the letter still tucked into her back pocket. Tyler's words. His warning. Her lifeline. The edges were soft now, smudged with fingerprints and last night's storm. She clutched it like it could anchor her.

Behind her, the deputy's voice crackled through his radio. "Dispatch, we've got a code seventy-one. Defacement with possible biohazard. Requesting backup and forensic. Scene not secured. Victim present."

She barely heard him.

Because her reflection stared back at her from the glass—warped, blood-smeared, broken. Her face was cut in half by the letter T. The word TRUTH slicing through the person she used to be.

This wasn't just a threat.

It was personal.

Deliberate.

Intimate.

A message meant for her alone. A warning soaked in blood; left on the place she was supposed to feel safest.

Someone out there didn't just want her scared.

They wanted her silenced.

And whoever they were—they knew she was reading. They knew she was close. They were watching.

She could almost hear Tyler again—his laugh echoing across the porch, teasing her about the "stubborn little farmhouse," calling it her fortress. Telling her to make it her second chance.

Now it looked like a battleground.

Her home—her whole damn world—was under siege.

And Savannah Blake knew, deep in the pit of her stomach, that this was only the beginning.

Savannah stood rooted to the spot, her gaze locked on the blood-red message scrawled across her front window for what felt like an eternity—five slow, torturous minutes where the world shrank into silence. The wind didn't blow. The trees didn't move. Even the birds had stopped singing, as if the land itself was holding its breath.

She should've been screaming—letting the fear claw its way out of her throat, wild and primal.

She should've been crying—giving in to the burn behind her eyes and letting the pain unravel her in thick, shaking sobs.

She should've been calling someone—Cassidy, anyone who could help make sense of this mess before it pulled her under completely.

But none of that came.

Instead, she just… stood there. Frozen in the unforgiving light of the sun, her body rigid, her heart thudding like it had nowhere to go.

Her eyes traced the jagged strokes of paint—no, not paint—blood. Red, raw, and deliberate. Every letter screamed louder than the last.

YOU DON'T WANT TRUTH.

The words didn't just threaten. They accused. Warned. Promised.

It wasn't vandalism.

It was a warning.

Her lungs locked, not from panic but something deeper. A cold, volcanic rage began to bloom in her chest—slow and pressurised. It didn't explode. It seethed.

Her boots scraped against the gravel as she walked numbly toward the porch and up the steps. Each step echoed like a dare. The same boards she and Tyler had once raced across now groaned beneath her weight as she lowered herself onto the top step.

She sat with her arms wrapped around her knees, the way she used to when she was little and trying not to cry after a scraped elbow or a hard day at school. Only this time, no one was coming with bandages or soft words. No one was going to fix this.

Her fingers trembled.

Not with fear.

With fury.

Who the hell did this?

Why now?

And why—why, after everything—did some part of her still believe Jace Calloway was innocent?

The name burned like a flare in her mind. She clenched her jaw, fighting the confusion that swirled alongside the dread. She wanted to hate him. Needed to. But Tyler's letter had cracked something open inside her—and now the truth was bleeding through.

Her phone buzzed sharply in her pocket.

She didn't have to look.

Cassidy.

Of course it was Cassidy. Probably calling to spin some version of the truth into something soft and harmless. To backpedal. To cry. To plead.

Savannah didn't answer.

Instead, she pulled the phone from her pocket and scrolled down. Past the newer names. Past colleagues and neighbours and friends who didn't really know her. Her thumb hovered over one contact. A name that hadn't been dialled in years.

Sheriff John Nolan.

The man who had once sworn to protect what was left of her family.

She hesitated for one long, shuddering breath.

Then tapped Call.

The line rang.

Once.

Twice.

Three times.

She didn't think he would answer.

But then—

"Savannah?"

His voice hadn't changed. Still low. Still sandpaper-rough, with the kind of wear that comes from too many long nights and too many regrets.

There was caution in it now. Hesitation. A tension that said he already knew this wasn't just a check-in.

"Yeah," she said. Her voice came tight and dry. "It's me."

A pause followed. Not long. But heavy.

"I heard one of my deputies responded out at your place," he said finally. "You alright?"

No. She wasn't. And the worst part was, she didn't even know what "alright" was supposed to feel like anymore.

"I'm not sure," she answered. "Can you come by?"

Another silence. This one longer. It stretched out until it felt like a rope between them—frayed and fragile, still holding, but barely.

She could almost see him now: behind his desk at the station, hand clenched around the receiver, staring out the window like he used to. Like he had the first time he came to tell her Tyler was dead.

Once upon a time, John had been more than just the sheriff. He'd been her father's best friend. Her protector. Her tether to something solid when everything else went sideways.

He used to stop by every Sunday after her adoptive parents died. Always with a grocery bag and a quiet joke. He'd sit at the kitchen table and ask about school, check the locks, making sure Tyler was doing well at work.

But after Tyler's murder… after the arrest… after the trial…

He stopped showing up.

Stopped calling.

Stopped looking her in the eye when they crossed paths in town.

Maybe it hurt too much.

Or maybe it was guilt.

Because he'd promised her father he'd take care of them.

And he hadn't.

"I'll be there in twenty," he said at last.

The line went dead before she could say thank you.

Savannah lowered the phone and let it rest in her lap, her thumb still brushing the edge like she didn't trust it to stay silent.

She stared out over her property, but the yard looked different now—like something had shifted in the bones of the land. It was quiet. Too quiet. Like the sky just before a tornado—still, heavy, and waiting to tear everything apart.

Her pulse beat slow and hard beneath her skin. Her bones ached like they remembered something her mind hadn't yet caught up to.

The truth wasn't coming.

It was already here.

And it had left a message on her window in blood.

Now, she was calling the sheriff not as the girl he'd promised to protect... but as a woman standing on the edge of a reckoning.

A storm was building.

And this time, she wasn't sure anyone—not Jace, not Cassidy, not even Sheriff John Nolan—could save her from it.

Not unless she faced it herself.

Not unless she wanted the truth... even if it destroyed everything.

Chapter Five

Jace Calloway hadn't been back in Cedar Ridge a full forty-eight hours, and already the town was trying to choke the air out of his lungs.

Everything looked the same. Too much the same. The diner still served coffee that tasted like burnt ash and broken promises. The gas station still had the same junkyard mutt that barked at every engine like it was guarding the gates of hell. The church bell still rang every Sunday morning—ten hollow tolls, always ten—as if the town could drown its sins in sound and pretend they never existed.

But nothing felt the same.

Cedar Ridge had once been home. Now it was a mausoleum dressed in nostalgia.

He'd spent a decade trying to scrub the town from his soul—the rust-coloured clay that clung to your boots, your bones, your name. Prison had taught him to disappear. To stay quiet. To wear stillness like armour. But all it took was one look at Savannah on that porch—same wildfire in her eyes, same steel in her spine—and every wall he'd built cracked like glass under pressure.

She still looked like fire wrapped in steel.

And she still didn't believe him.

He didn't blame her. Not after what she'd lost. Not after what he couldn't prove.

Now he stood on the ridge, leaning against the rusted hood of his old pickup, the paint chipped and sun-faded to hell. Below him, the cemetery stretched in rows of silence—headstones catching the last light of day like old secrets surfacing for air. The wind curled around him, carrying the scent of dry grass and coming rain.

His eyes locked on the far corner.

Tyler Blake.

Beloved brother.

Forever missed.

Jace scoffed. Forever missed, carved out of grief and clean-cut lies.

He scrubbed a hand over the stubble on his jaw. He hadn't planned to come here yet. Hadn't planned to see Savannah yet, either. But that plan had blown apart the second he learned that Tyler's belongings—the evidence—had conveniently disappeared. Moved. Sealed. Lost.

Someone was cleaning house.

And Savannah?

She was right in the middle of it. Whether she knew it or not.

A twig snapped behind him.

Jace didn't flinch. Didn't move. But every muscle went taut—shoulders tight, weight shifting just enough to anchor himself. The threat registered before the voice did.

"I figured I'd find you here."

The voice was sharp and smooth, like a knife dipped in honey.

He turned slowly.

Cassidy Kessler stood just inside the iron gate, arms crossed over her designer blouse, red heels biting into the earth like she belonged even here—among the dead. Her platinum hair was twisted into a perfect knot, not a single strand out of place. The silk scarf at her neck fluttered in the wind like a flag for the empire of secrets she ruled.

She looked like power bottled in perfume and glass.

He hadn't seen her since the trial.

"You've got some nerve," he said, voice flat.

"And you've got a death wish," she replied, walking forward without hesitation. "Strolling back into this town like you didn't split it down the middle."

Jace let out a low, humourless laugh. "Didn't expect a warm welcome. But I figured the truth might matter after ten years."

"Truth?" Cassidy tilted her head. "That's what we're calling it now?"

He studied her, eyes narrowing. "You nervous, Cassidy?"

Her posture didn't shift, but her grip on her elbows tightened.

"I'm not the one who served a decade for manslaughter."

"No," he said, stepping away from the truck, voice dropping to something razor-sharp, "you're the one who knew your daddy's business reeked of rot. The one whose best friend died the same night he tried to shine a light on it."

Her lips parted—just barely. "Careful, Jace."

"You think I care about careful anymore?"

He took a slow step forward. The cemetery swallowed the sound of their voices like it was listening.

"This morning," he said, "someone smeared a message across Savannah's window. Might've been written in blood."

That stopped her.

Cassidy's jaw twitched—just enough to confirm what he already suspected.

She knew something.

"You really think I'm gonna walk away from that?" he asked, stepping close enough that she had to tilt her chin to hold his gaze. "You think I came back to play nice?"

"If you're threatening me," she said coolly, "you'd better remember who still pulls strings in this town. You're on parole. All it takes is one slip."

His smile was cold and slow. "Then I'll make the slip count."

They stared at each other, still as the dead beneath their feet.

The wind whispered through the grass. Leaves skittered across the stones. A crow called in the distance—loud and lonely.

Cassidy moved first.

She stepped back with a breath that sounded like it scraped her throat. "You always thought you were the hero, Jace. But you're just the ghost that won't stay buried."

"She's not yours to protect," he said.

"And she's not yours to destroy," Cassidy snapped, eyes blazing.

She turned on her heel and strode away, her heels striking the path with a rhythm that felt too rehearsed. She didn't look back.

Jace didn't watch her go.

His gaze returned to Tyler's grave, jaw clenched.

Everything had started here.

And somehow, he knew—it would end here, too.

Only this time, he wouldn't walk away in handcuffs.

This time, he wasn't leaving without the truth.

Even if it killed him.

Jace stayed a while longer, staring at Tyler's grave.

His best friend.

His brother in every way that mattered.

The one person who ever truly had his back in this godforsaken town.

And maybe—just maybe—the only one who'd ever tried to save Savannah after all.

The cemetery was quiet. The wind stirred gently through the cypress trees, their limbs swaying like they knew how to keep secrets. Shadows stretched long across the grass, the golden slant of the late afternoon sun bathing the headstones in a hush of amber and sorrow. Somewhere in the distance, a mourning dove cooed low and steady, the sound almost reverent.

Jace's boots crunched over the gravel as he stepped forward, then sank to one knee. The stones bit into his jeans. Moisture from the ground crept through the denim and into his bones, but he didn't move. Dust clung to his palms as he reached out and brushed it from the engraved letters—like somehow, he owed that much. Like he couldn't let Tyler sit forgotten beneath dirt and silence.

TYLER BLAKE

BELOVED BROTHER

FOREVER MISSED

The words didn't feel like enough.

They never had.

Jace swallowed hard as a lump rose in his throat, sharp and bitter. It hadn't truly hit him until this moment—not in prison. Not even on the long drive here, not even when he stood in front of Savannah on her porch—that Tyler was really gone. Not hidden. Not holed up somewhere waiting for this all to blow over.

Dead.

Buried because of a truth no one had dared to tell.

Because of a secret too dangerous to survive.

Because Jace hadn't been able to stop it.

He rested a hand on the cold stone. His fingers curled over the edge like he needed something to hold on to. Something solid. Something that wouldn't disappear.

"I'm gonna find out what happened to you," he said, voice low. Raw. "I swear it."

The breeze shifted again, stronger this time, rustling the tall grass and stirring loose petals from a long-faded bouquet. And with it came the memories—rising like ghosts from the soil, uninvited but unshakable.

Tyler and Savannah, bickering over the last piece of peach pie on a sticky summer evening. Tyler had snatched it right off the counter while Savannah was still reaching for it, and she'd chased him barefoot through the backyard, laughing so hard she could barely breathe. Her hair flying, the screen door slamming behind her, the two of them glowing with youth and sunlight.

Or that one July night out at Brush Hollow Lake. All three of them sprawled across the dock, sweat-damp and happy, stars so bright it felt like the sky had cracked open. Tyler doing cannonballs off the edge while Savannah floated, arms spread wide, her face tilted toward the heavens. Her laugh had echoed across the water like a song only they knew.

Jace had sat beside Tyler that night, legs dangling off the dock, beer bottle sweating between his hands. They'd watched her together—Tyler with the protective eyes of a big brother, Jace with something quieter. Something deeper. Something he hadn't even had a name for back then.

"She's got that heart, man," Tyler had said, towelling off, water dripping from his hair. "Like, a real one. Break it, and I swear—I'll break your jaw."

Jace had laughed. Cocky. Young. Stupid.

"I wouldn't hurt her."

But he had. Not with his hands. Not with betrayal. With silence.

With ten years of distance and damn near nothing to show for it.

He'd hurt her by not being there when it mattered.

By letting the truth rot while the lie won.

His fists curled against his thighs, jaw clenched as he stared at the stone.

"I should've protected you," he whispered, voice breaking. "Both of you."

The silence that followed was suffocating.

Not empty—but full. Heavy with things unsaid—memories, guilt, broken promises. The rustling trees. The steady drone of insects. The pine-scented wind brushing over his skin like a hand from the past.

And beneath it all, the quiet ache in his chest that never quite went away.

He bowed his head. Stayed that way for a long moment, letting the weight of it all press down until he couldn't breathe through it anymore.

Then—slowly, like a man standing up from his own grave—he rose.

The sun had sunk lower now, casting long shadows behind him. The headstone glowed gold in the fading light, the name carved into it as sharp and final as a blade.

"Rest easy, Ty," Jace murmured. "I'm not walking away this time. Not until the truth comes out. Not until I bring the bastard who did this into the light."

He stepped back, his boots crunching softly against the gravel. The wind tugged at his jacket, like the past didn't want to let go.

He turned toward the path, eyes hard. Set.

The pain was still there—lodged deep in his chest—but now, something else moved beside it.

Purpose.

He'd come back looking for answers.

And now, standing in front of Tyler's grave, he knew—

He wouldn't leave without them.

Even if it meant tearing the whole town apart to get them.

Even if it killed him.

Chapter Six

Sheriff John Nolan had aged since she'd last seen him.

More lines carved into his face, the silver threading thick through the dark at his temples. He wore it with a quiet dignity—the kind earned from too many years spent holding back storms no man could stop. His khakis were still sharp, shirt tucked with military precision, but the man inside the uniform looked… heavier. Like something in him had sunk low and settled deep.

The jawline was still firm. The boots still polished. But the light in his eyes— the one that used to burn with certainty, with justice—had dulled to something quieter. Sadder. A light dimmed by too many unanswered questions, too many names etched into too many headstones.

He stood in front of Savannah's shattered sanctuary, staring at the message smeared across her front window like a challenge carved in blood. His shoulders stiffened beneath his uniform, and for a long, heavy moment, he didn't speak.

Then:

"You okay?"

His voice was quiet, but not soft—gravelly, steady. Like it had once been used to keeping people calm in chaos.

"No," Savannah said, almost too fast. Her arms crossed over her chest, her fingers digging into her sleeves. "Not even close."

John nodded slowly, his gaze never leaving the message.

YOU DON'T WANT TRUTH.

The words pulsed in red against the glass, jagged and brutal, as if they'd been scrawled in a rage too big for the person who wrote them.

"You got enemies I don't know about?" he asked, finally looking at her. His expression was hard to read—part suspicion, part concern. All exhaustion.

Savannah hesitated. The truth caught somewhere between her ribs and her throat.

"Jace Calloway was here last night."

That got his attention.

John's entire body tensed. His jaw flexed. His eyes narrowed—not in shock, but in something colder. Older. Like a switch had been thrown and a buried war was coming back into play.

"You let him in?"

"No," she said quickly. "He showed up on my porch. Uninvited."

"And?"

She looked away, lips pressing into a line. "He gave me something. A letter."

He waited, the air between them charged.

"He said it was from Tyler," she added, voice quiet but steady. "Said... he was framed."

John closed his eyes for a beat. The sigh he let out was long and low, like it came from somewhere deep in his bones.

"Jesus."

Savannah stared at the window, at the smear of violence left behind. The letters had started to dry and darken under the sun, but they still looked fresh—like they were watching her.

"I didn't say I believed him," she murmured.

"No," John said, rubbing a hand over his chin, "but you didn't throw the letter away either."

Silence fell again, thick as fog. The kind that settled in your lungs and made it hard to breathe.

The wind picked up. Dust curled around their boots. A lone magpie called once from the fence post, then went still—like even the birds knew this moment needed silence.

Savannah swallowed, throat dry. "Do you think someone would come after me to keep it buried?"

John met her eyes—and in his expression, she didn't see disbelief. She saw confirmation.

"I think someone already did," he said softly.

The words landed like a blow. Not loud. Not fast. Just solid and true—like a verdict.

For the first time in years, Savannah felt like a girl again, standing in front of a man who'd once promised to keep her safe. But the man in front of her now looked like he wasn't sure he could still keep that promise. Or worse—like he'd already failed once, and the weight of that failure was still sitting in his chest like a stone.

John turned back to the message. His fingers flexed at his sides.

"This wasn't just a warning," he said after a beat. "It was a signal. Whoever wrote that… they wanted you to see it. They wanted you to feel it."

Savannah nodded slowly. "It worked."

A gust of wind pulled at her hair. Somewhere far off, thunder grumbled in the distance. A storm was coming—one she wasn't sure any of them were ready for.

And in that moment, beneath the blood-red scrawl and the quiet dread curling around her ribs, Savannah understood something she hadn't before.

The past wasn't finished with her.

Not yet.

Not by a long shot.

Later that afternoon, Savannah stood at the nurse's station, her fingers drumming a restless rhythm against the corner of a patient chart. She'd been staring at the same page for over ten minutes and hadn't processed a single word. The words might as well have been written in a language she'd forgotten how to speak.

The trauma bay behind her pulsed with movement—monitor beeps, clipped commands, the shuffle of gurneys, the soft swish of curtains being drawn. She heard it all, but none of it registered. It was the rhythm of life in chaos, the clinical heartbeat of a place that never slept. Normally, the routine calmed her. Grounded her.

Today, it was the only thing keeping her from falling apart.

Her first shift back since the incident.

Since the blood-red warning on her front window.

Since everything she thought she knew started to crack down the middle.

Cassidy hadn't called.

Not once.

And that silence—sharp and echoing—spoke louder than any slammed door. Louder than any betrayal.

"Savannah?"

The voice was gentle. Erica, the charge nurse.

Savannah blinked and looked up, startled like she'd just surfaced from underwater.

"There's someone here for you," Erica said quietly, glancing toward the waiting area.

Savannah frowned. "Who?"

"Said it was personal. Didn't give a name."

Erica's tone held something extra—curiosity, maybe. Or caution.

Savannah set the chart down, the pages fluttering like wings. Her legs moved before her mind caught up, taking her down the short hallway that opened into the visitor's lounge.

The moment she rounded the corner; her breath caught like it had been punched from her lungs.

Jace.

He stood just inside the doors, tall and steady under the harsh fluorescent lights, as if he'd grown out of the shadows themselves. Worn black hoodie. Faded jeans. Boots scuffed by time and miles. The sleeves of his hoodie were pushed up, revealing forearms marked by sun and scars. He looked different—but not.

Older. Harder. More haunted.

But the same steady presence she remembered.

The weight of him hit her like memory, instinct, and longing, all at once. Her ribs tightened.

Their eyes met. His gaze softened—just a flicker—and for one suspended second, she could almost believe they were kids again. Back when the world hadn't burned to ash. Back when love hadn't been twisted by grief and silence.

"I shouldn't have come," he said, voice low and scraped raw. "But I heard what happened at your house."

She stayed frozen, every muscle locked.

Of course he'd heard. This town had always been lousy with whispers.

"I don't need your protection," she said stiffly, crossing her arms—armour against the way he still affected her.

He gave a faint shake of his head. "I'm not here to protect you."

She swallowed hard. "Then why?"

Jace looked at her like the answer lived in her eyes and he couldn't bear to search anywhere else.

"Because you deserve to know the truth," he said finally. "All of it."

Savannah stepped forward, slow and wary. "You think a letter changes everything?"

"No." His voice cracked at the edges. "But it's a start."

He reached into his back pocket and pulled something out. Not a weapon. Not more proof.

A photograph.

He held it out, and she took it without thinking.

Her breath hitched.

It was them. The three of them. Savannah, Tyler, and Jace—sitting on the hood of that old truck out by Brush Hollow Lake. Tyler in the middle, arms slung around them both, laughing like the whole world was still wide open. Savannah in cutoffs and a tank top, barefoot, her hair windblown. Jace, younger, less hardened, eyes softer—caught in a moment when none of them knew what they'd lose.

"I kept it," Jace murmured. "Ten years. Through everything. It's the only thing that made it through."

Savannah's fingers trembled slightly around the photo. The edges were worn, faded at the corners. Real. Proof that something good had existed once.

Her voice was barely a whisper. "Why are you really here, Jace?"

He looked at her then—really looked. And something passed between them that had no name. Only weight.

"Because Tyler didn't die for nothing," he said. "And whatever he found… whatever he was trying to stop… it didn't die with him. You're in the middle of it now. Whether you want to be or not."

Her heart stopped. "Are you saying I'm in danger?"

"I think you already know the answer to that."

His words hit like a slap—cold, clear, and impossible to ignore.

Before she could answer, the echo of heels on tile cut through the air like a gunshot.

Cassidy.

She appeared at the edge of the corridor like a storm in silk—blonde hair perfectly in place, tailored coat thrown over one shoulder, eyes burning with fury and something deeper.

"What the hell is he doing here?" she snapped, storming forward.

Savannah didn't flinch. "He was just leaving."

Jace didn't argue. He met Savannah's gaze one last time—steady, searching. "If you change your mind… you know where to find me."

And then he walked away—vanishing through the sliding doors, swallowed by the afternoon light. Like a ghost she'd almost forgotten how to believe in.

Cassidy turned to her, face pale and furious. "Are you out of your damn mind? He killed your brother."

Savannah's breath caught. Savannah's breath caught. The photo seared in her palm like it might brand her.

"What if he didn't?"

Cassidy blinked, stunned.

"That's not your job to figure out," she said, voice hard but shaking. "You testified, Savannah. You swore you heard them arguing that night."

"I did," she said, her voice cracking under the weight of her own doubt. "But maybe I didn't hear everything."

Cassidy's jaw clenched. Her veneer was cracking.

"This isn't you," she hissed. "You don't chase ghosts. You believe facts. Logic. You don't—"

"I'm not chasing ghosts," Savannah snapped, eyes wet and defiant. "I'm chasing the one person who might've died trying to protect me."

Cassidy took a step back, her breath faltering.

"There's something you're not telling me," Savannah whispered, the air thick with betrayal.

"I didn't know what he was involved in," Cassidy said quietly, the words dragging out of her like confession. "I didn't know it would cost him his life."

Savannah stared at her. "Did you know he was scared?"

Tears spilled down Cassidy's cheeks, silent and swift. "No. I didn't."

The silence that followed was brutal.

Savannah turned away, voice like steel laced with heartbreak. "I need to finish my shift."

There was nothing left to say.

Cassidy lifted her hand—then let it fall.

She left quietly.

And Savannah stood there—photo in hand, heart in pieces, certainty unravelling—while the weight of everything she'd ever known collapsed around her like a house with no foundation.

Chapter Seven

By the time Jace got back to his motel room, the sky had darkened to ink.

Thunder rolled low over the hills—distant but creeping closer with every breath of wind. Like everything else in this godforsaken town, it was coming for him, whether he was ready or not.

He locked the door behind him with muscle memory more than thought. Two deadbolts. Chain slid into place. His back hit the wood for a beat, shoulders tense, eyes scanning the room like the shadows might shift.

The motel stank of mildew and cheap disinfectant. A rattling A/C unit churned stale air through the vents. One bed. One chair. One flickering lamp.

His burner phone buzzed on the nightstand. Again.

Blocked number. No voicemail.

Second time tonight.

Jace stared at it until it stopped.

Didn't answer. Didn't flinch.

He didn't need a voice on the other end to know what it meant.

They were watching.

They knew he was getting close.

He crossed the room in three strides and flipped on the lamp. The bulb blinked once before casting the space in a sickly yellow haze, like it was trying to hide the cracks in the walls and couldn't quite keep up.

He dropped into the creaking chair by the desk and laid the file down with reverence. Like it was a weapon. Like it mattered more than sleep or safety or whatever piece of soul he hadn't already burned to ash.

He opened it slowly.

A chaos of documents spilled out across the desk—each one a thread in the noose he was tying, page by page, around Vaughn Kessler's neck. Court transcripts, arrest records, redacted witness statements. Property deeds with forged signatures. Tax forms tied to charities that only existed on paper. Every forged signature, every line of ink—bled corruption.

At the centre of it all, printed in bold black type:

VAUGHN KESSLER.

Jace picked up a pen. The weight of it felt heavy in his hand, like it knew what he was about to write.

He circled the name slowly. Pressed hard—harder—until the paper threatened to tear beneath it.

Then beneath that, in block letters, he added:

CASSIDY KESSLER.

He sat back; eyes fixed on the two names like they might blink first.

Cassidy had always been too polished. Too composed. Always three steps ahead, even in stilettos.

Savannah didn't see it.

Never had.

But Jace did. From the very beginning.

It hadn't just been guilt in Cassidy's eyes earlier at the hospital.

It was fear.

Fear of something coming apart at the seams. Of a truth she'd buried so deep she thought it would never claw its way out again.

He flipped to another page. A nonprofit tax form—Hands for Hope.

Supposedly a charity for underprivileged youth. Set up two years before Tyler died. Kessler's name at the top.

But the signature at the bottom?

Cassidy Kessler.

His jaw tightened.

She hadn't just been involved. She was embedded. Up to her perfectly-manicured neck.

He let out a breath through his nose—slow and sharp, like he was trying to exhale the fury threatening to explode in his chest.

This town had chewed up too many good people and spit them out with a smile.

Tyler.

Him.

Now Savannah.

No.

Not this time.

Jace leaned back in the chair. Let it creak under him. Let shadows shift across the walls. Let the truth hang in the air like smoke.

He didn't have the full picture yet—but he was close.

Close enough to taste blood.

And this time?

He wasn't walking away.

Wasn't letting the truth rot beneath dirt, politics, and power.

Not the town.

Not Cassidy.

Not even Savannah, no matter how much it hurt her to hear it.

Outside, the rain finally started—soft at first, then harder, hammering against the window like a warning.

A low hum of tyres passed outside on the wet road, then nothing. Silence.

But the feeling stayed. That itch at the back of his neck. The heaviness behind his ribs.

Someone was watching.

And whoever it was… they were starting to panic.

Because the truth was coming.

And this time, it had Jace Calloway's name all over it.

That night, Savannah stood in her kitchen, unmoving.

The wine glass sat untouched on the counter beside her, the deep red liquid catching the overhead light in glimmers—like spilled blood waiting to dry. It swirled lazily inside the glass with every subtle tremor of the house, but she couldn't bring herself to lift it. Couldn't bring herself to drink. Her hands were too restless, her nerves too raw.

The silence was deafening.

Every tick of the old clock on the wall felt like it scraped across her skin. Every creak of timber, every whisper of shifting pipes in the walls made her flinch. The house—once her safe haven—now felt foreign. Too quiet. Too still. Like it was holding its breath along with her.

The windows, freshly cleaned and stripped of that red, hateful message, looked too open now. Too exposed. The professionals who had scrubbed the words from the glass had been efficient and silent—men in gloves and masks who didn't ask questions. But erasing the message hadn't erased what it meant.

Savannah pulled every curtain tight. Checked every lock. Twice. She moved through the house with the methodical tension of a soldier checking for landmines. The chill in the air wasn't from the weather—it was something else. Something crawling just beneath her skin.

Still, the feeling remained: she was being watched. Hunted. Not in the physical sense. In the targeted sense. The intentional sense.

She paused in the hallway, her fingertips brushing the cool plaster of the wall like she could absorb strength from it. Her thoughts spiralled, each one sharper than the last.

Cassidy hadn't called. Not even a text. No sarcastic quip, no midnight check-in. Just… silence. And from Cassidy, that silence wasn't apathy. It was calculated.

Sophie, her college friend, was out of town—off-grid with her latest influencer boyfriend, likely somewhere on a beach without signal. The sheriff? He already looked like the past was eating him alive. And her coworkers? They were good people—but not this kind of good.

She needed someone who could stand in the fire with her.

Her hand slipped into her pocket and closed around something soft and worn.

The photograph.

She unfolded it slowly, her eyes finding the familiar image in the dim light. Tyler, beaming. That stupid reckless grin that always landed him in trouble. Arms slung around both her and Jace like nothing could touch them.

God, they'd been happy.

She could almost hear Tyler's laugh—wild and warm—and see the exact shade of orange the sky had turned that night at the lake. Could almost taste the watermelon they'd passed around, could almost feel Jace's arm against hers on the truck hood, casual but electric.

Tyler had always protected them. Even when they didn't know they needed protecting.

Maybe that's what he was doing before he died. Trying to shield her from something he couldn't outrun.

Trying to fix it before it killed him.

And maybe he hadn't succeeded.

A knock at the back door shattered the silence.

Savannah jerked so violently that the wine glass toppled—she caught it just in time. Her breath came short and shallow, chest tight.

Another knock. Slower this time. Deliberate.

The air changed.

Her legs moved before her mind caught up, each step cautious. She reached the back window and, with trembling fingers, eased the curtain aside.

No one there.

Her stomach dropped.

Then—tap.

Something struck the glass.

She jumped back, heart hammering in her throat. Her vision swam for a beat before focusing on the square of white taped to the pane.

Her feet carried her forward, even as every cell in her body screamed retreat.

The note was jagged—letters cut from magazines, pasted together like something out of a nightmare ransom film. No handwriting to trace. No fingerprints, surely. Just cold, calculated threat.

LEAVE IT ALONE OR YOU'LL JOIN HIM.

Savannah stared at the message until the edges of her vision blurred.

Her hands trembled. Her breath caught. Then something inside her snapped taut—not with panic this time, but with fury. She yanked the curtains closed.

You'll join him.

Her brother. Her best friend. The boy who had protected her from monsters under the bed and then monsters in real life.

Now they were threatening to make her the next body in the ground.

And that?

That was their mistake.

She moved slowly through the darkened house and into the living room. The photo still clutched in one hand. The other balled into a fist.

She stood steady now, heart thudding—not from fear, but from fury. The tremor in her limbs gave way to something cold and fierce—like steel tempered in fire.

They thought she'd back down.

They thought she'd crumble like the girl who had once shattered on a witness stand, voice breaking as she pointed to the boy she loved.

But they had underestimated her.

She had survived loss. Learned how to breathe through guilt. Stitched herself together one jagged memory at a time. And every scar she carried now? It was armour.

Let them come.

She was done being afraid of the dark.

Her eyes flicked to the window, to the spot where the note was still hanging.

Ten years of silence. Then Jace comes back, and everything detonates around her.

Was it coincidence?

She didn't believe in coincidence anymore.

No—someone knew Jace was hunting something buried deep.

And they knew Savannah might be the one piece of the puzzle he hadn't yet uncovered.

So, they tried to scare her.

To silence her.

To erase her.

But she wasn't going anywhere.

Not now.

She walked back to the kitchen, picked up the untouched wine glass, and emptied it down the drain.

No more numbing.

Only clarity. Only fire.

Because if they wanted war—they'd just declared it.

And Savannah Blake was ready.

This time, she'd burn the truth into daylight.

Even if it killed her.

Chapter Eight

Savannah didn't sleep.

She hadn't even tried.

She sat curled on the couch all night, legs tucked tightly beneath her, a blanket wrapped around her shoulders like armour she didn't believe in. Not because she was cold—she wasn't. In fact, her skin burned from the inside out, hot with adrenaline, nausea, and the sick, electric weight of dread. Still, she clutched the blanket tighter, like it might hold her together if the darkness tried to take something else.

Every light in the house was on—kitchen, hallway, bathroom, even the lamp in Tyler's old room she hadn't touched in years. Pools of yellow light lit up the spaces around her, casting sharp-edged shadows that danced every time she moved.

But it didn't help.

The house still felt haunted. Not by ghosts—but by intent. Malice. The kind of fear that sits beside you and waits for your resolve to break.

The note had already been removed, bagged, and taken as evidence. But its presence lingered, carved into the air itself. The spot where it had been taped to the window felt like it was glowing. A curse she couldn't scrub off.

Even now, she sat with her back to it, afraid to turn around. Not because it was still there—but because it wasn't. That was worse.

Leave it alone or you'll join him.

The words lived behind her eyelids. She'd blinked a thousand times and still couldn't erase them. It was like they'd branded themselves into the fabric of her home. Her mind.

She'd called the sheriff within minutes of finding it. Her hands had shaken so violently she could barely tap the screen, her thumb missing the numbers over and over again. John had come faster than she expected, headlights cutting through the night like a promise that might actually mean something. He didn't knock. Just let himself in and closed the door behind him with the quiet respect of a man who knew terror when he saw it.

He didn't ask questions. Didn't try to soothe.

He just gloved up, peeled the note from the glass, and sealed it in a plastic evidence bag. His face was grim, mouth a thin line, eyes shadowed by a weight that had never left since Tyler died. The words he finally gave her were clipped, quiet, careful:

"You need to be careful."

As if that was enough.

As if being careful had ever made a damn difference.

As if Tyler hadn't been careful.

As if Savannah—who had walked a tightrope her entire life, who had followed every rule and bit her tongue and played it safe—hadn't already done everything right and still ended up here.

Still ended up haunted.

She didn't respond. Just nodded like she was supposed to. Like the good girl she'd always been. And when John left, she locked the door behind him, leaned her forehead against the wood, and exhaled so slowly it felt like she was letting out a lifetime of grief.

Hours passed.

Or maybe minutes.

Time didn't behave normally in fear. It stretched and curled in on itself until every second felt like a wound.

The sky outside began to shift around 5 a.m.—from pitch black to deep blue, then to a hazy lavender that bruised the horizon. Birds began to chirp somewhere in the trees, tentative and uncertain, like even they weren't sure it was safe to start a new day.

And somewhere in that liminal space, Savannah changed.

She stopped shaking.

Not because she wasn't scared.

She was terrified.

But fear had given way to something colder. Heavier. Sharper.

Resolve.

It slid through her like a second spine. Something forged from ten years of guilt, a brother buried with more secrets than answers, and a lifetime of wondering if silence had cost her everything.

She moved slowly, deliberately.

Jeans. Old grey hoodie. Hair twisted into a knot that she didn't bother to perfect. She didn't care about appearances. Only armour. Only motion forward. She slid her phone and keys into her bag with mechanical precision, checked them twice. Grabbed the photograph from the coffee table—the one Jace had given her—and tucked it into her jacket pocket.

Her boots echoed against the floor as she walked out of the house.

The early morning air hit her like a slap. Cold. Clean. Unforgiving.

She didn't care.

The Jeep engine roared to life beneath her hands, headlights cutting across the drive. The rising sun bled orange over the horizon like it was warning her too— just like everyone else had.

Too late.

Savannah pulled out onto the road, gravel crunching beneath the tyres.

She was done sitting in the dark.

She was done waiting for answers to come to her.

Today, she was going to find them.

Even if she had to drag the truth out, screaming, from the mouths of people she used to trust.

She didn't know where the road would end—not yet.

But she did know where to start.

And she was already on her way.

Jace opened the motel room door before she could knock.

He stood barefoot in the doorway, hoodie wrinkled, hair damp like he'd just stepped out of the shower—or hadn't slept at all. His expression was unreadable, his jaw tight with something unreadable—but his eyes…

His eyes locked onto hers with something fierce. Something steady.

Like he'd been expecting her.

Like he'd known the moment she made up her mind.

"Hey," he said softly.

Savannah didn't answer. She just stepped past him into the room.

The door clicked shut behind her.

The room smelled like old coffee and something else—burnout, maybe. The kind of place that held its breath between disasters.

The air inside was warm and close, thick with the scent of stale coffee, mildew, and something sharper—like adrenaline that had settled into the carpet. A small table sat near the window, cluttered with papers and printouts and red-ink slashes that cut through names and numbers like wounds. Beside it: a half-finished bottle of water. A single chair. A duffel bag slouched at the foot of the unmade bed.

It wasn't a place to rest.

It was a place to dig in and fight.

Jace leaned against the door, arms crossed over his chest, watching her with something taut in his posture.

"You okay?" he asked.

Savannah turned to face him fully. Her voice came out flat. "No."

He nodded once—like that was exactly the answer he'd expected.

"Then you're finally seeing it."

"I didn't want to."

"I know."

Her eyes drifted to the table. Pages fluttered slightly beneath the breath of the heater. Names. Signatures. Bits of truth stitched together by desperation and fury.

"Someone taped a death threat to my back window," she said, voice quieter now. "Cut-out letters. Ransom-style. Told me I'd join Tyler if I didn't back off."

Jace straightened. The heat in his expression changed—went from coiled worry to something darker. Sharper.

"Did you tell the sheriff?"

"I did. He said he'd 'look into it,'" she muttered, the bitterness in her voice unmistakable. "Like it was a noise complaint."

Jace dragged a hand through his damp hair. "They don't want you asking questions. They never did."

Savannah stared at him. "Why now, Jace? It's been ten years. Why is this happening now?"

He was quiet for a long moment. Then: "I don't know. Maybe it's because I came back. Maybe someone thinks I'll dig too deep. But whatever Tyler uncovered back then—someone didn't bury it well enough. And now it's leaking back to the surface."

Her chest tightened. "Who?"

His answer came like a gunshot. "Kessler."

She froze. "Vaughn Kessler?" Her voice was suddenly thin. "Cassidy's father?"

Jace nodded, slowly. "Yeah."

"Why would Tyler go after him? He worked for him."

"I know, but I think he found something," Jace said. "Something dirty. Something Vaughn was tied to. That's what Tyler told me, back then. Said it was big. Said it could ruin people."

"And you think that's why he died?"

"I know that's why he died."

Savannah's fingers curled into fists. Her voice dropped. "Then why pin it on you?"

His smile was bitter and worn at the edges. "Because I was easy. The perfect scapegoat. Son of a convict, who had a record a mile long. I had no alibi that night. And I was the last person to see him alive. They didn't even have to try—they just had to point."

The silence that followed was thick enough to choke on.

Savannah lowered her eyes. "You say you didn't do it."

"I didn't."

Her voice cracked on the edge of it, like the truth might splinter her if she reached too fast. "I want to believe you."

He took a slow step closer. "Then believe me."

She looked up at him. Something cracked inside her. Something quiet, old, and aching. And there, in the middle of it—him. Not the boy he'd been. Not the ghost she'd feared. But the man who'd survived ten years of silence and still looked at her like she mattered.

"I don't know where to start," she admitted.

"Then let me," he said. "Let me help. We do this together. But I can't do it alone."

He gestured toward the table. "I need access. Tyler's storage unit. The clinic. Whatever records he kept—if he left anything behind. And I need you, Savannah. I need your memory. What you saw. What you missed. The things that didn't make sense back then but maybe make sense now."

She closed her eyes. That time in her life was a wound she'd never let scab. Ripping it open meant blood. Guilt. Doubt. All of it.

She thought of the note. The cut-out letters. The way it had sat on her glass like a curse. The way silence had crept in behind it, too still, too loud. The silence in Cassidy's voice. The hollow space where Tyler should've been.

She opened her eyes.

Met his.

And nodded.

"Okay."

Chapter Nine

They started with the storage unit.

It sat on the edge of town, tucked behind a chain-link fence and a row of wind-worn eucalyptus trees that creaked like old bones in the breeze. The gravel lot was half-swallowed by weeds, and the faded sign above the rusted gate still read Cedar Ridge Secure Storage—though the "secure" part was questionable. The bulbs in the 24-HOUR ACCESS marquee had long since given up, leaving only a dim, flickering promise behind.

Savannah hadn't set foot here in years, maybe since the funeral.

She kept paying the monthly storage fee, telling herself it was practical—just until she was ready.

But the truth was, she couldn't bring herself to let go.

Not of Tyler.

Not of the pieces he left behind.

And maybe, deep down, she'd always known this day would come.

The key had lived in the back of her nightstand drawer like a ghost—forgotten, buried under loose change and expired receipts, but never truly gone. It had waited in silence, its purpose dormant until now.

Now it felt heavier than it had any right to.

She stood in front of the unit, hand poised at the lock, heart thudding like it might try to warn her back. She slid the key into the weathered cylinder and paused—just long enough to hear her own breathing. Then she turned it.

Click.

The door groaned upward with a sharp, metallic shriek that echoed across the empty lot, loud enough to make her flinch. Dust poured out like memory—thick, dry, and heavy with the scent of cardboard, motor oil, mildew, and time.

Jace stood behind her, silent.

She didn't step inside right away.

She just stood there.

Looking.

Nothing had changed.

Boxes stacked in precarious towers. Tyler's battered red toolbox sat on the left, the one with the faded decal of their high school mascot—some kind of bird with a football helmet, peeling and sun-bleached. A slouched black duffel bag lay slumped in the corner like a sleeping dog. Football pads. A cracked guitar case. And on the back wall, still hanging from a bent nail like a ghost waiting to be remembered—

Tyler's leather jacket.

Her chest tightened painfully. The sight of it knocked the wind out of her, as if grief had reached across time just to sucker-punch her again.

Behind her, Jace muttered, "Jesus."

She nodded but didn't speak. Words would have shattered the fragile silence clinging to the space.

He stepped inside first and reached up to tug the chain on the single overhead bulb. It flickered once. Then again. Then buzzed to life, casting the unit in a yellow haze that made the shadows feel like they were holding their breath.

It didn't make the place feel any less like a tomb.

They moved without speaking.

Deliberate. Careful.

He took the right side. She took the left. The air was stale, the kind that settled into skin, hair, and memory. Savannah crouched beside a stack of boxes labelled in Tyler's scrawl—Misc, Garage, College Stuff—and began peeling back the layers of a life cut short.

Old tax forms. Loan applications. Receipts from a music store that had closed five years ago. One box held nothing but tangled cords and broken speakers. Another was filled with crumpled job applications he'd never submitted.

Then her fingers brushed a worn spiral notebook.

On the cover, written in bold, smudged Sharpie:

Don't forget this.

She froze. Her breath caught.

She didn't open it.

Not yet.

A full hour passed. Maybe two. The light above them buzzed in intervals, pulsing like a heartbeat. Her knees ached from crouching. Her hands were smudged with ink and dust, nicked by paper edges.

She was about to suggest a break—just a few minutes to breathe—when she heard him.

"Sav."

Jace's voice wasn't loud, but it cut through the silence like a blade.

She turned instantly, heart jerking in her chest.

He was kneeling at the back of the unit, half-hidden behind an old workbench where dust clung thick to every surface. His head was bowed slightly, one hand holding a weathered shoebox, the other braced against the floor. A rusted ammo box sat pushed aside near his knee.

His expression was tense. Focused.

She crossed the unit quickly.

He held the shoebox out to her like it might burn through his hands.

The lid was cracked but intact. Inside: a Ziplock bag. A flash drive. A folded letter. And beneath them—

A photograph.

Savannah reached for it with trembling fingers and drew it into the light.

It was a group shot.

Tyler stood in the centre, grinning, one arm slung over Cassidy's shoulder. Cassidy looked younger—sharper around the edges but still put-together, her smile too careful. On her other side stood Vaughn Kessler, stern and upright, dressed in a suit that looked tailored and expensive.

But Savannah's eyes locked on the fourth man.

Tall. Silver hair. A smug, practiced smile. Expensive suit. Hands folded neatly in front of him.

The kind of face you remembered—even if you wished you didn't.

"Who the hell is that?" she asked, voice tight.

Jace's jaw worked as he stared down at the photo. "Marcus Rourke," he said finally. "He was a lawyer back then. Handled some of Kessler's... arrangements."

Her stomach turned. "He's in politics now, isn't he?"

"Yeah," Jace said. "Some kind of federal appointment. Real slick operator. Don't know much about him. But if he gets his hands dirty, he never leaves prints."

She looked back at the photo, her pulse thrumming. "So, what—Tyler was digging into Kessler and Rourke both?"

Jace shook his head. "I think it was only Kessler. But whatever he found must've scared him. Bad."

Savannah reached for the flash drive. It was scratched. Slightly warped. Lighter than it should've been. But even through the plastic bag, she could feel it vibrating with tension. Like a time bomb waiting for a password.

She held it up. "What do you think is on this?"

Jace looked at her. The shadows under his eyes made him look older. Harder. But his voice was steady.

"Whatever it is—Tyler hid it for a reason."

Savannah's grip tightened. Her fingers curled around the flash drive like it was something alive.

She thought of the message on her window. The way it had stared back at her. Threatened her. Dared her.

Leave it alone or you'll join him.

No.

Not a chance in hell.

She turned to Jace, eyes hard.

"Let's find out what they didn't want us to see."

They went back to her farmhouse.

Savannah hadn't wanted to.

The house didn't feel like home anymore—it felt like a wound that refused to close. The lavender still lingered in the air, curling through the rooms like a memory trying too hard to comfort. But beneath it, something darker clung to the walls.

Grief.

Fear.

The kind that sinks deep and stays.

Tyler was everywhere.

In the hallway, where she could almost hear his laugh.

In the creak of old floorboards that used to mark his steps.

But those were ghosts now. And with Jace here… they felt louder.

So did the fear.

It lived in the drawn curtains, the silence pressing too tight, the faint outline of tape on the back window—where someone had stuck a threat like a signature.

She didn't want to be here.

Not with that message still fresh.

Not with Jace.

Not with everything he brought back.

But taking him anywhere else—out in public—was worse. This town lived for whispers. And Jace Calloway had never belonged in any sentence that didn't end in scandal.

She let him come inside anyway. Not because she trusted him.

Not yet.

But deep down, past the doubt and pain, one thing still stirred:

If anyone could help her understand what really happened to Tyler…

It was the boy she'd loved.

And the man who'd come back, ten years too late.

They sat at the kitchen table. The laptop between them like a ticking bomb.

Jace booted it up, his hands steady, eyes locked on the screen. Savannah folded into herself, arms crossed, clutching her hoodie like a shield.

The flash drive clicked in.

One folder.

IN CASE SOMETHING HAPPENS.

Her pulse skipped.

Tyler's voice in her memory: Just in case, Sav. You never know.

She'd rolled her eyes then.

She wasn't rolling them now.

Jace opened the folder.

Scanned documents. Bank statements. Wire transfers. Names she didn't recognise. But the numbers—large. Some highlighted. Others circled.

Then: one audio file.

Jace looked at her. She nodded.

He hit play.

Tyler's voice poured through the speakers—crackling with static, but unmistakable.

Her breath caught.

He sounded older. More worn. Less fearless.

'If you're hearing this, I'm probably already in trouble. Maybe worse.'

Her heart lurched.

'Kessler's using the nonprofit to run a laundering scheme. I found overseas accounts. Fake charities. Donations that go nowhere. But that's not the worst part—Cassidy might be involved.'

Savannah gripped the edge of the table.

'I tried to talk to her. She shut down. Maybe she's scared. Maybe she's protecting him. I don't know. I think Kessler knows I know. He has hinted that if he can't trust the people he works with that, they might disappear. Then he asked about Savannah.'

A pause. Then:

'Jace—if they go after Savannah… you protect her. I don't care what it costs.'

The audio cut out.

Silence fell like a curtain.

Savannah's lungs burned. Her hands were slick with sweat.

Across the table, Jace sat motionless. Staring at the screen like it might bring Tyler back.

Finally, Savannah spoke.

"Cassidy's dad… he might be behind this?"

Jace nodded. "And now he's a state senator. Clean image. Big following. Untouchable, if you believe the press."

Her voice was thin. "Would he still be doing this though. It has been ten years. He might have stopped. All the evidence could be gone."

"I don't know but we will have to try to find out."

"If we make one wrong move…"

"He'll crush us."

Savannah looked at the laptop.

At the audio bar.

At the voice that had come and gone like a ghost.

Her brother had died for this.

And the world had moved on.

But she hadn't. Not really.

Not ever.

For ten years, she'd buried her questions under duty. Her grief under logic. Her guilt under silence.

Now, the past was knocking.

And maybe—just maybe—she didn't have to answer it alone.

She looked at Jace. Her voice was steadier now.

"I'm in this."

Jace met her eyes. He didn't smile. But something shifted—something older than time, deeper than words.

Regret.

Respect.

Maybe even hope.

Maybe something that still remembered how to love her.

That night, as he left, she followed him to the door.

The air outside bit at her skin, a cold that carried rain in its bones. The porch light buzzed, casting a weak gold circle that barely held back the dark.

"I'm still not sure if I can trust you," she said, arms folded tight across her chest. Her voice barely rose, but it carried weight—sharp, deliberate.

Jace paused on the step. He didn't flinch. "That's fair," he said simply—no defence, no protest, just a quiet acceptance.

She hesitated, something catching in her throat. "But I trusted Tyler," she said, softer now. "And he trusted you."

He turned back, and for a moment, the porch light caught his expression—worn, raw, and real. "Then I'll earn your trust back—whether you let me or not."

And with that, he stepped into the dark.

Savannah stood in the doorway, unmoving—like some part of her still hadn't let him go.

She didn't close the door. Not yet.

Because deep down, beneath the layers of doubt and anger and everything she still couldn't name…

And for the first time in ten years, she wondered—what if she'd been wrong? What if she should have trusted him from the very beginning?

Because if he'd been innocent all along—then her silence had helped bury the truth. And that would haunt her longer than grief ever could.

Chapter Ten

Cassidy's townhouse was too perfect.

Trimmed hedges. A porch with pristine white wicker chairs, fluffed cushions, and cheerful planters bursting with pink and purple petunias. Wind chimes tinkled gently from the eaves. A wooden sign by the door declared, Home is where the heart is in curling script.

Savannah stared at it like it was a punchline to a cruel joke.

Everything about the place screamed curated charm. Comfort. Safety. Normalcy.

But Savannah knew better.

Behind those pastel flowers and picture-perfect windows lived the daughter of a man who had destroyed lives—including her brother's.

Beside her, Jace stood silent, hands buried deep in the pockets of his hoodie. The morning fog hadn't lifted—it hung low and cold, swallowing sound and wrapping the world in warning. Savannah's heart beat like a drum in her ears.

"You sure about this?" Jace asked quietly.

"No," she said. "But we're doing it anyway."

This wasn't going to be just a knock—it was a reckoning.

Savannah hesitated a fraction of a second but before fear could talk her out of it, she climbed the steps and knocked.

The door opened almost instantly. Cassidy stood there in leggings and a tank top, flushed like she'd just come from a run. Her blonde hair was piled into a messy bun. But her eyes weren't casual—they were guarded. Sharp. Her gaze flicked from Savannah to Jace, and her mouth thinned into a tight line.

"This isn't a good time."

Savannah stepped past her before she could be turned away. "We won't take long. You need to tell us what you know."

Cassidy shut the door harder than necessary. "You're going to have to be more specific."

"You lied," Savannah said flatly.

Jace's voice followed, cold and cutting. "Start with the part where Tyler told you your father was dirty—and you did nothing."

Cassidy's expression cracked, just a flicker. "Don't talk to me like I didn't lose someone too."

"You lost a friend," Jace said. "I lost ten years of my life."

Savannah cut between them, her voice sharp. "We found a flash drive. Tyler left a message—he tried to warn you."

Cassidy's jaw trembled. She folded her arms, suddenly looking smaller than she had in the doorway.

"I know," she whispered.

Savannah blinked. "You… knew?"

Cassidy leaned back against the wall. Her voice dropped. "He came to me the week before he died. Said he'd found something big. Something about my dad and offshore accounts. I thought he was exaggerating. Tyler was always chasing something. Always playing the hero."

Savannah's stomach turned. "He was the hero."

"I know that now." Cassidy's voice cracked. "But back then… I was scared. You don't understand—my father isn't just powerful, Savannah. He's dangerous. I knew if I turned on him, I'd lose everything. My job, my safety. Maybe even my life. That's why I stopped working for him after Tyler died."

"So, you stayed quiet," Jace said, his tone sharpened to a blade. "You let them frame me. Let Savannah bury her brother with no answers. And you walked away."

"I didn't know you were innocent!" Cassidy snapped. "Nobody did! And by the time I started to suspect, it was too late. I panicked. I told myself if I just kept my head down, it would all blow over."

Savannah's voice shook—not from weakness, but the kind of fury that burned clean through restraint. "You let me hate him. You let me believe he died chasing shadows while you stood beside me at his funeral, pretending to grieve."

Cassidy's eyes filled. "What would you have done? If it were your father? Gone public on a hunch? Risked everything with nothing but a maybe? You think people would've believed me? My father has the press, the party, and the entire state eating from his hand."

"I would've tried," Savannah said. "God, I would've tried."

The silence that followed was jagged and raw.

Then Jace stepped forward. His voice was calm, but urgent. "We need the truth, Cassidy. All of it. If there's anything left—anything that could help—we need it now."

Cassidy looked at them both, her bravado crumbling. What was left underneath wasn't pride or malice—it was exhaustion. Guilt. Shame that had lived too long in the dark.

"There's something," she whispered. "Tyler gave me copies of what he found the night he came to me. He said it was proof. Said it could bring everything down. I... I never opened it."

Savannah stared. "Why not?"

Cassidy's answer was a whisper. "Because I was a coward."

She turned away without another word. Crossed the room. Dropped to her knees in front of a white cabinet like it was a confessional.

From it, she pulled a thick, slightly wrinkled manila envelope and handed it to Savannah with trembling hands.

The paper felt too light in her hands. Like it shouldn't be able to carry this much weight. This much truth.

Inside—photographs. Surveillance-style. Time-stamped. A man in a suit passing off a briefcase in a dim alley. Another shot: Rourke, Kessler, and two others at a private fundraiser. Scribbled notes in Tyler's handwriting ran along the margins—dates, locations, initials.

Savannah flipped through the photographs, each one heavier than the last. "These... these could bury your father."

Jace leaned in, pointing at one photo. "That's Juno's Bar. Kessler used to do drops there."

Cassidy nodded. "I kept them hidden. Told myself the storm would pass. That it would be safer if no one knew."

Savannah looked at her. Her voice was steady now. Cold. "It didn't pass. And now it's here."

Her phone buzzed in her pocket.

She glanced down—and froze.

Jace straightened. "What?"

Savannah's voice dropped. "The storage unit. It's on fire."

Cassidy gasped. "What?"

"Someone torched it."

Jace was already moving. "Let's go. If we're lucky, the fire department beat the worst of it."

Savannah shoved the photos back into the envelope and followed.

The air was thick with smoke when they arrived.

Not fresh smoke—this was what lingered after. Damp. Acrid. Saturated with chemical stink and soaked dreams, clinging to skin and hair and lungs like a warning that had come too late.

Sirens still echoed faintly in the distance, a fading wail swallowed by the morning fog. The last fire truck was just pulling away, red lights strobing across scorched pavement. The silence left behind was heavier than the smoke.

Tyler's storage unit was gone.

Where there had been memories—boxes, files, a guitar case, old tax records and a life taken too soon—there was now only ruin. A mangled husk of metal and melted rubber. Twisted shelving, collapsed in on itself. Waterlogged ash pooled in the corners. A blackened hinge still clung stubbornly to the edge of a frame. Bits of scorched paper drifted in the puddles like ghosts, curling and dissolving as they touched the water.

Savannah stood frozen in the cracked parking lot, eyes fixed on the wreckage. Her heart felt like it had been scooped out and left in the fire. Every breath hurt—burnt air scraping the inside of her throat, smoke stinging her eyes even though there were no tears left.

There was nothing to say. No words that could capture this kind of violation.

Jace stood beside her, jaw locked, hands clenched into fists. His shoulders were tight; his whole body braced like he was ready to throw a punch but couldn't find a target. Smoke curled around him in wisps, the smouldering light of the embers flickering across his face and making his eyes seem hollow.

"This wasn't random," he said finally, voice gravelled and low.

Savannah gave a single, brittle nod. "Someone knew we were here."

Watched. Followed. Waited.

Someone had been paying close attention. Close enough to know what they'd found. Close enough to torch it before they could use it.

A tall man in fire gear approached from the ruins—bunker coat open, helmet tucked under one arm. His face was lined with exhaustion, his eyes shadowed. He looked like he'd been doing this job too long to be surprised by what he'd seen today.

"We got lucky it didn't spread," he said, voice hoarse from smoke and fatigue. "Started in the back corner. Accelerant was definitely used. Kerosene, by the smell. This wasn't accidental."

Savannah didn't flinch. She just nodded, like she'd been expecting that answer since the second the call came in.

Savannah stared past him, her eyes locked on the place where Tyler's voice had once existed—on flash drives, in scribbled notes, in the sharp edges of truths no one had wanted to see. She could still hear him.

If you're hearing this, I'm probably already in trouble…

Now there was nothing left but soot and silence.

"Thank you," she murmured, though her voice didn't sound like her own.

The fire chief gave a respectful nod and moved on.

Jace exhaled sharply and ran a hand through his hair, jaw working like he wanted to spit. "They're scared," he muttered. "That means we're getting close."

Savannah turned toward him, her voice hollow. "Close to what?"

Jace looked at her, and for a moment, something raw and ancient stared back at her from behind his eyes. Not fear. Not anger.

Resolve.

"To the people who killed your brother," he said. "And the reason they still want you silent."

Despite the heat still radiating from the scorched ground, Savannah shivered.

She folded her arms, trying to hold in the grief, the helplessness, the rage. The smell of smoke clung to her clothes, to her skin, to the back of her tongue. It was all she could taste.

Footsteps crunched behind them.

Cassidy emerged from the fog, coughing into the crook of her arm. Her skin was pale, almost waxen, her eyes wide and glassy. She took in the devastation slowly, like her mind couldn't quite process what she was seeing.

Her voice was thin, almost inaudible. "This is bigger than I thought."

Jace shot her a sidelong glance. "We can't do this alone anymore."

Savannah turned to him, voice sharper than she meant. "You trust her now?"

He didn't answer right away. The silence stretched taut between them.

"No," he said finally. "But we don't have a choice."

Savannah looked back at the ruins, blinking against the rising sting in her eyes. The shoebox. The notebook. The photo. The scribbled notes that might've been enough to crack something wide open.

All gone.

"How many times are they going to take him from me?" she whispered.

No one answered. There wasn't one.

Smoke curled in the air, bitter and thick. She inhaled and felt it burn her lungs, mix with the grief she'd never fully exhaled.

Then something inside her clicked into place.

A steel spine beneath the sorrow.

She turned to them, her jaw tight. "We go to the sheriff. We give him everything—Tyler's message, the photos, the timeline. We put it all on the table. Let the light do what the fire tried to erase."

Jace studied her. "You really think he'll help?"

"I don't know," she said. "But I'm done waiting for someone else to act. I'm done letting them set the rules."

Jace nodded slowly. The weight in his gaze shifted. Not lighter—but sharper. Like he saw her clearly now.

"Then we go full throttle," he said. "No more hiding. We burn them—before they burn us."

The three of them stood in the ash-laced silence, framed by smoke and ruin and the dying glow of what should've been proof.

And Savannah knew:

This was no longer about grief.

No longer just about justice.

This was war.

Chapter Eleven

That night, Savannah sat on the edge of her bed, laptop open on the quilted comforter. The pale blue glow bathed her face in sterile light, casting long, flickering shadows across the quiet room. The only sound was the low hum of the ceiling fan and the faint creak of old wood beneath her feet.

Her fingers hovered over the keys, unmoving.

Her eyes stayed locked on the screen.

The photo stared back at her.

Tyler. Cassidy. Kessler.

Three smiles. Three masks. Three pieces of a puzzle that never fit quite right—she just hadn't noticed until it was too late.

They looked so young in the image. Carefree. Relaxed. Tyler had that cocky half-grin he always wore when he thought he was getting away with something. Cassidy leaned in close, her hand resting on his shoulder like she belonged there. And Kessler stood behind them both, a drink in hand, smiling like a man who already owned the room.

It was a moment frozen in time.

And now it felt… tainted.

A trap disguised as friendship.

Savannah stared harder, as if she could see past the pixels, as if she could peel back the lies hiding behind the image. These were the people she'd grown up with. Trusted. Laughed with. Built her world around.

And now all she could see were the fractures.

The shadows.

The rot beneath the polish.

Who had they really been back then?

Who had she been?

Her chest tightened. The air in the room grew colder, sharper somehow, like it had turned against her.

She reached forward and slowly closed the laptop, the soft click sounding louder than it should in the stillness.

As if she'd silenced them.

As if silence could protect her now.

The moment stretched.

Then—her phone buzzed on the nightstand.

She jumped.

For a breathless second, she just stared at it. The screen glowed against the dark, a harsh white rectangle in the shadows. Her heart thudded, slow and heavy.

She reached for it with stiff fingers.

Unknown Number.

One new message.

YOU WERE WARNED.

Her stomach turned to ice.

Every nerve ending went tight.

A metallic taste filled her mouth—fear or adrenaline, she couldn't tell.

Another buzz.

This time, a photo.

She opened it.

And stopped breathing.

Her house.

Taken from the tree line behind it.

Not from the street. Not a drone.

Not something casual or accidental.

This was close.

Deliberate.

Real.

The angle was low. Human.

Grainy in the fading dusk—but unmistakable.

Her back porch. The screen door slightly ajar.

The porch light casting a soft halo on the steps.

The living room window glowing faintly behind closed curtains.

She stared at the photo, her pulse thundering in her ears.

They'd been there.

Maybe still were.

Her throat closed. She rose slowly, phone clutched tight in her hand, every step toward the window like walking across glass.

She yanked back the curtain.

Nothing but blackness.

The thick outline of trees.

A shifting wind.

Still—

She felt them.

Somewhere out there.

Watching.

Breathing the same air.

Waiting.

Another buzz.

YOU STOP NOW OR WE FINISH WHAT WE STARTED.

The world dropped out from under her.

Her knees buckled, and she caught herself on the windowsill, fingers leaving damp streaks on the wood. Her breath came short and shallow, every sound in the house suddenly louder. The creak of wood. The ticking of the clock. Her own panicked heartbeat, wild and feral in her chest.

Were they already inside?

Was she alone?

Was she next?

A flicker of movement caught her eye.

There—at the edge of the trees.

A figure. Still. Shadowed.

Half-hidden by branches.

Too still to be an animal.

Too large to be anything but human.

Watching.

Waiting.

Savannah staggered back from the window, yanking the curtain shut with shaking hands. Her back hit the wall, and she slid to the floor, knees drawn up, heart hammering like it might split her ribs from the inside.

This wasn't a threat anymore.

Not a warning.

This was a promise.

This was a clock ticking down.

And the countdown had already begun.

Savannah stared at the photo glowing on her phone screen.

Her breath hitched, like her body had forgotten how to inhale without trembling. Her thumb hovered above the glass, but she didn't touch it. Couldn't.

She read the message again.

YOU STOP NOW OR WE FINISH WHAT WE STARTED.

A fifth time. A sixth.

The words didn't change.

But something inside her had.

Her chest tightened, lungs squeezing like fists around nothing but smoke and panic. She felt the pulse behind her ribs hammering hard and uneven, like her heart wanted out.

The digital clock on her nightstand glared at her in unwavering red: 9:48 p.m.

Just minutes ago, she'd whispered lies into the dark.

It's over. It's slowing down. Maybe they're done.

But they weren't.

They were just getting started.

Her phone buzzed.

Another photo.

Her eyes dropped to the image—grainy and green, tinged with the eerie blur of night vision. It took her a second to register what she was looking at.

Then her breath caught.

Her stomach twisted.

Her bedroom window.

Not a neighbours. Not the porch.

Hers.

Taken tonight.

They'd been outside this room—this very room—mere feet away.

And she hadn't heard a thing.

Not a footstep. Not a creak. Not the soft rustle of leaves from someone moving through the trees. She hadn't sensed them. Hadn't felt the shift in the air.

They were ghosts.

Her voice broke before she even realised she'd spoken.

"Okay."

Just one word.

Small. Shaken.

But it cracked something inside her wide open.

Not fear. Not fully.

Surrender.

No more pretending.

No more waiting.

No more playing nice with shadows that clearly wanted her gone.

She tapped the screen with trembling fingers and attached the photos. Then typed a message to Jace, her hands unsteady on the keys:

They were here. Tonight.

She hit call.

He answered on the first ring.

"They were there?"

His voice was low. Steady. A calm laced with steel.

But she heard it—just under the surface.

The shift.

The weight.

Bracing for war.

Savannah nodded before remembering he couldn't see her. "Yeah," she whispered. "I think… I think someone's still out there. They were so close, Jace. Right outside my window."

Her voice faltered, then broke. "How did they get that close without me knowing?"

The silence that followed was brief—but sharp.

It felt like the whole world held its breath.

Then Jace said, voice dark with grim certainty, "They've been watching you longer than we thought."

The words landed in her chest like a weight.

Pressed the breath right out of her.

She closed her eyes and felt it rise—bile at the back of her throat. Shame. Rage. Grief. The primal, helpless terror of being hunted in your own home.

"They're not bluffing," she whispered.

"No," Jace said. "They're escalating."

The word echoed like a bullet ricocheting off the walls.

Escalating.

Everything in her gut twisted. There was no more guessing now. No more half-steps.

"What do we do?" she asked, her voice barely audible.

"Pack a bag. Essentials only. Nothing you don't need. You have twenty minutes."

A pause. Then, clipped, and final:

"I'll be outside."

"Jace—" Her voice cracked. She didn't know what she was going to say. She just needed something. Some promise that this wasn't spinning out of control. That she wasn't alone.

"Don't argue," he said, and his voice was gentle now. Fierce and warm, like armour wrapped in concern. "I'll explain on the road."

The line went dead.

Savannah sat frozen for one more second.

Then she moved.

Not in a daze.

Not in panic.

With purpose.

She shoved the phone into her back pocket, grabbed the bag she kept under the bed—the one never truly meant for this—and stood in a room that no longer felt like hers.

They'd come to her doorstep.

They'd watched her sleep.

They wanted to finish what they started.

But they didn't know her.

Not like Tyler had.

They didn't know what it meant to push her this far.

She wasn't running.

She was reclaiming her ground.

And the second she crossed that threshold, she wasn't prey anymore.

This time, she wasn't waiting for them to strike.

This time, Savannah Blake was coming for them.

She stood frozen for half a heartbeat. Then instinct kicked in.

She yanked open drawers and started packing fast—jeans, hoodies, socks, boots. Her laptop. The flash drive. Birth certificate. Whatever might matter if she didn't come back.

She reached for the nightstand—and stopped.

The revolver.

Her father's gun.

Cold steel gleamed faintly in the lamplight. It looked untouched, but it hummed with memory. Heavier than it should've been. Heavier than guilt.

She hadn't laid a hand on it since the verdict.

Back then, she hadn't been thinking about justice.

She'd been thinking about escape.

Because grief had hollowed her out.

Because silence had filled the space where hope used to live.

Now her fingers hovered above it, trembling.

She stared like it still held that possibility.

But tonight wasn't about disappearing.

It was about fighting.

She wrapped the gun in one of Tyler's old T-shirts—soft from a hundred washes, faded at the collar—and tucked it gently into her bag.

Just in case.

By the time she zipped it shut, the clock read 10:06 p.m.

Fifteen minutes gone.

Every second felt louder than the last—like time itself was pounding toward her.

She turned off the lights.

Took one last look at the house. The walls that used to make her feel safe. The corners where Tyler's laughter used to live.

Then she opened the door and stepped into the dark.

No hesitation.

No second glance.

She didn't look back.

Not tonight.

Not ever again.

Chapter Twelve

Jace was already waiting.

His truck idled at the curb, headlights off. He didn't get out. Didn't need to.

Savannah didn't ask where he got the truck. Didn't care.

He leaned across the seat and opened the door.

"You sure about this?"

She tossed her bag in and climbed up beside him.

"No," she said. "Let's go."

They didn't go far.

Twenty miles out, past the town limits and deeper into nowhere. Jace drove like he knew the path by memory.

Trees closed in around them, branches clawing at the windshield like the woods themselves wanted to keep them out. The road narrowed. Gravel gave way to dirt. Then nothing. Just tracks and darkness.

Savannah leaned forward. "Are you sure this is even—"

Then, through the shifting branches—dim, half-hidden—it appeared.

The cabin emerged like a secret—weathered wood, sagging porch, moss-covered roof. The air felt colder here. Sharper. Full of pine, damp soil, and silence.

He parked behind a thicket of brush, killed the lights, and grabbed the bags. "No one's used it in years," he said. "My uncle used to come out here during hunting season. Off-grid. No signal. No power. Just quiet."

It should've felt like safety.

But to Savannah, it felt like waiting. Like the kind of quiet that came before something terrible.

The inside was sparse—one room, two twin beds, a stone hearth, dust everywhere. Jace dropped her bag by the door, then crouched at the fireplace and started stacking kindling.

Savannah sat stiffly on the edge of a bed; arms wrapped around herself. "I shouldn't have gone back," she murmured. "To the storage unit. To Cassidy's. Any of it. I should've let it stay buried."

Jace struck a match. The fire caught with a soft crackle.

"If you had," he said, not turning, "then they win."

"They still might."

He stood and faced her, face shadowed by firelight, the hard angles of it looking older than his years.

"Why did you believe me?" he asked quietly.

She met his eyes. "Because when I looked at you… I saw him."

Jace's jaw clenched, throat working. "I didn't save him."

"No," Savannah said. "But you're trying to save me."

The fire had burned low now, casting soft orange shadows on the walls. But in its warmth, something fragile had survived the cold.

And for a long, charged second, neither of them spoke.

Then Jace stepped forward. Something raw in his face. "There's something I haven't told you."

Savannah tensed. "What?"

He didn't sit beside her. Instead, he dropped to the opposite bed, elbows braced on his knees, head lowered like it hurt to say it out loud.

"The night Tyler died… when you heard us argue it wasn't the last time I was supposed to see him. He called me after the argument. Asked me to meet him. After midnight."

Savannah's breath caught. "What do you mean?"

"He said he had proof," Jace said quietly. "The kind that would bury Kessler. Told me to meet him at the footbridge behind the clinic."

Her brows drew together. "That's where he was murdered."

Jace nodded, eyes lifting—haunted. "Yeah. But I never made it."

She froze. "Why not?"

"I was jumped. Two guys in ski masks—hit me from behind. Beat the hell out of me. Took my phone, my wallet… left me bleeding in a ditch off Route 6."

Savannah's heart slammed into her ribs. "Jesus, Jace."

"I woke up in a drainage tunnel. Couldn't walk straight."

His hand lifted briefly to his temple, brushing an old scar she hadn't noticed before. "Still get ringing in my ears when it rains."

He exhaled, voice tightening. "By the time I got to the clinic, it was already too late. There was crime scene tape everywhere. And Tyler… he was already gone."

He didn't have to say the rest. She saw it in the slump of his shoulders. In the pain buried behind his eyes.

Savannah stared at him. "Why didn't you tell anyone?"

"I tried. But who was gonna listen?" His voice turned bitter. "Nineteen years old, record already tainted from juvie, no phone, no ID, and bruised like I started the fight myself. Half the town already thought I was guilty."

Savannah stood slowly. The floor creaked beneath her.

"So, they planned it," she said, voice low. "Tyler's death. Your silence."

Jace nodded once, the movement tight. "It was never just about killing him. It was about silencing him. Making sure no one ever heard what he had to say."

Savannah's voice was barely a breath. "What was the argument about? The one I heard that night?"

He drew in a slow breath. "Tyler told me the man he worked for was dirty. Said things were getting dangerous. Then he told me they threatened you." His jaw clenched. "I lost it. I told him to stop digging. To get out before it got worse. I begged him to walk away—for your sake."

She crossed the small room without thinking and dropped to her knees in front of him, the firelight dancing across his face in flickering golds and shadows. It softened the lines but couldn't erase them—the pain carved too deep, worn too long. The kind of pain that came from bearing the cost of someone else's crime.

Her voice trembled. "Why didn't you tell me?"

Jace didn't look at her. His hands were clasped, knuckles white. "After they said they found my blood on Tyler's body… you stopped coming."

Her breath caught. "I'm so sorry."

His eyes stayed locked on the flames. "I'm not the one who died."

"No," she said softly. "But you lost everything because of it."

He didn't respond right away. When he did, his voice was low. Worn.

"I was the easy target. Wrong side of town. Juvenile record. They needed a villain, and I checked all the boxes."

Savannah looked down, her fists clenched in front of her. "The worst part is… deep down, I never fully believed you did it. Not really. Not you."

Her voice cracked. "But I didn't fight for you either. I didn't ask the right questions. I let the silence decide."

That made him turn. Really look at her.

And something behind his eyes broke—not with anger, not blame.

But grief. Raw and quiet.

Laced with something else.

Forgiveness.

"You lost him too," he said. "And I looked guilty enough."

Tears burned hot behind her eyes. "I should've known. I should've trusted the boy who used to climb onto my roof at midnight and swear I could count on him forever."

His mouth twitched—something like a smile. Cracked and tired, but real.

"You still can," he said. Then added, almost to himself, "Somehow, after everything… I didn't lose this."

She didn't ask what this meant.

She already knew.

And as the fire cracked and the silence held between them, for the first time in ten years… she didn't feel alone.

Not anymore.

Savannah stood slowly, the firelight casting her shadow long across the floorboards. She moved to her backpack, crouched, and unzipped it with deliberate fingers. For a moment, she just stared inside—like the object she was about to retrieve might change everything.

Then, without a word, she pulled out something wrapped in soft, worn cotton.

She turned, walked back across the room, and held it out.

Jace didn't move at first. His eyes flicked to the bundle, then to her face.

He took it gently from her hands, like whatever was inside might shatter. As he unwrapped the fabric—an old T-shirt, faded with time and grief—his brows pulled tight.

The revolver sat cold and matte in the soft folds, its steel catching the low orange flicker of the fire.

A box of ammunition was tucked beside it.

It looked too heavy for something so small.

His voice, when it came, was low. Measured. Almost too steady.

"What the hell, Savannah… You have a gun?"

"It was my father's," she said.

Her tone wasn't defensive. It wasn't anything at all.

Just… restrained. Like something was cinched too tightly inside her to allow for emotion.

She hesitated, just for a beat. Then added, "I haven't looked at it since your conviction."

Jace's gaze snapped to hers. Her face was in shadow, but he didn't need light to hear what her voice had just confessed.

His throat worked.

"What do you mean by that?"

She didn't answer.

She didn't need to.

The silence was more honest than any words could've been.

And when her eyes dropped, when her arms folded around herself like the memory had taken the breath from her lungs, he understood.

"You were going to use it… on yourself?"

She nodded once, barely perceptible.

Her voice came quiet and tight.

"After Tyler died. After you were convicted. You were both gone—and I didn't know who I was without you."

The air thickened between them. Not just with grief, but with everything unsaid for a decade.

"I'd lost everything," she continued, her voice softer now. "And there were days I couldn't function. Couldn't eat. Couldn't sleep. Couldn't breathe."

A pause.

"I would open the drawer and just… stare at it."

She looked down at her hands.

"For hours sometimes."

The silence that followed felt sacred.

Like interrupting it would ruin something too fragile to name.

Jace's hands curled around the revolver, the weight of it anchoring him to the floor.

He didn't speak.

Didn't move.

"But I never picked it up."

Her voice had changed—firmer now. The echo of choice, not chance.

A breath escaped him, slow and careful. Like it had been held in the space between them for ten years.

"Savannah…"

"I didn't," she repeated, meeting his eyes. "Because part of me still hoped I was wrong. About you. About everything. And if I was…" Her voice broke, just slightly. "I didn't want that to be the last thing I ever believed."

Something cracked open inside her then, but she didn't cry.

She just stood there, arms wrapped tight across her chest like a fortress that had only barely held.

Jace looked down at the weapon in his hands, then back to her—like he was seeing the whole of her for the first time. Not just the woman who'd held on to the fight, but the one who'd once nearly let go.

He moved quietly, reverently. Rewrapped the gun in Tyler's old T-shirt, smoothing the edges with fingers gentler than she expected.

Then he laid it down beside her bag.

His voice was quiet. Steady.

"You're not the one who should carry that kind of weight."

Her throat tightened. She swallowed hard.

"Neither are you."

Neither of them moved.

Then, finally, slowly, Jace reached for her.

No words. No explanations.

Just arms outstretched, an anchor in human form.

Savannah didn't resist. She stepped into him like he was gravity, like his warmth might keep her from breaking.

And for the first time in a decade, she let herself be held.

Not carefully. Not out of pity.

But tightly. Fiercely.

Like maybe he needed it too.

She buried her face in his shoulder and felt the fire at her back, the cold of the night held off only by this—this quiet, trembling moment of being seen.

She held on.

To him. To herself.

To something that felt like survival.

And in the stillness between heartbeats, she realised—

She wasn't falling anymore.

Chapter Thirteen

They barely slept.

Jace sat by the door, his back pressed against the rough wood, the revolver resting across his thigh. One hand curled loosely around the grip, but his finger never touched the trigger. He hadn't spoken in over an hour. Maybe more. His eyes kept moving—window to wall, shadow to fire, tracking every flicker like it might become threat.

The cabin was thick with the scent of wood smoke and unease. The fire was nearly out—just a soft pulse of red beneath crumbling ash. Each log gave a slow, reluctant crack as it broke apart, like it was resisting the inevitable.

The wind outside whispered through the trees. But inside, it was all breath and tension. No one moved. No one dared.

Across the room, Savannah lay curled on the narrow bed beneath a scratchy wool blanket that smelled like dust and time. It didn't touch the chill inside her. She stared at the ceiling, eyes unblinking, tracing the dark beams like they might spell out an answer she'd missed.

Sleep hovered just out of reach. Teasing. Cruel.

Every time her eyes slid shut, she saw flashes—Tyler's grin, that stupid lopsided smirk he used when he knew she was about to lecture him. Then came the image from her phone. The message. The photo of her house taken from the tree line. A hunter's gaze on a familiar target.

And always—Jace.

Jace in a courtroom. In cuffs. In chains.

Jace bleeding in her memory, alone and branded with guilt that never belonged to him.

Outside, something moved.

A sharp screech tore through the trees—a bird, high-pitched and jarring.

Then—crack.

A branch.

Close.

Too close.

Savannah's breath caught in her throat. Her fingers tightened around the edge of the blanket until her knuckles burned. Her head turned sharply toward Jace.

He was already up—silent, poised, gun in hand, his entire body wired like a trap about to spring.

He didn't speak. Didn't move.

He just listened.

And Savannah listened with him.

A long beat.

Two.

Then the wind again. Only the wind.

Leaves rustling like whispers.

A soft sigh from the fire.

No more movement. No more sounds. Just… silence. Watching them.

They didn't relax. They couldn't.

Even when the moment passed, the fear lingered like smoke. It settled into the cracks of the room, into their bones.

Savannah exhaled slowly, her chest tight. She rolled onto her side, back to the fire, eyes trained on the cabin's cold wall. The blanket scratched against her cheek, but she didn't shift.

She didn't need comfort.

She needed truth.

"You think they'll come tonight?" she asked softly, voice barely louder than the wind.

Jace didn't answer right away.

"They might," he said at last. "But they'd be stupid to."

A hollow pause.

"They've already done worse," she murmured.

"Yeah." His voice was quieter this time. "I know."

Another stretch of silence passed. The fire gave one last pop, like punctuation.

Then Savannah spoke again, surprising herself.

"Do you ever stop blaming yourself?"

Jace didn't answer immediately. She could picture him still—rigid, shadowed, jaw tight with things he hadn't said aloud in years.

"No," he said finally, his voice a rasp of honesty. "But it gets harder to hold onto the hate when I'm looking at the person I lost everything for. And realising… maybe it wasn't all for nothing."

Her throat clenched. A single tear slipped down her cheek and vanished into the wool. She didn't wipe it away.

"I'm sorry," she whispered. It came out raw. Fractured. "For not believing in you. For leaving you alone in it."

"So am I," Jace said.

For what, he didn't say.

Maybe for surviving when Tyler didn't.

Maybe for not getting there in time.

Maybe for everything silence had cost them both.

The floor creaked.

She didn't turn, didn't ask.

Then she felt him.

Jace sat on the edge of the bed behind her—close but not touching. Still holding distance like he didn't want to break whatever this fragile truce had become. But she felt the heat of him through the blanket. The quiet strength of his presence.

A silent offering.

A wordless shield against the dark.

She didn't speak again.

Neither did he.

But when her body finally eased and her breath came softer, it wasn't comfort that did it. Not exactly.

It was presence.

It was knowing that if the world came apart tonight, she wouldn't face it alone.

And maybe that—was enough to make it until morning.

The wind had kept them company all night, whispering against the cabin walls. By morning, it followed them still—ghosting through the cracked truck window like a warning not yet spoken.

The morning was grey and thin, the sky sagging low and colourless, like a secret not yet told. The world looked muted through the windshield—trees shivering in the wind, roads slick with mist, everything cold and unfinished.

They drove back into town with the heater off, windows opened just enough to keep the glass from fogging. The silence between them wasn't heavy—it was taut. Wary. Like the road itself might splinter beneath them if they said too much.

Savannah sat stiffly in the passenger seat, one hand curled in her lap, the other brushing against the flash drive in her coat pocket like it was a relic. A weapon. A truth too sharp to name. Her thumb ran over the smooth plastic shell in an endless rhythm.

She had what Tyler died for.

Now she had to decide what to do with it.

Cassidy was already waiting at the café.

She sat alone in the corner booth, hood pulled low, sunglasses on despite the overcast sky. A half-drunk cup of coffee sat cooling in front of her, the steam long since faded. She didn't look up when they walked in. Didn't wave.

She just sank lower into the booth, like she wished the vinyl could swallow her whole.

Jace scanned the room instinctively as they entered. Two old men at the counter. A waitress wiping down menus. A kid in a hoodie playing with his phone near the front window. Normal. Quiet. Too quiet.

They approached without a word.

He slid into the seat across from Cassidy, his shoulders squared. Savannah sat beside him, not touching, but close. Her posture was guarded—tight at the jaw, spine straight—but her hands were steady now. Steady like resolve.

Cassidy didn't offer a greeting.

"Where the hell did you two go?" she muttered, low and clipped.

"We went somewhere safer," Jace said. His voice was even, but his eyes didn't waver. "Someone threatened Savannah."

Cassidy's brows lifted above her sunglasses. "What?"

Savannah's voice was calm, but brittle at the edges. "They sent two photos. My house. The back door and my bedroom window. Said if I didn't stop digging, they'd finish what they started."

Cassidy's mask slipped—just for a moment. Her mouth parted. "Bloody hell."

No one moved.

No one drank. No one even breathed too deeply.

The silence between them wasn't just tense. It was full.

Stuffed with guilt. With memories. With ten years of regret finally pressing against the surface.

Then Cassidy reached slowly into her oversized tote bag. Her fingers shook as she rummaged, then stilled when she pulled something out—a flash drive, small and metallic, like a bullet in her palm. She held it out across the table.

"I scanned everything last night," she said quietly. "Everything Tyler gave me. Plus, the photo from the bar—time-stamped, geo-tagged. He labelled most of it himself. Some of it connects to offshore accounts. Shell companies. It's not just dirty—it's dangerous."

Savannah took it, turning the drive over in her hand.

The plastic warmed quickly in her grip.

Jace's jaw tensed. He didn't reach for the drive. Didn't speak. But Savannah felt the shift in the air beside her—the way his shoulders stiffened like he was holding something back. Not anger. Just the sharp edge of ten stolen years.

She looked up slowly, voice quiet but razor-sharp. "Why now, Cassidy?"

Cassidy flinched. She dropped her gaze to the table, tracing a scratch in the laminate with her thumbnail. "Because I finally stopped pretending I wasn't part of it."

Jace didn't speak.

Cassidy's voice cracked slightly as she went on. "I thought staying silent made me neutral. But it didn't. It made me complicit."

She looked up—eyes rimmed with red behind the sunglasses, though no tears fell.

"And because he trusted me," she added. "Tyler trusted me. And I let him die with the truth buried in my hands."

Savannah stared at her, the flash drive clenched between her fingers like something holy. Or damning.

Then, softer now, she said, "Let's make sure it doesn't stay buried."

Cassidy gave a slow nod. "My dad was here last week."

Both Jace and Savannah tensed.

Cassidy leaned in, lowering her voice. "No press. No entourage. He checked into the Harbour Inn under an alias. I traced his security detail. One night, he met someone behind the old courthouse. Military posture. The way he moved… he was giving orders. Like he owned the place."

Jace's head snapped up. "You get a name?"

"No. No surveillance footage. No receipts. They parked off-grid and walked the last block. But I tracked phone pings for the security detail. They left their phones in the car."

"Classic," Jace muttered. "Controlled. No digital trail."

Savannah's skin prickled. "You think the person he met is the same one who threatened me?"

"Yes," Jace said, without hesitation. His eyes didn't leave Cassidy. "He's not warning her. He's trying to shut her down."

Cassidy's mouth opened, then closed. Her next words came in a whisper. "I want to believe he's not behind it. I want to believe there's still a line he wouldn't cross."

Jace leaned forward, voice low and tight. "There's no line when a man starts hiding in the dark. He's either planning something… or trying to bury what's already been done. Either way, he's scared."

Savannah's voice cut through the thick air like a blade. "Then we make him more scared."

She turned to Jace. "We take it all to John. The flash drives. The bar photo. Tyler's letter—everything."

Cassidy hesitated. Her fingers twisted the edge of her sleeve again. "Are you sure you can trust him?"

Savannah didn't answer right away.

She remembered John at the funeral—grief etched into every line of his face. The way his hand had lingered on the casket like a final promise. His voice, hoarse with something close to guilt.

"I trust that he loved my brother," she said finally. "And that he's not part of this."

Jace looked unconvinced, but not combative. "If he is, we'll know fast."

Savannah nodded once. "And if he's not… then we finally have someone on the inside."

Cassidy pulled her hood a little lower, voice quiet as breath.

"Just be careful. My father never starts something he doesn't finish."

Jace reached across the table, took the flash drive from Savannah, and slipped it into his jacket pocket like it was something alive.

Then he looked at her—not Cassidy. Savannah.

And his words were a vow.

"Then let's finish it for him."

Chapter Fourteen

Sheriff John Nolan met them at the station.

The usual ease—the worn smile, slow drawl, that familiar lilt he wore like armour—was gone.

His jaw was clenched. His uniform jacket was buttoned wrong—one side askew like he'd thrown it on mid-call. A gun rested at his hip, but it was the weight behind his eyes that spoke louder. Something grim. Something old. Something he'd hoped would never resurface.

He remained standing.

"What the hell have you kids stirred up?" he asked, voice gruffer than they remembered.

Savannah didn't flinch. She stepped forward and laid two flash drives and a thick, rubber-banded folder on his desk. Her hand lingered—just a second—before pulling back like it burned.

"The truth," she said quietly.

John stared at the pile. For a beat, he didn't move.

Then he opened the folder.

Surveillance stills. Time-stamped photos. Bank statements. Shell company registrations. And faces he couldn't pretend not to recognise. Faces that had shaken his hand. Donated to his campaigns. Stood on courthouse steps and talked about justice.

Then came Tyler's handwriting—on pages scanned and stored like echoes from a grave.

Silence stretched, taut and trembling.

By the time he reached the end, John's posture had shifted. Suspicion drained from his face, replaced by something heavier—recognition, sick and cold.

He sank slowly into his chair and dragged a hand down his face. When he spoke, it was barely more than breath.

"I always knew Kessler was slick," he muttered. "But this? Laundering. Bribes. Suppressed testimony. Sealed warrants." His voice caught. "And Tyler…"

He didn't finish. Couldn't.

Jace stepped forward. His voice was low, tight. "We've been threatened. Twice."

John's head snapped up.

"Someone took photos of Savannah's house. From the woods. Sent her a message—said if she didn't stop digging, they'd finish what they started."

A flash of fury lit in the sheriff's eyes. He shot to his feet—sudden, sharp. "Jesus Christ. Why the hell didn't you come to me sooner?"

Savannah didn't blink. Her arms folded across her chest. Her voice was calm. Deadly precise.

"Because we didn't know if we could trust you."

It landed hard. John flinched like she'd slapped him.

Something shifted behind his eyes—regret, maybe. Or the realisation of how long he'd been looking the other way.

He gave a slow nod. "That's fair."

He looked down at his hands. They weren't steady.

"I failed Tyler," he said softly. "And I failed you. I promised your father I'd watch out for you both if anything ever happened to him." His voice cracked. "He was a damn good cop. Loyal. Honest. Loved you kids more than anything."

"I know," Savannah said, her voice low. But there was no softness in it. Not anymore.

John turned his attention to Jace, quieter now. "Looks like I failed you too, son."

Jace's jaw twitched. But he said nothing.

John stood again and began to pace—two steps forward, then back. Like the truth was too heavy to sit with. When he finally stopped, he planted both hands on the edge of the desk and leaned in.

"This is bigger than me. Bigger than this station. I'll take it to the DA, then the Bureau—but quiet. No press. No phones. No trail. We go loud too early; someone high up makes this disappear before it draws breath."

He looked up. His voice sharpened. "Until I call, you stay off the radar."

"We've got a place," Jace said. "Off-grid. No signal."

"Good. Stay there. No phones, no credit cards, no goddamn social media. Ghost yourselves."

John turned back to Savannah, something raw in his voice now. "And Savannah—whatever happens next… don't walk into it alone."

She gave a single nod. "I won't."

But deep down—she already knew.

She might not have a choice.

The fire crackled low in the cabin fireplace.

The room was quiet except for the whisper of sap hissing in the wood and the distant hum of wind pressing against the walls. Crickets pulsed outside, their rhythm broken only by the occasional rustle of dry leaves.

Jace slept light in the chair by the window. One arm folded across his chest, the revolver resting within reach on the windowsill. His head tilted forward, brows furrowed even in sleep. Like his mind never fully let go.

Savannah sat cross-legged on the bed. Awake. Still. Watching the night from behind tired eyes.

The last message glowed dim on her phone screen.

YOU STOP NOW OR WE FINISH WHAT WE STARTED.

No more photos. No more movement.

Just silence.

And it didn't feel like mercy.

It felt like a countdown.

She looked up. The fire was nearly out—just a faint pulse in the stone hearth, painting shadows across the walls like moving ghosts. The wind slipped through the cracks in the window frame, curling around her ankles, carrying the scent of pine and cold earth.

Outside, something moved.

Not loud. Not close. But there.

A shift. A whisper. A breath in the wrong place.

She rose quietly, walked to the window, and peered into the trees.

Just blackness.

Just branches and sway.

But deep in her gut, something stirred—an old fear. Not loud or sudden. Just present.

She couldn't see them.

But she felt them.

Somewhere out there—beyond the firelight, past the treeline where Tyler once stood—someone was watching.

Still waiting.

Still deciding.

She stepped back from the glass and sat slowly on the edge of the bed.

No sound. No scream. No knock at the door.

But this wasn't over.

Whatever was coming next—it was already on its way.

And this time… it wouldn't miss.

Two nights later.

They had spent the last two days staying awake—watching each other sleep but saying very little. The silence between them wasn't strained… just fragile. Like a bridge neither of them were ready to cross.

Savannah still didn't know what to say. Not yet.

The fire burned low—no more than a flickering hush in the hearth. Shadows slithered across the cabin walls, stretching long and strange. Outside, the moon hung low and pale, casting everything in that silver kind of silence—the kind that felt too still to be safe.

Jace sat by the window, half-swallowed by dark.

The revolver rested in his lap like an extension of his arm. One hand draped over the grip, relaxed but ready. His eyes scanned the trees—quiet, constant, calculating. Moonlight carved a slash across his face, catching on the sharp line of his cheekbone, the tension in his jaw. He looked like a statue built from battle scars and nights without sleep.

Savannah watched him from the bed. Her knees were tucked under the wool blanket, but the cold crept in anyway—settling somewhere deeper than skin.

The flickering firelight made him look unreal.

Like a man from a story no one wanted to remember.

The kind that never ends well.

"Do you ever relax?" she asked, her voice barely more than a breath.

Jace didn't move. His eyes didn't leave the window. "Not when someone wants you dead."

No hesitation.

No drama.

Just fact.

Finally, slowly, he turned to meet her gaze.

"Try to rest," he said. "I'll keep watch."

But she didn't lie down. Not yet. Couldn't.

"I keep thinking about that photo," she murmured. "How close they were. My house. My life… right there. Right outside."

"They wanted you to see it," Jace said. "Fear's a message. They're hoping you'll read it loud and clear."

She gave a dry, bitter laugh. "Well… it's working."

Jace stood. Crossed the room in three quiet strides.

He crouched beside the bed; eyes level with hers. The firelight caught the edges of him—his stubble, the scar near his collarbone, the tired lines around his eyes. But something in his expression shifted. Softened. Like the edge of a blade dulled by time, weather, and grief.

"Savannah."

She looked at him.

Really looked.

And her chest pulled tight.

"You're the bravest person I know," he said, steady and low. "You could've walked away. After Tyler. After everything. But you didn't. You stayed. You fought."

Her fingers moved before her words did—lifting, brushing the roughness of his jaw. "That doesn't mean I'm not scared."

"Good," he said, leaning into her touch, just enough. "Brave gets you killed. But scared… scared keeps you alive long enough to win."

She wanted to tell him not to be reckless. Not to go out there alone again. That she needed him.

That she didn't know how to survive another loss.

That she loved him.

But the words jammed in her throat, too raw to shape.

So instead, she whispered, "Be careful. Okay?"

His eyes didn't leave hers. Steady. Searching. Like he could feel every unsaid thing she was holding inside.

"I will."

And for now, that had to be enough.

CRACK.

A sharp snap split the quiet.

They both froze.

Another crack—closer.

Low. Deliberate. Not wind.

Jace moved like he'd been waiting for this exact moment. Silent, fast, coiled. Gun up. Shoulders squared. Eyes sharp.

"Back door," he said. "Go. Now."

Savannah didn't question. She moved—bare feet hitting the cold floor, heart in her throat, breath shallow. She yanked the back door open—

Blinding light.

A flashlight exploded across her vision.

"Don't shoot!" a voice barked. "It's me!"

She shielded her eyes, squinting. "John?"

The sheriff stepped into view, breath fogging in the cold night air. His badge caught the beam of light, glinting. He wasn't alone—two deputies moved behind him. One held a shotgun tight to his chest, eyes sweeping the tree line. The other scanned the shadows, hand near his belt.

Jace appeared beside her, weapon still raised.

Then, reluctantly, he lowered it. "Jesus Christ, John. Ever heard of a phone?"

"No service out here, remember," John said, tense. "Didn't have time to wait."

He stepped inside, boots heavy on the floorboards. "We need to talk. Now."

Savannah blinked at him, trying to slow her pulse. "What's going on?"

But the look in his eyes made her blood run cold.

This wasn't about the trees. It wasn't about the photos or the threats.

The fear in John's expression—the way his jaw flexed, the flicker of something behind his words—it wasn't aimed at the outside.

It was something else.

Inside the cabin.

The fire roared now, hot, and restless—its crackling too loud, its shadows too wild. The door was bolted. Curtains drawn. But the walls still felt too thin.

John didn't waste time.

He crossed the room once, the heavy thud of his boots matching the beat of Savannah's heart, then turned sharply. His face was pale under the brim of his hat, voice rough, barely more than gravel.

"The DA's dead."

The words dropped like a stone. The air went still.

Jace stood straighter. "What?"

John's eyes met his, grim and hollow. "Car crash. Bypass road just outside county lines. Brake line was cut."

Savannah's knees buckled slightly. She reached for the table beside her. "Oh my God…"

"She had the files," Jace said, barely above a whisper. "She was the first one you gave copies to."

John nodded. "She took them home last night. Said she'd go through everything, vet the chain, bring in the Bureau this morning."

Savannah pressed a fist to her mouth. Her voice cracked. "She didn't even get the chance."

"She didn't make it ten miles," John said. "No skid marks. No turn attempt. Just straight off the ridge."

Jace's jaw clenched. "They killed her."

"No doubt in my mind," John said. "This wasn't random. It was a message. And a warning."

"They're escalating," Jace muttered, pacing once. "This isn't a cover-up anymore. It's cleanup."

"Exactly," John said. "They're tying off every loose end. Fast. Quiet. Permanent."

Savannah's stomach turned. "If Kessler's behind this—"

"He is," John interrupted. "He's scared. Which makes him dangerous. He's not like the others. He doesn't make public mistakes. He's never had to."

Jace's fists curled. "So, what now?"

John didn't flinch. "We go federal. Full Bureau. But it has to be surgical. I need time. Time to vet agents I can trust, to set up witness protection, secure chain of custody on the evidence. If I screw up even one piece of that, this whole thing collapses. And Kessler walks."

"And if you wait too long?" Jace's voice was sharp. Unforgiving. "We die."

John didn't argue.

He slipped a hand into his coat and drew out a satellite phone. Small. Scuffed. Unmarked.

He held it out to Savannah.

"Pulled this out of evidence. Nobody knows I've got it—but if they ever check, they can trace it. So, keep it off unless you have no other choice. Life or death, that's it. No casual calls, no texts, no names. You don't get second chances with this. My number's already saved inside."

Savannah took it slowly. Her fingers curled around it like it might explode. It was light in her hand.

Too light to carry the weight of survival.

She looked up, voice tight. "What about Cassidy?"

John's face darkened.

"I don't know," he admitted. "She's giving you real intel. So far, she's been helpful. But her father—he's got reach. And power. If he even suspects she's turned on him, she's in danger."

He paused.

Then, bluntly: "Or she's already compromised."

Savannah recoiled. "You think she's playing both sides?"

"I think she's scared," John said. "And scared people are unpredictable. Sometimes they do the right thing. Sometimes… they try to survive."

It wasn't reassurance.

It was a warning.

A cold, necessary truth.

Jace crossed his arms. "Then we assume nothing."

"Exactly," John said. "From here on out, you trust no one unless they bleed for it. No updates. No digital trails. I'll come to you when it's time to move. Until then—you vanish."

"And if they find us?" Savannah asked.

John's eyes didn't blink. Didn't soften.

"Then you fight," he said. "And you don't stop."

Chapter Fifteen

John left just before midnight, vanishing into the woods with his deputies like ghosts. The silence that followed felt heavier. Meaner. Like even the trees were holding their breath.

Savannah stood in front of the fire, the burner phone still in her hand like a loaded weapon. She hadn't moved in minutes, her mind replaying every word John had said.

Behind her, Jace lingered in the shadows near the window, still keeping watch.

"You don't have to stay here," he said quietly.

She turned. "You're not getting rid of me."

"That's not what I meant."

"I know," she said, stepping toward him. "You still think this ends with you dying to protect me. Like if one of us has to go down… it should be you."

He didn't deny it. His silence said everything.

Savannah crossed the room until she was just a breath away. "But we're in this together, Jace. You and me. I didn't come this far to lose you now."

He looked at her for a long moment, eyes stormy and uncertain. Then his jaw tensed.

"There's something you should have."

Her stomach dropped. "What?"

He reached into his pocket slowly, like the weight of the object had been burning a hole there for days. When he opened his hand, a small, scuffed silver ring lay in his palm.

Simple. Worn. Familiar.

"I found it," he said quietly. "In Tyler's storage unit. It was with the drive."

Savannah's breath caught.

"That was my father's," she whispered. "Tyler wore it every day after our father died."

Jace nodded, eyes on the ring. "It belongs to you. But I wasn't ready to give it back. I thought… maybe I deserved to carry a part of him. But I don't. Not after everything."

She reached for it instinctively—but he closed his fist around it before her fingers could touch it.

Her breath caught.

"Before I give it to you," he said, voice low and steady, "there's something you need to know."

His eyes lifted to hers, sharp with unspoken weight.

"I've done things, Savannah. In prison. To survive. Things I'll never be proud of. If you knew half of it…"

She stepped closer, her breath hitching.

Then, gently, she placed her hand over his—over the closed fist, the ring hidden inside. Her other hand on his chest, her fingers rested against the steady thrum of his heartbeat beneath.

Strong. Uneven. Human.

Real.

Alive.

His.

"I don't need the whole story," she whispered. "I already know enough."

Jace looked at her—really looked. And for a moment, everything else fell away.

What passed between them wasn't just grief or guilt or the heavy ache of what they'd lost.

It was something deeper.

A wordless vow.

Not just to survive.

Not just to expose the truth.

But to begin again—with open wounds, and open hearts.

Slowly, he opened his hand.

The ring—Tyler's—gleamed dully in his palm, still warm from his skin. He didn't speak. Just offered it.

And when Savannah reached for it, her fingers brushed his. The contact sent a quiet shiver up her spine.

The ring slid into her palm like it had always belonged there.

And for a moment, surrounded by firelight and silence and the ghosts of people they'd both lost, something inside her steadied.

They weren't just fighting for justice anymore.

They were fighting for each other.

She didn't plan to move. Didn't think.

Her hand was still pressed against his chest when her eyes lifted to his—and what she saw there unravelled the last thread of distance between them.

A breath.

Then she rose onto her toes.

And kissed him.

It wasn't tentative.

It wasn't sweet.

It was heat and history and raw, aching need—a collision of grief and memory and the years they'd both survived without each other. It was a kiss born of grief, and longing, and all the things they'd never had the chance to say.

Jace didn't hesitate.

His hands came to her waist—firm, reverent—as he pulled her in like he'd been waiting a decade to touch her again. His mouth found hers with urgency, deepening the kiss until Savannah felt it in her chest, in her knees, in every part of her that had felt hollow for too long.

His hand slid up the curve of her back and tangled in her hair, cradling the base of her neck, holding her in place as if afraid she might vanish again. The press of his body was solid and warm, grounding her when the rest of the world felt like it could fall away.

Savannah gasped softly against his lips; the sound caught between a sigh and a moan. Her fingers curled into his shirt, anchoring herself to the thrum of his heartbeat—wild, steady, alive. She leaned into him, into the kiss, into the heat curling low in her belly and spreading like fire through her limbs.

He moved with restraint, but just barely—like control was something he wore thinly around her. Like the taste of her was both salvation and punishment.

And she gave in. Completely.

Because here, in this sliver of borrowed time, with the fire casting shadows and his mouth claiming hers, nothing else mattered.

When they finally broke apart, breathless, her hands were still fisted in his shirt, and his forehead dropped to hers, eyes closed, chest rising and falling like he'd just come back from the edge of something.

Neither of them spoke.

They didn't need to.

The silence between them pulsed with everything the words couldn't hold.

But Savannah knew—without doubt or hesitation—that if the world ended tomorrow, if the truth burned and the past bled out—

This would be the moment she carried with her to the end.

They slept for a few stolen hours, curled together in the too-small bed, her head rising and falling with each breath from his chest, his arm draped heavy and sure around her waist.

For the first time in what felt like forever, Savannah slept without waking in a jolt of panic. No dreams of blood or footsteps. No shadows clawing at the edges of her mind. Just warmth. Steady breath. The quiet rhythm of a man who had survived hell—and was still here. With her.

But peace never lingered in their world.

Morning came too fast—dragging light and dread in with it. And with it, the crunch of tyres over gravel.

Jace's eyes snapped open. He was upright in an instant, hand diving under the bed to grip the revolver. "That's not John," he said, voice low and sharp as steel.

Savannah pushed herself up, sleep still clinging to her bones, boots half-on from the night before. She crossed the room and tugged the curtain aside just an inch.

A black SUV crept into view, headlights dimmed, engine rumbling like a warning.

She stiffened. "It's Cassidy."

But Jace stayed locked in place, the gun still raised.

Moments later—Bang. Bang. Bang. A frantic knock at the door.

"It's me! Please—let me in!"

The panic in Cassidy's voice wasn't faked. It was cracked. Wild.

Jace moved fast, gun still in hand, checking the window, then the porch. He flung the door open wide—but kept his grip tight.

Cassidy stumbled through like she'd been running for her life. Hoodie up. Sweat beading her forehead. Her face pale and ghosted with fear. Hands trembling, chest heaving.

"They know," she gasped. "My dad—he knows I gave you the files. He's going to kill me."

Savannah rushed forward, catching her before she collapsed. "Cassidy, breathe. You're okay. Just slow down—what happened?"

Cassidy reached into her jacket with shaking fingers. Pulled out something crumpled.

A photo.

Not just any photo. A surveillance still. High angle. Grainy. But unmistakable. Cassidy walking into the café where they'd met. Her face in full frame. Timestamped.

Savannah's stomach turned. "Where did this come from?"

"It was on my windshield," Cassidy whispered. "No note. No message. Just… this."

Jace swore under his breath. He bolted the door behind her and yanked the curtains closed, sealing them back into their dark, flickering silence.

Savannah guided Cassidy to the bed and sat beside her, pressing a hand to her shoulder. "You're safe here. We won't let anything happen to you."

But Cassidy shook her head, eyes wide, skin clammy. "You don't understand. My father doesn't threaten. He erases. He's never gotten his hands dirty personally, not that anyone's seen—but he doesn't need to. People fear him because when someone gets in his way… they disappear."

She looked between them—eyes rimmed red, voice barely a breath.

"He doesn't just remove people. He enjoys it."

The words hung like smoke in the room—heavy, toxic, undeniable.

Then, after a breath: "And I think… I think he's the one who had Tyler killed."

The world stopped turning.

Savannah's heart stuttered. "Are you sure?"

Cassidy nodded, slowly, like every muscle in her neck resisted. "He hated Tyler. Called him weak. Said he 'betrayed the wrong people.' Said people like that didn't deserve second chances." Her voice cracked. "At the time, I thought it was just him being angry. But now—after what I've seen, what I know—he meant it."

Tears slipped down her cheeks. Silent. Hopeless.

Across the room, Jace stood frozen in place, hands clenched at his sides. Fury simmered under his skin, quiet and dangerous. He looked at Savannah—and in that look, she saw what they both already knew.

"No more waiting," he said. "This doesn't end in courtrooms or headlines. We move. Soon."

Savannah rose, her expression hardening into something sharper than fear. "We finish this."

Cassidy looked up, voice cracking. "How? You don't know what he's capable of. He has people everywhere. Money. Power. No one touches him."

Savannah's tone dropped low—measured, lethal. "Then we go straight to the source."

Jace stepped forward, quiet and resolute. "We use what we've got. The timeline. The files. The chain of command. We push it all into the light."

"And we make damn sure," Savannah said, her eyes gleaming, "that it burns."

Cassidy swallowed hard. "You're going to expose him?"

Savannah met her gaze without blinking.

"No," she said.

Her voice was cold. Final.

"We're going to destroy him."

Outside, the wind picked up—slow at first, then sharper. Harsher.

It hissed through the trees like something alive, dragging the dry scent of pine and ash behind it. Dead leaves scraped across the gravel like brittle bones, whispering warnings as they danced in frantic circles. The trees groaned under the weight of the coming storm, their limbs swaying like restless sentinels. The sky had turned the colour of old bruises—dark, swollen, full of something waiting to break.

And just beyond the thinning treeline, high on a wooded ridge, a figure crouched low.

Motionless. Patient. Camouflaged in dirt, bark, and darkness.

He moved like the forest—slow, deliberate, almost part of it. Binoculars pressed to his face; he adjusted the focus with the precision of someone trained not to blink. His breath fogged slightly in the early chill, but he didn't move. Didn't shiver.

Down below, the glow of the cabin fire flickered against the windows. Just a sliver. Just enough.

He watched the figures inside—three shapes now, all close, all unaware.

Then he lowered the binoculars slowly.

And pressed a finger to the earpiece tucked beneath his collar. The radio keyed with a soft click.

"You were right," he murmured. Voice low. Calm. "She led us straight to them. They're all inside. Together."

A long beat of static followed.

Not accidental.

A silence long enough to feel like it was waiting—for something. Or someone.

Then a voice cut through. Male. Cold. Smooth as silk stretched over broken glass.

"They don't know about me yet. Let them think they've won," it said. "If they don't stop, we'll bury them."

The man on the ridge didn't flinch.

But he paused. Just a breath.

"What about Kessler?" he asked.

"Let him dig his own grave. I look out for myself."

"And his daughter? If she dies—"

Another pause.

Flat. Final. "He won't care. Anyway, if he gets caught, he won't be around to see."

A longer silence followed. Deeper than before.

"He's no different. Disposable, like all the others."

The words landed like gunfire—quiet, but lethal.

The man on the ridge gave a slight nod, more to the silence than the voice in his ear.

"Understood," he murmured.

Then, with steady fingers, he reached into his coat, pulled out a cigarette, and lit it—the flame brief against the dark, the ember flaring like a warning.

Below, in the cabin, firelight danced across the windows.

Unaware.

Unprepared.

The wind howled louder now, threading through the trees like a scream muffled by distance. It clawed at the world with invisible fingers, rattling branches and stirring leaves that skittered like mice.

Nature itself seemed to shrink back.

As if it, too, knew what was coming.

Chapter Sixteen

The warehouse on Riverbend Avenue loomed like a ghost from a forgotten war—silent, scarred, and bracing for something it had seen too many times before. Once a hub of industry, now it sat rotting at the edge of the river, cloaked in shadow and silence.

Cassidy had said they might find something here. A lead. A thread to pull. Maybe more.

Savannah stared at it through the grime-caked windshield, her pulse a roar in her ears. Dust clung to the narrow, broken windows like ash from an old fire, and vines curled up the brick walls like nature itself was trying to strangle whatever secrets still lived inside.

Somewhere beyond that rusted steel door was the truth. Maybe justice. Maybe something colder. Sharper. Revenge.

Beside her, Jace checked the magazine in his gun—again. The click of metal was soft but deliberate. His movements were steady, almost too steady, but the tension in his shoulders told the real story. He was coiled. Controlled. One wrong sound from that warehouse and he'd explode into motion.

Savannah swallowed hard and reached for the door handle, her fingers trembling just enough to betray her.

"Last chance to back out," he muttered, not looking at her.

Savannah's grip tightened on the door handle. "Not a chance."

In the backseat, Cassidy sat rigid, hands clenched in her lap. "My father used to bring people here when he wanted them off the books. No staff. No cameras. No trail. Just men he paid too much and trusted too little."

Jace glanced at her in the rearview mirror. "Perfect place for a setup."

Cassidy's voice trembled, but she met his eyes. "You still don't trust me."

"No," Jace said, flat and unapologetic. Then, softer, "But I trust her."

He nodded toward Savannah.

Cassidy didn't argue. She just reached for the door handle and stepped out into the wind.

They entered through the side, slipping past a rusted chain-link fence and into a forgotten service corridor Cassidy had used years ago during one of her father's campaign shoots, before Tyler's death.

Inside, the air was stale and sharp—dust, oil, and something metallic that clung to the back of the throat.

The main warehouse floor opened before them like a cavern. Shafts of pale morning light broke through cracks in the ceiling. The space was mostly empty—except for a single desk near the far wall.

On top of it sat a folder.

Nothing else.

No guards. No voices. No movement.

Jace's hand hovered near his weapon. "This feels wrong."

Savannah edged closer, careful not to let her footsteps echo too loudly. "Too clean," she agreed.

They reached the desk together. Jace scanned the area while Savannah reached for the folder, her fingers trembling just slightly.

Inside were a half-dozen photos—surveillance stills of Tyler meeting with someone in the woods. Close-ups of documents. A signature.

V. Kessler.

Cassidy stepped forward, her face drained of colour. "That's my father's private signature," she whispered, pointing to the line at the bottom of the document. "He only uses it for covert contracts. Illegal ones."

Jace's jaw clenched. His voice went flat. "This ties him directly. No plausible deniability. No middlemen to blame."

Savannah stared at the file in her hands, the paper trembling. Her breath caught in her throat. The truth was here—ink on a page. Final. Undeniable.

Her fingers curled around it like a lifeline.

"We have enough," she said, trying to steady her voice. "This… this proves Tyler didn't die for nothing."

She turned toward the exit—

And the warehouse exploded with light.

Cassidy screamed as spotlights ignited overhead, searing-white, and sudden, slicing through the darkness. Shadows vanished. Every escape was now exposed.

From the far corners of the warehouse, men emerged. Four—no, six—dressed in black, tactical, silent but deadly in their precision. Faces obscured, rifles raised. They moved like they'd done this before.

"Move!" Jace shouted, shoving Savannah behind him as he drew his weapon.

A shot rang out. The sharp, deafening crack of a high-calibre round.

Glass shattered above them in a rain of shards.

Jace returned fire, his aim sharp, focused, two shots dropping one of the men to the ground. "Get behind the desk—go!"

Savannah grabbed Cassidy's arm and pulled her hard, heart thundering in her chest as bullets chewed through crates and sheet metal. The warehouse echoed with violence—gunfire, shouting, the high-pitched whine of ricochets.

Then a heavy metal door slammed open near the loading dock. Reinforcements. More boots. More guns.

A choked sob tore from Cassidy's throat. "They knew," she cried. "Oh my God, they knew—"

"Save it!" Savannah yelled, dragging her forward.

She spotted a stairwell to the right, the handle half-broken, the sign above it cracked and tilted. She didn't hesitate. She yanked it open and shoved Cassidy through. "Upstairs—go!"

Their boots pounded up the concrete steps, every breath a stab in the ribs, every turn of the stairwell echoing with the sound of pursuit. Two flights up, Savannah slammed into a rusted metal door. It groaned open under her weight.

They burst into an abandoned office space—windows shattered, furniture overturned, glass crunching underfoot. Mould clung to the walls. The air smelled like rot and dust.

Beyond the broken frame of one window, a fire escape clung to the outside of the building like an afterthought.

Jace turned and kicked the door shut behind them, locking it with a pipe jammed into the hinge.

"We're boxed in," he said, breathing hard.

"No." Savannah crossed the room fast, pointing. "We jump."

Cassidy's eyes went wide. "It's two stories!"

Savannah turned on her, eyes blazing. "Then stay here. See what they do to traitors."

Cassidy blinked—then scrambled for the window, clambering through the jagged glass without another word.

Jace helped her down onto the creaking metal steps, then turned back to Savannah, his voice urgent. "Your turn."

She nodded, adrenaline screaming through her veins, and climbed through the window, boots hitting the platform with a clang.

She was halfway down the second ladder when it happened.

A sharp crack split the air.

Pain tore through her upper arm like fire and lightning. She screamed, her hand flying from the rail, her grip slipping.

She nearly fell.

But instinct—or desperation—took over. Her other hand shot out, clutching the railing just in time.

Blood was already soaking her sleeve, warm and fast.

"Savannah!" Jace's voice cut through the chaos, raw with panic.

She couldn't answer. Couldn't breathe.

Teeth clenched, she forced herself down one rung at a time. Every step sent another jolt of agony through her arm. The world narrowed to pain and metal and the frantic beat of survival.

Her knees buckled as she hit the ground.

Jace caught her, one arm locking around her waist. His hand pressed to her bleeding arm, already slick with red. "You're okay," he said, voice low and fierce, trying to convince them both. "I've got you."

"Not really," she gasped, gritting her teeth. "Feels like someone shot me."

Cassidy was already in the SUV, the engine running, door flung wide, eyes wide with terror. Jace hauled Savannah into the backseat, slammed the door, and threw himself behind the wheel.

Shouts echoed behind them. More gunfire.

The windshield cracked as a bullet slammed into the hood—but they were already peeling away, tyres screaming, gravel spraying behind them like shrapnel.

The warehouse disappeared in the rearview mirror.

So did the light.

So did the men.

But Savannah knew this wasn't over.

Not even close.

Behind them, one of the attackers stepped onto the fire escape and raised a walkie.

"They got out."

A crackle. Then a voice—chillingly calm.

"Doesn't matter. We know where they're going."

They drove in silence—the kind that screamed.

The kind that filled every corner of the cab with things none of them were ready to say.

Outside, dusk clung to the trees like smoke, the sky bleeding from bruised purple to ink. The headlights cut through it in narrow beams, bouncing off gravel and empty road signs as the tyres chewed up miles like a countdown ticking too fast.

Savannah pressed her sweatshirt harder against the wound on her upper arm. Blood trickled steadily, soaking the sweatshirt, warm and sticky against her skin. Each pothole, each rut in the road sent another jolt of agony through her shoulder, but she didn't make a sound.

Didn't wince. Didn't flinch.

She'd bled worse. Felt worse. But this? This felt personal. This felt like they'd stepped into the open too soon.

Beside her, Jace's grip on the steering wheel was locked tight. His knuckles had gone bone-white, the tension winding through him like barbed wire. His jaw was clenched, eyes fixed ahead—but Savannah could see the storm just beneath the surface. Controlled. Contained. Barely.

He hadn't said a word since they'd sped away from the warehouse.

Didn't ask how bad the wound was. Didn't ask if they were followed.

Didn't ask if Cassidy had set them up.

Finally, after what felt like an eternity wrapped in engine hum and heartbeat, his voice cut through the dark.

"You okay?"

Rough. Tight. Like the words hurt to say.

Savannah exhaled slowly, the air hitching with pain she didn't want him to hear. "I've had better days."

That was all she gave him.

It was enough.

In the back seat, Cassidy sat hunched against the door, her eyes locked on the blur of passing trees. Her hoodie was damp with sweat, hands wringing the hem like she could twist her guilt out through the fabric.

"How did they know we were there?" She whispered. "The warehouse—it was supposed to be empty. Unwatched. I swear, I didn't know—"

Savannah turned her head slightly, just enough to catch Cassidy's reflection in the rearview. Her face was paper-white. Her voice? A thread.

"No one's blaming you," Savannah said quickly.

But the lie dropped like lead between them—heavy and sharp-edged. She didn't look at Jace as she said it.

Because she didn't have to.

He still hadn't spoken. Still hadn't looked back. His silence spoke volumes—more than fury, more than accusation.

It was a silence that knew how this worked. That knew betrayal often wore the face of someone begging to help.

Cassidy's eyes filled. She wiped at them with the edge of her sleeve. "I thought I was doing the right thing."

Still, Jace said nothing.

The road curved sharply, and his hands moved with it—precise, controlled—but Savannah saw the way his jaw flexed, like he was biting back everything he wanted to say.

Or maybe, everything he wanted to do.

Savannah shifted, wincing as pain tore through her again. She grit her teeth, lips paling.

Jace's eyes flicked toward her, just for a heartbeat. Just long enough to see the blood now dripping past her elbow, darkening the denim of her jeans.

"We'll be there soon," he muttered. "Five more minutes"

She nodded, jaw tight. "Fine."

Behind them, the warehouse disappeared. But what they'd seen inside—the name, the signature, the betrayal—came with them.

Chapter Seventeen

John was waiting by the time they pulled into the drive; his truck parked at an angle like he'd skidded in sideways and hadn't bothered correcting it. His coat hung open, holster strapped tight across his chest, the wind tugging at the hem like it was trying to pull him back into motion.

He was already halfway to the porch when Jace jumped out and opened the passenger door.

"What the hell happened?" John barked, eyes locking instantly on the blood staining Savannah's sweatshirt.

Cassidy stumbled forward, breathless, panic all over her face. "It was a trap—they knew. We barely made it out. They shot her—"

"Inside," John snapped, cutting her off with a sharp flick of his hand. "Now. All of you."

Savannah didn't argue. Her legs wobbled as she stepped down from the SUV, pain shooting up through her arm like white fire. But she walked anyway—face pale, jaw set in quiet defiance.

Inside the cabin, John cleared the table with one brutal sweep of his arm—papers, cups, a half-finished map scattering to the floor—and gestured for her to sit. He was already pulling a first aid kit from a weathered cabinet; his mouth muttering curses under his breath.

"Hold still," he grunted, grabbing the scissors and slicing through her sleeve. The fabric peeled back sticky with blood. "Through and through. Clean exit." He doused the wound with peroxide. "You're lucky."

Savannah hissed and jerked at the sting, gripping the edge of the table. "Try telling that to my jacket."

Jace stood nearby, pacing the length of the room like a panther in a cage, arms crossed tight, fury radiating off him in waves. His voice was low and controlled—but the edge in it was sharp enough to draw blood.

"That warehouse wasn't just compromised," he said. "It was rigged. They weren't watching from a distance—they were waiting. Armed. Organised. They knew every step before we took it."

John didn't ask how. He didn't have to.

He taped gauze over Savannah's arm and stood, wiping his hands on a rag. His expression was grim. "Then we're done playing defence. It's time we hit back."

He turned sharply to Cassidy. "You said he doesn't keep digital records. What about hard copies? Originals?"

Cassidy nodded, arms wrapped around herself. Her voice was quiet, but there was steel under the fear. "He keeps everything—ledgers, payment schedules, blackmail contracts, even old negatives from photo ops he never released. No computers. No servers. He doesn't trust anything he can't burn in ten seconds."

"Where?" John asked.

Her hesitation was brief—but telling. Then: "Crimson Hill. Our estate. Third floor study. The safe's behind a false panel in the west wall—bookcase, middle shelf. Push in Cicero. Hidden switch."

Jace's bitter laugh was hollow and sharp. "How poetic."

He faced her head-on now, eyes hard. "So, your grand plan is for us to break into the home of a sitting U.S. Senator—your father—who just tried to have us gunned down in a warehouse like rats?"

Cassidy didn't flinch. "Yes. Because that safe holds everything. Evidence. Names. The whole rotten tree, not just the branches." Her voice cracked—but she steadied it. "It's the only shot we have to expose him before he buries us for good."

Savannah pushed herself upright. She was still pale, sweat clinging to her brow, but her voice was solid. Unshaken. "She's right. If we want to end this... we have to take the fight to him. This time, we draw the lines."

John exhaled slowly, the weight of a dozen calculations crossing his face in a single breath. "Then we do it smart. Silent. Surgical. One entry. One team. In and out before security even knows we're on the property."

He looked to Jace. The question was implied—but the answer came anyway, hard, and unyielding.

Jace nodded once. "Try and stop me."

John's eyes narrowed, pleased. "We hit tonight. No delays. No second chances."

And across the room, Savannah's fingers curled around the edge of the table.

They were done running.

Now? They were going hunting.

Later, with the sun bleeding out over the hills in long, slow streaks of gold and bruised purple, Savannah sat curled on the front porch of the cabin, a blanket draped around her like armour she didn't quite believe in. A chipped mug rested between her hands, its contents long gone lukewarm. She hadn't taken a sip.

The air held that strange quiet that doesn't belong to peace—but to waiting. The kind of silence that lives in the seconds before the sky cracks open. A breath held by the world itself.

From inside, muffled voices drifted—John and Cassidy, talking logistics and timelines. Plans for tonight. Risks. Routes. Maybe regrets.

Jace stepped outside without a word, the screen door creaking shut behind him. His boots crunched softly over the old wood planks as he came to stand beside her. He didn't sit at first. Didn't speak. Just watched the tree line like it might move.

Like it would.

"You should be resting," he said finally, voice low and worn around the edges.

"I will," she murmured, eyes still fixed on the horizon. "When this is over."

He didn't argue.

After a pause, he lowered himself beside her—close, but not quite touching. The space between them buzzed with unsaid things. Fear. Guilt. Something older and harder to name.

"I should've seen it coming," he said. "I should've protected you."

She turned then, just enough to look at him. Her hair was a mess, her arm bandaged and tucked close, but her eyes were steady.

"You did."

"I got you shot."

"You got me out."

His jaw flexed. He looked away, down at his hands, fingers twitching like they wanted to ball into fists but didn't quite have the strength.

"I made a call," he said. "And you paid the price."

Savannah reached across the space between them and laced her fingers with his. He tensed—just for a second—then let himself hold on.

"You don't get to carry the weight of every broken thing, Jace," she said gently. "You're not a weapon anymore. You're a man. My man. And you're not alone."

That last word hung in the air between them like a promise she wasn't letting him break.

He turned to her slowly, his expression cracking at the seams. Behind the silence in his eyes was a lifetime of survival—of blood and metal and being used. But here, now, with her, the armour wavered.

And for a moment, he looked like a man trying to believe he was still allowed to feel something like hope.

His voice came quiet. Raw.

"If something happens at Crimson Hill—if I don't—"

Savannah cut him off the only way that mattered.

She leaned in and kissed him.

Not desperate.

Not frantic.

Just real.

Her hand slid up the front of his shirt, fingers curling into the collar like she needed to anchor him. The kiss was soft at first—a question asked in silence. Then deeper, warmer. Surer. A vow passed from mouth to mouth.

I'm still here.

You're not alone.

Jace froze, barely breathing.

Then he moved.

His hands lifted, rough palms cupping her face like she was something sacred, something breakable. And then he kissed her back—slow, intense, threaded with a thousand unsaid things. Grief. Fire. Fear. Devotion. Forgiveness.

The kind of kiss that tasted like old ghosts and new beginnings.

The kind that said I would burn down the world for you.

When they finally pulled apart, neither of them moved far. Savannah's forehead dropped gently against his, and her hand stayed fisted in his shirt like letting go might make this moment vanish.

Her breath brushed his lips when she whispered, "No more goodbyes."

Jace closed his eyes. Let the promise settle in his chest like something worth bleeding for.

His voice was steady this time. Certain.

"Then we make it count."

And in the space between heartbeats, they both understood.

Tonight wasn't about vengeance anymore.

It was about survival.

And love.

And the kind of war worth waging—for each other.

Somewhere far away, in a room wrapped in shadows and silence, Senator Vaughn Kessler poured himself a drink.

The scotch caught the light from the fireplace behind him—amber and slow, sliding into crystal like liquid spite. He didn't rush it. He never did. Power, after all, was best wielded by those who never seemed hurried.

Outside, the wind whispered against the tall windows, but inside, everything was still. Too still. Like the room itself knew better than to breathe in his presence.

Kessler stood with his back to the door, his silhouette framed by floor-to-ceiling glass. Beyond the pane, the estate stretched out across Crimson Hill— manicured gardens, rolling lawns, perimeter lights already blinking to life as dusk deepened into something heavier. The house gleamed gold against the darkening sky. Regal. Untouchable.

He lifted the glass to his lips, sipped once, and exhaled like a man enjoying the calm before the kill.

The door behind him creaked open.

He didn't turn.

"He told me they were coming for me," Kessler said, his voice a low, effortless command. "Tell security we could have visitors tonight."

The man who entered nodded once—no words, just obedience—and disappeared into the shadows as quickly as he'd come.

Kessler remained at the window; eyes fixed on the estate below. One hand cradled the glass, the other tucked neatly into his pocket. The weight of the silence around him was absolute.

Then, softly—like a snake uncoiling—he spoke.

"Let them come."

His reflection stared back at him in the glass: composed, cold, and entirely in control.

He took another sip of scotch; let it burn down slow.

"It's time they remembered who holds the leash."

A faint smile ghosted across his lips. Not amused. Not pleased.

Predatory.

Because he wasn't planning to run.

He was planning to hunt.

The gates of Crimson Hill loomed ahead—tall, black wrought iron laced with gilded initials, flanked by manicured hedges sculpted to brutal perfection. Two stone lions crouched atop marble pedestals, their mouths twisted in permanent snarls, as if daring anyone to trespass. Beyond the gates, the estate rose like a crown set into the bluff—sharp angles, towering columns, windows glowing faintly in the dark like watchful eyes. Regal. Imposing. Dangerous.

Jace eased Cassidy's SUV to a crawl, then killed the headlights and pulled off the private road, tucking them behind a dense line of trees where the shadows swallowed them whole. The engine ticked quietly as it cooled, a soft metallic exhale in a night otherwise suffocating with silence.

He stared through the windshield for a long moment; eyes fixed on the estate. Then he let out a slow breath.

"Last chance to turn around."

Savannah didn't even look at him. "Say that one more time and I'll hit you."

Cassidy, sitting in the backseat, leaned forward, pulling her hair into a tight ponytail. Her usual polished veneer was gone. No makeup. No earrings. Her designer heels had been left, replaced with black boots scuffed from years in the back of a closet. She wore a faded hoodie, two sizes too big, the sleeves shoved to her elbows. The senator's daughter was gone. What remained was something harder. Sharper. Stripped down to truth and loyalty—and a kind of quiet rage that hadn't fully taken shape.

"I know the layout," she said, her voice low but steady. "There's a side staff entrance behind the east wing. It's hidden by hedges, leads straight to the old wine cellar. From there, we go up through the laundry chute. It was sealed on the upper levels, but the west wing shaft was never closed off—my father forgot it existed. It opens just outside the hall that leads to his study."

She paused, glancing between them. "The safe's behind the third shelf in the built-in bookcase. You push the spine of Cicero. That unlocks it."

Jace blinked once. "Fancy."

Savannah checked the Glock John had handed her earlier, chambering a round with smooth precision. The metal snapped home with a sound that somehow echoed louder than it should have.

John hadn't come. If he got involved, the defence could argue unlawful entry by law enforcement. So, it was just the three of them. No badges. No backup. Just trust and necessity.

"Let's hope his ego hasn't changed his system."

Cassidy nodded. "Once we have the files—what's the plan?"

Savannah's tone was flat. "We expose him. No deals. No leaks. Full sunlight."

Jace's voice followed, darker. "We survive."

Cassidy met their eyes, a flicker of nerves in her expression. "And if something goes wrong?"

Jace checked his sidearm again, fingers moving with quiet finality. "Then you run. Don't wait for us. Don't be a hero. You run, and you don't look back."

Savannah looked at him then, something sharp and protective sparking in her eyes. "That includes you."

Jace held her gaze for a long second. "We'll see."

The moment stretched—unspoken things balanced on the edge—then broke.

All three slipped out of the SUV, doors clicking shut with barely a sound. The gravel crunched under their boots, muffled and deliberate. Savannah took the lead, her frame taut with purpose, pistol tight in both hands. Jace fell in at her side, silent and steady. Cassidy followed, steps quick but silent, her breath visible in the cooling air.

Above them, clouds crept across the moon like spilled ink, swallowing the light. Wind whispered through the trees—low and cold. The kind of wind that warned. The kind that carried stories of blood.

They approached the iron gates from the far edge where the fence was weakest—Cassidy's old shortcut from when sneaking out was her biggest crime. A hollowed-out section of hedge and a warped patch of fencing gave way to a narrow path.

Savannah ducked first, heart hammering.

Every step forward felt like a countdown.

Each second heavier than the last.

Somewhere inside that estate, a monster was waiting.

And this time—they were walking straight into its den.

Time to end it.

Chapter Eighteen

They crept through the tall hedge in single file, Cassidy leading the way. The trees thinned as they neared the edge of the estate, revealing the house in full—a sprawling colonial fortress of brick and glass, three stories high and impossibly wide, perched on the bluff like it owned the sky. Its windows glowed faintly behind sheer curtains—soft golden eyes, watching. Waiting.

Savannah's breath caught in her throat.

The Kessler estate wasn't just intimidating. It was theatrical. Built for power. A place designed to make you feel small—and remember it.

"Security cameras," Jace murmured, eyes scanning the perimeter. "Northwest corner. South tower. Front gate. Thermal rig on the east balcony."

Cassidy nodded grimly. "He upgraded after Tyler died. Paranoia makes for a hell of a contractor."

Jace raised a hand, signalling them to stop. From his jacket, he pulled John's compact jammer and flipped the switch. The device came to life with a faint hum, its small screen glowing green.

"Fifteen minutes of scrambled footage," he whispered. "That's all we get."

Cassidy glanced at her watch. "We won't get a second chance."

They moved.

The staff entrance was nestled behind a row of thick camellia hedges, almost invisible in the dark. It sat wedged between the shuttered greenhouse and the servant's quarters—an afterthought in architecture, but now, their only way in. Cassidy stepped forward and punched in a childhood code: 3-1-7-6. Her parents' wedding date.

The lock clicked.

Inside, the air shifted.

The scent hit Savannah like a memory—leather polish, cut flowers, cold marble. It was a curated kind of smell. Expensive. Masculine. Measured. Like power had a cologne.

The hallway was dim, lined with portraits of Kesslers through the generations—cloaked in pearls and pressed suits, their smiles smug and controlled. Gold frames, soft carpets, and quiet menace.

"This place gives me the creeps," Jace muttered under his breath.

Cassidy didn't answer.

She led them through a discreet side door and down a narrow staircase that spiralled beneath the house. Stone walls. Damp air. The temperature dropped with each step.

They reached the wine cellar.

Massive. Immaculate. Bottles arranged in obsessive rows, everything labelled and temperature-controlled. An antique tasting table stood to the side, flanked by leather chairs no one had used in years.

"This way," Cassidy said, moving quickly to the far wall.

She shoved aside a dusty rack half-obscured by crates of vintage cabernet. Behind it: a rust-rimmed laundry chute, tall and narrow, its mouth yawning like a throat.

Jace squinted. "You're kidding."

Cassidy arched a brow. "Welcome to the aristocracy."

Savannah gave a small, breathless grin. "Ladies first?"

Jace sighed. "If I see a spider, I'm blaming both of you."

He hoisted himself up.

The metal groaned beneath his weight. Every creak echoed like a warning in the narrow shaft. One by one, they climbed into the dark, pressing their bodies into cold, gritty walls. The air smelled of dust, old fabric, forgotten history.

With every pull upward, they slipped deeper into the house's bones—into the belly of a legacy built on secrets, silence, and blood.

They emerged into the west wing hallway, breathless and coated in cobwebs. The carpet beneath their boots was plush, muffling every step. Ornate sconces cast warm light along the corridor. The portraits here were even older—founding fathers, senators, judges. Their eyes followed. Silent. Condemning.

Cassidy didn't flinch. She led them forward, each step faster now.

They stopped at a heavy wooden door.

"The study," she whispered.

It was locked.

Cassidy crouched, pulled a slender pin from her waistband, and set to work. Her hands were steady. Her face was stone.

Savannah tightened her grip on the Glock. Jace turned his back to them, scanning the hallway, body tight with tension.

Click.

The door creaked open.

The study looked ripped from a royal dossier. Floor-to-ceiling shelves, deep mahogany panelling, an enormous Persian rug underfoot. A black marble fireplace gleamed at the far end, empty and immaculate. No warmth here—just display. Authority. Power.

A massive oak desk commanded the room like a throne. Behind it, the bookcase wall was too perfect.

Cassidy moved toward it with quiet certainty.

"Fourth shelf down. Fifth book from the left."

She reached for a leather-bound legal volume. Cicero.

She pushed.

Click.

The hidden panel slid open.

Behind it: a safe. Steel. Old-school. Manual dial.

Cassidy froze. "He changed it."

Jace cursed softly. "We don't have time for trial and error."

Savannah stepped forward. "Try your mom's birthday."

Cassidy blinked. "Why would he—?"

"Because he's arrogant. And sentimental. It's what I'd use."

Cassidy hesitated. Then turned the dial. "Zero-seven. One-two."

Click.

The safe opened.

Inside: Hell.

Files. USB drives. Bank ledgers. Surveillance photos. Hard copies. Every dirty secret kept like trophies. Payoffs. Kill orders. Evidence that could burn half the statehouse to the ground.

Savannah's voice caught. "This is it."

Jace was already stuffing everything into his pack.

"We're done. Let's mo—"

The lights snapped on.

The room froze.

A slow, deliberate clap echoed through the space, sharp as a shot.

They turned.

Senator Vaughn Kessler stood in the doorway, flanked by two armed guards.

He wore a tailored midnight-blue suit, his cuffs gleaming with gold. A pistol dangled loosely in his hand like a glass of wine at a dinner party. His smile didn't reach his eyes.

"Well done, Cassidy," he said, voice velvet-wrapped and venom-laced. "You brought them right to me."

Cassidy's face twisted—shock, confusion, betrayal.

"No," she breathed. "I didn't—I didn't know—"

Kessler tsked. "Of course you did." He stepped forward, slow, casual. "You always were predictable. Emotional. Weak. It's in your blood just like your mother."

Cassidy's eyes burned. "Go to hell."

Kessler smiled wider. "I've already built it."

Jace stepped forward, gun steady, voice low and lethal.

"Don't."

Kessler didn't flinch. If anything, he smiled—cold and knowing.

"Do you really think I'd leave something this valuable unguarded?"

He gave a small, deliberate nod.

One of the guards surged forward, grabbing Cassidy by the arm and yanking her down hard. She hit the floor hard, her hoodie snagging on the rug. The second guard swept his weapon across the room like a pendulum; eyes locked on Savannah.

Savannah's voice cracked through the air like a whip.

"Let her go."

But Kessler didn't look at her. His attention was locked on Jace with a predator's focus, lips curling into something that might've passed for a grin if it hadn't been carved from ice.

"You know," he said smoothly, almost amused, "I tried to have you killed in prison. Three times."

He tilted his head. "You just wouldn't die."

Jace's mouth twisted into a smile as cold as the steel in his hands.

"Sorry to disappoint."

Kessler's voice turned darker, meaner.

"I should've finished you myself."

"I'm right here," Jace said.

The air between them vibrated with tension—two men forged in fire, standing in the ruins of what they'd survived. One built on ambition and control. The other on pain and resolve. A hammer and a scalpel, sharpened to destroy.

Kessler finally turned to Savannah, his gaze glinting with something cruel and close to admiration.

"Tyler was a fool. I told him to back off. Let things settle. But no. He had to play the hero."

He gave a careless shrug. "He was going to destroy everything I built."

Savannah's breath caught. Her grip tightened on the Glock until her knuckles ached.

"You killed him," she whispered.

Kessler exhaled, unbothered.

"He gave me no choice."

Her voice cracked. "And me? Are you going to kill me too?"

Kessler raised his gun, levelling it at her chest with terrifying calm.

"Of course, I am. And Jace will take the fall—just like he did for your brother. You were warned, Savannah. But like Tyler, you don't know when to quit."

In a heartbeat, Jace moved—stepping in front of her, shielding her with his body. His gun came up fast, steady, unwavering.

His voice was low but lethal.

"Try it."

"Move," Kessler barked, tone losing its cool.

Jace didn't move. "You'll have to shoot through me."

Kessler narrowed his eyes. His lip curled.

"You'd die for her?"

Jace's voice was guttural. Final.

"I already did."

Kessler pulled the trigger—

Click.

Silence.

Just the cold, empty sound of a firing pin meeting nothing. A mechanical betrayal.

Jace lunged.

The room exploded.

Cassidy screamed, scrambling behind the desk as bullets tore into the shelves. Leather-bound books erupted into clouds of paper and splinters. A globe shattered against the far wall. Smoke curled through the air like breath escaping from the house itself.

Jace slammed into Kessler with all his weight, driving him backward. They hit the desk hard—wood groaning, pens scattering, drawers spilling open. Kessler's pistol skidded across the polished floor and disappeared beneath a chair.

Jace landed a punch. Bone crunched. Blood sprayed.

One of the guards turned, gun raised—

Savannah fired.

One shot, centre mass.

The second tore through his chest.

He collapsed without a sound.

The last guard bolted, footsteps retreating into the dark hallway beyond.

"Savannah!" Cassidy shouted from behind the desk. "The files!"

Savannah rushed forward, grabbing everything she could—folders, flash drives, ledgers—shoving them back into the duffel like it was the last lifeboat on a sinking ship.

Across the room, Jace had Kessler by the collar. The senator's nose was shattered, blood leaking freely. His face, once pristine and polished, was wrecked. Human. Beatable.

Jace slammed him into the bookcase.

"Let's see how you like a prison cell."

Kessler spat blood. "You think this ends with me?"

His voice rasped with venom. "You think I'm the only one?"

"No," Jace said. "But it starts with you."

Cassidy appeared beside him, panting.

"We need to go. Now. They'll send more."

"Help me with the bag," Savannah said, already moving.

Jace shoved Kessler down. The air rushed from his lungs in a grunt. He twisted, trying to rise, but Jace flipped him onto his stomach and yanked his arms behind his back.

"Hold still," he snarled.

Cassidy ripped a curtain cord from the nearest window and tossed it over. Jace caught it, wrapped it twice, then knotted it hard enough to bite into skin.

Kessler writhed. Blood in his mouth. Rage in his eyes.

"You'll regret this," he spat. "Every one of you. You don't know who you're dealing with."

Savannah stepped over him, calm and merciless.

"Maybe," she said. "But not tonight."

Jace hauled the senator upright.

"Move."

They fled the study down the hall—Cassidy with the bag, Jace dragging Kessler, Savannah watching their six—vanishing down the corridors of a house built on lies, now shaking under the weight of its truth.

Behind them, the once-imposing study lay in ruin. Books torn apart. Chairs overturned. Blood soaked into the rug like ink. The scent of gunpowder and fire lingered, a funeral dirge for power gone unchecked.

Ahead of them—sirens. Lights. The sound of a city waking up.

And for the first time in a decade… the future.

Chapter Nineteen

They ran.

Through the corridors of power turned battlefield—alarms screaming like sirens of the damned, crimson strobes slicing the dark, casting their shadows like ghosts that refused to stay buried. Footsteps thundered behind them. Muffled commands barked through radio static. A voice shouted for containment. For blood.

Cassidy led the charge, her breath ragged, her grip white-knuckled around the duffel that now weighed as much as guilt. Hard drives. Ledgers. Contracts soaked in silent screams. Every step sounded too loud. Every second they stayed alive felt stolen.

Jace dragged Kessler behind him, the senator stumbling, snarling, his designer suit smeared with blood and dirt. Power didn't look good on its knees.

Savannah brought up the rear, the Glock raised, sweeping every corner, every shadow. Her heart was a drumbeat inside her throat. The air was thick with smoke and adrenaline, and her limbs trembled with the memory of gunfire.

They burst through the staff entrance like fugitives in a dream. The cold slapped them across the face, raw and real. Breath steamed in the air. Their boots crashed through frost and brittle leaves, louder than they dared.

The woods didn't offer comfort. Only cover.

Branches clawed at them. The wind keened. The estate loomed behind them, monstrous and sprawling, silhouetted against the blood-orange sky like a relic of greed and rot.

The SUV waited where they left it—dark, cold, loyal.

Jace yanked the rear door open and shoved Kessler inside like a sack of garbage. "Lie down. Move, and I'll put you down."

Kessler coughed, blood flecking his lip. "You don't have the guts."

Jace met his eyes—flat, grey, unreadable. "I've got nothing but guts left."

He slammed the door shut so hard the frame shuddered.

Savannah slid into the passenger seat, hands trembling, chest rising and falling like a wave breaking over and over. Cassidy dove into the back, breath ragged, eyes wide and shining with everything she couldn't say. She slammed the evidence at her feet like it burned.

Jace climbed into the driver's seat, blood trailing from a cut at his temple. He didn't speak. Didn't look back. He turned the key.

The engine roared.

Tyres screamed against gravel. Dust kicked up behind them like ghosts trying to claw them back. They tore down the winding drive just as sirens crested the ridge—wailing like the death cry of an empire finally choking on its secrets.

No one spoke.

Not for miles.

The silence inside the SUV was louder than the storm they'd left behind. It filled every corner, every broken breath, every unspoken fear. Savannah's fingers curled around the Glock, resting it in her lap like it might still be needed. Her other hand never left the duffel bag. The weight of it was heavy, not just with proof—but with consequence.

Then, her phone lit up. John.

She answered. "We're out."

"Do you have it?" he asked, voice tight.

She looked down at the bag. "All of it. Every name. Every file. Every lie."

A long pause. The kind that held more history than words.

"And the senator?"

Her gaze shifted to the rearview mirror. Kessler sat hunched, hands tied and glaring. No more smugness. No more speeches. Just bruises, blood, and a silence that said everything.

"We have him too," she said.

Another pause. Then, John's voice, quieter now: "Good. It's over."

But Savannah didn't say anything. Because she wasn't sure it was.

They reached the sheriff's office just after dawn.

The horizon split open in streaks of grey and gold, the kind of morning that felt borrowed from another world. A quieter one. The kind that comes just before the world changes—or breaks.

Kessler was hauled from the vehicle by two deputies. He didn't fight, but he didn't falter either. He walked like a man still trying to pretend the crown was on his head.

As he passed Savannah, their eyes locked.

No words.

He didn't deserve them.

Inside, the evidence was logged. Bagged. Sealed behind glass and chain of command. Thousands of pages of corruption, cruelty, silence, stretching back more than a decade. Each file a loaded gun aimed at the old guard. Savannah signed her name beside every folder like she was writing the last chapter of someone else's reign.

Cassidy stood beside her, arms folded tight across her chest. Her eyes were swollen with exhaustion. Her mouth pressed thin, like if she said one word, she'd fall apart.

"They'll come for this," she said. "Lawyers. Media. Favours owed. He'll try to bury it all."

Savannah's gaze was still fixed on the hallway where Kessler had been taken.

"Let him," she said.

Cassidy turned to her. "You think he'll talk?"

Savannah's jaw clenched. "I hope he does. Because this time—we're the ones watching."

Behind them, Jace stood shoulder to shoulder with John, the older man's hand gripping his arm like anchor and comfort. Jace's shirt was torn, blood staining the collar, but his posture was iron. He didn't fidget. Didn't flinch.

He was no longer running from the past.

He was the reckoning.

When Savannah turned, their eyes met. He didn't speak. He just reached for her hand.

It was bloodstained. Shaking.

She took it anyway.

"We did it," he said.

She looked at him, eyes shadowed with fire, voice low.

"No. We survived it."

A beat passed between them. Quiet. Not empty. A silence filled with everything they hadn't said, and everything they no longer had to.

And in that fragile dawn, with justice finally in their hands, Savannah let herself believe that maybe—just maybe—survival could be enough to start again.

The world felt like it had been cracked open—jagged and raw, edges sharp enough to draw blood, with no promise of repair or rest.

Savannah stood on the courthouse steps, the morning sun stabbing through the heat haze, relentless and unyielding. The flashbulbs exploded like lightning, each burst searing an imprint behind her eyelids. Reporters swarmed behind barricades—an ocean of faces, voices, questions, each more invasive than the last, their microphones thrust forward like spears.

"...Did you believe Jace Calloway was innocent of killing your brother?"

"...Did you know about Senator Kessler's connection to money laundering?"

"...Was your brother investigating him before his death?"

"...Are you and Jace Calloway romantically involved?"

The questions came fast, bullets fired in rapid succession, the noise a tide rising, threatening to drown her. Words bled into each other, a fractured chorus of accusation and curiosity. The glare of cameras pressed down like a furnace, heat and scrutiny burning through her skin.

But Savannah did not flinch. Not this time. Not when the weight of everything she'd lost—and everything she'd won—was balanced on a knife's edge.

She did not answer. Could not. Her throat tightened into a constriction, heartbeat drumming deafeningly in her ears. Every breath was deliberate, every moment a test of will.

Then, like a sudden calm in the storm, Jace stepped forward, sliding quietly beside her. His presence wrapped around her—not to shield her from the storm, but to steady her within it. A quiet strength anchored in his steady gaze and the firm touch of his hand settling gently at her lower back.

He didn't rise to the bait, didn't snap back at the questions. He just stood there, calm, and unshakable—a man stripped of pretence, with nothing left to hide and everything left to protect.

Slowly, he guided her down the steps, each footfall carrying them away from the chaos. The crowd's roar faded into a distant thunder; the flashing lights dimmed to a soft glow. Inside, the storm quieted, leaving a hollow silence that filled the space between them.

The waiting black car promised sanctuary. The moment the doors closed, the cacophony vanished, replaced by a heavy, welcome silence—a curtain falling, closing the world out.

Cassidy sat curled in the far seat, posture rigid, face a mask of porcelain smoothness. Her eyes, dark and weary, met Savannah's with a depth that spoke of nights spent wrestling ghosts.

"I thought I'd feel relief," she murmured, voice brittle like dry glass. "Like I could finally breathe again."

Savannah leaned forward, voice low, coaxing. "But?"

Cassidy looked away, her gaze distant, hollow. "Instead, I just feel... empty. Like something's been ripped away—something I didn't even know I was holding onto. Like I tore off the bandage too fast, and all that's left underneath is raw bone."

Savannah's fingers pressed to her temple as a slow, aching pulse bloomed behind her eyes. "That's what the truth feels like sometimes. It doesn't free you at first. It empties you. Strips you bare. Before it lets you breathe."

Jace said nothing. He sat in the shadows beside them, jaw clenched tight, eyes fixed on the window as if searching for a way out—or perhaps a way forward. His breaths were shallow, measured. He hadn't exhaled since they left the courthouse steps.

Savannah reached across the seat, her hand brushing against his. He looked down, startled by the contact, then met her eyes—steady, raw, honest.

No words were needed. Not now.

Behind them lay the shattered remnants of their past—the lies, the pain, the secrets.

Ahead, the world was watching.

Whatever came next, they would face it side by side.

Not fugitives anymore.

Not just survivors.

But something stronger.

Something forged in fire and tempered by loss.

And finally—free.

Chapter Twenty

The last twenty-four hours since Crimson Hill blurred past them like a storm they barely survived—interviews, interrogations, relentless meetings with lawyers and officials. There hadn't been a single quiet moment. No space to breathe. No chance to just be.

Now, the cabin wrapped around them like a cocoon—steeped in a golden hush that felt sacred after the chaos. The kind of stillness that pressed down with weight but also offered fragile refuge.

Outside, the wind whispered softly through the pines, carrying secrets from afar. Inside, John dropped a battered cardboard pizza box onto the rough-hewn wooden table, then followed with a tray of gas station coffee, his grimace telling them everything. "Don't thank me," he muttered, voice heavy with exhaustion. "It's cold and probably poison."

No one moved to argue.

John sank into a chair with a long, weary sigh, rubbing the back of his neck as if trying to knead the tension out of his bones. "The Feds have the drives. The media's looping the footage like it's the trailer for some damn justice thriller. Kessler's donors are bailing faster than rats off a sinking ship. At least three investigations will be official by morning."

Jace stood by the window, arms crossed, his silhouette framed by the dying light fading into dusk. He didn't turn.

"It's a start," he said quietly.

John's eyes flicked toward him; scepticism and hope tangled in the glance. "You'll be cleared. Officially. The governor's prepping a statement. Says he wants to 'restore public faith in the justice system.'"

He snorted, bitter. "Like he wasn't first to throw you to the wolves."

Jace's voice was low but sharp, stripped of anger, layered with fatigue. "Too little. Too late."

It wasn't bitterness. It was a deep, weary kind of exhaustion—the kind that didn't come from sleepless nights, but years of clawing just to stay afloat.

Savannah sat on the worn couch, knees pulled to her chest, watching him quietly. He hadn't truly exhaled since Crimson Hill. Not even when Kessler's cuffs clicked shut. Not even when the press turned their cameras away. He had won. But the war had carved deep trenches in him, scars hidden beneath his skin.

John looked between them, then stood slowly. "You two should talk," he said softly, voice low with regret—or maybe a flicker of hope. "You earned this. Don't waste it."

Then, quieter still: "Some of us never got the chance."

He grabbed his coat and left, the door closing with a gentle finality.

Cassidy lingered for a moment, her hand brushing Savannah's arm. "I'll go with him. Give you space."

Savannah nodded. Cassidy left without another word, the door clicking shut behind her.

The cabin sank into silence, painted in the amber hush of twilight.

Jace still hadn't moved from the window.

Outside, the light faded to silver-grey, the trees casting long, skeletal shadows. His reflection in the glass looked back at him—a man carved from pain, remade in rage, now hollowed by something dangerously close to hope.

Behind him, Savannah stood near the fireplace, arms wrapped tightly across her chest, as if holding herself together from the inside out.

"You've barely looked at me since yesterday," she said quietly.

His shoulders stiffened. "I've been… processing."

She let out a brittle laugh—thin, sharp, a cracked veneer on fragile skin. "Processing? You were willing to die for me. But now you can't even look me in the eye?"

He turned just enough for her to see the storm raging in his eyes.

"You think that was easy? Watching him raise a gun at you—knowing that might be the end?"

"I lived it too, Jace," she said, voice trembling but fierce. "Don't pretend you were the only one bleeding."

He winced but held his silence. The space between them stretched wide—a fault line waiting to fracture.

"I know you should hate me," she whispered. "For walking away. For not believing you when it counted."

"I didn't blame you for thinking I was guilty."

"But I do," she said, voice raw. "I blame me. Every single day."

His jaw clenched, muscles tight with unshed words. "So, what happens now? I go back to a life I barely survived—and you go back to a name soaked in blood and lies?"

Her eyes burned with quiet fire, voice steady. "Is that really what you think I care about? My name?"

"No," he admitted, bitterness low and bitter. "I think you care about safety. About control. About always having a way out. And I'm not safe. I never was."

She crossed the room, stopping just a breath away from him.

"You're wrong."

He didn't move.

"You're not the boy they locked up. And you're not the man they tried to break. You're the one who stood between me and a bullet. You're the one who brought down a monster. You didn't run, Jace. You stayed."

His voice cracked, barely a whisper. "I still have blood on my hands."

"So do I."

That truth settled like a stone between them—heavy, undeniable. But it didn't crush them.

"I believed the lies because they felt safer," she confessed. "I held everyone at arm's length, thinking that was the way to survive."

He finally looked at her—really looked.

"But you let me in."

"Not enough," she whispered. "Not when it mattered most."

His shoulders sagged with the weight of it all. "I don't know how to be what you need."

"You don't have to be anything," she said gently, placing her hand over his chest, over his heart. "Just stay."

He blinked, caught off guard. "Stay?"

She nodded. "With me."

He hesitated—the long pause of someone learning how to hope again.

"I don't know if I deserve that."

"I do," she said. "And I want you. Not as a second chance. As the choice I should've made all along."

Then she reached up, her fingertips curling gently behind his neck, pulling him closer as if she could anchor herself in this moment forever. When their lips met, it was not a desperate grasp for lost time, nor an apology whispered in the dark. It was a kiss forged in quiet certainty—a vow spoken without words.

It was a choice.

Choosing each other. Still. Now. Always.

The kiss carried everything they hadn't dared say aloud—love, yes, but deeper still: trust born from shared scars, survival woven through every breath, the fierce ache of belonging finally claimed. This wasn't the fire of passion that burned and consumed. It was the slow, steady glow of something real, something rebuilt from ruins.

He cupped her face with reverence, as if memorising the softness of her skin, the curve of her cheek, the tremble beneath his touch. His thumbs traced light paths, gentle where the world had been anything but. Savannah leaned in, deepening the kiss, her breath hitching, their bodies aligning in a slow, deliberate rhythm. There was no rush—only the sacred stillness of knowing.

Her hands slid up into his thick hair, fingers threading into the nape of his neck, holding tight, seeking anchor. He kissed her again—softer this time—as if relearning the taste of hope itself. His mouth traced down to her jaw, her throat, warm breath fanning over skin that fluttered beneath his lips. Savannah's hands roamed over his chest, slipping beneath the hem of his shirt, hungry for skin, warmth, truth.

He undressed her without haste, eyes locked on hers—silent questions in every brush of knuckles along her ribs, every slow uncovering of skin. She answered with soft sighs, steady gaze unwavering. Her own hands moved with trembling need across his body, not frantic, but claiming—curious and raw with desire and reverence.

They sank onto the bed in a tangle of limbs and whispered breaths, the covers bunching beneath them like a nest woven from every hard-fought battle they'd survived. Jace laid her down as though placing something sacred, hands mapping her like a constellation charted by a traveller finally home—ribs, hips, thighs—each touch a quiet prayer, an ache made flesh.

His mouth followed the map—collarbone, the swell of her breast, the softness of her stomach—each kiss a confession, a promise. She arched toward him, breath hitching, every movement a dance of discovery, not conquest. It was a homecoming.

When she pulled him closer, it was more than want. It was surrender. A trembling, conscious yes.

Their bodies moved in a slow, molten rhythm—tender, earned, alive. Savannah's fingers clawed at his shoulders, nails pressing into flesh as her body opened, welcomed, and held on like she had waited a lifetime for this moment.

Every breath was a vow. Every touch, a remembering. Every heartbeat, a resurrection.

They spoke no words. They needed none.

Their love lived in the language of skin, in the fierce hold after the storm passed—tight, unyielding, a silent promise that letting go was impossible.

Afterward, Savannah rested her head against his chest, her hair spilling over him like a sigh finally released. His arm curled around her, strong and protective. His thumb moved in slow, lazy circles along her spine, grounding them both.

The cabin breathed around them, its quiet vast and full.

For the first time in a long time, Savannah did not feel like she was falling.

He pressed a gentle kiss to the crown of her head, voice thick with sleep and something softer still. "Still with me?"

She kissed the spot just over his heart, where steady beats pulsed beneath her lips.

A smile touched her mouth, soft and real. "Always."

And for the first time, always wasn't a fragile hope whispered into the dark.

It was something real.

Something worth fighting for.

Something they might actually get to keep.

Neither spoke again. They didn't have to.

For once, the silence wasn't a threat.

It wasn't loss, regret, or abandonment.

It was rest.

It was peace.

Savannah drifted to sleep like that—warm, held, finally safe.

And in her dreams, Tyler was there.

Standing barefoot on the edge of a sun-warmed dock, the light catching his grin—bright and easy—the same way it used to be when summer stretched ahead, endless, and untouched.

He was happy.

And so was she.

Chapter Twenty-One

The next morning, they returned to the farmhouse. No more hiding. No more running. It was time to come home.

Jace moved with steady determination, carrying their belongings into the house—his bag slung over one shoulder, hers tucked firmly beneath his arm. The worn leather straps creaked softly, the only sound in the quiet morning. Savannah trailed behind, her steps slower, drawn by a pull she couldn't resist— the ancient oak tree that stood sentinel just beyond the back porch.

The early light poured across the land in waves of gold, the sun inching higher and stretching shadows long and lean over the dew-soaked grass. Everything around her was still, reverent—as if the earth itself was holding its breath, waiting for a new chapter to begin.

The tree was as steadfast as ever. Tall and weathered, its thick, gnarled branches reached skyward like arms embracing the morning light. Deep, knotted roots curled beneath the soil, gripping the earth with an unspoken promise of endurance, a tether to a past that neither time nor sorrow could sever.

This tree had seen everything.

It had borne witness to storms that had raged, and quiet days bathed in sunlight. It stood firm through heartbreak and hope alike. It had watched Tyler teach her to climb, his laughter ringing through the air as she clung to branches with trembling hands. It had sheltered her and Jace in the secret place where they had shared their first kiss beneath its sprawling leaves. It had held space for her grief when she returned from the funeral, chest tight, breath shallow, unable to face the world.

It had even seen the day Jace was taken—handcuffed, fighting for his innocence.

And now, the oak stood witness again. Not to a girl fleeing shadows, but a woman stepping forward—scarred, stronger, alive.

Savannah reached out, her palm grazing the rough bark. It was cool under her fingers, solid and unwavering. The touch grounded her—anchored her to something enduring beyond pain and loss.

This tree had cradled two childhoods beneath its branches. It had kept their secrets safe—comic books hidden inside a rusted tin box, notes folded and tucked away, petty dreams and whispered promises etched like invisible scars in its bark. And it had endured—still here long after Tyler was gone.

She knelt in the grass, feeling the dampness seep into her jeans, cool against her skin. In her hand was a folded newspaper, its edges softened and worn from being opened and read over and over. The headline stared back at her, stark and undeniable:

KESSLER IN CUFFS: POLITICAL GIANT FALLS.

Her fingers trembled as she opened the old tin box nestled among the roots. The comics that had once lived inside were gone, claimed by years and weather, but the hollow remained—a hollow carved by memory.

Carefully, she laid the newspaper inside.

Then, from her coat pocket, she pulled out a second item—a worn, creased photograph.

Her and Tyler, side by side.

He was in his graduation robe, grinning, his arm slung around her shoulders like he had the whole world ahead of him—and so had she.

She remembered that day. The pride in her chest so big it barely fit behind her smile.

Now, she stared down at the image, the years folding in around her like mist.

Then, gently, she laid it beside the newspaper.

With slow, deliberate hands, she gathered a scoop of soil—soft, fragrant, forgiving—and covered them both.

Not to forget.

But to remember, in a different way.

"I'm sorry," she whispered, voice fragile, breaking like a thread pulled too tight. "I should've seen it sooner. I should've known something was wrong."

A gentle breeze stirred the leaves overhead, soft as a breath against her cheek.

"And I forgive you," she said, throat tight with the effort it took. "For leaving me. For trusting the wrong people. For not saying goodbye."

She closed the tin, smoothing the earth over it, her hands resting lightly on the ground—a silent prayer, an offering.

She stayed there a long moment, waiting for the ache inside to quiet, to settle into something bearable.

A warm hand rested gently on her shoulder.

She didn't startle. She knew without looking who it was.

Jace stood behind her—solid and silent—the wind tugging at the edges of his jacket, the soft light catching the quiet truth in his steady eyes.

"You okay?" he asked softly.

Savannah rose, brushing soil from her jeans. She didn't answer immediately.

Her gaze drifted back to the oak, then to the farmhouse—its windows catching the morning light, promising safety once more. Then she looked at Jace, the man who had walked through fire with her, who bore scars like badges of survival, not defeat.

"I think…" she began, drawing in a deep breath. "I'm ready to stop surviving."

He studied her, cautious but hopeful. "And start living?"

She nodded, feeling the warmth of possibility seep into her bones.

"With you."

A slow, relieved smile spread across his face—not triumphant, but soft, like the first quiet dawn after a long, dark night.

He reached for her hand.

She didn't hesitate.

She took it.

Together, they turned toward the future—not perfect, not unscarred, but theirs.

The next morning, Savannah and Jace lay wrapped in the hush that followed lovemaking—legs tangled beneath thin summer sheets, skin warm and slick from the heat they'd made together. The quiet between them was gentle, almost sacred, a fragile pause after so much storm.

The window stood open, inviting in the soft breath of dawn. A warm breeze stirred the curtains, lifting them like whispers, carrying the scent of dew-soaked earth and the rustle of leaves. Somewhere beyond the trees, the steady hum of crickets began—a lullaby only the wilderness knew how to sing.

Lavender from the garden drifted in, sweet and heady, weaving through the subtle mix of sweat, skin, and something quieter. Something softer. Something that smelled like home.

Savannah curled against Jace's chest, her fingers tracing lazy, familiar paths over the curve of his ribs—memorising him not just with thought, but with touch. His heartbeat thudded steady beneath her cheek—slower now, calm. Grounding.

Each breath he took lulled her deeper into stillness.

The kind of stillness that only arrives when the danger has passed. When the world, for once, isn't pressing in from all sides.

Jace shifted slightly, his arm tightening around her—not to pull her closer, but to remind her she was there. And so was he.

Outside, the sky was blooming gold when the phone rang—sharp and sudden, slicing through the quiet like a blade. The sound felt wrong, intrusive, breaking the delicate bubble of peace, they'd found.

Jace reached out, muscles flexing beneath her cheek as he grabbed the phone off the nightstand. Savannah watched him sit up slowly, rubbing a hand across his face, heavy with sleep.

"Yeah?" His voice was rough, layered with the haze of just waking.

Then he stilled.

Something in his posture—too still, too quiet—made Savannah's breath hitch. A cold prickle crawled down her spine.

She sat up cautiously, pulling the sheet tighter around her, instinct coiling tight in her chest.

"What is it?" she asked, voice low and wary.

Jace lowered the phone without answering, fingers clenched tight around it. When he finally turned to face her, his expression was already different—closed off, armoured.

"It was John," he said quietly.

The knot in Savannah's stomach tightened—sharp and immediate, primal. Because nothing good ever followed a voice like that.

She gripped the sheet tighter as Jace ended the call and stood, running a hand through his hair like the gesture could somehow shake loose the weight of the news.

"What happened?" Her voice trembled, already braced for the worst.

He hesitated, just a fraction, then turned toward the window. The early light caught the tension in his shoulders as he stared out, as if distance could dull the blow.

"Kessler's dead," he said finally, the words falling heavy in the still air.

Savannah blinked, stunned. "What?"

He exhaled slowly, deliberately—but the breath brought no relief. "Found hanging in his cell this morning. No noise. No witnesses. Just... gone."

Her pulse jumped, sharp and relentless. "Suicide?"

He looked back over his shoulder, gaze colder than she'd ever seen—icy, detached. "That's what it looks like."

She swallowed hard, throat tight. "Was there... a note?"

Jace nodded, eyes unreadable. "Yeah. Said he was sorry. Admitted to killing Tyler. Claimed he covered it up, manipulated evidence, buried the truth. Blamed pressure, mistakes, guilt—the usual coward's confession."

Savannah sank onto the edge of the bed, fingers curling into the sheets. Her mind reeled, trying to fit the word sorry beside the man who'd shattered her family, nearly destroyed Jace.

"So... it's over?" she whispered, barely daring to believe it.

Jace's body sagged beside her on the mattress, the weight of years pressing down with him.

"Yeah," he said softly. "It's finally over."

She turned toward him, searching for peace, anger, release—something, anything—but found only exhaustion. Deep and bone-weary, the kind that doesn't come from sleepless nights but from carrying a truth too long, too alone.

Savannah's hand moved gently to his knee. "It should feel like a victory," she said quietly.

"It doesn't," he admitted. "Feels like an ending that came too easy for him. Like he escaped without ever facing what he did."

She nodded, understanding. "But the world knows now. He didn't get to rewrite the ending. You did."

His eyes softened, and he nodded once—barely, but enough.

For the first time in ten years, there was no lie hanging over them. No shadow of doubt. No open wound demanding answers.

Just truth.

Raw. Final.

Outside, the wind stirred the branches of the old oak tree—watching, waiting. Still a witness.

Chapter Twenty-Two

Jace was on his knees in the front room of the farmhouse, replacing a warped floorboard near the hearth. The hammer rested beside him, the scent of sawdust and pine thick in the air. Dust clung to his forearms, and the sweat-darkened collar of his shirt clung to the curve of his neck. The morning sun streamed through the windows, cutting shafts of gold across the old wooden floor.

He liked the rhythm of it—the press of nail to wood, the familiar give of the grain, the weight of each swing. There was a kind of truth in this work. Honest. Simple. After everything, there was something healing about fixing what was broken with your own two hands.

Savannah was back at the hospital—her first full week since everything had unravelled… and then slowly, miraculously, settled again. She'd kissed him that morning on her way out, her breath warm with coffee, her fingertips brushing his jaw with quiet promise.

He could still feel it.

The house was quiet now, settled into the kind of silence that felt lived in, not lonely. Only the creak of the floorboards and the steady hum of cicadas drifted through the open windows. Even the wind seemed softer here, more forgiving.

So, when the knock came, it sounded louder than it was. It echoed through the stillness like it didn't belong.

Jace pushed to his feet, wiping his hands on a rag as he crossed the room. He opened the door to find Sheriff John Nolan on the porch—hat in one hand, an envelope in the other.

"Morning," John said, his voice quiet. Measured.

"Hey," Jace replied, eyes narrowing slightly. "Everything okay?"

John didn't answer immediately. He held out the envelope instead. Government letterhead. Crisp and white, official in the way only bureaucracy could be. Jace's name was typed neatly across the front. Simple. Final. The kind of paper that held more weight than it seemed to deserve.

"This came through officially this morning," John said. "I figured… you deserved to hear it in person."

Jace took the envelope with cautious fingers, like it might break open if he breathed too hard. His eyes scanned the front, then lifted back to John's.

"What is it?"

John met his gaze directly. "You're exonerated, Jace. Fully cleared. The state signed off this morning. You're no longer a convicted felon. You're free."

The words landed with a strange kind of stillness. Jace didn't speak. Didn't move. He just stood on the porch, staring down at the envelope like it might disappear if he blinked.

His fingers tightened around the edges. A muscle jumped in his jaw. His throat worked, but nothing came out. For ten years, he'd told himself it didn't matter—that he didn't need a piece of paper to tell the world who he was. That the truth had always been enough.

But hearing it… holding it…

It split something wide open.

He sat down slowly on the edge of the porch step, the envelope resting on his lap like something sacred—or radioactive. The wood was warm beneath him, the world impossibly bright.

John stayed where he was, arms crossed, eyes steady. He didn't speak. He just let the silence fill the space between them.

Jace stared out at the road. The trees swayed in the wind, tall and slow. The gravel shimmered in the heat. Everything looked the same—but felt different.

For the first time in ten years, he could breathe without someone else's lie pressed against his chest.

"She would've wanted to see this," Jace said finally, his voice hoarse. "Savannah."

John nodded. "I figured. But I thought you might want a minute. To feel it before you had to explain it."

Jace looked up at him, and for a second, the man he'd once been—before the trial, before the years, before the prison walls—flickered across his face.

"Thank you," he said quietly.

John gave a slight nod, though his expression didn't soften much. "You don't need to thank me," he replied, voice low. "Truth is… I feel like I failed you."

Jace blinked. "What?"

John's gaze drifted toward the yard, where the sun stretched long shadows through the grass. "Hell Jace. I was the one who arrested you," he said. "Put the cuffs on like I knew something. Like I was doing the right thing."

Jace swallowed hard, the memory slicing through the morning light. The sound of the cuffs. The look on Savannah's face. The press of gravel against his knees.

"You weren't the only one who thought I was guilty," he said quietly.

"Doesn't make it better," John murmured. "Doesn't make it right."

A heavy silence settled between them. Not bitter. Not angry. Just honest.

"No," Jace said after a moment. "It doesn't."

"I should've asked more questions," John continued. "Should've pushed back. Looked harder. I let pressure make the call. And you paid the price for it."

Jace stood slowly, the envelope still folded tight in his hand. He stepped off the porch, the gravel crunching beneath his boots. The morning sun caught the edge of his face, shadow, and light mingling in sharp relief. He looked older now. Worn. But stronger, too. Refined by fire.

"You can't change what happened," Jace said. "Neither can I. But you're here now. You believed me when it counted. That has to be enough."

John exhaled slowly. "You're a better man than me."

Jace gave a small, humourless smile. "No," he said. "Just a man who ran out of choices."

Another beat passed. Then John cleared his throat and straightened. "The official statement goes out within forty-eight hours. Press'll be hungry. You don't owe them anything—but if you want a voice, you've got one."

Jace shook his head slowly, a dry laugh escaping. "They ignored the truth for a decade. They don't get to profit off the ending."

John gave a half smile. "Then tell them your beginning."

He turned to leave, boots heavy on the porch boards, but paused at the bottom of the steps. "You ever need anything—anything—you call me. Doesn't matter what it is."

Jace nodded. "Thanks, John."

The sheriff tipped his head, then walked down the gravel path and climbed into his cruiser. The engine turned over, tyres crunching slowly down the drive until the sound disappeared into the breeze.

Jace stood there in the quiet, envelope still in hand.

The farmhouse behind him.

The world in front of him.

And for the first time in a long time, the weight—the guilt, the doubt, the injustice—was his to set down.

He looked down at the envelope—creased now, smudged by calloused hands. But clean. His name, his truth, finally unshackled.

He looked back at the road.

Waited for the sound of Savannah's car.

She'd want to see it for herself.

She deserved to.

And this time, he'd be the one to give her the truth.

With no more shadows left to hide in.

The screen door creaked open just as the last sliver of sunlight disappeared behind the tree line, painting the sky in bruised shades of lavender and ash. Savannah stepped into the farmhouse, her every movement weighed down by the long hours behind her.

Her scrubs were wrinkled and streaked with dried blood, the knees scuffed from kneeling beside gurneys, the sleeves rolled up just enough to show the faint press of bruises where the day had demanded too much. She moved on instinct—dropping her bag by the door, toeing off her shoes with a tired grunt.

The house met her with stillness, broken only by the low hum of the ceiling fan and the distant hush of wind brushing through the pines outside. It was a kind of silence she didn't get at the hospital—clean, undemanding. But tonight, something in it felt different. Tense. Expectant.

She called out, voice quiet, careful. "Jace?"

"In here," came his voice from the living room.

Steady. Controlled.

But there was something beneath it—a ripple, a tightness she knew too well. Savannah's heart kicked up as she followed the sound.

She found him standing near the fireplace, haloed by the dim amber glow of the table lamp. He was barefoot, wearing a worn T-shirt and jeans dusted with sawdust. A letter in his hands trembled ever so slightly, the way paper does when a man is holding more emotion than he wants to show.

He turned as she entered.

Their eyes met.

And something shifted in her chest.

"What is it?" she asked, instantly alert, the fatigue of the day falling away like an old coat.

Jace didn't answer at first. Instead, he crossed the room slowly, like he was approaching a fragile edge neither of them could see. When he reached her, he didn't speak. He simply held out the letter—offering it with both hands, reverent, like it might dissolve if he let go too soon.

Savannah took it, brows drawing together in confusion. She unfolded the paper, scanned the header—and stopped breathing.

Her heart lurched.

The words blurred slightly, but she didn't need to read them twice. She knew. Felt it in her bones.

Her lips parted, her voice cracking. "Jace…"

He finally spoke, voice low and quiet, like if he said it too loud, the world might undo it. "It's official. I'm exonerated."

Her knees nearly buckled.

He steadied her with a hand at her elbow.

"The governor signed it this morning," he continued. "John brought it by himself."

Savannah stared at the letter, then back at him, her eyes brimming. Tears slipped free before she could stop them, cutting warm trails down her cheeks. It wasn't just joy or relief. It was the rush of surviving long enough to witness something that once felt impossible.

She pressed the paper to her chest, as if holding it there might let it sink beneath her skin. "It's over."

Jace nodded slowly. But the look in his eyes said it wasn't that simple. Relief, yes. But also, disbelief. Grief. Ghosts.

She reached for him, and he came into her arms with the weight of everything he'd carried for ten years. They folded into one another, her arms wrapping around his shoulders, his around her waist. His face pressed into her neck, and for a long time, they just stood there, breathing the same air, anchored only by the silence between them.

No news crews. No courtroom. No spotlights or shouting.

Just the woman who had walked through hell beside him—and the man who had refused to let it burn him down.

"I didn't think it would feel like this," he murmured into her shoulder, voice rough.

"Like what?"

He drew back slightly, just enough to look into her face. His eyes shimmered—not just with unshed tears, but with something rarer. Hope. "Like something I never dared to hope for… actually came true."

Savannah cupped his face with both hands, her touch gentle, grounding. "You deserve this, Jace. Every word in that letter. Every breath of freedom."

His hands found her hips, pulling her closer—not possessive, but needing to feel something solid. "I stopped believing in justice a long time ago," he said. "But I never stopped believing in you."

Her breath caught, and she leaned in until their foreheads touched. "And I will never stop believing in you," she whispered.

A pause.

Then he said it again, like he needed to hear it from his own mouth to believe it.

"I'm free, Savannah."

She smiled through her tears, a slow, radiant curve of her lips. "Then let's start living like it."

Outside, the last of the light filtered through the windows in soft gold, stretching across the worn floorboards like a blessing.

And inside, they stood wrapped in each other, two people who had been bent, but not broken—scarred but not defined by it.

They had stood in the ashes of everything they'd lost.

Now, finally, they could build something new.

Together.

Free.

Chapter Twenty-Three

The next morning, soft light spilled across the farmhouse floor in slow golden ribbons, catching on the worn wood and the steam rising from two untouched mugs. Savannah and Jace sat at the small kitchen table, shoulders relaxed but quiet stillness between them—not from discomfort, but contentment.

The radio murmured low in the background, some old blues tune drifting lazily through the space, weaving between the clink of ceramic and the gentle groan of the old house settling into a new day.

Savannah's feet were tucked beneath her, chin resting on one hand as she watched Jace over the rim of her coffee cup. His hair was damp from a quick shower, curls still tousled, and his T-shirt was soft with age—something that made her chest ache with a kind of peace she hadn't realised she'd craved for years.

It was the kind of morning that felt rare and borrowed—unhurried. Undemanding. A breath between storms.

Until the knock came.

It was firm. Deliberate. Not the uncertain tap of a neighbour. Not the casual rattle of delivery.

Jace looked up, his brow tightening as he set his mug down. Savannah straightened slowly, the stillness cracking just slightly at the edges.

They exchanged a glance.

He rose, the chair scraping softly against the floor, and moved to the door.

When he opened it, a man in a courier uniform stood on the porch, clipboard in one hand and a thick, sealed envelope tucked beneath the other arm. His face was impassive. All business.

"Delivery for Mr. Calloway," he said, tone clipped.

Jace signed his name without a word and accepted the envelope. No questions. No unnecessary pleasantries. The man was already turning back down the steps as Jace closed the door behind him.

He turned the envelope over in his hands, frowning. There was no return address. No markings beyond his name—typed in crisp black letters, centred perfectly. Clean. Cold.

He walked slowly back to the kitchen, the weight of it heavier than paper ought to be.

Savannah stood now, her hand resting on the back of her chair. "What is it?"

Jace tore the seal and unfolded the letter inside. His eyes scanned the page, and his frown deepened.

"It's from the State Attorney's Office," he said, voice slow, unreadable. "They're requesting I attend a meeting tomorrow morning at the Cedar Ridge Law Chambers."

Savannah moved to his side, taking the letter when he offered it. Her gaze skimmed the page.

"There's no reason listed," she murmured, brows pulling together. "No subject. Just the time, the location, and the word confidential twice."

"Yeah," Jace said, his jaw tightening slightly. "Feels like a chess move."

She looked up at him, her voice quieter now. "You think it has to do with the press release?"

He exhaled, rubbing a hand across the back of his neck. "Could be. Maybe fallout from Kessler's death. Or questions about the original trial. Or… something else. Something they don't want in writing."

Savannah folded the letter carefully and set it on the table between them. The kitchen seemed a little cooler now. The music on the radio had shifted, the blues guitar fading into silence before another song could begin.

"Do you think you should go?" she asked after a beat, her tone even, but her eyes searching.

He met her gaze. For a second, the weight of everything—the exoneration, the public attention, the quiet suspicion that nothing was ever truly finished—pressed between them. But then his spine straightened, his jaw set.

"Yeah," he said simply. "I'll go. But I don't want to walk in there alone."

Savannah didn't hesitate.

She reached for him, her hand curling gently around his wrist, grounding him. "Then you won't," she said, voice sure. "I'll be right there beside you."

His shoulders eased, just a fraction—but it was enough to see. Enough to feel.

"Thank you," he said softly, that quiet vulnerability he rarely showed slipping through the cracks.

Savannah smiled, tired but resolute. "Always."

Jace looked down at her hand in his. Then to the envelope again, still lying on the table like a sealed secret waiting to shift their world one more time.

But this time, they would face it together.

No shadows.

No lies.

Just truth. Whatever came next.

The room smelled like old coffee and panic.

Jace sat stiffly at the long mahogany conference table, the kind that gleamed too perfectly under the recessed lighting—sterile, heavy, expensive. Savannah was beside him; her hand rested lightly on his knee beneath the polished surface. She didn't speak—she didn't need to. Her touch said everything: I'm here. I've got you.

Across from them sat two attorneys from the State's Office—one mid-forties, sharp suits, tighter expressions. Polished, professional, forgettable. Between them sat a third man, older and sharper, with slicked-back silver hair and a tailored suit that likely cost more than Jace had earned in a year before prison. He hadn't introduced himself. He didn't need to. Power never did.

Without a word, the man slid a folder across the table. Not with hesitation—but with precision. Like he'd done this a hundred times before. Like lives could be condensed to paper, signed, stamped, and buried.

"We'll be issuing the press release shortly after this meeting concludes," one of the attorneys began. His tone was clipped, courteous, and completely devoid of warmth.

"We're prepared to offer a financial settlement," the other added. "In exchange, Mr. Calloway will waive any future claims against the state and agree to full confidentiality moving forward."

Jace stared at the folder. He didn't touch it.

The words landed like a gavel. Not an apology. Not justice. Just… cleanup.

Beside him, Savannah remained quiet. Her hand on his knee didn't falter. A quiet anchor in a room built to disorient.

"How much?" Jace asked, his voice even, but low.

It was the silver-haired man who answered. "Eight point six million. Paid in full within thirty days."

Savannah's eyes flicked toward Jace, but she didn't speak. She could feel it— the storm building in him. He was weighing fire against forgiveness.

Jace's jaw clenched. "That's what ten years costs?"

The attorney shifted slightly. "It's not about cost. It's about resolution."

"No," Jace said, his voice colder now. "It's about damage control."

One of the attorneys across the table opened his mouth, but he cut him off.

"You knew what Kessler was," he said, his voice rising, steady but sharper. "Maybe not all of you. But someone did. And now he's dead, the cover-up's collapsing, and you want to make sure I keep my mouth shut before the public starts asking who let it happen."

The attorneys exchanged quick, uneasy glances.

"I don't want it," Jace said flatly.

Savannah's brow lifted—but she stayed silent, trusting him to follow the path he needed to walk.

"I don't want blood money for something you can't give back," Jace continued, his voice raw now. "You stole ten years. Ten years of my life. Of everything I could've been."

"Mr. Calloway," one of the attorneys began, trying to regain control.

"It's not justice," Jace said. "It's politics. A payout to quiet the problem. You're not offering this because it's right. You're offering it because you're scared."

He paused, his shoulders tense. Then, he turned to Savannah.

His voice dropped. Not weak—never that. Just... honest.

"What do I do?" he asked her quietly.

Savannah leaned forward, her hand sliding up to rest over his shoulder, her fingers brushing the edge of his jaw.

"I can't tell you what to do," she said gently. "I didn't live those years. You did."

He looked at her, searching for something—clarity, maybe. A reason to say yes. Or no.

She didn't waver.

"They're not paying you for your silence, Jace. They're paying you because your life terrifies them. Because after everything they did to bury you, you're still standing. You spoke up. You fought back. You survived. And that… that scares the hell out of them."

Her thumb brushed the curve of his cheekbone—soft, grounding. "So, if you take it, don't let it be for them. Let it be for you. Because you earned every damn cent. Because you're going to use it to build a life, they never thought you'd live long enough to have."

Jace turned back toward the table.

His spine straightened, slow but sure. The steel was back.

He didn't nod. Didn't smile.

He just said, "Then let's make them regret ever thinking I'd stay broken."

He reached for the pen.

"I'll sign your papers," he added, voice flat. "But don't think it makes us even."

The folder opened with a soft click. Inside: pages of sterile legal jargon. Lines of indemnity. Terms of silence. Dollar signs that didn't look real. His name. His case number. His life, reduced to lines.

He signed.

One page. Then another.

Until it was done.

The silver-haired man leaned forward and collected the documents, flipping through them with the detachment of someone confirming a box had been checked. He folded his hands, tone smooth as silk.

"You're free to speak publicly about your arrest. Your trial. Your exoneration. But any content relating to the investigation of government officials—particularly former Senator Kessler—must remain strictly off the record."

Jace didn't flinch.

"That includes names, files, internal communications, and the settlement amount," the man continued. "You can speak your truth. But everything else—stays buried."

"Buried," Jace echoed, the word sharp in his mouth. "Like it never happened?"

The man gave a small, impassive nod. "As far as the public is concerned, justice was served. You were cleared. That's the story."

Jace leaned back in his chair, his expression unreadable.

"Neat little bow," he muttered. "For a decade of hell."

One attorney flinched slightly but said nothing.

The man across the table shrugged faintly. "Sometimes silence is the price of peace."

Savannah's hand found Jace's again. Her voice was steady as stone. "Peace should never come with a price tag."

For the first time, the suited man looked directly at her. His face was blank, eyes unreadable. "And yet… here we are."

He rose to his feet.

He tucked the pen into his pocket like a weapon sheathed for later. The folder held between his fingers like a bomb that had already gone off.

The papers were signed.

The deal was done.

But as Jace stood—shoulders squared, eyes calm—it wasn't with defeat.

It was with defiance.

Because the truth still lived inside him.

And in the quiet that followed, Savannah's hand in his was all the truth he needed.

Chapter Twenty-Four

The drive home was quiet.

Not uncomfortable—just full. Brimming with everything they couldn't quite say yet.

Everything signed away under fluorescent lights. Sterile legal jargon. Empty checkboxes. Everything waiting in the silence between them.

The countryside blurred past in streaks of green and gold, the gravel hum beneath the tyres loud in the absence of words—steady, like a heartbeat. Jace's hands stayed fixed on the wheel, his jaw tight. Not angry. Not uncertain. Just… processing.

Savannah didn't press. She understood this silence. Respected it. Some truths needed time to settle before they could be spoken aloud.

When they pulled into the drive, the farmhouse stood in warm light, the porch catching the last golden slant of afternoon. Familiar. Safe. It had seen them through worse. It would hold them through whatever came next.

Inside, the air was still and cool, smelling faintly of sawdust, coffee, and old wood. Savannah dropped her bag by the door and toed off her shoes with quiet ease. She turned to say something—to offer something—but paused when she saw Jace still standing with his hand on the doorknob.

He didn't look at her right away.

"What do you want to do with the money?"

His voice was low but direct. No hesitation. No lead-in. Just the question, laid bare between them.

Savannah stilled, watching him.

"That's your decision," she said gently. "It's yours."

He turned then, eyes meeting hers across the room. His brows drew together, a flicker of hurt or confusion there, too faint to name.

"No, Savannah," he said quietly. "It's ours. We're a team."

There was an edge to it—not anger, but vulnerability disguised as assertion. A fear that maybe, after everything, there were still things left unspoken. Unshared. Unclaimed.

His voice softened, but the undercurrent of doubt lingered.

"Aren't we?"

She didn't answer right away. Instead, she walked to him slowly, the soft creak of the floorboards the only sound in the room. When she reached him, she placed a hand flat against his chest—right over his heart. Her touch was warm, steady. Grounding.

"Of course we are," she said. "I'm not going anywhere."

Her eyes held his, unflinching. Honest.

"But you need to understand something. I'm with you for you. Not for what you can give me. Not for a payout. Not for a name in a headline or a zero on a check."

She brushed her thumb gently across the soft cotton of his shirt, where his heartbeat pushed steady beneath.

"I chose you when you had nothing, Jace. And I'll keep choosing you—whether you keep every cent, give it all away, or burn it in the backyard."

A pause.

"What matters is you. Us. That's all I've ever wanted."

Jace let out a slow breath, something shifting behind his eyes—something deeper than relief. Not quite joy. But maybe the first trace of peace. Of being seen. Of being enough.

He didn't smile, but he stepped closer, lowering his forehead to hers, their bodies aligned in that small, quiet way they'd learned to lean on each other.

"I just needed to hear it," he murmured.

"Then hear it again," she whispered. "I love you. I'm not here for the money. I'm here for the man who walked through hell and still came out with his soul intact."

His hand came up to cradle the back of her neck, his fingers threading gently through her hair.

"Then let's make this count," he said quietly.

"We already are," she replied.

And for a moment, the rest of the world faded.

The papers were signed. The past recorded.

But this—this quiet, steady heartbeat between them—was the only thing that felt real.

Later that afternoon, Savannah stood barefoot in the kitchen, the sink half-full of soapy water, the sun streaking across the floor in warm gold. But the stillness didn't settle right.

There was a pressure in her chest she couldn't name—like something was about to snap.

Peace, she realised, always felt like a borrowed thing. Something fragile. Temporary. Never entirely theirs to keep.

She didn't know what the rest of the day would bring.

But when the press release dropped, they felt it before they heard a single word.

It was in the shift—a sudden weight in the air, the way animals sense a storm.

The buzz started as a low hum. Then came the whine of tyres on gravel. Doors slamming. Voices. Cameras clicking in a staccato rhythm like distant gunfire.

Jace was the first to move.

He crossed to the front window, peeling back the curtain with two fingers.

"Shit," he muttered.

Savannah joined him, peering over his shoulder.

Reporters. Photographers. Microphones hoisted in the air like weapons.

A dozen cars now lined the road—some still idling, some parked haphazardly on the grass. A news van pulled up behind them. Another.

Camera flashes fired like lightning. Voices called his name. Someone yelled, "Mr. Calloway! Do you have a statement about the press release?"

It was chaos disguised as curiosity. And it landed on the farmhouse like a swarm of locusts.

"Back door," Jace said suddenly, turning. "They're gonna try it."

Savannah moved quickly, locking the kitchen door just as someone pounded on it from the other side. She flinched. Another knock followed—this time more aggressive.

She grabbed her phone with trembling hands and dialled the one person she trusted to respond fast.

"John? It's Savannah. We need help. Now."

Her voice was tighter than she meant it to be. But the look in Jace's eyes told her she wasn't wrong.

From the bedroom window, a drone zipped past, its mechanical whine cutting the air like a scalpel. It hovered for a moment—then turned and disappeared.

They couldn't leave.

Every window framed another stranger. Every door another breach. The quiet they'd fought so hard to rebuild was being devoured—by headlines, by lenses, by every hungry stranger outside.

Jace stood stiff at the window, his arms crossed, his body braced like he was ready to go back into battle. But there was nowhere to swing. No courtroom. No cell door. Just noise.

He didn't speak. Didn't blink.

Savannah stood beside him, her hand brushing against his, trying to remind him he wasn't alone.

Within twenty minutes, the piercing wail of sirens cut through the cacophony. Sheriff John Nolan arrived with three deputies, each moving like men who knew how to part crowds with calm force.

Barricades went up. A perimeter was established. The push of bodies was redirected toward the road. Voices protested, cameras jostled, but they no longer had free rein. The chaos was held at bay.

The moment the front door closed behind the last uniform, the silence hit hard—too sudden. Too heavy.

Jace sat down on the edge of the couch, his elbows on his knees, hands locked together so tightly his knuckles went white.

John stepped into the living room, his hat in one hand, sweat on his brow, concern in his eyes.

"You two okay?"

Savannah nodded slowly. "We will be."

Jace didn't answer. He stared at the floor, jaw tight, breathing through his nose like he was trying to keep himself from breaking something.

John didn't push. He took the offered coffee with a quiet nod and settled into the worn armchair across from them, his eyes tracking every flicker in Jace's body like a man who'd once worn that weight himself.

For a long beat, only the soft clink of mugs, the ceiling fan's low hum, and the muffled sound of the press beyond the barricades filled the room.

Then John spoke.

"I wish I was just here to handle the media."

Savannah stiffened. "What is it?"

He leaned forward, elbows resting on his knees, his mug cradled between weathered hands.

"I just got a call from a friend in Sacramento. Works in Records Management."

Jace's eyes lifted, wary now.

John's jaw tightened.

"The files," he said. "The ones we handed over. The ones from the investigation. Evidence logs, backup drives, sealed records—all of it. They're gone."

Savannah froze. "Gone? What do you mean gone?"

"There was a fire," John said, his voice low. "At the off-site storage facility. Last night. The whole place went up."

Jace straightened. "You've gotta be kidding."

"Wish I was," John said grimly. He set his mug down with a quiet clink. "No alarms tripped. No cameras caught anything. Fifteen minutes flat. The arson team's calling it an electrical fault, but..." He shook his head slowly. "It smells wrong. Too convenient. Too clean."

Savannah's heart pounded. "Everything's gone?"

"Drives. Paper records. Backup logs. Even the chain-of-custody files. Nothing but ash."

A cold silence swallowed the room.

Jace stood again, pacing toward the window, then away. Then back. Like the walls were closing in.

"So, they buried it," he said. "For good this time."

John's gaze was steady. "Or someone's making sure it never comes up again."

Jace turned to Savannah. His eyes had sharpened—no longer wide with disbelief, no longer just exhausted. They were lit from somewhere deeper now. Older. Darker.

A few days later, a letter arrived in a plain manila envelope.

No postage date. No return address.

Just Jace Calloway's name printed in stark, black block letters, and in the upper-left corner, the embossed seal of the California Office of Criminal Justice Reform—clean, official, and quietly ominous.

It wasn't the kind of envelope that screamed trouble.

But it whispered it—cool and careful, like something that didn't want to be noticed until it was too late.

Jace found it wedged halfway through the mailbox, the paper stiff and untouched by weather. He didn't open it on the porch. Or inside the door.

He stood in the kitchen and stared at it for ten full minutes.

By the time Savannah came in, the coffee in his mug had long since gone cold. The kettle on the stove had cooled, and the silence was so thick it felt like the house itself was holding its breath.

The envelope lay open on the table. One edge of the letter fluttered in the breeze from the cracked kitchen window.

And Jace's hand—fist clenched loosely around the pages—was pale with tension.

His face didn't give much away. But his jaw…

His jaw told the story of a man who had just heard the rules shift again.

Savannah froze at the doorway, reading the room before the words.

"What is it?" she asked softly, already bracing.

He didn't look up.

He didn't have to.

"They want me to speak at a conference next week," he said finally, his voice rough and low. "About wrongful convictions. About mine."

She stepped further into the room, her brow tightening.

"The state invited you?"

"California Office of Criminal Justice Reform," he muttered. "They're calling it a 'Restorative Justice Summit.'" He snorted, no humour in it. "Policy makers. Law enforcement. Judges. Survivors. A couple of other exonerees."

He finally looked up, his expression tired. "I guess I'm one of those now."

Savannah pulled out a chair and sat across from him, her movements slow and deliberate, like trying not to spook a man standing on the edge of something invisible.

"What do they want you to say?"

Jace exhaled, jaw flexing as he looked back down at the letter.

"That justice works," he said. Bitter. Controlled. "That the system caught its mistake. That the process held. That somehow, everything that happened to me was the unfortunate exception—not the proof that the whole damn thing's broken."

He looked at her again, and this time there was fire behind the weariness.

"They want me to tell people the fire didn't burn everything down."

"And does it feel that way to you?" Savannah asked, her voice low, steady.

Jace didn't answer.

Instead, he dragged a hand through his hair, the letter crackling as he finally loosened his grip. The paper slipped from his fingers and landed back on the table, face up—like a dare.

"I signed the deal," he said after a beat. "I can't talk about Kessler. Or the payout. Or what was destroyed in that fire. Not publicly."

"But you can talk about what they did to you," Savannah said gently, reaching across the table for his hand.

Her fingers closed around his—warm, steady, grounding.

His eyes flicked to hers. Searching.

"You can talk about the nights you didn't sleep," she continued. "The sound of cell doors. The way people stopped calling. The way you started to forget what real life felt like."

Her voice didn't tremble. "You can talk about the years you lost, Jace. Because that's your truth. And no NDA can touch that."

Jace stared down at their hands—hers wrapped around his like a tether to something real.

"They're not asking you to lie," she added after a moment. "But if you choose to speak—don't do it for them. Don't give them a neat headline or a feel-good closing panel. Do it for the ones still sitting behind bars. The ones nobody's listening to."

A beat passed. Then two.

And still, he said nothing. Just sat there, the silence stretching like a fault line.

But his shoulders eased.

Not much. But enough to see.

Savannah didn't push. She knew better than to rush a man whose entire life had been built on waiting.

Eventually, Jace looked toward the window, where the wind moved through the trees like a whisper of something almost remembered.

Then he looked back at her.

And slowly—without bravado, without certainty—he nodded.

Not because the wound had healed.

Not because forgiveness had come.

But because purpose… purpose was beginning to grow in the ashes.

Chapter Twenty-Five

The ballroom gleamed with polished wood and politics. Gold trim edged the towering white columns, and crystal chandeliers rained fractured light across a sea of designer gowns, tailored suits, and the carefully neutral expressions of people who knew how to smile without ever showing their teeth.

Every inch of the space reeked of money and performance. Waiters moved like shadows—silent, swift, holding silver trays with flutes of champagne that probably cost more than Jace's truck. The conversations were light on substance and heavy with self-congratulation. Laughter punctuated the air like stage cues, and every face looked rehearsed.

Jace hated it already.

He tugged at his collar for the third time, the starched fabric foreign against his skin. His suit fit perfectly—Savannah had insisted—but it still felt like wearing someone else's life. A costume. A version of himself he hadn't earned.

Or didn't want to earn.

Across the room, a camera flash sparked, and his body instinctively tensed.

Savannah's hand came up, smoothing his lapel with gentle precision. Her fingers paused for just a moment longer than necessary, grounding him.

"You look perfect," she said, her voice low but sure.

He gave a short, humourless huff. "I feel like a fraud."

"You're not," she said, gaze steady. "You're the most honest man in this room."

He glanced around—at the senators, the bureaucrats, the eager-faced interns trying to climb toward influence. Then back to her, voice quiet but laced with unease.

"Like walking into a lion's den in a sheep mask."

Savannah leaned in, her lips brushing just beneath his ear. "Except you're not the sheep."

He didn't smile, not really, but the tightness in his shoulders loosened. A fraction.

"I'd rather be back at the farmhouse," he murmured. "Covered in dirt. Fixing the door you broke."

She gave him a sideways look, equal parts amused and exasperated. "I didn't break it. I tested its structural integrity. It failed."

That earned a twitch at the corner of his mouth. Almost a laugh. Almost.

But it faded quickly.

"This is the part I'm bad at, Savannah," he said, glancing at the polished crowd. "The stage. The cameras. Pretending I'm not just waiting for someone to pull the rug out from under me again."

Her hand slid into his, fingers lacing with quiet certainty.

"That's why I'm here," she said, eyes locked to his. "No more rugs. No more running. No more hiding from who you are, Jace."

He held her gaze—longer this time. Searching it. Steadying himself in it.

"You're not here to convince them of anything," she added. "You're here to remind yourself that you survived. And they can't touch that."

He didn't answer right away. But his fingers tightened around hers.

Then, with a breath that tasted like nerves and resolve, he nodded.

And together, they stepped into the crowd—shoulder to shoulder, hearts aligned, bracing not for applause, but for truth.

Whatever came next, they would face it the way they always had.

Not as headlines or footnotes.

But as the storm and the anchor. The survivor and the witness.

Unpolished. Unapologetic.

Undeniably real.

Jace's name was called.

A ripple of polite applause followed—measured, curious, the kind reserved for someone not entirely understood.

He climbed the stage with the gait of a man walking into a courtroom—not with fear, but with the deliberate caution of someone who had spent too long learning how quickly the floor beneath you could vanish. Every step held the echo of ten years behind bars. Every breath was measured, controlled.

The lights were hot. The silence expectant.

Savannah watched from the wings, hands clasped tight in front of her, breath caught behind her ribs. She could see the way Jace's jaw set. The tension in his shoulders. The invisible weight he carried like a second skin.

He stepped to the podium, paused, and scanned the room. No notes. No tremble in his voice when he began.

"My name is Jace Calloway. I spent ten years in prison for a crime I didn't commit."

The room stilled. Forks were set down. Eyes lifted. The kind of silence that holds its breath.

"I was nineteen when I was arrested. Twenty when I was sentenced. Thirty when I walked out with a plastic bag of state-issued clothes and a decade I'd never get back."

A rustle of discomfort moved through the crowd. Someone cleared their throat. A woman looked away. A man adjusted his tie like it might change the weight of his guilt.

"I was scared," Jace said simply. "The first night in prison, I didn't sleep. Not because of the noise, or the cold, or the steel bars—but because I knew I didn't belong there. And no one cared."

He let that land. No bitterness. Just truth.

"Every day after that was a fight—to be heard, to stay safe, to keep from becoming someone I didn't recognise. I wasn't surviving time. I was surviving a system that decided I didn't matter."

His voice didn't rise, but his words struck like hammer blows.

"I lost everything. My best friend—the one they said I murdered. My freedom. My family. My faith. I missed birthdays. Funerals. I forgot what laughter sounded like without fear. I forgot what it felt like to be touched without suspicion."

A beat. A breath.

"My name became a number. My future became a cell. And my truth became something no one wanted to hear."

He looked down for a moment, then back up—steady now, more steel than sorrow.

"When I got out, all I had were questions—and silence waiting on the other side. No job. No home. No apology. Just ten years of silence and a world that had already moved on."

From the wings, Savannah felt the ache in his words like a bruise beneath her ribs.

"But I'm not here to assign blame," he continued, voice lower now. "I'm here because someone refused to let the silence win. Savannah Blake believed in me when no one else did. She fought for my truth like it was her own."

He looked toward her, and the connection in that moment eclipsed everything else in the room.

"I learned something in those ten years. Justice doesn't mean punishment. It means accountability. It means listening to the voices we've already dismissed. It means understanding that real justice starts when we admit we got it wrong."

He leaned in slightly, both hands braced on the podium, not to steady himself—but to drive it home.

"We don't need a perfect system. We need a brave one. One that's willing to say, 'We failed'. One that listens, not just when it's convenient—but when it's uncomfortable. Because if it can happen to me, it can happen to anyone."

Silence stretched.

And then, slowly, the applause began.

Tentative. Then fuller. Louder. No longer polite or curious.

Not out of pity.

Not out of politeness.

But because truth had a pulse again—and it was standing at that podium.

Jace stepped down from the podium, the applause following him like a tide. His shoulders were squared, his head high—his posture straighter than it had been in years.

He didn't smile.

He didn't have to.

Because for the first time in a decade, he hadn't been asked to defend himself.

He'd been asked to speak.

And they'd listened.

Savannah found him near the back wall, half in shadow, holding a glass of water like it was the only thing tethering him to the floor. His posture was still—shoulders straight, expression unreadable—but his gaze had the far-off look of someone still standing behind a podium, still hearing the echo of his own words even as the applause had faded.

She started toward him, heart softening at the sight of him alone in the crowd, when a man intercepted her path—like smoke sliding under a door.

Tall. Polished. Unsmiling.

His presence chilled the air around them, cutting through the hum of conversation and clinking glassware like a sudden gust through an open window. Savannah stopped short, something in her gut twisting with the unmistakable click of instinct: danger.

He extended a hand toward Jace.

"Mr. Calloway," the man said, voice smooth, sharp-edged. "Impressive speech."

Jace didn't take the hand.

Didn't even glance at it.

He stared at the man like he was a ghost he'd half expected to see. One he hoped he wouldn't.

Savannah watched a quiet shift ripple through him—small, subtle, but sharp. His grip on the glass tightened just slightly. His jaw ticked once.

"I'm sorry," Jace said coolly. "Do I know you?"

The man let his hand fall with a slight shrug, unbothered. "Not yet."

He smiled—but it was the kind that came with conditions. "Marcus Rourke. Special liaison to the Governor's Office of California. I oversee private security reform. Discretionary parole oversight. Other… sensitive matters."

Savannah's blood went cold.

Rourke.

The name didn't ring loud to her, but the way Jace's shoulders went rigid beside her told her everything she needed to know.

Jace's voice stayed flat, unreadable. But Savannah could feel the tension gathering under the surface like a wire pulled too tight.

"Strange," Jace said, sipping his water like it was scotch. "I spent ten years behind bars. You'd think I'd have heard your name at least once."

Rourke gave a laugh, polished, and practiced. "That's because you were never meant to be in the rooms that matter."

Then his eyes slid to Savannah.

His gaze didn't just settle—it lingered. Cool. Measuring. Memorising.

"Ms. Blake," he said, his tone faux-pleasant, the kind reserved for opponents disguised as guests. "A pleasure."

Savannah stepped forward without hesitation, her spine straight, voice clipped and deliberate. "Likewise."

She didn't offer her hand.

Didn't smile.

Didn't blink.

There was something too rehearsed about him—like a man who practiced smiling in mirrors until it stopped looking human. He wore confidence like armour, but Savannah could feel the rot behind the shine. The smell of a man used to hiding things in locked drawers and untraceable memos.

He let the silence linger—too long. Just enough to test control. To remind them this wasn't a meeting. It was a message.

"Well," Rourke said finally, his lips curling into something that only looked like a smile. "I do hope your new life lives up to your expectations."

Then he was gone.

No goodbyes. No backward glance.

Just turned and disappeared into the throng of donors and dignitaries, his expensive shoes silent against the marble like he'd never been there at all.

Jace didn't move. His eyes stayed on the crowd, scanning for Rourke even as the man vanished like smoke into the folds of political theatre.

Savannah waited a beat, then stepped closer, her hand finding his arm. "Do you think he was still working with Kessler?"

Jace didn't answer right away. He just kept looking.

Looking for the ghosts he knew were still here.

"Back then?" he said finally, voice low. "Yeah. I'd bet everything on it."

Her brow furrowed. "But the files are gone. No proof. Just ashes."

"Doesn't mean the threat is," Jace replied. His jaw was tight again. But this time, it wasn't fear behind it—it was clarity. "People like Rourke don't disappear when the fire goes out. They just shift to higher ground."

Savannah's pulse quickened, but she didn't show it. She placed her hand over his, firm and warm. "So, what do we do?"

He finally looked at her.

And for the first time since stepping off the stage, the hard edge behind his eyes softened.

"We live," he said. "Loudly. Publicly. Together. That's what they hate most. People like him thrive in silence. So, we make sure they never get it again."

She nodded slowly; eyes locked to his. "I can do that."

He exhaled, the last of the tension draining from his frame like a slow leak from a long-held breath. His fingers laced with hers.

They turned toward the exit—toward the clean air and the honest dark.

Behind them, the ballroom buzzed on, all glitter and masks and champagne-laced diplomacy.

But ahead, the road was quiet.

And it started to feel like theirs.

Chapter Twenty-Six

By the end of the week, the media frenzy had finally burned itself out. The reporters who once crowded the fence line like vultures eventually packed up their cameras and moved on to the next headline. The vans left first, easing off down the gravel road with nothing new to shoot and no one left to corner. Then the drones stopped buzzing the rooftop. The shouting died. The tension loosened.

And overnight, the world lost interest.

No more knocks at the door.

No more shouted questions from the driveway.

No more strangers pointing long lenses through the trees like hunters in waiting.

What had once felt like an unrelenting siege faded into silence.

But Jace didn't celebrate.

Savannah didn't either.

There was no toast. No exhale of victory. Just a strange, heavy quiet—like the air after a storm, when everything's still damp and too still, and you don't know whether to hope or brace for more.

But that Friday night, when they sat side by side on the porch with their hands wrapped around mugs of tea and nothing but the cicadas for company, it felt like the first real breath in weeks.

The sky was dark velvet above them, pricked with stars. The porch light cast a warm, soft glow, catching the rim of Savannah's mug and the curve of Jace's profile. Neither of them spoke for a long time.

They didn't need to.

The silence between them wasn't empty—it was full. Full of everything they'd weathered. Full of questions they didn't need to ask out loud. Full of the knowledge that peace like this—quiet, real, hard-won—wasn't something the world handed out easily. You had to protect it. Guard it like fire in a high wind.

Savannah leaned her shoulder gently against his.

He didn't move, but his thumb brushed hers where their hands rested against the mug. A small thing. But she felt it.

"You sleep at all last night?" she asked, her voice barely above a whisper.

Jace gave a quiet huff. "Some."

She looked over at him. "Lie again and I'll make you drink chamomile with valerian root."

That earned a flicker of a smile. Barely there. But it was something.

"I slept a little," he admitted. "Still get that feeling sometimes… like they're gonna come back. That I'll look out the window and see another van."

"They won't," she said softly, with more conviction than she felt.

He nodded, but his eyes didn't leave the trees.

Another long stretch of quiet passed between them. The cicadas droned. A breeze moved the wind chimes with a lazy clink. Somewhere in the distance, a dog barked once, then stopped.

"I used to think silence was the enemy," he said finally. "Back inside… it meant isolation. Solitary. Being forgotten."

Savannah turned slightly toward him, listening.

"But out here…" He paused, then looked at her. "This kind of silence—it feels different. Like maybe it's what healing sounds like."

She didn't say anything right away. Just reached out and slid her fingers through his—warm, steady, sure.

"It is," she said. "It's also what staying feels like. And you're allowed to stay now, Jace."

He looked down at their joined hands, then up at the stars overhead—clear and endless and out of reach for far too long.

And for the first time in days, maybe weeks, maybe longer than he could name, he let his eyes close.

Just for a moment.

Just to feel what peace might be like if it ever got the chance to last.

That Saturday, Cassidy showed up in oversized sunglasses and a designer hoodie two sizes too big, like armour she hadn't figured out how to take off yet. Her hair was tied in a low knot, her sneakers scuffed and mismatched, as if she'd dressed in the dark—or stopped caring somewhere around Tuesday.

Her sarcasm arrived before she did.

"Don't worry, I come bearing pastries and deeply repressed emotions," she called, stepping onto the back porch with a bakery box balanced on one hand and a forced smile that didn't come close to touching her eyes.

Savannah crossed the porch in two steps and wrapped her in a hug anyway.

Cassidy didn't flinch, but she didn't quite return it either. Her arms hovered, then dropped—like she wanted to lean in but didn't trust herself to.

Inside, Jace looked up from the kitchen table as Cassidy entered. The moment froze—just briefly—but it was sharp, brittle, and too full of things unsaid.

There had been history there. Not anger. Not blame. Just grief. Complicated. Muddied by proximity and guilt and the shared weight of a truth that had broken more than it mended.

"I brought carbs," Cassidy said, setting the bakery box down on the table with too much energy. "That's practically an apology."

Jace didn't blink. He just watched her for a long moment. Then:

"Apology accepted. What kind?"

"Cinnamon," she replied. "The expensive kind. Don't make me say I care."

He opened the box, took one, and gave a single, measured nod. "Good choice."

And just like that, the tension broke—not all the way, not forever, but enough to let the air move again. Enough to breathe.

They didn't unpack the past. Not that day. Cassidy wasn't ready, and neither of them pushed. But she stayed. She sat down. She let Savannah make tea and didn't mock it. She let Jace ask how she'd been and gave him actual answers—brief ones, but real.

She didn't cry, but her sarcasm was duller around the edges. Less of a defence mechanism. More of a muscle memory she hadn't figured out how to put down yet.

She was still reeling. From her father's death. From the unravelling of the myth, she'd lived under her whole life. From the reality that Vaughn Kessler—once the backbone of her world—had orchestrated so much rot beneath a polished surface.

Cassidy hadn't touched the estate. Hadn't returned calls from his attorneys. She'd shut off her old phone after the third message from a senator's aide offering 'deeply felt condolences and professional opportunities'.

She didn't want sympathy.

She wanted space.

Instead of stepping into his legacy, she'd taken a job no one would post about. A small nonprofit in Sacramento—something about re-entry programs and youth rehabilitation. Quiet work. Underpaid. Unseen.

She coordinated paperwork. Set up intake appointments. Sent reminder emails. Answered phones under a first name only.

She didn't want to be known.

She wanted to be useful.

Now, in the farmhouse garden, the sun slanted low through the trees, casting long golden shadows over the table. Iced tea sweat in their glasses. The cicadas hummed like background music to a summer that hadn't asked for permission to keep going. Cassidy pulled off her sunglasses for the first time since arriving.

Her eyes were red-rimmed, but dry.

"I'm starting to realise," she said quietly, "that blood doesn't buy loyalty. It just… complicates it. Gives people cover to do damage you don't see until it's done."

Savannah reached across the table, her fingers brushing lightly over Cassidy's. "You're not him, Cassidy. Not even close."

Cassidy didn't respond right away. Just stared at their joined hands. Her voice, when it came, was almost too soft to hear.

"You're not just Tyler's sister, either."

The words hit like a thread stitching something back together—tentative, imperfect, but real.

They sat with that truth for a long moment. Each holding space for the other. Each still bruised, still stitched up inside—but not bleeding anymore. Not today.

And maybe that was enough.

From the porch, Jace stepped into view, wiping his hands on an old rag, his presence quiet but grounding. He didn't interrupt. He didn't speak. He just leaned against the post, watching the two women with a peace in his eyes that hadn't been there even a few weeks ago.

He'd learned when to step in. And when to simply witness.

The garden smelled like mint and warm soil. A bird fluttered low across the yard. And for the first time in a long time, Cassidy didn't look like she was preparing to run.

Not from the past.

Not from herself.

Not anymore.

The money had cleared. Jace Calloway was a millionaire. No headlines. No fanfare. No check handed over in a dramatic courtroom. Just numbers on a screen and a call from a lawyer confirming what Jace already knew: the state had finally put a price on his lost decade.

It didn't feel like justice.

It didn't feel like relief.

It felt like confirmation that his life had been weighed, measured, and monetised. That someone, somewhere, had written a number on a piece of paper and decided ten years in a cell was worth that much.

He would've given it all back in a heartbeat—for one missed birthday, one morning in the sun, one hug from his mother before the cancer took her.

But that wasn't on the table.

So, he did the only thing he could.

He started building something new.

One quiet afternoon, not long after Savannah finished a long shift at the hospital, she walked out into the early golden light, exhaustion curling around her shoulders like an old shawl.

And there he was.

Leaning against his brand-new truck—clean, silver, shining like a promise—with that glint in his eye she hadn't seen in weeks.

"Come with me," he said simply, opening the passenger door before she could argue.

She blinked at him. "Jace, I'm—"

"Come with me," he said again, softer now, like he already knew she'd say yes.

She was still in her scrubs, hair twisted up in a clip, a faint stain of coffee on her sleeve. Her feet ached. Her brain fogged. But something in his expression pulled her forward. Hopeful. Sure.

She slid into the seat, heart rising just slightly above the fatigue.

He didn't say much on the drive—just kept stealing glances at her like he was holding a secret between his teeth. Like he couldn't believe what he was about to share.

They passed the familiar parts of town first—gas stations, small shops, traffic lights blinking lazily in the afternoon sun. Then the scenery changed. Lawns turned manicured. Trees grew taller. Houses sat farther apart, each one framed by iron gates or stone pillars or sprawling wraparound porches that looked pulled from glossy real estate magazines.

Savannah frowned, watching out the window. "Where are we?"

He didn't answer.

And then he pulled into a driveway.

The tyres crunched softly over the gravel, and she looked up—and forgot how to speak.

The house was… breathtaking.

Craftsman style. Stone and wood, soft and warm, with a wide porch that wrapped around the front like open arms. Tall windows gleamed beneath ivy-draped eaves. Lavender and rosemary lined the walkway. Wind chimes danced in the trees.

It wasn't the biggest house on the street. But it was the kind of place that looked like it remembered how to breathe—and was ready to teach them how.

Jace turned off the engine, then circled around and opened her door, offering a hand.

She let him help her down, her heart thudding louder than her thoughts.

"What is this?" she asked, blinking. "Why are we here?"

He didn't answer at first.

Instead, he pulled a small envelope from his jacket and handed it to her.

She opened it with shaking fingers. Inside was a single sheet of paper.

An address.

A transaction record.

Her name.

She stared. Looked up at him. Stared again.

"It's yours," Jace said quietly.

Her voice caught. "What?"

He exhaled, smiling in that slow, vulnerable way that always wrecked her more than he knew. "Ours, technically. But the deed's in your name."

She just kept blinking. "You bought us a house?"

"I bought us a home," he corrected. "You gave me something no one else ever did. A future. A reason to believe I could have one. I wanted to give us something real. Permanent. Safe."

Her throat tightened. "Jace…"

"I know it doesn't fix anything," he said gently. "I know money doesn't undo what happened. But this—" he gestured around them, his voice thickening slightly— "this is something we get to build. Not survive. Not defend. Build."

She didn't speak. Couldn't.

He stepped closer, brushed a hand against her cheek. "And now, if you ever break a door again, I promise not to hold it against you."

She laughed—wet, breathless, stunned. "You idiot," she whispered, her arms already around his neck. "I love you."

"I know," he murmured, hugging her back with both arms tight around her waist. "That's why I did it."

They stood like that for a while, surrounded by silence and late-afternoon light. Her scrub top wrinkled. His shirt still carrying the scent of sawdust from a project he hadn't told her about yet. And between them, the future stretched out—not clean, not perfect, but theirs.

Eventually, they walked the path to the front door, hand in hand.

Not afraid.

Not uncertain.

Just steady.

Because sometimes, healing didn't arrive with fanfare.

Sometimes, it came wrapped in cedar beams and soft stone.

In the creak of a porch swing.

The clink of tea mugs.

The quiet knowledge that this time, no one could take it away.

And for Jace and Savannah, that was everything.

Chapter Twenty-Seven

The late afternoon light streamed through the farmhouse windows in soft golden streaks, landing on half-filled boxes and the ghost of old memories. Dust motes floated in the air like they had nowhere better to be, catching in the beams that stretched across the floorboards. The scent of cedar lingered beneath it all—faint, familiar, like the house itself was remembering along with them.

The silence was only broken by the occasional thud of drawers being opened, the low rip of tape, the gentle rustle of packing paper. Every sound felt too loud. Too final.

Jace stood in the hallway, a roll of bubble wrap tucked under one arm and his shoulders squared like he was bracing for something bigger than just moving day.

"You sure you want to give away the old armchair?" he called, tipping his head toward the living room.

Savannah poked her head out from the kitchen, a small smile curling at the corners of her mouth. "You hate that chair."

"I hate how it squeaks every time I sit down. Feels like it is tattling on me."

She huffed a soft laugh. "You said it was cursed."

"It is. But you still love it."

She shrugged, trying to keep the weight out of her voice. "It doesn't match the new house."

He gave her a mock nod, lips twitching. "Design over sentiment. Got it."

They were almost done. Most of the furniture had been tagged—some pieces destined for charity pickup, others wrapped carefully to follow them to the new house. Jace had insisted on starting fresh. No more 'haunted furniture', he'd said, like exorcising the past could be done with new upholstery.

Now they stood at the threshold of Tyler's room.

Savannah paused in the doorway.

The room hadn't changed. Not really. The bed was neatly made; the shelves still lined with books and old trophies. His jacket still hung on the back of the desk chair; a pair of headphones looped around the armrest like he might walk in and put them on. It still smelled like him—like clean cotton, faded cologne, and the faint hint of the cedar-scented soap he always used.

Savannah hadn't stepped inside for longer than a minute or two since the funeral. Just enough to dust. To keep it from feeling forgotten. But not enough to feel it fully.

Today, she had no choice.

They were giving the bedroom set to a local outreach program that helped young men aging out of foster care. It was the right thing. Tyler would've approved.

Still, her hands trembled slightly as she reached for the sheets.

Jace knelt by the nightstand, quiet but steady. "This one's stuck," he said, giving the drawer a tug.

Savannah glanced over. "It always was. He kept too much junk in there. Old receipts, guitar picks, a rock he swore was from the Grand Canyon."

Jace gave another tug. The drawer gave with a sudden lurch, and a handful of loose papers fluttered to the floor.

Then something small hit the hardwood with a soft clack.

Jace stilled.

He reached down, fingers closing around the object. A small, black USB drive.

He turned it over slowly in his palm. It was nondescript. Ordinary. But the air in the room changed anyway.

He looked up, his voice lower now. "Savannah."

She froze mid-fold, the sheet sliding from her hands. There was something in the way he said her name. Careful. Weighted.

He held out the drive. "It was taped to the bottom of the drawer."

She stepped forward, taking it gingerly between her fingers. It was cold. Lighter than she expected. She stared at it like it might bite.

"I… I don't understand," she said quietly.

Jace stood, brushing his hands on his jeans, but his gaze didn't leave the device. "Do you think it's connected to Kessler?"

Savannah's pulse kicked. "I don't know. Maybe?" Her voice faltered. "Tyler was careful. He might've made a backup… in case something happened."

Jace's jaw tightened. He nodded once, then gently plucked the drive from her fingers, and held it up to the light. "We should see what's on it."

Savannah swallowed hard, her throat suddenly dry. The light coming through the window didn't feel warm anymore. It felt sharp. Distant.

The nostalgia drained from the room. In its place: unease. Possibility. A door creaking open to something they thought had ended.

She looked around—at the bed, the shelves, the posters still taped to the walls. A boy's room frozen in time.

Except maybe Tyler hadn't frozen everything. Maybe he'd left something behind on purpose.

Not just a trace.

A warning. A truth. A final breadcrumb.

She looked at Jace her voice small. "Do you think this changes anything?"

He looked back at her, expression unreadable. But his voice was steady.

"I think we're about to find out."

And as they left the room—USB drive in hand, boxes forgotten—the air felt heavier. Charged.

Because some memories didn't fade.

Some waited.

And some had teeth.

Savannah set her laptop on the dining table, the afternoon light casting long slants across the wood. She opened the screen, pulled the USB from her pocket, and hesitated for just a breath.

"This is what Tyler left behind," she said quietly, slipping it into the port.

Jace stood behind her, arms folded tightly across his chest, eyes locked on the screen as it blinked to life.

Folders began to populate—dozens of them. Each labelled with innocuous titles that didn't match the weight they carried: "Vendor Logs," "Clearance Memos," "Client Transfers," "Project Archive."

And inside those folders—PDFs. Scanned documents. Photographs. Audio files. Some marked with state seals. Others with timestamps, bank logos, even surveillance snapshots.

Jace leaned in, brow furrowed. "He wasn't just gathering dirt."

"No," Savannah murmured. Her throat felt tight, dry. "He was building a case."

She clicked on the first file—an internal memo stamped with official California state letterhead, dated nearly eleven years ago. A bold red header burned across the top:

CLASSIFIED: PROJECT PERSEUS

Directive: Expedited clearance for political containment operations.

Tactics include Controlled disinformation, selective prosecution, and media reframing.

Objective: Eliminate threats to administrative cohesion and long-term power consolidation.

Authorising Agent: Marcus Rourke

Office of Security Affairs

Savannah's hand hovered over the trackpad, frozen.

"Tyler uncovered a machine," she said, barely above a whisper. "A political weapon. Designed to erase people who got in the way."

Her stomach turned. This wasn't just a scandal. It was an entire covert operation sanctioned by the Office of Security Affairs.

Jace sat back, the colour draining from his face. "They used this on me."

Savannah nodded. "Do you think they are still using it? If it was this big ten years ago. How big is it now?"

She clicked into another folder. This one held spreadsheets—thousands of lines of offshore account activity. Transactions routed through shell corporations with generic names. One spreadsheet was tagged with a name in the corner: Senator Vaughn Kessler.

Savannah scrolled, her breath catching as she scanned the columns: wire transfers, laundering routes through a dummy nonprofit in Nevada, massive deposits timed just days before major prosecution drops.

She opened a photo next. It showed Kessler shaking hands with Rourke, both men grinning. In the background, a blurred podium banner read: California Justice Initiative—2015 Annual Donor Gala.

"These weren't just bribes," Jace said, voice low and tense. "This was infrastructure. Kessler's legal reforms—they were smoke and mirrors. They buried people like me while cleaning their money on the side."

Savannah clicked on another file—an audio clip.

Tyler's voice crackles softly through the laptop speakers. His tone is steady, but you can hear the weight behind every word—the kind of fear that's long since turned into resolve.

'If you're hearing this… I'm dead.

Let me be clear—I didn't overdose. I didn't kill myself.

That's the story they'll push. Kessler and Rourke will make it look clean—they always do.

But it's a lie.'

Savannah's breath catches. Jace stays still, jaw tight.

'He found out I was going to the press. I had everything—sources, scanned documents, payment trails, audio, names. I was ready to blow the whole thing wide open.

And then he came after Savannah.'

The pause here is longer. The breath that follows is heavier.

'He said if it didn't disappear… she would.

So, I stopped. I waited. I backed off. But I didn't run.

I knew I couldn't protect her forever—not the way they were coming. So, I made sure the truth would survive me.'

His voice breaks slightly—just enough to feel it before he clears his throat.

'Sav, I love you. You were always more than a little sister. You were my anchor. My conscience. My reason to fight harder.

And Jace…'

There's a long breath. The emotion swells.

'You're my brother, man. Not by blood, but by every damn thing that counts. You were the best part of my life before everything fell apart. I trusted you with everything.

So, I'm asking you now—if I'm gone… look after her. Keep her safe. Don't let this machine swallow her the way it tried to swallow me.'

Another beat. The voice steadies again, but now it's razor-sharp.

'Burn it down, Sav. All of it.

Whatever it takes.

Don't stop until the truth screams louder than their lies.'

The audio clicks off.

The silence that follows is deafening.

Jace reached for her hand. "You okay?"

Savannah didn't answer right away. She covered her mouth, tears stinging her eyes.

She looked up at him—eyes red, throat tight, grief and fury braided into something harder than steel.

"No," she said. "But I'm ready."

Jace stood silent for a long beat. Then: "We have to finish what he started."

She nodded. "This isn't over. Not even close."

And in that farmhouse, with sunlight dimming around them and the past crackling through a USB drive, they realised something terrifying—and galvanising:

Tyler hadn't just found the rot.

He'd left them the match to burn it down.

In Sacramento, behind the soundproofed glass of a penthouse office lined in steel and shadow, Marcus Rourke ended a secure call with a flick of his finger. The line cut off with a quiet beep—clinical. Absolute.

He didn't move at first. Just stood there, the city lights below flickering like dying stars. Traffic crawled through the arteries of downtown, unaware of the quiet violence humming behind the glass.

"The surveillance team just informed me," he said at last, his voice cool as ice water over a blade. "She found it."

Across from him, a man in a charcoal suit leaned forward to light a cigarette, the flame briefly catching in his eyes. He exhaled slowly, deliberately. Smoke curled toward the ceiling like a warning no one would heed.

"Then it's time," the man said, his voice flat, "we remind Ms. Blake what happens when you dig up graves we've salted shut."

Rourke didn't reply at first. He turned toward the window, adjusting his cufflinks like a man preparing for a eulogy.

"She just became a liability," he said finally. The smile that ghosted across his lips held no amusement—only intent.

The man tapped ash into a crystal tray, unbothered. "And the ex-con?"

Rourke's tone dipped, colder than before. "Collateral."

Outside, the wind howled against the glass like a distant scream. Inside, everything stayed still.

"I erased Kessler. I burned the files. I handed them silence on a silver platter," Rourke continued, quiet now. Too quiet. "I thought they'd know better than to test what's left. I thought they would finally let it rest and move on."

He turned from the window, eyes like ice beneath polished steel. "They didn't."

A beat of silence stretched, heavy and lethal.

"Get rid of her."

The man across from him stood and gave a single nod.

Rourke's voice followed him to the door—cool, final, without a flicker of regret.

"I don't care about the convict. Without her, no one's listening. But if he gets in your way…"

A pause.

"Make it fast. Make it clean. And this time—don't miss."

Chapter Twenty-Eight

The first person they called was the sheriff.

There wasn't even a discussion—it was instinct. John Nolan was the only person in Cedar Ridge they trusted without hesitation. He'd risked his badge to help them before, had stood toe-to-toe with power and refused to back down. If anyone needed to see what was on that USB, it was him.

He arrived in just under twenty minutes, his county truck rumbling up the driveway like a promise no one had to speak aloud.

No pleasantries. No small talk. He stepped through the front door and scanned the room with the alertness of a man who already knew the ground was shifting beneath them. His eyes landed on the laptop, still open on the kitchen table.

"What did you find?" he asked, his voice flat, edged in tension. No hello. No wasted breath.

Savannah looked at Jace, then nodded. "You need to see this."

She turned the screen toward him. PROJECT PERSEUS glared at the top of the folder like a threat waiting to breathe.

John leaned in. Scrolled.

Internal memos stamped with state seals. Transaction records. Asset transfers linked to foreign banks. Sealed court dockets. Digital fingerprints tied to shell corporations that looped back to campaign donations and nonprofit grants. One name surfaced again and again like a watermark burned into every page.

Rourke.

Jace spoke low. "Tyler must have downloaded everything before they came for the originals."

John's expression didn't shift at first—but his silence changed. It thickened. Darkened.

He clicked through three more files, then another. His jaw flexed. A muscle ticked in his temple.

Then he straightened slowly, like someone dragging himself up out of quicksand.

"Jesus Christ," he muttered.

Savannah folded her arms, hugging herself as her stomach flipped. "He was building a case, wasn't he?"

John nodded once, tight and controlled. "This isn't just a cover-up. This is a damn operation. Financial laundering. Political targeting. Rigged prosecutions. Fabricated evidence. And media control to mop up after. This is…" He stopped. Swallowed hard. "This is treason dressed up in law-and-order rhetoric."

He turned to them, and for the first time since they'd known him, the steely calm cracked. Just a hair.

"They killed people to protect this," he said hoarsely. "And if they know you found it, they'll come for you. No trial. No warning. Just silence."

Jace met his eyes. Steady. Certain. "We know."

John exhaled slowly, bracing his hands on the back of a kitchen chair like it was the only thing holding him upright.

"We need to make backups. As many as we can. We need to get this to someone who can push it up the ladder—outside the state. Outside the system."

"I already did," Savannah said, sliding a small case across the table. "Three copies. One's yours. One's in Jace's pocket. The last one stays with me."

John took the drive, holding it like it might detonate. His fingers curled around it tight.

"Good," he said. "I'll make some calls. Not from the station. I've got a burner I trust. But you need to lay low. Now. Tonight."

He turned toward the door, his stance urgent, his voice shifting from worry to command.

"You two just became targets. Again." His eyes flicked back. "Now we hit back."

That's when the hum of engines broke the stillness.

Low. Smooth. Too smooth.

Then headlights flared—three sets. Bright. Blinding. Predatory. Coming down the quiet street.

Jace didn't hesitate. "Sav."

She froze.

He didn't have to explain. She understood.

"He already knows," she whispered.

The words hung like ice in the air.

Then chaos ignited.

Jace grabbed her wrist, yanking her toward the front door. "Move!"

John was already sprinting, keys in hand. Rain was starting to fall—fat drops hitting the porch like warning shots.

Then came the first SUV, sliding into view like a shark nosing into shallow water. It blocked the drive.

A second cut off the gate. The third idled behind them, attempting to box them in.

No plates. Lights now off. No hesitation.

"John—" Savannah's voice cracked with panic.

"I see them," he snapped, diving into the cab of his truck.

He jammed the gear into reverse and hit the gas—gravel screaming under his tyres, flinging rocks into the dark. The truck surged backward.

Pop-pop-pop.

Suppressed gunfire. Quick. Precise.

The rear window exploded—glass shattering in a sharp spray. Cold air rushed in. Savannah screamed.

Jace flinched—blood streaking down from a graze at his temple—but he shoved her down between the seats, covering her with his body.

John didn't flinch. "Hold on!"

He swung the truck into drive and veered off the main road, barrelling toward a narrow trail that cut behind the property.

The truck bucked hard, jostling over ruts and dips. Mud splashed up the sides. The trees grew denser.

Behind them, the black SUVs surged forward. Engines roared. Headlights now cut through the trees like blades.

"They've been watching us," Jace growled. "They knew the second we opened the files."

A bullet pinged off the side mirror—it exploded in a spray of glass and sparks.

"Where the hell did they come from?!" Savannah shouted, breath ragged with terror.

John jerked the wheel hard left, narrowly missing a rusted-out water tank. "Doesn't matter. We're not stopping."

One of the SUVs hit a low ditch and fishtailed, tyres screeching in the mud.

The other two held back—uncertain in the uneven terrain.

"We've got a window," Jace said. "Take it—now."

John floored it.

They hit an old cattle gate—John didn't even slow. The truck blew through it, wood and rusted chainlink scraping across the hood like metal claws.

The road dipped—steep, curving, tight—and they vanished into the ravine, swallowed by the trees.

Branches whipped the sides. Mud sprayed across the windshield. The wipers struggled to keep up.

And then—silence.

No headlights. No gunfire. Just the growl of their own engine—and the pounding of three hearts in sync.

John kept driving.

Jace finally sat up, still breathing hard, checking Savannah for blood. "You okay?"

She nodded, barely. "You?"

"Just a scratch."

John's hands stayed locked on the wheel, his jaw rigid, voice gravel. "This wasn't a warning."

"No," Jace said grimly. "This was their final move."

And in the hush that followed, as the truck pushed deeper into the dark woods, all three of them knew:

This war just went loud.

Three hours later, they were buried deep in the forest, hidden inside John Nolan's off-grid cabin—a decommissioned ranger station turned survivalist bunker.

The place was nothing but wood, stone, and shadow. The air inside smelled of old pine, oil, and smoke—like a place that remembered storms and secrets. No electricity. No cell signal. No roads for miles. Just kerosene lanterns casting low, flickering halos of light, and the constant creak of the wind moving through timber.

Silence pressed down like a second roof.

Savannah sat curled on a threadbare loveseat, legs tucked beneath her, a chipped enamel mug cradled in both hands. The coffee inside was bitter, black, and barely warm, but she couldn't stop sipping it. She needed the burn, needed to feel something that wasn't panic or dread. The ceramic clinked softly against her teeth. Her fingers wouldn't stop shaking.

The fear hadn't faded.

It had just settled deeper—woven into her muscles, her breath, her bones. A shadow stitched beneath her skin. A phantom heartbeat she couldn't quiet.

Jace stood near the narrow front window, his silhouette tall and tense. The dried blood on the side of his face had cracked like old paint, crusted into his stubble. He hadn't spoken much. Every few minutes, his eyes swept the dense tree line, watching for movement that hadn't come yet. Not yet.

He hadn't touched the coffee.

Savannah glanced over, her gaze snagging on the smudge of red near his temple. "You should let me clean that," she murmured.

Jace didn't turn. "Later."

John poured himself two fingers of bourbon into a dented tin cup—no ice, no water, just the harsh comfort of habit. He didn't sit. Just leaned one shoulder against the heavy post by the hearth, his stance rigid, his eyes unreadable.

"They weren't feds," he muttered finally, as if picking up a thread none of them had dropped. "Too quiet. Too surgical."

"Then who?" Savannah asked, her voice raw from adrenaline and exhaust. "Mercenaries?"

"Private contractors," John confirmed, taking a slow sip. "Black-budget types. Off-book. Probably hired through one of Rourke's shell companies. Clean credentials. Fake names. No paper trail. No fingerprints. Corporate ghosts."

"They shot to kill," Jace said flatly. "Not to scare."

John nodded. "That's how you know they're not government. The feds want leverage. These guys wanted a clean slate."

Jace finally turned from the window and crossed the room, his boots echoing hollow on the old plank floor. He sank down beside Savannah on the loveseat, his body close, his presence solid and grounding in a way no words could match. He didn't touch her, but his nearness steadied her more than the coffee ever could.

"This doesn't stop," he said quietly. "Not unless we stop him."

Savannah looked up at him, her eyes glassy from exhaustion, but there was steel beneath the sheen. "We can't go to the media. Not yet. They'll twist it. They'll smear us. Or make us disappear."

John's expression hardened. "They're already watching every phone tower, every license plate reader, every traffic cam in the region. I'd bet money Rourke's got someone inside every local outlet, too."

"We need to be smart," Jace added. "Surgical. We have the truth, but right now that makes us vulnerable, not powerful. They know we have it, and that makes us dangerous."

Savannah's fingers curled tighter around the mug. Her knuckles turned white. "Then let's be dangerous."

For a second, no one spoke.

Outside, the wind picked up, rustling the trees with a sound like whispers just out of reach. The lantern on the table flickered. Somewhere deep in the woods, a branch cracked like a gunshot.

John finally pushed away from the beam. "I've got a stash of gear here. Backpacks. Burner phones. We lay low tonight. At first light, we move."

"Where?" Jace asked.

John looked between them, jaw tight. "Somewhere they won't follow. Somewhere we can plan the next move without ending up in a shallow grave."

Savannah stood slowly, the tremble in her legs barely noticeable now. She walked to the small window on the opposite wall and stared into the black. No headlights. No movement. Just trees and stars.

"They tried to silence Tyler," she whispered. "They may have had him killed, but now they're going to learn something the hard way."

Jace met her eyes, his voice steady and low. "What's that?"

She turned back to them, eyes burning with something sharper than fear.

"That we're not running. Not anymore. And Tyler's voice is going to be heard."

The words hung there, fierce, and final, like an oath neither of them needed to repeat. Outside, the forest held its breath.

Inside, the lantern sputtered quietly.

After a long moment, Savannah crossed the room and knelt in front of Jace, where he sat on the edge of the loveseat, elbows braced on his knees. The dried blood at his temple had begun to crack and flake, and she could see now how deep the graze had been. It was ugly. Angry. Still seeping in one spot near the hairline.

She dipped the corner of her sleeve into a nearby tin cup and wrung it out with practiced hands. "Hold still," she said gently, and without waiting, reached up to touch his face.

Jace didn't move. Didn't flinch. His eyes stayed on hers, unreadable, but he let her clean the blood—slowly, carefully—like the world outside wasn't falling apart.

The cloth trembled in her fingers, just barely.

She swiped again, tracing the edge of the wound, biting the inside of her cheek when she saw him wince. "Sorry."

"It's fine," he murmured.

"No, it's not," she said, a ghost of a smile tugging at the corner of her mouth. "You're bleeding. I'm shaking. We're hiding in the woods like fugitives. Nothing about this is fine."

Jace's lips curved, but it didn't quite reach his eyes. "Still better than prison."

She gave a quiet huff of air. Almost a laugh. "Low bar."

The cloth lingered against his cheek for a beat longer than necessary. Her thumb brushed away a smear of dried blood near his jawline. When she pulled her hand back, his fingers caught hers, just for a second.

Warm. Solid. Steadying.

"Thanks," he said quietly.

She nodded, not trusting her voice. The air between them crackled—not with romance, not yet—but with something real. Raw. Human.

Chapter Twenty-Nine

The lights of the city shimmered against the glass like a lie dressed in gold—bright, glittering, hollow. From twenty stories up, everything looked clean. Orderly. Obedient.

Just how Marcus Rourke liked it.

He stood motionless before the floor-to-ceiling windows of his penthouse office, a crystal tumbler in one hand, half-filled with amber scotch that caught the city glow like fire in a cage. The skyline stretched before him like a kingdom, a monument to control—his control.

Behind him, the private elevator chimed softly. The hiss of the doors opening was followed by footsteps—measured, tentative, chosen with care.

He didn't turn.

"Well?" Rourke's voice was velvet wrapped around a scalpel—quiet, but unforgiving.

The man in the suit stopped precisely three feet behind him. He smelled of too much cologne and too little courage. Slick hair. Spotless shoes. Eyes that flinched before the verdict was spoken.

"They escaped," he said. The words landed like pebbles in a glass ocean.

Silence. Cold. Waiting.

"How?" Rourke asked without shifting his gaze.

"They used the riverbed. There was a—an unmarked trail. No aerial visibility. The team lost them near the south fence line when one of the SUVs hit mud."

Rourke's jaw ticked. He lifted the glass and took a slow sip, savouring nothing.

"How many vehicles did we deploy?"

"Three," the man replied. "Two trailed the target route. One held the perimeter. We assumed they'd take the paved access roads—"

"And how many people did they have?"

The man hesitated. "Three."

Rourke turned. Slowly. Deliberately. The kind of turn that made the air heavier just by existing in it.

"And yet," he said, his gaze locking on the man like a hawk sighting prey, "she's still breathing."

"Yes, sir."

He placed the tumbler on a glass end table with surgical precision. Walked forward. Each footfall was nearly soundless, but they rang louder than any voice in the room.

"When I give an order to erase a problem," Rourke said, voice steady as frostbite, "I don't expect a chase. I expect silence."

"We didn't anticipate Nolan's involvement. His truck was off grid. They bypassed every monitored junction. We believe they've gone fully dark—no traceable signals, no device activity. We didn't have a tracker on the sheriff's personal truck."

Rourke paused. "Of course they went dark."

He stepped closer, until he stood just inches from the man—close enough to see the pulse ticking in his throat, the sweat shining just behind his collar.

"You underestimated all of them," Rourke said softly. "The nurse. The convict. And now the sheriff."

The man stood frozen, breathing through his nose, trying not to tremble.

Rourke tilted his head, his voice dipping into something glacial.

"Tell me—why do I fund surveillance that only shows me hindsight?"

The man said nothing. There was nothing safe to say.

Rourke smiled—a fraction too wide. A flicker too empty.

"That's what I thought."

He turned away, returning to the glass, to the glittering skyline and the illusion it offered. He lifted the glass again, took another sip, and let it burn.

Behind him, the man waited, still and pale.

"Send someone else," Rourke said. "Not a cleaner. Not a contractor. I want someone who enjoys it."

The man blinked. "You mean… him?"

A pause. A beat of silence like the world exhaling before a storm.

"Yes," Rourke said. "Bring in Kane."

The man's throat bobbed. "He's not… predictable."

"He doesn't need to be," Rourke replied. "He just needs to get rid of her."

He turned slightly, just enough for the man to catch the edge of a smirk that wasn't meant for amusement.

"They think they've slipped the leash," he said. "Let them believe it. Let them rest. Let them feel safe."

He stepped closer to the glass, the city's reflection rippling across his image like water.

"Then we remind them—freedom isn't real. It's just time between mistakes."

He finished the scotch in one long, deliberate swallow. Set the glass down.

"And this," he said softly, "was their last one."

John unrolled a topographic map across the scarred table, weighing it down with a hunting knife, a dead battery, and half a glass of bourbon.

"Three ways out of here," he said, stabbing his finger toward the faded terrain. "North—steep ranger trail, no cameras, no roads. West—fire road, fast but exposed. South—the dry riverbed. Rugged as hell, but we might get lucky."

Jace hovered over the map, eyes narrowing. "Rourke's people will be watching for a group on the move. If we split, we triple our chances."

John looked up sharply. "Exactly what I was thinking."

Savannah set down her coffee, her voice steady despite the tremble in her hands. "We each take a copy of the files—one USB per person. We go to different sources. Trusted ones. In-person only. This isn't just backup," Savannah said. "It's insurance. In case they come for us before we get there."

"That way," Jace added, "if one of us gets intercepted, the others still have a shot. Someone will get through."

John nodded. "I've got a former federal prosecutor in Oakland. She's clean— retired early when the corruption started to stink. I'll head west. No electronics. No trails."

"I'll go south," Savannah said. "There's a whistleblower group near Mariposa. Tyler had it on the USB drive—off-grid, no ties to law enforcement. I think that's where he was going to take it himself. If anyone knows how to take down a political machine, it would be them."

Jace folded his arms, his jaw tight. "I'll go north. There's a journalist in Sacramento—independent, no corporate strings. She reported on Kessler years ago, got shut down. She'll listen."

John looked between them, the gravity of it settling in. "Three routes. Three targets. Three chances."

"No backups. No texts. No calls," Savannah said. "We check in only when it's safe."

Jace touched the flash drive in his jacket pocket, then looked to Savannah. "We move at dawn."

"This is war," John said, his voice low. "Once we go, there's no hiding. Rourke won't send mercs next time. He'll burn down whole counties if it means burying this. His survival depends on it."

Savannah looked at them both. "Tyler died trying to shine a light on what they're doing. We finish what he started."

John gave a tight nod. "Then God help anyone who tries to stop us."

The fire in the stone hearth crackled low, its amber glow casting restless shadows across the weathered floorboards. Outside, the forest lay silent and vast, wrapped in the kind of stillness that made every creak inside the cabin feel louder—like the trees themselves were holding their breath.

John was asleep in the bunk; his snores barely audible over the soft pop of the embers.

On the threadbare couch, Savannah sat curled beneath an old wool blanket, her knees tucked to her chest, arms wrapped tight around them. Her eyes flicked toward the fire, unfocused, her thoughts far from the room.

Jace moved carefully as he eased down beside her, wincing as his muscles protested. The gash on his temple had been cleaned and bandaged, but the ache ran deeper—bone deep, soul deep—the kind that came after a fight you weren't sure you'd survived.

The blanket shifted as she leaned slightly into him, seeking warmth or comfort or maybe just proof that he was still there.

"You okay?" he asked softly.

She didn't answer right away. Just let her head rest lightly against his shoulder.

"I don't know," she murmured. "I think I'm waiting for the sound of tyres again. Or gunfire. Or… something."

He took her hand beneath the blanket—anchoring her, lacing his fingers through hers. "Then let me wait with you."

She didn't look at him right away. Just stared at the fire, her voice soft. "I keep thinking about the recording. Hearing his voice like that. So certain. So scared."

Jace nodded slowly. "He was trying to protect you. Even with his back against the wall."

"He died alone." Her voice cracked. "And I didn't even know what he was carrying. All this time, I thought he just… gave up."

"He didn't," Jace said gently. "He made a plan. He left it for you. For us."

She looked at him now, eyes glassy. "What if we can't finish what he started?"

Jace squeezed her hand. "Then we go down trying. Together."

For a long moment, neither of them spoke. The only sound was the fire, the whisper of wind brushing against the cabin walls.

Then Savannah leaned in, resting her head against his shoulder. "You know what scares me most?"

"What?"

"That after this is all over… there won't be anything left of me… or us… that isn't bruised or broken."

Jace kissed the top of her head, holding her tighter. "Then we build something new. From the ashes. Stronger. Real."

She let herself believe it. Just for a moment.

And in the quiet wreckage of everything they'd survived, the embers of hope glowed just enough to hold the night at bay—for now.

Chapter Thirty

The sun had just begun to rise, casting pale streaks of gold through the dense canopy overhead. The forest held its breath, still wrapped in mist, as if unwilling to wake fully. Fog clung to the edges of every tree, softening the world into something quiet and waiting. Dew slicked the leaves, shimmered like glass on spiderwebs, and soaked the laces of their boots. Every step on the forest floor left a dark print in the damp earth.

Behind them, the ranger cabin stood silent and watchful—half-swallowed by shadow and pine—as though the woods themselves were trying to hold onto them for just a little longer. A last refuge before the world turned hostile again.

Their packs were light. Stripped down to the essentials: cash, maps, untraceable phones powered off and wrapped in foil, water, protein bars—and the most important item, each one carrying a USB drive sealed in a waterproof sleeve and tucked into the lining of their bags like a secret they weren't allowed to forget.

John adjusted the straps on his backpack, his movements slow and deliberate, then looked toward the paling sky. "We split at the crossroads," he said. "No matter what happens, no matter what you see or hear—you don't stop. Don't look back. We keep moving."

He waited a beat, then added, "Phones stay dark. No contact until you're somewhere safe and off-grid. We don't risk the signal. Not even once."

Savannah nodded, her eyes fixed on the narrow gravel path like it might vanish if she blinked. "If we all get caught… we lose everything."

"We won't," Jace said. His voice was steady, but there was tension in his jaw, a flicker of something wild beneath the calm. "One of us makes it. That's the mission."

They stood in silence a moment. The kind of silence that came just before something broke—like the pause between a heartbeat and a flatline. The weight of it pressed in from every side. This was the edge. Beyond this, nothing was guaranteed.

John looked to each of them, his face hard but his eyes fierce with something unspoken. "Watch your backs," he said. "Don't try to be heroes. Just get the truth to someone who can run with it."

He didn't wait for a reply. Just gave one nod, then turned west, his boots crunching on the damp ground as he disappeared into the mist.

Savannah inhaled sharply, ready to turn south—but then—

"Hey."

Jace's voice was soft, but it stopped her like a hand to the chest.

She turned back to him. He hadn't moved. His eyes were locked on hers, shadowed with things he hadn't said and might not get another chance to. Around them, the forest was quiet but listening.

"Just…" he said, taking a slow step toward her. "Wait a second."

Her lips parted, her breath catching in her throat. "Jace… I don't know what's going to happen out there," she said, her voice shaking around the words. "I want to believe we'll all make it, but if something goes wrong—if I don't make it—"

"Don't," he cut in, voice low but firm. "Don't say it like that."

"I have to," she whispered. "Because I love you. I do. I think I have since that first time I saw you with Tyler in the school library… and every day after. And if this is the last time, I see you, I need you to know that. Not wonder. Not guess."

Jace stared at her like she'd cracked something open inside him. His defences— so well-practiced, so worn-in—faltered. His mouth opened once, closed again, and then—

He reached for her, cupping her face in both hands, his palms warm against her chilled skin. His thumbs brushed at the tears that hadn't fully fallen yet.

"I love you too," he said. Simple. Unshakable. "I didn't know how to say it. Hell, I didn't even think I was allowed to feel it. But I do. And I'm not letting that go."

She leaned into him, like her ribs had finally unclenched, like she was breathing for the first time in days. His forehead touched hers.

The kiss came slow, reverent, like something sacred in a world falling apart. It wasn't rushed. It wasn't frantic. It was steady and deep and full of everything they hadn't had time to say before now. Not goodbye—but come back.

When they broke apart, her fingers lingered on the front of his jacket, like she was memorising the shape of him.

"You get that drive to the journalist," she said. "You deliver it. Then you come back to me."

"I will," he whispered, brushing a strand of hair behind her ear. "You better be waiting."

"I will be."

He let his hand fall from hers, slowly, like parting from gravity itself.

And then—he turned. Without looking back.

She watched him disappear into the trees, until his shape vanished between the shifting light and fog.

Then she turned south, toward her own trail—toward danger, and hope, and the war they were still trying to win.

The forest closed around them, silent and vast.

But behind them, in the shadow of that old cabin, something stronger than fear had taken root.

And it was not done burning.

The fire road shimmered under the morning sun—dusty, cracked, and carved like a wound through the mountainside. It twisted down into the lowlands like a scar that never healed, exposed to sky and satellite, with no trees to offer cover. No shadows to slip into. Just heat rising off the gravel, the echo of footsteps, and a hundred ways to die if the wrong eyes were watching.

Sheriff John Nolan stood at the trail's edge, boots planted in dry soil, thumb brushing the edge of the USB drive tucked in the hidden seam of his uniform jacket. It was warm from his body heat, the plastic casing smooth and unremarkable.

But what it carried could raze a kingdom.

His badge caught the sun—a dull glint off tarnished brass. Not a relic. Not a memory. A warning.

He'd kept it pinned through every lie, every closed-door threat, every body shoved under bureaucratic silence. He wore it now not because it gave him power, but because it reminded him who he was before the fear set in. Before the compromises. Before the truth became a currency you paid for in blood.

He adjusted the pack slung over one shoulder, the straps biting into overheated skin. Checked the revolver at his hip, then the hunting knife strapped against the back of his belt. Not just for show.

His eyes scanned the ridgeline—every exposed bend, every outcrop of dry brush that could hide a scope or a silencer. Nothing yet. But quiet didn't mean safe.

He started walking west.

The old ranger cabin disappeared behind him within minutes, swallowed whole by forest and fog. Jace and Savannah were already gone, vanished in opposite directions with their own slices of the truth. No radios. No cell towers. No lifelines. If even one of them made it to the right hands, the lies would start unravelling.

But this road—his road—was the gamble with the longest odds.

The fire trail wound through BLM land and former government testing ground—decommissioned, sure, but still laced with monitoring systems, and probably tagged in whatever satellite grid Rourke's people had access to. If someone had picked up their signal during the escape, if they had time to mobilise—

This is where the trap would be waiting.

Good.

Let them come.

His truck—no plates, no VIN, scrubbed clean—was stashed two miles back, buried beneath brush and a collapsed redwood. From here, it was Oakland by backroads and trails. Forty-eight hours of walking if luck tilted his way. Closer to sixty if he had to deviate from him direct route.

He kept his pace stead. Not too fast. Not slow enough to look like he was scared.

Dust rose with every step, clinging to his boots, his cuffs, the sweat trailing down his neck. A hawk wheeled overhead, screeching once before vanishing behind a slope of burnt pine. The wind shifted—high and sharp. He caught the scent of something… off. Engine oil? Metal?

Or just memory.

His instincts twitched, but he didn't stop.

Ten years ago, Tyler Blake had been murdered for this information—the son of a work colleague, a friend, a kid John had promised to protect… and hadn't. But if they made it, if even one of them reached the truth's end, then Tyler wouldn't have died for nothing.

John reached a ridge where the trail narrowed—two hundred yards of exposed bend, no cover, high on the canyon wall. He slowed, scanning the rocks above and the valley below. Still quiet.

But his gut whispered again.

He touched the USB through the jacket, grounding himself in it.

Names. Dates. Signatures. Transaction logs. Ties to shell companies in Zurich, Doha, and Beijing. Rourke's private militia logs. The death orders on so many. The successful hits on judges, lawyers, and law enforcement. A campaign fuelled by corporate laundering and rewritten justice.

Project Perseus. One name to bury them all.

John squared his shoulders.

"I'm still standing, Rourke," he muttered, voice like gravel. "And I'm not going down quietly."

He moved on, jaw tight.

Every mile west was a threat made real. Every step was a funeral march—for the corruption, for the fear, for the empire of silence they built out of other people's bones.

He didn't care if they came for him.

He'd walk through hell with a target on his back and a badge on his chest, as long as that truth made it through the smoke.

He was still the sheriff of Cedar Ridge.

And now he was coming to burn the rot out by hand—with fire, grit, and nothing left to lose.

Chapter Thirty-One

The ranger trail narrowed into little more than dirt and stone, winding through towering pines and jagged switchbacks that carved across the mountainside like scars etched by time. Loose shale slipped beneath Jace Calloway's boots as he climbed, each step steady, deliberate. His breath fogged in the crisp morning air, the weight of the pack on his shoulders nothing compared to what rode inside his jacket pocket.

The USB drive pressed against his chest like a second heartbeat—small, plastic, and world-ending.

The early light filtered through the treetops, soft and golden, catching on dew-laced needles and casting fractured shadows across the path. It was beautiful, almost holy—but Jace didn't look up. He wasn't here for serenity. This wasn't pilgrimage.

It was war.

And this was the front line.

Sacramento was days away by foot, and he would take every one of those days if it meant staying off the grid. No cars. No signals. No easy paths. Every road had eyes now. Every plate reader and drone-fed camera could turn him into a red dot on Rourke's surveillance feed. One mistake, and the silence would swallow him just like it had Tyler.

Maya Ortiz was the only journalist he trusted with this. A truth-digger, not a headline chaser. She'd exposed Kessler's prison contracts years ago and paid for it with her career. But she hadn't stopped. She'd gone underground. Built a platform no one could buy. She'd disappeared from the networks—just like him.

Jace tightened the straps on his pack as he reached a narrow bend, the trail sloping upward, the valley yawning wide to his left. Pines towered like sentinels above him, still as statues, their shadows long and watchful. He paused for a breath, scanning the woods for movement.

Nothing. Just the wind threading through the branches and the sound of his pulse in his ears.

He moved on.

Every step was a reminder: of what he'd lost, what he'd endured, and who he was now. He'd been a prisoner. A ghost. A man locked behind bars and behind grief. But Savannah had seen through that. She'd seen the pieces he hadn't even known were still salvageable.

Tyler had seen it too. Had trusted him with the truth. Had died for it.

Now that truth sat in Jace's coat, encrypted and burning like a fuse.

At a narrow ledge, he paused. Sweat cooled on his back as he took out the flash drive—just long enough to look at it. Nondescript. Forgettable. The kind of thing a person might overlook at the bottom of a junk drawer.

But this drive had teeth. Names. Ledgers. Black sites and black budgets. It was the bullet Tyler never got to fire.

This was his shot now.

Jace slid the drive back into its sleeve and zipped the pocket shut, pressing it flat to his chest like a shield.

He thought of Savannah.

Of her eyes in the morning light, tired but bright. Of the way her voice had cracked when she told him she loved him—not desperate, but defiant, as if daring the world to take her down before she got the words out.

He'd never said those words to anyone. Not before prison. Not during.

Even after Savannah had told him she loved him—eyes steady, heart wide open—he hadn't said them back.

He didn't think he was allowed. Didn't think he deserved to.

But he knew better now.

She was it. The one thing that had never wavered, even when everything else fell apart.

And now, with no one listening but the trees and the wind threading through the silence, he said it again—softly, reverently, like it mattered more now than it ever had.

"I love you, Savvy."

A promise.

A prayer.

A battle cry.

Then he kept moving—through brush, over rock, deeper into the wilderness that swallowed sound and light. The trail narrowed again ahead, disappearing between two ridges cloaked in shadow.

No shortcuts. No safety net.

Just one man.

One chance.

One shot at redemption wrapped in a drive barely bigger than his thumb.

And Jace Calloway wasn't stopping until the truth reached the light—no matter how far, how steep, or how bloody the climb.

The sun had barely cleared the horizon when Savannah Blake stepped into the dry riverbed, boots crunching over jagged stones bleached white by time and drought. The morning air was thin and sharp, filled with dust that coated her lungs and clung to her flannel like a second skin. There was no trail here—just a gash in the earth, raw and forgotten, carved by centuries of storms and silence.

It wasn't a path.

It was a reckoning.

She adjusted the straps of her backpack, cinching them tight against her spine. Every muscle in her body protested. Her shoulders ached. Her calves burned. Her hands still bore faint tremors from the adrenaline crash. The night before had been a blur of gunfire, shattered glass, and a kiss she hadn't wanted to end. But there was no room now for fear. Or longing.

Only forward.

This was the only way south without being seen. No road signs. No signal towers. Just a stretch of barren wash that wove between canyon walls like a forgotten vein, winding toward the last people Tyler Blake had ever trusted.

The Mariposa Network.

She'd memorised the note he'd had on the USB drive the night before—she didn't know why she did, she just had a feeling it would be important. And she was right.

They were ghosts. Burned-out feds. Data analysts gone dark. Journalists who wouldn't shut up when the system told them to. Tyler had whispered their names once, over beers and music and midnight fears she couldn't explain.

Now she knew why.

If anyone could blow open Project Perseus—if anyone could turn those files into fire—she'd find them here.

The USB was stitched into her jacket's lining. She kept touching it—not from fear, but because it tethered her. To her brother. To what he'd given up.

To what she refused to let die.

Burn it down, Sav. All of it.

She stumbled once, slipping on loose gravel. Her palm scraped hard against a jagged boulder, tearing the skin. Blood welled up, stinging in the dust. But she didn't stop. She didn't curse. She just straightened, wiped her hand on her jeans, and kept moving.

This wasn't a path that forgave hesitation.

By midmorning, the heat had arrived in full force—radiating off the canyon walls, turning every breath into effort. The sun burned overhead, unrelenting. The air shimmered like a mirage. Her flannel clung to her like wet paper, and her skin itched with sweat and grime. She hadn't seen another human since she left Jace this morning. But that was the point.

Every step was a test. Every stretch of sun-blasted earth asked her the same question:

How far are you willing to go for the truth?

Her answer stayed the same.

As far as it takes.

She thought of Jace.

Of the way his hand had lingered against hers before they split. The way his voice had cracked when he said, 'Then come back to me'.

The way he'd said 'I love you' like it was something sacred.

They didn't get to have a future. Not yet.

But maybe—if she survived this—she could build one with him out of the wreckage.

Savannah crested a steep ridge of cracked earth, her legs trembling, her breath ragged. Below her, the canyon opened into a narrow gorge—twisting like a serpent between the southern hills. Somewhere beyond it: forest. Dirt roads. A ranger station turned safehouse that Tyler had mapped in detail.

The last known drop point for the Network.

She braced her hands on her knees, trying to catch her breath. Her lips were cracked. Her throat raw. But in her chest, beneath all the fatigue and fear, something steadier burned.

Resolve.

She looked south—toward the shadows, the thorns, and the silence—and started down the ridge.

One woman.

One drive.

One truth no bullet could bury.

And no matter what waited ahead—Savannah Blake wasn't turning back.

Chapter Thirty-Two

The hills outside Oakland stretched like burned bones beneath the rising sun—cracked, dry, and humming with heat. The asphalt shimmered like water, but there was no mercy in it. Sheriff John Nolan kept one hand steady on the wheel, the other brushing against the sweat-soaked fabric over his chest pocket. The USB drive was still there, pressed against his sternum like a second heartbeat.

So close.

The city skyline floated in the distance—faint, silver-blue against the haze—but it was real. One hour more. Maybe less if the backroads held.

The truck—old, borrowed, by a law-abiding citizen trying to help—rattled over the pavement with every bump. It had no plates, no records. Because Nolan had stripped it too clean to be lucky. And deep down, he knew luck didn't stick around this long without wanting something in return.

He adjusted the revolver on his hip and checked the mirror again.

Empty road.

Still—

His gut twisted before his eyes caught up.

Movement.

Fast.

Controlled.

A black SUV peeled out from a side road and fell in behind him. Too clean. Too quiet. Then another. One behind. One on the flank.

John's jaw clenched. His pulse spiked.

"Damn it," he muttered, and shoved his foot down.

The truck groaned like it knew it wasn't built for this. But it surged forward.

Then the shots came—sharp and fast. The rear windshield exploded in a spray of glass. Shards glittered in the sun before clattering across the seat.

He ducked low, swerved hard. Tyres screamed. Gravel spat.

Another shot tore through the side mirror. A third punched clean through the passenger door and slammed into the glovebox.

He veered off the road, cutting onto a narrow utility trail barely visible through the weeds. Rusted fencing flashed past. Dead branches clawed at the windows.

The SUV followed without hesitation—engine snarling like a dog that had tasted blood.

The tree line loomed ahead—thin coverage, but just enough to break a clear shot. He took the chance. Gunned the wheel. The truck fishtailed over dirt and roots, bounced off a stump, and slammed into a ditch with a crunch of metal and a burst of smoke.

John's head cracked against the window. Stars flared in his vision.

Pain bloomed in his ribs. But there was no time to check.

He was already moving—grabbing the revolver, jamming the USB deeper into his jacket, and kicking the door open.

The forest swallowed him in a rush of shadow and birdsong.

Behind him, the SUV's tyres screeched to a stop. Doors slammed. Voices barked orders.

Then came the chase.

John crashed through underbrush, his lungs burning, the stitch in his side sharp enough to blind him. But he didn't stop. Couldn't. Every step was a gamble. Every heartbeat was a countdown.

Then a bullet whipped past his ear. Another clipped a branch above his head. A third hit home.

His thigh lit up with agony—hot, deep, and immediate.

He collapsed hard, skidding behind a fallen log. Blood soaked through his pants, dark and fast. He bit back a scream and drew the revolver with a shaking hand.

Shadows moved.

Two men, dressed for war. Tactical gear. Sunglasses that hid everything.

He fired—once. The first man staggered back with a shout, clutching his arm.

He fired again—missed.

Click.

Empty.

John stared down at the revolver like it had betrayed him. His hand trembled. His vision blurred.

A boot crunched through the leaves.

Then the forest went black.

The woods had gone still again. A bird called somewhere up the slope. The sun pressed down like a weight.

The black SUV reversed onto the trail. Dust kicked up behind it like smoke after a fire. Then it was gone—leaving only skid marks and the coppery scent of blood.

Hours later.

John Nolan lay motionless, one hand clamped over the bullet wound in his thigh, the other curled against the soil. The revolver was gone. So was the drive.

His jaw clenched. His breath came shallow.

He was still alive.

Barely.

They had taken the USB. One third of the evidence—gone.

But not all.

Hope divided by three, Jace had said, back when this plan had only been paranoia and paper.

And John had believed him. Had counted on the redundancy. Savannah had a copy. So did Jace.

He didn't know where they were. Didn't know if they were still breathing.

But he was.

And as long as he was—

This war wasn't over.

He let his eyes close for a second. Just a second. Then, with a groan of pain and a grit of teeth, John Nolan dragged himself toward the brush, one inch at a time.

The badge on his chest caught a shard of sunlight.

Still shining.

Still fighting.

Because no matter how much blood this truth cost—

It was worth every damn drop.

The foothills north of Sacramento sprawled like a sunburned wasteland—dusty, exposed, broken only by twisted scrub trees and skeletal barbed-wire fences. No shelter. No shadows. Just open ground and a sky so bright it felt like judgment.

Jace Calloway moved fast, boots dragging through loose earth, breath shallow and sharp. Dust caked his jeans, his throat, the creases of his clenched hands. His pack thudded against his spine with each stride, the USB drive tight against his chest, wrapped in a waterproof sleeve and stitched into the inner lining of his jacket like a secret too dangerous to leave behind.

Because it was.

Two days of climbing; a night sleeping in a ravine and dodging every potential drone sweep, had left him raw. His legs burned. His ribs still ached from an old bruise. But this—this was the last stretch. A few more miles, and he'd reach the edge of the city. The rendezvous point: an abandoned print warehouse just outside the grid. Concrete, anonymous, and off the books.

And inside—Maya Ortiz.

The last real journalist left in the state. Blacklisted. Unbought. Unbroken.

The only one Jace thought might actually finish what Tyler started.

Jace ducked beneath a ridgeline of scorched rock and flattened against the slope, catching his breath. His heartbeat thundered in his ears, louder than the wind scraping over the hills.

A few more miles, and the fight would be in Maya's hands. A professional. A truth-digger. He just had to make it to the door.

Then—

Crunch.

A single, deliberate footstep behind him. Not an animal. Not a slip.

An ambush.

His head snapped toward the sound, but—

Too late.

A figure exploded from the brush, slamming him back against the rocky incline. Another grabbed him from behind, strong, and silent. Gloved hands wrenched his arms. He kicked, twisted, shoved—

"Get the hell off—!"

An elbow connected—one attacker grunted—but the second drove a hard jab into his stomach, knocking the wind out of him. A fist followed, sharp and unforgiving, splitting the skin across his cheekbone. The world tilted.

He hit the ground, knees first, choking on dirt and blood.

A boot collided with his ribs—twice.

White-hot pain lanced through his side. His body folded.

Rough fingers clawed through his jacket. He fought back, snarling, biting, blind—but they were fast. Trained. Coordinated. Government, or worse.

One let out a sharp grunt of victory. "Got it."

Jace tried to lunge—tried to reach for the drive—but he was too slow, too disoriented. A knee smashed up under his chin, and the impact sent fireworks across his vision. He collapsed again; arms limp in the dirt.

Footsteps shuffled beside him. Then someone crouched low.

Jace forced his eyes open.

The man wore black tactical gear. Mirror-shade sunglasses. No insignia. No name.

His voice was gravel wrapped in silk.

"You're lucky, convict."

Jace coughed. Blood mixed with spit as he glared upward. "Try me again, asshole."

The man's mouth curled into a smile—cool, dismissive. "You're not priority anymore."

He held up the USB drive like a trophy.

"But your girlfriend?" he added, tilting his head, voice dipping quieter. "The nurse?"

A pause. Deliberate. Cruel.

"He wants her dead. No matter what."

Jace's heart stopped.

Savannah.

The name didn't even leave his lips, but it ripped through his chest like shrapnel.

The man straightened. Then—a boot to the ribs. Hard. Jace cried out, folding in on himself.

"Enjoy the sunset," the man said, turning away.

The SUV's engine roared to life in the distance. Gravel crunched. Tyres spun.

They were gone in seconds—swallowed by the haze and heat like ghosts.

Jace lay still, cheek pressed to the dirt, blood seeping from his mouth, his ribs screaming with every breath.

But he wasn't done.

Not even close.

He let the pain anchor him. Let the rage sharpen him. Savannah was still out there. Alone. Walking into danger she didn't even know was coming. And he'd be damned if he let Rourke touch her.

They thought taking the drive would stop him.

They didn't understand who he was now.

Jace Calloway had spent ten years buried by a system that wanted him silent. But he'd crawled out of that grave with purpose in his bones and fire in his blood.

And now they'd taken the only thing keeping her safe.

Big mistake.

He shoved himself upright, trembling, bleeding—but moving.

Step by step, fuelled by nothing but adrenaline and a promise.

One way or another, he'd get to her.

One way or another, the truth was still getting out.

And if Rourke wanted a war—

Then he'd just made it personal.

Chapter Thirty-Three

The sun hung low in the sky, slanting gold through the dust-streaked foothills like firelight filtered through smoke. The air shimmered with heat. Everything smelled of sunburnt sage and dry earth. Savannah Blake's boots scraped over loose rock as she crested the final ridge, her legs shaking beneath her. Her throat was raw, her lips cracked, and blood caked her scraped knees, but she didn't stop.

She couldn't.

Not when, through the haze and between the trees, she finally saw it.

A rusted water tower—its legs splintered with age, the paint almost gone—but still bearing a faded red triangle barely visible beneath layers of grime and weather.

Her breath caught.

The mark.

Exactly where Tyler had written it would be, typed in a file in the USB drive that she was carrying to tell the world of the corruption within their government, he'd written, 'look for the triangle. Mariposa. They'll help; they will know how to get it out'.

She staggered forward, blinking tears. Her heart thudded like it was trying to punch through her ribs.

Then—

A rustle.

A shadow.

From behind a sandstone boulder twenty yards ahead, a figure emerged. Tall. Lean. Dust-covered clothes in neutral tones, one hand hovering near the pistol holstered at his hip. A woman followed, younger, compact, rifle slung low— not aimed but not relaxed either.

They didn't move fast.

Didn't need to.

Their stillness spoke of training. Of readiness.

The man lifted a hand. "Name."

Savannah raised both hands slowly, her body screaming in protest. Her fingers trembled as she unzipped her jacket pocket and pulled out a small object wrapped in waterproof casing.

"Savannah Blake," she rasped, voice barely there. "I was told to find the Mariposa Network. My brother—Tyler Blake—he thought you would help."

The name landed like a stone dropped in still water.

The woman lowered her rifle slightly, her eyes flicking to the man.

Recognition.

Something in their stance shifted—not relaxed, but no longer hostile.

"You walked the riverbed?" the man asked.

"All the way from Cedar Ridge," Savannah replied, swaying on her feet. "I have something. You need to see it."

She held the drive up; the casing smeared with dirt and sweat. The weight of it seemed to radiate heat now—more burden than object. A piece of her soul lived in that plastic.

The man studied her for a breath, then gave a small, clipped nod.

"Come with us. Slowly."

She followed them down a narrow switchback trail barely visible from above, hidden by twisted oaks and overgrown brush. Her boots stumbled once. Twice. But they didn't wait—just moved forward, sure of every step.

And then—the canyon opened.

Low-profile tents reinforced with aluminium. Makeshift solar panels lashed to plywood frames. A satellite dish wrapped in camo netting. Cables running through crushed gravel like veins beneath skin. Everything tucked into the earth like it had grown there.

It didn't look like a base.

It looked like a secret.

And everyone stopped when she entered. Conversations halted. Heads turned. The air buzzed with silent questions.

They led her through the camp to a converted shipping container tucked beneath a stand of cedar trees. It was cool inside, dimly lit by a single lamp. The scent of old books, ozone, and something herbal filled the space. A soldering station blinked quietly in one corner.

At the centre of the room, a woman stood.

Late fifties. Iron-grey braid. A black fleece jacket patched at the shoulder. Sharp eyes—cut from flint, not fear.

She didn't smile.

She didn't need to.

"I'm Evelyn Hart," she said. "Founder of the Mariposa Network."

She stepped forward.

"You're Tyler's sister."

Savannah nodded. The weight of it all caught up at once—grief, exhaustion, adrenaline. Her knees buckled, but she locked them out of sheer will. One more step. Just one.

"Tyler was going to give us information before he died. I thought it was all lost."

"I found it. Everything Tyler found," she said, voice breaking. "The money trails. The assassinations. The names. Rourke's orders. It's all here."

She held out the USB.

Evelyn took it with both hands, like it was holy.

She turned immediately to the young woman who'd followed them in. "Download it all. Air-gapped system only. Now."

The tech didn't hesitate—gone in seconds.

Evelyn turned back. "You walked that whole way with that?"

Savannah nodded, barely able to stand. "Jace Calloway went north. Sheriff John Nolan went west. We split up to increase the odds. I don't... I don't know if they made it."

Evelyn didn't flinch. "We've had no intercept chatter. That's a good sign. And you made it. Which means someone still has a fighting chance."

Savannah swayed. Evelyn caught her elbow, steady and firm.

"You're safe now," she said. "Let's get you water. Food. You've done more than enough."

"I just need a minute," Savannah whispered, sinking into a battered old armchair someone slid behind her. She slumped back, eyes half-closed. "Just… a second to breathe."

Evelyn crouched in front of her, resting a hand on her knee. Her voice was quieter now, but fierce. "You did the impossible, Savannah. You brought the match to the powder keg."

She looked toward the door.

"Now we light it."

Outside, the camp shifted back into motion. Quiet. Focused. Controlled chaos with purpose.

Inside, Savannah leaned her head back, her hand curled unconsciously toward the spot where the drive had been.

She had made it.

The drive had made it.

And somewhere in the world, the first sparks of truth were about to fly.

Jace's fingers shook as he powered on his phone, his back pressed tight to the base of a crumbling concrete pillar beneath the abandoned overpass. Dust clung to the sweat on his neck. Every second the screen lit up felt like a flare against the sky, a digital scream that could draw eyes—drones, interceptors, trackers.

He knew it.

Didn't care.

He had to reach her.

Savannah.

The home screen flickered on. No signal bars at first. Then one. Two. Enough.

His heart slammed against his ribs as he scrolled through the contacts—just two numbers stored. He stopped at the second number…

Her name blinked up at him: Savannah Blake.

He tapped it. Hit call.

Put the phone to his ear, breath ragged.

Nothing.

Straight to voicemail.

He yanked the phone back, stared at the screen like sheer will might change the outcome. Tried again. Another hollow click, then the automated voice. Still dark. Still unreachable.

The breath that left his lungs came out in a shudder—half fury, half helplessness. The kind that burned worse because there was nothing to swing at. No enemy. Just silence.

He switched to the message thread. Her name lit up at the top like a ghost. The last text she'd sent was days old— 'Be home soon. Love you.'

His fingers hovered over the keypad. Then typed.

Please, Savvy. Call me the second you get this. I'm begging you. Just let me know you're alive.

He read it twice, hit send.

The message hung for a heartbeat—buffering. Searching.

Then—

Delivered.

But no read receipt. No typing dots. Just silence.

Jace closed his eyes. His jaw tightened until it ached. He scrubbed a hand down his face, smearing dirt, and blood.

"Come on, Savvy," he whispered into the air, voice frayed at the edges. "Come on."

A long silence. The wind kicked dust along the cracked pavement. In the distance, a hawk cried once.

He looked at the phone again. Nothing yet.

His pulse wouldn't slow.

Neither would the ache in his chest.

Because she was out there.

And they had said Rourke wanted her dead.

And if anything had happened to her…

Jace shoved the phone into his jacket and stood, wincing at the fire in his ribs.

He wasn't waiting.

He wasn't stopping.

Because now, every second without her voice was one second closer to hell.

And he was going to burn the whole system down to get her back.

Savannah sat on a rickety chair in front of a folding table inside the mess tent, the canvas flap muted the wind, wrapping her in half-light. Her fingers curled around a chipped tin cup of water that tasted faintly of iron and old wood smoke—cold relief she gulped down like a prayer. A volunteer slid a steaming bowl of rice and beans in front of her. Simple, nourishing, and too quiet in the aftermath of everything.

She ate slowly, each spoonful as deliberate as a meditation, eyes unfocused on the swaying rows of cots beyond. Her feet throbbed where the riverbed had ground blisters into her heels; every step felt raw in her bones. The weight of the last two days—running, hiding, the suns burning glare—pulled her shoulders low. In that riverbed, she'd almost let the sun burn her into nothingness. Here, she was something again.

"Cot?" a soft voice offered—a young woman in olive drab, brown hair pulled back under a bandana.

Savannah pressed her lips together, shook her head once. "I'm fine," she whispered, voice brittle.

Evelyn Hart stood nearby, arms folded, taking her measure. Then she nodded. "Shower first. Then you rest."

Fifteen minutes later, Savannah huddled under the trickle of tepid water in a narrow makeshift stall. The stream was more drizzle than downpour, but it was heaven. She let it run down her back in cold rivulets, scrubbing at the grit and dried blood until her skin stung pink and the water sluiced away clean. She closed her eyes and felt layers of fear and fatigue peel off with each soapy rinse.

Dressed in freshly issued clothes—soft joggers, a plain grey tee, thick wool socks—she emerged into the pre-sunset chill of the main tent. An old leather couch sat near an unlit wood stove, its cushions cracked and well-worn. She sank into the corner, curled onto her side, head resting on the armrest like a child folding into a parent's lap.

All she wanted was to hear Jace's voice. She imagined it: low and rough with worry, but alive. Alive.

Her phone lay face-down on the floor beside her—silent and powerless with its battery removed. No calls. No contact. That was the pact. Not until the Mariposa Network had released the files and the world was listening. Every beep, every ring could be a trap.

She reached out, fingertips brushing the smooth phone, then withdrew. Risk. Not yet.

She drew the blanket up to her chin, the coarse wool scratchy but warm against her cheek. Beneath it, her heart slowed, easing into the promise of safety— temporary, fragile, but enough.

Sleep came quickly, without fanfare. Her last thought before her lids fluttered shut was of Jace walking that narrow trail north, each footstep carrying his promise to return. And Savannah let herself believe it.

In the hush of the scattered penumbra, she slept—at last free, if only for a night.

Chapter Thirty-Four

The story broke at 8:04 a.m.

At first, it was just another notification. Another buzz on a lock screen. A headline flashing across the bottom of a quiet morning broadcast.

But by 8:05, the ripple had turned into a tidal wave.

Traffic outside the Capitol screeched to a halt as though the city itself had slammed on the brakes. Drivers pulled over mid-commute, coffee forgotten, hands trembling around steering wheels as their eyes locked on glowing screens. Office workers stopped mid-step, staring down at phones, mouths parted in stunned silence. In cafés, trains, and classrooms, conversations died mid-sentence.

Tyler's files—released in full.

Encrypted archives unlocked and dumped on a mirrored network of sites impossible to scrub.

Bank statements. Surveillance logs. Flight manifests. Internal memos bearing Marcus Rourke's digital signature.

And the voice recording.

Chilling. Crystal clear.

A private meeting—Rourke speaking in clipped, arrogant tones, naming names, outlining bribes and extortion, orders to eliminate witnesses, silence whistleblowers. Evidence of secret detention sites, off-book budgets, and a conspiracy that reached every corner of the state's justice system.

The truth laid bare.

By 8:15, #PerseusFiles was trending worldwide.

By 8:17, civil rights groups and journalist watchdogs issued official statements.

By 8:18, a U.S. Senator retweeted the leak with one word: 'Enough'.

By 8:20, every major news outlet had picked it up—CNN, BBC, Al Jazeera, Reuters—all calling it the biggest political scandal of the decade. Some were already dubbing it 'Watergate West.'.

Anchors on live broadcasts looked shell-shocked, stammering through segments as producers shouted in their earpieces and new footage rolled in by the second.

And by 8:30, Marcus Rourke's face was everywhere.

On phone screens.

On news tickers.

On smart TVs that auto-updated breaking alerts.

On digital billboards along I-80 and Route 50—some of which were already being defaced by protestors.

Spray-painted words slashed across his face like accusations:

LIAR. TRAITOR. MURDERER.

Crowds were forming outside federal buildings and courthouses across the state—angry, unified, loud. Some carried signs. Some just came to bear witness. But all of them knew, now.

The silence had been broken.

The lies exposed.

And somewhere in an undisclosed location—beneath the shadow of a rusted water tower marked by a faded red triangle—Savannah Blake slept.

Not from comfort.

From sheer exhaustion.

Her body was still, curled in the corner of a plain, nondescript room, the weight of the last few days pressing down like lead. She'd done it. She'd gotten the drive into the right hands.

Outside, radios crackled. Voices rose in stunned disbelief, then louder—half-shocked, half-cheering.

It had worked.

The truth was out.

And at last, after years of silence and cover-ups—

Tyler's voice was heard.

John watched it unfold from a hospital bed, half-propped up by stiff pillows and the slow drip of morphine humming through his veins. The room smelled like antiseptic and overcooked eggs. A heart monitor beeped steadily beside him, each pulse too loud in the quiet.

He'd managed to crawl far enough from the ditch, blood soaking his jeans, the revolver long gone. Found a signal. Dialled emergency. Said just enough before he blacked out. When he woke, he was here—patched up, sedated, alive.

The bullet had missed the femoral artery by a whisper. "Clean exit," the surgeon had said. "You're lucky."

He didn't feel lucky.

Not with the USB gone. Not with the dull ache in his leg or the heavier one in his chest, where failure pressed like a second wound. That drive had been everything. His part of the mission. His debt to Tyler. To Savannah. To Jace. To justice.

And he'd lost it.

The nurse had left the TV on—muted. But the banner caught his eye around 8:05, crawling across the bottom of the screen in urgent red.

BREAKING: WHISTLEBLOWER LEAK EXPOSES STATEWIDE CORRUPTION.

Then the video package rolled in. A flurry of headlines. Tyler's name.

John reached for the remote, fumbling with stiff fingers, and turned up the volume just as the anchor's voice steadied:

"—in a sweeping exposé now known as the Perseus Files, a cache of classified documents and audio recordings obtained by whistleblower Tyler Blake has confirmed a systemic conspiracy spanning multiple state agencies. Blake, a former government analyst, was murdered ten years ago, and a Jace Calloway was wrongly convicted of the crime but has since been released. Tyler's his evidence—painstakingly researched and delivered posthumously—has now reached the public."

A photo appeared on screen. Tyler, laughing, holding a guitar in one hand and a beer in the other. Young. Alive. Before it all went dark.

John's throat tightened.

The anchor's voice softened, reverent. "Tyler Blake risked everything. And though he didn't live to see it—his truth will reshape the course of this state's history."

John closed his eyes.

For a long breath, he let the silence inside him settle. Not just grief—but release. Relief.

Tyler had made it. Not in body, but in legacy. They hadn't silenced him after all.

Despite the bullets, despite the erasures, despite the blood spilled in shadows—they hadn't won.

The system had cracked wide open.

John exhaled, slow and heavy.

And for the first time in a long time, he let himself believe in something more than survival.

He believed in justice.

Jace sat in a roadside diner just outside Sacramento, tucked in a cracked vinyl booth that smelled like old coffee and older regret. The place was nearly empty—just a trucker hunched over eggs at the far end and a waitress who hadn't asked many questions when she saw the bruises on his face. He'd ordered coffee out of habit, not intention. It sat in front of him now, long since cold, untouched except for the steam that had ghosted away minutes ago.

Above the counter, an ancient television flickered with static at the edges. No sound. Just a muted news anchor mouthing gravity while the red crawl at the bottom of the screen said everything that mattered:

BREAKING: PERSEUS FILES EXPOSE FEDERAL CORRUPTION RING.

The words burned into his vision, bold and irrevocable. His jaw clenched, chest tight with disbelief and something dangerously close to hope.

They'd made it.

The world finally knew.

But knowing didn't make her safe.

The system was bleeding now, exposed for the rot it was. Tyler's truth—their truth—had finally clawed its way into the light.

But that wasn't the only truth clawing at Jace Calloway.

What he didn't know—what hollowed out his ribs more with every breath—was who had made it.

John?

Savannah?

Had it been her drive? Her voice?

If it had been John's drive…

Then Savannah might be gone.

The not knowing was a slow kind of agony.

Worse than the cracked rib.

Worse than the pain lancing through his side every time he inhaled.

Because pain meant he was alive.

Ignorance just meant he was helpless.

And that was unbearable.

His phone buzzed against the table. He snatched it like a drowning man grabbing a rope—but it was just a weather alert. He swiped it away, hand trembling.

No missed calls.

No messages.

No Savannah.

He checked again anyway. Opened the thread. Stared at the last message he'd sent her hours ago:

Please, Savvy. Call me the second you get this. I'm begging you. Just let me know you're alive.

Delivered. But not read.

He rubbed a hand over his jaw, rough with days-old stubble, and stared blankly at the formica tabletop. Time moved weirdly in here. Too slow. Too loud. The ticking clock on the wall felt like a countdown. To what, he didn't know. Maybe the moment when someone walked through the door and told him she was gone.

His foot bounced restlessly beneath the table.

His hand stayed curled around the phone like a lifeline.

She should've called by now.

He couldn't shake the last words that bastard in the black shirt had whispered before the SUV vanished in a spray of gravel:

'The nurse. He wants her dead. No matter what.'

He hadn't said her name, but he didn't have to.

Jace had seen it in his eyes. Cold. Certain.

That was the last thing he remembered before the world tilted sideways and he hit the dirt with blood in his mouth and fire in his ribs.

Now here he sat, still breathing, but barely holding it together.

Frozen. Trapped in a loop of waiting.

Please, Savannah. Just call. Just text. Just… something.

He didn't know if the silence meant safety.

Or if it meant he was already too late.

The truth was out. The story was out.

But stories don't stop bullets.

And Jace knew better than anyone: Marcus Rourke didn't lose quietly.

He looked down at his phone again.

Still dark.

His reflection stared back in the screen—cut, hollow, raw.

And he prayed.

Not to any god that ever answered him before. But to her. Please, Savannah. Please be alive. Say something. Anything.

Chapter Thirty-Five

The first thing Savannah registered was warmth.

Sunlight poured through the cracked blinds in narrow bands, brushing across her face like a soft hand. It was a gentle kind of light—quiet, golden, almost apologetic in the way it kissed her skin. For a moment, she stayed still, eyes closed, letting it soak into her bones.

The second thing she noticed was silence.

But not the sharp-edged, listening kind she'd carried with her for days—not the silence of hiding, or holding your breath because every noise could mean danger. This was different. This quiet felt earned. It felt like safety.

She blinked awake slowly, the stiffness in her body surfacing all at once. Every muscle protested as she shifted, her limbs heavy from too many hours curled on the old couch. Her flannel shirt was twisted around her waist, one sock missing, hair tangled and unbrushed. She looked a complete mess—and felt like one.

A faint trace of lavender soap clung to her skin, the only remnant of a shower she could barely remember taking. Someone—Evelyn, probably—had draped another wool blanket over her while she slept.

That small gesture—quiet, thoughtful—hit harder than she expected.

Not because it was grand.

But because it reminded her, she wasn't alone anymore.

She sat up slowly, legs over the edge of the couch, toes brushing cool floorboards. Her throat was dry, her eyes gritty, but her heartbeat had slowed to something normal, something human. For the first time in what felt like forever, her body wasn't braced for flight.

The room buzzed with low voices and quiet motion. Two techs hunched over workstations near the back, monitors flickering with code, data streams, mirrored file transfers still churning. The hum of solar-powered servers filled the space with a quiet energy. Across the room, Evelyn Hart stood with her arms crossed, watching one of the screens with the sharp, focused calm of someone who'd seen revolutions born before breakfast.

When Evelyn turned and saw Savannah awake, something shifted in her expression. A smile. Small, rare. But real.

"It's done," Evelyn said, her voice low but certain.

Savannah blinked, brain still climbing out of sleep. "What?"

"The story broke just after eight this morning. We hit five encrypted networks simultaneously. It went live across the dark net, scrubbed versions on major media forums. Journalists picked it up in minutes. Mirrored across thousands of IPs before breakfast. Rourke. Project Perseus. The death squads. The money trails. The memo. Your brother's voice."

She stepped closer, crouching beside Savannah like she didn't want to break the moment.

"It's all out there now."

Savannah didn't respond at first. Her mouth opened, but no words came. A breath escaped her—half-sob, half-laugh—as something inside her finally let go. She shook, just a little, her fingers curling into the blanket like it was the only thing tethering her to the moment.

"It worked," she whispered. "Tyler... he did it."

Evelyn reached out and gripped her hand, firm and warm. "You did it. He trusted the right person. And you got it across the line."

Savannah swallowed hard, blinking away tears. The knot that had lived in her chest for days—tight and twisting—was finally unravelling. She let herself lean into it. Just for a moment.

Then she remembered.

Her hand shot to her backpack. She unzipped it with shaking fingers and pulled out her phone. She hadn't powered it on yet—hadn't dared. They'd told her not to. No calls. No signals. Not until the story went live.

But now...

Her thumb hesitated over the button.

Then she pressed it.

The screen lit up. Signal bars blinked into place. Time updated.

Immediately, a message flashed onto the screen.

A single line.

Time-stamped from the day before.

Please, Savvy. Call me the second you get this. I'm begging you. Just let me know you're alive.

Her breath caught in her chest. Her fingers fumbled as she opened the thread, hit Call.

It rang once.

Twice.

Then—

"Savvy?"

His voice hit her like a jolt of electricity, straight through the ribcage.

"Jace," she breathed. "Oh my God. Are you okay? Where are you?"

"You're alive," he said, rough and breathless, the words tumbling out like a prayer. "God, Savvy. I thought they—I thought I lost you."

"I was lucky, no one tried to stop me," she said, pressing the phone tighter to her ear. "I made it. I'm safe. I'm at the Mariposa base. Evelyn Hart's team—Jace, they got it out. All of it. The files. The voice recording. Tyler's work. It's everywhere. We did it."

"I saw the headlines. I didn't know whose drive made it through. I didn't know if you—" His voice cracked, then steadied. "Every hour I didn't hear from you—I thought…"

Savannah closed her eyes, let his voice wash over her. "It was mine," she said. "But it could've been yours. Or John's. We planned for this. We planned for this, Jace. It worked."

He exhaled hard, like he'd been holding his breath for a week. "Where are you exactly? Tell me."

"I'm still here. Still safe. They're watching over me."

"Are you okay?" he asked, voice softer now. "Really okay?"

"I am now," she whispered. "But Jace… are you?"

"I will be," he said, and she could hear the truth in it. "Now that I know you're alive."

She smiled, tears blurring her vision again. "Then come find me."

There was a pause. And when he spoke again, his voice had changed—low, steady, sure.

"I will. And this time, Savvy… I'm not letting you go."

She didn't answer right away. Just sat there in the quiet hum of the room, clutching the phone to her ear, her heart pounding with something too big to name.

For the first time in days, the fear was gone.

The fight wasn't over—not by a long shot—but for now, in this fragile moment between battles, Savannah let herself believe in peace.

And she let herself believe in him.

The sun was high and bright, casting sharp gold light across the canyon as a dust-covered Jeep rolled to a slow stop just beyond the edge of the Mariposa Network's hidden camp. The engine ticked as it cooled, the sound too loud in the stillness. Around it, the forest hushed again—birdsong warbling from the trees, dry wind whispering through brittle leaves, and the low hum of solar rigs vibrating faintly in the heat.

A guard stepped out from behind a shaded checkpoint—cautious, steady, one hand resting near his sidearm but not drawing. The man who climbed out of the Jeep was limping slightly, favouring his left side. His shirt was torn, stained with blood and dirt. His face bore days-old bruises, one eye still shadowed with purple and yellow, but his eyes—dark, glassy with exhaustion and fire—were sharp.

"Name?" the guard asked.

"Jace Calloway," he said, the words scraping past dust-dry lips. "I'm here for Savannah Blake."

The name moved faster than the wind.

A voice crackled over a nearby comm. Then, through the layered rise of tents and gear, a figure came running—swift and sure-footed down the slope. Evelyn Hart emerged from the shadow of the mess tent, her fleece jacket pushed back, hand lifted to shield her eyes from the sun.

She scanned him once—head to toe—and nodded once, short, and sure.

"He's clean," she called to the guard. "Let him through."

Jace didn't wait for a second nod. He was already moving—stumbling past tents, past cables coiled like snakes in the dirt, past startled volunteers, and watchful eyes. His boots kicked dust with every uneven step, his heart thudding like a war drum trying to outrun the last three days.

And then—

He saw her.

Savannah stood in the open doorway of the communications trailer; one hand wrapped around her phone. Her hair was damp, pulled into a low braid, her clothes loose and unfamiliar. Her face was thinner than he remembered. Paler. Tired.

But her eyes—when they met his—lit up like sunrise after a month of storms.

They froze.

Just for a heartbeat.

The world narrowed to a tunnel between them.

And then she ran.

Her phone hit the ground with a dull thud, forgotten. Her boots slapped hard against the packed earth, arms pumping. Jace didn't care about the pain in his side or the crack in his rib—he ran too.

They collided at full force, both winded, both trembling, both half-laughing, half-sobbing. Savannah's arms wrapped tight around his neck, her fingers digging in like she didn't trust the ground to hold her. Jace caught her around the waist and held on like he'd found the edge of a cliff and refused to fall.

He buried his face in her shoulder, breathing her in. Sweat, dust, and something unmistakably her.

"Thank God, Savvy," he breathed. "You're safe."

She pulled back just enough to cup his face in both hands. Her thumbs skimmed over the cut on his cheek, the bruise near his jaw. "I thought I lost you," she said, voice shaking. "When the files hit—I didn't know if you made it. I didn't know if—"

He didn't let her finish.

He kissed her.

Hard. Desperate. Real.

It wasn't the kiss of reunion—it was the kiss of survival. The kiss of two people who had run through fire and somehow met at the other side. Her mouth parted under his. Her fingers curled in his shirt, holding tight. He cradled the back of her head like he was afraid she'd vanish if he let go.

When they finally pulled apart, she rested her forehead to his, breathing in sync with him. Her eyes were wet, lashes thick with tears that didn't fall.

"I told you to come find me," she whispered.

"And I told you," he said, voice rough and raw, "I wasn't letting you go."

They stood there for a long moment, arms wrapped tight, the whole camp moving softly around them—quiet footsteps, low murmurs, respectful distance.

Because this wasn't just a reunion.

It was a vow made in flesh.

It was love, tested and proven, found in the wreckage.

And nothing that came before—or would come after—could ever take this from them.

Chapter Thirty-Six

By mid afternoon, word came through the secure channel:

John Nolan was alive.

Savannah let out a sob the second Evelyn relayed the message, her hands flying to her mouth as her shoulders crumpled with relief. Tears sprang to her eyes without warning—sharp, grateful, unstoppable.

Jace, sitting beside her, exhaled hard and slumped forward, elbows on his knees like the weight of a mountain had finally been lifted off his back.

"He's stable," Evelyn said, scanning the message again with a rare softness in her voice. "Recovering at a hospital in Oakland. Looks like emergency responders got to him just in time. He's tough. Stubborn, too. Tried to discharge himself already."

Jace let out a low huff of disbelief. "Of course he did," Jace muttered, a crooked smile breaking through. "That's John."

Savannah laughed through her tears, pressing a hand over her heart. "God, I'm glad he made it. I thought we'd lost him."

They didn't move for a long moment, just sat in the charged quiet that followed the news. The kind of quiet that came after hurricanes. After miracles.

Eventually, they drifted toward each other on instinct, no need for words. They spent the rest of the day barely a foot apart—curled together on the old leather couch in the heart of the communications tent. Jace's arm slung protectively around her shoulders, his thumb drawing slow circles over the curve of her arm. Savannah rested her hand over his chest, not for comfort but to feel him—his heartbeat steady under her fingers, the quiet rise and fall of his breath proof he was still real, still here.

They didn't say much.

They didn't have to.

The truth was out.

John was alive.

And—for now—they were safe.

By late afternoon, Evelyn returned, a rare glint of satisfaction in her flint-grey eyes. She held a tablet in one hand like it was something sacred.

"You'll want to see this," she said, crossing to them.

Jace and Savannah leaned in together as Evelyn tapped the screen. A muted video clip rolled out: grainy but clear.

Marcus Rourke.

Arrested.

On the tarmac of a private airfield just outside Sacramento.

He was flanked by federal marshals, hands behind his back, his expression somewhere between disbelief and fury. He wore a tailored suit, silver cufflinks flashing in the sun, but the power in his posture had vanished. His hair whipped in the wind. A small, black bag was zipped at his side—too little, too late.

The voiceover filled in the details.

Attempted international flight. Diplomatic jet flagged. Denied clearance. Taken into custody without incident.

For now.

Savannah's lips parted as she watched the screen, breath hitching. "It's really happening," she whispered.

Jace's arm tightened around her. "The walls finally closed in."

He didn't sound smug. Just tired. Wary. Like a soldier waiting for the second wave.

They thought maybe—just maybe—they'd be able to rest now.

To eat something real.

To sleep without one eye open.

Maybe even think about what came next. A courtroom. A future.

Each other.

But an hour later, Evelyn returned. This time, her face was unreadable.

"There's a call for the two of you," she said carefully. "DOJ. Department of Justice. High-level. They're patching in through our secure relay."

Savannah straightened immediately, pulse quickening. "About what?"

Evelyn didn't blink. "They didn't say. Just that it's urgent. And they're sending a car."

Jace's hand found Savannah's without hesitation. His fingers locked with hers, firm and steady.

He didn't look surprised. Neither did she.

Because they both knew:

Yes, the truth was out.

Yes, Rourke was in cuffs.

Yes, they'd made it to the other side of the storm.

But this wasn't the finish line.

It was just the next threshold.

And the story wasn't over.

Not yet.

The sun had begun its slow descent behind the canyon ridge, spilling gold, and rust across the treetops as the jeep rumbled up the gravel path. Dust hung in the warm air, catching the fading light like ash in a breeze. It was the kind of dusk that made the world feel suspended—caught between what had been and whatever came next.

Savannah and Jace stood just outside the main tent, fingers tightly laced, shoulders brushing. Neither spoke. There was nothing left to say here—only what waited beyond.

The old jeep came to a slow stop in front of them, its engine idling low.

Savannah turned first. Without hesitation, she stepped into Evelyn's arms and held on. "Thank you," she whispered, voice cracking. "For everything."

Evelyn hugged her back just as fiercely, her hands gripping tight, like she was sending off more than an ally—like she was letting go of family. "You held the line when it mattered," she said, her voice thick. "Don't let them twist it now. You earned this truth."

Jace stepped forward next, reaching for Evelyn's hand. The handshake was firm, grounded in mutual respect.

"We'll be careful," he said quietly.

"I'm counting on it," Evelyn replied. Then she pulled a slim manila envelope from beneath her arm and handed it to Savannah. "Printed copy of the files. For your records. Trust no one until they earn it."

Savannah took it with both hands, clutching it to her chest like a relic.

As they climbed into the jeep, Evelyn watched them from the edge of the clearing—arms crossed, eyes sharp. She didn't wave. She didn't need to. Her silence was a benediction.

Twenty minutes later, the jeep pulled into a nearly abandoned fuel station carved out of nowhere. The scent of hot oil and sunbaked asphalt hung in the air. Waiting in the shade beside the pumps was a black SUV, sleek and spotless against the dusty backdrop.

As Savannah and Jace climbed out, two clean-cut federal agents approached. Their jackets were crisp, their badges clipped in plain view, their expressions neutral—polished, but not unkind.

"I'm Agent Reynolds," the taller one said. "This is Agent Torres. We're with the Department of Justice. We'd like you both to come with us."

Savannah's body tensed on instinct, her pulse spiking. Jace's thumb brushed across her knuckles, steady and grounding.

Reynolds held up a hand, voice calm. "You're not under arrest. This is off the record—for now. They just want to hear your story. From the source."

Jace nodded once. No hesitation. "Then let's go."

Inside, the SUV was cool and quiet. The blast of air conditioning made Savannah shiver, the leather seats stiff beneath her. Outside, the forest faded like a dream in the tinted windows—gone as if it had never existed.

Jace slid in beside her, his arm coming instinctively around her shoulders. Savannah leaned into him, her head resting against his chest, his heartbeat slow and steady beneath her cheek.

Her eyes closed, the exhaustion finally catching up to her—bone-deep, soul-heavy. She let herself drift. Safe. Not free yet. But getting there.

"I can't believe it's really over," she murmured, barely audible over the sound of gravel under the tyres.

"Not over," Jace said gently, brushing his lips against her temple. "But we're through the worst of it."

She didn't answer, but her fingers tightened over his. A silent agreement. A promise made in exhaustion.

The road wound on. The forest gave way to scattered farms, then city outskirts. But neither of them made it far before sleep claimed them. Savannah's head stayed tucked against his shoulder; Jace's hand never left hers—even in dreams.

They arrived in Sacramento just after ten that night.

City lights shimmered across the windshield, casting long reflections on the glass. Government buildings rose in clean lines, sterile and looming, floodlights making everything feel brighter than it should have been. Surreal. Unforgiving.

The SUV rolled to a stop at the edge of a federal complex. The moment the brake clicked into place, a man in a tailored grey suit stepped forward from the shadows, clipboard in hand, ID clipped neatly to his lapel.

He opened the back door.

"Savannah Blake? Jace Calloway? I'm Agent Drummond, Department of Justice." His voice was clipped but polite. "We've been expecting you."

Jace blinked away sleep, straightening. Savannah rubbed her eyes, heart ticking up again as she sat upright beside him.

"We're ready," she said.

Drummond nodded once. "Then let's get started. There's a lot to discuss."

They followed him through a maze of quiet, sterile corridors. The building pulsed with hushed urgency—keycards beeping, phones ringing, muffled voices behind closed doors. Everything smelled like cold air and burnt coffee. Paper and bureaucracy.

They passed a row of darkened offices, a newsfeed scrolling silently on a wall-mounted screen. Rourke's face flashed across it, grainy and angry in custody. Savannah didn't stop walking.

The hallway seemed to stretch forever, institutional, and cold. Savannah's boots echoed on the linoleum. Her stomach churned—too empty, too tight. But she didn't slow.

Finally, they reached a heavy steel door labelled Interview Room 3B. Drummond opened it and gestured them inside.

The room was sparse—fluorescent lighting, a long table with three metal chairs, a pitcher of water, and a single recording device already lit with a quiet red glow.

Inside, another agent was already seated.

She looked up as they entered. Late forties. Crisp navy pantsuit. Cool, clear eyes. An air of calm authority that needed no introduction.

"This is Agent Nadine Keller," Drummond said. "She'll be conducting the interview."

Agent Keller nodded. "This conversation will be recorded for internal review only. You are not under arrest. You're here voluntarily. Do you both consent to being recorded?"

Savannah and Jace exchanged a glance.

"Yes," they said, almost in unison.

Keller opened a slim file and adjusted a small mic on the table.

"Then let's begin. Start at the beginning," she said. "Tell me everything you know about Project Perseus."

For the next two hours, they told her everything.

Every hour. Every name. Every place.

From the morning Jace walked out of the prison gates, about Kessler, about finding the USB drive, to the last encrypted upload at Mariposa.

Savannah spoke slowly at first, voice brittle, but steady. She told them about Tyler. About his work. About his death. The drive. The fail safes.

Jace picked up when her voice caught. His jaw clenched through the part about the black SUV. About the threats. About the attempts on their lives. And how close they'd come—so many times—to losing everything.

They gave her facts. No embellishment. No dramatics. Just the raw, harrowing truth.

Keller took notes, stopping occasionally to ask sharp, precise questions—pausing on names, dates, inconsistencies. She never raised her voice. Never doubted. Just listened. Professional, but not detached.

When they finished, Keller closed the file slowly and looked up.

"You did the right thing," she said. Nothing more. Nothing less.

Drummond stepped forward. "We're moving you both to a secure hotel for the night. Under protective custody until we're sure the threat has passed. A U.S. Marshal will be stationed outside your room."

Jace nodded, jaw tight. "And John Nolan?"

"He's safe," Drummond confirmed. "Still under heavy guard at a secure facility. He'll recover. He's already given a full statement. Backed everything up."

Savannah sagged against the chair, the tension sliding off her bones like melting ice. "And Rourke?"

"In federal custody," Keller said. "No bail. No immunity deals. No backdoor escape routes. This time, he faces trial."

Jace reached across the table, took Savannah's hand again. Their eyes met. The current passed between them—grief and relief and something like belief.

"You'll be safe tonight," Drummond added. "We've arranged for fresh clothes and supplies. Food's already waiting at the hotel."

There was nothing left to say.

They stood.

The walk back through the corridor was slower this time. Heavy with exhaustion. But also… lighter somehow.

Their fingers brushed.

Then linked again.

The nightmare hadn't ended.

But the story had changed.

And somewhere in that shift—between the arrests and the confessions, the truth, and the fallout—something new had taken root.

Not just survival.

But the possibility of a life beyond it.

Chapter Thirty-Seven

They didn't say much during the ride.

The SUV cut through the night streets of Sacramento, city lights flashing across the windows like faint echoes of chaos left behind. Jace kept one arm around Savannah, the other hand resting on his knee, his thumb twitching with nerves he couldn't quite shake.

Savannah leaned against his shoulder, the hum of the engine and the last of the adrenaline lulling her into a kind of quiet daze. Neither of them had eaten. Neither had really slept.

But they were alive. Together. And—for tonight—that was enough.

The vehicle pulled into a private underground garage beneath a nondescript hotel. A U.S. Marshal met them at the door, scanned their faces, and gave a short nod.

"Top floor. End of the hall," the agent said. "Room's secure. We've got the hallway sealed. No one gets through without our say-so. If anything shifts— you'll hear it from us first."

They were led through a back elevator, not the lobby. No check-in, no signatures, no curious eyes. Just mirrored walls, quiet hums, and the soft ding of arrival.

By the time Jace helped her into the hotel suite—one careful, agonising step at a time—the worst of the adrenaline had faded, replaced by the dull ache of survival. Her body screamed with each movement, a sharp reminder that danger wasn't over, only delayed. Outside, the night was too quiet. Inside, the stillness hummed with the weight of everything unsaid.

The suite was larger than expected—spare, quiet, untouched. A king-size bed. Two chairs. Blackout curtains drawn tight. A tray of warm food waited: grilled chicken, rice, bottled water. Towels stacked beside fresh clothes folded at the foot of the bed.

Savannah stood just inside the doorway, still and wide-eyed.

Jace closed the door gently and locked it. Twice. Then he turned to her.

"Come here," he said softly.

She didn't hesitate. Just walked into his arms.

They stood there for a long time. No danger. No running. Just two people held together by exhaustion and the need to feel someone still breathing beside them.

Eventually, he kissed the top of her head. "We should eat."

She nodded but didn't move.

"We should shower."

Another nod.

"We should sleep."

"Yeah," she whispered, and finally let go.

They ate side by side on the bed, more picking than devouring. Words felt unnecessary.

Later, they showered—separately. Not from distance, but because their bruised bodies weren't ready for closeness just yet.

When Savannah stepped out of the bathroom, wrapped in an oversized T-shirt, Jace was already in bed. He reached for her immediately.

"You still with me," he whispered. The same words from the night they first held each other, back when they weren't sure tomorrow would come.

She didn't even bother with the blankets at first. Just curled into him like she'd never left. His arms locked around her like a vow.

"Can I ask you something?" she whispered against his throat.

"Anything."

"Do you think it's over?"

He paused. "No," he said honestly. "But I think it's close."

She nodded. "Close is good."

"Close is better than dead."

She gave a small, hoarse laugh—raw and real. "You always know how to sweet talk a girl."

"I aim to impress," he murmured, kissing her temple.

Within minutes, her breathing evened out. And soon after, so did his.

Outside, the world spun on. Headlines unfurled. Statements were drafted. Charges filed.

But inside the hotel suite—lights dimmed, bodies warm, hands laced together—there was something else.

Not peace. Not yet.

But something close enough to dream on.

The knock came just after nine.

Jace stirred first, blinking against the soft grey light filtering through the curtains. His arm tightened around Savannah's waist before he realised what had woken him. Her head was tucked beneath his chin, her hand pressed flat against his chest, like she was still making sure he was real.

The second knock came—gentle, but firm.

He untangled himself carefully, rubbing sleep from his eyes as he padded barefoot to the door. He checked the peephole—instinct now.

Agents Drummond and Keller waited in the hall.

He opened the door a crack. "Morning."

"Apologies for the early hour," Drummond said, holding a clipboard and slim folder. "Just a few follow-ups. Won't take long."

Savannah was already awake, her voice thick with sleep. "Everything okay?"

Keller offered a reassuring smile. "No threats. Just clarification. The perimeter's still secure."

They settled at the table. Savannah pulled the hotel blanket around her shoulders like armour, her hair tousled. Jace sat beside her, grounded but guarded.

The questions were standard. Clarifications. Timelines. Minor details. They answered everything without hesitation.

Keller took neat notes, then looked up. "You two have been remarkably consistent."

Jace gave a tired smile. "We lived it."

There was a pause before Drummond set the clipboard down. "We also brought an update."

Savannah sat straighter.

"As of this morning," he said, "seven of Rourke's people are in custody. Two more are being tracked. Raids happened overnight in three states. It's moving fast."

Savannah's voice was tight. "The ones who went after Jace?"

"Some," Keller confirmed. "Others were tasked with suppressing the truth. But the circle is breaking."

Jace let out a slow breath. "That's more than we expected."

"It's not over," Drummond added. "But the tide's turning."

They stood to leave. Drummond paused at the door. "We'd advise one more night. Just precaution."

"Fine by us," Jace said.

"We'll check in tonight. Secure line only," Keller added.

When the door clicked shut, Savannah handed Jace a mug of hotel coffee.

He bumped it gently against hers. "One more day."

Savannah smiled, quiet and sure. "We can do one more day."

And they could.

Because now, they weren't just surviving.

They were finally beginning.

The day passed slowly, wrapped in quiet and comfort—a rare, fragile luxury after everything they'd endured.

Sunlight filtered in through the thick hotel curtains, casting soft gold onto the carpet and bedspread, illuminating dust motes that drifted lazily in the still air. Somewhere far below, traffic moved along the streets of Sacramento, life resuming as if the world hadn't tilted off its axis only days ago.

But inside the suite, time didn't move. Not really.

The television murmured quietly from across the room—muted commentary, looping headlines, familiar names. Rourke. Federal custody. Scandal. Fallout. Conspiracy. The phrases came and went like background static.

Jace sat on the plush hotel couch, one arm draped over the backrest, Savannah curled into his side. Her legs were drawn up, feet tucked beneath her, her cheek resting on his shoulder. A cooling cup of coffee sat abandoned on the table in front of them, long forgotten.

They didn't need caffeine.

They needed stillness.

Jace couldn't stop watching her.

The way her hair spilled over her shoulder, slightly damp from her earlier shower. The way the sunlight skimmed across her skin, softening the edges of her face, making her look almost ethereal. He watched her chest rise and fall, calm now. No fear. No edge of panic.

Just peace.

"I love you," he said softly, like a secret he couldn't hold in any longer.

Savannah tilted her head, a small, sleepy smile blooming at the corner of her lips. "That's the fourth time you've said that today."

He kissed her temple. "Doesn't mean it's lost any weight."

She laughed quietly—low and sweet—and nestled in closer. Her fingers toyed absently with the edge of his T-shirt. "You keep saying it like you're afraid I'll forget."

"I say it," he murmured, "because I never thought I'd get to."

She looked up at him, eyes shining with something raw and real. "You have it now, Jace. All of it. Me. This. Us."

He leaned down and kissed her—slowly, like he had nowhere else to be for the rest of his life. His hand cupped the side of her face, thumb brushing the soft skin just beneath her eye. Her hand found his chest again, resting over his heart, feeling it beat beneath her palm like proof.

"I love you too," she whispered, voice barely audible. "So much it scares me."

He touched his forehead to hers, drawing in a breath that felt like the first in years.

"I used to think I didn't get to have this," he said, his voice barely above a whisper. "That after prison, after the silence, after everything that was taken from me… I didn't get this kind of ending."

Savannah cupped his cheek, her thumb brushing the line of his jaw. "It's not the end," she murmured, soft and sure. "It's the beginning."

Jace closed his eyes for a moment, soaking in her nearness, the warmth of her hands, the scent of her skin. But there was something else—something raw he hadn't let himself say until now.

"When I got out," he said quietly, "I was afraid to see you. Afraid to ask about you. I kept picturing a ring on your finger, a husband, maybe kids. A life I wasn't part of anymore."

Her expression softened, eyes glassy but clear. She reached up and threaded her fingers through his hair, pulling him just a little closer. "There's never been anyone else, Jace."

He blinked, startled. "Savannah…"

She smiled—gentle, steady. "You're the only man I've ever loved. The only one I ever wanted."

The silence between them deepened—not heavy, but sacred. Like something that had been waiting years to breathe.

Jace swallowed hard, emotion catching in his throat. "You waited…"

"I loved you," she said simply. "There was never room for anyone else."

He touched her then like she was something holy. His lips brushed hers again, slow and aching, reverent in a way that made her eyes close, and her fingers tighten in his shirt. There was no urgency. No fear. No shadows creeping in from the edges of the room.

They kissed like they had time now. Like the world could wait.

And for once—it could.

Hands wandered slowly—curious, tender. Fingertips traced the shape of backs, hips, collarbones. Shirts lifted. Blankets shifted. But there was no rush, only reverence. As if every movement whispered thank you for surviving. Thank you for staying. Thank you for still being here.

They made love the way only people who've nearly lost each other do—with aching care, with quiet devotion, with gravity in every touch. The kind of intimacy that doesn't just speak desire, but trust. Healing.

Afterward, the sheets were tangled, and the light in the room had turned softer, pink at the edges with the approaching dusk.

Jace lay half on his side, half across her chest, head resting against her shoulder, his arm flung across her stomach. One of Savannah's hands stroked his hair, the other tracing lazy circles across his back. The silence wrapped around them like a blanket.

"I'm not going anywhere," he murmured into her skin. "Not ever."

Savannah smiled, eyes closed, body heavy with the kind of safety she hadn't felt in years. "Good," she whispered. "Because I don't ever want to be without you again."

He lifted his head, just enough to meet her gaze.

"Say it again," he asked softly. Like a prayer.

Her hand came to cup his cheek. "I love you."

He leaned in and kissed her shoulder. "I'll never stop saying it."

Outside, the world still reeled. Phones rang. Prosecutors prepared statements. Somewhere, someone was still running scared.

But inside that hotel room, wrapped in warmth and quiet and love, none of it reached them.

They didn't talk about what came next. Not tonight. Not yet.

They didn't need plans or promises or timelines.

They had each other. Finally.

And that was enough.

Chapter Thirty-Eight

The knock at the door came just after ten the next morning.

Savannah was tucked beneath the covers, half-asleep, the sunlight warming the edges of her hair. Jace was already up, pulling on jeans and a T-shirt, barefoot as he crossed to the door. He glanced through the peephole, always careful, always expecting ghosts.

Agent Keller stood in the hall with a small folder tucked under her arm, her expression calm but purposeful.

"We've finished the sweep," she said quietly. "It's time."

Jace stepped aside and let her in. Savannah sat up slowly, blinking the sleep from her eyes as Keller entered.

"Good morning," Savannah said, voice still thick with sleep.

"Good morning. I've got news," Keller replied. "We've confirmed the last of Rourke's private enforcers are either in custody or in federal wind-down procedures. No further credible threats have surfaced. Your phones are clean. Your names are being kept out of the press, for now. And your statement has already helped secure the groundwork for a federal indictment."

Savannah pulled the blanket tighter around her chest. "So, we're free to go?"

"You're free," Keller voice softened, like she understood the weight of the word. "You can check out whenever you're ready. There's a vehicle waiting to take you anywhere you need—home, another city, witness transition if that's something you want to discuss."

Jace shook his head. "We're not running anymore."

Keller nodded once, a small smile on her lips. "Didn't think you would."

She handed Jace the folder. "Contact information. A DOJ liaison in case anything changes. And this—" she pulled out a separate page "—is from John Nolan."

Savannah was already sliding out of bed, her eyes wide. "John?"

"He's awake and stable. Still recovering, but lucid and stubborn as ever. He's been asking for you both."

Jace opened the page. A short, handwritten note in John's messy scrawl was taped to the bottom:

Still here. Still breathing. Can't believe you did it, you crazy kids. When you're ready, get your asses over here—room 308, Oakland General. I'm not going anywhere. —JN

Savannah pressed her hand over her mouth, eyes welling. "He made it," she whispered. "He really made it."

Keller stepped back toward the door. "We'll escort you out when you're ready."

When the door clicked shut behind her, Jace looked at Savannah. "You want to go see him now?"

She nodded without hesitation. "Let me shower."

They packed quickly—what little they had—then dressed and stepped out of the hotel room that had held their world still for one precious day.

The drive to Oakland was quiet but light. No shadows chased them this time. No fear clung to the corners of their silence. Savannah kept her hand in Jace's the whole way, the city unfolding ahead like something waiting to be claimed.

At Oakland General, they were led through a side entrance and up to the third floor. Nurses smiled quietly, nodding like they knew who they were.

John lounged upright in bed, remote in one hand, untouched Jell-O wobbling on a tray nearby. His leg was elevated, stitches still visible beneath the hospital gown. But his eyes—sharp, stubborn, alive—lit up the moment they walked in.

"Well, damn," he said with a grin. "Didn't think they'd let you two lovebirds off the leash this fast."

Savannah crossed the room in two steps and threw her arms around him carefully. He grunted but didn't complain, one arm wrapping loosely around her back.

"I thought you were gone," she whispered.

"Yeah, well," he muttered. "So did I. Guess I'm harder to kill than I thought."

Jace stepped closer, clasping John's free hand. "You saved us, man. The files, the drive—it worked because you didn't quit."

John gave a tired smirk. "Wasn't about me. It was about finishing what Tyler started. You two just… made sure it mattered."

For a moment, all three sat in silence—no need to say more.

Then John nodded toward the hallway. "Nurse said there's decent coffee down the hall. If one of you loves me, you'll go get me some."

Savannah laughed, wiping at her eyes. "We love you. But we're still gonna make you suffer a bit."

"You're damn lucky I can't chase you," he grumbled.

But his smile never faded.

And for the first time in what felt like forever, it felt like life was beginning again.

Ten days after they left the hotel suite, Jace and Savannah stood in the entryway of their new home—a modern, sunlit house tucked into one of the quiet, tree-lined streets of Cedar Ridge's most sought-after neighbourhoods. The kind of place Jace had never imagined himself in.

The floors gleamed. The paint was fresh. Not a single thing needed fixing.

Jace looked around, still trying to believe this quiet, clean life was really his. He didn't have much in the way of possessions. A bag of clothes. A well-worn duffel. Some books. Everything else had been packed alongside Savannah's things, folded into a future they'd built together.

"I feel like I should fix something," he said as they stepped into the airy living room. "A leaky faucet. Squeaky door hinge. Anything."

Savannah smiled, slipping her arms around his waist. "We don't have to fix anything anymore. We just get to live here."

And that's exactly what they did.

There was no clutter, no mess to sort through, no ghosts hiding in the walls. Just sunlight spilling across hardwood floors and the soft hum of quiet that felt earned.

They hung only a few pictures at first—one of Tyler, one from when they were young, and a candid shot Evelyn had taken of them at the Mariposa camp, laughing despite the exhaustion.

Jace didn't say much about the neighbourhood, but Savannah saw it in the way he kept glancing out the window, still half-waiting for something to go wrong.

He was used to surviving.

This—peace, comfort, security—was still something he was learning to trust.

At night, they lay in bed with the windows cracked open, the breeze carrying the scent of pine and warm pavement. No alarms. No sirens. Just crickets and stillness.

"Feels too good to be real," Jace murmured one night, his arm tucked beneath her, hand brushing lazy circles on her hip.

Savannah kissed his chest, her voice soft. "It's real. We made it."

And day by day, they settled in. They made grocery lists. They tried new recipes. They sat on the back deck and drank wine at sunset.

It wasn't about forgetting what they'd been through.

It was about finally letting it go.

Jace had once told her he didn't believe he was allowed to have a life like this. That peace, love, and stability were for other people.

But every morning he woke up with Savannah wrapped in his arms, in a home he bought for Savannah, he let that belief fade just a little more.

The late afternoon sun bathed the back deck in golden light, catching in the leaves of the tall trees that surrounded the house. Savannah sat curled into one of the lounge chairs, barefoot, a glass of iced tea sweating on the small table beside her. Jace was nearby, barefoot as well, tinkering with the old charcoal grill they'd rescued from the farmhouse.

The air smelled like warm pine and cut grass—peace, distilled.

They didn't talk much about what had happened. Not anymore. Not because they were ignoring it, but because they didn't have to. The silence between them now wasn't heavy. It was healing.

The knock on the front door came around four.

Savannah looked up, brows lifting slightly. "You expecting anyone?"

Jace shook his head, already moving toward the house.

When he opened the front door, John Nolan stood there, dressed in jeans and a worn button-down, his leg still bandaged under his jeans, but his posture strong. Whole. Alive.

Jace let out a breath. "John."

"Hope this isn't a bad time," John said.

Jace stepped aside. "Never."

Savannah was already on her feet by the time John walked through the sliding doors. She crossed the room and hugged him tight without hesitation.

"You look better," she said.

"I feel better," he replied, giving her a soft smile. "You two doing okay?"

"We are now," Jace answered simply, his hand brushing Savannah's lower back.

John nodded once, then exhaled. "I didn't just come to check on you. I've got news."

They sat inside, the evening shadows beginning to stretch across the hardwood floors. Savannah and Jace listened as John leaned forward, his hands resting on his knees.

"Rourke's trial starts next week," he said. "It's all moving faster than I expected. DOJ wants to make a statement with this—open proceedings, full press coverage, no redactions. They want the country to see all of it."

Jace gave a slow nod. "And us?"

"They're calling us all in to testify," John confirmed. "You, me, Savannah. Evelyn too. They want the firsthand accounts. No summaries. No deals. Just the truth, from the people who lived it."

Savannah's fingers curled around Jace's.

"And after that?" she asked, voice quiet.

John's gaze softened. "That's it. The last hurdle. After eleven years of silence, hiding, threats… this is it. We get to close the door. For good."

The room stilled, the weight of his words falling like dust in sunlight.

Jace leaned back in his chair, his hand still wrapped tightly around Savannah's. "Then we'll be there. Whatever it takes."

John's jaw tightened, but there was a flicker of peace in his expression. "We're almost there."

Savannah nodded, her voice steady. "Let's finish it."

Outside, the wind rustled through the trees.

Inside, three survivors sat together, bound not just by what they'd endured, but by the promise of what still lay ahead.

Justice. Truth. And finally… closure.

Chapter Thirty-Nine

Savannah stood at the top of the courthouse steps three days later—no podium, no statement, no shield.

No carefully crafted statement to the reporters crowding the sidewalks with cameras lifted and microphones thrust forward.

Just stone beneath her feet, the morning sun climbing over the Sacramento skyline like a quiet sentinel, and the truth sitting heavy in her chest—sharp, cold, and undeniable.

She wore black.

No makeup. No jewellery. No mask.

Only the gravity of what had been stolen.

Only the fire of what she had left to give.

The crowd buzzed below, press badges flashing, headlines already writing themselves.

Wrongfully Imprisoned Man to Testify Today.

Explosive Corruption Trial Unfolds in Sacramento.

But she didn't look at them.

She looked ahead.

Inside, the air was colder than she remembered. Stale, almost sterile. The kind of chill that seeped into your bones when the stakes were too high and the walls had seen too much.

Marcus Rourke sat at the defence table, still dressed like power—tailored charcoal suit, silk tie, gold cufflinks—but none of it fit quite right anymore. The polish couldn't cover the cracks. His eyes were bloodshot. His jaw clenched and unclenched. His fingers drummed faintly against the table, a restless, anxious tic he didn't seem aware of.

He looked like a man watching the walls close in.

Like a monarch mid-fall, still pretending the crown was intact.

As Savannah passed, he leaned slightly forward. The security officers at his side didn't blink.

His voice, low and venom-laced, slithered through clenched teeth.

"This won't stick," he said. "People forget. They always forget."

Savannah stopped.

She turned just enough for only him to see her expression.

Her voice was calm. Measured. A scalpel, not a sword.

"They don't have to remember you," she said. "They'll remember what we did. What we said. And I'm not done."

She walked on, unflinching. Each step toward the witness room another vow. Another refusal to let fear steer the ending.

When her name was called, she entered the courtroom with her spine straight, her chin high, and her pulse thundering behind her ribs. Her hands didn't shake. Her voice wouldn't either.

She raised her right hand. Swore to tell the truth, the whole truth, and nothing but.

She thought of Tyler. Of Jace. Of Evelyn and John. Of the farmhouse and the fear and the nights she thought she might never make it out. Of hope, stubborn and burning like a flame she refused to smother.

And then—Savannah Blake spoke.

She told them about her brother.

About the day he died.

About the silence that followed.

About the man who was blamed—Jace Calloway—and how his conviction became a convenient shield for everyone involved. She told them about the cover-up. About Vaughn Kessler admitting that he killed Tyler, then Kessler committing suicide. About the missing evidence. About the hidden files that Tyler died trying to expose. About the digital drive John, Jace and her risked everything to deliver.

About Project Perseus—how Rourke weaponised fear, how people disappeared, how the justice system turned into something twisted and unrecognisable beneath his grip.

She told them about Jace walking out of prison with nothing but scars and silence.

She told them about what it took to survive after.

Every word landed like a match against dry kindling.

She didn't cry. She didn't rage.

She didn't have to.

Her voice was steady. Clear. Carved from loss and conviction.

And when she was finished, the courtroom fell still.

No murmurs. No coughing. No clicking of pens.

Just silence.

Sharp and sacred.

Because sometimes, the truth doesn't have to scream.

It just has to endure.

And Savannah Blake made sure it did.

When she stepped down from the stand, her hands were cold, but her heart was fire.

And across the courtroom, Jace looked at her like she'd just moved a mountain with nothing but the weight of her truth.

Because she had.

And somewhere, beneath the weight of indictment and consequence, Marcus Rourke finally looked afraid.

When Jace Calloway took the stand, the silence in the courtroom shifted.

He didn't wear a suit.

Just a plain white shirt, sleeves rolled to his elbows, and the weight of ten years in his eyes.

He raised his right hand, voice low but unwavering, as he swore the oath. Then he sat—every movement measured. Steady. Like a man who'd long since learned not to flinch.

The prosecutor stepped forward. "Mr. Calloway, do you swear that the testimony you're about to give is the truth?"

"I do."

"Please state your full name for the record."

"Jace Henry Calloway."

"And you understand why you're here today?"

"I do," he said again. "Because the truth matters. Even when it's ten years too late."

The courtroom held still. Not even a breath out of place. At the defence table, Marcus Rourke sat stiff and pale, his jaw clenched tight enough to crack.

The prosecutor gave a single nod. "Can you confirm the testimony Savannah Blake gave earlier?"

"Yes," Jace said simply. "Every word of it."

He looked to the jury—not pleading, not performing. Just telling them what they needed to hear.

"I spent ten years in prison for a murder I didn't commit. For the death of my best friend, Tyler Blake."

He let the words land. No dramatics. No spin. Just truth, unadorned.

"I was twenty when I was convicted of manslaughter. Thirty when I got out. I lost more than a decade. I lost my name, my future. I was branded a killer. Treated like I was nothing. And it wasn't just my freedom they stole—it was my faith in everything that's supposed to stand between a man and injustice."

"Mr. Calloway," the prosecutor said, "can you tell the court what you now know about the person who actually committed the crime?"

Jace nodded once. "Vaughn Kessler. Tyler worked under him. Kessler was laundering money—millions—for Rourke's off-the-books project. When Tyler discovered it, he did what a good man would do. He tried to expose it."

He looked directly at Rourke now.

"He never got the chance."

Jace leaned forward slightly, voice steady.

"They killed him. And they pinned it on me. Because I was convenient. Because I had no connections. No power. I was close enough to make the lie believable."

"And who ordered Tyler Blake's murder?" the prosecutor asked.

Jace didn't hesitate. "Marcus Rourke. He gave the order. Kessler carried it out. Everything after that—the tampered reports, the falsified evidence, the intimidation—was designed to protect Rourke and silence the rest of us."

A ripple moved through the courtroom. The judge's gavel brought it to heel, but the damage was done. The truth was out.

"Do you have any doubt that Rourke was behind it all?"

Jace shook his head. "None. Tyler got too close to the truth. I got turned into a scapegoat. Savannah spent the next decade carrying the weight of not knowing what really happened to Tyler. And Rourke stayed clean. But he built this machine. Every piece of it."

He paused, jaw set—not from anger, but from clarity.

"And I'm not here for sympathy. I'm not even here for justice for me. I'm here because Tyler never got to speak for himself. And because for ten years, Rourke counted on our silence. On our fear."

He glanced at Savannah in the front row. Then back to the jury.

"But we're not afraid anymore."

The prosecutor stepped back, satisfied.

The defence declined to cross-examine.

And when Jace rose from the stand, he didn't glance at Rourke. Not once.

Because for the first time in over a decade, the truth wasn't buried.

It was standing tall.

And so was Jace Calloway.

When Sheriff John Nolan took the stand, his badge wasn't pinned to his chest—but the weight of his oath came with him all the same.

He wore a dark button-down, sleeves rolled to the elbow, a bandage still visible on his left forearm—a silent reminder of how close the truth had come to being buried for good.

He raised his hand, swore his oath, and settled into the witness chair with the calm steadiness of a man who'd seen too much—and who finally had the chance to put it right.

The prosecutor approached. "Sheriff, please state your name and occupation for the record."

"John Nolan. Sheriff of Tuolumne County."

"And how long have you served in that role?"

"Just over twenty years."

"Sheriff Nolan, can you tell the court when you first became involved in this case?"

He nodded once. "It was shortly after Jace Calloway was released on parole. Miss Blake and Mr. Calloway came to me with evidence—photos, documents, names. All of it pointing to Vaughn Kessler's involvement in Tyler Blake's murder. Evidence that proved the wrong man had been convicted."

"And how did you respond?"

"I took it seriously. Every piece they gave me checked out. I was going to obtain a warrant to arrest Kessler. But the situation escalated fast. The original evidence was stolen. Savannah and Jace risked their lives to retrieve a new copy."

His voice stayed even, but there was something cold behind it. Controlled fury.

"Kessler confessed to killing Tyler Blake while in custody," Nolan continued. "He never named who gave the order—but before he could, he died by suicide in his cell."

He paused. Let the weight of it sit.

"At the time, we thought it was over. Savannah and Jace had finally found justice. Or so we believed."

The tension in the courtroom thickened like a held breath.

"But it wasn't over, was it?"

"No, sir," Nolan said. "A few days later, Savannah called me again. She was packing up her house to move and found something hidden in Tyler's old room. A USB drive, taped to the underside of one of his nightstand drawers. She knew right away it was important."

He glanced toward Savannah in quiet respect before continuing.

"She didn't wait. She called me immediately, and I met them as fast as I could. We were just trying to get the drive to safety when everything fell apart."

"Can you explain what happened?"

"We were ambushed. Shot at while trying to get away. It was planned—deliberate. We knew then that someone still had eyes on us. We took cover and made the call to split up and deliver the evidence to multiple sources, just in case only one of us made it through."

His voice dipped, rough now. Not from fear—but from the memory of how close it had all come to ending.

"Savannah reached her contact. The evidence made it through. That's the only reason we're here."

"And what was on the drive?"

"Everything. Internal documents. Audio recordings. Transaction ledgers. It confirmed what we suspected: that Vaughn Kessler was working under direct orders from Marcus Rourke. The drive detailed the financial shell companies, black-ops tasking, money trails—everything that tied Rourke to the murder, the cover-up, and the years of silence that followed."

Nolan shifted slightly in the chair, his gaze steady and unflinching.

"I've worn this badge a long time. I've seen corruption before. But this? This was something else. This was rot from the top down. And if Savannah Blake hadn't found that drive—if she and Jace hadn't risked everything to get it into the right hands—none of us would be sitting in this courtroom."

The prosecutor nodded. "Sheriff, do you believe Marcus Rourke ordered the attack that nearly killed you?"

"Yes," Nolan said, without the slightest pause. "He wanted the evidence destroyed. And he didn't care who had to die to make that happen."

A ripple of noise stirred in the gallery, quickly silenced by the judge's gavel—but the damage was done. The truth had landed.

"And do you believe Miss Blake and Mr. Calloway were telling the truth from the beginning?"

"I don't just believe it," Nolan said. "I know it. I lived it. I bled for it."

He turned to the jury, gaze unwavering.

"They were the ones who kept going. Who didn't break. Who didn't back down—no matter what it cost them. And if this country still stands for anything—if we still believe in justice—we owe that to them."

The prosecutor stepped back. The defence declined to cross-examine.

Nolan stood slowly, adjusted his jacket, and stepped down from the stand—no drama, no theatrics. Just the weight of truth, finally unshackled.

And for the first time in a decade, it wasn't being buried. It was being heard.

And across the courtroom, Marcus Rourke didn't just look afraid—he looked like a man the world had already left behind.

Chapter Forty

The atmosphere in the courtroom had shifted.

It no longer felt like a trial.

It felt like an unmasking.

The prosecution didn't have to push anymore.

Didn't have to argue or dramatise or wrestle the spotlight.

Now, they simply had to show.

And piece by piece, they did.

The truth bled into the open—slow, deliberate, undeniable.

A former junior staffer—barely older than Savannah had been when she'd first walked into the Marcus Rourke's office—took the stand, hands trembling, voice thin with restraint.

She spoke of closed-door directives. Manila envelopes labelled "off-books correspondence" and "Perseus entries."

She told them about the day she was ordered to shred half a filing cabinet's worth of internal memos.

The order had come directly from Rourke's inner office.

She hadn't questioned it then.

But the weight of what she'd helped conceal will never leave her.

Next came the digital forensics expert. Calm. Precise. Clinical.

With methodical ease, he traced the origin of the Project Perseus memo.

Authored on a government-issued laptop.

Logged in under Marcus Rourke's credentials.

Timestamped. IP-verified.

The draft history—complete with tracked edits, auto-saves, and internal timestamps—carried Rourke's digital fingerprints like blood at a crime scene.

The gallery held its breath.

The project had been initiated over twelve years ago. The data Tyler Blake had uncovered only scratched the surface—covering the first eighteen months. But now, the full scope of Project Perseus was beginning to emerge from the shadows.

For years, it had lived in whispers. Rumours traded behind closed doors. Hushed conversations that died the moment they reached sunlight.

But this wasn't a theory anymore.

It was evidence.

And it was damning.

At the defence table, the once-formidable legal team sat in stunned silence—no objections, no strategies, no spin. Just the quiet unravelling of everything they thought they could contain.

The polished smiles were gone.

The arrogance drained from their posture.

Their eyes dropped. Their shoulders stiffened.

Even they knew—this couldn't be salvaged.

By mid-afternoon, they requested a private conference in the judge's chambers.

The murmurs started before the door even closed.

Ten minutes later, when court resumed, the judge's voice struck like a bell.

"The defence has requested to enter negotiations for a plea agreement."

Gasps. Audible. Disbelieving. Vindicated.

The tension that had held the courtroom hostage cracked like ice.

But at the defence table, Marcus Rourke didn't move.

Didn't argue.

Didn't look to his attorneys.

Didn't lift his head.

He sat frozen—hands clasped in front of him like a man praying to a god he no longer believed in.

His expression was hollow.

Not fury. Not regret.

Just the brittle, sinking awareness that the empire he built—stone by stone, lie by lie—was collapsing in real time.

There would be no fixer this time.

No spin. No secret panel.

No backdoor escape.

Not now.

Because the ghosts he thought he'd buried had names.

Had voices.

Had evidence.

And they dragged the truth into the light—

Where even he couldn't escape it.

Outside, the late afternoon sun spilled across the courthouse steps.

John Nolan stood with Savannah and Jace near the edge of the plaza, just outside the barricades.

Behind them, reporters packed up cameras.

Officers waved traffic through.

And disbelief still hung in the air like smoke.

"He's being taken to the law offices," John said, squinting toward the doors.

"Starting negotiations," Jace muttered. "Unbelievable."

Savannah said nothing.

Her arms were folded tightly across her chest, jaw locked, eyes fixed on the courthouse like she was bracing for something no one could name.

Then the doors opened.

Marcus Rourke emerged, handcuffed, flanked by two officers.

One on either side—close, but not rough.

He still wore his tailored charcoal suit, but it looked smaller now. Rumpled. Weary.

His tie askew. Cuffs unbuttoned. His spine not quite straight.

Behind him, two of his attorneys followed, murmuring in low tones. Their briefcases hung like dead weight at their sides.

Photographers raised cameras.

Reporters shouted over one another.

Savannah didn't blink.

Then—

A loud pop.

Sharp. Clean.

Too clean.

Screams tore through the crowd.

Gasps. Chaos. A camera hit the pavement with a crack.

Someone yelled "Gun!"

Another screamed "Sniper!"

And then—

Rourke collapsed.

Forward. Hard.

Blood spilled down the courthouse steps.

John shoved Savannah behind him, already reaching for his weapon.

Jace pulled her lower, shielding her behind a concrete pillar.

Officers' dove for cover. Radios erupted. Sirens howled.

But it was already over.

Rourke wasn't moving.

One officer crouched beside him, checked for a pulse, then looked up.

A single shake of the head.

"No pulse!"

Time fractured.

The reporters backed away, stunned.

One of Rourke's attorneys knelt beside him, hands shaking, mouth moving—but no sound came.

The medic arrived way too late.

High above, officers swept the rooftops—

But the shooter was already gone.

Like a ghost.

Marcus Rourke's story didn't end with a trial.

It ended with a bullet.

In public.

On the very steps he once climbed to claim power.

Savannah exhaled shakily, her hand pressed to her chest. "He's really gone."

John scanned the skyline, jaw tight. "This wasn't justice," he muttered. "This was retribution. Or cleanup."

Jace stared at the body. "Someone didn't want him talking."

And in the quiet that followed, there was no verdict.

No closing argument.

No gavel strike.

Just blood on the courthouse steps—

And the shadow of a man who vanished without ever being seen.

A day had passed since Marcus Rourke bled out on the courthouse steps.

The headlines were brutal.

Power Broker Executed Before Plea Deal Finalised.

Sniper Ends Rourke Trial in Shocking Turn.

Justice or Silence?

Inside a secured federal building in downtown Sacramento, the air felt sterile—too clean, too quiet.

Fluorescent lights buzzed faintly overhead, casting a flat, cold glow across the conference room.

Savannah Blake sat between Jace and Sheriff John Nolan at a long, polished table, each with a sealed bottle of water in front of them—untouched, forgotten.

The adrenaline from the last forty-eight hours had burned off, but something else lingered beneath the surface: a question no one wanted to say out loud.

Across from them sat Deputy Director Elaine Fields, Public Corruption Division, DOJ.

Mid-fifties, steel-grey suit, hair pulled back tight. Sharp-featured. Sharper eyes.

Her laptop sat open beside a neatly stacked trio of manila folders, but the authority in her voice didn't come from the files. It came from a career built on knowing when to be polite—and when to stop pretending.

She'd already thanked them, already said words like 'heroism' and 'national impact'.

But now, as she leaned forward and folded her hands on the table, her tone shifted—more clipped, more serious.

"Do you know who killed Rourke?" John asked. The words were quiet but direct.

Fields didn't hesitate.

"We have a theory," she said.

She tapped one manicured finger on the top folder.

"After Rourke's arrest, several of his private security contractors—enforcers, mostly—began cooperating. Some flipped fast. Others took pressure. But a few of them mentioned the same name."

She looked up. "A name they said they were afraid to say out loud."

Jace narrowed his eyes. "Who?"

"Ezra Kane."

Jace blinked. "Never heard of him."

Fields nodded slightly. "That's what we expected. We believe it's an alias. There's no official record—no photo, no known address. But the name came up multiple times in independent interviews. Always with the same kind of hesitation. One of them said saying his name was like inviting a ghost through your door."

Savannah glanced toward John, her voice low. "What did they say he did?"

Fields met her gaze without blinking.

"He wasn't part of Rourke's regular crew. He didn't run intimidation or cleanup. He was… a specialist. A ghost."

She paused.

"They said Rourke only used him when something needed to be done quiet. Final. And permanent."

"A hitman," John said flatly.

"Yes," Fields confirmed. "But not just any contractor. Based on descriptions, we're looking at someone with military-grade training. Possibly ex-special forces. One witness called him Rourke's 'insurance policy.'"

Jace's jaw worked silently, eyes fixed on the centre of the table.

"You think he took Rourke out."

Fields didn't flinch. "We do."

"Because Rourke was about to talk," Savannah said, voice just above a whisper.

"Exactly. He was ready to negotiate. That meant naming names—associates, donors, contractors. If Kane had reason to believe his identity, or his work, would come to light… then yes, it's likely he acted pre-emptively."

"But you can't prove it." John's voice was calm, but there was steel behind it.

Fields gave a slow, deliberate nod.

"Not yet. There's no footage. No traceable sniper position. The angle was high, the shot clean—surgical. Whoever pulled that trigger was in and out before we even secured the scene. This wasn't a protestor or a vigilante. It was a message."

"Message from who?" Jace asked.

Fields didn't answer at first. Then:

"Could be someone further up the chain. Could be self-preservation. Either way—Rourke didn't order his own execution. And Ezra Kane… if that's even his real name… made sure there'd be no plea. No confessions."

The room settled into silence, each of them thinking the same thing—

That justice, for all its victories, sometimes came just inches short of the truth.

John leaned forward, elbows braced on the table.

"Do you think he'll come after us?"

Fields exhaled slowly through her nose.

"No. We don't believe so."

She tapped once more on the folder.

"Kane's profile—what little we have—suggests he's not a cleaner in the traditional sense. He finishes threats to his employer. That employer is dead. The leash is cut."

But no one relaxed.

Then Savannah spoke, her voice steady, but distant:

"So… what happens now?"

Fields closed the folder gently, as if putting a period on everything they'd just heard.

"We keep going. Rourke's assets have been frozen. We're tracking shell corporations, offshore accounts, encrypted transfers. Everything he tried to bury—we're going to dig up."

"And Kane?" Savannah asked, her eyes never leaving Fields'.

"If he's real, we'll find him."

John gave a quiet nod. "And in the meantime?"

Fields looked at each of them in turn, her voice softer—but no less firm.

"In the meantime… live your life. Go home. You earned that right."

Savannah didn't look away.

"You'll let us know if you find him?"

"Absolutely." Fields said. "You started this. You deserve to know how it ends."

Chapter Forty-One

It had been a week since Marcus Rourke collapsed on the courthouse steps, and though headlines still snarled for space, Cedar Ridge possessed a talent for quieting noise. Here, the air tasted of turned soil and pin-drop stars; the pace was slow enough to hear your own heart settle.

Inside Savannah and Jace's new home, the kitchen smelled of rosemary chicken and Cassidy's pecan pie. Savannah, still in navy scrubs, had a faint wine-flush on her cheeks; Jace's sleeves were rolled, forearms dusted with flour from 'supervising' dessert.

They lingered around the scarred pine table long after the plates were clean, basking in the peculiar comfort of people who'd seen each other shattered— and stayed anyway.

Cassidy swirled her Merlot, one brow arched. "So, let me get this straight: you finally have more zeros than nightmares in your bank account, and you choose to push wheelchairs?"

Jace grinned. "Radiology transport is glamorous. Last shift I was crowned 'Keeper of the Warm Blankets'. Respect the title."

Savannah tipped her head, fond exasperation in her smile. "He spent ten minutes convincing Mrs. Hanley that chocolate pudding outranks lime gelatine."

"Objectively true," Jace said. "Dessert shouldn't wobble like guilty testimony."

John Nolan barked a laugh, reaching for another slice of pie. "Only you, Calloway."

Jace lifted his coffee cup in solemn salute. "Justice for pudding."

They laughed—full-bellied, unguarded—until the pecan pie was all gone.

After dishes, they migrated to the living room. Cassidy tucked herself into an armchair, knees hugged to her chest. John leaned against the couch arm, mug in hand, gaze half-on the flames, half-on Savannah—like a father making sure the world behaved.

Savannah folded cross-legged on the couch cushion. When Jace returned with fresh coffee, he didn't sit. He set the mugs down, wiped suddenly damp palms on his jeans, then knelt.

The room froze, breath held.

"Jace—?" Savannah's voice trembled with surprise more than fear.

He pulled a velvet box from his pocket, thumb worrying the hinge. "Fourteen years ago, you loaned me your lucky pencil so I could pass chemistry." His smile was crooked with nerves. "I've been writing plans around you ever since."

Her hand went to her heart.

"You believed in me when no one else did. You fought for me when most people would've walked away. I know the world's still messy, but if you'll have me—if you'll say yes—I want to spend whatever comes next loving you the way you've always deserved."

He opened the box. Firelight caught on a simple, elegant diamond solitaire ring.

"I'm asking, Savannah Blake… will you marry me?"

For a moment, she couldn't breathe. Cassidy clutched her mug with both hands, eyes misty. John looked down and smiled—a quiet witness, content to let the moment belong entirely to them.

Tears blurred her sight. "You're absolute menace," she whispered, laughter laced with wonder. "Yes—yes, of course, yes."

Air rushed back into the room as Cassidy squeaked, John cleared his throat, and Jace slid the ring onto her finger. He rose and gathered her into an embrace that felt like sunrise after a ten-year night.

For a heartbeat, the earth kept spinning, but inside their home it tilted just for them.

Later, after Cassidy and John drove off down the gravel lane, the house settled into the hush that follows great joy. The fire was mostly ash; moonlight silvered the floorboards. Savannah traced the ring, then curled her fingers into Jace's collar and kissed him until language felt redundant.

When she finally spoke, it was a breath against his lips: "I still can't believe you had that speech in your pocket."

He touched his forehead to hers. "I had a version of it scribbled on prison notebook paper. This was the edit that ends happier."

She smiled, gentle. "You taught me how to breathe again too, you know. Tyler used to tap the porch light twice when he got home safe. You became my porch light."

Soft silence: then he kissed the centre of her palm. "Then I'll keep flickering."

Peace—earned, fragile—settled with them on the couch.

Two weeks later a Thursday sky spilled clean light over the Tuolumne County registry office. No aisle, no organ music, just tile floors echoing quiet vows.

Cassidy, in pale blue, clutched tissues; John stood straighter than any honour guard. Savannah's knee-length white dress swayed when she promised to walk beside Jace 'in riots, in recess, and in boring Tuesdays with burnt coffee'. Jace's hands shook only once—when he said she'd 'replaced every prison wall with windows'.

Rings exchanged, paperwork sealed, and that was that—except for the way he cradled her face like a miracle outside the courthouse doors.

Sun warmed the steps. Savannah laced her fingers through his. "Confession," she teased, brushing her thumb over his ring, "I almost asked for a rooftop string-light wedding."

"I'd have hung the stars if you'd wanted them." He slipped an envelope into her hand.

She opened it—flight itinerary, names spelled correctly this time. Her laugh broke bright and incredulous. "Malé?" she gasped. "You're kidnapping me to the Maldives?"

"Rescuing," he corrected. "Private villa, over-water bungalow. No reporters, no alarms. Just you, me, and water clear enough to see tomorrow coming."

She shook her head, wonder and gratitude warring on her face. "You rushed our passports."

"Forged your signature on the expedited form," he confessed. "Consider it my last crime."

Her eyes shimmered. "You know I've never seen water that blue."

He cupped her cheek, thumb skimming the edge of her smile. "You've seen enough red. Time for blue."

Gold sunlight caught the new band around her finger, and Savannah realised paradise wasn't palm trees or turquoise seas.

Paradise was the man who knew the colour she needed next.

Epilogue

Two years later...

The rain had started soft—just a whisper against the slate roof, steady and rhythmic, like the world was catching its breath.

Inside their home in Cedar Ridge—warm lights glowing against the grey sky—Savannah gripped the edge of the marble kitchen island and drew a long, shaky breath through her nose.

Then exhaled. Then swore. Loudly.

"Jace!"

Nothing.

She closed her eyes, another wave tightening across her abdomen. This one didn't roll—it crashed.

"Jace Calloway, get in here!"

From somewhere upstairs came a startled clatter, followed by the unmistakable thud of socked feet on hardwood and a door creaking open.

"What? What's wrong? What happened?" His voice echoed down the hallway—panicked, winded, and slightly too high-pitched for someone who used to chase down corrupt politicians.

Savannah braced her palm against the counter and stared down at the puddle spreading beneath her feet. "My water just broke," she said. "And unless you want to welcome your son in the middle of this very expensive kitchen, I need help. Now."

Jace appeared in the doorway seconds later, shirt half-buttoned, hair sticking up in every direction like he'd fought the closet and lost. Phone in one hand, hospital bag in the other.

"You're early," he said, blinking.

She shot him a look. "I'm thirty-nine weeks and four days. That's not early. That's right on time. Which is more than I can say for you."

Jace crossed the room in two long strides, already slipping one arm around her waist like muscle memory. "Okay. Okay. Breathing. We're breathing. The bag is packed. The car is gassed. The playlist is queued—wait, did you change the playlist?"

"I took off the Enya," she said, gritting her teeth as another contraction hit. "We're bringing a life into the world, not opening a day spa."

He kissed her temple anyway. "You're radiant, even when you're threatening to throw me out the window."

"Save the charm for the delivery room," she muttered, clinging to him as they made their way toward the front door.

The rain had picked up outside, tapping against the glass like soft applause. Through the floor-to-ceiling windows, Savannah caught a glimpse of their street—wide, tree-lined, quiet. Porch lights glowed warm against the storm. The kind of neighbourhood where people waved from driveways and baked too much at Christmas.

Their neighbours—teachers, doctors, sweet retirees—had no idea that everything was about to change inside the house on the hill.

On the porch, Jace helped her down the steps carefully, holding her hand with the same steady grip he'd given her since the day she let him back in.

"You good?" he asked, opening the passenger door.

Savannah nodded, breath hitching as the next contraction began to roll through her like a freight train. "I'm ready," she whispered. "I just want to meet him."

Thunder rumbled low in the distance, not threatening—just steady, like a drumbeat.

She settled into the seat with a groan that was half pain, half awe.

"Jace?"

"Yeah?"

"When he gets here… don't look at the clock. Don't look at the doctor. Just… look at me first."

He paused, one hand braced on the roof of the car, rain trailing from his lashes.

"I will," he said, soft and sure. "Every time."

She smiled, even as another wave hit, and he climbed in beside her, reaching instinctively for her hand before turning the key in the ignition.

They pulled away from their home under a silver sky, red taillights cutting through the mist. Behind them, the house stood waiting—warm, quiet, full of everything that had come before.

And just before they turned the corner, the porch light flickered—once, twice—then burned steady.

Just like Tyler used to do.

Later That Night…

The hospital room was dim, cocooned in the soft blue glow of monitors and a single bedside lamp. Rain still tapped the windows—no longer urgent, just soothing. Like the sky had exhaled.

Savannah lay propped against the pillows, damp curls clinging to her forehead, the weight of labour still draped across her shoulders like a fading storm. But in her arms, she cradled something far more powerful than exhaustion.

Jace sat beside her, one hand wrapped around hers, the other resting gently on their newborn son's back. A bundle of pale green cotton and impossibly soft skin.

Red-faced. Sleepy. Perfect.

"I think he has your mouth," Savannah whispered, voice raw with wonder. "And your ridiculous ears."

"I'll take that as a win," Jace murmured, grinning. "But that nose? That's all you."

The baby stirred, let out a tiny sigh that made both of them still. Savannah smiled through the tears she hadn't bothered to wipe away. She didn't want to miss a second of this.

They'd counted his fingers twice. Then again. Just to be sure. Just to marvel.

"He's heavier than I expected," Jace said softly. "Feels like… the whole world."

Savannah reached out, fingertips brushing her son's cheek. "That's because he is."

They sat in silence, wrapped in the kind of peace you only earn after losing everything and choosing—desperately—to build again.

Finally, Jace shifted a little in his seat. "So… I know we talked about names."

Savannah tilted her head. "We never quite landed."

"I didn't want to decide until he was here," he said, gazing down. "Didn't feel right naming a future I hadn't held yet."

Then he looked up, eyes glassy.

"But I was thinking… what if we named him Caleb Tyler Calloway?"

Savannah stilled.

"Caleb," Jace said gently. "For 'faithful'. For the boy who never gave up on hope."

She swallowed. Her throat was suddenly too tight for words.

"And Tyler…" His voice broke. "Because he led us here. Because he was our beginning. He should always be part of our family."

Savannah blinked hard, tears spilling fresh.

"Jace…"

"I know it's a lot. We don't have to decide now, I just—"

"Say it again," she whispered.

"Caleb Tyler Calloway."

She let out a long, shaky breath. Then smiled, wide and sure.

"That's his name."

Jace leaned in, kissed her temple, then brushed his lips against the downy crown of their son's head.

"Welcome to the world, Caleb," he murmured. "You're already the best thing we've ever done."

And as Caleb blinked up at him—wide-eyed, new to everything—Savannah wrapped her arms around both of them and finally, finally, felt whole.

No headlines. No chaos. No grief clawing at the door.

Just love.

Just them.

Just everything.

The End

Quiet Danger

Alison Reid

A complete standalone romance

Previously published individually

Chapter One

Annie Spencer, a 25-year-old art gallery director, was a striking figure, embodying both elegance and beauty. Standing at five feet seven inches, her svelte frame was filled with a quiet strength that belied her size. Her dark, long wavy hair framed her face, the strands catching the soft light of the bar as she moved. Her bright blue eyes sparkled with intelligence and passion, reflecting her love for the world of art and the vibrant community she had cultivated within the gallery.

Tonight, she was dressed impeccably in a stylish black blazer that exuded professionalism while also highlighting her keen sense of fashion. Underneath, she wore a silky blouse that added a touch of sophistication, its smooth fabric gliding against her skin. Her sleek trousers, tailored to perfection, complemented her silhouette, while her heeled boots gave her an air of confidence as she navigated the bustling atmosphere of the bar.

It was a Friday night, the culmination of a long week filled with the demands of managing exhibits, collaborating with artists, and attending to the diverse clientele that frequented her gallery. After a series of meetings and phone calls, Annie relished the opportunity to unwind with her colleagues, to let the stress of the week melt away amidst laughter and good conversation. The bar was a local favourite, known for its eclectic decor and vibrant ambiance, providing the perfect backdrop for an evening of conversation and laughter.

As she entered the bar, the familiar sounds of clinking glasses and animated chatter enveloped her. She spotted her colleagues gathered around a large table in the corner, their smiles welcoming her to join in the festivities. Annie felt a wave of warmth wash over her as she approached, the energy of the night sparking excitement within her.

"Annie! Over here!" Sarah Banks her new gallery assistant called out, waving her over enthusiastically. She made her way through the crowd, her heart lightening with each step. Conversations flowed easily, and Annie found herself laughing at jokes, sharing stories, and toasting to the end of a productive week. Each sip of her drink filled her with a sense of relaxation, allowing her to momentarily forget the pressures of her responsibilities.

As the night wore on, they shared insights about the art world, discussing upcoming exhibitions and the challenges of engaging new clients. Annie thrived in this environment, her passion for art and connection with people shining brightly. She cherished these moments, where her professional life seamlessly blended with personal friendships, fostering a sense of belonging within her team.

However, as the clock ticked on and the lively atmosphere continued to pulse around her, Annie couldn't help but feel the weight of exhaustion creeping in. The days had been long, and while she loved her work, it was refreshing to have a night off to simply enjoy the company of friends.

After several hours filled with laughter and storytelling, Annie realised it was time to head home. She exchanged hugs and goodbyes with her colleagues, feeling grateful for the support and friendship they shared.

Stepping outside into the crisp night air, she took a deep breath, savouring the moment. The moon hung low in the sky, casting a soft glow over the dimly lit parking lot. Annie pulled her blazer tighter around her shoulders, her heels clicking softly against the pavement as she made her way to her car. Each step echoed in the stillness, heightening her awareness of the world around her.

As she approached her car, she fumbled in her purse for her keys, her fingers brushing against the familiar items within. The night felt peaceful, yet a subtle tension lingered in the air, a reminder of the long week she had just navigated. Unbeknownst to her, the tranquility of the evening was about to shatter.

Out of nowhere, a masked man rushed toward her, his silhouette emerging from the shadows like a phantom. Time seemed to freeze for a split second as he closed the distance, and then he was upon her, grabbing her from behind with a force that stole the breath from her lungs. Panic surged through Annie like a tidal wave, flooding her senses and overwhelming her with fear. The world around her blurred, and all she could focus on was the oppressive grip of this stranger.

Before she could comprehend what was happening, he was pinning her against the cold metal of her car, the sharp chill seeping through her stylish blazer and making her acutely aware of her vulnerability. The shock of the moment coursed through her, disorienting her as adrenaline pulsed in her veins. She fought instinctively, her body thrashing against the unyielding strength of her attacker, but he was too powerful, his hold unrelenting.

"Let me go!" she screamed, her voice a mixture of desperation and defiance. The sound echoed in the emptiness of the parking lot, her cries swallowed by the stillness that surrounded them. Annie's heart raced furiously in her chest, the pounding matching the frantic rhythm of her thoughts. She couldn't believe this was happening; just moments ago, she had been enjoying a night out with colleagues, laughing, and sharing stories, and now she was trapped in a nightmare.

In her struggle, she twisted her body, desperately trying to escape his grasp. Panic threatened to cloud her mind, but somewhere within her, a flicker of determination sparked. She couldn't just submit to fear; she had to fight back. With every ounce of strength she could muster, Annie kicked out, her heel connecting with the man's shin, hoping to create even a momentary distraction.

"Please, don't hurt me!" she gasped, her breath coming in quick, shallow bursts as she fought to remain calm amidst the chaos. The weight of the situation pressed down on her, but she refused to succumb to it. She needed to think, to act. Her bright blue eyes scanned the darkened lot, searching for any sign of help, for any passerby who might hear her cries.

The cold metal of the car dug into her back, reminding her of the reality of her predicament. She had to escape, had to find a way to break free from this terrifying grip. "Get off me!" she shouted again, each word laced with a fierce determination that surprised even her. The fight within her was ignited, fuelled by a refusal to be a victim. In that harrowing moment, as her heart raced and her mind raced faster, hoping that she would survive this encounter.

William Banks, a 32-year-old partner at a prestigious law firm, exudes a quiet confidence that commands attention without him even trying. Standing six foot two inches tall with an athletic build, he carries himself with an air of assurance, his sharp features softened by a steady, thoughtful gaze that can put clients and colleagues alike at ease. His dark hair is cut short and neatly trimmed, complementing his crisp white shirt that fits perfectly, with the sleeves rolled up to reveal strong forearms that hint at both discipline and an active lifestyle. After a long day of back-to-back meetings, he has loosened his tie, the fabric hanging carelessly around his neck, signalling a moment of relaxation as he heads out to pick up his younger sister, Sarah, from a night out with her new work friends.

As he drives into the dimly lit parking lot in his sleek black sedan, William reflects on the day's challenges, mentally shifting gears from the world of legal negotiations to the light-hearted banter he anticipates with Sarah. The soft hum of the engine is a soothing backdrop, but as he pulls into a parking spot, a sudden commotion catches his attention. His heart races as he scans the scene and spots a masked man grappling with a woman against a car, the struggle frantic and chaotic.

Without a moment's hesitation, William's instincts kick in, honed by years of dealing with high-pressure situations in the courtroom. Adrenaline surges through him as he throws open the car door and dashes toward the attacker, every fibre of his being focused on stopping the assault. His mind sharpens, filtering out the noise around him as he zeroes in on the threat.

With a swift motion, he drove his shoulder into the assailant, slamming into him and knocking him off the woman. The force sent the man sprawling across the cold pavement. The woman's shocked gasp cuts through the tense air, but William's focus stayed locked on the man sprawled on the ground. He grabbed the assailant by the collar and landed a hard punch to his face, snapping the masked figure's head back. Desperation flickered in the man's eye as he struggled to escape. Despite William's strength and determination, the assailant wriggled free, slipping from his grasp and disappearing into the shadows of the parking lot like a ghost.

William stood seething with frustration, the bitter taste of defeat lingering in his mouth as he scanned the darkness for any trace of the man who had threatened the woman's safety. Anger pulsed through him, mingling with a deep sense of helplessness. He felt a fierce protectiveness for those who cannot defend themselves, a trait deeply ingrained in his character.

Breathless from the adrenaline of the confrontation, William turns to the woman he has just rescued. Her face is a mixture of fear, confusion, and gratitude, the shock still evident in her wide eyes. Taking a moment to steady himself, he approaches her slowly, his protective instincts kicking in as he checks for any signs of injury. "Are you okay?" he asks gently, ready to offer her any support she needs.

Annie's wide eyes, filled with fear and shock, lock onto William's, and before he can utter another word, she instinctively clings to him. Her svelte frame trembles in his arms, and without thinking, he wraps his arms around her, pulling her close. "You're safe now," he murmurs, his voice calm and soothing, meant to quell the storm of fear swirling within her. He felt her body shaking against him, and his heart raced, not just from the adrenaline of the encounter, but from the undeniable chemistry crackling between them.

Annie's delicate features were illuminated by the dim parking lot lights, and in that moment, William couldn't help but notice her beauty. She had an allure that drew him in, vulnerable yet resilient, a captivating combination that stirs something deep within him. As he held her, he felt the warmth of her body against his, and a quiet realisation begins to take shape in his mind: he likes the way she looks and feels in his arms.

He brushed a hand gently along her back, feeling the tension begin to ease as her shaking gradually subsides. His touch tender, almost protective, as he focused solely on calming her down. "Take a deep breath," he encouraged, his words laced with a sincerity that he hoped would penetrate the fog of panic that enveloped her. She nodded slightly, still nestled against him, her head resting against his chest.

Time seemed to stretch in the embrace, the chaotic world around them faded into the background. For now, all that existed was the two of them, the warmth of their bodies, the rhythm of their heartbeats syncing in a moment of shared vulnerability. William's thoughts drift, momentarily lost in the connection they share, and he revelled in the feeling of being her shield, the one who was there at just the right moment to protect her.

As she finally began to regain her composure, he felt a sense of relief wash over him, grateful that he was there when she needed him most. The bond they had formed in this fleeting moment was palpable, as Annie pulled back slightly to meet his gaze, he sees the gratitude shining in her eyes, mingled with something deeper, something that ignites his curiosity about who she is.

"Thank you," Annie whispered, her voice still trembling but laced with sincerity. Her eyes, though shaken, locked onto his with gratitude. "I don't know what would've happened if you hadn't shown up."

William offers her a soft smile, trying to steady his own racing heart. The reality of how close this woman had come to harm lingered in his mind, a mix of relief and concern flooding him. "I'm just glad I was here," he said, his gaze holding hers for a moment longer than necessary. There was something about her, a quiet strength beneath the fear, which spoke to him.

He hesitated, then asked, "Are you sure you're okay?" His voice carried an edge of concern as he studied her closely.

With a small nod, she replied gently, though there was a hint of uncertainty in her voice. "I think so..."

William frowned, still unsure. "Do you need anything? Do you want me to drive you home?" he offered softly, his tone full of quiet reassurance.

"No, I'll be okay... thank you so much for your help," she replied, her gratitude evident in her eyes.

William suddenly realised he was still holding her, his arms gently wrapped around her. Reluctantly, he let her go, a surprising sense of loss washing over him as the warmth of her body slipped from his grasp. She was the first woman he had held in six months, and he savoured the feeling, a stark contrast to the emptiness he had felt since Susan.

Annie stepped back, her eyes meeting his. "Thank you," she whispered, her voice filled with sincerity. Turning toward her car, she still looked shaken, but there was a quiet determination in the way she squared her shoulders, trying to regain her composure.

William watched her turn away, the sense of disappointment deepening in his chest. He sensed something about her had stirred a deeper interest. There was a vulnerability and strength in her that pulled at him.

As she got into her car, he took a slow, measured breath, reluctantly forcing himself to let her go.

Chapter Two

William turned back to his own car. His footsteps felt heavier, weighed down by the lingering thoughts of the brief but intense connection he'd felt with that woman. He walked to his car, the door was still open, he just stood there, staring blankly at the dashboard. The memory of her trembling in his arms, the softness of her voice, and the way she looked at him, all swirled in his mind. With a sigh, he locked his car, shoving his keys into his pocket.

He headed toward the bar, the hum of distant chatter reaching him as he got closer. Inside, the familiar sounds of laughter, clinking glasses, and the murmur of conversations pulled him out of his thoughts. His eyes scanned the room until they land on his sister, Sarah, seated at a table near the back, surrounded by her colleagues. She's in the middle of a lively conversation, her laughter ringing out across the room.

When Sarah saw him, she waved enthusiastically, her bright smile lighting up the room, completely oblivious to the chaos he just faced outside. William forced a smile in return, slipping effortlessly into the role of the protective older brother, but his thoughts were elsewhere. Part of him was still outside with the woman he'd just saved. He kicked himself for forgetting to ask her for her name, replaying the fear in her eyes, the hesitation in her voice, and the overwhelming need he'd felt to protect her.

He effortlessly weaved through the noisy bar crowd, making his way toward his sister, the memory of that brief encounter lingered.

Sarah was still laughing and chatting with her colleagues as he reached her, she stood and gathered her things. "Hey, big bro!" she grinned, her tone a little tipsy but full of cheer. "Ready for the weekend at Mum and Dad's?"

William nodded, though his thoughts remain half-anchored in the parking lot and the woman he'd just rescued. The adrenaline from the moment still thrummed faintly in his veins. "Yeah, let's get going," he said, gently steering Sarah toward the exit. Ever the social butterfly, Sarah waves goodbye to her coworkers, clearly reluctant to leave the lively atmosphere behind.

As they step into the cool night air, Sarah sighs and leans into her brother's side as they walk toward his car. "I'm so bummed you didn't get to meet my boss tonight," she said with a hint of disappointment in her voice. "She's amazing, and I've been wanting you two to meet for over a month now, but she left early."

William's stomach tightened at her words, a flicker of realisation forming, though he quickly brushed it aside as irrational. The odds that her boss was the same woman from the parking lot seemed too coincidental to even consider. Shaking the thought from his mind, he offered a small, reassuring smile. "Maybe next time. You'll have to introduce me properly then."

Sarah nodded absentmindedly, oblivious to the thoughts swirling in his head as she chatters on about work and their weekend plans. Her carefree words were a stark contrast to the unease lingering in William's mind. He listened, but part of him was still fixated on what had just unfolded in the parking lot. He decided not to mention the attack to Sarah; there was no need to worry her, especially since they were heading home for what was meant to be a relaxing weekend with their parents, a tradition they upheld once a month.

When they finally reached his car, William helped her inside and closed the door. As he rounded the car to the driver's side, he couldn't shake the memory of the woman's wide, frightened eyes, her trembling body pressed against his, and the vulnerability she'd shown in that fleeting moment. The thought of her ordeal weighed heavily on his mind. If they ever crossed paths again, he wouldn't let her slip away a second time.

For now, though, he forced himself to focus on getting to his parent's estate in Sleepy Hollow. He slid into the driver's seat, glancing at his sister's relaxed form beside him as she continued to talk. His mind, however, was miles away, silently wondering if fate would ever bring him and that mysterious woman together again.

As Annie drove away, her hands gripped the steering wheel tightly, knuckles white from the pressure. Her heart was still racing, the adrenaline from her fear still coursing through her veins. She glanced nervously at the rearview mirror, half-expecting the masked man to reappear from the shadows. But the parking lot behind her was eerily still, except for one figure, her drop dead gorgeous rescuer.

He was walking back to his car, his confident stride cutting through the quiet. The sight of him sent a fleeting sense of safety through her, easing her nerves momentarily. But it isn't just the fear fading. Her chest tightened for a different reason, one she hadn't expected, an undeniable attraction to the man who had just probably saved her life.

The way he had held her, strong yet gentle, had left a mark on her in ways she hadn't anticipated. His touch, his steady voice, the calm in his eyes, it had been years since her heart had beaten that fast for reasons other than fear. She hadn't meant to feel anything but relief, yet here she was, her thoughts fixated on the man who had stepped in just in time. A rush of gratitude mingled with confusion as she sped down the quiet street, the image of his handsome face still fresh in her mind.

Annie's pulse gradually slowed as the distance between them grew, but the memory of his arms around her lingered, leaving her unsettled in a way she couldn't quite place.

She pressed her lips together, attempting to push the thought from her mind. It didn't make sense. She had just broken up with a man she had been dating for a few weeks, months ago, who had completely turned her off from dating. The idea of getting involved with anyone felt unappealing, and more than likely, she would never see her rescuer again. Yet, that realisation left a small ache in her heart.

Annie's mind wandered back to the man who had soured her view on dating, Jeremy Spears, a 34-year-old construction worker who had initially seemed like everything she wanted. However, after just three dates, the easy charm he had displayed began to morph into something darker. He developed an obsessive need to know where she was, what she was doing, and who she was with. His constant texts and relentless demands for her time and attention smothered her, leaving her feeling trapped and scared. She had ended things before they could spiral further, but then the incident at the gallery happened. Annie shiver at the memory.

As she drove through the quiet streets, the weight of that incident still pressed on her, leaving her conflicted. Her rescuer had made her feel something completely different, safe, grounded, and inexplicably drawn to him in a way she hadn't expected. It unsettled her, how his presence had calmed her so thoroughly in the aftermath of the attack, but also how she'd felt more than just relief when she was in his arms.

She shook her head, forcing herself to take a deep breath, trying to rein in the whirlwind of emotions swirling inside her. She wasn't ready for anything new, not after what had happened with Jeremy. And yet, she couldn't stop thinking about the way her rescuer had held her, the warmth of his voice, and how she'd felt a flicker of something, something more than just gratitude.

"Not now," she whispered to herself, pulling into her apartment carpark. As she parked the car, she tried to quiet the thoughts racing through her mind, but the feeling lingered, unsettling, and undeniable.

Annie stepped into her small but inviting apartment, the tension from the night still clinging to her like a second skin. She sighed heavily, kicking off her boots by the door and shrugging off her blazer. The weight of the evening pressed down on her shoulders, her thoughts still racing from the attack. She made a beeline for the bathroom, craving a moment to escape it all.

The soft glow from the bathroom lights cast a soothing warmth over the space as she filled the tub, adding a generous amount of lavender-scented bath oil. The fragrance filled the air, slowly easing the tight knot in her chest. She slipped into the steaming water, letting out a breath she didn't realise she was holding. The heat seeped into her skin, melting away the tension in her muscles, the weight on her mind.

With her eyes closed, Annie allowed herself to drift, the fear from the parking lot slowly fading as the warmth enveloped her. Her body relaxed, but her thoughts remain stubborn, circling back to her rescuer, his steady presence, his protective hold, and the calm in his voice that had soothed her panic. She shook her head, trying to push the thoughts away.

She wasn't ready for that. Not after Jeremy. The whole ordeal with him had left her wary, and the idea of letting someone else in right now felt too complicated, too risky. She couldn't afford to get swept up in the feeling of safety someone else provided, no matter how genuine it seemed.

Annie sank deeper into the water, telling herself to let it go. This night was already more than she'd bargained for. She wasn't ready for anything more, not now.

After what felt like hours of soaking away the tension, Annie finally stepped out of the tub, her skin warm and relaxed. She towelled off and slipped into a silk nightgown, the fabric cool against her freshly bathed skin. Her body felt lighter now, the stress of the evening having melted away, and she looked forward to the comfort of her bed. But just as she's about to crawl beneath the covers, her mobile phone rings.

She frowned, glancing at the clock, too late for anyone to be calling. As she approached her phone on the kitchen counter, she noticed an unknown caller highlighted on the screen. She hesitated for a moment before answering. "Hello?" she asked softly, her voice still heavy with the lingering calm of her bath. But there's no response, only silence on the other end.

Annie's brow furrowed, and she listened more intently, the stillness of the room amplifying the faint sound of breathing coming from the other side. "Hello?"

she repeated, this time with more urgency, her voice firm but edged with unease.

The breathing continued, slow and deliberate, sending a cold ripple of discomfort down her spine. The eerie silence pressed in on her, and for a moment, she felt frozen, unsure of what to do.

After a few long seconds, she shook her head, annoyed now, and quickly ended the call. Dismissing it as a prank or perhaps just a wrong number. Too tired to give it much thought, she went to her bedroom, slipped between the sheets of her bed, pulled the blankets up to her chin, trying to shake off the strange feeling that lingered.

As her body sank into the mattress, her eyes flutter closed, and sleep claimed her within minutes. She had no way of knowing that the unsettling call was only the beginning, a warning of the disturbing events that lie ahead.

William and Sarah drove along the winding country roads, the scenery transitioning from the bustling city to the serene landscapes surrounding their parents' estate. Nestled amidst rolling hills, the estate boasts an elegant old house framed by lush, manicured gardens, a place steeped in comfort and tradition where they spent countless weekends growing up. The familiar sight brought a sense of nostalgia as they approach the sprawling property.

As they pulled into the long, tree-lined driveway, Sarah's face lit up with excitement, eager to unwind after a busy week. William felt a weight pressing down on him. The events of the evening echoed in his mind, the memory of the attack still vivid, even as he attempted to push thoughts of the woman he rescued to the back of his consciousness for the sake of family time.

Their parents, Helen and Henry Banks, greeted them warmly at the door, enveloping them in the familiar embrace of home. Their weekend unfolded pleasantly, filled with long, leisurely breakfasts where laughter mingled with the aroma of freshly brewed coffee, afternoons spent strolling through the gardens, and evenings rich with good wine and lively conversation. Both William and Sarah relished the chance to disconnect from the pressures of their careers, enjoying the moments that reminded them of their childhood.

On Sunday afternoon, William found himself alone with his mother and father on the terrace as the sun began to descend, casting a warm glow over the estate. His father, a distinguished man with the same sharp, handsome features as William, sipped his whiskey thoughtfully, while his mother sipped her tea.

"You seem quieter than usual," his mother observed, glancing sideways at him, a hint of curiosity in her eyes.

William hesitated, the knot in his chest tightening. After a moment, he decides to share the details of the attack. He recounted the frightening encounter, the masked man, the struggle in the parking lot, and how he intervened just in time to save the woman. His tone remained casual, yet he deliberately omits the deeper impact she's had on him, the way she clung to him had stirred something unsettling within him.

Henry and Helen listened intently, nodding as William shared his story. After a moment of reflection, Henry said thoughtfully, "Good thing you were there. You did the right thing, son. I'm proud of you."

Helen chimed in, a knowing smile on her face. "This woman has left an impression on you." It was more half-question half-statement, but the implication was clear.

William turned to his mother, a hint of annoyance in his voice. "Mum don't get any ideas. I'm not interested in women right now."

His mother looked exasperated. "William, not all women are like Susan."

"I know, Mum, but it's just too soon."

Henry interjected, "It's been six months, son."

William let out a heavy sigh. "Finding your girlfriend in bed with another man is hard to get over, especially when I was thinking about asking her to marry me."

Just then, Sarah walked out onto the terrace. "And thank God you didn't. I never liked that woman," she said with disgust in her voice.

William glanced at Sarah, recalling how much she had disliked Susan. She had sensed something was off long before he did.

Sarah looked at William, clearly aware of his thoughts. "You should have listened to me. She was a terrible person."

William grimaced and nodded, defeated. "I know."

Helen quickly shifted the topic. "So, did this woman you rescued catch your interest, William?"

Sarah's eyes widened after her father filled her in. "Oh, did you like her? Did you get her number?"

William shook his head. "No, that's not really something you do after an incident like that."

"Did you at least get her name?" Sarah pressed.

William shook his head, disappointed in himself.

Exasperated, Sarah said, "William?"

William said, "I'm not interested in getting involved with anyone right now."

Sarah's expression brightened. "You know, I have the perfect person for you! My boss, she's lovely, kind, hardworking, and beautiful."

"Sarah, no," William replied, shaking his head. "I'm not interested, and I definitely don't want matchmaking help from my little sister."

Sarah pouted. "You're no fun! Just wait until you meet her; you'll change your mind."

William replied firmly, "No, I won't!"

Their parents exchanged proud glances at their children, and then Henry chimed in, "Never say never, son. I had no idea I was interested the day I met your mother." He smiled at Helen.

Helen blushed, a testament to their enduring love even after thirty-five years of marriage.

His mother smiled sweetly at William and said, "It's clear this woman has made you think. Perhaps it's time to move on and start dating again. Your father and I aren't getting any younger, and we would love some grandchildren."

Henry lifted his whiskey and said, "Hear, hear!" William just shook his head in disbelief, while Sarah flashed him a cheeky smile, clearly enjoying the moment.

As William drove Sarah and himself out of his parents' driveway later that evening, his thoughts drifted to the woman he had rescued. He imagined her in his bed, heavily pregnant with his child, and surprisingly, a sense of happiness washed over him. Shaking his head, he reminded himself that he wasn't ready for that yet, with anyone.

Chapter Three

Annie spent a quiet weekend alone, as was her routine, finding solace in the solitude that comes with a life devoid of family. Since losing her parents at just eighteen, she has learned to find comfort in her own company. Though loneliness sometimes crept in, she often sought refuge in activities that allowed her to escape reality, whether it was going to the movies, losing herself in a good book, or immersing herself in her work at the art gallery.

At twenty-five, Annie is strikingly beautiful, her delicate yet confident presence captivating those around her. Her bright blue eyes sparkled with curiosity, revealing a depth of thought and feeling. Dark hair fell in soft waves around her shoulders, framing her face and highlighting her fair skin. Though she is svelte, she carries herself with effortless grace, often drawing attention wherever she goes. However, beneath this exterior lies a wariness about the attention she attracts, especially after her recent dating debacle.

On Saturday afternoon, Annie prepares for an outing, selecting a casual yet chic outfit: a fitted white sweater that accentuates her figure, paired with dark jeans and ankle boots. She grabs her purse and heads out, determined to enjoy the day despite the weight of her recent experiences. At the theatre, she buys a ticket for a romantic comedy, craving a light-hearted escape to lift her spirits.

Settling into her seat, she can't help but feel a twinge of longing for the kind of love depicted on screen. Although she never had trouble finding a date, men are often drawn to her beauty and charm, but her recent dating experience has left her cautious and reflective. She only dated Jeremy for a short while, but it was enough to make her feel wary of men.

As the movie plays, Annie lost herself in the story, laughter bubbling up at the comedic moments and softening the edges of her worries. However, even as she enjoyed the film, her mind drifted back to thoughts of the masked man and the handsome stranger who had saved her. She hoped to forget about the chaos of the previous night, even if just for a little while.

After the credits rolled, she reluctantly left the theatre, still reflecting on her feelings but grateful for the quiet moments that helped her recharge. The sunlight greeted her as she stepped outside, and takes a deep breath, enjoying her peace and solitude, even amidst the emotions of the past days.

On Sunday, Annie focused on finalising details for the art exhibit scheduled for Friday night. The gallery would showcase Michael Godard's distinctive martini art, featuring playful olives, grapes, and other whimsical characters. Annie was thrilled about this exhibit, as Michael typically reserved his works for display in Las Vegas and rarely showcased them in galleries. However, he had agreed to do this as a favour for the gallery owner, Irene. Annie felt confident that New York would appreciate his unique style.

On Monday morning, Annie woke up feeling surprisingly refreshed, a sense of calm washing over her. The quiet, peaceful, and productive weekend had worked wonders, helping her regain her composure after the attack on Friday night. Taking a moment to appreciate the gentle morning light streaming through her window, filling her small apartment with warmth and hope.

Annie prepared for work, carefully selecting her outfit, a tailored blouse paired with a flowing skirt that showcased her professional style as an art gallery director. The vibrant colours lifted her spirits, bringing a hint of brightness to her mood. She decided to embrace the day ahead with a positive outlook, determined to leave the unsettling events of the past week behind her.

After parking her car, Annie strolled toward the gallery, the crisp morning air invigorating her senses. Each breath felt refreshing, grounding her further and pushing the memories of the attack into the background. Yet, despite her efforts to stay focused, her thoughts occasionally drift back to the man who saved her. His presence lingered in her mind, not just as her rescuer but as someone who had provided a fleeting sense of safety and warmth during a moment of fear.

Shaking her head slightly, trying to clear her thoughts and remind herself that she needed to concentrate on her work. After all, she doesn't even know him, and getting caught up in thoughts of a stranger could only distract her from the tasks at hand. Taking a deep breath, she stepped into the gallery, ready to embrace the challenges of the day.

Annie's week unfolded smoothly, brimming with productivity and the joy of collaborating with her colleagues at the gallery, especially Sarah, her new gallery assistant. At just twenty-one years old, Sarah is a delightful presence, her infectious enthusiasm brightening the space. The two women quickly forged a strong bond, sharing laughter and brainstorming ideas as they curate exhibitions and engage with visitors. Annie cherished Sarah's fresh perspective, feeling grateful for the companionship in her often solitary work life. Annie thrived in the vibrant atmosphere of the gallery, where the walls are adorned with striking artworks that ignite her creativity.

As Friday morning dawns, Annie walked toward the gallery with a hopeful mindset, eager to begin hanging the Godard pieces for that evening's exhibition. She knew Irene would stop by to check on her progress, so distractions need to be kept at bay. The sun filters through the clouds, casting a warm glow on the pavement, further lifting her spirits. But as she nears the gallery, her optimism wavers. Something feels wrong. Her heart sinks as dread pools in her stomach. Scrawled across the once-pristine exterior wall in stark black graffiti is a single hateful word: *'Bitch.'*

Shock rippled through her, and she quickly glances around to see if anyone else is nearby. Just then, Sarah emerges from the carpark, her cheerful demeanour faltering as she takes in the unsettling word. "What happened?" she asked, her eyes wide with disbelief.

Annie assessed the situation, her instinct telling her to brush it off. "I think it's just kids messing around," she replied, striving to maintain an air of calm. "We'll get it cleaned up. It's just silly graffiti."

Despite Sarah's obvious worried expression, Annie focuses on practicality. She swiftly calls in a cleaning crew, ensuring that the offensive message is removed as soon as possible.

As Annie directed the gallery assistants on where to hang the artworks, a simmering discomfort gnaws at her. She keeps telling herself it's just a random act of vandalism, but the word sticks in her mind, unsettling her. Even after the wall is restored to its former state, the unease lingers. Still, Annie dons a brave face, refusing to let the incident overshadow the excitement of tonight's exhibition. This is an important event, and she's determined to focus on making it a success.

Irene arrived at the gallery a little after two in the afternoon. As soon as Annie saw her, she smiled and said, "Hello, Irene! How are you today? I hope you like what you see," gesturing toward the exhibits on the walls.

Irene, always warm and affectionate, greeted Annie with a kiss on the cheek. "It looks magnificent," she said, her eyes scanning the gallery with approval. "You've all clearly worked very hard."

They walked together, taking in the full effect of the carefully arranged artworks. Annie then updated her, "The catering will arrive at five, and the doors will open at six. It's a formal affair, so I'll head home soon to change into my gown and then come back. I'm planning to take a taxi, so I won't have to drive. These events tend to involve quite a bit of champagne."

Irene chuckled softly. "Smart thinking."

Irene left shortly after, giving Annie a warm smile. "I'll be back at five to help organise the caterers," she said.

Annie nodded, her excitement evident. "I'm really looking forward to it."

William's week has been a whirlwind of meetings and court appearances, leaving him mentally drained by Friday afternoon. His law firm, one of the most prestigious in New York State, is always bustling with activity. Pouring himself a strong cup of coffee, he decides to call Sarah, hoping to check in on her and hear about her week. As the phone rings, he leans back in his chair, grateful for a brief escape from his hectic schedule.

"Hey, big brother!" Sarah's voice was bright and cheerful as she answered. They chatted for a few minutes, catching up on their lives. William listened intently while Sarah shared lively stories from her week at the art gallery, her excitement spilling over as she talked about the upcoming exhibition and the interesting visitors they'd had.

"Don't forget, you promised to be here tonight for my first exhibition," she reminded him, her tone playful yet serious.

"Yes, I wouldn't miss it for the world. I'm looking forward to it," William replied.

"And don't forget, it's formal," Sarah added with a teasing lilt.

William chuckled, "Got it. I'll be there."

With that, they said their goodbyes and hung up.

By six o'clock, the gallery was buzzing with activity as the exhibition was about to open. Irene, dressed in her signature orange, was fussing over the caterers, making sure every detail was perfect. Annie glanced at her fondly, grateful for the woman who had hired her straight out of college and given her the break she needed.

Sarah arrived, looking elegant in a light blue dress and heels. "Hi, Annie! What do you need me to do?"

Annie smiled at her, taking in how lovely she looked. "You look beautiful, Sarah."

Sarah grinned, giving her a playful look. "Thank you, but everyone's going to be looking at you tonight, not the artwork."

Annie blushed slightly. She was wearing a snug ruby red, off-the-shoulder satin gown that hugged her figure, her dark hair swept up with loose tendrils framing her face.

"I hope not," Annie laughed, then instructed, "Just stick close to Irene tonight. I want her to relax and not stress over anything. If you need my help, don't hesitate to come to me, no matter what I'm doing, okay? The other gallery assistants will be mingling, so if anyone has questions, they'll be ready to step in."

Sarah nodded confidently. "Leave it to me, Annie. I won't let you down."

Annie smiled warmly. "I know you won't."

At precisely six o'clock, the gallery doors swung open, welcoming the first wave of guests. The soft hum of conversation filled the space as the caterers, dressed in crisp uniforms, began circulating trays of hors d'oeuvres and flutes of champagne. The clinking of glasses and polite laughter added to the atmosphere of sophistication.

Annie stood near the entrance, watching the crowd with a mix of anticipation and nerves. She took a glass of champagne from a passing tray and had a small sip, hoping to settle the butterflies in her stomach. These events always made her anxious, hoping everything would run smoothly. She scanned the room, making sure the art was displayed perfectly, and prayed that the night would go off without a hitch.

By the time seven o'clock rolled around, the gallery was alive with guests admiring the artwork, sipping champagne, and engaging in lively conversations. Annie found herself speaking with a tall, distinguished gentleman, his silver hair and sharp suit adding to his air of sophistication. His eyes, however, seemed to linger more on Annie than on the artwork that adorned the walls.

As he complimented her on the exhibition, his words carried a tone that suggested he was far more interested in her than in the art. But Annie, ever graceful, handled the situation with poise. She smiled politely, steering the conversation back to the pieces on display, expertly shifting the focus without missing a beat. Her charm and professionalism never faltered, even as she felt his gaze linger.

Despite his clear intentions, Annie kept the conversation light and respectful, making sure to keep the evening's purpose, the exhibition, at the forefront.

William walked into the gallery around seven, greeted by a bustling scene of well-dressed guests sipping champagne and chatting in lively clusters. The space was alive with energy, the clinking of glasses and soft hum of conversation blending into the background as he made his way through the crowd.

He moved from exhibit to exhibit, admiring the vibrant artwork but also keeping an eye out for his sister. As he stood in front of one of the larger pieces, taking in its detail, he overheard a nearby conversation. A gentleman's voice, suave yet slightly predatory, was making overtures toward a woman. Her response, however, caught William's attention. She gracefully deflected his advances, skilfully steering the conversation back to the art with a poise that impressed him.

Though he couldn't see them, the woman's voice struck him, it was warm, like honey, carrying a calm strength that soothed his senses. Instinctively, William felt a spark of protectiveness; the gentleman's tone suggested he was more of a leech than a genuine admirer. Curious and slightly concerned, he subtly shifted his position, hoping to catch a glimpse of the woman behind the voice.

Just as William was about to catch a glimpse of the woman whose voice had captivated him; he heard Sarah's cheerful call. "William, you made it!"

He turned, a bit disappointed by the distraction, and smiled at his sister. "Of course I told you I would." He leaned down to kiss her on the cheek, feeling a warmth in their bond. "It looks like a very successful affair."

"Yes, it is! Annie has worked very hard on this exhibition. I want to introduce you to her," she said, a cheeky smile playing on her lips.

"Sarah, no matchmaking," he replied, recalling their conversation from last Sunday and the playful warnings he had given her.

She looked at him with feigned innocence, batting her eyelashes. "Of course not," she said, suppressing a grin, clearly enjoying the moment.

Annie burst into laughter at something the lecherous gentleman said, her melodic laugh ringing through the gallery. Sarah, standing nearby with William, caught the sound and turned to her brother with excitement. "She's close! I just heard her laugh."

William's interest piqued as he recalled that enchanting sound, it was the same laugh that had drawn him in moments earlier. "Really?" he said, his curiosity intensifying. "Lead on."

With a firm grip on his hand, Sarah guided him around a pillar. Then, in an instant, he spotted her. Annie looked absolutely stunning in her off-the-shoulder ruby red gown, the fabric hugging her figure perfectly. Her hair was elegantly swept up, revealing her long, graceful neck, and William felt an overwhelming urge to lean in and kiss it.

"Annie!" Sarah called out.

The woman in ruby red turned at the sound of her name, her stunning smile lighting up the room and twisting William's stomach with an unexpected mix of desire and admiration.

Annie, looking relieved to finally have someone divert her attention from the lecherous gentleman, glanced at Sarah with concern. "Is everything okay?" she asked, unaware that William stood right behind her.

"I want you to meet my brother, William," Sarah said, stepping aside to reveal the man who had come to her aid just days earlier.

William extended his hand toward Annie, a warm smile on his face. Without thinking, she took his hand, and an electric shock of connection ran up her arm, causing her to momentarily freeze.

William's voice was soft as he spoke, "We meet again."

Sarah glanced back and forth between William and Annie, sensing the charged atmosphere. Noticing Annie's moment of hesitation, she cleared her throat, her curiosity piqued. "Have you two met before?" she asked, a hint of mischief in her tone, completely oblivious to the subtle tension that had blossomed between them.

William couldn't take his eyes off Annie, captivated by the way the soft glow of the gallery lights highlighted her features. Turning slightly toward his sister, he said, "This is the young lady I told you about last weekend."

Sarah's eyes widened in realisation, a mischievous grin spreading across her face. "Oh, okay," she replied, clearly intrigued.

Annie finally tore her gaze from William's, a blush creeping up her cheeks. "Your brother saved me last Friday," she admitted, her voice barely above a whisper, warmth flooding her cheeks as she recalled the intensity of that moment.

"William Banks," he said, flashing a charming smile as he realised, he still held her hand. "It's a pleasure to be introduced properly."

"Annie Spencer," she replied, her voice steady despite the flutter of nerves in her stomach. "Yes, it is." The warmth of his touch lingered on her skin, and for a moment, the bustling gallery faded away, leaving just the two of them in their own world.

Sarah gave her brother a cheeky grin, her eyes twinkling with mischief. "Well, I better get back to Irene. I'll see you later, big bro."

William barely registered her words, his mind entirely captivated by the enchanting creature in front of him. "Yes, okay, Sarah," he replied absently, his gaze locked onto Annie. The vibrant atmosphere of the gallery buzzed around him, but all he could focus on was the warmth in her eyes and the way her smile lit up the room.

Chapter Four

Annie gently pulled her hand back from William's grasp, and he reluctantly let go, a hint of regret crossing his face. "How are you, Annie? After the ordeal of last week?" he asked, genuine concern lacing his voice.

Annie smiled, a warm blush creeping onto her cheeks. "Thanks to you, I'm well, thank you," she replied, glancing at him through her long lashes, feeling a touch self-conscious under his admiring gaze.

"I must say, you look stunning," William said, his eyes sparkling with admiration as he took in her elegant figure in the ruby red gown.

"Thank you," Annie replied, her cheeks still slightly flushed from his compliment. "What brings you here tonight?"

William smiled, his expression shifting to one of fondness. "Sarah has been very excited about her first exhibition, so she made me promise I would make an appearance." He paused, then added sincerely, "I'm glad I did."

His gaze lingered on her, and for a moment, the noise of the exhibition faded away, leaving just the two of them in their own little world.

William frowned slightly as he referred to the gentleman she had been talking to earlier. "Do you have to deal with men like that often?" The protectiveness in his voice was evident, and he didn't like the thought of her being pursued by someone like him.

Annie smiled, brushing off his concern. "Unfortunately, it comes with the territory. I think I get asked out at least twice a week by some male client." She shrugged, her tone light and dismissive, as if the unwanted attention didn't bother her. But underneath her casual demeanour, there was a flicker of wariness about the kind of attention she attracted.

William frowned at her words, a protective instinct rising within him. "You need to be careful; there are some men who don't take 'no' for an answer." His voice held a seriousness that contrasted with the light-hearted atmosphere of the gallery.

Annie met his gaze, her expression unyielding. "Believe me, I know." The fervour in her voice hinted at past experiences, a depth of understanding that resonated with him. He could see the strength in her determination, but it only intensified his concern. He wanted to shield her from any man who would dare to disregard her boundaries.

William's mind raced as he considered the intense feelings surging within him. He had always had a protective instinct, especially towards the women in his life, but the overwhelming urge he felt for Annie was different. It wasn't just a brotherly concern or a friendly inclination; it was something deeper, something that made his heart race and his thoughts scatter.

He couldn't quite pinpoint why she stirred such fierce emotions in him. Perhaps it was the vulnerability he had sensed in her after her recent ordeal, or the way her eyes sparkled with determination despite the challenges she faced. There was a strength beneath her gentle demeanour that captivated him, drawing him in like a moth to a flame. The thought of anyone threatening that strength ignited a fire of protectiveness he hadn't anticipated, leaving him questioning what it was about her that stirred such profound feelings.

William chuckled lightly, trying to keep the mood relaxed. "You sound like you have had experiences in that regard."

Annie smiled ruefully, a hint of pain in her eyes. "Unfortunately, yes. I seem to attract attention for some reason, which can be quite annoying at times."

Her tone was serious, but there was an undercurrent of pain in her words. She glanced away for a moment, recalling the unwanted advances she'd faced, then returned her gaze to William, her expression a mix of amusement and resignation. William admired her ability to navigate those challenges with such grace, even if he felt a pang of concern for what she had endured.

William shifted gears, eager to steer the conversation toward a lighter subject. "The exhibition seems to be a great success," he remarked, surveying the lively crowd around them. "I have to admit, I hadn't heard of this artist until Sarah mentioned him to me. His work is quite remarkable."

Annie's face lit up at the compliment. "Isn't it? Michael Godard has such a unique style. I love how he blends humour with artistry, making his pieces both fun and thought-provoking." She gestured toward one of the exhibits, her passion evident in her animated expression.

William followed her gaze, taking in the vibrant colours and whimsical designs that adorned the walls. "I can see why Sarah was excited. It's refreshing to see art that sparks joy rather than just contemplation," he said, genuinely impressed. The conversation flowed easily between them, the earlier tension easing as they shared their thoughts on the artwork and the atmosphere of the event.

As Annie and William continued their conversation, she was suddenly knocked off balance by a flurry of activity nearby. A woman, clearly caught up in her excitement, accidentally bumped into Annie, sending her staggering toward William. In an instant, he instinctively reached out, catching her in his arms before she could fall.

"Whoa, I'm so sorry!" the woman exclaimed, her cheeks flushed with embarrassment as she quickly stepped back, realising the situation.

Annie found herself once again enveloped in William's embrace, his strong arms steadying her. The warmth of his body sent a jolt through her, and she couldn't help but feel a rush of surprise and confusion. It was mind-boggling how easily he had caught her; how natural it felt to be held by him.

"Are you okay?" William asked, concern lacing his voice as he looked down at her, his grip still gentle but firm.

Annie nodded, her heart racing. "Yes, I'm fine. Just a little startled," she replied, her breath slightly unsteady. The proximity between them was electric, and she could feel the intensity of his gaze on her, stirring something deep within her that she struggled to comprehend. "It seems you've saved me again."

William chuckled lightly. "It's an occupation I'd gladly take on," he said, a playful smile dancing on his lips.

Annie looked at him, stunned by his easy charm and the warmth radiating from him. She felt a flutter of something unexpected in her chest, a mix of gratitude and an undeniable attraction that left her momentarily speechless.

As Annie removed herself from William's embrace and straightened her dress, she felt a slight flush creeping up her cheeks. Just then, Irene approached from behind her.

"Annie?"

"Oh yes, Irene, what can I do for you?" she replied with a smile.

Irene gave William an appreciative glance, her eyes sparkling with interest. "First of all, you can introduce me to this handsome young man."

Annie felt the heat of embarrassment rising within her. "Irene Howard, this is William Banks, Sarah's brother."

Irene extended her hand, and William took it, raising it to his lips to kiss her knuckles with a charming grin. "It's a pleasure to meet you, Irene."

The gesture was smooth and graceful, leaving Annie momentarily captivated by the warmth of his demeanour.

Irene's face lit up with delight as she beamed at William. "Oh, Sarah is a lovely girl, one of Annie's many successes," she said, her voice full of pride.

William turned to Annie, raising an eyebrow in curiosity. "Really? You must tell me more."

Irene giggled, her laughter light and infectious, reminiscent of a schoolgirl's delight. "You are charming, aren't you?" She gave him a playful pat on his chest, clearly enjoying the banter. The atmosphere between them felt warm and inviting, making Annie's heart flutter with a mix of excitement and apprehension.

Irene, clearly fishing for a reaction, raised an eyebrow and asked, "So, where is your wife?"

William smiled wryly. "Alas, I am single, no wife, no girlfriend."

Irene's interest piqued as she leaned in, her eyes sparkling with mischief. "Really? Maybe you should ask our beautiful Annie out. After that horrible Jeremy, Annie deserves someone charming like you."

Annie felt a wave of shock wash over her, but she quickly masked it with a laugh, trying to push the idea aside. "Oh, come on, Irene. Let's not go there," she said, her tone light yet laced with a hint of embarrassment. The thought lingered in the air, making her pulse quicken.

William seized the opportunity, a playful smile spreading across his face. "I would love to take Annie on a date," he said, turning his gaze to her. "Would you do me the honour of saying yes?"

Annie felt heat rise to her cheeks, completely embarrassed by the sudden attention. But before she could formulate a response, Irene chimed in with enthusiasm, "Of course she will. Won't you, Annie?"

Caught off guard and left with little choice, Annie nodded, her heart racing. "Yes, of course," she managed to say, feeling a mix of annoyance and trepidation at the unexpected turn of events.

A broad smile spread across William's face. "Wonderful! Does next Saturday suit you?"

Irene turned her attention to Annie, noticing her reluctance. "Annie, not everyone is like that horrible Jeremy, dear. William here is a completely different class," she said, patting William's chest with an encouraging smile. "Aren't you, dear?"

Annie felt backed into a corner, her heart racing at the thought of dating again. "Next Saturday will be lovely, thank you," she replied, her voice slightly shaky as she tried to mask her nerves. The prospect of a new relationship filled her with excitement and apprehension in equal measure.

Irene looked at William with a sense of pride, her smile warm and genuine. "You make sure you look after our Annie. She is a special girl," she said, her voice firm yet affectionate.

William met her gaze with sincerity. "You have my word," he replied, his tone earnest.

Irene beamed at him. "Lovely." She then turned to Annie. "Well, dear, I must be off. Are you okay to finish off the night?"

Annie smiled, feeling a mix of excitement and apprehension. "Yes, of course, Irene. I will look after it."

"You're a gem. It has been a pleasure to meet you, William," Irene said, then looked back at Annie with a playful glint in her eye. "You let me know if he doesn't treat you like you deserve, Annie."

Kissing Annie on the cheek, she added, "Have a lovely night. Goodbye, William." With that, Irene left the gallery, leaving Annie feeling utterly dumbfounded by the whirlwind of events.

Once they were alone, Annie turned to William, her heart racing. "You don't have to take me out. Please don't feel obligated." The words tumbled out, revealing her mix of nerves and uncertainty about stepping into the world of dating again.

William smiled, a playful glint in his eyes. "Wild horses could not stop me," he declared confidently, leaning slightly closer. His tone was light-hearted, but there was an underlying sincerity that made Annie's heart flutter. The warmth in his gaze reassured her, cutting through her anxiety like a knife. She couldn't help but smile back, feeling a rush of nerves.

William leaned in, genuinely interested. "So, tell me about the 'horrible Jeremy,'" he prompted, his brow furrowing slightly.

Annie sighed, the memories surfacing reluctantly. "He was horrible," she replied, her tone laced with frustration.

William raised an eyebrow, pressing for more. "Is that it?"

"He was a guy I went out with a few times," she explained, her voice steadying. "Let's just say, he wasn't worth my time."

"Clearly," William remarked, a hint of amusement creeping into his voice. "Irene certainly didn't like him. Why was that?"

Annie shifted slightly; her nervousness evident as she gathered her thoughts. "He was a little obsessed with me," she admitted, her gaze dropping to the floor. "That made me very uncomfortable."

William's expression darkened with anger as he processed Annie's words. "I'm sorry," he said firmly, his voice low and steady. "No man should do that."

Annie looked into his eyes, the warmth of his gaze a stark contrast to the terrible feelings Jeremy had invoked. "He scared me," she admitted softly, her voice trembling slightly. "I haven't dated since him, because of him."

Seeing the pain in her eyes, William felt a surge of protectiveness. He reached out, gently running a finger down her beautiful cheek, his touch tender and reassuring. "I promise," he said, sincerity evident in his tone, "you're safe with me."

Annie felt a flicker of warmth at William's words, but a nagging doubt crept into her mind. *Physically safe, perhaps*, she mused, but *emotionally*? That was a different story. Memories of Jeremy's obsession echoed in her mind, casting a shadow over her budding feelings for this charming man before her.

She wanted to believe William, to trust that he wouldn't hurt her like Jeremy had, but the scars from her past were still fresh, making it hard to fully open her heart. *What if I let my guard down and he becomes just like him?* The thought chilled her, leaving her torn between the thrill of possibility and the fear of vulnerability.

As she searched William's eyes for reassurance, a part of her longed to take that leap of faith, but the other hesitated, uncertain if she was ready to risk her heart again.

Sarah spotted them from across the gallery, a bright smile spreading across her face as she approached. "There you two are! Have you seen Irene? She was looking for you before she left."

Annie returned her smile, feeling a warmth in her chest. "Yes, she found me. If you want to leave, Sarah, you can, I'll lock up."

Sarah hesitated, a flicker of uncertainty crossing her face as she studied her boss. "Are you sure?"

Annie nodded, noticing the exhaustion etched into Sarah's features. "Yes, Sarah, I'll be fine. You've had a long day."

With a reluctant sigh, Sarah finally relented, knowing Annie's determination. "Okay, but text me when you get home. I'll worry otherwise."

Annie chuckled lightly. "I promise." As Sarah turned to leave, Annie felt a wave of gratitude for her assistant's support.

Sarah leaned in and kissed William on the cheek. "See you, big bro. I'll call you tomorrow."

William smiled back. "Okay, have a good night, Sarah."

Once they were alone, Annie looked at him and said, "I'm sure you have a better place to be. It was lovely to meet you William, again," she added, starting to move away, but he gently placed a hand on her arm to stop her.

"How are you getting home? You're not driving, are you?"

"No, I never bring my car when we have exhibitions. The champagne," she said with a smile. "I just take a taxi home."

William replied, "No, I'll take you home."

Annie looked surprised but quickly nodded. "Thank you. I might be another hour, though."

William smiled reassuringly. "I don't mind. I have plenty to look at. Just find me when you're ready."

Annie hesitated for a moment, then asked, "Are you sure?"

"Yes," he confirmed, his tone steady and sincere.

Forty minutes later, Annie approached William, who was still intently gazing at a piece of artwork.

"You've been looking at that for a while now," she remarked, a teasing lilt in her voice.

Without turning to her, William replied, "I like it."

Annie tilted her head slightly, curiosity piqued. "Oh? What do you like about it?

William finally turned to Annie, his eyes bright with enthusiasm. "What I really love about this piece, is how he incorporates hidden messages. Like the leaves of the trees shaped like a heart, and the way the olives are forming a heart with their hands. Even the title, Falling for You, has that romantic touch."

Annie nodded in agreement, her smile widening. "You're absolutely right. Godard has a unique way of layering meaning into his art, making you look closer to uncover those details." She studied the painting again, feeling a sense of connection to both the artwork and William's keen eye for observation.

William gazed at Annie's radiant smile, captivated by the warmth it brought to the room. "Your smile is stunning," he remarked, his voice softening, "and your eyes are like sapphires."

Annie felt a rush of warmth flood her cheeks. "Thank you," she replied, her voice barely above a whisper.

With a gentle touch, William slid his finger down her cheek, his gaze never wavering. "I love the way you blush," he added, a hint of nostalgia in his tone. "My mother does that."

Annie glanced at William, her heart fluttering slightly. "Are you ready to leave?" she asked, her voice steady despite her excitement. "I just have to lock up on the way out."

William nodded, a smile playing on his lips. "Well, lead on," he replied, his tone encouraging as he fell into step beside her. The atmosphere felt charged with anticipation as they moved toward the gallery's entrance together.

Annie walked into her small office, William following closely behind. She quickly grabbed her bag, her mind still buzzing from the night's events. As she turned to set the alarm, she felt William's gaze on her, adding a layer of warmth to the moment. Once the alarm was set, she moved to lock the front door, the soft click echoing in the quiet gallery.

"I just have to text Irene," Annie said, pulling out her phone. She typed quickly:

Just locked up, alarm is set. Have a lovely weekend, Annie.

Almost immediately, her phone buzzed with a reply:

Looking up from her phone, she smiled at William. "Okay, all set," she said, her heart racing a bit. "Thank you for taking me home."

William met her gaze, his expression sincere. "There was no way I was going to let you try to get a taxi by yourself this time of night," he replied firmly.

Annie laughed, the sound light and genuine, sending a flutter straight to William's heart. "You're very protective, aren't you?"

He shrugged, a hint of a smile on his lips. "Yes."

They walked together to William's car, the night air cool and refreshing. He opened the door for Annie, and she slid into the plush passenger seat, feeling a mix of apprehension and nervousness. William closed the door gently and made his way around to the driver's side, getting in and settling behind the wheel.

After starting the car, he turned to her with a curious smile. "So, where to?"

Annie took a moment to gather her thoughts, then provided him with the address. As she spoke, she felt a sense of comfort in his presence, the nerves from earlier fading away. William nodded, engaging the gear and smoothly pulling away from the curb. The soft hum of the engine filled the quiet space between them, and as they drove into the night, she couldn't help but steal glances at him, captivated by the way his focus was entirely on the road ahead.

As they arrived at Annie's apartment block, the building loomed elegantly in the soft glow of the streetlights. She directed William to a parking spot, and he smoothly manoeuvred the car to a halt. The night felt still and filled with unspoken anticipation.

Once out of the car, Annie turned to William with a smile. "Would you like to come up for a coffee?" she asked, her stomach full of butterflies.

"I'd love to," he replied, returning her smile with warmth.

They made their way inside, and once in her apartment, Annie kicked off her heels, revelling in the immediate comfort of being barefoot. She glanced back at William, who was admiring the space, taking in the art pieces and décor that reflected her personality.

"I'll just make us some coffee," she said, heading into the kitchen. As she moved about, she felt a flutter of nerves. The simple act of preparing coffee felt intimate, and she hoped it would ease the tension between them.

William leaned against the kitchen doorway, watching her with a faint smile. "Can I help?" he offered, his voice light.

"No, just relax. I've got this," she replied, glancing over her shoulder at him, feeling both grateful for his presence and a bit shy under his gaze. She turned her focus back to the task, pouring water into the coffee maker and savouring the moment.

Annie finished brewing the coffee, glancing over her shoulder at William. "How do you take yours?" she asked.

"White, two sugars, thanks," he replied.

She smiled, "Same as me." With a sense of comfort in their shared preference, she prepared their coffees, carefully pouring the rich liquid into two mugs. Once done, she handed him his cup with a soft smile.

They made their way to the living room, where William settled into one end of the sofa. Annie placed her cup on the coffee table, turning to him with a playful glint in her eye. "Would you mind if I changed out of this dress?"

William raised an eyebrow and smiled. "If you have to."

Annie chuckled, appreciating his easy-going nature. "I'll be right back," she said, disappearing into her bedroom, feeling a little nervous about the change in atmosphere.

Annie quickly slipped into her bedroom, the soft lighting casting a warm glow over the space. She pulled off her elegant dress, revelling in the comfort of her fitted shorts and a snug shirt that hugged her figure just right. The fabric felt soft against her skin, a welcome change from the formality of the gown.

After taking a moment to smooth her hair and gather her thoughts, she returned to the living room, a sense of ease washing over her. Sitting on the sofa, she tucked her legs beneath her, feeling more relaxed in her casual attire.

With her coffee cup cradled in her hands, she took a sip, savouring the warmth and richness of the brew. The familiar taste grounded her, and she glanced at William, a smile playing on her lips as she settled into the moment.

Annie looked at William, curiosity dancing in her eyes. "Is the coffee okay?" she asked, hopeful for his approval.

"Yes, thanks! Just the way I like it," he replied, his smile warm and genuine, making her feel at ease.

Feeling a spark of intrigue, Annie leaned in slightly. "So, what do you do for a living?"

William met her gaze, his expression shifting to one of pride. "I'm a lawyer," he said, the words carrying a weight of responsibility.

Annie raised her eyebrows, impressed. "Really? That sounds interesting! What kind of law do you practice?"

William took a sip of his coffee, considering his answer. "Mostly civil law. It can be challenging, but I enjoy it."

Annie nodded, intrigued by his dedication. "I can imagine. It must be rewarding."

William smiled, appreciating her interest. "It has its moments. What about you? What made you decide to work in the art world?"

Annie took a moment, her expression softening as she spoke. "My mother was an artist. She taught me to appreciate art from a young age. It's always been a passion of mine."

William leaned in, intrigued by her story. "Are you close to your parents?"

Annie's smile faded slightly, and she looked down at her coffee for a moment. "I was. They died in a car accident when I was eighteen."

A shadow crossed William's face, his heart sinking with sympathy. "Oh, I'm so sorry," he said gently, meeting her gaze with sincerity. "That must have been incredibly hard for you."

Annie nodded, feeling the weight of the memory. "It was. I had to grow up quickly after that. I don't have any siblings, unfortunately."

William's brow furrowed in concern. "That sounds tough. I can't imagine how lonely that must feel."

Annie offered a small, appreciative smile. "It had its challenges, but I've learnt to enjoy my own company, and I keep busy."

"I'm glad to hear that," William replied, his voice sincere. "What about boyfriends?"

Annie felt a warmth spread across her face, "I wasn't interested while I was at college, I only started dating after I got settled into the gallery job then Jeremy happened."

"Do you mind if I ask what this Jeremy did?" William asked carefully, sensing the weight behind her earlier words.

Annie took a deep breath, clearly gathering her thoughts. "It was about three months ago. He was a construction worker, handsome and funny, so I agreed to go out with him," she paused, as if revisiting the memories. "By the third date, I knew something was off. He must've noticed me pulling away, but I had no intention of seeing him again."

Her voice wavered slightly as she continued, "He started texting, calling, sending me flowers... turning up at my work and even here at all hours, demanding to know who I was with or what I was doing. It was suffocating. One day, he showed up at the gallery when I was in my office on a call. Irene was out front. I had told her a few days before how scared I was of him, so when he showed up, she refused to let him see me. That's when he went ballistic. He started threatening everyone in the gallery."

Tears welled in her eyes, and she fought to keep her composure. "Then he barged into my office and locked the door before I even realised what was happening."

Tears streamed down her cheeks, and William, without hesitation, placed his cup on the coffee table and moved closer to her. He gently took her hand, his touch warm and reassuring, silently offering his support. Annie gave him a small, tearful smile, grateful for his presence during this painful recollection.

"He grabbed me," she continued, her voice trembling. "Started kissing me, telling me he loved me. I tried to push him away, but... I'm no match for a 34-year-old construction worker. He was so much stronger than me." She paused, her breath shaky. "For a moment, I really thought he was going to rape me. I was terrified."

Annie continued, her voice barely above a whisper, "Luckily, the police arrived just before... you know..."

William's expression darkened with concern, and without thinking, he gently wrapped his arms around her, pulling her into a comforting embrace. "I'm so sorry, Annie," he murmured, his voice filled with sincerity. "No woman deserves that. No one should ever go through something like that."

Annie leaned into his warmth, finding solace in his words and presence, the weight of her pain slowly lifting as she allowed herself to softly sob in his arms. After a few moments, her tears subsided, and she pulled away, her cheeks flushed with embarrassment. "I'm so sorry," she whispered, avoiding his gaze as she wiped her eyes.

William gently tilted her chin, meeting her gaze. "Don't be sorry," he said softly, his voice filled with sincerity. "I'm the one who's sorry this happened to you. No one should ever have to go through that." His eyes held hers, offering a silent promise of understanding and protection.

Annie looked up at him, her voice barely above a whisper. "Thank you," she said, pausing as if gathering the strength to continue. "I haven't dated since… too scared." Her eyes flickered with vulnerability.

William met her gaze, his tone steady and full of assurance. "I promise you," he said, his voice soft but firm, "I will treat you with the utmost respect." His words hung in the air, a quiet vow that seemed to ease some of the tension she carried.

"I believe you will," she whispered, her voice barely audible.

William leaned in, softly brushing his lips against hers in a gentle kiss. Pulling back slightly, he smiled. "I better go; you need your beauty sleep." He kissed her again, just as softly. "Thank you for the coffee."

He stood up, walking toward the door with Annie following closely behind. "Thank you for bringing me home," she said, her voice warm.

"You're welcome," William replied, turning to face her. "I'll see you next Saturday."

"Okay," she nodded.

"I'll let you know what time during the week," he added before giving her one last smile and stepping out the door.

Chapter Five

As William stepped out of Annie's apartment and into the cool night air, his mind was racing with what he had learned about her. The thought of her being in such a terrifying situation stirred a deep protectiveness within him. He had always been careful with women, but with Annie, he knew he'd have to tread even more gently.

Her fear, her vulnerability, it was all still so raw. He could see it in her eyes, hear it in her voice. He needed to be patient, to give her space while also showing her that she could trust him completely. She had been through enough, and the last thing he wanted was to rush anything and scare her off.

As he walked toward his car, William resolved to make sure Annie felt safe, respected, and valued, things she deserved after what she'd endured. He would be careful, but also steady. If he wanted to truly be part of her life, he'd need to show her he was different, that he was someone she could count on without fear.

But then, his thoughts drifted to Susan. She had been nothing like Annie. Susan was unkind, manipulative, and untrustworthy, the complete opposite of Annie's warmth and sincerity. Yet, the pain Susan had caused still lingered in his heart. Could he trust Annie with his heart after that betrayal? Would she hurt him the way Susan had, or was she the one person who might finally heal the wounds he kept hidden?

William's phone rang early on Saturday morning, and when Sarah's name flashed on the screen, he sighed, already expecting some teasing. He answered, "Hi, Sarah."

"Hello, lover boy," Sarah giggled on the other end.

"Don't start," he replied, his tone playful but trying to rein her in.

"I told you that you'd like Annie. Was I right?" she asked, a hint of triumph in her voice.

William downplayed his feelings, keeping it cool. "She's… okay."

"Oh, come on, big bro! You couldn't keep your eyes off her," Sarah teased, her laughter bubbling through the phone.

William rolled his eyes, though a smile tugged at his lips. "You're imagining things," he muttered, but Sarah wasn't buying it.

Sarah chimed in, "She couldn't keep her eyes off you either."

"Do you think?" William asked, his curiosity piqued despite himself.

"I knew it! You like her," Sarah said, her tone gleeful and victorious.

William chuckled, trying to maintain his composure. "I wouldn't go that far," he replied, though the flutter in his chest suggested otherwise.

Sarah pressed on, "So when are you seeing her again?"

"Who said I was?" William replied, feigning nonchalance.

"You can't be serious! She's one in a million," Sarah exclaimed, her enthusiasm unwavering. "You need to make a move before someone else does!"

"What makes you think she would go out with me? After Irene told me about 'horrible Jeremy,'" William said, scepticism lacing his voice.

Sarah fell silent for a moment, the gravity of the conversation settling in. "Did she? Everything?"

"What do you mean?" William asked, needing clarification, a sense of urgency creeping into his tone.

"That day was terrible, William. Annie didn't deserve that," Sarah said quietly, her voice tinged with concern.

"Were you there that day?" he pressed, his heart tightening at the thought of Annie's ordeal.

"Unfortunately, yes," Sarah replied, her voice heavy with the memory. "It's something I would never wish on any woman. He cornered her in her office and locked the door; he was seriously out of his mind. By the time the police got there…" She paused, her voice reflecting the pain of the recollection. "She was practically naked… I don't think I will ever forget her screams for help, or the fear in her eyes when they finally broke in… it was horrific."

William felt a wave of anger surge within him. "I can't believe that happened. How could someone do that?"

"People like him think they can control others," Sarah said, shaking her head. "You know, she came in the next day as if nothing had happened and has never talked about it. The only thing she said to Irene and me, was that she vowed never to date again, but she deserves someone who will treat her right."

William admitted, "She is very nice."

Sarah's eyes lit up with excitement. "I'll convince her to give you a chance, big bro!"

"It's okay, Sarah," William said with a grin. "I'm already going out with her next Saturday."

"That's amazing!" Sarah cheered, her excitement bubbling over. "How about you come over for dinner tonight? I'll make your favourite."

"Okay, what time?" William asked, feeling his sister's infectious enthusiasm.

"Around six," she replied happily. "I'll see you then."

They said their goodbyes and hung up.

William arrived at exactly six o'clock, as Sarah opened the door, he breathed in the delicious aroma wafting from the kitchen.

"Hey, that smells amazing!" he exclaimed, a smile breaking across his face.

"Thanks! I hope you're hungry," Sarah replied.

They settled at the dining table, and Sarah served generous portions. As they caught up on the week's events, the conversation flowed easily. William felt a wave of relief wash over him in his sister's warm presence.

As they enjoyed their meal, Sarah brought up the date with Annie. "So how did you manage it?"

"Manage what?" William asked, feigning ignorance.

"Convince Annie to go out with you. I was surprised when you said you had a date with her."

"Why? Am I that grotesque?" he laughed.

"Of course not! It's just…" Sarah paused, choosing her words carefully.

"What is it?" he prompted.

"William, you've seen her," Sarah paused, her expression serious. "She gets asked out nearly twice a day by some very attractive, wealthy men, but she politely declines every time."

A pang of annoyance shot through William. "I can thank Irene for the date," he replied, his voice tinged with frustration.

"Oh?" Sarah was intrigued.

"Yeah, she practically forced Annie to go out with me," William said, a smile spreading across his face at the memory.

Sarah giggled. "Good on Irene! How did Annie take it?"

"She tried her best to politely decline, but Irene wouldn't have it," William replied, a triumphant glint in his eyes.

Sarah laughed, clearly pleased with Irene's intervention, but then her expression grew more serious as she remembered something. "Did Annie tell you about the graffiti outside the gallery?"

William's expression immediately shifted to concern. "No, what happened?" he asked, his voice tense with worry.

"When Annie got in on Friday, there was graffiti on the wall just outside the gallery," Sarah explained, her tone more serious now.

"What did it say?" William pressed, his concern deepening.

Sarah paused for a moment, her fork hovering above her plate. "It said *'Bitch.'* Annie was a little freaked out by it," she admitted. "She tried to hide it, but her eyes gave it away."

"Really?" William raised an eyebrow. "What do you think she was worried about?"

"Not sure but I think it shook her up more than she wants to admit," Sarah said, leaning back in her chair. "She's been really calm about everything that has happened, but..."

William nodded, absorbing her words. "It's not just the graffiti itself; it's the feeling of being threatened, especially after what she went through."

"Exactly. I think the gallery used to be her safe space," Sarah added. "I can tell it has been bothering her."

As they finished their meal, William pondered the implications of Sarah's observations. He respected Annie's strength, but an uneasy feeling lingered in his mind. The conversation hung in the air as they cleared the table, both aware of the challenges that lay ahead.

It was Tuesday afternoon, after a busy morning in court, William wrapped up early and decided to stop by the art gallery to see Annie and his sister. As he walked through the front doors of the art gallery the scent of paint and soft music greeted him, instantly putting him at ease.

The gallery full of bursts of colours and textures, but William's eyes immediately search for Annie, but he only found Sarah, arranging artwork, a smile spread across his face.

She looked up, her expression lighting up with delight. "William! I didn't expect to see you here!" she exclaimed, rushing over to give him a quick hug.

"I had some free time and thought I'd check in on my favourite art gallery assistant," he teased, a playful grin on his face.

Sarah beamed, clearly pleased to have him there. "You just missed Annie; she had to run out for a bit," she informed him, a hint of mischief in her voice. "I'm sure that's why you're here."

"I wanted to see you too," William replied, but deep down, he knew it was Annie he really wanted to see.

After a few more minutes of light conversation, he decided to take his leave, promising to return soon to catch up with Sarah and see Annie.

As he stepped outside, the late afternoon sun cast a warm glow over the pavement. He was just about to head toward his car when he caught sight of Annie walking across the road toward him. His heart started to race. She hadn't notice him yet, her focus was on her phone as she walked with purpose.

William watched her as she walked towards him, a sense of excitement filling him. Suddenly, his focus sharpened when he spotted a car speeding toward her, veering off course and heading directly for her. Time seemed to slow as he realised the driver was deliberately aiming for her. Adrenaline surged through him.

Without a second thought, William sprint forward, his heart racing as he reached out and pulled her toward him just in time. Causing her to stumble into his arms, barely avoiding the car that sped past them with a screech of tires.

"Are you okay?" William breathes, holding her tightly, his heart pounding in his chest. Gazing down at her, searching for any signs of injury.

Annie's expression shifted from surprise to recognition, and her breathless response barely registered through his own adrenaline. "What just happened?" she stammered, visibly shaken.

"I saw that car coming straight for you," he replied, his voice steadying as he held her close, realising how close she had come to being injured, or worse, killed. "Are you hurt?"

"No, I'm fine, just… I think I'm okay. Who was that?" Annie replied, still processing the moment, her voice trembling slightly as the adrenaline began to fade.

William quickly glanced back at the road, scanning for the vehicle, but it had already disappeared down the street, leaving behind only the echo of screeching tires. "I don't know, but we should probably get you somewhere safe," he suggested, his voice steady but filled with concern. The protective instinct he felt earlier surged within him, now fully awakened, and a gnawing feeling in his gut. *What the hell is going on, that was no accident.*

He studied Annie's face, noting the lingering shock in her bright blue eyes and the way she instinctively kept hold of him. "We need to get you inside," he urges, his tone firm but gentle. "You shouldn't be out here, not after that."

Annie nodded slowly, her expression still a mix of disbelief and fear as they both released their hold on each other. "Yeah, you're right," she said, her voice trembling slightly. "I didn't even see it coming."

William took her arm, guiding her away from the street and toward the entrance of the gallery. As they walked, he scanned their surroundings, his senses heightened.

"William! Annie! Are you guys, okay?" Sarah called out, opening the gallery doors and rushing toward them, her worry evident in her voice.

Annie could only nod, momentarily speechless as she processed what had just happened. The shock of the near miss left her feeling unsteady, and she instinctively tightened her grip on William's arm, seeking comfort in his presence.

"Just a close call," William reassured Sarah, casting a quick glance at Annie, who was still trying to catch her breath. "I saw a car coming right for her."

"What? A car?" Sarah gasped, her eyes wide with disbelief. "Did you get their plate number?"

"No, it happened too fast. I barely got there in time to pull her out of the way," William explained, his voice steady but edged with urgency.

Sarah exchanged a quick, grateful glance with her brother before turning her full attention to Annie. "I'm so glad you're okay," she said softly, her concern palpable.

As the reality of her safety began to sink in, Annie took a deep breath, gathering her composure. "I'm fine, just a little shaken," she managed, releasing her grip on William but staying close, her heart still racing from the adrenaline.

"Thank you for saving me, again," Annie said, her voice steadier now but still tinged with the remnants of fear. "This seems to be becoming a habit..., you saving me."

William waved off her gratitude with a modest smile. "I'm just glad I was there, but I think we should get you inside." He glanced around to ensure there were no lingering threats before leading her back into the gallery.

"Right, come on," Sarah urges, guiding them back toward the gallery's entrance. As they walk, Annie can feel her heart rate slowly returning to normal, but the encounter had definitely left an imprint.

As they step inside the art gallery, the atmosphere shifted from the chaos of the street to the calming presence of colour and soft music. The soft lighting highlighted the beautiful pieces on display, creating a sense of safety that wrapped around them. William glanced at Annie, who appeared to be regaining her composure, though he can still see the lingering shock in her eyes.

Sarah, ever the energetic spirit, hurried off towards the kitchen area. "I'll make you some tea, Annie! Just sit tight!" she called over her shoulder, her voice bright despite the tension that just unfolded.

Annie nodded appreciatively but felt the need to sit down and collect her thoughts. She headed towards her office at the back of the gallery, with William following closely behind. "You don't have to worry about me," she assured him, forcing a smile as she opened the door to her office.

"I know," William replied, leaning against the doorframe as she stepped inside. "I just want to make sure you're okay. That was pretty intense out there."

Annie took a deep breath, "I'm starting to feel better," she admitted, looking around her office as if grounding herself in her space will help dispel the lingering unease.

William studied her for a moment, wanting to delve deeper into the situation but sensing that this isn't the right time. He wrestled with the knowledge he had about the graffiti, the carpark attack and now this; he knew there's more going on than Annie realised. However, he decided to keep that information to himself for now, wanting to shield her from unnecessary fear.

"Do you need anything? Water? Something to eat?" he offered, shifting the focus away from the incident.

"No, I'm okay for now," Annie replied, moving to her desk and starting to organise a few papers. "Just give me a moment to settle down."

"Alright," he said, leaning back slightly against the door. He felt a strange mix of concern and admiration as he watches her regain her composure. "I'll be right here if you need anything."

Just then, Sarah returned with a steaming cup of tea. "Here you go, Annie! I made it just how you like it," she said, handing the cup to her with a warm smile.

"Thank you, Sarah," Annie replied, taking the mug and letting the warmth seep into her hands. She took a sip, letting the familiar taste soothe her further.

Sarah glanced at the clock, realising she needed to tend to the gallery. "I'll be right back, Annie. Just keep resting," she said, her voice laced with concern. "If you need anything, just call me."

Annie nodded, still sipping her tea, grateful for the brief moment of respite. "Thanks, Sarah. I will."

Before heading out, Sarah turned to William, her expression serious. "William, can you keep an eye on her for a little while? I just want to make sure she's okay."

"Of course," he replied without hesitation. "I'm happy to stay."

"Thanks, I appreciate it," Sarah said, giving Annie a reassuring smile before stepping out to manage the gallery.

Once they were alone the atmosphere shifted slightly, leaving a comfortable silence between William and Annie. He took a seat in the chair opposite her desk, watching as she sipped her tea. The warm liquid seemed to be doing its job, helping to calm her down after the chaotic events outside. As Annie gradually relaxed, William's thoughts drifted back to the moment when she was in his arms. Despite the intensity of the situation, there had been something wonderful about the way she felt, her warmth, the softness of her body pressed against his, and the scent of her hair that had enveloped him, even if only for a fleeting moment.

Annie set her cup down and looked up at him, her eyes meeting his. The warmth of her smile catching him off guard, and he found himself staring. William couldn't help but admire her full lips, which curved naturally into that gentle smile.

In that moment, he realised just how captivating she truly was, and his heart beat a little faster. It's a strange blend of emotions, admiration for her strength, appreciation for her beauty, and a fierce desire to protect her from whatever dangers lurk outside.

"Are you sure you're okay?" he asked, breaking the silence, his voice softer than intended.

"I'm getting there," Annie replied, her smile widening slightly. "Thank you for being here."

"Just doing what I can," he said, leaning forward slightly.

Annie looked down at her tea, taking a deep breath as if to anchor herself in the moment. William noticed how her fingers gently wrap around the warm cup, and he felt an inexplicable urge to draw closer, to share more of himself with her. The room was filled with a comfortable silence, as it stretched comfortably between them, Annie decided to break it, eager to shift her focus from the earlier incident. "You know, Sarah has been such a wonderful addition to the gallery," she began, her eyes lighting up as she talked about his sister. "I'm really glad I hired her. She has this incredible sunny outlook on life that just brightens the place."

William nodded, a smile creeping onto his face. "Yeah, she really does," he replied, appreciating Sarah's natural charisma and positive energy. "We're quite close. I'm proud of her for how she is taking to her new job."

Annie smiles back, her admiration for Sarah evident. "You should be. It's refreshing to work with someone so enthusiastic. She is always bubbling with ideas and excitement," she commented, taking another sip of her tea. "I feel lucky to have her on my team."

"Seems like you both feel the same way," William observed, leaning back in his chair, genuinely interested in her perspective. "So, what's your favourite part about running the gallery?"

Annie paused, considering her answer. "Honestly, I love sharing art with people. It's amazing to see how different pieces resonate with different individuals. When someone finds joy or inspiration in a piece I've chosen, it makes all the hard work worth it," she explained, her passion for her job shining through.

"That's a beautiful way to look at it," William replied, genuinely impressed. "You clearly have a gift for it."

"Thanks! I try my best," Annie said, her cheeks flushing slightly at the compliment.

William felt an unexpected ease talking to Annie, drawn in by her thoughtful insights and genuine interest in what he had to say. The more they talked, the more he realised how much he enjoyed her company.

As their conversation continued, the earlier tension seemed to dissolve completely, replaced by a warm bond that felt promising. They both found themselves laughing and sharing more about their lives, each discovering unexpected connections between them that deepened the budding relationship.

As Annie finished her tea, she took a moment to savour the warmth of the mug before setting it down on her desk. A sense of calm had settled over her, and she felt grateful for the conversation and the company. Standing up, she stretched slightly, the tension of the day beginning to ebb away.

"Thank you for being here, William," she said, a soft smile gracing her lips as she walked around her desk. She approached him, and he stood up instinctively, feeling a shift in the air between them.

Before he could process what was happening, Annie lent up and gently kissed him on the cheek. The gesture was sweet and sincere, her gratitude palpable. "Thank you for saving me, again," she added, her voice barely above a whisper, but filled with warmth.

William was taken aback, his heart raced at the unexpected affection. A mixture of shock and delight washed over him, but he tried to maintain a composed demeanour. He couldn't help but feel a surge of happiness at her gesture, warmth spreading through him as he processed the moment.

"Of course, I'd do it again in a heartbeat," he replied, his voice steady despite the flutter of emotions inside him. He looked into her eyes, wanting her to see how much he meant it.

Annie pulled back slightly; her cheeks flushed as she realised the intimacy of the moment. She seemed to hesitate for just a second, her smile lingering as she met his gaze. "I really appreciate it," she said softly, the sincerity in her tone deepening.

William can't help but smile back, feeling a connection that seems to transcend the chaos they both faced just a little earlier. "I'm just glad you're okay," he assured her, his heart still racing from the simple kiss.

As they stood there, the air between them felt charged, a subtle shift in their dynamic that both of them could sense. He watched as Annie stepped back, her demeanour still warm but now slightly shy, and he knew they had crossed a threshold into something more personal.

Just as the warm moment between Annie and William began to settle, Sarah stepped inside the office, her expression brightening the room. "Hey, Annie! Your two o'clock client is here," she announced, her energy infectious.

"Thank you, Sarah," Annie replied, turning to her assistant with a grateful smile. "If you want to visit with your brother for a little while, feel free to use my office."

William watched as Annie placed her hand gently on his arm. The light touch sent a small jolt of warmth through him, and he found himself instinctively leaning into her touch. "Thank you again for everything," she said, her smile radiant. She squeezed his arm softly before moving to the door, and William couldn't help but smile at her, his heart lifting at her kindness.

"Anytime," he replied, his voice steady but full of warmth as he met her gaze.

With that, Annie turned and headed towards the door, leaving William and Sarah alone in the office. As she walked away, he watched her, captivated by the way she carried herself, confident yet tender. However, as soon as she disappeared from view, a frown crossed his face.

He felt a sudden heaviness settle in his chest. Thoughts of the today's incident, the carpark attack and the graffiti swirl in his mind, a stark reminder of the danger that still lurked around Annie. The contrast between their light-hearted conversation and the reality of her situation ate at him, and he couldn't shake the concern that had begun to take root.

William ran a hand through his hair, trying to clear his thoughts. He knew he needed to figure out how to protect her while navigating his feelings for her. The kiss on the cheek still lingered in his mind, but the worry for her safety cast a shadow over his thoughts. He sighed, mentally preparing himself for whatever might come next, determined to be there for Annie.

Chapter Six

Annie stepped into the gallery's main space, where the bright, airy atmosphere enveloped her as she approached Mrs. Higgins, a distinguished-looking woman with a keen eye for art. Mrs. Higgins stood near one of the walls, admiring a vibrant landscape painting that captures the serene beauty of a rolling countryside bathed in golden light.

"Good afternoon, Mrs. Higgins!" Annie greets her warmly, a smile spreading across her face. "I'm so glad to see you again. Are you ready to take a closer look at that landscape we discussed?"

"Oh, Annie! It's absolutely stunning," Mrs. Higgins replied, her eyes sparkling with enthusiasm. "I can't wait to have it in my home."

Annie leads Mrs. Higgins closer to the painting, pointing out the intricate details that make it so special. "The colours are so rich, and the way the light interacts with the landscape is just breathtaking, don't you think?" she comments, watching as Mrs. Higgins lean in closer, captivated by the brushwork.

After a little discussion, during which Annie highlighted the artist's background and inspiration behind the piece, Mrs. Higgins nods decisively. "Yes, I'll take it! It's exactly what I was looking for."

Annie's heart swelled with pleasure at the positive response. "That's wonderful to hear! When would you like it to be shipped?" she asked, jotting down notes in her planner.

"Oh, I'd like to have it shipped next week, if possible," Mrs. Higgins replied, her voice filled with excitement. "I want to get it hung up before my dinner party."

"Perfect! And do you have a spot in mind for it?" Annie asked, genuinely interested. "Or would you like me to assist you in choosing the right place?"

Mrs. Higgins thinks for a moment, tapping her chin thoughtfully. "I have a large wall in my living room that would be perfect, but I'd love your expert advice to make sure it's displayed to its full potential," she said, her appreciation for Annie's expertise evident.

"I'd be happy to help with that!" Annie assures her, her enthusiasm visible. "I can come by next week before the shipping date and help you find the best place for it."

"Thank you, Annie! You always know how to make these decisions so much easier for me," Mrs. Higgins replied, her gratitude genuine.

Annie beamed at the compliment, feeling a sense of accomplishment as they finalise the details. The interaction reaffirmed her love for her work and the joy she finds in connecting art with people. As they wrap up the conversation, she felt energised, ready to take on the rest of the day with renewed purpose.

As Annie continued her interaction with Mrs. Higgins, explaining the nuances of the painting and answering her questions with ease, William and Sarah step out of the office. Sarah lent slightly toward her brother, her voice barely above a whisper. "You know, Annie is incredible at her job. I'm learning so much from her every day," she remarked, her pride evident.

William glanced over at Annie, watching her animatedly discuss the artwork. He can see how engaged Mrs. Higgins is, her smile widening with every word Annie spoke. "I can see that," he replied, genuinely impressed. "The way she communicates with her clients is remarkable. She makes them feel valued and understood."

Sarah nodded in agreement, her eyes following Annie as she gestured toward the painting. "She has this calm confidence that draws people in. I think it's why her clients keep coming back," Sarah added, her admiration for Annie clear.

William watched as Annie lent in closer to Mrs. Higgins, her demeanour warm and inviting. He noted how she effortlessly balanced professionalism with genuine care, making the interaction feel personal and meaningful. "You're right," he said thoughtfully. "It's not just about selling art for her; she truly loves sharing it with others."

As they continued to observe, William felt a sense of pride for Annie's abilities and realised how much he admired her. He couldn't help but think about the potential she had to influence others through her passion for art. The way she connected with her clients only deepened his appreciation for her, solidifying the spark he felt during their previous conversations.

"You're lucky to work with someone like her," William concluded, turning to Sarah with a smile.

"Totally," Sarah agreed, her enthusiasm matching her brother's. "I hope I am as good as her at my job one day."

As the two watch Annie with Mrs. Higgins, the air was filled with a sense of admiration and hope, both siblings feeling fortunate to be part of her life.

Sarah glanced at William, a teasing smile forming on her lips. "You know, William, she will be good for you," she predicted, her tone light but playful.

William, caught off guard by his sister's sudden matchmaking, blinked in surprise. He shot her a sideways look before replying, "Maybe." The word came out casually, but there was a hint of something thoughtful behind it.

As Annie's conversation with Mrs. Higgins wrapped up and she prepared to leave, William turned to Sarah, who's been eagerly watching her boss. "Well, I should get going," he said, glancing at his watch. "I have a few things to take care of."

"Alright," Sarah replied, her expression a mix of reluctance and understanding. "Thanks for coming by big bro. It's always nice to see you."

"Of course. I enjoyed visiting," he responded, a warm smile crossing his face. "I'll call you this weekend, alright? We can catch up properly then."

"Sounds great!" Sarah replied, her enthusiasm evident, before shooting him a playful sidelong glance. "But will you even have time? You might be a little too preoccupied," she teased with a knowing grin.

William shook his head, feeling grateful for their close bond. "You're not going to stop teasing, are you?" he added playfully.

"No," Sarah assured him with cheeky grin. "You know I love you."

Before he stepped away, William gave Sarah a quick hug, holding her tightly for a moment before releasing her. "See you soon," he said, turning to head towards the exit. He glanced back one last time, catching a glimpse of Annie wrapping up her discussion with Mrs. Higgins.

With a mix of thoughts swirling in his mind about Annie and her safety, William left the gallery, feeling a sense of purpose to protect her while enjoying the connection that's begun to grow between them.

As the week progressed, a sense of normalcy returned to Annie's life. She enjoyed her work at the gallery, time with Sarah and engaging with clients without any incidents. The unsettling events from the beginning of the week faded to the background, allowing her to feel more at ease. However, as Thursday night rolled around, she arrived home from work, the familiar comfort of her apartment wrapping around her like a warm blanket.

As soon as she stepped inside, her phone rang, cutting through the quiet ambiance. Annie hesitated, glancing at the screen displaying an unknown caller, contemplating whether or not to answer. With a sense of unease creeping in, she picked up the phone. "Hello?" she said, but all she heard was heavy breathing on the other end.

"Hello? Please, just leave me alone!" she finally exclaimed; her voice firm yet tinged with anxiety. The breathing persisted, sending a chill down her spine. Frustrated and unnerved, she hung up and tried to shake off the unsettling feeling.

She headed to the kitchen, grabbing a bottle of water from the fridge, hoping it would help calm her nerves. Just as she twisted the cap off, the phone rang again, startling her. Another unknown caller. With a weary sigh, she answered, gripping the water bottle tightly. "Please, just leave me alone," she said, her voice tinged with desperation, expecting yet another prank call.

"Annie?" a familiar voice responded, making her heart skip a beat.

"William?" she replied, surprised.

"Yeah, it's me," he said, his tone a comforting mix of concern and warmth. "What's wrong?"

Annie hesitated for a moment before finally explaining, "I've been getting these prank phone calls. They're really unsettling."

William's voice sharpened, his protective instincts kicking in. "On your mobile?"

"Yes. It comes up as an unknown caller, but that's pretty normal for me since I don't have all my clients' numbers saved. I just got one right before you called."

"I'm really sorry to hear that. Are you okay? Do you feel safe?" he asked, trying to keep his tone calm so as not to worry her further.

"I'm fine, just… a little on edge," Annie admitted, her voice softening with gratitude for his concern.

"How did you get my number?" she asked, curiosity flickering in her tone.

"Sarah gave it to me," he replied smoothly. "I hope you don't mind. I thought it might be a good idea to check in on you."

Annie smiled, touched by his thoughtfulness. "That's sweet of you," she said, her heartwarming at his concern.

"I also wanted to let you know I'll pick you up at six on Saturday night," William continued, his tone shifting to something more hopeful. "Is that okay?"

Annie's breath caught in her throat, a wave of nervousness washing over her. She hesitated for a moment, her apprehension clear, but finally said, "Oh… um, okay," a small smile forming despite the fluttering in her chest.

"Great! Just so you know, it's a formal affair," he added, his voice slightly tense, as though holding his breath, awaiting her reaction.

"Formal? That's fine," she reassured him, excitement beginning to replace her nerves. The thought of dressing up for the occasion gave her a thrill. "I'll be ready."

"Awesome. I'm really looking forward to it," he said, the relief in his voice palpable, grateful she hadn't tried to back out of their date.

They chatted a bit longer, their conversation flowing naturally as they discussed the day they had. With each passing moment, Annie found comfort in William's presence, even over the phone, and the tension from earlier slowly began to fade.

"Thanks for calling, William. It was nice talking to you," she said sincerely as they prepared to say goodbye.

"Anytime, Annie. Just remember, I'm here if you need anything," he replied, his voice warm and reassuring.

"Goodbye, William," she said softly, feeling a sense of calm after their conversation.

"Goodbye, Annie," he echoed before hanging up.

As Annie set her phone down, a mix of emotions swirled within her. Though the prank calls had left her shaken, the thought of her upcoming date with William filled her with a quiet sense of anticipation. She took a deep breath, deciding to focus on the positive and look forward to what the weekend might bring.

The next morning, Annie arrived at the art gallery feeling a mix of excitement and lingering anxiety from the previous night's prank calls. As she walked through the doors, the familiar scent of paint and polished wood welcomed her, instantly soothing her nerves. She found Sarah already at her desk, her bright smile lighting up the room.

"Morning, Annie," Sarah greeted her cheerfully.

"Morning," Annie replied with a smile.

"William called yesterday and asked for your number," Sarah said, beaming. "I gave it to him. I hope you don't mind."

Annie's heart fluttered at the mention of William. "No, of course not! He did call me," she said, her smile growing wider.

Sarah flashed a cheeky grin. "He's really looking forward to Saturday."

Annie thought for a moment. "So am I."

Sarah's expression softened. "He'll treat you right, Annie."

"I know. It's okay, Sarah. I feel safe with your brother."

Despite the lingering fear from the prank calls and other incidents, the anticipation of spending more time with William helped chase away her worries. She couldn't shake the feeling that perhaps this new relationship was exactly what she needed to move forward.

On Friday afternoon, William sent her a text confirming:

I'm looking forward to Saturday, see you at six.

Her heart skipped a beat at the thought of their evening together. She quickly replied:

I can't wait.

Chapter Seven

Saturday arrived, and Annie spent the day in a flurry of excitement and nervous energy. As the clock approached six o'clock, she meticulously prepared herself for the night ahead. After trying on several outfits, she finally decides on a stunning navy-blue satin floor length gown. The off-the-shoulder design highlighted her graceful collarbone, while the small sleeves added a touch of elegance. The gown had a daring slit on one side, which gave a glimpse of one of her shapely legs as she walked, which she planned to accentuate with colour matched high heels.

Annie applied her makeup with care, focusing on enhancing her features rather than overshadowing them. A touch of mascara brought out her eyes, and a soft pink lipstick complemented her natural beauty. When she glanced in the mirror, she couldn't help but smile at her reflection, feeling beautiful and confident.

At exactly six o'clock she heard a gentle knock on the door. With one last deep breath to steady her nerves, she opened the door, William was standing there, looking impeccably handsome in a tailored tuxedo. His eyes widen in surprise as he took in her appearance, and he stumbled over his words. "You look… wow! Absolutely stunning," he said, his voice filled with genuine admiration.

Annie felt her cheeks heat up as a blush spread across her cheeks. "Thank you," she replied softly, a shy smile gracing her lips.

William stepped inside, his gaze still lingering on her, clearly impressed. "That dress looks amazing on you."

"Thanks! I was hoping you would like it," she replied, her heart racing at the compliments.

He offered her his arm, as she placed her hand on it, she felt a rush of warmth, a mix of thrill and comfort as they stepped out into the evening together. The anticipation of the night ahead filled her with a sense of joy, knowing that they will share this experience together.

William opened the passenger door of his sleek black car for Annie, offering her a warm smile as she slid into the seat. He gently helped her adjust her dress, ensuring that she was comfortable before closing the door and making his way to the driver's side. The car hummed to life as he navigated the streets, the city lights twinkling like stars against the darkening sky.

As he drove, the conversation flowed easily between them, laughter punctuating their exchanges. William admired how the soft glow of the dashboard illuminated Annie's face, highlighting her sparkling eyes. With every shared smile and playful remark, he found himself even more drawn to her charm and grace.

Arriving at the venue, they pulled up to the grand entrance, where elegant valets stood ready to assist. William stepped out first, then walked around to help Annie. As he opened the door, he extended his hand toward her, and she took it, feeling the warmth of his grip as he helped her navigate the car's low seat.

"Thank you," she said softly, her heart racing as he offered his arm to her. The valets greeted them with nods, taking care of the car while William guided Annie toward the entrance.

Inside, the ballroom was a breathtaking sight. Crystal chandeliers hung from the ceiling, casting a soft, golden light over the elegantly set tables. Each table was adorned with fresh flowers and flickering candles, creating an inviting atmosphere. In front of them, a polished dance floor awaits, and a stage stands proudly at the far end, ready for the evening's festivities.

"What's the occasion?" Annie asked, glancing up at William with curiosity.

"It's a retirement party for one of the original partners at the firm," he explained, his voice filled with pride. "He's been with the firm for over thirty years, and we're all here to celebrate his contributions and say goodbye."

Annie nodded, impressed by the significance of the event. "That sounds wonderful," she replied, excitement bubbling within her at the thought of the celebration.

William led her further into the ballroom, their fingers brushing together as they walk, igniting a spark between them. As they found their seats, Annie couldn't help but feel that this evening was the beginning of something special, not just a formal affair but a moment shared between two people who have found a connection amidst the chaos of their lives.

Seated at the head table, William and Annie found themselves in the company of the other partners of the law firm, each engaged in lively conversation. The atmosphere was filled with laughter and the clinking of glasses, a perfect blend of professionalism and camaraderie.

As they settled in, Annie lent slightly toward William, her voice low and playful. "I didn't realise you were a partner," she whispered, her eyes sparkling with intrigue. "You didn't mention it."

William chuckled softly, a hint of pride in his smile. "I must have forgotten," he replied, stealing a glance at her. In that moment, he was utterly captivated by her beauty, the way her hair fell gracefully over her shoulders, the soft glow of her skin in the ambient light, and the genuine warmth of her smile.

While William was still looking at Annie, several of the other partners approach the table, their presence commanding attention. One of them, a distinguished man with greying hair and an amiable demeanour, looked at Annie and raises an eyebrow playfully. "Who is this beauty you have with you, William?" he asked, a wide grin spreading across his face.

William stands, straightening his posture as he introduces Annie. "This is Annie Spencer," he said, his voice steady and confident. He extended his hand to her, to help her to rise beside him. "Annie, this is Mr. Thompson, our senior partner."

Annie shook Mr. Thompson's hand with a charming smile, feeling the warmth of William's presence beside her. As the introductions continue, William confidently presented the other partner, shaking hands and exchanging pleasantries. "And this is Mr. and Mrs. Carter," he said, gesturing to a couple who exude an air of sophistication.

Throughout the introductions, Annie's poise, and grace impress everyone at the table, and William felt a swell of pride at her side. "William is the youngest and only single partner of the firm," Mr. Thompson added with a knowing glance at Annie, eliciting a few chuckles from the group.

As the evening progressed, William and Annie engaged with the partners and their wives, Annie charmed everyone with her wit and elegance. Amidst the lively discussions and laughter, William's gaze often drifted back to Annie, captivated by the effortless way she fitted into this world. He realised that, despite the formal setting, this evening felt more like a celebration of their budding relationship than just a professional gathering.

The dinner unfolded beautifully, each course more delightful than the last. The atmosphere was warm and inviting, with engaging conversations flowing around the table. Laughter punctuated the air as stories were shared, and Annie found herself effortlessly fitting into the lively dynamic of William's colleagues and their spouses. She listened intently, contributing her own thoughts, and William couldn't help but admire her charm and intelligence.

As the last course was cleared away, the lights dimmed slightly, signalling the beginning of the speeches. One by one, the partners took to the stage to express their gratitude and share fond memories of the retiring partner, Mr. Thompson. Annie clapped enthusiastically after each speech, her smile infectious, and William found himself captivated not just by her beauty but by her genuine enthusiasm and warmth.

Once the speeches concluded, the atmosphere shifted as soft music began to play, inviting guests to the dance floor. William's heart raced as he turns to Annie, his eyes sparkling with excitement. "Would you like to dance?" he asked, a hint of nervousness in his voice.

Annie's face lit up as she nodded. "I'd love to!"

They made their way to the dance floor, and William wrapped one arm around her waist, pulling her close, holding her other hand against his chest. The moment their bodies connected, he felt an undeniable sense of belonging, as if they were always meant to be together. The music swelled around them, a slow and romantic tune that seemed to echo the emotions swirling in his heart.

As they swayed gently to the rhythm, William couldn't help but wonder what Annie was thinking. He studied her face, noticing the way her eyes shone with happiness and her lips curved into a soft smile. His mind raced with thoughts of how incredible she felt in his arms and how their bond seemed to deepen with each passing moment.

Yet, a cautious voice in the back of his mind reminded him that it might be too soon to think about how he was feeling. For now, he savoured the intimacy of the dance, the way her body fit perfectly against his, and the electric current that flowed between them. As they move together, William knew he wanted to explore this relationship further, but for this moment, he focused solely on the joy of having Annie close, cherishing every second of their dance beneath the shimmering lights of the ballroom.

As the music played on, Annie found herself twirling around the dance floor, gracefully moving from partner to partner. She danced with several of the partners, her laughter mingling with their jovial banter, and a few of the younger lawyers joined in, eager to share a dance with the stunning art gallery director. Each time she stepped away, William couldn't help but feel a twinge of envy and pride. He watched as she charmed everyone with her radiant smile and effortless grace, the attention she received making her all the more captivating.

Finally, after what felt like an eternity, Annie returned to William's side. He pulled her in close on the dance floor, eager to feel her warmth once more. As they swayed to the music, he lent down slightly to whisper, "You know, everyone seems to gravitate toward you. It's almost like you're a magnet."

Annie smiled, a hint of mischief sparkling in her eyes. "It can be a curse sometimes," she replied playfully. "I love people, but sometimes it feels like they expect too much."

William raised an eyebrow, intrigued. "What do you mean, a curse?"

She laughed lightly, brushing a loose strand of hair behind her ear. "I'm not sure why I attract so much attention. It's often unwanted."

William's grip tightened slightly at her words. "Like the gentleman at the exhibition?" he asked, genuine concern lacing his voice.

"Yes, exactly. They seem to think that because I'm single, I'm fair game," Annie responded, her expression turning thoughtful. "Especially the wealthy ones. They act like every woman should swoon at the sight of them just because of their bank balance."

"I am surprised you're single," William said with a cheeky smile. "You're a beautiful woman, smart, hardworking, funny, charming, sexy…"

Annie laughed, shaking her head. "Please stop! I'll get a big head."

William admired her modesty, appreciating the way she deflected compliments.

As they continued to dance, the world around them faded, leaving just the two of them in their own little bubble. William's mind filled with gratitude for having her in his life, and he couldn't help but feel a deeper bond forming between them.

The night unfolded wonderfully, filled with laughter, lively conversation, and the soft glow of chandeliers illuminating the elegant ballroom. Annie was in her element, her warm personality drawing everyone in. She danced, mingled, and shared stories with the partners and their wives, genuinely enjoying the company and the celebration of Mr. Thompson's retirement.

As the evening wound down, the partners and their spouses approached Annie to say their goodbyes. Each of them expressed how much they enjoyed meeting her, and the wives enthusiastically mentioned their plans to visit the gallery soon. "We'll definitely pop in to see your collection!" one of the partners' wives exclaimed, her eyes sparkling with excitement. Annie beamed at the prospect, graciously thanking them for their support and enthusiasm.

William stood nearby, watching Annie's interactions with pride. Mr. Thompson, the retired partner, caught his eye and gave him a knowing smile. "Don't let this one get away William," he advised, nodding toward Annie. "She's a keeper."

Annie's cheeks flushed at the compliment, and she glanced at William, who met her gaze with a bright smile. "I won't," he replied confidently, his voice steady. "I think so too."

Laughter filled the air as the group shared the moment, Annie's embarrassment gave way to joy. The warmth of William's words lingered between them, and the connection they've built that evening felt stronger than ever. As they all parted ways, Annie's heart raced with excitement, not just from the lovely evening but also from the growing bond she shared with William.

With a final wave and a few more kind words exchanged, the partners and their wives headed out into the night. William and Annie lingered for a moment longer, the ballroom now emptying around them, the lingering music faded into a gentle hum. The night had been magical.

As William and Annie left the ballroom, the night air felt refreshing after the warmth of the elegant event. They stood side by side and waited for the valet to bring the car around, their conversation flowing easily between them. William stole glances at Annie, who glowed under the soft streetlights, her navy-blue gown shimmering as she shifted slightly.

When the car arrived, William opened the door for her, his gentlemanly demeanour shone through. "After you," he said with a smile, and Annie slid inside, feeling grateful for the care he shows her. As he settled into the driver's seat, a comfortable silence enveloped them, only broken by the sound of the engine humming.

The drive to her apartment is filled with soft music playing on the radio, and they share the occasional smile, both reflecting on the enjoyable evening they've had. When they finally arrive, William walked Annie to her door, their fingers entwined with each other's as they walked, sending electric sparks through both of them.

At her door, Annie turned to William, her heart fluttering. "Thank you for such a lovely evening," she said sincerely, her eyes sparkling with warmth.

Without thinking, William gently pulled her into his arms, holding her as if she were delicate glass. He leaned down, and their lips met in a tender kiss, savouring the moment. Annie kissed him back, lost in the sweetness of the gesture. When they finally pulled apart, a rush of warmth flooded her cheeks, and she couldn't help but blush under his gaze.

"Goodnight, William," she whispered, a smile lingering on her lips as she fumbled for her keys.

But the blissful moment was short-lived. As she opened her door, her heart sunk at the sight before her. Chaos… in her apartment, furniture was overturned, and the walls were marred with spray paint. The word *'bitch'* stood out glaringly, a stark contrast against the walls that once felt like her safe haven.

Annie's breath caught in her throat as panic gripped her. "Oh my God," she whispered, stepping inside to take in the devastation. William, strolling away, heard her and immediately sensed her distress. He quickly turned back and followed her into the apartment, his protective instincts kicking in. "Annie, what's wrong?" he asked urgently, his eyes scanning the room to assess the chaos and the hateful word painted across the wall.

Annie stood frozen, shock and fear written across her face. "I… I don't know what happened," she stammered, her heart racing. William stepped closer, wrapping his arm around her shoulder, offering her comfort in the midst of the chaos.

"We need to call the police," he said firmly, his voice steady as he guided her back toward the door. "Let's make sure it's safe first." As they stood together, the joy of the evening, overshadowed by the unsettling reality of this moment.

William swiftly pulled out his phone, his fingers trembling slightly with anger as he dialled the police. While he spoke to the operator, his voice remained calm and authoritative, but inside, a surge of concern for Annie consumed him. He watched her standing in the middle of the chaotic room, her expression a mix of shock and distress. She fought to maintain her composure, but he could see tears pooling in her eyes, threatening to spill over.

"Annie," he said softly, putting his phone back in his pocket, "I'm right here. It's going to be okay." He stepped closer, wrapping his arms around her in a comforting gesture. She leant into him, seeking solace in his presence as soft sobs escaped her lips.

"I just don't understand why this is happening," she murmurs, her voice shaky. "What have I done to deserve this? It feels like everything is falling apart."

William tightened his grip around her, wishing he could take away her pain. "You're strong, Annie. You'll get through this. You're not alone." He brushed a stray tear from her cheek with his thumb, trying to offer reassurance through his touch.

After what felt like an eternity, the sound of sirens pierced the night, followed by the arrival of the police. Two officers stepped into the apartment: their expressions serious yet compassionate. "Good evening. I'm Officer Grant, and this is Officer Lee. We received a call about a break-in?"

Annie nods, her voice barely above a whisper. "Yes, I came home to find everything like this."

William remained by her side, providing silent support as the officers started taking notes and assessing the damage. They asked Annie questions about what happened, how she discovered the break-in, and whether she saw anyone suspicious in the area.

"I… I was out to dinner, and when I came home…" she trails off, her eyes welling up again. William squeezed her hand, silently urging her to continue.

The officers exchanged glances, understanding the gravity of the situation. "We'll need to take some photos and check for fingerprints. Is there anywhere else you might have seen suspicious activity recently?" Officer Grant asked gently.

"I… no, not that I can think of," Annie replied, her voice trembling as she wiped the tears from her face with the back of her hand.

As the officers began to document the scene, William stayed close to Annie, feeling the weight of her fear and vulnerability. He lent in, whispered, "You're doing great. Just focus on the officers; I'm here with you."

She nodded, taking a deep breath to steady herself, trying to push down the waves of anxiety threatening to overwhelm her. As the officers worked, they carefully examined the walls and doors for fingerprints and documented the damage, but Annie couldn't shake the feeling of violation that lingered in the air.

Once the officers finished gathering evidence and taking their statements, they reassured Annie that they would do everything they could to find whoever was responsible. "If you think of anything else, please don't hesitate to reach out," Officer Lee said before preparing to leave.

That's when William spoke up, recalling the graffiti incident at the gallery. "And she was attacked in a parking lot," he added. "Not to mention, you almost got hit by a car."

The officers exchanged concerned glances, clearly unsettled by these revelations. "These events might be related," Officer Grant said, looking directly at Annie. "Do you think someone might be targeting you?"

Annie's heart raced at the thought. "Why would anyone want to hurt me? It makes no sense." Her voice trembled as she tried to process the implications.

The officers pressed on. "Have you had any trouble with anyone recently?"

Annie shook her head. "No, not that I can think of…"

But William interjected, "What about Jeremy?"

Annie turned to him, a shiver running down her spine. "Jeremy?"

"Jeremy attacked Annie at her place of work," he clarified. "It should be documented."

The officers immediately perked up, eager to gather more information. "Can you tell us this person's name?" Officer Grant asked.

Annie took a deep breath, recalling the nightmare. "His name is Jeremy Spears."

"Were the police called when this incident occurred?" Officer Lee inquired.

She glanced at William before responding simply, "Yes." Annie's expression grew puzzled and increasingly worried, her brow furrowing. "Do you think he might be involved?" she asked, a hint of fear creeping into her voice.

The officers exchanged glances, then Officer Lee spoke again. "It's possible this Jeremy Spears could be connected to what's been happening. We'll need to check on him and see where he was tonight."

Then Officer Grant added, "In the meantime, do you have somewhere else to stay? You'll need to arrange to have the locks changed and the door repaired."

Annie hesitated, her mind racing as she considers her options. Just then, William gently took her hands in his, his grip reassuring. "You can stay in my spare bedroom at my apartment if you'd like," he offered, his voice calm and steady.

Annie looked up at him, unsure if she should accept. "I don't want to impose," she replied softly, her heart fluttering at his kindness.

"You wouldn't be imposing at all," he assured her, sincerity in his eyes. "I want to make sure you feel safe."

After a moment of contemplation, Annie nodded, grateful for his offer. "Thank you, William. I appreciate it," she said, her voice barely above a whisper. She felt a mix of relief and apprehension, knowing she'll be in good hands, even if the circumstances were less than ideal.

After the officers gather the necessary contact details from both William and Annie, they assured them that they will be in touch regarding their investigation. "Stay safe, and don't hesitate to reach out if anything else happens," Officer Lee said, his tone firm but sympathetic.

Once the officers left, William turned to Annie. "Why don't you pack a bag with everything you'll need for a couple of days?" he suggested gently.

Annie nodded, grateful for his support. Headed to her bedroom, changed into comfortable slacks and a soft blouse. She took a moment to collect herself, fighting back tears as she gathered the essentials, clothes, toiletries, and anything else she thought she might need. After a few minutes, she emerged from her bedroom with a suitcase in tow.

William waited patiently in the living area, his expression warm and reassuring. As she approached, he smiled and took the suitcase from her. "Let's secure the door as best we can," he said, helping her lock up and ensuring everything is in order.

Together, they walked to his car, and William placed her suitcase in the boot before helping her into the passenger seat. Annie settled in quietly, the weight of the evening settling heavily on her chest. Silent tears began to slide down her cheeks as she grappled with the fear and uncertainty of the situation.

Noticing her distress, William reached over and gently held her hand, offering comfort as he started the engine. "You're not alone, Annie," he reassured her softly. "I'm here for you." As they drove towards his penthouse apartment, he glanced at her, wishing he could alleviate her fears and bring her some peace amidst the chaos.

Chapter Eight

William pulled his car into the parking garage of his building, glancing over at Annie, who was still lost in her thoughts. He parked the car and turned off the engine, offering her a reassuring smile as they both stepped out. They walked toward the elevator, and as the doors closed, the tension in the air seemed to ease slightly.

When they reach the penthouse floor, William led her down a short hallway before unlocking the door. As he opened it, Annie stepped inside and gasped softly, taken aback by the stunning view that greeted her.

The apartment was beautifully furnished, with a modern yet cozy aesthetic. Floor-to-ceiling windows frame the skyline, allowing the soft glow of the city lights to filter in. The living area featured elegant furniture, tasteful artwork adorning the walls, and an inviting warmth that made it feel like a home.

"Wow," Annie breathed, taking in the breathtaking view and the elegant decor. "This is amazing."

William chuckled softly, pleased by her reaction. "Thanks. I tried to make it comfortable," he replied. He watched as she walked further into the space, her eyes wide with wonder. The sight of her amazement lifted his spirits, even if the circumstances that brought them here were far from ideal.

"Make yourself at home," he encouraged, stepping aside to let her explore. Annie walked to the window, gazing out at the twinkling lights of the city below, feeling a sense of calm wash over her, even amidst the lingering worry from the night's events.

She turned to William with a playful grin. "You might never get rid of me," she joked, her laughter light as she glanced back at the view.

William's stomach tightened, an unexpected warmth settling in. He watched her for a moment, her laughter lingering in the air, and thought to himself, *I'm happy for you to stay forever.*

William gently led Annie down the hallway to the spare bedroom, opening the door to reveal a large bedroom adorned with soft linens and warm lighting with an ensuite at one end of the room. He placed her suitcase on the bed, ensuring she has everything she might need during her stay.

"Here you go," he said, gesturing to the room. "Make yourself at home. If you need anything, just let me know."

"Thank you," she replied, gratitude in her voice.

"Would you like some coffee?" he offered, hoping to create a more relaxed atmosphere.

"Yes, please," she responded, a small smile breaking through her earlier distress.

They headed to the kitchen, and William prepared the coffee, the aroma quickly filling the space. He handed her a steaming cup and gestured toward the sofa in the living area. They settled in, sitting side by side, the warmth of the mugs comforting in the midst of the chaos outside.

After a few moments of silence, Annie takes a deep breath and said, "I'm so sorry about this. I really don't have anyone else to turn to." Her cheeks flushed slightly as she spoke, the vulnerability evident in her tone. "Most of my friends live in one-bedroom apartments and I don't have any family left. It's times like these is when you miss them the most."

William's expression softened and looked at her with empathy. "I'm so sorry, Annie. It must be incredibly hard for you." He paused, glancing away for a moment, then added, "Don't you have any uncles or aunts?"

Annie shook her head, her eyes downcast. "No, my parents didn't mention any aunts or uncles."

William nodded, feeling a weight in the air as he absorbed her words. "That must be really tough, feeling isolated like that."

"Yeah, it has its challenges," she admitted, her voice barely above a whisper. "But I've learned to rely on myself. I just... I didn't expect to need help like this."

William placed a comforting hand on her shoulder. "You're not alone anymore, Annie. I'm here for you."

Annie offered a small, appreciative smile, her eyes brightening slightly despite the heaviness of the evening. "But you've done so much for me already," she said softly, a hint of guilt in her voice. "I feel a bit of a nuisance."

William shook his head firmly, his expression earnest. "Please don't say that," he replied, leaning in slightly to emphasise his point. "Sarah thinks the world of you, and I like you too. You must know that."

Her heart skipped a beat at his words, and she met his gaze, sensing the sincerity behind them. The warmth of his compliment wrapped around her like a comforting blanket, easing some of her anxiety.

"I appreciate that, really," Annie said, her voice more assured. "It just feels strange to rely on someone else."

"You're not a burden, Annie," William reassured her, his tone gentle yet firm. "We all need help sometimes, and I'm glad I can be here for you. You're more than welcome to stay as long as you need."

Annie smiled again, the weight on her chest feeling a little lighter. "Thank you, William. It means a lot to me."

William nodded, his heart swelling with warmth between them. He hoped she could see how much he genuinely cared, and that this situation might bring them closer together.

They continued to talk for a little while longer, sharing light-hearted stories and comforting words, the tension of the evening slowly dissipating as they settled into each other's company. The conversation flowed easily, with laughter punctuating their exchanges, until they finally placed their empty cups on the coffee table.

Annie stood up, the exhaustion from the day catching up with her. "I should go have a shower and get some rest," she said, her voice soft.

William stood as well, a slight hesitation in his demeanour as he gently touched her arm. "Annie…," he said, searching her eyes, "may I kiss you?"

She looked at him, a mixture of surprise and warmth flooding her features. After a brief moment, she nodded slightly, her heart racing. William stepped closer, his hands gently cupping her face, and then he leaned in, pressing his lips against hers.

The kiss was soft and comforting, a balm for both their spirits, but Annie felt a yearning within her that pushed her to want more. She wrapped her arms around his neck, pulling him closer as she ran her fingers through his thick, soft hair.

William wrapped his arms around her, deepening the kiss and igniting a fierce warmth within her. The world outside faded away, leaving only the two of them wrapped in each other's embrace.

Annie parted her mouth, she welcomed the invasion of his tongue, sending waves of longing coursing through her and stoking the fire building inside.

Eagerly, she pressed against him, feeling heat flood her veins as his hands glided down her back, pulling her closer with a slow and deliberate intensity.

Annie let out a low moan, the sound escaping her lips as the kiss deepened, overwhelming her senses. William murmured her name against her lips, "Annie," his voice a husky whisper that sent a thrill through her. The way he said her name was both a caress and a promise, wrapping around her heart and making her ache for more.

William pulled back slightly, his breath warm against her skin as he whispered, "Annie, I like kissing you." The sincerity in his voice sent a shiver down her spine.

In response Annie made a soft, lingering *'mmm'* noise, a sound of both agreement and desire that ignited something within him. Unable to resist the pull between them, William captured her lips again, kissing her passionately, as if he was trying to erase the distance between them and seal the moment forever.

William's hand slid from her back to her chest, cupping her breast gently through the fabric of her blouse. Annie let out a soft moan, her desire rising as she instinctively pressed herself closer, seeking the warmth and connection of his touch.

William paused, his forehead resting against hers, his breath uneven. "Annie," he whispered again, his voice thick with desire and restraint. He searched her eyes, waiting for a sign, wanting to be sure she was comfortable with how far they were going.

Annie met his gaze, her own heart racing, but in her eyes was the same desire, tempered by trust. She leaned in pressing a tender kiss to his lips, reassuring him that she was with him every step of the way.

William let out a deep, involuntary moan, the sound rumbling from his chest. His restraint shattered as he took her mouth again, this time with an intensity that sent a shiver down Annie's spine. The kiss was devastating, filled with passion and longing, leaving no space between them. His lips moved urgently against hers, pouring all the emotions he had been holding back into the embrace.

Annie's body responded instantly, her hands gripping the fabric of his shirt as she kissed him back just as fiercely, completely lost in the moment. The heat between them was undeniable, and for a brief moment, the world outside of their embrace seemed to fall away.

The kiss deepened, their emotions intertwining as they lost themselves in the moment. The warmth between them grew, igniting a spark of passion that made Annie's heart race. But just as the kiss intensified, Annie pulled away slightly, her breath quickening as she sought clarity amid the whirlwind of feelings.

William noticed her pulling back, and a flicker of disappointment crossed his face. He released her gently, wanting to respect her boundaries while still holding on to the lingering warmth of their embrace.

Annie's cheeks flushed and a shy smile on her lips. "William, I need to tell you something, but I'm not sure how," she said softly.

William's expression shifted to one of concern. "What is it, Annie?"

Annie looked down, unable to meet his gaze. "I have… never been with…" She hesitated, her cheeks growing hotter. "You know."

At first, William looked confused, but then realisation dawned on him. "Oh, okay." A smile began to form on his face.

She met his eyes, searching for reassurance. "You don't mind?"

"Why would I mind?" he replied, a grin spreading across his face. "I won't pressure you into anything, Annie. I feel privileged that you want to be with me."

"Really? You're not upset?" Annie asked, her voice tinged with uncertainty.

"No, Annie, I'm not upset, but I want you to be sure," he replied, taking a deep breath. He knew he might regret what he was about to say, but he needed to make sure she felt confident in her decision. "I think you should take a shower, and if you still want to be with me afterward, come to my bedroom. If you don't feel ready, you can sleep in the spare room. No pressure."

Annie looked a bit unsure and hurt. "Don't you want to be with me?"

William's expression shifted to shock and remorse. "No, it's not that, Annie. Please believe me. It's taking all my willpower not to pick you up and carry you to my room." Sincerity was clear in his eyes. "But this is a big step for you, and I don't want you to feel pressured into anything."

She stood there for what felt like an eternity, William holding his breath. Then, she gave him a small nod and a shy smile, tinged with uncertainty. "Thank you, William." With that, she turned and walked toward the spare room, closing the door softly behind her.

As the sound of the latch clicked shut, a whirlwind of emotions swirled within her, gratitude for his respect and thoughtfulness, confusion about her feelings, and a hint of excitement for what might come next. Alone in the dimly lit room, Annie took a deep breath, trying to calm her racing heart.

Stepping into the shower, she let the warm water cascade over her, hoping to wash away the tension. She lingered under the steam, allowing it to envelop her and ease her troubled mind. When she finished, she wrapped herself in a soft towel, her skin still glistening from the moisture.

Rummaging through her suitcase, she found a delicate nightie, simple yet elegant, it felt soft against her skin. After slipping it on, she padded into the spare bedroom, the cool air sending a slight shiver down her spine.

Sitting on the edge of the bed, Annie thought about William. She had never felt this way about anyone before. The desire to genuinely be with him thrilled her, yet it also filled her with fear. *Should she go to him? Did he truly want her to? Would she regret her decision in the morning?* No, she wouldn't—she wanted him. She was certain he was the one. When she was in his arms, she felt safe and cherished.

With her mind made up, she stood and walked to the door. Taking a deep breath, she opened it and made her way to William's bedroom. She knocked softly, holding her breath and trying to steady her trembling hands.

William watched as Annie walked toward the spare room, his heart pounding in his chest. He needed her to make the decision, to take that leap of faith. He knew what he wanted; he wanted her. Yet, he also understood that she needed to feel safe and secure in her choice. He wanted her to know that he wouldn't pressure her into anything, she could trust him.

His mind drifted back to her confession, the way she had nervously admitted she was a virgin. He hadn't expected it, but now that he knew, a wave of protectiveness washed over him. It wasn't that he felt pressure or anxiety about it, quite the opposite. He felt honoured. Annie had chosen to trust him with something so personal, something that showed just how deeply she cared for him.

With a heavy sigh, he turned and walked to his room. Once inside, he stepped into the shower, letting the warm water cascade over him as he tried to clear his mind. Thoughts of Annie consumed him, her smile, her laughter, the way she looked at him with both curiosity and uncertainty. After finishing his shower, he slipped on a pair of loose boxers. Normally, he preferred to sleep without anything on, but he figured that if Annie did come to him, opening the door in just his skin might frighten her away.

As he dried off and dressed, he couldn't shake the feeling of anticipation mixed with a hint of nervousness. He hoped she would come to him, but he also respected her space, willing to wait as long as it took for her to feel ready.

William sat on the edge of his bed, his heart racing as he waited, hope and anxiety swirling within him. The anticipation felt almost unbearable, each minute stretching into what felt like an eternity. He replayed their earlier conversation in his mind, recalling how he had reassured her that she could take her time. But now, with each passing moment, he couldn't help but wish she would come to him.

Then, just as he was about to second-guess everything, there was a soft knock at his door. His heart raced faster, pounding in his chest as if it might burst. He stood up abruptly and walked to the door. Pausing for a moment, he took a deep breath to steady himself, then slowly opened it.

There stood Annie, illuminated by the soft light from the hallway. She wore a delicate, almost sheer nightgown that clung softly to her curves, its fabric whispering against her skin as she shifted slightly. William's breath caught in his throat at the sight of her. The vulnerability and beauty radiating from her left him momentarily speechless. All of his earlier apprehension melted away, replaced by a profound sense of longing and tenderness. This was the moment he had hoped for, and seeing her there, so close yet so fragile, filled him with an overwhelming desire to cherish her.

William stepped aside, his heart pounding as he gestured for Annie to enter the room. He watched her glide past him, each movement filled with grace and uncertainty. As the door clicked softly shut behind them, he couldn't help but marvel at her beauty, how the delicate fabric of her nightgown caught the light, highlighting her figure in a way that made his breath hitch.

His palms itched with the urge to reach out and touch her, to draw her closer, but he reminded himself to tread lightly. He needed to be careful, understanding of the emotions swirling between them. Every instinct urged him to take her into his arms, to feel the warmth of her body against his, but he resisted the impulse, wanting her to feel safe.

"Annie," he said softly, his voice low and steady, filled with warmth. He took a step closer, his gaze locking onto hers, searching for any sign of hesitation. "Are you sure you want to be here?" The sincerity in his tone was clear; he wanted her to know she was in control.

As she looked up at him, her eyes filled with a mix of determination and vulnerability, he felt a surge of affection. He wanted this moment to be perfect for her, and he would do everything in his power to ensure she felt cherished and respected.

Annie didn't say a word; instead, she took a step closer to William, her gaze locked onto his. The air around them was thick with anticipation as she gently placed her hands on his bare chest, feeling the steady beat of his heart beneath her palms. Her touch sent a rush of warmth through him, igniting something deep within.

Slowly, she slid her hands up, her fingers gliding over his skin like a whisper, sending shivers down his spine. As her hands linked behind his neck, William felt his breath catch in his throat, overwhelmed by the intensity of the moment. Her touch was electric, like fire coursing through his veins, igniting a glorious sensation that left him breathless.

He could feel the warmth radiating from her body, her presence enveloping him in a way that felt both exhilarating and comforting. With her hands resting on the back of his neck, he leaned in slightly, his heart racing, captivated by the connection between them. In that moment, everything else faded away, leaving just the two of them in their own world, where desire and trust intertwined.

They locked eyes for what felt like an eternity, the air between them thick with anticipation. Slowly, William leaned in, their lips meeting in a kiss that instantly ignited a surge of passion. The kiss was gentle, reassuring, filled with the unspoken promise that she was safe with him. Through that touch, he tried to convey all the care and tenderness he felt for her.

He pulled away from her lips just long enough to lift her nightgown over her head, letting it slip down her body and fall to the floor. He gazed at her with undeniable desire in his eyes, his voice coming out in a breathless whisper, "My God, you're beautiful."

She didn't feel self-conscious, only consumed by desire and need. The need to feel his arms around her again, the need to lose herself in him, to spiral together in the intensity of the moment.

He lifted her effortlessly into his arms, carrying her to the bed and laying her down gently. In one smooth motion, he removed his boxers and joined her, the space between them disappearing as he settled beside her.

Lying on their sides, they gazed into each other's eyes, the room filled with a quiet intensity. William lifted his hand, gently brushing a stray strand of hair from her face, his touch tender and filled with unspoken emotion.

He moved closer, their bodies almost touching, the heat between them building. Then, he captured her lips with his, trying to control the fierce desire surging through him. Every moment was a struggle to hold back, to be gentle, yet his yearning for her was undeniable.

She heard him curse softly, a groan escaping as he pulled her closer, the intensity between them growing. The sensation of his body pressed up against hers was exhilarating, a feeling entirely new to her. Every touch every breath they shared sent waves of excitement coursing through her, awakening something she had never experienced before.

"William," she whispered softly, her voice trembling with anticipation. "I want you to show me how to love you."

William let out a deep, involuntary moan, the sound rumbling from his chest, his restraint shattered as he took her mouth. She parted her lips, welcoming the insistent, heated exploration of his tongue, the sensation both fiery and intoxicating.

His lips moved on hers with controlled expertise. She was heated and desperate to have his hands on her. Her body, her sensual curves, pressed to him as time and the kiss spun out of control with desire.

Beneath it all, the shock of lust burned through her, igniting every nerve and vein so she burned with a passion she had never felt before. Everything within her centred on the raging need for him.

His hands moved down her body to rest on her hips pulling her even closer so she could feel his urgent arousal. "Annie, I want you so much," he murmured against her lips.

She let out a soft moan before whispering, "Touch me…, please."

With that, he gently pushed her onto her back and positioned himself half above her, capturing her mouth in a searing kiss as he slid his hands up her body. Her breath came on a strangled cry as he cupped her breast. With a groan he slid his thumb over her ripe nipple, then did it again when she sobbed, and he felt her body arch for more. In the heat of their kiss, their mouths fused, and tongues intertwined. Her arms wrapped around him; her body moulded to his in a bold invitation. He took his time, intent on giving her as much pleasure as possible.

His tongue danced with hers heating their desire even more. Her mouth ravenous as his hand found the silken curve of a rounded thigh and stroked. He tore his mouth from hers and placed his hot wet tongue on her hard erect nipple, licked, and teased as she cried out and sobbed with pleasure.

He shifted to the other nipple, teasing it with the rasp of his tongue against the hard peak. The soft sobs and moans escaping Annie only spurred him on further.

Slowly his mouth and tongue trailed down from her fully erect nipples to her stomach. He slowly travelled further down, kissing and licking to prolong her pleasure. He slowly travelled further down until his tongue found her, warm and slick with pleasure. Knowing that she was so aroused, aroused him even more. Sliding his tongue over her wet folds, she cried out breathlessly, "William… please."

He found her core, hot and slick, he licked, gently sucked. A long moan escaped her lips.

He whispered, his voice thick with desire, "Annie… you taste so incredible."

As his hands held her hips, he increased the pressure of his tongue, causing her writhing beneath him, and moan with pleasure. New sensations were building within her, a yearning for something she couldn't quite define. She had never experienced anything like this before; no other man had touched her in such a way.

The pressure inside her intensified, leaving her feeling hot and slick with desire. Her hands gripping the sheet beside her to try to anchor herself to reality, but all she could focus on was William's mouth and the exquisite feelings he was creating. Annie didn't think it was possible to feel any better until her body exploded in sensations, she didn't think were possible. She gasped his name as she climaxed. "William!"

He continued to suckle gently until her convulsions subsided. Then began to slowly kiss his way up her body, making sure he paid homage to every curve, worshipping her with his hands and warm mouth.

When he settled between her thighs, the moment shifted—charged, delicate, trembling with everything unspoken. She felt him, his arousal hot and heavy, as he gently cupped her face.

"Annie," he whispered, his heart racing as he rested his forehead against hers. "Are you sure? It might hurt the first time."

"I'm sure." Her voice shook, but not with fear. "Please, William."

William bent his head and kissed her passionately on the mouth. She could taste her scent on his lips as he pressed forward. She was ready for him, hot and wet, with one long, smooth thrust, he entered her sweet, tight centre.

"Oh…!" A sharp pain shot through Annie.

William froze immediately, his breath warm against her throat, holding her as though she were breakable.

"I'm sorry," he murmured into her skin, his voice ragged with want and restraint.

He waited a moment longer before tentatively easing back, driving into her deeply—slow, deliberate—so she felt every inch of him, carving pleasure through her.

"William…"

Hearing his name like that… raw, breathless, worshipful… it overwhelmed him—too fierce, too deep—and her name slipped from him in a hoarse, broken whisper that was almost a plea, "Annie!"

He began to move slowly at first savouring the feel of her welcoming body. Increasing his pace, his breathing uneven and harsh as he felt the honeyed warmth that surrounded him. Annie's enjoyment turned to disbelief at the feelings that flooded through her.

Waves of electric excitement coursed through her and the wild cries she heard were hardly recognisable as her own. Her fingers tightened on his shoulders as William's body forced hers into a matching rhythm.

Their mouths crashed together, ravenous, helpless. He devoured every gasp, every trembling moan, losing himself in the way she moved under him—like she was made for him, like she wanted him just as fiercely.

Pleasure detonated through her, white-hot and violent, her tightening body dragging him straight into the heart of her climax as she screamed his name.

"William…"

"Annie—" His voice broke into a groan against her throat as the world ripped open inside him. His hands clamped on her hips, holding her to him as he buried himself to the hilt. Her tight, honey-slick heat pulled him past the point of return.

A guttural, primal growl tore from his chest as he spilled into her, shuddering hard, every breath stolen by the force of it. He stayed there, locked deep inside her, heartbeat hammering with hers, knowing nothing had ever felt this right.

After their breathing slowly returned to normal, William gently withdrew from Annie's warm, yielding body and rolled onto his back, drawing her with him until she nestled comfortably in the crook of his arm. The lingering heat of her skin against his was both soothing and intoxicating, grounding him in the intimacy of the moment. As he adjusted their positions, he caught the soft sighs escaping her lips—a delicate, almost unconscious sound that spoke of deep contentment.

Annie let out a quiet moan, her eyelids fluttering as sleep began to claim her. With a drowsy murmur, she shifted closer, her body moulding perfectly to his side as if she belonged there. Within moments, she surrendered to blissful slumber, her breathing slow and even, the gentle rise and fall of her chest pressing rhythmically against him.

As William slowly surrendered to sleep, his mind racing even as his body begged for rest. The depth of their connection overwhelmed him, sending shockwaves through his very core. Every touch, every whispered breath between them had ignited something deep inside him—something raw, unfamiliar, and undeniable. He had never felt anything like this before. It wasn't just physical; it was something more, something that reached beyond desire into a realm far more profound. Holding her now, feeling the steady beat of her heart against his, he knew one thing with absolute certainty: Annie had just changed everything.

Chapter Nine

Annie woke to the gentle glow of the sun filtered through the curtains, casting warm rays across her face. As she blinked away the remnants of sleep, she became aware of her surroundings, she was naked in William's bed. A wave of contentment washed over her, mixed with a hint of soreness that reminded her of the previous night. Sitting up, she instinctively held the sheet against her breasts, the cool fabric contrasting with the warmth of the sun in her skin. A soft smile played on her lips as memories flooded back, filling her with a sense of happiness.

Annie spotted her nightgown on the floor and slipped it over her head, the smooth fabric gliding softly against her skin. Feeling the gentle weight of the gown, she made her way to the kitchen, hoping to find a warm cup of coffee to start her day.

As Annie walked into the kitchen, the rich aroma of brewing coffee filled the air. Her eyes found William standing by the counter, pouring the steaming liquid into a mug. He heard her footsteps and turned, a warm smile spreading across his face. Annie felt her cheeks flush as their gazes locked.

William approached her, wrapping his arms around her waist and pulling her close. He leaned down to plant a soft kiss on her lips, his touch sending a delightful shiver through her. "Good morning," he said, his smile brightening the room. Annie's heart fluttered at the warmth of his embrace.

Annie smiled up at William, her eyes sparkling with warmth. "Good morning," she said softly, her voice still tinged with sleep. She wrapped her arms around his neck, feeling the solid strength of him beneath her fingertips.

"Did you sleep well?" she asked, her brow slightly furrowed with curiosity. The closeness of their bodies and the lingering warmth from the night before wrapped around them.

William's eyes sparkled in response, a blend of affection and contentment evident in his gaze. "Yes, I did. Did you?"

"Oh yes," Annie replied, her smile widening as she recalled the warmth of their night together.

William looked at her intently, his expression serious yet searching, as if he wanted to read her thoughts. "No regrets?" he asked, his voice low and steady.

Annie met his gaze, a soft smile playing on her lips. "No," she affirmed, the certainty in her voice ringing clear.

William let out a sigh of relief, the tension in his shoulders easing. "Good," he said, a smile breaking across his face. "Because I thought last night was amazing." His eyes sparkled with warmth and genuine admiration, reflecting the depth of his feelings for her. The memory of their intimate moments lingered in his mind.

Annie leaned in, her heart fluttering with affection as she pressed her lips gently against his. The kiss was soft and tender, filled with the warmth of her feelings for him. She pulled back slightly, searching his eyes for reassurance, and smiled. "I did too," she whispered, her voice barely above a breath.

William watched Annie with a fond smile, then asked, "Would you like some coffee?"

"Yes, please," she replied, her eyes lighting up at the thought.

He moved to the coffee maker and poured another cup, the rich aroma filling the air. After adding a splash of cream, he turned and handed the steaming mug to her.

Annie wrapped her hands around the warm cup, taking a sip. "Mmm, that's good," she said, a satisfied smile spreading across her face as she savoured the first taste of her morning.

The peaceful morning was abruptly interrupted by a loud knock on the door, shattering the silence.

William's expression shifted to one of recognition. "That's Sarah's knock," he said with a hint of exasperation.

Annie raised her eyebrows, a mix of surprise and curiosity. "Oh?"

William glanced at her, weighing their options. "It's up to you. If you want to keep us a secret for now, we can."

Annie nodded, her expression thoughtful. "Yes, I think that might be a good idea for now."

He smiled in agreement, relieved at her choice. He didn't want to deal with Sarah's teasing just yet. "Okay, you go have a shower and get changed. I'll get the door," he said, leaning in to give her a lingering kiss that ignited the warmth from earlier.

With a last glance at him, Annie slipped away, and William turned toward the door, preparing for whatever Sarah had in store.

William opened the door to find Sarah standing there, a bright smile lighting up her face. "Hi, big brother! How are you this morning?" she greeted cheerfully, stepping inside without waiting for an invitation.

"I'm good, thanks. How about you?" he replied, trying to keep his tone casual.

"Good! Just came to see how last night went?" she said, her eyes sparkling with mischief as she leaned against the side of the sofa, clearly eager for details.

William felt a rush of anxiety at her question, but he masked it with a nonchalant shrug. "It was fine," he said, keeping his response vague while mentally preparing for any probing she might attempt.

Sarah raised an eyebrow, a playful smirk on her lips. "Just fine?" she echoed, her tone teasing as she leaned forward slightly, clearly not buying his casual response.

William quickly deflected, feeling the pressure of her curiosity. "Do you want some coffee?" he asked, hoping to steer the conversation away from last night.

"Yes, please!" Sarah replied, her attention shifting as she settled onto the sofa, crossing her legs and watching him with an amused glint in her eye.

William took his time making the coffee, the rhythmic sound of the machine providing a brief reprieve from the weight of Sarah's gaze. He focused on the task at hand, trying to maintain his composure while his mind raced with thoughts of Annie.

William finally walked over to the sofa, balancing a steaming mug of coffee in his hands. He handed it to Sarah with a smile, trying to play it cool despite the tension lingering in the air.

She wrapped her hands around the warm cup, taking a sip before her eyes met his. As the rich flavour registered, she raised an eyebrow, a knowing smile spreading across her face.

"What's with that look?" William asked, feigning innocence, but he could feel his heart racing under her scrutinising gaze.

"Oh, nothing," Sarah replied, her tone dripping with playful sarcasm. "Just thinking about how 'just fine' you are this morning."

William turned away, feeling heat creep into his cheeks as he realised, she had seen right through him. The teasing glint in her eyes suggested she suspected there was more to the story, but he remained resolute in keeping their secret for now.

Just then, Annie emerged from the spare room, dressed in shorts and a T-shirt. "Morning, William," she said, and then, pretending to just notice Sarah, added, "Oh, morning, Sarah!"

Sarah glanced between the two of them, a sly smile forming on her lips. "Oh, I'm just fine," she said, her tone playful, clearly enjoying the moment.

William turned to Sarah, trying to sound casual. "It's not what you think."

Sarah raised an eyebrow, a teasing smile playing on her lips. "Oh, really?"

William's expression shifted to one of seriousness. "It's not." He paused for a moment, then realised he had the perfect distraction to steer the conversation away.

Sarah's grin faltered as she noticed the serious expressions on both William and Annie's faces. "What's going on?" she asked, her teasing tone replaced with concern.

William sighed and gestured for Annie to sit down. "It's not what you think," he repeated, this time more sombrely. "Annie's staying here because someone broke into her apartment last night."

Sarah's eyes widened in shock. "What? Are you okay?" she asked, turning to Annie.

Annie gave a small nod. "I'm alright, just a bit shaken. They spray-painted something on my wall... William called the police, and they suggested I stay somewhere else until I can get things sorted. So, William offered me his spare room."

Sarah's face softened with sympathy. "That's horrible. I can't believe someone would do that. Do you have any idea who it could be?"

Annie glanced at William, then back at Sarah. "You know about the other things that have happened... the graffiti at the gallery, the prank calls, the carpark attack, and that near miss with the car. We're not sure if they're connected, but the police think they might be."

Sarah looked between them, her worry deepening. "Annie, I'm so sorry. If you need anything, please let me know. I'll help in any way I can."

Annie smiled faintly, appreciating Sarah's kindness. "Thank you, Sarah. I really appreciate it. I just want this to be over."

William nodded, his expression serious. "We'll figure this out. But for now, you're safe here."

A little later, William and Sarah moved around the kitchen, working together to prepare breakfast. The sound of bacon sizzling and the aroma of fresh coffee filled the air. Annie offered to help, but they insisted she relax, so she settled onto the sofa, waiting patiently.

As they all gathered at the table to enjoy a pleasant breakfast, sharing laughter and conversation that lightened the mood.

When their meal was finished, Sarah smiled brightly. "We're going to our parents' place next weekend," she began. "Why don't you come with us, Annie?"

"Oh no, I don't want to intrude," Annie said quickly, looking between the siblings.

William and Sarah exchanged a glance, both of them shaking their heads. "You wouldn't be intruding," William insisted. "We want you to come."

Sarah nodded eagerly. "Our parents will be happy to have you, I promise."

Annie hesitated for a moment before finally smiling. "Alright, I'd love to come. I just hope your parents won't mind."

"They'll be thrilled," Sarah assured her, beaming.

After breakfast, Sarah stood up, grabbing her bag. "I have to run," she said cheerfully. "I've got a BBQ lunch with a friend."

William hugged his sister tightly. "Have fun. See you later."

Annie smiled warmly at Sarah. "Enjoy your day, Sarah."

"Thanks, Annie! I'll see you soon," Sarah said with a wave, before heading out.

As the door closed behind her, Annie started tidying up the breakfast dishes. William joined her in the kitchen to help. As they worked side by side, Annie glanced at him and said, "I think it's lovely how close you and Sarah are. You don't always see that with such a big age gap between siblings."

William smiled, drying a plate. "Yeah, I'm lucky. We've always been close. She's more than just my little sister; she's my best friend." He paused for a moment, then added, "She keeps me grounded."

Annie looked thoughtful, "It's really nice. Not everyone has that kind of relationship with their family."

As they finished cleaning up, William set the last dish aside and turned to Annie, a curious look crossing his face. "Annie, I know you mentioned your parents… but did you ever have any contact with your grandparents? Or maybe uncles or aunts? Did they exist, or was it really just the three of you growing up?"

Annie paused, leaning against the counter as her expression softened. "No, it really was just my parents and me. My dad's parents passed away when I was really young, and my mum… well, her family kind of disowned her when she married my dad. I'm not even sure if her parents are still alive, probably not. She didn't talk about them much. It really hurt her, the way they treated my dad."

She smiled, a bit of warmth creeping into her voice. "You see, her parents were wealthy, and my dad was from the wrong side of the tracks, as they used to say. But my parents were so much in love." Annie's smile turned wistful. "They loved me dearly, and they would've loved to have more children, but my birth was hard on my mum, and she couldn't have any more. So, it was always just the three of us, in our own little world. And now… well, now it's just me."

William nodded, his expression soft. "I can't imagine what that must've been like. You're incredibly strong for getting through it."

Annie met his gaze, her eyes soft with gratitude. "Thanks, William. It wasn't easy, especially after my parents died." Her voice wavered slightly. "The car accident happened when they were on the way to my graduation."

Tears welled up in her eyes as the memory surfaced, and she blinked, trying to keep them from spilling over. "I was so excited for them to be there, to see me walk across that stage. But they never made it." She swallowed hard, her voice barely a whisper now. "I didn't even get to say goodbye."

William's expression darkened with sympathy. He reached out, gently placing a hand on her arm, his thumb brushing her skin in a comforting gesture. "Annie, I'm so sorry. That's… heartbreaking."

Annie nodded, wiping away the stray tear. "It was. But I've done my best to move forward, to live a life they'd be proud of." She offered a small, bittersweet smile. "It just gets a bit lonely sometimes."

But then, as if pulling herself out of the sadness, she gave William a brilliant smile. "I know they would be proud of me."

William returned her smile warmly. "I'm sure they would be." His eyes softened, his voice sincere. "I know I am."

Annie smiled, touched by William's words. "Thank you," she said softly, her eyes lingering on his for a moment before shifting the conversation. "So, what do you plan to do today?"

William shrugged casually. "I'm not sure," he replied, leaning against the counter. "What about you? Would you like to do something together?"

Annie's smile widened. "That sounds nice. I wouldn't mind getting out of the apartment for a bit. Maybe we could go for a walk or grab some lunch somewhere?"

William grinned. "Sounds perfect. Let's make a day of it."

William and Annie arrived at Coney Island, the vibrant atmosphere buzzing with laughter and excitement. As they stepped onto the boardwalk, the salty ocean breeze welcomed them, and Annie's eyes sparkled with anticipation.

Their first stop was the iconic Ferris wheel, a towering structure that offered breathtaking views of the coastline and the bustling beach below. They climbed into a brightly coloured gondola, and as it began to ascend, Annie squealed with delight. William laughed, enjoying her infectious enthusiasm. At the top, they shared a moment of awe, gazing out at the expansive ocean stretching to the horizon.

"Can you believe how beautiful it is?" Annie said, her voice filled with wonder.

William nodded, stealing glances at her radiant smile. "It's perfect," he replied, feeling a sense of happiness wash over him.

After their exhilarating ride, they strolled hand in hand along the boardwalk, taking in the sights and sounds of Coney Island. The air was filled with the scent of popcorn and cotton candy, and the joyful shouts from carnival games added to the festive ambiance. They stopped to take pictures by the colourful murals and enjoyed the playful atmosphere.

Eventually, they decided to grab lunch at one of the boardwalk restaurants. They settled at a cozy outdoor table overlooking the beach, where the sound of waves crashing provided a calming backdrop. Annie ordered a classic lobster roll, while William opted for a crispy fish sandwich.

As they enjoyed their meal, they shared stories and laughter, the warmth of the sun complementing their growing connection. "This is so much fun," Annie said, taking a bite of her lobster roll. "I can't believe I've never been here before!"

William smiled, pleased to be sharing this experience with her. "I'm glad we came. It's nice to escape the usual routine."

After finishing their lunch, they lingered a little longer, savouring the moment before continuing their adventure at Coney Island.

As they settled onto the warm sand after lunch, Annie looked out at the waves gently lapping the shore. She turned to William, curious about his background. "So, where do your parents live?" she asked, brushing a strand of hair behind her ear.

William leaned back on his elbows, his gaze drifting toward the horizon. "They live in an estate in Sleepy Hollow. That's where Sarah and I grew up." There was a hint of pride in his voice as he mentioned his hometown.

Annie's interest piqued. "An estate? That sounds beautiful."

"Yeah, it is. It's been in the family for generations," William explained. "My parents are both lawyers, but they come from what you'd call 'old money.' You know, families that have had wealth for a long time. It's a different world, really."

Annie could sense the complexity in his words. "What's it like growing up in that environment?" she asked, genuinely intrigued.

William chuckled lightly. "It has its perks, for sure. We had a lot of opportunities, private schools, trips abroad, but there are expectations that come with it, too. Sometimes it felt like you're living in a fishbowl, constantly under scrutiny."

Annie nodded, absorbing his words. "I can understand that. It must be hard to find your own identity when everyone has their own expectations."

"Exactly," William replied, glancing at her. "But I try to focus on what makes me happy. Like this." He gestured around them, taking in the beach, the sun, and the moment they were sharing.

Annie smiled, warmth spreading through her. "I'm glad we came here today; it's been a lovely day," she said softly.

William sat up and gently kissed her on the cheek. Annie felt a rush of warmth and instinctively put her fingers to the spot he kissed, smiling at him. "What was that for?" she asked, her voice a mix of surprise and delight.

"Just felt like it. Hope you don't mind," William said with a casual grin.

"No, not at all," she replied, her cheeks flushing again as she turned her gaze toward the water.

William took her hand, his thumb brushing over her skin. "I love the way you blush."

Annie laughed, shaking her head playfully. "I'm not fond of it."

William leaned back smiling. "So, how does someone become an art gallery director at twenty-five? That's quite an accomplishment," he asked, his eyes flickering with genuine interest.

Annie smiled, a hint of pride tugging at the corners of her lips. "Well, I did my diploma, and we had gallery owners come in for guest lectures. Irene was one of them. She took a liking to me, and after I got top marks, she offered me a job. When she was really happy with my work, she decided to promote me to director so she could retire."

William raised his eyebrows, clearly impressed. "That must've been a lot of hard work."

"It was," Annie admitted, her voice soft but steady. "But it was also incredibly rewarding. That's one of the reasons I hired Sarah. I believe young people should be given a fair go when they prove themselves."

William smiled at that, a spark of admiration deepening in his gaze. "It sounds like you've already become that kind of mentor to others. That's... pretty incredible." William paused then continued, "I noticed how you interacted with your clients the other day at the gallery. It looks like you're very good at your job," he complimented, his voice warm and sincere.

Annie felt a blush creeping up her cheeks at his praise. "Thank you, William," she replied, her smile brightening. "I really enjoy what I do, and I like connecting with people."

William smiled back at her, then stood up and gently helped Annie to her feet. Once she was standing, he wrapped his arms loosely around her waist and kissed her softly on the lips. Surprised but delighted, she put her arms around his neck and kissed him back, deepening the moment between them.

William pulled back slightly, resting his forehead against hers. He looked deeply into her eyes, his expression earnest as he whispered softly, "I really like you, Annie."

Annie felt warmth spread through her at his words, a blush creeping up her cheeks. She smiled, her eyes sparkling as she murmured back, "I really like you too, William."

William took Annie's hand, intertwining their fingers as they made their way back to his car. The warmth of his touch sent a flutter through her heart, and she smiled at him as they walked. Once inside the car, the atmosphere shifted to a comfortable quiet, the soft hum of the engine and the rhythm of the tyres on the pavement creating a soothing backdrop.

Annie gazed out the window, enjoying the passing scenery as it blended into a blur of colours. The sun began its descent, casting a golden glow over everything and wrapping them in a serene warmth. She felt content, the day they'd shared lingering in her thoughts. The peacefulness of the drive allowed her to reflect on how much she was enjoying William's company, and she stole glances at him, admiring the way he focused on the road with a calm, assured demeanour. The quiet was comforting, filled with unspoken understanding and growing bond between them.

When they arrived at William's apartment, Annie turned to him with a radiant smile. "I had a wonderful day," she said, her eyes sparkling with happiness. William felt a warmth spread through him at her words, glad that their outing had brought her joy.

Annie headed to the spare room and took a quick shower, letting the warm water wash away the remnants of the day. She slipped into a soft silk nightie, then laid onto the bed just to rest for a little while but before she knew it the weight of the day's excitement pull her into a restful sleep.

A couple of hours later, William softly knocked on her door, calling out gently, "Annie, would you like some dinner?" When there was no answer, he pushed the door open slowly, peering inside to find her peacefully asleep on top of the bed, her hair fanned out like a halo around her face.

Quietly, he walked in and grabbed the throw rug draped over the chair, carefully laying it over her to keep her warm. He paused for a moment, admiring her serene beauty as she slept, her expression tranquil and content. Unable to resist, he leaned down and pressed a soft kiss to her cheek before quietly exiting the room, leaving her to rest peacefully.

Annie stirred slightly as she felt a gentle warmth on her cheek, pulling her from the depths of her dream. Her eyelids fluttered open just enough to register the dim light in the room and the comforting presence of the throw rug covering her. A soft sigh escaped her lips, a mixture of contentment and confusion.

As she drifted back into a dreamlike state, she felt a lingering sensation of warmth where William had kissed her. A small smile graced her lips, and her heart fluttered at the memory of his tender gesture. The warmth spread through her as she settled back into the pillows, the world around her fading into the background once again.

With a soft sigh of contentment, Annie nestled deeper into the mattress, allowing the comfort of the moment to lull her back into sleep, her dreams now tinged with the sweetness of his kiss.

Chapter Ten

Annie woke up on Monday morning, blinking against the soft light filtering through the curtains. She hadn't meant to fall asleep in the spare room. She had wanted to sleep in William's bed, but she must have been exhausted that she hadn't even made it there.

She stretched, her body still aching slightly, and sighed. Pushing back the covers, Annie got up and headed for the shower, letting the warm water cascade over her. It cleared her mind and soothed the tension in her muscles. After getting dressed, she stood in front of the mirror, blow drying her hair until she finally felt ready to face the day.

Stepping out of the room, Annie made her way down the hallway. The comforting scent of coffee greeted her as she entered the kitchen, where William was already up, moving around by the counter with his back to her. Without a word, she silently walked up behind him and wrapped her arms around his waist, resting her head against his back.

"Good morning," she whispered softly.

He turned in her embrace, wrapping his arms around her in return, a smile spreading across his face. "Good morning," he replied, his voice warm and gentle.

William bent down, his lips brushing softly against Annie's in a lingering kiss. He held her close, the warmth between them making the moment stretch just a little longer. When he finally pulled back, his eyes searched hers with a smile.

"Did you sleep well?" he asked, his voice low and tender.

Annie nodded, though a slight flush crept into her cheeks. "I did, but I would've slept better if I was with you," she admitted, biting her lip slightly. "Sorry, I must've been more tired than I thought and accidentally fell asleep in the spare room."

William chuckled softly, running his thumb across her cheek. "No need to apologise. I missed you, though."

Annie looked up at William, her eyes softening. "I missed you too," she whispered, her arms tightening around him.

William smiled, the warmth in his gaze deepening. "Would you like some coffee?" he asked.

Instead of answering right away, Annie hugged him tighter and leaned in, her lips finding his in a slow, tender kiss. As she pulled back just slightly, her lips still brushing against his, she murmured, "First, I want a proper good morning."

William grinned against her mouth, his arms wrapping around her as he kissed her back, giving her exactly what she wanted.

Annie pulled back, breathless from William's kiss, her cheeks flushed. "Now that was a good morning," she giggled softly, her eyes sparkling with affection.

William chuckled, though he, too, seemed reluctant to let go. They slowly released each other, the warmth of their embrace still lingering between them.

He turned to make her coffee, moving with ease around the kitchen. A moment later, he handed the steaming cup to her, a smile playing on his lips. "Here you go."

"Thanks," she said, her fingers brushing his as she took the cup.

"Do you want some breakfast?" William asked, glancing at her with a playful smile.

"I'll just make a piece of toast," she replied, sliding a slice of bread into the toaster.

He raised an eyebrow, his voice teasing. "Is that all?"

"Yes," she smiled back, catching his amused expression.

"Okay," he said with a nod.

With her toast ready, Annie spread some butter on it and took a quick bite. "I need to get to work," she said between bites and sips of coffee. "Will you be late tonight?"

"I don't think so. I have court this morning, but after that, I'll just be at the office."

"Alright, have a wonderful day," she replied, leaning in to kiss him goodbye before grabbing her things and heading out the door.

Annie arrived at the gallery before Sarah, taking a moment to enjoy the quiet atmosphere as she settled into her office. She was organising her desk when Sarah walked in.

"Good morning, Sarah!" Annie greeted her as she stepped out of her office.

"Morning, Annie!" Sarah replied, her bright smile lighting up the room. "How's living with my brother? Have you got sick of him yet?" she laughed.

Annie chuckled, shaking her head. "No, not yet," she said, then quickly changed the subject. "Are you going to lunch with the other gallery assistants today?"

"Yep, is that still okay?" Sarah asked, raising an eyebrow.

"Absolutely. I just want to make sure I'm here before you leave," Annie replied, feeling a sense of relief at the thought of having the gallery to herself for a little while.

Annie had a productive morning, meeting with several clients and discussing potential exhibitions. The energy in the gallery was positive as she worked closely with a talented new artist whose works they were considering for an upcoming show. They exchanged ideas and visions, and Annie felt a spark of excitement about the possibilities.

As lunchtime approached, Annie finished up her notes, feeling accomplished. Just then, Sarah popped her head into the office, her expression bright and eager. "Hey, Annie! The assistants are leaving now," she said, a hint of excitement in her voice.

"Great! Enjoy your lunch," Annie replied with a smile. "I'll see you when you get back."

"Okay, bye!" Sarah waved cheerfully as she headed out.

With the gallery quiet once more, Annie settled back into her work at her desk, surrounded by the peaceful ambiance. Time flew by as she focused on her tasks. Suddenly, the door buzzer rang, signalling a customer's arrival. She glanced at the clock on the wall, expecting Sarah and the others to return any moment.

Just as she prepared to greet them with a smile, the office door swung open. Annie looked up, but her smile faltered as a chill ran down her spine. It wasn't Sarah standing there; it was Jeremy, his expression twisted into a smug grin that sent a wave of panic crashing over her. "Hello, Annie," he said, his voice oozing malice. "I noticed you've replaced me with some rich guy."

Her heart raced, and she instinctively tensed as she met his gaze. "What are you doing here?" she managed to whisper, fear tightening her throat. "You can't be here."

Jeremy stepped further into the room, closing the door behind him with a soft click that echoed ominously in the silence. "Oh, but I can," he replied, his tone dripping with mockery. "I think it's time we rekindled our relationship."

Annie stood up from her desk, her instincts screaming at her to create distance. She took a cautious step back, keeping the desk between them, her heart pounding wildly in her chest. She felt trapped, terrified of what he might do next.

Before she could move again, Jeremy darted around the desk with lightning speed, grabbing her tightly. "Oh, you feel good," he sneered, his arms wrapping around her as she struggled.

"Let me go!" Annie shouted, her voice trembling with fear as she fought against him.

Ignoring her pleas, Jeremy lowered his head and forced a kiss on her. His grip tightening as Annie desperately tried to break free, but he held he so tight she couldn't move.

As Sarah and the other gallery assistants made their way back from a delightful lunch, the sun shone brightly, casting a warm glow over the street. Sarah animatedly recounted a funny story, her laughter echoing through the air when she suddenly spotted William approaching. "Hey, big bro! What are you doing here?" she called out, then quickly added with a laugh, "Don't answer that… Annie's probably in her office."

William leaned down to plant a kiss on her cheek, a warm smile spreading across his face. "I came to see you too."

Sarah chuckled, a cheeky grin crossing her face. "Yeah, sure you did!"

They entered the gallery together, the familiar scent of paint and canvas wrapping around them like a comforting embrace. As Sarah headed to the back to put away her bag, William made his way toward Annie's office, confident that she wouldn't mind his unannounced visit.

He pushed the door open, but as he stepped inside, he froze. There was Annie, wrapped in the arms of another man, sharing a kiss. A jolt of confusion and disbelief surged through him, his heart sinking. Not again… another Susan! He turned on his heel and walked out, the painful image seared into his mind.

Sarah appeared just as he exited. "Annie not in there?" she asked, noticing his stricken expression. "What's wrong?"

"Annie's busy," he replied, his voice laced with bitterness and hurt.

Sensing something was seriously wrong, Sarah rushed into Annie's office. As she caught sight of the scene unfolding, she screamed, "Jeremy! Let her go!"

William was nearly out the gallery door when he heard Sarah's panicked shout. Jeremy! Oh my God! Annie! His heart raced as he sprinted back to Annie's office, every instinct urging him to reach her. The sight that greeted him sent a surge of adrenaline coursing through his veins. Sarah was desperately tugging at the man, trying to pry him away from Annie. Jeremy's lips were still pressed against Annie's, but now William could see the fear in Annie's eyes as she struggled to break free from his grip.

"Let her go!" William shouted, urgency lacing his voice as he charged into the room. He could see the panic in Annie's eyes, her struggle growing more desperate with each passing second. Jeremy lifted his lips from Annie's, his grip tightening as he glanced over his shoulder, a mocking smile twisting his lips. "What are you going to do about it?" he taunted, clearly relishing the chaos.

William felt a surge of anger wash over him. "I said let her go!" he repeated, stepping forward and grabbing Jeremy by the shoulder, yanking him away from Annie. She stumbled back as William threw a punch that connected with Jeremy's face, sending him crashing to the ground.

Sarah held Annie, trying to soothe her as she sobbed, tears streaming down her face. William seized Jeremy by the collar and delivered another powerful punch to his face, sending him sprawling to the ground, unconscious.

William turned to Annie and gently took her from Sarah's arms, pulling her close to him. He looked at Sarah, his voice urgent. "Call the police, now."

Sarah quickly grabbed her phone and called the police, urgently asking them to hurry.

Meanwhile, William tried to soothe Annie in his arms, his voice filled with regret. "I'm so sorry, Annie. I thought…"

Sarah knew exactly what William thought was happening here, she shot him an angry look, her voice sharp. "Annie is *not* Susan!"

William met her gaze over Annie's head, regret, and pain evident in his eyes. "I know."

"Do you?" she snapped, frustration boiling over. With that, she stormed out of the office to wait for the police.

Guilt consumed William as he held Annie close, her sobs echoing in his ears. She remained oblivious to the tense exchange between him and Sarah, lost in her own anguish as she clung to him for comfort.

The sound of sirens pierced the air as the police arrived, their lights flashing brightly. Sarah directed them to the office where William remained soothing Annie, who still trembled in his arms.

As the officers entered the office, one of them, Officer Daniels, immediately recognised Jeremy, who was just beginning to regain consciousness on the floor. The officer's eyes narrowed, recalling the previous incident in which Jeremy had been arrested for similar aggressive behaviour towards Miss Spencer.

Quickly assessing the chaotic scene, Officer Daniels approached Jeremy, motioning for another officer to assist. Together, they moved swiftly to handcuff him, ensuring he was secured before he could attempt to resist.

Officer Daniels approached Annie, his expression serious but compassionate. "Miss Spencer, I assume you want to lay charges?"

Annie was too shaken to respond, her voice lost in the wave of emotions. William, standing protectively by her side, answered for her, his tone filled with determination. "Damn right she does."

The officer turned his gaze to William, nodding slightly. "When she has regained her composure, she'll need to come to the police station to give us a statement."

William nodded in understanding, his jaw set with resolve. "I'll bring her," he assured him.

Annie gradually began to calm down, though the memory of the confrontation with Jeremy lingered in her mind. The ride to the police station was quiet, filled with unspoken thoughts and a heavy tension that hung in the air. William stayed close to her, his presence offering comfort and reassurance.

Once inside the station, they settled into a small waiting area. Annie took a deep breath, trying to steady her racing heart. She glanced at William, who gave her a reassuring smile, though the worry in his eyes was hard to miss.

When they were called into the interrogation room, Annie felt a surge of anxiety mixed with determination. She knew she had to share her experience to ensure Jeremy wouldn't hurt anyone else. As she spoke to the officer, William stood nearby, his gaze unwavering, a silent promise to never doubt her again.

Yet guilt gnawed at him, the guilt of thinking Annie was just like Susan and for not being there to protect her when it mattered most. He wished he could take away her fear and erase the memories that haunted her. As Annie recounted her story, he felt a sense of helplessness wash over him, wishing he could somehow alleviate the pain that Jeremy had inflicted. Despite his internal turmoil, William remained steadfast, ready to defend her against any lingering threats.

When they finished at the police station, Annie insisted that William take her back to the gallery. He wanted to stay with her, but she reassured him that she could manage on her own for the rest of the day, and he needed to return to his work.

The drive back was subdued, the air heavy with unsaid words. Upon arriving at the gallery, Annie turned to William, sensing the worried look etched on his face. "William, I will be okay. You don't have to worry," she said, trying to sound more confident than she felt.

William grimaced, the weight of guilt pressing down on him like a stone. "Yes, I do," he replied, his voice low. It wasn't just worry that troubled him; it was the guilt of having doubted her and the lingering fear that he hadn't done enough to protect her.

After telling Annie he would see her at home, he stepped out of her office, only to be met by Sarah. Her expression was fierce and accusatory, as if he were the devil himself.

He raised a hand, bracing himself for her anger. "I know, Sarah, I shouldn't have ever thought Annie was anything like Susan."

Her eyes burned with frustration. "I am so angry with you, William!" Her voice cut through the stillness of the gallery, sharp and unyielding. It was a level of confrontation that was rare between them.

William opened his mouth to reply, but the pain in Sarah's gaze left him momentarily speechless. He felt the weight of her disappointment heavy on his shoulders, and for once, he knew he deserved it.

Annie navigated the rest of the day in a daze, grateful for Sarah's support. They spent the afternoon discussing the gallery's upcoming exhibition, but Annie struggled to concentrate. Each time her thoughts drifted to the confrontation with Jeremy, a wave of anxiety washed over her.

When the clock finally indicated it was time to leave, she didn't hesitate. With William still at work, she drove home, the quiet of the car offering a much-needed escape from her racing mind.

Upon entering the penthouse, she headed straight for the master ensuite, filling the bathtub with warm water. Steam rose gently, wrapping around her like a soothing embrace. As she sank into the tub, the heat enveloped her, melting away some of the tension from the day.

The bathroom door opened, and William stepped inside, concern etched across his face. "How are you?" he asked softly.

Annie opened her eyes and met his gaze, feeling a wave of comfort wash over her at his presence. She extended her hand toward him, a sweet invitation. "Join me," she said.

William took a step closer, his eyes searching her expression. "Are you sure?"

"Yes, I need you," Annie replied, her voice sincere.

William hesitated for a moment, then slowly began to strip off his clothes, to reveal his strong physique. He stepped into the warm water behind Annie, he wrapped his arms around her, pulling her close against him. The warmth of the water enveloped them, and Annie melted into his embrace.

Annie sighed softly, leaning back into William. "That feels nice," she murmured, relishing the warmth and comfort of the moment.

"Yes, it does," William replied, his voice low but laced with tension. "But Annie, I need to tell you something, and I'm not sure how you're going to take it."

"What is it, William?" she asked, concern creeping into her voice.

William took a deep breath, struggling to find the right words. "Today, when I came to your office, I thought you were kissing Jeremy, not that he was forcing you."

Annie spun around to face him, her expression a mix of disbelief and hurt. "You thought I was cheating on you?"

His eyes reflected pain and regret. "Yes."

"Why would you think that?" Annie asked, hurt lacing her voice, searching his eyes for understanding.

"It's happened to me before, so it's hard to trust," William said, his voice faltering. "I'm sorry. I know you're nothing like Susan, but I…" He struggled to find the right words, his emotions swirling inside him.

"Did this Susan cheat on you?" Annie asked, her voice laced with concern.

"Yes," William replied, his gaze dropping as he recalled the memory. "I found her in bed with another man."

"Oh, William, that's terrible," Annie said, her heart aching for him.

William couldn't help but think how she was more worried about him than angry at him, and that realisation only deepened his sense of guilt.

Annie looked into William's eyes and said, "You know I would never do that… don't you?"

"Yes, I do," he replied, his voice filled with regret. "You're not like that. I feel so terrible for even thinking you would." William lowered his head and kissed her gently, pulling back, he said softly, "I am so sorry."

Annie then got up and straddled his hips. "I know…," she said, her voice full of trust as water splashed to the bathroom floor.

She cupped his face, bringing her lips to his with a sense of urgency. William's hands glided up her back, then down, to pull her closer, before they found their way to her breasts, gently kneaded them, his thumb brushing over the hardened nipples.

"William… please," she moaned against his mouth.

Their kiss deepened with fervour.

William pulled away briefly, their eyes locking in an intense gaze. He lifted her hips, positioning himself before slowly guiding his arousal into her warm, inviting centre, he entered her slowly, deliberately, until he was buried deep inside her.

William watched as a look of wonder and pleasure spread across Annie's face, her lips parting in a soft "oh."

William gazed deeply into her eyes and murmured, "I don't think I'll ever get enough of you."

He guided Annie's hips upwards before thrusting back into her, water splashing to the floor.

"Oh… William," she gasped.

William murmured against her neck, "I love hearing you say my name."

Annie began to move in a steady rhythm, water splashing around them, but neither cared. Her movements were slow at first, gradually increasing in speed, drawing them both closer to the edge.

William's mouth closed possessively around one hard nipple, licking and gently sucking before shifting to the other one, sending waves of pleasure through her.

"William, please," she moaned.

Their rhythm quickened as William kissed her fiercely, his mouth ravenous against hers. He slid his hand down between their bodies, his touch driving her to the brink. She shattered, her body trembling with release.

William let out a low, guttural groan as he climaxed with her, his voice filled with raw emotion as he called out her name, "Annie!"

They remained entwined as William gently stroking her back.

"I don't deserve you," he whispered, his voice soft. "You're incredible."

Annie flashed a playful grin. "That… was incredible."

He smiled and kissed her gently on the lips. "I'm sorry, Annie. I hope you can forgive me."

"There's nothing to forgive," she said. "I understand; it just brought back some painful memories."

William hugged her tightly, marvelling at how unbelievable the woman in his arms truly was.

Annie quickly settled into a routine living in William's apartment, finding comfort in the rhythm of their shared life. After long days at the gallery, she returned to the warmth of William's home, where the familiarity of the space and his presence eased the tension of her day.

Their evenings unfolded with a natural ease, allowing them to enjoy each other's company without always needing conversation. Some nights were filled with laughter as they swapped stories about their day, while other evenings found them sitting side by side on the couch, each immersed in their own world, Annie curled up with a book and William focused on legal briefs. Yet, their quiet companionship spoke volumes.

Occasionally, they would watch a show together, sharing snacks and exchanging comfortable glances that needed no words. It was a calm, steady bond, one that brought joy in the simplest ways. They didn't feel the need to fill the silence with chatter or forced interactions; instead, they found peace in simply being near each other, a reminder that they could exist together without pretence.

Each night, they would sleep in William's bed, filled with passion and to William's surprise and pleasure, Annie began to grow more adventurous, embracing their intimacy with an enthusiasm that deepened their connection.

William found his connection with Annie to be the most profound he had ever experienced with a woman. It transcended the physical, though that aspect of their relationship was undeniably mind-blowing. She fulfilled him in ways he hadn't realised were possible, making him feel alive and whole. This feeling overshadowed every past relationship, including his time with Susan, which now seemed trivial by comparison.

Annie made him feel cherished, understood, and accepted; emotions he had longed for but never truly found until now. In her presence, he experienced a unique blend of completeness and vulnerability that was both exhilarating and terrifying. Each laugh they shared, every intimate moment, and the quiet evenings spent together only deepened his understanding of what they had. William realised that this was something extraordinary, a bond he had never thought possible.

Thursday afternoon, they were lounging in the living room of the penthouse when a firm knock echoed through the space. William opened the door to reveal two police officers standing outside, their expressions serious, yet professional, a stark contrast to the tranquility that had enveloped the apartment moments before.

Annie's heart sank, sensing that something was amiss. She sat up straighter, her instincts kicking in as she glanced at William, whose demeanour shifted instantly from casual to concerned.

"Good evening, Mr. Banks. May we come in?" officers Grant asked.

William nodded and stepped aside to let the officers in. Annie, sitting on the sofa, gestured for them to take a seat. Officers Grant and Lee exchanged glances before settling across from her. Their expressions were serious but calm, and Annie's own face reflected a mix of concern and hope as she waited for them to speak.

"We have some important updates regarding your case," Officer Grant began. "We're confident that Jeremy Spears is responsible for the break-in at your apartment and the graffiti on the gallery's exterior wall."

Annie's eyes widened at the mention of Jeremy. "Did he confess to everything?" she asked, her voice steady but tinged with anxiety.

Officer Lee took a deep breath before responding. "No, he denied the break-in until we showed him the CCTV footage of him entering your building. He's still in custody, awaiting a court hearing, and with the assault charges and these new charges, we believe he'll be locked away for quite some time."

Relief washed over Annie's face as she glanced at William sitting beside her, taking her hand in his. She smiled at him, a flicker of hope brightening her eyes. "It's over," she said softly, her voice a mix of gratitude and resolve.

William gently squeezed her hand, sensing the weight of her ordeal beginning to lift as a wave of relief washed over them. Officer Lee continued, "We're pressing new charges later today for the break-in. You'll likely need to testify if he pleads not guilty, but hopefully, he'll plead guilty, which would save everyone a lot of time."

As the officers finished their notes and prepared to leave, Annie and William expressed their gratitude. "Thank you for everything," Annie said sincerely, her voice steady.

"Take care," the officers replied before stepping out.

Once they were gone, William wrapped his arms around Annie, and they both finally relaxed, knowing her nightmare was over.

Chapter Eleven

Friday arrived, and as William and Annie sat down for breakfast, he casually reminded her, "Don't forget, we're heading to my parents' estate after work tonight, I will pick you and Sarah up from the gallery." His tone was light, but there was an undercurrent of excitement. It was clear that William was looking forward to the weekend, and Annie could sense how much it meant to him for her to meet his family.

Annie smiled, grateful for the consideration, but she hesitated before responding. "I've been looking forward to meeting your parents," she began, her voice softening with regret, "but I won't be able to join you tonight."

William raised an eyebrow, his expression shifting slightly. "Why not?" he asked, trying to keep the disappointment out of his voice.

"I have to stay at the gallery late," Annie explained. "We're getting a shipment of artworks tonight, and I need to be there to make sure everything goes smoothly. I won't be able to leave until it's all sorted."

William nodded, understanding. "I get it. Work comes first. You can come up in the morning, though, right?"

"Yes, definitely," Annie reassured him. "I'll drive up first thing on Saturday. I wouldn't miss meeting them for the world."

William's smile returned, though more subdued. "Alright, we'll save you a seat at the breakfast table. Just let me know when you're on your way."

Annie gave him a warm look, feeling relieved that he understood. She was genuinely excited to meet his parents, but the demands of the gallery couldn't be ignored. "Thank you for understanding," she said. "I'll see you tomorrow."

Annie arrived at the gallery just as the morning sun cast a soft glow through the large windows. Inside, she found Sarah already there, adjusting a new display. Sarah looked up and smiled as Annie approached, Annie could see the familiar energy in her movements, a sign that Sarah was already thinking ahead to the weekend.

"I'm glad you're here," Sarah said cheerfully, stepping back from the artwork. "You ready for tonight. Are you excited to meet Mum and Dad."

Annie hesitated, a small sigh escaping her lips. "Actually, I won't be able to make it tonight," she said, her voice filled with a tinge of disappointment. "I've got to stay here for the shipment coming in. I'll have to come up tomorrow morning instead."

Sarah's expression shifted, her smile softening into understanding. "Oh no, that's a shame! I know they were looking forward to meeting you, but I get it." She placed a hand on Annie's arm reassuringly. "The gallery comes first. That shipment is important."

Annie nodded, grateful for Sarah's understanding. "I've been looking forward to meeting them too. I'm really disappointed I can't come tonight, but there's no one else to handle it. I'll head up early tomorrow, though."

Sarah gave her a supportive smile. "Don't worry about it. It'll be fine, and we'll all have plenty of time together over the weekend. My parents will completely understand."

Annie felt some of her disappointment ease. "Thanks, Sarah. I just didn't want them to think I wasn't excited to meet them."

"They won't," Sarah reassured her. "I'll make sure they know how much you're looking forward to it. Besides, William can't stop talking about how great you are. You'll be the star of the weekend, even if you're fashionably late." She winked, making Annie laugh despite her earlier frustration.

Feeling lighter, Annie glanced around the gallery, refocusing on the work ahead. "Alright, let's get everything ready for this shipment, then. The sooner it's done, the sooner I can head up tomorrow."

Sarah nodded, understanding that tonight's work had to come first, but knowing that tomorrow would bring the long-awaited introduction to William and Sarah's parents.

At precisely five o'clock, William walked into the gallery, his tall frame casting a shadow as the door swung open. The soft sound of his footsteps echoed across the polished floor as he entered, immediately spotting Sarah and Annie at the far end of the gallery, busy with their final preparations for the evening.

Sarah was the first to spot him, her face brightening into a grin as she waved. "There you are, right on time!" she called out, her voice warm and inviting. William and Sarah had reconciled after he shared that he had apologised and explained everything to Annie.

William smiled in return and walked over, his gaze flitting between the vibrant artwork adorning the walls and the two women at the centre of the room. "Of course, always," he replied casually as he approached them. "Hi, Annie," he added, his voice softening slightly as he addressed her. They hadn't revealed their relationship to Sarah yet, and there was something exhilarating about keeping that secret just between them. Sarah had her suspicions, but she didn't know for certain.

Annie looked up from the paperwork she was holding, a smile playing on her lips. "Hi, William," she greeted, her expression brightening despite the long day. She tucked a strand of hair behind her ear, feeling a small flutter in her chest at his presence.

William's gaze lingered on her for a moment before turning to Sarah. "Ready to go?" he asked, glancing at his sister.

Sarah nodded and tossed her clipboard onto a nearby table. "Yep, just wrapping up here. But I'm sad Annie won't be coming with us tonight," she said, throwing a playful pout in Annie's direction.

Annie chuckled, shaking her head. "I'll be there tomorrow morning, I promise," she reassured them. "Just have to handle the shipment tonight."

William nodded, understanding but slightly disappointed. "We'll save you a seat at breakfast," he teased gently, before looking around the gallery. "This place looks amazing, by the way. You two have been busy."

"Always," Sarah replied with a proud smile. "But I think I'm done here for the day."

William gave a quick glance at his watch, then back at Annie. "We'll see you tomorrow then?"

"Definitely," Annie replied, feeling the warmth of their company as they prepared to leave.

As Sarah and William waved goodbye, Annie stood by the gallery entrance, offering them a warm smile. She watched as they disappeared into the evening, feeling a slight pang of envy but also excitement for the busy night ahead. Turning back inside, she focused on the task at hand. She needed to make sure there was plenty of space for the incoming shipment.

The gallery felt quiet as she moved around, rearranging pieces and clearing an area for the large crates she was expecting. She double-checked the space, ensuring everything was ready. At exactly 7p.m., the shipment arrived, right on schedule.

The removalists worked efficiently, unloading crate after crate, the sounds of their movements filling the once-quiet gallery. Annie directed them with a calm professionalism, making sure the delicate artworks were handled with care. It took a full hour to unload all the pieces, and by the time she had inspected the shipment and signed the paperwork, it was already 9 p.m.

Finally, she locked up the gallery, letting out a long breath of relief. As she stepped outside into the crisp evening air, she glanced at her watch. It wasn't that late. She could still drive to William and Sarah's parents' estate and arrive at a reasonable hour. After all, it was less than an hour away.

Pulling out her phone, Annie quickly texted William:

I have finished with the shipment, wondering if it's too late to come now?

She didn't have to wait long. William replied almost instantly:

No, not too late. I will look out for you.

Smiling at the response, Annie texted back:

Okay, see you about 10p.m.

With a sense of excitement bubbling inside her, Annie hopped into her car, thankful she had packed her suitcase that morning so she wouldn't have to return to the apartment. The thought of finally joining the family gathering filled her with anticipation. After the busy evening at the gallery, the drive felt like the perfect way to unwind, and she was eager to meet William and Sarah's parents for the first time.

Sliding into the driver's seat, she started the engine and set off on the long drive to their estate. The road stretched out before her, the quiet hum of the car blending with the calming sounds of the night. As she neared her destination, the time seemed to pass effortlessly, and before she knew it, she was only a few miles away.

But just as she approached a bend in the road, she pressed the brakes, and nothing happened. Panic surged through her as the car continued forward, her foot desperately pumping the pedal. "Oh my god," she gasped, her heart racing. The car veered sharply off the road, the world spinning as she lost control.

The last thing Annie saw was the blur of trees rushing past before everything went black.

William paced the length of the terrace, his phone clutched tightly in his hand. His parents' home was quiet, too quiet for his liking, and the clock on his phone read 10:30 p.m. Annie was supposed to have arrived half an hour ago.

He had been calling her for the past fifteen minutes; each unanswered call tightened the nerves in his gut. The line would buzz, the ringtone echoing through the silence, but there was no answer, no reassuring voice to ease his growing fear.

He tried to focus, telling himself that she was probably just late, that maybe she had lost track of time or hit traffic. But the unease in his chest was building, creeping into his thoughts. Something felt off.

William sat down on the edge of a chair and dialled her number again, his thumb hovering over the call button as he stared at his phone. The ringing felt endless, each unanswered tone only adding to his worry.

"Come on, Annie... please pick up." His voice was barely a whisper as he pressed the phone to his ear, his heartbeat loud in the stillness of the room.

When the call went to voicemail again, William stood abruptly, running his hands through his hair in frustration. He had to try again. He wasn't going to stop until he knew she was okay.

Annie slowly regained consciousness, the world around her spinning as she blinked her eyes open. Her head pounded, and a deep ache throbbed in her ribs. She felt disoriented, her mind struggling to piece together what had happened. The last thing she remembered was her car careening around the sharp bend, the brakes completely unresponsive. Then... the crash.

Her phone's persistent ringing finally pulled her fully into the moment. Groggy and dazed, she fumbled for it with trembling hands, her vision blurry as she answered the call.

"Annie?" William's voice came through, a mix of relief and fear. "Thank God, I've been calling for ages! Are you okay?"

She swallowed hard, her voice faint as she tried to speak through the dizziness. "William… I… I've had an accident… the brakes… they didn't work." Each word came out slowly, her mind still struggling to catch up.

"Where are you?" His voice was frantic now, clearly terrified.

"I don't know… a bend, I think. I'm so dizzy…" Annie's head spun, and she could feel herself fading in and out.

"Stay with me, Annie. I'm coming to find you. Just hold on." William's voice was firm, filled with urgency.

William's heart pounded as he hung up the phone, panic tightening in his chest. Annie had been in an accident, and she sounded weak… too weak. He needed to move, but first, he had to let his family know.

He rushed down the hallway to where his parents, Henry and Helen, were sitting in the living room, Sarah lounging nearby with a magazine.

"William?" Helen looked up, noticing the alarm in his face. "What's wrong?"

"Annie has had an accident," he said, the words tumbling out quickly. "Her brakes failed on a bend. I need to go and find her."

Henry stood up immediately, his brows furrowed in concern. "Do you know where she is?"

"Not exactly, but she mentioned a sharp bend. I think I can track her down." William grabbed his jacket, his movements quick and frantic.

"I'm coming with you," Sarah declared, already on her feet, grabbing her bag without hesitation.

William glanced at her; his urgency mirrored in her expression. "Okay, let's go," he agreed, not wasting a second.

Henry stood by his face tight with concern. "Take care of her, both of you. And call us the minute you find her."

"We will," William promised, his voice taut with the weight of the moment. With Sarah at his side, they rushed out the door, hearts pounding, both driven by a single purpose… finding Annie and bringing her home safe.

William and Sarah hurried to the car, the tension between them evident. As soon as they buckled in, William turned the key, the engine roaring to life. The silence in the car was heavy, both of them lost in their anxious thoughts.

Five minutes into the drive, Sarah's sharp intake of breath cut through the stillness. "William, stop! Over there!" She pointed toward a car barely visible through the trees, its dark shape resting at an odd angle just past the guardrail.

William's heart raced as he slammed on the brakes, his eyes following where Sarah pointed. "Oh, God..." he muttered, his stomach knotting in fear. The car was partially hidden, the front crushed against a tree. It was Annie's.

Without thinking, William pulled the car to a stop, his hands shaking as he threw open the door. "Stay here," he said, but Sarah was already unbuckling, her determination matching his as they hurried toward the wreck.

William sprinted toward Annie's car, his heart pounding in his chest, every second stretching painfully as he closed the distance. Sarah was right behind him, but all he could focus on was getting to her. He reached the car and yanked the door open with force, the hinges creaking under the pressure.

"Annie!" he shouted, his voice trembling with panic. Annie was slumped over in the driver's seat, her head leaning against the window. Her eyes fluttered open and closed, groggy, barely registering his presence.

"Annie, stay with me," William urged, his hands gently cupping her face. She was dazed, blood trickling from a cut on her forehead. Her breaths were shallow, and her body seemed limp, as if struggling to stay conscious.

Sarah came up behind him, gasping as she saw Annie's state. "Oh my God... William, is she okay?" she whispered, fear gripping her voice.

"I don't know," William muttered, his throat tight. He gently checked her pulse, his fingers trembling. "Annie, hang in there. We're getting you help."

William's hands shook as he cradled Annie's face, her shallow breathing causing his heart to ache. "Sarah, call an ambulance... now!" His voice cracked with desperation, not taking his eyes off Annie.

Sarah fumbled for her phone, her fingers trembling as she dialled the emergency number. "Yes, we need an ambulance," she said quickly, her voice urgent. "There's been a car accident. My friend is injured... She's in and out of consciousness. Please hurry!"

As soon as she finished giving the operator their location, Sarah immediately called their parents. "Mum, Dad, it's Annie... we found her... We've called an ambulance, but she's hurt. I will call you back when we know where she goes."

William glanced at Sarah, his face pale with fear, but his focus quickly returned to Annie, stroking her cheek softly. "Hold on, Annie," he whispered, his voice raw. "Helps on the way."

The sound of sirens pierced the still night air as the ambulance finally arrived, its lights flashing across the darkened road. William stood by Annie's side, his hands gripping hers tightly, whispering reassurances even though she was barely conscious.

Two paramedics rushed out, their movements quick and efficient. One of them, a man with a calm but focused demeanour, immediately approached William. "Sir, we need to take over now," he said firmly but gently, guiding William back a few steps.

The other paramedic, a woman with short hair, leaned into the car, checking Annie's vital signs and assessing her injuries. "She's got some serious bruising, possible rib fractures," she called to her partner. "Oxygen mask, now."

Within seconds, they had placed the oxygen mask over Annie's face, carefully securing her head and neck in a brace. "She's in and out of consciousness," the male paramedic noted, checking her pulse. "We need to move her, but carefully. We can't risk any internal injuries worsening."

The paramedics moved with practiced skill, carefully easing Annie out of the wreckage onto a stretcher, all while Sarah stood to the side, nervously watching. William's heart raced as he hovered nearby, watching helplessly as they worked.

"She's stable for now, but we need to get her to the hospital immediately," the female paramedic announced. They lifted the stretcher and wheeled her towards the ambulance. William moved closer, his voice shaky. "Can I come with her?"

The paramedic gave a brief nod. "You can ride with us. Let's go."

William turned to Sarah, his face lined with urgency and worry. Without hesitation, he pulled his car keys from his pocket and tossed them to her. "Go home," he said firmly. "I'll call as soon as I know something."

Sarah caught the keys, her expression tense. "Okay," she replied, her voice trembling slightly, "but call me the minute you find out anything, William. Don't leave me in the dark."

"I won't," he promised, his eyes already focused on the ambulance where the paramedics were securing Annie inside. He turned and hurried toward the open doors, climbing in just as they finished strapping Annie to the stretcher.

The paramedics worked swiftly, checking Annie's vitals again as the ambulance doors shut behind him. William sat down beside her, his heart pounding as the vehicle roared to life.

In the back of the ambulance, William sat close to Annie, gripping her hand tightly. His thumb gently brushed over her knuckles, desperate to offer her any comfort he could as she drifted in and out of consciousness. The steady beep of the heart monitor filled the small space, but his focus never wavered from her pale face.

"Hang in there, Annie," he whispered, his voice thick with emotion. "I'm right here. You're going to be okay."

The paramedics worked around him, securing oxygen and monitoring her vitals, but all William could do was hold her hand, silently willing her to wake up and give him some sign that she would be all right.

After what felt like an eternity, the ambulance finally pulled into the hospital. The doors swung open, and the paramedics rushed Annie out, pushing her gurney toward the emergency entrance. William followed, never letting go of her hand until he was forced to step aside as they wheeled her into the ER.

He stood there, helpless, as the hospital staff took over.

William paced anxiously in the sterile waiting room, his heart racing with worry as the minutes ticked by. He glanced at the clock on the wall, willing time to move faster, but it felt as if each second stretched into eternity. His mind was a whirlwind of worst-case scenarios, replaying the moments leading up to the accident, and the sight of Annie's unconscious form haunted him.

Finally, after what felt like an age, a doctor in scrubs approached him. The doctor's expression was serious but calm, and William felt a surge of hope as he stood up to meet him.

"Mr. Banks?" the doctor asked, his voice steady.

"Yes, that's me. How is she?" William asked, his voice trembling slightly.

The doctor took a breath, choosing his words carefully. "Annie is stable now. She suffered a concussion and some bruising, but she's conscious and responsive. We're keeping her for observation, but her vitals are good."

A wave of relief washed over William, loosening the tension in his shoulders just a bit. "Can I see her?" he asked, his heart racing with a mix of anticipation and anxiety.

"Of course. Follow me," the doctor replied, leading William through the bustling hospital corridors, his mind swirling with thoughts of Annie.

As they walked down the bright, fluorescent-lit hallway, the sterile scent of antiseptic filled the air. The doctor paused outside a room and turned to William, offering a reassuring nod. "She's resting but awake. When you go in, just keep your voice low and let her know you're here."

Taking a deep breath, William pushed the door open and stepped into the room. The sight of Annie lying in the hospital bed made his heart ache. She looked pale, a patch on her forehead, and the monitors beeped softly beside her, their rhythmic sounds a comforting reminder that she was still with him.

Annie turned her head slightly at the sound of the door, her eyes fluttering open as she recognised him. A weak smile broke across her face, though it was tinged with exhaustion. "William…" she murmured, her voice barely above a whisper.

"Annie…" he replied, rushing to her side and gently taking her hand in his. As their fingers intertwined, he felt her warmth, and a wave of relief flooded over him. "Thank God you're okay."

She blinked slowly, struggling to focus, but the recognition in her eyes was enough to calm his frayed nerves. "What happened?" she asked, her voice trembling slightly.

"You were in a car accident," William explained softly, brushing a loose strand of hair away from her face. "But you're okay now. The doctors are taking care of you."

Annie nodded, her expression shifting as she processed his words. "I… I had no brakes…" she trailed off, confusion and fear flickering in her gaze.

"It's all right," he reassured her, squeezing her hand gently. "You're safe now. I'm right here."

William settled into the chair beside Annie's hospital bed. He pulled his phone from his pocket, taking a moment to steady himself before dialling Sarah's number.

When the line connected, he could hear Sarah's voice immediately, filled with concern. "William? Is she okay?"

"Hey, Sis," he replied, striving to keep his voice steady despite the tumult of emotions swirling inside him. "Annie is awake. She's stable. I'm going to stay with her for now, and I'll call you again in the morning."

There was a brief silence on the line as his words sunk in. "Okay, I'm really glad she's okay," Sarah said, urgency creeping into her tone. "I'll let Mum and Dad know."

"Thanks," he said, glancing at Annie, who was watching him intently with a look that mixed gratitude and concern. "I'll keep you updated."

"Tell her we're all thinking of her," Sarah said before hanging up, leaving William feeling a bit more grounded as he turned his attention back to Annie.

Annie and William chatted softly for a little while, their voices a soothing presence in the sterile room. Eventually, Annie's eyelids grew heavy, and she drifted off to sleep. William settled into the chair beside her bed, resting his head against the wall as the dim light from the bedside lamp cast a warm glow around them. The gentle sound of her breathing lulled him into a light sleep.

Chapter Twelve

As dawn broke, the first rays of sunlight crept through the window, illuminating Annie's peaceful face. William stirred awake, blinking against the brightness and feeling the stiffness in his body. He reached out to take her hand, a wave of relief washing over him as he watched her breathe steadily.

Moments later, the door opened softly, and a doctor entered the room, clipboard in hand. He smiled at the sight of William awake. "Good morning," he said, glancing at Annie. "I have good news. We're discharging her today."

William sat up straighter, hope flickering in his chest. "Really? That's great!"

"Yes," the doctor continued, nodding. "But it's important she gets plenty of rest. She may experience some headaches for a little while, and if she has any severe head pain, you need to bring her back to the hospital immediately."

William nodded, absorbing the information. "What about her forehead?" he asked, concern etching his features.

"You can remove the patch on her forehead, but make sure the stitches stay dry," the doctor instructed. "Keep an eye on her, and don't hesitate to call us if anything seems off."

William thanked the doctor, relief flooding through him as he glanced at Annie, who was beginning to stir awake. She blinked slowly, taking in the morning light and the familiar sounds around her.

"Hey, sleepyhead," he said, squeezing her hand gently. "You're going home."

A small smile spread across her face. "That's great."

After the discharge papers were signed and they prepared to leave the hospital, Sarah appeared in the doorway, a bright smile lighting up her face.

"Hey, you two!" she greeted cheerfully, stepping into the room. "Ready to get out of here?"

William returned her smile, grateful for her presence. "We are!"

"You look much better," she said, glancing at Annie. "Let's get you home."

Annie smiled back, feeling a wave of relief. William helped her sit up and then eased her off the bed. Together, they gathered her belongings, with William gently guiding her toward the door, keeping a steadying hand on her arm.

When they finally reached the entrance, Sarah was waiting by William's car.

"Here we are," she said, holding the door open for them. William carefully helped Annie into the back seat, ensuring she was comfortable before sliding in beside her.

Once Sarah settled into the driver's seat and started the engine, she pulled away from the hospital. Annie leaned against William, feeling a sense of safety and comfort wash over her.

As they arrived at his parents' estate, William carefully helped her out of the car, steadying her as she stepped onto the driveway. Just then, Henry and Helen Banks emerged from the house, their faces lighting up with relief and warmth upon seeing Annie.

"Annie!" Helen exclaimed, wrapping her arms around her in a warm embrace, being careful not to hurt her bruised ribs, Henry followed suit, giving her a comforting hug as well.

"We're so glad to have you here," Helen said, her voice filled with genuine affection.

Annie smiled, feeling genuinely welcomed by Sarah's and William's parents. "It's so nice to meet you both," she said warmly.

Helen and Henry exchanged pleased glances, both responding in unison, "We're happy to finally meet you too."

Helen stepped back slightly, studying Annie with a nurturing gaze. "Have you eaten yet?" she asked, concern evident in her tone.

Annie shook her head slightly, feeling a bit embarrassed. "Not yet. I didn't really feel up to it in the hospital."

"Oh, we can fix that!" Henry said enthusiastically. "We've got plenty of food prepared. Let's get you settled in and fed."

Annie felt a wave of gratitude wash over her as they ushered her into the dining room. The sight before her was inviting, with a beautifully set table laden with an array of pastries, fresh fruit, toast, and an assortment of condiments. "Wow!" she exclaimed, laughter bubbling up. "I don't think I'm that hungry."

Sarah, already seated in the dining room, chuckled at Annie's reaction. "My parents always go a little overboard," she said.

William gently helped Annie into a chair at the dining table, settling in next to her. Henry took his place at the head of the table, while Sarah and Helen sat across from them, all eyes on Annie.

Helen smiled brightly. "William and Sarah didn't eat this morning either, so we can all have brunch together," she said, her voice filled with warmth.

"That's so kind of you. Your home is beautiful," Annie replied, feeling the atmosphere envelop her like a comforting blanket.

Henry nodded, his eyes twinkling with enthusiasm. "I have a few original paintings that you might be interested in seeing later, Annie. I'd love to get your opinion on them."

"Oh, that would be wonderful!" Annie replied, genuinely excited at the prospect. She felt a sense of belonging wash over her, a welcome feeling after the tumultuous events of the past few days.

As they settled into their brunch, Henry and Helen leaned in, eager to learn more about Annie.

"So, Annie," Helen began with a warm smile, "tell us about your family. Do you have any siblings?"

Annie took a sip of her drink, feeling the warmth of their interest. "No, unfortunately, and my parents passed away when I was eighteen," she said softly.

Helen's expression shifted to one of sympathy. "That must be lonely," she replied gently.

Annie hesitated briefly before responding. "Yes, it can be sometimes, but I try to keep myself busy, especially with work."

Helen's eyes lit up. "Speaking of work, we've heard a bit about your job at the gallery. What's that like?"

Annie smiled, her enthusiasm for her work shining through. "It's really exciting! I get to curate exhibits, work with various artists, and connect with the clients. It's fulfilling to help others appreciate art and its impact on our lives."

"That sounds amazing," Henry said, nodding appreciatively. "What's been your favourite exhibit to work on so far?"

Annie thought for a moment, recalling a particularly memorable project. "There was an exhibit dedicated to local artists, highlighting their stories and the challenges they faced. It was incredibly moving to see how art can express personal experiences and connect people."

Helen exchanged a glance with Henry, clearly impressed. "You have such a thoughtful perspective on art, Annie. It's inspiring," she said.

Annie felt a warm glow at their compliments. "Sarah is very talented too; she's impressed me since I hired her. She's a delight to work with."

Sarah smiled at the compliment. "Annie is being too nice. She's teaching me a lot," she said, a hint of pride in her voice.

As they all chatted, the atmosphere in the dining room was warm and inviting. Henry and Helen shared stories about William and Sarah, and laughter filled the air, making it feel like a celebration. The food on the table looked inviting, but Annie found herself picking at her food rather than diving in.

William watched her closely, noting her small bites and the way she pushed a few items around on her plate. Concern flickered across his face as he leaned in slightly. "Hey, are you feeling okay?" he asked, his voice low and filled with genuine worry.

Annie looked up, her eyes meeting his. She gave a small nod, a reassuring smile touching her lips. "I'm fine, really. I just haven't gotten my full appetite back yet," she replied, trying to sound more upbeat than she felt.

William relaxed slightly but remained observant. "Just make sure you don't overdo it," he said softly, his gaze lingering on her as if he could sense her struggle.

She appreciated his concern and tried to push herself to eat a bit more, but her body had just started to recover. Despite that, she felt comforted by the warmth of the family around her and William's unwavering support. The pleasant brunch continued, filled with laughter and conversation, but Annie remained aware of the love and care she was surrounded by, thinking how lucky William and Sarah were.

After brunch, William led Annie out to the terrace, mindful of the doctor's orders for her to rest. As they stepped outside, a gentle breeze greeted them, carrying the sweet scent of blooming flowers from the expansive gardens below.

Annie paused, her breath catching at the stunning view. The meticulously landscaped gardens stretched out before her, vibrant with colours and alive with the sound of chirping birds. There were pathways winding through lush greenery, dotted with benches that invited quiet reflection. "Wow," she breathed, a smile spreading across her face. "This is absolutely beautiful."

William glanced at her, his heart swelling at the sight of her delight. "I thought you might like it," he said, stepping closer to her side. The intimacy of the moment felt special, with just the two of them sharing the tranquility of the garden view.

As Annie leaned on the railing, soaking in the scenery, William took a moment to admire her. The sunlight highlighted her features, casting a warm glow around her, even with the patch on her forehead, she was still beautiful.

"Thank you for bringing me out here," Annie said, turning to him. "It's nice to get some fresh air."

"Of course," he replied softly. "You need to take it easy, but I wanted you to enjoy this while you can."

They stood silently gazing over the garden bathed in the golden glow of the sun. The tranquil beauty of the flowers and the soft rustling of leaves created a serene backdrop for their quiet moment. William stood behind Annie, his presence warm and protective as he admired the view.

Carefully, he wrapped his arms around her, being mindful not to disturb her bruised ribs. His touch was gentle, conveying both affection and caution. He moved a strand of hair away from her neck, his fingers brushing against her skin, sending a shiver of warmth through her. With a soft sigh, he leaned in and placed a tender kiss on her neck. Annie closed her eyes, leaning back slightly into him.

Annie turned in William's arms, a slight wince escaping her as she adjusted her position. Instantly, William withdrew his arm from her waist, taking her hands gently in his. "I don't want to hurt you," he said, concern etched on his face.

"I know you wouldn't hurt me, William," she replied, offering him a reassuring smile.

"Annie…" he whispered, his voice low and intimate.

He leaned down, gently capturing her lips in a soft kiss, and she melted into him, kissing him back. William brought his hands to her face, cradling it tenderly as he gradually drew her closer, deepening the kiss with a growing intensity.

Sarah stepped onto the terrace, she paused for a moment, taking in the sight of her brother and Annie. Clearing her throat to announce her presence, the sound cut through the intimate atmosphere. Annie instantly pulled away from William's embrace, her cheeks burning with embarrassment as she buried her face in his chest, overwhelmed by a rush of heat. The moment had been electric, and now the blush spread across her cheeks, deepening as she tried to regain her composure, acutely aware of Sarah's watchful gaze.

Sarah raised an eyebrow at her brother with a teasing smile. "Why don't you show Annie her room?" she suggested, her tone light but knowing.

Turning to Annie, she added, "We got your suitcase from your car this morning, so it's in your room, all ready for you."

With a cheeky grin directed at William, Sarah turned on her heel and sauntered away, leaving the two of them alone again. The air between Annie and William was thick with unspoken words, their earlier moment still lingering as they exchanged glances, both unsure of what came next.

William gazed at Annie; her cheeks still flushed from their kiss and leaned in to press his lips gently against hers. The sweetness of the moment quickened his heart, and he entwined their fingers as he took her hand. "Let's go," he murmured, leading her inside.

As they made their way through the house, William guided Annie up the elegant staircase. The soft carpet cushioned their footsteps, and the warmth of the home enveloped them like a comforting embrace. He sensed her nervousness as they approached the door to her room. With a gentle push, he opened it to reveal a beautifully decorated space filled with soft colours and a lovely view of the gardens outside.

"Oh, this is lovely," Annie exclaimed, her eyes lighting up as she walked to the window to take in the vibrant blooms and lush greenery beyond.

William looked at Annie, a warm smile spreading across his face. "Yes, it is," he replied, his gaze lingering on her. Annie turned to face him, sensing the deeper meaning behind his words, and a blush crept across her cheeks.

William took her hands and gently guided her toward the bed. "Come lay with me," he said softly, his voice filled with concern. "You need to rest; you promised the doctor."

Annie nodded, feeling exhausted but grateful for his care. She sat on the edge of the bed and lifted her shirt slightly to reveal the dark bruises where her ribs were injured. "It looks worse than it feels, I think," she said, her fingers tracing the edges of the discoloured skin.

William's eyes darkened with worry as he knelt beside her. He reached out and gently touched her uninjured side. "That looks painful, Annie... I hate seeing you hurt." His voice was thick with emotion as he carefully helped her settle onto the bed.

Annie offered a small smile. "It'll heal," she whispered, reaching for his hand as he lay down next to her, pulling her close but mindful of her injuries.

"I was so scared when you didn't arrive at ten last night," William whispered, his voice heavy with emotion. He tightened his grip on her hand, as if reassuring himself that she was really there.

Annie gently caressed his face, offering him a sweet smile. "Thank you for saving me… again."

"Thank God, I found you," he replied, relief washing over him.

Annie giggled. "I remember you saying that saving me was an occupation you'd gladly take on. How do you feel about it now?"

William smiled back. "I would still gladly take it on." Then his expression turned serious. "I'm getting your car checked to find out why the brakes failed."

"It was just an accident…" she tried to reassure him.

His expression shifted, concern furrowing his brow as he met her gaze. "I need to be sure," he said firmly but gently. "I can't let anything happen to you, Annie." Leaning closer, he lowered his voice to a whisper. "I promise, I won't let anything happen to you."

Annie smiled softly, tears shimmering in her eyes as she looked at him. "William, ever since I met you, you've protected me. I don't doubt you now." Her voice trembled slightly with sincerity.

William's heart swelled at her words. "Thank you for your trust," he replied, his tone warm and earnest. He reached out to brush a tear away from her cheek, feeling a deep sense of responsibility to keep her safe.

Annie gazed into his eyes and whispered, "I trust you more than anyone." She closed her eyes for a moment from exhaustion.

"You're tired. I should let you rest," he said gently.

"No, please stay with me, just for a little while," she replied, her voice softly pleading.

As Annie's eyelids grew heavier, she nestled against William, her breathing becoming slow and steady. A peaceful smile graced her lips as she gradually slipped into a blissful sleep.

William watched her, his heart swelling as he took in the softness of her features and the serenity that enveloped her. In that moment, he felt an overwhelming urge to express the depth of his feelings. "I love you, Annie," he whispered softly, knowing she wouldn't hear him.

The words hung in the air, a mix of vulnerability and warmth. He wasn't entirely ready to confront the reality of his feelings, but saying them out loud felt necessary, almost freeing. He knew that one day he would share this truth with her, but for now, he simply grateful to have her in his life.

William gently slid off the bed, grabbing the throw from the nearby chair. He laid it over her and pressed a soft kiss to her forehead before quietly leaving the room.

Chapter Thirteen

William made his way downstairs and stepped onto the terrace, where his parents and Sarah were seated, enjoying cool drinks in the afternoon sun.

Helen looked up as he approached, her expression warm and welcoming. "Oh, there you are! Where's Annie?" she asked.

William replied, trying to keep his tone casual, "She's lying down; she is very tired."

Sarah shot him a knowing smile, her eyes twinkling with mischief. "I bet she is."

Caught off guard, William shot her a surprised look, his eyes narrowing slightly as he silently warned her not to mention the incident she had witnessed earlier on the terrace.

William's parents remained blissfully unaware of the unspoken tension between him and Sarah. Henry leaned back in his chair, a thoughtful expression on his face. "I must say, William, she is lovely…, smart, too," he remarked, nodding in approval.

Helen, however, had a hint of sadness in her voice as she added, "It's a pity about her family. Not having her parents around so young must have been horrible."

William sat down on a nearby chair, took a deep breath, collecting his thoughts before he spoke. "Apparently, when her parents were married, her mother's family disowned her because they didn't approve of the match," he explained, glancing at his parents for their reaction. "So, she could actually have some family out there that she doesn't even know about."

His mother's brow furrowed with concern. "That's so sad," she said softly.

William nodded, continuing, "But Annie has no interest in finding them. She told me that her parents were very happy and in love, and as far as she's concerned, that's all that matters. She doesn't want to dig into the past or chase after people who rejected her parents."

William respected her choice to focus on the love her parents had shared rather than the pain of their loss.

Henry and Helen exchanged glances, their expressions a mix of empathy and understanding.

Annie slowly woke up, the sunlight filtering through the curtains and casting a warm glow in the room. She stretched, feeling the softness of the bed beneath her, and smiled as she recalled the peaceful sleep she'd had. Glancing at the clock, she realised she had slept for a couple of hours. She thought it was time to wash her hair and finally remove the uncomfortable patch on her head.

With determination, she got out of bed and made her way to the ensuite. As she stepped into the shower, the warm water cascaded over her, instantly soothing her sore muscles. She took a moment to relish the sensation before focusing on her hair and body, carefully washing herself while being mindful of the stitches on her forehead.

As she lathered her hair, her thoughts drifted to William, and how profoundly he had changed her life, it was more than a physical attraction, it was also deep and emotional connection. Well… it was on her part; she wondered if he felt the same.

After rinsing off the last of the soap, Annie took a deep breath and enjoyed the moment of calm. The thought of William in her mind, makes her heart race and cheeks flush. She found herself looking forward to seeing him again.

After her shower, Annie stepped out and wrapped a soft towel around herself, relishing the warmth and comfort it provided. She carefully patted herself dry, taking her time to ensure she didn't hurt her ribs or irritate the stitches. As she blow-dried her hair, she caught a glimpse of herself in the mirror and paused to examine the area where the patch had been.

With a sense of trepidation, she inspected the stitches. The cut was still visible, but the swelling had subsided significantly, allowing her to breathe a sigh of relief. A wave of gratitude washed over her as she realised that her long, wavy hair would help conceal the injury. The ability to hide the remnants of her ordeal allowed her to feel less self-conscious about her appearance.

As she smiled softly at her reflection, Annie took a moment to ensure her hair framed her face and hid the stitches as best as she could.

She turned to her suitcase, rummaging through it until she found a pair of knee-length shorts and a fitted shirt along with underwear. After slipping into her outfit, she turned back to the mirror. The reflection that greeted her was a pleasant surprise, while she was still a bit pale, she felt a sense of joy at how much she resembled her old self. The bright colours of her clothes added a cheerful touch, she felt a glimmer of confidence return.

Annie opened her bedroom door and stepped out into the hallway, the soft carpet cushioning her footsteps. As she took in her surroundings, she felt a mixture of curiosity and apprehension, unsure of where everyone was in the large house. Just as she was about to head down the stairs, Henry appeared from around the corner.

"Hello, Annie! You look much more refreshed now," he greeted her with a warm smile.

"Thank you! Yes, I feel so much better," she replied, returning his smile with genuine gratitude.

Henry's eyes lit up with enthusiasm. "I'd love to show you those original paintings I mentioned earlier. I'd really appreciate your thoughts on them."

Annie felt a thrill of excitement at the idea. "I'd love to see them," she replied, eager to engage in a conversation about art, something she was truly passionate about.

With that, Henry gestured for her to follow him, leading her further down the hallway. They arrived at a beautiful painting that depicted a serene landscape, complete with rolling hills and a majestic horse grazing in the foreground. The colours were vibrant, capturing the warmth of a golden sunset that bathed the scene in a soft glow.

Annie stepped closer, admiring the technique. "The colours are stunning! It looks like it was done with a palette knife," she remarked, her eyes sparkling with appreciation. "I love how the texture adds depth to the painting. It really brings the landscape to life."

Henry smiled, clearly pleased with her feedback. "I thought you'd appreciate the technique. It's one of my favourites."

After their discussion about the landscape painting, Henry led Annie into a well-lit room where an original Thomas Kinkade painting hung on the wall. It depicted an old shack nestled in a beautiful garden at twilight, the soft glow of lights shining through the windows, inviting and warm. The garden was filled with vibrant flowers and lush greenery, perfectly capturing the tranquility of the scene.

Annie was instantly captivated. "This is incredible," she said, stepping closer to examine the details. "The way the light spills from the windows creates such a cozy, nostalgic atmosphere. You can almost feel the warmth coming from inside the shack."

Henry nodded, appreciating her insight. "Kinkade had a unique ability to capture light and its effects on the landscape. It's like he painted the essence of home and comfort."

Annie continued to admire the painting, tracing her fingers along the frame. "It feels like a moment frozen in time," she mused. "You can imagine the stories that could unfold in that little shack."

Henry smiled, clearly enjoying the conversation and the connection he was building with Annie. Their discussion about art had flowed easily, creating a comfortable atmosphere between them.

Just then, Helen walked in, her warm presence brightening the room. "There you two are," she said cheerfully, glancing between them. Her gaze landed on Annie, and she smiled warmly. "Oh, you look much more refreshed! I bet you were glad to get that patch off."

Annie returned her smile, her cheeks flushing slightly. "Yes, my head feels much better now," she replied, a hint of relief in her voice. The lingering discomfort had been weighing on her, but the simple act of washing her hair and changing into fresh clothes had made a significant difference in her appearance and mood.

Helen's motherly instinct kicked in as she approached Annie, a genuine concern shining in her eyes. "I'm so glad to hear that. Now, you missed lunch, but you must come downstairs and have some afternoon tea on the terrace. William and Sarah are waiting for us."

With that, Helen took Annie's arm and started leading her to the terrace via the stairs, their footsteps echoing softly in the grand hallway.

As they arrived on the terrace, Helen called out to Sarah and William, "Look how wonderful Annie looks now!"

William stood up, his eyes lighting up as he admired her. "You do look so much better," he said, a warm smile spreading across his face. He moved to help Annie onto a chair at the table.

Annie settled into her seat, basking in the warmth of the sun and the comfort of William's family surrounding her. The weekend flew by, and she cherished every moment spent with them. William was attentive and kind, Sarah was fun and cheerful, and their parents were loving and welcoming.

When they returned to William's penthouse Sunday night after dropping Sarah off at her apartment, William turned to Annie, his expression a blend of softness and determination. "You should get some rest," he suggested gently, guiding her toward their bedroom. "I have a bit of work to finish, but I'll be in soon."

Annie smiled playfully. "Yes, sir," she laughed, lightening the mood.

William's gaze softened further. "I missed sleeping next to you," he confessed.

"I missed it too," Annie replied, her heartwarming at his words.

Annie stirred awake on Monday morning, the soft light filtering through the curtains. As she rubbed the sleep from her eyes, she noticed the stillness of the apartment around her. She sat up and glanced at the small note on the bedside table. It was neatly written:

Gone to work. Rest. If you need anything, call me. William.

A smile tugged at her lips at his thoughtfulness.

After enjoying a piece of toast for breakfast, Annie picked up her phone, her fingers trembling slightly as she dialled Sarah's number. After a few rings, her gallery assistant answered, her voice cheerful but laced with concern. "Hey, Annie! How are you feeling?"

"I'm okay," Annie replied, her voice steadier than she felt. "I just wanted to check in and make sure everything is running smoothly at the gallery."

"Everything is fine. I rescheduled your appointments for later this week," Sarah assured her. "Just focus on resting. You promised the doctor you'd take it easy for at least three days."

"Yeah, I know," Annie sighed, grateful for Sarah's support. "I'll be back to work tomorrow."

After hanging up, Annie tried to spend the day reading, hoping to lose herself in the pages of a book, but it didn't take long for her to realise it was pointless. Remembering she needed more things from her apartment, she called William.

He answered, concern evident in his voice. "Annie, are you okay?"

Annie laughed softly. "Yes, William, I'm fine. Stop fussing," she said, taking a breath. "I just wanted to let you know I'm taking a taxi to my apartment to grab some things."

"Can't it wait until tonight? I'll take you," he urged.

"I'm going out of my mind with boredom. I need something to do, and Jeremy is still locked up, so no one is going to hurt me," Annie pleaded.

William could hear her frustration. "Okay, just be careful. Let me know when you get home, I want to make sure you're safe."

"I promise," she replied.

Annie stepped out of William's apartment building, the crisp air brushing against her skin as she spotted the taxi waiting at the curb. She walked over quickly, nodding to the driver before slipping into the back seat. As the car pulled away, her mind wandered, the familiar city streets passing in a blur until they reached her own apartment building.

When they arrived, Annie thanked the driver and stepped out, her eyes drifting toward the building's entrance.

She took a deep breath before heading inside, stopping to pick up her mail before climbing the stairs, her footsteps echoing in the stillness of the hallway. As she reached her door, she hesitated, her hand hovering over the key. The door and frame had been repaired since the break-in, a faint reminder of the chaos that was now behind them.

With a steady hand, Annie unlocked the door, the quiet click of the lock breaking the silence as she stepped inside. She tossed her keys and the mail on the table. The apartment was neat and intact, back to its usual state. Moving through the rooms, she quickly gathered what she needed. Once she had everything, she sat down at the table and began sorting through her mail.

Her gaze landed on a thick envelope, its weight and the law firm's letterhead catching her attention. Curiosity piqued, she sat down and carefully tore it open. She unfolded the papers; her eyes scanned the first few lines of the cover letter. Her eyes widened in astonishment, her breath catching in her throat. The contents were shocking, something she had never anticipated.

Before Annie could fully process what she was reading, a sudden knock at the door startled her from her thoughts. She walked over and pulled it open. Standing before her was a man, his face twisted with rage and eyes ablaze with anger. Her blood ran cold, and in that instant, she realised the mistake she had made by opening the door.

Instinctively, her body tensed with fear. She tried to slam the door shut as quickly as her trembling hands would allow, but it was too late. The man shoved his way in, the force of his body slamming against the door, sending her stumbling backward. The door crashed shut behind him with a menacing thud, trapping her inside with him. Annie's heart pounded wildly in her chest as the room seemed to close in on her, the air thick with danger.

The intruder's voice was a harsh growl, dripping with rage. "You bitch; you need to come with me." His eyes were wild, the anger in them fierce and terrifying.

Annie's breath caught in her throat, her instincts screaming at her to move. She spun on her heels and darted past the table and chairs; her body fuelled by pure adrenaline. Behind her, she could hear the man barrelling after her, his heavy boots crashing into furniture, knocking over her table and chairs in his furious pursuit.

Her heart pounded in her ears as she dashed into the living area, her eyes scanning desperately for an escape. "Who are you? What do you want?" she cried, her voice shaking with fear.

But the man said nothing, his sole focus was on catching her, his face twisted in a mask of rage as he closed the distance between them.

The man lunged at her, his body slamming into hers with brutal force. Annie crashed against the wall, the impact knocking the air from her lungs, pain slicing through her already bruised ribs. A picture on the wall fell, shattering on the floor with a loud crash, glass scattering across the hardwood. Pain shot through her back, but she twisted desperately, slipping free from his grasp before he could tighten his hold.

Gasping for breath, she bolted toward the kitchen, her mind racing. She wasn't going to let him take her. She wasn't going to give up without a fight. Her hands shook as she yanked open a drawer, searching for anything, something to defend herself.

Just as Annie's fingers brushed the handle of a knife in the drawer, she felt a powerful grip seize her from behind. Her heart leapt into her throat as the intruder yanked her against his chest, his breath hot and ragged in her ear. The cold, sharp edge of a knife pressed against her throat, and she froze instantly, her body going rigid.

"Don't move," he hissed, the menace in his voice chilling her to the core. The blade bit lightly into her skin, she felt a drop of blood trickle down her neck, a clear warning of what would happen if she resisted. Annie's pulse pounded in her ears, fear surging through her as she stood there, trapped, her mind racing for a way out.

As the intruder adjusted his grip, Annie felt the slight loosening of his hold and seized her chance. She twisted her body sharply, trying to break free, but as she moved, he reacted with a violent swing of the knife. The blade swung through the air and caught her arm, slicing through her skin.

A sharp pain shot up her arm as the blade made contact, and Annie let out a gasp, stumbling back. Blood began to stream from the wound, dripping onto the kitchen floor in bright red drops. Her breath came in ragged gasps as she clutched her arm, backing away from him, the terror in her chest now mixed with the burning pain.

The intruder glared at Annie, his voice low and menacing as he advanced on her again. "Stop resisting, or you'll get hurt worse," he snarled, his eyes dark with fury. He held the knife out, its blade slick with her blood, a warning that he was ready to strike again if she didn't comply.

Annie's heart pounded, her body trembling from both fear and pain. She pressed her wounded arm against her chest, trying to stop the bleeding, but her mind raced, frantically searching for a way out.

"Don't run or I will hurt you again," the intruder growled, his tone ice-cold as his eyes flicked towards her bleeding arm. "Get a towel or something for your arm," he ordered, his voice now edged with impatience.

Annie, still in shock and trying to steady her shaking hands, nodded numbly. She turned toward a drawer, her mind racing but unable to come up with an escape plan. She pulled out two tea towels, her movements robotic, and clumsily wrapped them around her arm, trying to stifle the steady flow of blood.

In a strained, almost threatening voice, the man spoke again. "Now you're coming with me. Don't even think about running, or I won't be responsible for what happens next."

Annie's heart sank, realising how dire her situation had become. She glanced around the apartment but saw no way out. Nodding reluctantly, she felt a wave of cold fear wash over her as he grabbed her, pushing the knife into her back just enough to remind her of the danger she was in. He kept close to her body, hidden from view so that if anyone passed by, they wouldn't see the weapon.

With every step she took, she felt the cold steel of the blade and the oppressive weight of helplessness. She had no option but to follow his instructions, her mind frantically trying to understand why this was happening.

The intruder directed Annie toward a parked black van, his knife pressing into her back as they walked. The street was eerily quiet, with no one passing by to witness her predicament. Each step felt heavier than the last, her mind racing for a way to escape, but no opportunity presented itself.

When they reached the van, he roughly pushed her inside, following closely behind. Annie barely had time to brace herself before she was shoved to the cold metal floor. Panic surged through her as he quickly zip-tied her wrists and feet, the tight bindings digging into her skin. She winced as her injured arm began to throb, the lack of pressure causing the wound to bleed again.

Annie's breath coming in shallow gasps, fear tightening around her chest as the van door slammed shut, leaving her trapped and helpless.

The van roared to life as the man climbed into the driver's seat, his rough movements shaking the vehicle. Annie lay on the cold, hard floor, her body aching from the restraints, her injured arm burning with pain. The engine's growl filled her ears as the van pulled away, and she had no idea where he was taking her.

Fear gripped her, making it hard to think clearly. Her thoughts drifted to William, the man who had been so worried about her, she needed him now more than ever. A wave of longing and terror washed over her as she wished desperately for his protection. Her chest tightened, and she swallowed hard, trying to suppress the panic threatening to overwhelm her. *Was she ever going to see him again?*

The drive felt endless, every bump in the road jarring Annie's bound body. Time lost all meaning as she lay there, fear clutching her insides. The van finally came to a halt, and her heart pounded painfully in her chest. She heard the man's footsteps as he got out, and the door slid open with a grating screech.

Annie's breath hitched, terror consuming her. It was dark outside now, the last traces of daylight long gone. The man climbed back into the van, rough hands grabbing her. She tried to steel herself as he forced a scratchy sack over her head, her world plunging into blackness. Her pulse quickened, every nerve in her body screaming in panic.

He cut the zip ties from her ankles with a quick slash. "Get out," he ordered, his voice cold and emotionless.

Annie's body trembled as he yanked her to her feet, the zip ties still biting into her wrists. She could feel the tightness of the restraints digging into her skin. She stumbled as he shoved her out of the van, her sense of direction completely lost. Fear coursed through her veins, and she knew she had no choice but to follow his commands, every step making her feel more helpless.

Annie was pulled into a dimly lit house that reeked of mould and decay. The air was thick with a musty odour that made her stomach churn. The intruder dragged her through a narrow hallway, his grip unyielding, and pushed her into a small room.

As she stumbled onto an old, threadbare sofa, the fabric felt damp and grimy against her skin. He quickly zip-tied her ankles once more, the rough plastic biting into her flesh, ripped the sack off her head.

Before he left, he turned to her and said roughly, "Scream all you want; no one will hear you." The finality of his words sent a chill down Annie's spine. With a final shove, he slammed the door shut, the sound echoing ominously in the silence. As she heard the unmistakable sound of a slide bolt engaging, sealing her in the darkened room, a wave of panic washed over her. The reality of her isolation sank in, tightening its grip around her throat as she struggled to catch her breath. Just then, she heard the van start up and drive away, and a chilling thought crept in, she was utterly alone.

Chapter Fourteen

Shortly after William hung up with Annie, his phone rang again. Glancing at the screen, he saw it was the mechanic who was inspecting Annie's car. He answered quickly, still treating the brake failure as a precaution. With Jeremy in custody, the immediate danger seemed to have passed, but William wanted to be thorough, just in case.

As William brought the phone to his ear, he answered, "Hey Charlie, how's it going?"

Charlie's voice sounded tense. "William, I've got some news about Annie's car."

William's interest piqued. "Yes?"

"It wasn't an accident," Charlie said, his tone grim.

William felt a wave of dread wash over him. "What... what do you mean?"

"Someone cut the brake lines," Charlie explained. "Not all the way through, but just enough for the brake fluid to leak out slowly."

A sick feeling settled in William's stomach. "Are you seriously saying this was done on purpose?" He paused, the realisation hitting him like a punch. "Someone tried to hurt Annie?"

Charlie answered, "Yes, it had to have been cut that night. Based on the damage, it would've taken just about the time from the gallery to where the accident happened."

"But that can't be right," William replied, his mind racing. "Jeremy was in custody. He couldn't have cut it that night."

"William," Charlie said firmly, "it had to have been done that night. I'm certain of it."

"That means someone else is trying to hurt Annie," William muttered, the realisation hitting hard. Then it dawned on him, Annie had gone to her old apartment. Panic surged through him. "I've got to go, Charlie," he said urgently.

"Okay, but..." Charlie started, but William had already hung up.

William slipped his phone into his pocket and stood up from the desk, snatching his car keys. Without another thought, he left his office and told his secretary he needed to go out. His heart was pounding, and his mind raced he needed to find Annie.

As he stepped into the lift, the familiar hum of it descending felt oddly slow, heightening the tension building inside him. When the doors opened, he ran to his car and got in, gripping the steering wheel for a moment before starting the engine. The streets blurred past him as he drove, his thoughts solely focused on Annie.

William pulled into Annie's apartment block, he quickly made his way up to her apartment, feeling the trepidation in his chest.

When he reached her door, he knocked, but it swung open with the weight of his knock. He froze, staring at the slightly ajar door, a sinking feeling settling in his gut. *Why would she leave it open?* That wasn't like Annie.

Cautiously, William pushed the door open a little more, the heart feeling heavy. He was about to call out her name, but the word caught in his throat as his breath hitched. The apartment was completely trashed, furniture overturned, picture frames shattered, books and personal items strewn across the floor. His heart pounded in his chest, panic clawing at him.

William rushed through Annie's apartment, his heart racing as his eyes scanned the chaotic mess. His mind reeled, fear coursing through him as he frantically searched for her, calling her name, "Annie!" The overturned furniture and broken glass only fuelled his panic, but there was no sign of her.

Then, in the kitchen, he froze. His stomach churned as he saw a dark, crimson stain on the floor.

Blood.

His breath came in shallow gasps, his mind struggling to comprehend the scene. He dropped to his knees beside the blood, his hands shaking, trying to grasp what had happened. Annie was gone, and the blood told him something terrible had taken place.

William shakily pulled his phone from his pocket, his fingers trembling as he dialled the police. His voice was barely steady as he explained what he'd found, his gaze never leaving the pool of blood on the kitchen floor. "There's blood, Annie's not here, I don't know what happened," he stammered, his throat tight.

He didn't move after that. His legs felt rooted to the spot, the fear gripping him like a vice. Kneeling there, he could barely process anything beyond the persistent dread that something horrible had happened to Annie. Time seemed to stretch painfully, every second feeling like an eternity.

Finally, the sound of footsteps approached. Officer Grant and Officer Lee arrived; their faces set in concern as they entered the apartment. They found William still on the kitchen floor, his eyes wide and haunted. Officer Grant knelt beside him, gently placing a hand on his shoulder. "Mr. Banks, we're here now. We'll find out what happened. We'll find her."

William, still kneeling, felt the gravity of those words settle over him as he nodded numbly, hoping against hope they were true.

William slowly rose to his feet, his legs shaky beneath him, but his eyes sharp with fear and confusion. "Is Jeremy out of custody?" he asked, his voice tight.

Officer Grant shook his head firmly. "No, he's still in custody. There's no way he could've been involved in this."

William's heart sank as he ran a hand through his hair, frustration bubbling to the surface. "That means it wasn't him," he muttered, pacing as the weight of the realisation hit him. "It was someone else…" His voice cracked, and he put his head in his hands, feeling the crushing sense of helplessness.

"We thought she was safe," he said, his voice barely above a whisper. "That's why she come back here… we thought the danger was over." The words hung in the air, heavy with regret and fear.

Officer Grant stepped forward, his expression serious but compassionate. "Mr. Banks," he said gently, "we need to get you out of here. The crime scene team is on their way, and we need to gather evidence."

William looked up, his eyes clouded with worry, reluctant to leave the space where Annie had been last. "But what if she's…" he began, his voice faltering.

"We'll do everything we can to find her," Officer Grant assured him, his voice firm but calm. "But right now, we need to secure the scene. The sooner we can get to work, the sooner we'll have answers."

William hesitated for a moment, glancing back at the blood on the floor, then gave a slow nod. Reluctantly, he let Officer Lee guide him toward the door, feeling the crushing weight of uncertainty press down on him as they left the apartment.

William finally returned to his apartment after the police finished questioning him. The weight of the world pressed down on him, leaving him feeling lost and numb. Each thought was consumed by the desperate hope that Annie was okay. He sank onto his sofa, his heart heavy with worry, and pulled his phone from his pocket, his hands trembling slightly as he dialled.

When Henry answered, William's voice cracked, "Dad."

Recognising the pain in his son's voice, Henry immediately sensed something was wrong. "What's wrong, son?"

"Annie…" William choked out, "she has been kidnapped."

"What? Why? I thought they had the guy?" Henry's concern deepened.

"We were wrong. It's obvious someone else is involved because he's still in custody," William replied, his voice laced with anguish.

"Hang tight. We'll be there in an hour," Henry said firmly before hanging up, not waiting for a response.

With urgency, Henry called Helen, his voice quick and panicked as he relayed the news. Shock washed over her, but she quickly shifted into action. She rushed to their bedroom, gathering essentials in a flurry, knowing they needed to be with their son. Within five minutes, they were on their way, determination driving them through the night.

William's heart raced as he dialled Sarah's number. When she picked up, her voice was bright, filled with anticipation. "Hey big bro, what's up?"

But the weight of the moment crushed any hint of hope in his chest. "Sarah…," he said, his voice heavy with despair. "Annie… she's been kidnapped."

Silence fell on the line, her initial excitement evaporating into disbelief. "What! Are you serious?"

"Yes," William replied, his voice barely above a whisper. "Jeremy didn't take her. Someone else took her."

"Oh my God," Sarah breathed, the gravity of the situation hitting her like a freight train. "What do we do?"

"I don't know," William admitted, running a hand through his hair in frustration. "I'm just waiting for updates from the police."

"Hold on, I'm coming over," Sarah said, her tone shifting to one of determination. "I will be there soon."

William nodded even though she couldn't see him. "Thanks, Sarah."

As he hung up, he felt a flicker of comfort in knowing he wouldn't have to face this nightmare alone, but the fear for Annie's safety remained, a dark cloud looming over him.

Within fifteen minutes, Sarah arrived, her urgency evident as she rushed up to William's apartment. When he opened the door, the moment felt electric, heavy with emotion. Without hesitation, Sarah stepped inside and wrapped her arms around him, pulling him into a tight embrace. Tears slipped silently down her cheeks, soaking into his shirt.

"I can't lose her, Sarah," William said, his voice breaking under the weight of his fear. "She's the one."

"I know," Sarah replied, pulling back slightly to meet his gaze, her eyes glistening with tears. "I've known for a while."

William's heart ached at her words, the reality of their situation crashing down on him. He felt the warmth of her support, but the fear of losing Annie overshadowed everything else. Sarah squeezed his hand reassuringly, her presence grounding him in the chaos.

As Sarah moved about the kitchen, she busied herself with making a pot of coffee, her hands working mechanically as she tried to maintain a semblance of normalcy amidst the chaos. She watched the dark liquid drip and rise in the pot, the familiar ritual bringing her a momentary sense of calm. She felt the tension radiating from William as she handed him a cup of coffee and settled onto the sofa beside him, silently letting him know that she was there for him.

Forty minutes later, there was a knock at the door, shattering the silence that enveloped the apartment. Sarah rushed to answer it, her heart pounding as she opened the door to reveal their parents. Helen stepped inside first, her expression a mix of concern and love. Without hesitation, she moved straight to William and enveloped him in a tight embrace, holding him close as if to shield him from the weight of the world.

Henry followed closely behind, placing a reassuring hand on William's shoulder. "We're here, son," he said softly, his voice steady but filled with unspoken worry.

William stood frozen in their embrace, his eyes dry, his heart heavy. He hadn't cried yet; he felt numb, as if he were trapped in a nightmare he couldn't wake from. The warmth of his mother's arms was comforting, yet it did little to penetrate the cold dread that had settled deep in his chest. All he could think about was Annie and the terrible uncertainty of her fate.

All four of them sat in the living room, the weight of uncertainty heavy in the air. Words seemed inadequate, but their presence offered a comforting solidarity. Helen sat next to William, gently rubbing his back, while Henry maintained a steady hand on his shoulder. Sarah, across from them, kept stealing glances at her brother, wishing she could ease his pain.

As the clock ticked toward midnight, the tension grew thicker. Just when it felt like the silence might consume them, the sound of a knock on the door echoed in the room, Sarah rushed to open it. The door opened, revealing two detectives, their expressions serious yet purposeful. The room fell still, all eyes turning toward the newcomers as hope and fear mingled in the air, each of them bracing for the news they desperately needed but dreaded to hear.

The detectives settled into their seats across from William, their expressions serious as they prepared to deliver information that might change everything. "Mr. Banks," one of them began, his tone professional yet urgent, "we need to ask you some more questions. We're hoping you can shed some light on some new information that has come to our attention."

William straightened in his seat, a mix of anxiety and determination washing over him. "Yes, anything," he replied, his voice steady despite the turmoil swirling inside him.

"Are you aware that her maternal grandmother has left her a substantial estate in her will?" the detective continued, watching William closely.

"What?" William exclaimed, confusion flooding his features. "Annie didn't even know if she was still alive. She didn't even know her!" His heart raced as he processed this unexpected revelation, the implications swirling in his mind. *What could this mean for Annie? For her safety?*

The detectives exchanged glances, then one of them continued, "As we were searching for evidence, we came across some paperwork sent to Miss Spencer. It informs her that she is now an extremely wealthy woman."

William's brow furrowed as he processed this new information. "What do you mean?" he asked, his voice tight with concern.

"It appears this letter was only received by her today," the detective explained. "We contacted her grandmother's lawyer, who revealed that she discovered Annie's existence in the last year of her life. In light of that, she changed her will to leave everything to Miss Spencer."

William shook his head in disbelief. "Annie didn't even know her grandmother. She thought she was long dead," he said, his mind racing. The idea that Annie had inherited such wealth from someone she never knew added another layer of complexity to her already precarious situation. *How would this news affect her? What if it played a role in her kidnapping?*

Henry leaned forward, his eyes narrowing with concern. "Do you think this has something to do with her disappearance?" he asked, his voice steady despite the turmoil churning inside him.

The detectives exchanged glances, their expressions turning serious. "Yes," one of them replied, "it seems that Miss Spencer's grandmother was leaving her fortune to her nephew before she discovered knowledge of Miss Spencer's existence. We haven't been able to contact him, but when he found out he wasn't the beneficiary, he was reportedly furious."

William's heart sank as he absorbed this information. "So, he could be involved?"

The detective nodded grimly. "It's possible. He expressed intentions to contest the will, but the lawyer assured us that it's ironclad. Regardless, his anger could have driven him to act out, especially if he felt entitled to that inheritance."

Henry ran a hand through his hair, frustration and worry etched across his face. "We need to find Annie before this gets worse."

William's voice trembled with a mix of frustration and determination as he leaned forward, his fists clenched. "Annie wouldn't even care about the money," he insisted, his eyes blazing with conviction. "She's not like that. She wouldn't care."

The weight of his words hung in the air, a stark reminder of who Annie was, a woman driven by passion and kindness, not by wealth. He knew that deep down, her heart was far more valuable than any inheritance.

The detectives exchanged glances before one of them spoke, his tone serious yet measured. "We are still in the process of trying to locate Mr. Summers, but we haven't had much luck yet. We're also searching all the properties that her grandmother owned, hoping he might be using one of them as a hiding place."

William listened intently, his heart racing at the implications. The idea of Annie being at risk because of a family dispute made his stomach churn. He couldn't shake the feeling that time was running out, and every moment they spent searching was a moment Annie could be in danger.

Suddenly, one of the detectives' phones buzzed loudly, breaking the heavy silence in the room. He glanced at the screen and quickly answered, his expression shifting from serious to urgent. "Yes, this is Detective Marshall," he said, his voice steady as he listened intently.

After a moment, he straightened up, a spark of hope igniting in his eyes. "You found him? Where is he? At the police station?" He nodded as he absorbed the information, his mind racing with the possibilities.

Turning back to William, Henry, and Sarah, he announced, "We've located Mr. Summers. He's at the police station right now." The room filled with a mix of anxiety and anticipation, each family member's heart pounding at the prospect of uncovering new leads.

"Let's go," he urged, motioning for his partner to follow. The urgency in his voice propelled everyone into action as they prepared to leave the apartment, fuelled by a renewed sense of purpose.

William sprang to his feet, the urgency in his voice cutting through the tense atmosphere. "What about Annie?" he demanded, his eyes wide with desperation. "Was she with him?"

The detectives exchanged glances, the weight of their silence sending a chill through the room. William's heart raced as he waited for an answer, each second stretching out painfully. He needed to know that she was safe, that she hadn't been harmed.

Detective Marshall took a step forward, his expression sombre yet steady. "No, she wasn't, but we're going to try to find out as much as we can from Mr Summers. We'll keep you updated as soon as we have more information."

William clenched his fists, frustration and fear battling within him. "You have to find her. Please," he implored, his voice strained with emotion. The thought of Annie in danger was unbearable, they needed to bring her back.

The detectives nodded, their expressions resolute. "We're doing everything we can, Mr. Banks," Detective Marshall assured him, his voice firm. "We'll get to the bottom of this. You have our word."

With that, the detectives stepped out of the apartment, leaving a heavy silence in their wake.

Henry turned to William; concern etched on his face. "This is truly unexpected," he said quietly, his tone a mix of confusion and worry.

Helen's voice trembled with disbelief as she processed the shocking revelation. "She's an heiress? Annie didn't think she had any family. This is unbelievable." Her brow furrowed, a mixture of confusion and concern washing over her. She glanced at William, searching his face for any sign that this news could somehow change the gravity of their situation. "How could she not know? And now, with all this… it's just so overwhelming." Helen shook her head in disbelief, struggling to reconcile the image of the woman her son loves with the sudden complexities of wealth and family.

William sank back into the sofa, frustration boiling inside him. "She wouldn't care; she wouldn't even care about the money," he spat, his voice edged with anger. The realisation that someone could use Annie's newfound wealth as a motive for her abduction ignited a fierce protectiveness in him. "He took her because of the money," he continued, the words laced with bitterness as he ran a hand through his hair. "She wouldn't care about any money!" Each thought felt like a punch to the gut, amplifying his helplessness and fear. William's mind raced with a mix of worry and rage, picturing Annie in danger, exploited for something she had never even wanted.

Henry, Helen, and Sarah exchanged worried glances, their expressions a mixture of concern and fear. They knew William to be an even-tempered man, steady in the face of adversity. But now, as he seethed with anger, it was clear that the situation was taking a toll on him.

Henry's brow furrowed, contemplating how to reach his son and calm the storm brewing within him. Helen's heart ached for William; she could see the anguish in his eyes, the way his fists clenched at his sides. Sarah, sensing the tension, leaned slightly forward, placing her hand on his knee to try to absorb some of his turmoil.

Chapter Fifteen

Annie stirred from a fitful sleep, her body aching and her mind clouded with confusion. The dim, dingy room surrounded her like a suffocating shroud, the stale, disgusting smell clawing at her throat and making her stomach churn. She blinked against the darkness, straining to remember how she had ended up in this hellhole, but her thoughts were foggy and scattered.

The man hadn't returned, leaving her in a state of anxious anticipation mixed with despair. Long hours of being bound had caused her hands and feet to lose feeling, the zip ties biting into her skin, and she couldn't remember the last time she had felt normal. In a futile effort to keep the blood flowing, she wiggled her toes and fingers, desperate for any sensation that would remind her she was still alive.

An urgency to relieve herself twisted in her gut, but there was no way to escape her situation. It was painfully clear that if she couldn't hold it any longer, she would have to go where she sat, adding humiliation to her already unbearable predicament. As the reality of her captivity sank deeper, Annie's mind spiralled into a frantic search for answers. Why was this happening to her? What had she done to deserve this? The questions echoed in her mind, intensifying her sense of helplessness.

As the sun began to rise, its faint light seeped through the grimy boarded window, casting a muted glow in the dingy room. Annie squinted at the sliver of illumination, realising with a sinking feeling that she had been trapped here for at least twelve hours. Time had become meaningless in her captivity, but the light signalled another day without her freedom.

Panic surged within her as she pondered her situation. *Were they looking for her? Did anyone even know she was missing?* William would surely wonder where she was if she didn't show up at home. She had vanished without a trace.

Her mind raced with possibilities. *Had William sensed something was wrong? Did he suspect that something terrible had happened?* She yearned for his presence more than ever, wishing he could come and rescue her from this nightmare. The realisation that she was utterly alone tightened its grip around her chest, leaving her breathless and afraid.

The detectives arrived back at William's apartment at noon the next day, their expressions serious as they entered the living room filled with a heavy tension.

William stood immediately, his heart racing with hope and dread. The lead detective wasted no time, his tone firm as he addressed William and the others.

"We've questioned Mr. Summers," he began, locking eyes with William. "We found blood in the back of a van he owns. So he admitted to taking Annie, but at this stage, he refuses to divulge her location."

William felt a surge of frustration, his fists clenching at his sides. "What do you mean he won't tell you?" he demanded, his voice strained. "He has to tell you! You have to find her!"

The detective nodded, understanding the desperation behind William's words. "We're doing everything we can. Our team is currently searching each property that her grandmother owned. There are quite a few, so it's taking some time to go through them all thoroughly."

Helen gasped softly, covering her mouth with her hand as she absorbed the weight of the situation. "How could he do this? Why would he take her?" She murmured, her voice trembling.

Henry placed a reassuring hand on her shoulder, his expression grim. "We need to stay strong and focused," he urged. "We have to trust that they'll find her."

As the detectives exchanged glances, William's heart sank. Each passing moment felt like an eternity, and the thought of Annie suffering alone only fuelled his anger and fear.

As the detectives prepared to leave, one of them moved toward the door, his phone buzzing insistently in his pocket. He pulled it out, glancing at the screen before answering. "Detective Harris," he said, his voice steady but alert.

A moment later, his expression shifted from routine professionalism to a mix of disbelief and urgency. "What? You're sure?" he asked, his eyes widening. "Alright, we're on our way."

He quickly turned back to the room, his voice cutting through the heavy atmosphere. "We found her! She's alive!"

William's heart surged at the news, his breath catching in his throat. "Where is she?" he asked, desperate for more details.

The detective raised a hand to calm him, urgency in his tone. "We're still gathering information, but we've located her at one of the properties. We need to head out now to secure the area and ensure her safety."

"Please, just get her home," William urged, his voice cracking with emotion.

"Hang tight," the detective assured him, and with that, the officers rushed out, leaving William and his family in a whirlwind of hope and anxiety.

Helen grasped Henry's hand, her eyes glistening with tears of relief. "Thank God, they found her," she whispered, disbelief colouring her words.

Sarah let out a breath she didn't realise she was holding, whispering, "Thank God," as she collapsed onto the sofa. Her body sagged with relief, the weight of worry finally lifting as hope began to seep back into the room.

William stood frozen for a moment, processing the news, the weight of his worry lifting slightly. "We need to go with them," he said, determination flooding his veins. "I can't just sit here."

Henry placed a firm hand on William's shoulder, halting him in his tracks as he was about to follow the detectives out the door. "William, we can't go with them. We'd only be in their way. You have to trust them to do their job," he urged, his voice steady but gentle.

William's frustration bubbled beneath the surface. "But what if they don't get there in time? What if…"

"Stop," Henry interrupted, his grip tightening slightly. "You have to believe that they're doing everything they can. If we go, we'll just be another distraction. We need to stay focused and wait for updates."

With a heavy heart, William reluctantly agreed, sinking back onto the sofa, his head in his hands. The familiar feeling of helplessness washed over him, eating at his insides. "I'm terrified, Dad," he admitted, his voice breaking. "Nothing can happen to her."

Henry moved to sit beside his son, the weight of his own worry etched on his face. "She's strong, William. And they've found her. That's the most important thing. We have to believe she's going to be okay."

As William stared blankly at the floor, a whirlwind of anxiety and dread twisted in his stomach. The silence in the room felt suffocating, amplifying his fear for Annie, the woman he loved. All he could think about was the possibility of losing her, and it terrified him more than he could articulate.

Helen looked at William with a mix of concern and determination. "You need to take a shower and change," she urged gently.

He shook his head. "No, I can't," he replied, his voice heavy with worry.

She softened her tone, knowing how much Annie meant to him. "William, when we need to go to her, you don't want her to see you like this," she said, gesturing to his unkempt appearance. "You need to be strong for her. Please, just a quick shower."

He hesitated, the desire to stay rooted in the moment battling with the realisation that he needed to pull himself together. With a reluctant sigh, he finally nodded. "Okay, fine. Just give me a minute."

Annie sat huddled on the grimy floor, her body weak, and her spirit fading as the stench of her confinement surrounded her. It had to be midday, though she couldn't be certain, time had blurred into an endless nightmare. Her hope had begun to dwindle, replaced by a sinking feeling of despair.

Then she heard it, faint at first, but unmistakable. Footsteps. Her heart lurched in her chest, panic rising. *Was it the man coming back? Or someone else?* She held her breath, straining to listen.

The footsteps grew louder, closer. She tensed, every nerve on edge, ready to face whatever was coming. Then, cutting through the oppressive silence, she heard a voice.

"Annie! Annie Spencer!"

Her heart raced as hope flickered back to life. It wasn't him. It wasn't her abductor. It was someone looking for her, someone trying to save her.

Annie's heart pounded as she gathered every ounce of strength she had left. "Help! I'm in here! Help!" Her voice cracked with desperation, but it was loud, carrying through the silence of the house.

A moment later, she heard a response. "Annie, we're on our way!" Relief flooded through her, tears welling in her eyes.

The sound of the bolt sliding open was like music to her ears. The door creaked, and light spilled into the dingy room, momentarily blinding her. Squinting against the brightness, she saw a figure standing in the doorway, a policewoman, her face full of concern.

"It's okay, you're safe now," the officer said softly, stepping toward Annie.

The policewoman quickly knelt beside Annie, pulling out a small knife to cut the zip ties around her ankles. The bindings fell away, and then she moved to Annie's wrists, slicing through the ties there as well. The moment her hands were free, excruciating pain hit. Annie gasped, feeling a sharp, burning sensation in her hands and feet, like pins and needles multiplied a thousand times.

A male officer entered the dim room, his voice steady but gentle. "We have some people who will be very happy to know you're safe."

Annie instinctively tried to stand, but the female officer placed a calming hand on her shoulder. "No, you need to wait for the paramedics," she said firmly. "We need to make sure you're okay."

Annie nodded, her body trembling from relief and exhaustion. Tears streamed down her face, her chest heaving as the weight of the past hours began to lift.

About five minutes later, the paramedics arrived, their movements swift and efficient. One of them knelt beside Annie, gently taking her arm to check the deep gash. "This looks nasty," he muttered under his breath, before carefully cleaning and dressing the wound. Meanwhile, another paramedic examined her hands and feet, checking for circulation and treating the raw cuts on her wrists and ankles where the zip ties had bitten into her skin.

"You're going to be okay," the paramedic reassured her, applying bandages. Once they were confident, she was stable, they moved her carefully onto a stretcher. Annie lay back, feeling the weight of the ordeal slip away as they lifted her and began carrying her out of the dark, foul-smelling room.

The sunlight hit her face as they stepped outside, a burst of fresh air filling her lungs as she was finally taken out of her prison.

Annie was gently lifted into the ambulance, the paramedics securing her as the doors closed with a soft thud. The vehicle began moving, the sound of the siren fading into the background as Annie's mind drifted in and out of exhaustion. The paramedics continued monitoring her, offering quiet reassurances, but the world felt surreal, as if it was happening to someone else.

When they arrived at the hospital, she was wheeled straight into the emergency room. The doctor quickly examined her arm, noting the deep cut. "We'll need to stitch this," he said softly. Annie nodded, watching as he cleaned the wound, the sensation sharp but distant. After a quite a few careful stitches, he looked up and asked, "Would you like a shower before I treat the rest of your injuries?"

Annie's voice was hoarse, but she managed, "Yes, please."

The doctor gestured to a nurse. "Take her to the showers, but don't leave her alone. Once she's done, let me know so I can take care of the cuts on her ankles, wrists, and neck."

The nurse helped Annie up slowly, guiding her to a nearby room. As the warm water hit her skin, Annie felt a sliver of relief wash over her, cleansing both her body and some of the fear that had gripped her for so long.

After the shower, Annie was dressed in two hospital gowns for modesty and comfort. The nurse carefully wheeled her back to her room, where the doctor was waiting. He methodically cleaned the cuts on her wrists and ankles, the antiseptic stinging as it touched her raw skin.

"You're doing great," he said gently, applying bandages over the worst of the wounds. When he reached the cut on her neck, he placed a small patch over it, ensuring it was protected from infection. Once her ankles and wrists were wrapped securely, the nurse inserted an IV drip into her arm, explaining that it was to help with her dehydration.

Finally, Annie was settled in the hospital bed, her body heavy with exhaustion. The room was quiet, save for the soft beeping of machines monitoring her vitals. As her eyes fluttered open and closed, she drifted in and out of sleep, her mind still reeling from everything that had happened but her body finally beginning to find some much-needed rest.

Annie was startled awake by the soft knock on the door, followed by two detectives stepping into the room. Their expressions were calm but serious. "Miss Spencer," one of them said gently, "I'm Detective Harris, and this is Detective Young." They both offered her a kind but professional smile.

Annie nodded, her mind still foggy from sleep. "We need to ask you some questions about what happened," Detective Harris said, pulling out a small notepad.

Annie took a deep breath and began to recount everything, her abduction, the drive, being held in the filthy room. The detectives listened carefully, nodding as they took notes. When she finished, there was a brief pause before Detective Young spoke again.

"We've discovered who was behind this. It was your cousin."

Annie's heart sank. "Because of the inheritance?" she asked, already knowing the answer but needing to hear it out loud.

The detectives exchanged a glance before Detective Harris confirmed, "Yes, that's right. He was angry about being cut out of your grandmother's will. He wanted the fortune, and when he realised it wasn't his, he decided to take matters into his own hands."

Annie stared at the ceiling, her voice barely a whisper as she muttered, "I don't even want it…" Her words hung in the air, heavy with exhaustion and disbelief. She hadn't asked for any of this, the money, the danger, the betrayal by a family member she didn't even know.

The detectives exchanged a glance before Detective Harris gave her a soft, reassuring smile. "We understand, Miss Spencer. Rest now. You've been through a lot."

Without another word, they quietly gathered their things and left the room, the door closing with a gentle click behind them, leaving Annie alone with her thoughts.

Chapter Sixteen

A knock at the door, Sarah quickly opened it, her heart pounding. Two detectives stood on the other side, their faces calm yet serious. She stepped aside, letting them in.

They made their way to the living room, where William sat on the edge of the sofa, his hands clenched tightly in his lap. The detectives took seats across from him.

Detective Harris spoke first, his tone steady. "Mr. Banks, we've found Annie. She's safe."

William's breath caught, his entire body sagging in relief. "Is she okay?" he asked, his voice shaky with emotion.

"She's been taken to the hospital. She has some injuries," Harris continued, "but nothing life-threatening. She's going to be alright."

William closed his eyes for a moment, overwhelmed by the news. "Thank you," he whispered, his voice thick with gratitude. "Thank you so much."

"What hospital?" he asked quickly, his need to see Annie taking over.

The detectives told him, and after a round of handshakes, Henry and William both expressing their deep gratitude, the detectives left quietly, leaving the family to process the news. William stood, already mentally preparing to rush to the hospital.

Henry stood up and looked at his family, his voice calm but urgent. "Okay, let's go. I'll drive."

They all nodded in agreement, grabbing their coats and heading for the door. The ride to the hospital was tense, with everyone focused on getting there as quickly as possible.

When they arrived at the emergency department, William rushed to the reception desk. "I'm here for Annie Spencer," he said, breathless with anticipation.

The nurse glanced at the chart, then nodded. "Yes, she's here. But only one visitor at a time, I'm afraid."

Without hesitation, everyone looked at William, silently understanding he should be the one to see her first. He didn't waste time, following the nurse down the hallway, his heart pounding. When they reached Annie's room, the nurse opened the door, and William stepped inside.

Annie lay on the bed, asleep, her face pale, her body wrapped in hospital gowns. His gaze immediately locked onto the patch on her neck and the bandages around her wrists. A surge of anger flared in him. *How could someone hurt her like this?* But he forced it down. She didn't need his anger right now.

He walked quietly to her bedside and bent down, pressing a gentle kiss to her forehead. As his lips touched her skin, Annie stirred, her eyes fluttering open. For a moment, they locked eyes, her weary gaze meeting his, filled with relief and something unspoken.

"William…" she whispered, her voice weak but filled with emotion.

"I'm here," he whispered back, his voice soft but full of promise.

As Annie gazed up at William, tears filled her eyes, spilling over as she took in his familiar, comforting presence. It felt surreal to see him here, alive, and safe, after everything that had happened.

"Shh, it's okay. You're safe now," William reassured her, his voice low and soothing.

Annie blurted out, "I was so scared."

William's heart ached at her words. "Annie, I'm so sorry. It's all my fault. I promised I'd keep you safe…"

His statement lingered in the air, the weight of it heavy. Annie met his gaze and said softly, "Please don't, William. Don't blame yourself."

"But…" he started.

"No 'buts.' We had no idea about my grandmother or cousin. Please, don't do this. I'm begging you."

"Okay," he said reluctantly. "How do you feel? Where does it hurt?"

"My arm is cut; I'll probably have a scar. My wrists and ankles are pretty scraped up. But I don't care, as long as I'm here with you."

William bent down and kissed her gently on the forehead. He explained, "The mechanic who was looking at your car called me after you left for your apartment and told me your brake lines were cut. Jeremy couldn't have done it. I rushed over to your apartment, but I must have just missed you," his voice thick with emotion, "I was terrified when I found your apartment all smashed up." He shuddered, then continued. "When I found blood on the kitchen floor, at that moment, I thought my life was over."

Annie shivered as she recounted her terrifying ordeal. "I was so scared. I had no idea why he took me. He didn't tell me anything; he just grabbed me and locked me up."

"Shh, it's over now," William reassured her, his voice firm yet gentle. "And you're not going back to that apartment alone, ever. I'm not letting you out of my sight."

Annie managed a soft laugh despite her lingering fear. "That might be a bit hard when you have to go to court."

William chuckled softly, the warmth of his affection filling the room.

Annie lifted her arms weakly toward William, her longing for his embrace overwhelming her pain. With a gentle touch, he gathered her into his arms, careful not to upset her injuries. The warmth of his body enveloped her, and she felt a sense of safety.

William leaned in, pressing his lips softly against hers, a tender kiss filled with unspoken promises and relief. He then peppered kisses across her forehead, her cheeks, and the bridge of her nose, his heart swelling with gratitude that she was alive and safe.

Annie let out a soft, joyous laugh, her eyes sparkling with relief.

"Unfortunately, I have to leave and send Sarah in; they are only allowing one person in at a time," William said reluctantly, his arms still around her holding her gently.

Annie opened her mouth to protest when the door swung open. William's arms remained around her as Sarah, along with their parents, walked in.

"Finally," Sarah exclaimed, a grin spreading across her face. "I told the nurse we weren't waiting any longer. Annie had to see her family *now*."

Helen chuckled, "She is very persuasive when she wants to be."

William released Annie and stood up, allowing his parents and Sarah to move in closer to Annie. They enveloped her in warm hugs, their expressions a mix of relief and love, as they surrounded her with support.

Annie took a deep breath, gathering her thoughts as she looked at William's family. "I... I don't even know where to start," she said, her voice trembling slightly. "He just took me, locked me up, and never said why."

Helen's eyes widened in concern, and Henry's jaw tightened with worry, but Annie pressed on. "Just before he arrived, I opened an envelope from a lawyer and it said that my maternal grandmother left me everything she owned, her entire fortune… she apparently passed away six weeks ago. I didn't even know she existed."

She paused, searching their faces for understanding. "Then he turned up and forced his way in, I fought him off, but I wasn't strong enough. Why would he want to hurt me over money I never even wanted?" Her voice broke at the end, the weight of the revelation settling heavily in the room.

Henry said, "Money makes people do some bad things."

Helen and Sarah nodded in agreement.

Then Sarah asked cheerfully, "So, how rich are you?"

Helen and Henry responded in unison, "Sarah!"

Annie laughed, then revealed the figure the estate was worth. The room fell silent as all four looked at her in astonishment.

Annie looked at them, her expression steady despite their reaction. "It's not going to change me," she said firmly, her voice calm and resolute. She could see their shock, but she wanted them to understand that no matter the fortune left to her, she remained the same person.

Sarah finally regained her composure, a soft smile spreading across her face as she looked at Annie. "We know, Annie," she reassured her, her voice steady. Laughter filled the room, a balm for the tension that had hung over them.

Soon after, Henry, Helen, and Sarah took their leave, relief evident on their faces as they departed, grateful that Annie was safe and sound.

William settled onto the side of the bed, gently holding Annie's hand. She looked up at him, concern flickering in her eyes. "You're not worried about this inheritance, are you?"

William shook his head, a soft smile on his lips. "No, why would I be? It's yours."

Annie sighed, her expression a mix of frustration and sorrow. "Honestly, I wish I never got it," she admitted. "But I can't leave it to my cousin, not after what he did."

William's expression darkened, anger flashing in his eyes. "No," he said firmly, his voice steady but fierce. "The only thing he deserves is to be in jail."

Annie felt an overwhelming fatigue wash over her, her eyelids heavy as she spoke. "Do you know when I can get out of here?"

William glanced at her; concern etched on his face. "I can go ask if you'd like."

But as Annie studied him, she noticed the dark circles under his eyes and the weariness in his posture. "You need to go and get some rest," she urged softly.

William opened his mouth to protest, but Annie cut him off. "When is the last time you slept?"

"Sunday night," he admitted, guilt creeping into his tone.

"Then you should go home," Annie insisted, her voice gentle yet firm.

William shook his head, his expression a mix of concern and affection. "I don't want to leave you," he said, his voice low.

"That's sweet," Annie replied, offering a small smile, "but you need to get some sleep, and so do I."

Reluctantly, William sighed. "Okay, but I will be back in the morning."

Annie nodded, her heart lifting at his promise. "I look forward to it."

He stood up, leaning down to press his lips against hers in a tender kiss.

William stepped out of the hospital, the brisk evening air hitting him as he made his way to the nearest taxi stand. His mind was still racing, thoughts of Annie flooding his consciousness, but he forced himself to take a deep breath and focus on getting home.

Once he arrived at his apartment, he found Sarah and his parents bustling about in the kitchen, the smell of something comforting wafting through the air. "You're back!" Sarah exclaimed, relief evident on her face.

"Yeah," William replied, a weary smile breaking through.

"How is she?" Helen asked.

"They're taking good care of her," William said, his voice steady with reassurance. Then, after a brief pause, he added, "I'm going to ask Annie to marry me."

Helen's face lit up with joy. "That's wonderful, William," she beamed.

Henry clapped his son on the back, pride shining in his eyes. "Well done, son."

Sarah, practically bouncing with excitement, squealed, "I knew it! I told you you'd love her!"

The atmosphere was warm but tinged with exhaustion as they sat down for an early dinner. Plates of steaming pasta and fresh salad filled the table, and they ate in companionable silence, each lost in their own thoughts.

After the meal, William helped clear the table, the fatigue settling in deeper now. They all exchanged quiet goodnights, and one by one, they retreated to their rooms, the weariness of the day weighing heavily on them.

William finally collapsed onto his bed, the events of the past few days flooding back. But despite the fatigue, a small flicker of hope ignited within him, knowing that Annie was safe and that he would see her again in the morning.

"Good morning, Annie. How are you feeling today?" the doctor asked cheerfully as he walked into the hospital room.

"I'm feeling okay this morning, thank you," she replied with a smile.

The doctor's expression shifted slightly as he glanced at her chart. "I have some blood test results we need to discuss."

Annie's smile faded. "Is everything alright?"

"Yes, yes," the doctor reassured her, "but there's something you need to know." He paused, his tone gentle. "You're pregnant."

Annie stared at him, her voice barely a whisper. "Really?"

"Yes, congratulations," the doctor said with a warm smile.

"Thank you, doctor," Annie replied, her face glowing with the news.

"Now, you're cleared to go home today. I'll have your discharge papers ready soon," he continued. "Make sure to rest and take care of those wrist and ankle wounds. You'll need to get your stitches out in seven to ten days, and your local doctor can handle that." He paused, looking at her kindly. "And of course, you'll need to follow up with your doctor about the pregnancy as well."

"Thank you, doctor," she said sincerely.

"You're welcome, dear. Take care of yourself," he replied, gently patting her hand.

As the excitement of the news settled in, Annie's mind began to race. How is William going to take this? she wondered, her heart skipping a beat. They hadn't talked about anything this serious. She didn't even know if William loved her, she knew he cared, but does he love me...? *Does he even want children?*

But then, a wave of warmth washed over her. I love him, she realised, the truth of it filling her with a quiet sense of joy. And now, she was carrying his child.

I'm so happy I'm pregnant, she thought, her hand instinctively resting on her stomach. Wow. The reality of it all was overwhelming yet beautiful. I'm going to be a mum.

William felt a renewed sense of energy after a restful night's sleep, the worries of the past few days temporarily lifted as he drove to the hospital. The morning sunbathed the streets in a warm glow, and he couldn't help but smile as he thought of seeing Annie again.

Upon arriving at the hospital, he made his way to her room, his heart racing with anticipation. When he walked in, he was greeted by an unexpected sight: Annie was out of bed and sitting in a chair by the window, looking out into the sunlight. The sunlight illuminated her face, casting a soft halo around her as she turned to look at him.

"Good morning, sweetheart," William said, his voice warm and full of affection.

"Morning," Annie replied, a smile breaking through her fatigue, her eyes sparkling with life.

He walked over and leaned against the bed, his gaze never leaving her. "How are you feeling this morning?" he asked softly.

Annie's eyes sparkled with excitement as she looked up at William. "I can go home today!" she exclaimed, her voice filled with joy. "The doctor just has to sign my discharge papers. I just have to look after my wrists and ankles and get the stitches out in a week."

William's heart swelled at her enthusiasm, and a smile spread across his face, relief washing over him. "That's amazing, Annie! I can't wait to get you home," he said, stepping closer.

"I can't wait to be back too," Annie replied, her smile soft and dreamy.

Chapter Seventeen

After Annie was discharged from the hospital William insisted on taking her to her apartment to collect some of her belongings. He knew it would be hard for her, but they couldn't avoid it forever. As they pulled up in front of the building, Annie grew quiet, her hands tightening in her lap. William noticed the shift in her mood, reaching over to give her hand a gentle squeeze.

When they reached the door, the sight of the police tape still stretched across it hit Annie hard. Her breath caught in her throat, and she felt a rush of fear and sadness. Memories of that day, the confusion, the terror, flooded back. Tears stung her eyes as she stood frozen in the hallway, staring at the tape.

William stepped in front of her, his presence a grounding force. "You can do this," he said softly, brushing a hand across her cheek.

Annie blinked back tears and shook her head. "I know, I thought I was fine, but…seeing this…" She trailed off, feeling the weight of everything crashing back.

William wrapped his arms around her, pulling her close. "We'll just grab what you need and get out of here. You don't need to stay long." His voice was calm, soothing, and it gave her the strength to nod in agreement.

Together, they carefully stepped inside. The apartment felt cold and unfamiliar now, like a space invaded by darkness. Annie looked around at the mess, the broken glass, the overturned furniture, and a sob escaped her. This place had once been her sanctuary, and now it was a crime scene. William stayed by her side, silently offering his support.

As they walked through the rooms, gathering her clothes and essentials, Annie couldn't help but feel the weight of what had happened here. But with William's steady presence, she managed to keep it together, knowing that as long as she had him by her side, she wouldn't have to face it alone.

After gathering Annie's belongings from her apartment, William drove them to his penthouse, his hand resting gently on her knee as a silent reassurance throughout the drive. The weight of the past few days lingered, but with every passing moment, Annie felt more at ease knowing she wasn't facing any of it alone.

When they arrived at William's penthouse, the warmth of the place hit Annie immediately. It was a stark contrast to the cold, eerie feeling of her apartment.

As soon as they stepped through the door, Henry and Helen were waiting with open arms. Helen was the first to rush over, pulling Annie into a gentle but heartfelt hug.

"We're so glad you're safe, sweetheart," Helen said, her voice thick with emotion. Henry stood behind her, offering Annie a kind smile as he nodded in agreement.

Annie smiled weakly, still processing everything. "Thank you," she whispered, feeling grateful for their support.

"Sarah is at the gallery," Henry explained, stepping forward. "But she'll be back later. She wanted to make sure everything's running smoothly."

"That sounds like Sarah," Annie replied with a small laugh, the tension in her chest easing slightly in the familiar comfort of William's family.

Helen stepped back, looking her over with a mix of relief and concern. "Are you alright, dear? Do you need anything? Food, water, just let us know."

"I'm okay, really," Annie assured them, though exhaustion still clung to her. She glanced over at William, who smiled at her with a look that made her feel safe.

"You're home now," William said softly, wrapping an arm around her shoulder. "Let's get you settled in."

After Henry and Helen exchanged knowing glances and headed out to the terrace, William turned to face Annie, gently took her hand, and led her to the bedroom. The atmosphere in the room felt quieter, more intimate now that they had a moment alone.

Annie looked at William and softly said, "I think I'd like to take a bath. Could you help me with these bandages?"

William nodded; his face serious as he guided her to the bathroom. He carefully began to peel away the bandages from her wrists and ankles, his hands gentle but his expression darkening with each layer he removed. The raw, red marks left behind from the bindings filled him with a quiet anger, the reality of what she'd been through settling heavily on him.

When he reached for the patch on her neck, his movements slowed. As he peeled it away, revealing the deep cut beneath, William's breath caught in his throat. The wound was a painfully stark reminder of how close he had come to losing her. The anger in his eyes softened into something deeper, an overwhelming fear that gripped his heart.

He gently touched the skin around the cut, his voice low and gravelly, "Annie…"

She looked up at him, her eyes tired but steady. "It's okay, William. I'm here."

But William couldn't shake the image of her lying there, hurt, and vulnerable. The thought of what could have happened made his chest tighten. "I almost lost you," he whispered, the words filled with a mixture of fear and relief.

Annie reached out, placing her hand on his to reassure him. "But you didn't. I'm here, and I'm safe, with you."

William moved to the bath, turning the hot water on to fill the tub. The sound of rushing water filled the air, and steam began to rise, creating a warm and inviting atmosphere. He tested the temperature with his hand, ensuring it was just right, then stepped back to wait for the tub to fill.

Once the tub was ready, William returned to Annie, taking her hand and guiding her toward the bath. As they stepped into the warm water together, Annie winced slightly at the pain from her wounds on her ankles. William settled in behind her, wrapping his arms around her as they both sank into the soothing embrace of the water. He lathered a washcloth and began gently washing Annie's shoulders.

"Mm, that's nice," Annie moaned softly, leaning into his touch.

William continued to wash her arms, being particularly careful around her wrists. "You're so beautiful," he said, his voice filled with warmth and admiration.

Annie leaned back against William, her heart racing as she felt the warmth of his body enveloping her. The comforting embrace of the water made her feel safe and vulnerable all at once. After a moment of silence, she took a deep breath, gathering her courage.

"William," she began softly, her voice trembling with emotion. "I need to tell you something…"

"What is it, Annie? You can tell me anything," he replied gently, encouraging her with a warm smile.

"I love you." The words hung in the air between them, a blend of fear and relief washing over her.

William paused, his breath catching as he processed her confession. He turned her slightly to face him, searching her eyes for sincerity. "You really mean that?" he asked, his voice barely above a whisper.

"More than anything," Annie affirmed, her gaze steady and earnest.

A smile spread across William's face, lighting up his features. "I love you too, Annie," he confessed, his heart swelling with joy. "I fell in love with you that night in the parking lot, the very first night."

"Really?" Annie asked, her eyes wide with surprise.

"Yes, really," he replied, his voice filled with warmth. "I love you more than life itself. You're my world, Annie. I can't imagine my life without you."

Annie looked at him shyly, a blush rising to her cheeks. "There's something else I need to tell you," she said softly.

William regarded her with a hint of confusion. "What is it, sweetheart?"

"I hope you're not angry with me," she added, her voice trembling slightly.

"I could never be angry with you. Please, just tell me," he urged gently.

Annie turned to face him fully, locking her gaze with his. "I'm pregnant."

William's eyes widened in shock, the words hanging in the air between them. A mix of emotions flooded his face, surprise, joy, and an overwhelming sense of protectiveness. He took a moment to process the news, his heart racing as he searched Annie's expression for any hint of fear or uncertainty.

"Pregnant?" he echoed softly, a smile slowly breaking across his face as realisation set in. "Are you serious?"

Annie nodded, a blend of excitement and apprehension flickering in her eyes.

William's heart swelled with joy as he wrapped his arms around her, his voice filled with warmth. "This is incredible, Annie! I can't believe it!" He pulled her close, his expression turning earnest. "Are you okay? How do you feel about this?"

Annie glanced at William, her voice barely above a whisper. "I'm a little scared. I only found out this morning from the blood tests they did at the hospital."

William's brow furrowed with concern. "You do want the baby?"

Annie glanced at him, her eyes wide. "Yes, yes, of course! I can't wait to have your baby. It's just... it's a little scary."

"I'll be there every step of the way," he promised, his voice filled with reassurance.

Annie asked, "Are you sure you're okay with this?"

"I'm more than okay, Annie. I'm ecstatic! I think it's amazing. I love you, and I want to spend the rest of my life with you."

"I feel the same way. I love you, William."

William leaned down and kissed Annie softly on the lips. "Does that mean you'll marry me? As soon as possible?" he urged gently.

Annie's eyes widened in shock as she looked at him. "Really?"

With conviction, he replied, "Yes, Annie. I want you to be my wife."

"Oh, William! Of course, I will! I love you!" she exclaimed.

"Thank God!" He whispered in relief, "I promise I'll make you happy."

"I know you will. You've already made me so happy."

William carefully climbed out of the bath, water dripping from his skin as he turned back to Annie. He reached down, lifting her gently out of the water and cradling her in his arms. With great care, he began to dry her off, taking extra precautions around her injuries, making sure not to cause her any discomfort. He gently wrapped her wrists and ankles with new bandages.

Once they were both dressed, William turned to Annie, his expression serious but filled with warmth. "Are you ready to tell our family?"

Annie looked up at him, tears glistening in her eyes. William gently wiped a tear from her cheek, concern etched on his face. "Why are you crying?" he asked softly.

"I haven't had a family for a very long time," she admitted, her voice trembling with emotion.

William smiled tenderly, placing his hand on her flat stomach. "You have one now, sweetheart," he reassured her. "And it's only going to get bigger."

William and Annie made their way to the living room, where Sarah was already seated on the sofa, chatting animatedly with their parents, Helen and Henry. As they entered, the lively conversation came to a halt, and all eyes turned to them.

With a sense of pride swelling in his chest, William spoke up, his voice steady but filled with excitement. "Annie has agreed to marry me."

Instantly, the room erupted in joy. Helen jumped to her feet, her eyes sparkling with happiness, while Henry clapped his hands together, a broad grin spreading across his face. Sarah was already up, wrapping her arms around both William and Annie in a tight embrace. "Congratulations!" she exclaimed, her voice full of warmth.

After the initial excitement settled, William looked at his family, his expression shifting to something even more significant. "There's more," he said, pausing for dramatic effect.

Everyone turned their attention to him, curiosity etched on their faces. "We're having a baby," he announced, a beaming smile breaking across his face.

The reaction was instantaneous. Gasps of surprise and delight filled the air as their family processed the news. Helen's hands flew to her mouth in shock, while Henry reached out to pull Annie into another joyful hug. Sarah jumped up and down, her excitement contagious as she congratulated them once again.

Epilogue

Annie was putting the final touches on her latest art exhibition when Sarah approached, her reassuring smile as warm as ever.

"Everything is ready, Annie," Sarah said, her voice steady and confident.

"Thank you, Sarah. You've truly outdone yourself," Annie replied, her gratitude shining through.

The past few years had been a whirlwind for Annie and William. Their love story reached a pinnacle when they exchanged vows in a breathtaking ceremony in the lush garden of William's parents' estate. The setting had been nothing short of magical, with vibrant flowers in full bloom and twinkling fairy lights casting a soft glow over the celebration.

Three months pregnant at the time, Annie radiated joy in her elegant, flowing wedding gown. Every smile reflected her happiness, and William had been utterly captivated by her the entire day. His gaze, filled with awe and love, never left her. Beneath a floral arch surrounded by their closest family and friends, they made heartfelt vows, binding their futures together.

The celebration had stretched long into the night, filled with laughter, dancing, and dreams of the life they were building together. Now, standing in her art gallery, Annie felt that same surge of excitement she'd experienced on her wedding day.

Six months ago, Annie had purchased the gallery from Irene, using part of her inheritance. It was one of many milestones she and William had achieved together. They had also bought a beautiful, expansive home nestled on a sprawling piece of land, equipped with a state-of-the-art security system—a non-negotiable decision William had made after everything Annie had endured. His top priority was the safety of his family.

As for William's old penthouse, it had become Sarah's. He had gifted it to her for her birthday, knowing how much she loved it. Sarah had transformed it into her personal haven, a gesture that brought her immense joy.

"Guests will start arriving soon," Sarah said, snapping Annie out of her reverie.

Moments later, the gallery came alive. Guests mingled among the artworks, their admiration evident in hushed murmurs and appreciative smiles. The soft clink of champagne glasses punctuated the hum of conversation, while trays of canapés weaved through the crowd, adding to the elegant atmosphere. Annie stood back for a moment, soaking in the scene, her heart swelling with pride. She couldn't help but smile, thinking about how far she and William had come and how much they had to look forward to.

"Hello, Mrs. Banks," came a familiar voice, whispered in her ear. Annie started slightly, then laughed as William's warm tone registered. "You're looking as ravishing as ever tonight," he added playfully.

"You're biased," she teased, turning to face him. Her heart melted at the sight of her husband holding their nine-month-old son, Derek, cradled in his arms.

Annie leaned in, kissing William lovingly on the lips before pressing a gentle kiss to Derek's sleeping head. "How has Derek been today?" she asked, her voice soft with affection.

"Karen says he's been perfect as usual," William replied, his pride evident.

Karen, their middle-aged nanny, had become an indispensable part of their lives, a steady presence they both deeply appreciated.

Annie smiled at her husband, her eyes reflecting her happiness. "We've been blessed with a very well-behaved child," she said warmly.

William nodded, his gaze full of love as he looked at her and their son. "That we have," he agreed, his tone carrying a quiet gratitude.

Annie glanced up at him and asked, "Are your parents here yet?"

"Yes, they're talking to Sarah at the moment," William replied with a knowing smile. "I'm sure they'll find me soon enough to kidnap our child."

Annie laughed softly. "They do love Derek to distraction. I think it's wonderful."

William grinned at his stunning wife. "So do I. It gives me the perfect excuse to whisk you away for a few minutes and have my wicked way with you."

Annie chuckled, shaking her head. "That's good because I need to discuss something important with you."

William's brows lifted in curiosity. "Oh? Anything wrong?"

"No, sweetheart," Annie assured him, her smile growing. "Quite the opposite." She glanced over his shoulder and spotted his parents approaching. "Ah, here are Helen and Henry now."

Helen and Henry greeted Annie warmly, each embracing her and planting a kiss on her cheek.

Helen turned to Henry, who gently took Derek from William's arms, and said, "Everything seems to be running smoothly as always, Annie. We just came to steal your little man for a bit."

Annie laughed. "As you always do."

"Of course," Henry said with a broad smile. "Our grandson is an absolute delight to be around."

William crossed his arms, a playful glint in his eyes. "We wouldn't know. You're always stealing him from us," he teased good-naturedly.

Helen waved a dismissive hand, her eyes sparkling with humour. "Well, someone has to spoil him properly."

Annie exchanged a loving look with William, her heart full as she watched his parents dote on their son. Moments like these reminded her how blessed they truly were.

As Henry and Helen walked away with Derek, Henry called back with a grin, "We'll bring him back soon enough." Helen smiled warmly, following her husband into the crowd.

Annie turned to William, grabbing his hand. "Come with me," she said, a mischievous glint in her eyes.

William chuckled as she tugged him toward her office. "Are you planning to have your wicked way with me instead?" he teased, closing the door behind them.

Annie wrapped her arms around his neck, her lips just inches from his. "Would you object?" she asked playfully.

"Not a chance," William replied, his voice low and full of desire. He pulled her close and kissed her passionately, his arms tightening around her as if he never wanted to let go.

Eventually, Annie broke the embrace, though she kept her arms around him. Her cheeks were flushed, and her eyes sparkled as she looked up at him. "I have something to tell you, husband," she said softly.

William raised an eyebrow, his curiosity piqued. "Oh? And what might that be, wife?"

Annie smiled, her voice breathless. "You're going to be a father again."

William froze for a moment, his eyes widening in awe. "Are you pregnant?" he asked, his voice filled with wonder.

She blushed, her smile turning playful. "Well, that's usually how you become a father."

William laughed, his joy radiating as he scooped her into his arms and spun her around. "You've made me the happiest man alive, Annie," he whispered, holding her close as they shared a moment of pure bliss.

Annie laughed, her eyes dancing with mischief. "You know what that means, don't you?"

William tilted his head, curiosity flickering across his face. "What?"

She grinned. "It means your parents will have one each to kidnap."

William burst out laughing, then cupped her face and kissed her tenderly. "I love you, Annie Banks."

She smiled up at him, her voice soft and full of devotion. "And I love you, William Banks. Forever."

Eight months later, Annie and William's life blossomed once more as they welcomed a healthy baby girl into the world. William stayed by Annie's side through every moment, holding her hand and whispering words of encouragement.

When their daughter was finally placed in their arms, tears of joy filled their eyes. She was perfect, with delicate fingers, tiny toes, and a soft tuft of dark hair that mirrored William's.

As they cradled their newborn, Annie and William exchanged a tender smile, their hearts brimming with love. Their journey had been filled with both trials and triumphs, but now, as parents of two beautiful children, they felt a bond deeper and more unshakable than ever before.

Together, they embraced their growing family, filled with hope and excitement for the future. No matter what challenges lay ahead, they knew they would face them as a family, united by love and the promise of all that was yet to come.

The End

ʼore You Go...

ʼr these characters and want more love stories filled with passion, and second chances, my newsletter is where I share ʼirst.

You'll receive:

💕 Early access to new releases

💕 Exclusive reader-only content and extras

👉 **Join my reader list here:** https://alisonreidauthor.com

I'd love to welcome you.

Alison Reid

Thank you for reading Hearts in Pe

If you enjoyed this collection of irresistible heroes and heroines, keep
eye out for more upcoming romance collections by Alison Re
including:

Alpha Kings - *A Billionaire Alpha Male Romance Collection*

Cautious Hearts - *A Trust-After-Heartbreak Romance Collection*

Dark & Dangerous - *Brooding Heroes Romance Collection*

Final Surrender - *Alpha Heroes Yielding to Love Collection*

Forbidden Hearts - *A Forbidden Love Romance Collection*

Forever Mine - *A Longing-for-Love Romance Collection*

Guarded Hearts - *A Surrender to Love Romance Collection*

Hearts & Secrets - *Small Town Romance Collection*

Hidden Truths - *A Secret Identity Romance Collection*

Lies & Hearts - *A Lies, Secrets & Betrayal Romance Collection*

Love After Regret - *A Second-Chance Redemption Romance Collection*

Misjudged Hearts - *A Love After Judgement Romance Collection*

Torn Between Hearts - *A Love Triangle Romance Collection*

All of Alison Reid's books feature standalone stories, swoon-worthy
heroes, and guaranteed happily-ever-afters.

oks by Alison Reid

A Billionaire for Christmas

A Heart in Florence

After The Storm

Always You

Before I Fell

Before the Thaw

Beneath the Lies

Billionaire Bodyguard

Billionaire Rancher

Blueprints of the Heart

Branlow

Collide

Echoes of Deception

Falling for the Billionaire

Forever Yours

Heart of the Outback

Hearts on the Line

Hidden Gem

Kept Promises

Mended Hearts

Mistaken Hearts

New Year's Eve Kiss

Quiet Danger

Reckless Hearts

Reflections of Deception

...d all my books on Amazon:

https://www.amazon.com/author/alisonreid1970

About the Author

Alison Reid writes contemporary and small-town romance filled with heart, passion, and second-chance love stories. Her novels often feature strong heroines, irresistible heroes, and the happily-ever-afters readers adore. When she's not writing, Alison enjoys reading, spending time with her family, and imagining new love stories. She hopes her books give readers a few hours of escape, joy, and swoon-worthy romance they won't forget.

www.ingramcontent.com/pod-product-compliance
Lightning Source LLC
Chambersburg PA
CBHW050952180726
48291CB00006B/1800